THE LAMP OF THE WICKED

Phil Rickman was born in Lancashire. He writes and presents the book programme *Phil the Shelf* for BBC Radio Wales and has won awards for his TV and radio journalism. His sixth novel, *The Wine of Angels*, introduced the Revd Merrily Watkins, whose fraught baptism as a diocesan exorcist was chronicled in *Midwinter of the Spirt*, followed by a *Crown of Lights* and *The Cure of Souls*. He is married and lives on the Welsh border.

'A cracking mystery – characters drawn with such realism that they step out of the pages and perform for you in your mind's eye' Professor Bernard Knight, *Tangled Web*

Phil Rickman

THE LAMP OF THE WICKED

PAN BOOKS

First published 2003 by Macmillan

First published in paperback 2003 by Pan Books
an imprint of Pan Macmillan Ltd
Pan Macmillan, 20 New Wharf Road, London N1 9RR
Basingstoke and Oxford
Associated companies throughout the world
www.panmacmillan.com

ISBN 0 330 49032 X

1 3 5 7 9 8 6 4 2

A CIP catalogue record for this book is available from
the British Library.

Printed and bound in Great Britain by
Mackays of Chatham plc, Chatham, Kent

The light of the righteous rejoiceth, but the lamp of the wicked shall be put out.

Proverbs 13.9

October 1995

Just about every door on the top landing of that three-storey house had a hole bored in it, for crouching at and watching. Holes and watching. Watching through holes. It would always start like that.

'You *still* doing it?'

He realized he'd shouted it down the valley, which was wide and shallow and ambered under the late afternoon sun.

It was a lovely place. It ought to be grim and stark, with scrubby grass and dead trees. The reality – the actual beauty, the total *serenity* of the scene – he couldn't cope with that, didn't want any kind of balm on the memories that had brought him out here.

Oh, aye, a lovely place to be buried, beneath the wide sky and within sight of the church tower. But not the way the two women had been buried, chopped like meat and stowed in vertical holes. Not, for God's sake, like that.

And now he had to turn away, with the weary knowledge of how futile this was, because there was still too much hate in him.

What had happened – what had started him off – was spotting one of those neat holes that appeared sometimes in the clouds, as if the sun had burned through, like a cigarette through paper, and then vanished. He'd at once imagined a bright little bulging eye on the other side of it. And that was when he'd screamed down the valley, this great mad-bull roar: '*You* still *doing it? You still watching?*

Now he was looking all around, in case someone had heard, but there was nobody, only his own car in this pull-in area right by the field gate, near the fingerpost after which the field was named.

One of the signs on the fingerpost was light brown with white lettering, signifying a site of historic interest and pointing, up a narrow road to his left, towards a church that was not visible. The one that you could see, looking down the field, must be the village church, where the ashes of the monster had been scattered.

They should've been flushed down the bloody toilet.

He shut his eyes in anguish. *Get a grip!*

The county boundary apparently ran through the field, but he didn't know exactly where. Should've brought an OS map, but he wasn't really sure what he was looking for. Didn't really know why he'd come, except for the usual problem of not being able to settle, not being able to stop anywhere for long before it all caught up with him again. He'd be walking in and out of his house, driving to places and coming home without remembering where the hell he'd been, and then going into his own church and walking out of it again, uncomforted and fearful for his faith.

And still wanting *confrontation*. It was anger that brought him here, and he'd have to be rid of that before he could make any kind of start. If you were dealing with something that had been human, no matter how low, how depraved, it was incumbent upon you to operate in a spirit of consideration and sympathy and . . .

. . . love?

Oh, bugger *that*. He punched his own thigh in fury, thinking about old comrades – survivors and relatives of the war dead – who had made pilgrimages to battlefields aglow with poppies. How much love had *they* been able to summon for the bloody killers?

Not that this was really *like* that. The pity and the waste, oh aye. But the evil here had been slow, systematic, intimate and concentrated – some of it ending in this field, with the hacking and the dripping of blood and offal into the holes. The horror had been intensely squalid, and the hatred . . . well, there didn't seem to have *been* any particular hatred.

That, in some ways, was the worst thing of all: no hatred.

Except his own.

He'd left his car and climbed over the gate, near two black, rubberized tanks. There was a mature oak tree on his right. There'd been references in the statements to an oak tree. But was this one too near the road?

Now, he kept his eyes shut listening. It was said that no birds sang at Dachau, but the little buggers were singing away here. He'd never been able to identify types of birdsong, though, only the mewling of the buzzards in the rough country where he lived.

Where he lived, the countryside was scarred by hikers and by soldiers training. Not so very long ago, this field had been lacerated by police with spades. But it had healed now, was already back to being a beautiful place. Was that so bad?

Only for me.

He found himself patting his pocket, in case it had fallen out. He knew the words – ought to after all this time – but there was also a notebook in his pocket with it all written down, in case he got *resistance*, something bent on wiping it from his head, and he had to read it from the page, shouting it out into some dark wind.

But there was no wind. It wasn't even cold. He wanted challenge, he *wanted* resistance, he wanted to see the gloating in those little glittering eyes. Feel the watching. Experience the demonic. It didn't matter what else he'd become, at the bottom of it he was a man and he couldn't cope with it any other way.

Finally, in his desperate need for discomfort, he actually sat down by the hedge, letting the dampness soak through his pants. Which was daft and childish, but it sent him spinning back into the pain. It did that, at least.

And it started the memory like a silent film, black and white, ratchet click-clicking in the projector, no stopping it now. Here he is raging into Julia's bedroom, throwing himself down, sobbing, both hands on the bedclothes either side of where she's lying, feeling the still, waxy atmosphere in the bedroom and smelling the perfumed air.

She obviously sprayed perfume around first, to make it less unpleasant for whoever found her, if her body betrayed her, relaxing into death.

3

Typical, that.

He feels dampness. The dampness by the side of her. What must have happened, she swallowed a couple of handfuls of the pills and then, maybe half asleep, thought *Not enough*, and took some more, another handful. She was likely so far gone by then that the glass simply fell from her hand, spilling the rest of the water on the quilt and rolling away into the corner of the room, where he finds it. And then his gaze is tracking slowly around the bedroom with its mid-blue walls and its Paul Klee prints, noting, in the well of the pine dressing table, the vellum envelope.

Picking up the glass first, though, and laying it on the bedside table, a few inches from Julia's hair – she must've combed it first, you can tell. *Oh Christ, oh Christ.* Turning away, moving slowly towards the envelope until he can read his own name written on the front.

Inside, on the creamy notepaper she always used – her one constant luxury; she never could *abide* cheap notepaper – it says, in big looping handwriting that soon becomes blurred:

I'll keep it short, Shep.

I'm so, so sorry about this. But I do believe there is somewhere else – you showed me that – and that Donna needs me there now. She so needs someone to comfort her, I feel this very strongly. I'm so very sorry, because I love you so much, Shep, you know I do, and it's only thinking of you and sensing your arms around me that's going to give me the last bit of strength I need for this, so please don't take your arms away and please, please forgive me, and please go on praying for us. I'm so SORRY.

He'd no idea how long he'd been there, when the farmer found him: sitting with his back to the hedge, staring down the valley at the sunlight over the church tower. Sitting there up against the hedge like a bloody old tramp, with his eyes wet and his wet pants sticking to his arse.

Conceding afterwards that perhaps it was just as well the farmer did find him.

For now, anyroad.

Part One

*Be sober, be vigilant, because your adversary the devil
as a roaring lion walketh about, seeking whom he may devour.*

The First Epistle of Peter 5.8

1

Foul Water

It was a crime, what he was doing, this Roddy Lodge, with his wraparound dark glasses and his whipped-cream smile.

The stories had kept filtering through, like foul water out of sludge, and Gomer Parry had felt ashamed to be part of the same profession. Plant hire was the poorer for shoddy operators like Roddy: wide boys, duckers and divers and twisters and exploiters of innocent people, rich and poor – mostly incomers to the county that didn't know no better.

Too many blind eyes had been turned, this was it. Too many people – even so-called public servants, some of them – looking the other way, saying what's it matter if a few Londoners gets taken down the road; they got money to burn.

Bad attitude, sneering at the incomers, ripping them off. They were still people, the incomers. People with dreams, and there was nothing wrong with dreams.

Mostly.

What about Gomer Parry, though? Would he have backed off like the rest or looked the other way, if he'd had any suspicion of how deep it went? What about Gomer? Just a little bloke with wild white hair and wire-rimmed glasses and a sense of what was right and honourable: the plant-hire code, digger chivalry.

No point in even asking the question, because, the way it started, this was just a drainage issue. Just a matter of pipes and shit.

It had seemed odd sometimes to Gomer that his and Roddy's trenches had never crossed, even allowing for the fact that they operated from different ends of the county. Plant hire: big machinery in a small world.

But it was happening now, no avoiding it on this damp and

windy Sunday – a weary old day to be leaving your fireside, and if Minnie had still been alive likely Gomer would've put it off. But the old fireside wasn't the same no more, and she'd sounded near-desperate, this lady, and only up here weekends, anyway.

A Londoner, as you'd expect. Londoners were always looking further and further west in the mad rush to get country air down their lungs, like it was some kind of new drug. Rural properties in Herefordshire never stayed long on the market nowadays, especially the ones that really *looked* like rural properties, even if there were clear drawbacks.

Take this one. Classic example, see. What you had was this lovely old farmhouse, with a couple of acres, on the A49 between Hereford and Ross. Built in the rusty stone you got in these parts, and from the front there were good long, open views over flat fields to the Black Mountains.

But before that there was the A49 itself.

Gomer put a match to an inch of ciggy, October rain sluicing down on his cap, as another five cars and a big van came whizzing past – and this was a Sunday. All right, fair play, he spent his own days bouncing around on big, growling diggers, but no way Gomer could live so close to a main road like this, with fast cars and all the ground-shaking, fume-belching, brake-screeching juggernauts heading for the M50 and the Midlands.

Yet for this Mrs Pawson, in her tight white jeans, it was some type of peace, after London. '*Oh, we'd had enough of it, Mr Parry. Or, at least, I had. We couldn't hear ourselves think any more, and I was convinced Gus had the beginnings of asthma. I told my husband that if we didn't get out now we never would, not this side of retirement. We desperately needed peace, above all. Somewhere to walk.*'

Walk? Pretty soon, in Gomer's view, you'd give up going for walks, being as how there was a good two hundred yards of no-pavement between you and the nearest public footpath. For half the price, the Pawsons could've got theirselves a modern place, with no maintenance headaches, up some quiet lane.

But modern places weren't part of the dream. *This* was

8

the dream: eighteenth-century, a bit lopsided, no damp-proof course, dodgy wiring.

And private drainage.

The FOR SALE sign lay in the damp gravel at the side of the driveway. Gomer reckoned it'd be back up in the hedge within the year. They'd get their money back, no problem at all – the way Hereford prices were going these days, they'd likely get it back twice over. Even allowing for what it was going to cost them to put this drainage to rights, after what Roddy Lodge had done to it.

Gomer tramped back up the drive, past his bottle-green van. It had GOMER PARRY PLANT HIRE on the sides and across both back doors in white. Nev's idea, this was – '*You gotter advertise, Gomer, gotter put it about, see. Your ole clients is dyin' off faster 'n you can dig their graves.*'

The other side of the van, Gomer could see the top of the installation poking out of the grass not two yards from the property.

Efflapure: state-of-the-art sewerage.

Gomer had never even heard of an *Efflapure* before. Nev was likely right about him losing touch. He was well out of touch with the kind of rip-off junk getting unloaded on city folk who thought all they had to do was flush the lavvy and the council did the rest.

As for where Lodge had put it – un-bloody-believable!

'Mr Lodge showed us several brochures,' Mrs Pawson had told him earlier, 'and gave us the telephone numbers of two other people who'd had these particular models installed.'

'Phone 'em, did you?'

Mrs Pawson hadn't even looked embarrassed. 'Oh, we had far too much to think about.'

'Woulder made no difference, anyway,' Gomer conceded. 'Both be stooges, see. Friends of his, telling you you couldn't get no finer system anywhere in the country. Load of ole wallop.'

He started scratting about in the fallen leaves, uncovering a meter-thing under an aluminium shield, with another one like it inside the house, to tell you where the shit level in the processing tank was at. Waste of time and money. Folk had got along happily for centuries without knowing where their shit level was at.

Presently, out she came again, under a big red and yellow golfing umbrella.

'So what's the actual verdict, Mr Parry?' Attractive-looking lady, mind, in her sharp-faced way. Fortyish, and a few inches taller than Gomer, but weren't they all?

'You wannit straight?' Gomer took out his ciggy. Mrs Pawson was looking at it like he'd got a bonfire going with piles of old tyres. She took a step back.

'It's the reason we came to you, Mr Parry. Our surveyor said that you, of all people, would indeed give it to us . . . straight.'

Gomer nodded. This surveyor, Darren Booth, he was a reputable boy. He'd said these Pawsons could be looking at trouble, and he wasn't wrong. Gomer looked over at the Efflapure, blinking through his rain-blobbed glasses.

'All your ground's to the far side of the house, ennit? That orchard?'

'We did try to acquire some more, but—'

'And how far's *he* from the house?' Gomer nodded at the Efflapure. 'Four foot? Five foot? Bugger-all distance, ennit? You don't *do* that, see, Mrs P. Should've been set back, that thing, *well* bloody back. Likely Lodge done it this way to save a few yards o' pipe and having to go into the old orchard, mess with roots and stuff. But you *never* digs it in that close to a house, specially—'

'We specifically . . .' Mrs Pawson all but stamped her nice clean trainer in the mud. 'We specifically *told* him that cost was not an issue.'

'Ah . . .' Gomer waved a hand. 'Some folk, they'd cut corners for the sake of it. Don't reckon he'd've passed on no savings to you, mind. So, er . . .' Holding back a bit, because this wasn't good. 'What exackly did young Darren say could happen?'

'He didn't.' Mrs Pawson shivered under her umbrella. 'He just said it could become a problem and advised us to get a second opinion, and he suggested you, as . . . as the most honest contractor he knew. For heaven's sake, Mr Parry, what *does* it mean?'

Staring at him, all wild-eyed. She was up here on her own this weekend – husband still in London, kiddie with the nanny – and she was finding out, in the mud and the rain and the wind, how country life wasn't always a bowl of cherries. She looked thin and lost under the big brolly, in her white jeans and her clean trainers, and Gomer felt sorry for her.

He sighed. Nobody liked jobs like this, where you had to clean up after another outfit. But this time it was Roddy Lodge, and Roddy Lodge had it coming to him.

He went over to the house wall. No way you could be entirely sure, see, but . . .

'See this bit of a crack in the stonework?'

'Is that new?'

'Sure t'be. What he's done, see, is dug hisself a nice pit for this article, eight, nine feet down, right up against the ole foundations.'

'You're saying' – her jaw trembling – 'it could cause the *house to collapse*?'

Gomer thought about this, pushing back his cap.

'Well,' he said, 'not *all* the house.'

They agreed it needed moving, this Efflapure, to a safer location. If you accepted that such an object was actually needed at all.

'See, I wouldn't've advised you to get one o' them fancy things,' Gomer said. 'Waste o' money, my view of it. You got a nice, gentle slope to the ground there. Needs a simpler tank and a soakaway, like there was before. Primitive, mabbe, but he works, and he goes on workin'. No problems, no fancy meters to keep checking. Low maintenance, no renewable parts. Get him emptied every year or two, then forget all about him. Tried and tested, see, Mrs P. Tried and tested.'

A gust of wind snatched at the brolly. Mrs Pawson huffed and stuttered. 'So what on earth are we supposed to do with the . . . Efflapure?'

'Get your Mr Lodge to take the whole kit back, I'd say. Tell him what your surveyor said. He'll know Darren Booth, see, know how he puts hisself around the county, talks to the right people, so if you and your husband puts it over to Lodge, tackful-like, that it wouldn't look so good if it got out he'd been cutting corners to save hisself a few quid, you'd have most of your money back off him pretty quick, I'd say.' Gomer nodded seriously, figuring this was good advice – at least let Lodge know there were a few folk onto his games. 'Who was it told you to go to the feller in the first place, you don't mind me askin'?'

'He . . .' She brought out some folded paper from a back pocket of her jeans and handed it to Gomer. 'Somebody . . . pushed this leaflet through the letter box.'

Gomer opened it out. There was a drawing on the front of a roses-round-the-door Tudor cottage. Cartoon man in a doublet-thing with a ruffle round his neck and a cartoon woman in a long frock and an old-fashioned headdress. They both had big clothes-pegs on their noses. Underneath the drawing, it said:

In days of olde,

days before . . .

Efflapure

Gomer tried not to wince.

Mrs Pawson said in a panicky voice, 'It was a *local* firm. We thought—'

Gomer shook his head. 'Not what I'd call a *firm*, exackly. Lodge, he operates out of a yard, back of Ross-on-Wye, what I've yeard, with a coupler part-timers on sickness benefit.'

'But he's an authorized agent for . . . for Efflapure.'

'Agent for more dodgy outfits than you can shake a stick at,' Gomer said.

'So you . . . You know him.'

'Well . . . I knows *of* him. Seen him around.'

Roddy, with his baseball cap and his wraparound dark glasses. Roddy and his big, whipped-cream smile.

'Can you . . . ?' Mrs Pawson gripped the shaft of the umbrella with both hands, knuckles white. 'Can *you* take it away?'

'Me?'

'You could probably make some money out of it, couldn't you?'

'Well . . .' Gomer scratched his cheek. 'There *are* places one o' these might be suitable. Working farm, light industrial, mabbe. We could likely come to an arrangement. But I gotter say, you'd be better off going back to this Lodge and—'

'No!' Her whole body a-quiver now. 'I don't want that. I don't want him here again.'

Traffic swished past, all mixed in with the wind. There was a sudden thump in the leaves near their feet. Gomer saw that a big, ripe Bramley had tumbled from one of the trees, but Mrs Pawson jumped and looked behind her like it could be something a deal bigger than that. Now she was actually clutching his arm, the umbrella all over the place.

'Mr Parry, how soon could you do it?'

'You sure you don't wanner talk this over with your husband?'

'How *soon*?'

'Well, you won't be yere, will you, 'less it's a weekend?'

'It doesn't matter whether we're here or not. Could you do it tomorrow?'

'*Tomorrow?*' Gomer was more than doubtful. 'I'd have to put it to Nev – my nephew, my partner in the business . . .'

'Look,' Mrs Pawson said, teeth gritted, shivering seriously now, 'I just want it out of the way. We're new to the area and we made a mistake. It was a mistake and we're paying for it. I want it out and I don't want . . . *him* doing it, do you understand?'

Likely this was when Gomer should have spotted something. The look on her face: this kind of . . . well, *fear*, really. No getting round that.

The up-and-down of it was that he was sorry for this London woman, alone in her farmhouse with no farm attached, husband likely bored with it already. Smart-looking, educated woman washed up here, marooned in the flat fields with the traffic blasting past.

After what happened, he'd often think what else he might have said, how else he could've handled it – like stalling a while, taking advice, checking Roddy out a bit more. But what was to check out? What else was there to know about an operator, a wide boy, a conman, a ducker and diver, a bit of a poser?

'*Please*,' Mrs Pawson said.

Gomer wished he knew what else was bothering her but he figured she was never going to tell him. He nodded. 'All right, then.' What else could he say? 'Tuesday. What about Tuesday?'

It didn't feel right, even then.

2

Pressure

Sometimes, you just wanted to shake her. You wanted to get her into a corner and scream, *Why don't you just get on with it? You are a mature woman, you are unmarried. Like, being a priest is supposed to condition your hormonal responses or something? It's the only life you've got, for Christ's sake . . . whatever else you might think.*

Jane was leaning forward, across the kitchen table, making no secret about trying to listen.

It was getting dark now in the big, beamed kitchen and Mum was partly in shadow, standing in the corner by the door, taking the call on the cordless. She looked very small but quite ghostly in her grey alb. Her expression hadn't changed. Normally, when she picked up the phone and found out who was on the line, she'd *react* – like smile in relief, look curious, or maybe grimace. Like, she'd instinctively make a face if it was, say, the Bishop or – worse – Uncle Ted. The fact that there was no reaction at all this time meant that she was working seriously hard at concealing something she didn't want Jane to know about. Most of the time, Mum was an open book – and it wasn't by Proust or Joyce or anybody difficult.

So it was Jane who made the face. Like, was this ridiculous, or what?

'OK. Fine, let's leave it at that,' Mum said, and stubbed out the line. She put the cordless on the dresser and stood looking at it for a fraction too long before turning back to look into the room. In the lamplight her face was soft and in the long linen alb she looked, for a moment, like a little girl waiting to go to bed. Just needed the teddy.

'Cold call?' Jane raised both eyebrows. 'Emma from Everest? Stacey from Staybright?'

Mum came back to the table. She *did* look tired. Well, it had to be getting her down, this bobbing and weaving, covering her tracks.

'You don't have to do this, you know, Mum. Not with me.'

'What?' *Now* an expression: wariness.

'I'm on your side. I *like* Lol. I mean, in other circumstances – like not involving my ageing parent – the twenty-something age gap between him and me would be as nothing. But, you know . . . if *I* can't have him . . . What I'm saying is, if you want to arrange a little *tryst*, you have my blessing. And, er . . .' jabbing a thumb towards the ceiling. 'His too, I'd guess. He's not inhuman. Presumably.'

Jane sat back, arms folded. For a moment, Mum was almost smiling. Then she said brusquely, 'Don't you have homework?'

'Done it. Double free period this afternoon. However, if that's code for you want me to leave the room so you can call back, exchange a few steamy intimacies, I'd be happy to—'

'Don't push it, flower,' Mum said mildly.

'Push it? Jesus, if anybody ever *needed* a good push . . .' Jane subsided into her chair, drumming her fingers on the refectory table. This was not the time.

'Look at the time.' Mum closed her eyes, the childlike bit dropping away. She was thirty-seven now, no getting around that – heading for the rapid slide into cronehood, with her prospect of happiness, which had seemed so close, receding again. 'Parish meeting at half-seven, and we haven't eaten yet.'

'Not a problem.' Jane stood up. 'Why don't I go down the chippy?'

'I thought you were boycotting the chippy.'

'They're now claiming they've stopped using animal fat. I can live with that.'

'Would you?' Mum looked grateful, dragging her bag from the dresser, pulling out her purse.

'You want mushy peas, too?' Jane asked.

After the kid had left, Merrily went into the scullery-office, closed the door, switched on the Anglepoise and sat down, pulling her black woolly cardigan over her alb. She thought about calling Lol back but then – *parish meeting: income, cash flow . . . pressure* – phoned Huw Owen instead.

'You know everything,' she said. 'What line do I take on a mobile-phone mast in the spire?'

Huw said, 'Cold over there, is it?'

'Not by your criteria.' Huw's rectory was well up in the Brecon Beacons, above the snowline, where spring and autumn would wave to each other from either side of July.

'I were only thinking about you earlier,' he said. 'You and your rock star. Serious, is it, or just a fling?'

Rock star: a touch of irony, there. She didn't rise to it. 'We're permitted flings now?'

'Merrily,' Huw said, 'these are the days of sex-change clergy, transvestite clergy, bondage clergy, cocaine clergy. I'd say, as long as it doesn't involve Alsatian dogs . . . What's Bernie Dunmore's view?'

'Up to the individual conscience. Between the individual and God.'

'Nice. You can tell why he made bishop. And what's God say?'

'He says to get on with it or Jane'll be back with the chips.'

She pictured Huw slumped, shoeless and shaggy-haired, in front of his fire of coal and logs, the uncurtained window a cold blue square in the whitewashed wall. From the edge of his sheep-shaven lawn, you could see the site of the cottage where Huw had been born a bastard, as he liked to phrase it, two years before his mother took him off with her to Sheffield, to grow up a Yorkshireman with a weight of Welsh on his back.

Huw Owen: the mongrel come home to the hills. Merrily's Deliverance-tutor, her spiritual director.

'Aye, go on, then,' he said. 'Mobile-phone masts? The tips of the Devil's horns.'

Crossing the market place in the damp dusk, Jane looked back once. Through the heavy, dripping autumn trees, the lights of Ledwardine Vicarage were blurred, as though seen through tears, and she was wondering about Mum and Lol and how it could possibly be going wrong so soon.

All through the late summer, Mum had seemed brilliantly

light and girlish, maybe for the first time since she'd been ordained. Twice, she'd actually worn this provocatively low-cut top Jane had brought back from a summer sale in Hereford as kind of a joke.

Jane had imagined the skimpy thing lying on the floor of Lol's loft and was entirely cool about the notion. Mum had been a widow for over six years now and, although the crash that had killed Dad on the M5 had been a drastic kind of reprieve from a marriage gone bad, it was time to dump the guilt for ever.

It had to *be* guilt, didn't it? Mum had always been good at guilt, on any level. During the summer, Lol had written this song, 'The Cure of Souls', about the problem women priests might have loving God while also loving a man.

Which was only a problem if you believed that God *was* a man. If you believed that God was anything.

And if this thing – this *faith* in something unknowable, unprovable and very possibly bollocks – was likely to screw it up for Mum and Lol, there was no way Jane could live with that . . . like, even if she had to stand out here in the square and publicly burn Bibles on the cobbles.

The violence of the thought disturbed her a little. Pulling her beret down over her headphones, she switched on the Super Furries' *Rings Around the World* to blow it all away, crossing now into Church Street, with its lamplit black and white façades, moving under the dimly lit windows of the former Cassidys' Country Kitchen. At least the Cassidys had tried to serve traditional local produce, whereas now the place was charging an arm and a leg for two bits of squidge cradled in a red lettuce leaf. Gourmets were said to travel from three counties to eat here, but local people only ever came once – probably calling at the chippy on the way home.

This was typical of the way the village was going. With another overpriced antique shop and poor Lucy Devenish's old Ledwardine Lore turned into some rip-off, designer-trivia emporium pretentiously called Ledwardine Fine Art, it was close to becoming unbearably chic, with coachloads of French and Japanese tourists, like in the Cotswolds.

At least the chippy was still in business. Jane slipped into Old

Barn Lane, where its single window gleamed grease-yellow in the drizzle. This year, autumn had come down hard and fast, like some dank, grey roller blind. No Indian summer, no golden October days, and too late for all that now.

She bought cod and chips, twice. She and Mum didn't eat meat at all any more, but occasionally relapsed into eating fish. After all, Jesus had eaten fish, hadn't he? Jesus, in the right mood, would double your catch. Jane stepped down from the shop doorway, holding the chip package away from her fleece.

'Jane – tell your mother not to be late tonight, won't you?'

Uncle Ted Clowes stood there, merging with the greyness, bulky and stupidly sinister in his wide-brimmed Mafia hat. Until his retirement, Uncle Ted had been a solicitor, and you still couldn't trust the old bastard. He didn't like Mum being Deliverance consultant because it regularly took her out of the parish, out from under his thumb – which was probably the only truly worthwhile aspect of the whole crazy Deliverance thing.

Jane looked up. 'What's the problem . . . Ted?' In the light from the steamy window, his wide face looked like ridged sandstone; he hated it when she talked to him like an equal. She grinned. '*Not* . . . the great Commercialization-of-the-House-of-God storm?'

'It's a contentious issue,' Ted said heavily, 'and it needs to be resolved before it starts to split the village. Your mother knows that.'

Meaning he didn't want it dividing the ever-diminishing percentage of villagers who actually went to church. Not much of an issue at all, then. Jane converted the grin into a sweet and sympathetic smile. 'I'll get her bulletproof vest out of the airing cupboard.'

'One day, Jane,' said Uncle Ted, 'you'll learn to take some things seriously.'

'And the day *after* that, they'll bury me.' Jane refixed the headset. 'Better split or the chips'll be cold.'

Get a life, Ted.

She walked back through the village, its windows like Christmas lanterns. So far this year, it had been featured in three national-newspaper holiday supplements. Among the cars parked on the square – and taking up enough space for two – was this great long blue and cream Cadillac.

Ridiculous, really. Soon, it was going to be like living in one of those pottery villages that Ledwardine Fine Art was too upmarket ever to sell. Maybe each pottery village should have its own bijou pottery lady vicar. So much more tourist appeal than a crumpled old priest with a frayed dog collar and breath that smelled of communion wine.

'Once upon a time,' Huw said wistfully, 'folk believed the world were surrounded by angels, wing-tip to wing-tip. Interesting concept, eh? Everybody under the protection of vast, angelic wings, like newborn chicks.'

'Bit claustrophobic, though, when you think about it,' Merrily said.

'Also, the ultimate communication system. Safe, reliable . . .'

'Ah. Right. I see where you're coming from.'

'But where do they go now, the angels? No room left up there for the poor buggers, with all them signals clogging up the atmosphere – radio waves, satellite TV, daft sods in supermarkets ringing home half a mile away.' Huw put on a whiny Home Counties drawl. *'Darling, I'm at the cheese counter now – do we want Emmental or smoked Cheddar?'*

'So it's fair to say you're against masts, then.' Merrily wondered if Huw ever visited a supermarket, the way she often wondered why no woman appeared to have shared his life. He'd mentioned one once, in passing – just the once – but she'd sensed there was sadness attached.

'It's easy money, lass,' he said. 'Lot of space doing nowt inside church spires. No maintenance costs. Ten grand a year or more in the parish coffers. Environmentally friendly, too, on one level. Saves putting up them unsightly steel things on the hills.'

'But on another level, it could be causing cancer, damaging people's brains, et cetera. A lot of evidence piling up there.'

'Aye.'

'However, we're likely to get a mast anyway. Some farmer or other's going to give permission sooner or later for one of your unsightly steel things. So that's still bad health all round *and* a spoiled view.'

'You'd be reluctantly in favour, then,' Huw said.

'Well, no. I'm instinctively against it. But we could use the money, and Uncle Ted's smart. He knows that if he backs down on mobile phones, it'll be much harder for me to resist his plans for putting a gift shop in the vestry. I'm in a corner, Huw, and the meeting starts in about forty minutes.'

Merrily glanced at the scullery window, where the climbing rose used to knock against the glass in the night wind. Although she'd pruned it last spring, she half expected it to have grown back: *tock . . . tock . . . tock . . .*

'*And* the *Hereford Times* is hovering, because the mobile phone company looks like it's one of those about to start transmitting soft porn to new-generation handsets. I don't want to wind up in the papers again.'

'Stay out of it,' Huw said. 'Let the parish council take the decision, but make sure you nobble a few of them first.'

'Politics. I hate all that.' Merrily gazed into the Anglepoise circle of light enclosing the Bible, her sermon pad and a volume of the Alternative Service Book, 1980. *In His Presence*, it said on the front. 'Erm . . . would there be a Deliverance angle?'

'On mobile phones?'

'Transmissions. Signals . . . all that. I suppose that's why I'm ringing, really.' She heard footsteps on the kitchen flags; the chips had come.

'Spirits in the air?' Huw said.

'Something like that.'

'Or you could say the spire, which should be pointing to heaven, would be acting instead as a conductor for all kinds of shit thrown up from the earth.'

'You put these things so elegantly,' Merrily said.

'Stuff the Parish Council. Say *no* to it, lass.'

'Right.'

3

Something Ancient Being Lost

'*I mean, let's face it, nobody comes to church just to hear* me *preach . . .*'

It had just slipped out, and now they were all staring at her, as though she'd blasphemed in public or something.

Whatever you said always sounded more strident in the parish hall, the one building in mellow, timber-framed Ledwardine without a soul. The hall had been built in 1964. Its pink bricks and white tiling put you in mind of a disused abattoir; its caged, mauvish ceiling lights made faces gleam like raw meat.

'What I meant' – Merrily almost squirmed in her plastic chair – 'is that I've never really thought of myself as much of an orator. I'm . . . not always entirely comfortable in the pulpit. Like, who am I to step up there and lay down the law?'

Now she'd made it worse. She looked quickly around the table from face to face, aware that she was blushing because it could have been taken as a reference to her private life. She wondered if any of them knew about her and Lol. Maybe they all did. Maybe it was all over the parish. *Harlot.*

'Well, since you ask, Mrs Watkins . . .' The chairman, James Bull-Davies, looked half-amused. 'My understanding of the situation was that, for this short period every Sunday, the vicar was supposed to be some sort of mouthpiece for the Almighty. Suffused with the Holy Spirit. Or have I got that wrong?'

Merrily felt in need of a cigarette. She also felt like laying her head on the table and covering it with her arms.

'That's a little unfair, Mr Davies.' The soft, mildly Irish voice of Mrs Jenny Box drifted like scented smoke from the far corner. 'Mrs Watkins was displaying simple humility, and if that isn't part of God's core agenda for us all, then I don't know what is.'

'Oh Gord!' James Bull-Davies leaned back abruptly, to vague

splintering sounds from his carved wooden chair. 'Shut your damn mouth, James.' He waved a hand in exasperation. 'Anyone object if we drag this discussion back to *our* agenda? Or else we'll be here till the pubs've closed.'

James was chairing the meeting on military lines, eight tables arranged into a square. You felt that there should be sand trays and little model tanks. But it was good, Merrily had reflected, to have him back. He'd been out of village life for over a year, gathering his private affairs into some kind of order. Now, he and Alison were breeding horses professionally, and Upper Hall farmhouse was getting its leaking roof retiled.

In the semi-feudal past, it had been understood that the Bull family fortune should also maintain the fabric of the parish church; nowadays it was accepted that the odd crumpled tenner in the collection was going to be James's limit. The church was on its own now. It needed more income, short and long term.

'Sorry,' Merrily said. 'My fault.' In a roundabout way, she'd been attempting to make the point that, while incorporating a gift shop could be a good idea, the parish church should also be available simply as a quiet, sacred place – that it wasn't only about hymns and preaching. It wasn't only about Sunday.

'Look, I'm not . . .' Uncle Ted Clowes raised himself up. He looked irritated. 'I'm not entirely getting this. How does running a small shop in the church prevent it being a place of sanctuary? No one's suggesting the proposed outlet should be open for business all day and every day.'

'No,' Merrily said, 'but the church *itself* should be. . . . within reason. But what I'm really saying is . . .'

And then she lost the thread. The problem was, she was still in two minds about this. She was all for the church becoming more open, less formal. Hadn't she fought Ted's plan to lock the doors nightly at six p.m.? Hadn't she held out against parish purists outraged when she'd let Rex Rosser's sheepdog, Alice, lie on a back pew next to Rex?

The harsh lights hurt Merrily's eyes. There'd been no mention yet of the mobile-phone mast. Maybe Ted was thinking that if he could push the shop through without a struggle then he could slip the mast in near the end or save it for a future meeting

– one even more poorly attended than this, with its handful of delegates from local societies: the Women's Institute, the Young Farmers' Club, the tourism association. A couple of shop owners had shown up to voice mild fears about competition if the church went into the giftware business. But nothing serious, nothing likely to cause undue worry for Ted Clowes and the *pro* faction.

'I think the point is, Mr Chairman . . .' Again, it was Jenny Box, née Driscoll, one of the few with no obvious reason to be here, who came to Merrily's aid. 'The real point is that commercial enterprise would surely conflict with the sanctity and peace that the church must be allowed to provide at all times. If I want to go in and say a prayer, I may not wish to do so in front of a coachload of holidaymakers choosing picture postcards.'

And Jenny Box *did* go into the church and pray alone. Merrily had seen her several times and walked delicately past with a quiet smile, making herself casually available, in case this woman needed help. No particular response so far, and she didn't want to be thought of as courting the newest Ledwardine celeb.

The truth was that, while much of the village – especially the growing retired faction – recognized Mrs Box from daytime *lifestyle* TV or had shopped at *Vestalia*, Merrily had never even seen daytime TV, except by accident, and couldn't afford Vestalia. She was faintly embarrassed because the face of Jenny Box, from the start, had meant nothing to her.

'But . . .' Ted was looking pained. 'If you look at Hereford Cathedral, it's had a sizeable shop for years, virtually next to the nave.'

'But not *in* the nave,' Merrily said. 'And the cathedral's just a tiny bit bigger than Ledwardine church, and if you do want to pray there you can always find a quiet corner somewhere, or an empty chantry.'

'Well, if . . .' James Bull-Davies pushed fingers through his thinning hair. ' . . . If you're talking about a *quiet* place, there's always the Bull Chapel, isn't there?'

Merrily said nothing. Even she had found it hard to pray in the Bull Chapel.

Again, Mrs Box dealt with it. 'I accept it's your family's traditional resting place, Mr Chairman, but I don't think I'm alone in finding that chapel just a tiny bit sinister, with that forbidding old tomb and the effigy of the man whose eyes seem to follow you around. Sorry, I suppose that's silly of me.'

James gazed at Jenny Box, as he had several times tonight because, although he'd probably never seen her on TV either, Mrs Box was magnetic, her beauty soft and blurred under red-blonde hair just short of shoulder-length. There was very little make-up on her pale, regretful face, but even the livid lighting couldn't insult her skin. She lived in a narrow, three-storey house on the edge of the village, near the river – alone, it seemed, although there was said to be an estranged husband somewhere.

'Right, OK,' James conceded surprisingly. 'Point taken. We require a degree of separation, so I think we have to come back to Ted's suggestion of the vestry. Reasonable enough size. Not as if we're going to be selling country clothes or picnic hampers or what have you.'

'Well . . . it's a possibility.' Merrily had already thought about it; she didn't use the vestry much any more, not since the night it had been broken into. Now she kept all her clerical gear at the vicarage, and there was a cupboard in the body of the church for communion wine and stuff. 'I mean, I suppose I could spare it, but I can't speak for a future minister.'

'Not our problem,' James snapped. 'Future chap can sort him*self* out. Or herself. Be many years, anyway, before you think of moving on, I trust, vicar. Nothing to stop us sticking a couple of counters and a till in the vestry meantime, is there?'

'It'd need better lighting for a start, James. And some structural alteration, I'd guess. Costly?'

'But it's an *option*,' said James. 'At last we have an option. Thank Gord for that. We'll get it costed out, report back. Yes?' He looked at Merrily; she shrugged.

When they came out, half an hour later, without anyone having raised the possibility of installing a mobile-phone mast in the spire, Merrily wasn't entirely surprised to find Jenny Box, in a brown Barbour and a white scarf, waiting for her on the cindered forecourt.

'Look, thanks for . . .' Merrily gestured vaguely at the hall behind them. She felt short and inelegant in the old navy-blue school duffel coat that Jane had rejected as seriously uncool. 'I get a little flustered in there sometimes. I think it's the lighting, but if I turned up in sunglasses, somebody'd be putting it around that I'd been beaten up.'

Jenny Box didn't smile. Uncle Ted Clowes came over and put a patronizing hand on Merrily's shoulder. 'I think you'll find it makes a good deal of sense, my dear. Tourism's going to be very much the future of Ledwardine, we all have to accept that.'

'Not the whole of the future, I hope, Ted.'

'Well, there *is* another possibility.' He glanced warily at Jenny Box. 'But we'll talk about that again. Goodnight, ladies.'

Ted put on his hat and strolled away. A walkover, then. Merrily was aware that Jenny Box's expression had stiffened. For the first time tonight, in the thin light from the tin-shaded bulb over the doors of the village hall, she looked her probable age: forty-three, forty-four?

'Crass auld fool.' An unexpected venom thickened her accent. 'Sell his own grandmother.'

Merrily said nothing. The two of them walked away from the hall, into Church Street and up towards the square. The air glistened with moisture and the deserted village centre looked film-set romantic under a mist-ringed three-quarter moon.

'So how much are you thinking you'd need?' Mrs Box's voice had softened again without losing any of its insistence. 'For the church.'

'Well, I can't really . . .' Merrily hesitated. It was the first time she'd spoken more than superficially to this woman.

'Per year, say. How much per year, to maintain the church without the need of this tourist shop?'

It was a serious question, and there was no walking away from it. Merrily shook her head. 'I don't really know what a shop would turn over in a year.'

Mrs Box stopped on the edge of the deserted square. 'Tell me, have you asked God?'

'Sorry?'

'For the money. For the resources. Have you asked God?'

'Erm . . .'

Jenny Box smiled faintly, indicating that she wouldn't pursue it now. Directly in front of them, the small medieval building known as the Market Hall squatted on its stocky oak pillars. Mrs Box stood with her back to it, hands thrust deep into the pockets of her Barbour, a firmer, tougher proposition than she'd been in the hall.

'You were absolutely right, of course,' she said. 'Women, as a rule, aren't terribly good at preaching. Listening is what we do best. That's why women priests are so important. Women listen, and so women *receive*. I'm not talking feminist nonsense, but the time's come. Don't you feel that?'

'I think we can all receive, women *and* men,' Merrily said carefully. They were alone on the square, lit by bracket lamps projecting from gable ends. Mrs Box glanced over her shoulder.

'That man – Clowes. What he said about us all having to accept that tourism's the future, it makes me feel quite ill. Look at this place . . . it's getting like the Cotswolds – most of the people here born elsewhere, virtually all the businesses owned by outsiders.'

Merrily said nothing. Across the square, the lighted panes in the leaded windows of the Black Swan seemed as comfortably irregular as the moon-washed cobbles. She used to think of Ledwardine as an indestructible organism that ate and gradually digested change.

'Oh, I know I'm *part* of the invasion,' Jenny Box said. 'I can't help that. But when I see them trying to make this lovely old church into just another arm of the tourist industry . . . and I watch men like Clowes, who must be at least *half* local, just sitting there on their fat, complacent behinds and inviting it in, for short-term gain, I see something ancient being lost . . . and something insidious and inherently filthy creeping in. I want to go up in the tower and ring the bells and scream a warning. Don't you?'

'I don't know,' Merrily said honestly. 'In one way, I do want to get lots more people into church. I like the idea of these villages in parts of Italy and places, where the church is the natural centre of everything, people wandering in and out, hens laying under the pews. And yet . . .'

She looked up at the woman she vaguely recalled as a fashion model in the 1980s, pale and waiflike then, and a little damaged-looking, like an orphan taken in by Vivienne Westwood. Jane had said that once, when she was off school with flu, she'd seen Jenny Driscoll – newly arrived in the village then and a talking point – on some daytime chat show discussing fame, how shallow it all was. On the other hand, as Jane had pointed out, there were few aspects of modern life more shallow than daytime telly.

'I suppose you think I'm just some bored neurotic looking for a cause, to get noticed. Just say if that's what you think.'

'Oh, everybody here gets noticed. The real trick is to be anonymous.' Merrily smiled tiredly. Normally, she was invigorated by this kind of searching approach by an actual parishioner; she just didn't feel up to it tonight. 'I'm sorry, I should have got to know you better by now. I admit I haven't spent as much time in the parish as I should have, due to one thing and another.'

'Like being an exorcist,' Jenny Box said, all whispery sibilance.

'Deliverance Consultant is the preferred term these days.'

'Well, I prefer the old word. How often are you called on to exorcize people?'

'I never have.'

'*Never?*'

'Well, I've only had the job for just over a year. I've never encountered a . . . confirmable case of demonic possession.'

'But you believe it can happen?'

'Of course.' Merrily wasn't used to this. If local people ever talked about what she did outside the parish, it was never to her face.

'What about houses? You exorcize houses, do you?'

'Occasionally.'

'And would you agree,' Jenny Box asked, 'that whole communities are sometimes in need of it? Whole establishments, situations . . . whole *milieux*?'

'I'm not sure what you mean.' Merrily was thinking of last winter and the fundamentalist, Father Nicholas Ellis, who'd exorcize anything you could shake a cross at.

'Cleansing. The expulsion of evil. You probably know that the business I was in – when I was modelling – all that's pretty damn repellent to me these days. And though I'm well out of it all now, it's like when you give up some bad habit – smoking – you can't bear to be near smokers any more. You can smell them a mile off, and it's unbearably obnoxious, all the worse because it's tinged with this . . . foul desire.'

'Right.' Merrily was instinctively feeling the outside of her coat pocket, the familiar bulge made by her mobile phone . . . and the packet of Silk Cut and the Zippo.

'So coming out here was like going into detox for me. But why would I come *here*, you're asking, to this particular village, to be cleansed?'

'No, I wouldn't ask that. I try not to be nosy.'

'All right, then, why are *you* here?'

'Oh, I ask that all the time.'

Mrs Box laughed lightly. 'Vicar, tell me, have you ever had what you might call a visionary experience?' Merrily stared at her; Jenny Box raised both hands. 'I know, I know, it depends on how you'd define *visionary*. Oh, the clergy, you're so cautious these days, even the women.'

'Especially the women. We still feel we're on probation.'

Jenny Box regarded her solemnly. 'But you're the future. You must know that. Look, I'd like to discuss this and . . . some other things with you sometime . . . if you have an hour or so to spare – I mean, not now. I can see you're anxious to be off.'

'Well, it's just that my daughter—'

'No husband, though,' Mrs Box threw in quickly.

'He died. Some years ago.'

'A young widow, remarried to the Church.'

It was what people often said, and it was irritating. It began to rain again.

'Which is a wonderful thing,' Jenny Box said. 'You were . . . saved.' She smiled. 'It's hard to avoid the old clichés, isn't it?'

Merrily heard a voice calling from somewhere down Church Street.

'I'm learning all about that because I'm writing a book,' Mrs Box said. 'About some things that happened to me.'

'Oh?' No big surprise. *Jenny Box: the heartache I left behind.*

Serialized in one of the Sunday papers, a women's magazine. If it was sensational enough, if there were 'revelations'.

'*Mum!*'

Merrily turned, saw the kid running up the street. 'I'm sorry . . . that's Jane . . . my daughter.'

Jenny Box took a step back, and Merrily had a sudden powerful sense of something around this woman making small, anxious flurries in the air: disorientation, loneliness.

'I'd . . . like to hear about your book sometime.'

'It isn't finished yet. It isn't over, you see. What the book's about . . . those things aren't over. Those things have hardly begun.' Jenny Box shook her head and began to move away. Then she stopped beside one of the pillars of the market hall, turning her face to Merrily. 'You said we could all receive . . .'

'Yes.'

'Well, that . . .' She looked at Jane stumbling to a stop, shook her head with finality. 'Goodnight, Mrs Watkins.'

Pulling her scarf over her head, Jenny Box walked quickly away across the cobbles into the shadows behind the hanging lamps.

And here was Jane, the kid's face shining with rain and sweat.

'Oh *God*, Mum, I've run all the way down to the sodding hall. Tried to call you on the mobile.'

'It was switched off. Didn't want it going off in the middle of the meeting. What's the problem, flower?'

Jane said, 'Gomer.'

Merrily felt her stomach tighten. 'What's happened?' She'd been half expecting Gomer at the meeting: the only parishioner you could always count on for support against the village establishment.

'It's awf—' The kid was still struggling for breath. 'Awful.'

'*What?*' Remembering the night last January when Minnie had had her heart attack, the hospital vigil with Gomer, the final silence of the side ward.

'He came banging on the door. Didn't know where else to go. He'd been in the pub and he'd had a few pints and he didn't think he was safe to drive, so he was hoping you—'

'Where?' The rain was coming down harder. Jane had no coat, she must've gone rushing out in panic. 'Drive *where*?'

'He'd just got back from the Swan, OK, and . . . when he gets in the phone's ringing and ringing. The police'd been trying to get him for, like, ages. He was hoping you could take him, but now he's gone for his van, and he's probably way over the limit.'

'*Police?*'

'It's his yard in the Radnor Valley. His big shed. Mum, it's on fire. The shed with the diggers and the bulldozer? It's just all on fire. Gomer Parry Plant Hire . . . burning up.'

'Oh God.'

'He's gone like really manic. You know how he gets. Even if he was sober, he wouldn't be safe.'

'When was this?'

'Just a few minutes ago. He went tearing back for his van.'

'OK, he'll have to pass this way.' The village was silent – no vehicle sounds. Merrily pulled out her mobile and switched it on. 'Go back home, flower. I'll call you.'

'I'll come too.'

'No, you won't. I'll call you. Just go home and get dry. OK? I'll call.' Merrily pocketed the phone, put both hands on the kid's shoulders and pointed her at the vicarage. 'Go.'

She watched Jane walking across the empty street and into the vicarage drive, where the kid stopped and looked back.

'And bar . . . Jane, bar the door, OK?'

Merrily stepped into the road and waited.

4

A Good Name

'Sorry,' she muttered. Thorny branches in the hedge were scoring the side of the van. '*Sorry.*'

The problem was that although she could reach the pedals – just about – the driver's seat was sunken with wear and the heavy old van was hard to control on bends and steep hills when you couldn't fully see over the bonnet. Especially at night, in the intermittent rain, on these greasy country roads leading down to the Welsh border.

'Should've gone back for your own car, vicar,' Gomer murmured round his ciggy. 'I'd've waited.'

'No,' she said. 'You wouldn't.'

He said nothing. Hadn't he nearly run her down, before he'd spotted the dog collar in the headlights and braked so hard he'd stalled the engine?

Gomer Parry stalling an engine – unheard of. He'd been as close then as she'd ever seen him to coming apart. The night Minnie died, his anguish had flared publicly, just once, in a twilit street near Hereford County Hospital, before he'd subsided into bleak acceptance.

Tonight, however, there was no sign of him coming down from whatever emotional ledge he was clinging to, and the ciggy was glowing red and dangerous between his lips. He wore his cap and his old tweed jacket and, underneath that, a green sweatshirt with GOMER PARRY PLANT HIRE on it in white. This had been his nephew and business partner Nev's idea. Gomer had had two extra ones printed – a serious honour – for Jane and for Merrily, whose churchyard hedges he cut, whose ditches he cleared and not a penny charged for any of it. He even came to church, maybe every other Sunday. But plant hire was Gomer Parry's religion.

'They don't know how it started?'

Had she asked him this before? There were only so many things you could say en route to the ruins of a man's whole identity.

'If they knowed, they wasn't sayin'. You know what cops is like. Plus, nobody seen it at all till the whole shed was well alight. Four fire engines called out. *That* big.'

Poor Gomer, hunched gnomelike on the edge of the passenger seat, his wire-rimmed bottle glasses opaque in the dimness of the van. Merrily guessed that what Gomer and Nev did probably didn't even qualify as plant hire in the strictest sense. Mostly, they dug field drains and soakaways for septic tanks. They had two tractors, a lorry, a bulldozer and a couple of diggers, Gwynneth and Muriel, stored in a former aircraft shed, twenty minutes away, near a long-disused airstrip just across the Welsh border. Where the fire was happening.

'What about insurance, Gomer?'

'Oh, we're insured, sure t'be. But that en't the point, is it, vicar?'

'No. I guess not.' A couple of years ago, Gomer had been pressed by Minnie into semi-retirement and he'd let Nev more or less take over the business. But after Minnie's death, he'd gone grimly back, full-time. Plant hire: now it was all he had left.

'En't the point at all,' Gomer said sadly. They were held up by temporary traffic lights at roadworks on the edge of Kington town centre.

'Does Nev know?'

'Ah, he'll still be out on the bloody piss – apologies, vicar. Nobody knowed which pub the bugger was in.'

Unlike his nephew, Gomer didn't drink much at all these days. But earlier tonight, it seemed, he'd arranged to see a certain bloke in the Black Swan, about some job or other, and this particular bloke was a big boozer, and Gomer had felt obliged to keep up with him. '*Mabbe four pints, vicar,*' he'd confessed, surrendering the wheel. '*Tonight of all bloody nights.*'

When Jane had run up to Merrily on the square and said, '*It's Gomer,*' her first thought had been that he'd had a stroke or a heart attack like Minnie, who would have loved to mind the souvenir shop in the church – nobody better, except possibly Miss Lucy Devenish who'd kept Ledwardine Lore. Both of them dead now. All the things that might have been. Everything changing before you were ready, like pages of a favourite book ripped out to reveal a different story and new characters you were supposed to relate to instantly, the old ones suddenly gone for ever.

The traffic lights changed at last, and Merrily drove through the damp and empty small town and out of England.

Most of the leaves around here must have come down in last week's high winds. Between the stripped trees, you could see blue lights turning in the Radnor Valley below, beating at the mist, as though the night itself was strobing. No visible flames, only these gaseous blue lights and the off-white, misshapen moon bobbing in the mist over the border hills.

'Take a left by yere, vicar.' At the sight of the emergency beacons, Gomer's voice had gone flat. 'And keep slow.'

Merrily turned into a minor road, a fenced field on one side – stoical sheep-eyes in the headlights – and what looked like a quarry on the other. She drove on, in low gear, for about two hundred yards before the headlamps found a high wire fence and two metal wire-meshed gates, both hanging open. A police car, engine running, blue beacon revolving, was blocking the entrance. When Merrily wound down her window, there was the throb of other motors, a haze of headlights and a smell that filled up the van like poison gas: acrid, hostile.

A policeman walked over. 'Gomer.' And then he saw it was a woman behind the wheel. 'Oh.'

Gomer was shouldering open the passenger door. 'Couldn't bring that torch from under the dash, could you, vicar? Your side.'

The policeman said, 'You've brought the *vicar*?'

'Little vicar brought *me*, Robbie.'

The policeman sniffed the air around Gomer and nodded, getting the message. Gomer would know most of the coppers around here, and their dads and grandads, too.

Merrily found the torch and climbed out of the van. Her legs felt weak. She'd never been to Gomer's depot before. Looking around for the famous former aircraft shed, she saw only the harsh headlights of fire appliances and some other vehicles, and puddles swirling with beacon blue. A couple of firefighters were moving slowly around with hoses, amid eddies of smoke. They seemed to be spraying the earth, as if they were trying to stimulate growth, and she realized, shocked, that this was because much of the building must have fallen in around its contents. No flames were left anywhere; the firemen were just damping down, to make sure it didn't reignite.

She saw the husk of a tractor or maybe a bulldozer, its windows all gone. Gomer spat his cigarette into a pool of rainbowed water and walked away from the policeman towards a pyramid of twisted galvanized roof-panels, about ten feet high and wreathed in stinking smoke. Merrily started to follow him, then gagged on a mouthful of the searing air – no autumn-bonfire scents here; this was chemical, astringent. She doubled up, coughing. Gomer looked back; she waved him on, pulling out some tissues to mop her flooded eyes.

When she was over it, she could see him talking to two coppers and a senior-looking fireman inside a steamy mesh of headlamp beams. There were other people around, another blue light. She straightened up, began to move towards them, and another fireman bawled at her.

'Stay *back*!'

'OK . . .' Putting up her hands, backing off. The three-quarter moon gleamed off the flank of a digger lying tragically askew, like a great shirehorse with a broken neck.

Gwynneth, or Muriel. Merrily felt close to tears. She saw the policemen leading Gomer back towards the van, the senior fireman following them, snapping questions.

' . . . Oil tanks? Diesel?'

'Tank was inside,' Gomer said. 'Locked up.'

'Just the one?'

'Ar. Locked up. Good locks.'

'Who else had keys, Gomer?' An older policeman: grey moustache and sergeant's stripes.

'*Nobody* else had bloody keys, Cliff! Me and Nev, just me and Nev. You saying some bastard let hisself in? 'Cause you'd need a bloody oxyacetylene torch to break in yere, take it from me.'

'Far's I can gather, Gomer, there was no sign of a break-in when the fire brigade got here. No doors hanging open, nothing like that, nothing obvious. However—'

'When was this, Cliff?'

'Two hours ago, round about. It was well away by then.'

''Cause if you boys reckons this was done deliberate –' Gomer turned to the older policeman, a forefinger waving '– then I can give you a name, straight off.'

'Gomer, listen, we en't saying nothing like that at this stage.'

'A bloody *good* name, Cliff.'

Merrily blinked, confused. How could he possibly give them a name? Was there something she didn't know about, something Gomer hadn't told her? It went quieter suddenly, and she realized the hoses had been turned off.

'Gomer, listen to me,' Cliff said quietly, 'before you start throwing accusations around . . . you seen Nev tonight?'

'Eh?'

'*Nev.*'

'I never sees Nev at night.' Gomer calmed himself down, bringing out his cigarette tin. 'All right to smoke, is it?'

'Rather you didn't,' the fireman said.

The younger copper, Robbie, put a hand over Gomer's tin. 'Because we can't find him, see.'

'He lives at Presteigne. Lot of pubs in Presteigne. You go round the bloody pubs, you'll find him, all right.'

'We know all that,' Robbie said. 'We know Nev's been drinking heavy lately. Including tonight.'

'Depends what you means by heavy,' Gomer said guardedly.

'The thing . . .' The sergeant, Cliff, hesitated. 'The thing is, Gomer . . . Nev got hisself thrown out of the Royal Oak earlier on. Been on the beer, gets into a barney with Clem Morris's boy, Jordan, on account of Jordan thinks Nev's after his girlfriend. Something and nothing, as usual, but it all gets overheated, and we get sent along to calm things down. And we strongly suggested to Nev that he oughter go home directly and sleep it off.'

'Stupid fat bastard,' Gomer said.

'Only, we know Nev didn't go home, see, or he didn't *stay* home, because when we goes to his flat over the paper shop, after the fire was reported, Nev en't there.'

'What you saying?' Gomer snapped a glance over his shoulder towards the pyramid of smoking debris, his fists clenching. Merrily saw that, behind the collapsed shed, a small building was still standing, probably because it was made of concrete blocks. In the distance, below the moon, she could see a conifered hillside, the view of which the aircraft shed must once have concealed.

'What we want to ask you, Gomer,' Cliff said, gently enough to make Merrily very worried, 'is where might Nev've gone? A mate's . . . a girlfriend's?'

'What you saying?' Gomer turned slowly, the blue light flaring in his glasses. 'What you bloody *saying*, Cliff Morgan?'

Some more people were gathering around, firemen with their helmets off, like a sign of respect. Gomer suddenly spun away and pushed through them, disappearing into a hollow of darkness beyond the milky confluence of vehicle lights.

Merrily found him standing outside the concrete building. The air smelled of oil and charred wood. She felt slightly sick. From behind, she heard Cliff saying wearily, 'Don't let the little bugger go in, for Christ's sake.'

'Lend me the torch, vicar.'

But it was only holding tight to the heavy, rubberized flashlight that kept Merrily's hands from shaking. Drawing a long breath, she shone the light inside the building to where the water was still an inch deep, from the damping-down. And then the beam was all over the place as she pushed her sleeve into her face because of what the breath had brought in with it.

She started to cough again. Amid the diesel vapour and the wet wood-ash was an odour you could taste. The torch beam found its own way down scorched plasterboard walls, over a dented grey metal desk, a wooden chair that now looked like it was made of hollow columns of ash. The remains of a wooden partition hung in grotesquely ornate strands, like the rood screen in some abandoned church.

Biting down on her lip, Merrily shone the light back onto Gomer, standing there with his cap gone and his white hair springing up, an unlit roll-up between his teeth. As she watched, he seemed to sag, as if what she saw was just his clothes, and the living essence of Gomer was deflating inside them. She let the beam follow his gaze to what had been a mattress, reduced now to lumps of scorched fabric and exposed springs.

And *Oh God. Oh, sweet Jesus.* Like a prayer opening up.

Was that what she was supposed to do at this moment – offer up a prayer for what lay on the mattress, for the soul that had vacated the blistered, split skin, the flesh cooked in blue denim and left to congeal, the legs burned back to the bone, the feet fused into the Doc Martens by their melted rubber soles?

Merrily's stomach lurched

Hands gripped her shoulders. Gomer was alive again and turning her around, snatching the torch from her, but even when she was away from the smell, standing in a puddle, letting the cold water seep into her shoes, she was still seeing the spindle of an arm thrown protectively across the swollen, football face so that all you could make out underneath was the grimace of teeth.

She heard Gomer saying hoarsely to Cliff, 'You want that name? You want the name now, boy?'

5

Denial of the Obvious

It was raining again, the moon hidden. Cliff Morgan said, 'I know how hard this is, so if you're not one hundred per cent certain then you should say so.' His grey moustache covered most of his lips and his eyes suggested that he was more than ready for retirement. 'And frankly, Gomer, I don't see how you *can* be certain. I'm sorry. I think this is going to be a dentist job.'

He offered them shelter in the police car, holding open one of the back doors, but Gomer stood defiantly in the rain, rubbing hard at his glasses without taking them off. 'You bloody write this down,' he was insisting, as if he hadn't heard anything Cliff had said to him. 'You get it wrote down official, boy. I wannit in the report, black and white.'

'I en't writing anything down just now, Gomer. I think you're very much in shock.' Cliff looked at Merrily. 'Mrs Watkins, right?'

She nodded. She didn't think she'd seen him before, but he seemed to recognize her. Dyfed-Powys Police; maybe one of the cops involved in the Old Hindwell conflict last winter.

'Gomer been with you all night, has he?'

Merrily was startled. 'What's that mean?'

'I'm just pre-empting other people's questions, Mrs Watkins. People who don't know him as well as I know him.'

'Right,' she said. 'Of course. Sorry.' When a building on its own in the middle of the countryside got burned down at night, police inquiries were always going to start with the owner.

'At this moment, it's a suspicious death, Reverend. CID have been informed, the pathologist sent for, the scene-of-crime people. We don't yet know whether we've *got* a crime, but procedures are stricter now. Infantrymen like us, we're not allowed to touch anything any more. We're not clever enough, see.'

'All the same, you've obviously seen this . . . kind of thing before. Do you think . . . I mean, do you think he was dead before the fire?' She swallowed; she was still feeling sick, was somehow still smelling that awful smell – like roast pork – as though grease and fumes were in her hair. She knew why Gomer didn't want to come out of the rain.

The senior fireman said, 'I would *think* . . . although he must've been close to the seat of the fire, I would say he was overcome with smoke before it got to him. I don't think he would have suffered, if that's what you're asking.' He turned to Gomer. 'That mattress, Mr Parry – has that always been in the back room there?'

'Ar.' Gomer had his tin open and his fingers were at work on a new ciggy whether he knew it or not. 'Boy used to sleep there sometimes when things was bad between him and Kayleigh.'

'And sometimes not on his own, what I heard,' Cliff said.

'Mabbe. Her once locked him out best part of a week. Turned a blind eye, I did. He had enough problems back then. I never figured he was still kipping yere, mind. Mabbe there'd be nights when he's walking into the ole flat, and it just comes down on him that her'd gone and left him for a biker and a bloody ole squat in Cornwall. And he just . . . he couldn't stay there.'

Gomer stopped rolling the paper and tobacco, as if his fingers had gone numb, and he stared at the ground. Merrily wondered how often, since last January, he'd walked into his own bungalow and experienced that same cold dismay.

'But if you was thinking . . .' Gomer looked up at Cliff. 'If you was thinking that mabbe Nev Parry come in yere tonight pissed out of his head, and set all this off by accident or bloody carelessness, you can forget it now, boy.'

'Not my job to decide, Gomer.'

''Cause I'm giving you this other name now, and don't you forget it.'

'Gomer—'

'Roddy Lodge,' Gomer said. 'Roddy Lodge, plant-hire cowboy from up by Ross. You go over there and you talk to that bastard about this. Now. Tonight. 'Fore he can wash the bloody oil off his clothes. Roddy Lodge. You write that down.'

Cliff wasn't writing anything down. Another car was pulling in behind the police car and Gomer's van. 'CID, I do believe,' the younger copper, Robbie, said. 'Just in time for breakfast.'

Merrily put a hand over her mouth.

What you said to the bereaved, usually in hospitals, was something like, *Would you like me to say a prayer? Would you like us to pray together?*

It was not always appropriate.

Merrily drove Gomer's van for three or four miles before pulling into a lay-by, a mile or so over the hill from Kington Cemetery. Overhanging trees were dripping on to the bonnet, an all-night bulb was glowing outside a cottage across the empty road. As she killed the engine, a barn owl glided low, almost at windscreen level, seemed almost to hover for moment.

'Why've you stopped, vicar?' It was the first time Gomer had asked a question since they'd left the yard. He'd sat stiff-backed in the passenger seat, staring through his glasses and the windscreen.

'Ought to ring Jane,' she said.

'Her'll be in bed.'

'I don't think so, Gomer, somehow.'

'You gonner tell her?'

'I think so.'

She fumbled for her phone. Nev: she hadn't really known him. Yet she had.

No problem, vicar, I'll get Nev to do it, see . . .

That bloody Nev . . . digged a whole trench, got called away, come back and filled it in and forgot he en't put the bloody pipes down . . .

Daft bugger. Bloody sweatshirts. Never live it down. Gotter laugh, though. You gotter laugh . . .

Be meeting Nev on the site at eight – say this for the boy, no matter what he's put away the night before, he en't never late . . .

Probably because Nev would have been sleeping on the premises.

There was nobody for them to tell immediately about Nev. His mum and dad – Gomer's elder brother and his wife – were both dead. His ex-wife, Kayleigh, was presumably still in a squat in Cornwall with a biker. And the police had advised Gomer not to inform anyone more peripheral until there was confirmation.

Dentist job.

The quizzing of Gomer by a dishevelled detective constable had been brief and routine; they'd want to talk to him again tomorrow when they knew more. This time he hadn't mentioned Roddy Lodge, whoever *he* was . . . perhaps just a name thrown up by the shock, a convenient focus for Gomer's uncomprehending anguish, his denial of the obvious.

Merrily called up the vicarage number and was starting to get anxious when it rang six times before Jane picked up.

'Sorry.' The kid sounded muzzy. 'Think I kind of fell asleep in the chair.' A pause. 'It's bad, isn't it?'

Merrily told her most of it. No point in dressing it up. Jane was silent for a while, then she said, her voice pitched high and querulous, 'Couldn't it be like a tramp or something? I know that's just as like— just as bad for *somebody*, but it . . .'

'We have to wait for official confirmation, flower.'

'I just like *knew* there'd be something like this. It's that kind of year – anything that could possibly be bad is always worse. Starting with Minnie . . . What will you do now?'

'Come home, I suppose.'

'Mum . . .' Another pause as the wider implications sank in. 'This is going to screw him up completely, isn't it? It's not like he can revive that business on his own, not at his age. But if he doesn't, he won't know what to do with himself. He'll just fade into—'

'We won't let that happen,' Merrily said quickly. 'Go to bed this time, flower, or you won't be fit for school.'

'It's half-term.'

'Of course it is.'

'Holiday time,' Jane said. 'What fun.'

Merrily had been holding the phone tight to her ear and didn't think Gomer had heard any of Jane's side of the conversation at all. But when she pocketed the mobile and started the van's engine, he turned to her, green dashboard lights reflected in his glasses. Whatever small amount of light was available, Gomer's glasses always seemed to reflect it.

'En't gonner pack in, vicar. En't gonner walk away.'

'Never thought you would.'

'Gotter put it all back together. Somehow.'

'Yes.'

'Kind of memorial would that be for the boy, the business went down the toilet?'

'We should talk about that.'

'Put me outer the picture,' Gomer said. 'It's what he wanted.'

'Who?'

'Roddy Lodge.'

'Well, we can talk about that, too.' Merrily let out the clutch too quickly – the van lurched and the engine stalled. 'When we've got clearer heads. When we're not so—'

'You're bloody well fobbin' me off, ennit?'

'No, I'm not, but . . .'

'Poor ole bloody Parry! Shock of it turned his mind, done his ole brain in! Won't face up to the truth: the boy had a drink problem. Comes in out of his bloody head, sets light to the mattress. Always been a liability. Accident waitin' to happen. That's what they're gonner say, ennit?'

'No.' Merrily restarted the engine. 'No, they're not. Everybody liked Nev. Everybody who knew him.'

'Ar. Well, that's true. That's dead right. But it weren't Nev he was after. Me he wanted to get at, see. Poor bloody Nev, he just got in the way.'

'Gomer—'

'Can't back away from this, vicar. Gotter take my piece o' the blame. I never thought, see. Even after what I yeard in the Swan tonight, I never thought anybody in his right mind would . . .' He shook his head. 'But he *en't*, see. That's the point. En't in his right mind. I never really reckoned on that.'

It was something about his voice this time. And the realization that he must have been going over this, in a kind of mental mist, all the time she'd been talking at him. Merrily switched off the engine and then the lights, watching the green glow fade from Gomer's bottle glasses.

She slid a hand under her hair, undid her dog collar, pulled it off and put it on top of the dashboard.

She lit a cigarette.

'All right,' she said. 'Who's Roddy Lodge?'

6

Demonizing Roddy

Gomer borrowed Merrily's mobile and rang his home number. He wanted her to hear a message on his machine, which, if you didn't use the skip signal, would relay everything recorded since you last wound back the tape. He sat there for about four minutes with the mobile at his ear before thrusting it back at her.

'Listen . . .'

The moon was back in the sky, two of them back in Gomer's glasses: animation.

Merrily listened.

'*Mr Parry, it's Lisa Pawson. I'm back in London. Listen, I'm afraid I've had Lodge on the phone . . .*'

Private drainage: for serious country-dwellers there was no other kind; you had a septic tank, and when the smell got too bad you had it emptied. For some incoming city types, however, having to take responsibility for your own waste could be a perpetual source of fear. What if it overflowed? What if it all started oozing back up your lavatory, in the middle of a dinner party?

It was the fear of sewage that kept firms like the Birmingham-based Efflapure in business. After meeting Lisa Pawson, Gomer had spent a couple of hours on Sunday evening making inquiries about the firm. Apparently, an Efflapure was an overpriced, over-complicated, high-maintenance piece of junk that was supposed to turn your liquid waste into something you could safely add to your whisky. It would be smoothly and expensively installed for you by any one of a number of teams of so-called skilled sub-contractors all over the country.

Mostly cowboys, Gomer said. Like Roddy Lodge, of down by Ross-on-Wye.

' . . . *And somehow, he knew you'd been to see me. It was awful. I really think he must be slightly off his head. He insists there's absolutely nothing wrong with his positioning of the Efflapure and that you and the surveyor are "in it together", trying to discredit him. Naturally, I don't believe a word of this . . . but please will you call me as soon as you return.*'

Bleep.

Merrily passed the phone back to Gomer. 'How on earth did this Lodge know you'd been to see the woman?'

'Somebody seen the van, sure t'be.' Gomer put the mobile to his left ear and carried on listening to the sequence of messages. 'No big surprise. It's so near the main road, that place. Scores of motors going past, anybody could've seen me, even Roddy Lodge hisself. Anyway, vicar, shouldn't surprise *you* how fast word d'get around in this county.'

'No. I suppose not.'

'Also, see, there's a lot o' folk . . .' His voice faded; she saw the moons beginning to shake in his glasses.

'What's wrong?'

Gomer handed her the mobile again. He took off his glasses, turned away.

' . . . *never woulder believed it, Gomer. Wanted one and a half mile of track clearin', right up to the top of the Garth, and would we do it for two hundred? Bloody hell, I says, there's at least five days' work there, Mr Pugh!*'

Nev.

'*I says he could argue it out with you, he wanted to. So if you hears from Frankie Pugh, that's what it's about, all right?*'

Bleep.

Gomer coughed and looked out through the windscreen. Now that the sky had cleared again, you could see the lights of Eardisley village. Merrily put a hand on his arm. He'd become almost his old self, telling her about Efflapure and Roddy Lodge.

Now Mrs Pawson's angsty voice was back in her ear.

' . . . *I'm sorry, this is getting ridiculous. He's just phoned again.*'

This time he says he doesn't want any trouble and, while he isn't admitting that it was wrongly positioned, he says he's now prepared to come and take it away and return our money in full. In fact he . . . he was absolutely insisting that he should be the one to take it away. I'm sorry, one moment . . .'

Muted voices: Mrs Pawson in hurried conversation with someone in the room. Then she was back.

'My husband agrees that no way should that man be allowed back on the premises, so I'm hoping that you're going to be able to keep to the schedule and remove the . . . appliance tomorrow, as we arranged. I propose to telephone Lodge and tell him that you'll be handling everything. If there's a problem, please call me as soon as you can. Thank you, Mr Parry.'

Bleep.

Merrily lowered the phone. 'Both these calls were this morning?'

'Last one 'bout two this afternoon, I reckon,' Gomer said. 'No problem about lifting the unit. Me and Nev, we was gonner go over there first thing. But I still wanted to call her back, see. Some'ing puzzling me – why didn't her take him up on this offer to shift the thing hisself? Save 'em paying me to do it. Save me trying to flog it for 'em second-hand. Didn't make no sense.'

'Unless she wasn't convinced Lodge *would* give them their money back.'

Gomer shook his head. 'More'n that.'

'What did she say when you called her back?'

'Her wasn't in. So after tea I gets on the phone to young Darren Booth – that's the local surveyor called me in in the first place – and Darren . . . well, you ever met Darren, you'd know he's terrible loud – rugby club, male-voice choir, that's Darren. But today, the boy's gone dead quiet on me. "Gomer," he says, "my advice is, leave it a while. Let it lie. Likely her'll change her mind, you know what these Londoners is like." Now is that funny, or what, vicar?'

'It's odd.'

'Ar. "What kind of ole wallop is this, Darren?" I says. He says, "He en't right, that's all." '

'Lodge?'

' "En't stable," Darren says. "Very protective of his business," he says. And wouldn't say n'more. Comes on about how he has a hurgent appointment, rings off. Soon as I puts the phone down, it rings again. Voice goes, "Gomer Parry?" I says, "Ar, that's me." Voice says, "We don't like the – pardon my French, vicar – we don't like the fuckin' Welsh . . . we don't like the fuckin' Welsh pinchin' our business. You're gettin' a warnin' tonight. You comes south of Hereford, you're finished, Gomer Parry, you're a dead man." Then the line cuts off.'

'That was him – Lodge?'

'Held back his number, so I looks him up in the phone book, calls the number and nobody picks up. I reckon he wasn't calling from home, see – that's how it seems to me now. I reckon he was on a bloody mobile from down by my bloody depot, figuring out how he was gonner torch it. *You're gettin' a warnin' tonight* – how much clearer you wannit?'

Merrily sighed. 'If he was on a mobile, it might not be that easy to trace the call. And unless you have it on tape . . .'

'Course, I din't think that much about it – only made me more determined to do the job. Anyway, a bit later, I was gonner go to the parish meeting, thinking you might be in need of a spot of back-up, see, and I'm going across the square when Jumbo Humphries rolls up in his Caddy, says how about a quick one in the Swan, and I'm figuring if anybody know about Lodge it'll be him, so—'

'Jumbo?'

'Humphries. Drives this ole Caddy?'

'Ah.' Merrily got out another cigarette. 'I did notice this big, long American car on the square.'

'That was him. Bloody ole thing that is, vicar – does about eleven miles a gallon on a long run. You en't come across Jumbo? Got this place the other side o' Talgarth – second-hand motors, stock fencing, animal feed, newspapers. And a snack bar. Harrods, they calls it.'

Merrily smiled and thumbed the Zippo, illuminating Gomer's face. Seeing what might be small tear marks, she lit her cigarette quickly and put out the flame.

'And also a private investigator,' Gomer said.

'You're kidding.'

Gomer sniffed. 'En't that bloody brilliant, tell the truth, but he's cheap. Checks out stuff for farmers, mostly. Stuff the NFU won't do for free. Spyin' on neighbours in feuds . . . land disputes, stock-thievin'. Goes around with a video camera. Mickey Mouse operation, you ask me, but Jumbo, he thinks he's bloody Humphrey Bogart.'

'Hang on, this is the man you were keeping pace with on drinks? You and he each drank four pints in the Swan and then he drove off in this huge, conspicuous American limo?'

'Charmed life,' Gomer said. 'Plus he do weigh over twenty stone. Reckons it don't affect him the same.' He paused. 'Come to think of it, he had a couple of whiskies as well. We had a good ole chat – catchin' up, you know. And he told me a good bit about Lodge.'

'Oh,' Merrily said.

It was after midnight now and she was cold and tired. But Gomer was sounding increasingly focused and rational, and that was good. And if he needed to talk, well, women were good at listening – who said that? Never mind. Merrily smoked and listened.

It had been a rare case for Jumbo Humphries, the one that brought him up against Roddy Lodge. Probably routine for city private eyes, Gomer said, but rare for Jumbo: divorce.

What he'd previously failed to mention about Roddy was the boy's legendary success with women. Gomer said he'd found this hard to believe: flash bastard, but not much to look at. Anyway, Jumbo Humphries had been retained by a farmer from down near Welsh Newton, who'd employed Roddy for field-drain work and come to regret it big time.

First off: tools, equipment. Things disappearing – a hay-fork, a stainless steel spade – whenever Roddy had been. Which he couldn't believe at first, this farmer, as he knew the Lodge family: honest, straight, religious – Baptists. Couldn't believe it was down to Roddy, this petty thieving, so he didn't say anything.

And then, a couple of weeks after Lodge had finished the job and left, the farmer got word in the pub that his wife, who seemed to have made a lot of extra shopping trips lately, had been seen getting out of a white van in a lay-by where her own car was parked. When the shopping trips continued to increase, the farmer hired Jumbo Humphries to follow the wife.

Merrily found it hard to imagine how a twenty-stone man in a Cadillac was going to operate undercover in the vicinity of sparsely populated Welsh Newton, and this turned out to be a valid point. Although Jumbo Humphries had used one of the Land Rovers from his used-vehicle lot to follow the farmer's wife one afternoon to a disused quarry, where a man was indeed waiting in a white van, he evidently had, at some stage, been spotted.

'The van man – this is Lodge, right?' Gomer said. 'Jumbo recognizes him soon as he seen the dark glasses. So he parks out of sight – he thinks – on the edge of this quarry, gets out his video camera, starts creeping up on the van, figuring he might film 'em through the back window, get his evidence. Then . . .'

Gomer got out a roll-up, and Merrily lit it for him, noticing his hands were a long way from steady. He had two good drags before continuing.

'Then just as he comes around the side o' the van . . . bloody thing starts up, see. Spins round, comes after Jumbo – big empty space this is, the ole quarry yard – and Jumbo's running for his bloody life. Van's coming straight at him, near takes his foot off, and Jumbo, he stumbles and drops the camera. Van runs over it. Four hundred quids' worth of camera!'

'Occupational hazard, I suppose, for private eyes,' Merrily said.

'Not round these parts it en't. But there was more to come, see. Lodge knowed Jumbo. Everybody does. He knowed where to find him, where he goes, where he drinks. That night, Jumbo comes out the pub at Llyswen, just on closing time, finds all four of the Caddy's tyres slashed. Had to call a taxi to get home, come back with a low-loader next day to pick up the ole Caddy.' He looked at Merrily expectantly. 'See?'

'Well . . . Gomer, it's one thing running over a camera and slashing four tyres. I mean, it's *bad* . . . But a major arson attack on a competitor's yard involving . . . loss of life . . .'

'Vicar, you yeard what that woman said on the phone. And Darren. And *You're gettin' a warnin' tonight.*'

'How did Jumbo know that it really was Lodge who slashed his tyres? Could've been pure coincidence, couldn't it?'

Gomer snorted. 'Put it together, vicar. Darren says he en't stable. Somebody tells Lodge Gomer Parry Plant Hire's been on his patch, Lodge goes straight round there and leans on Darren. Then he's on the phone trying to put the frighteners on Mrs Pawson, only she's in London . . .'

'Didn't Jumbo take it any further?'

'Vicar, we en't talkin' about bloody Peter Marlowe yere. No, he didn't take it no further. He backed off. What he says to me, he says, "Mess with Lodge, Gomer, you en't dealin' with a normal human being n'more." '

'In what way?'

'Mental, vicar. Lost it, blown it. Works on his own all night sometimes – been witnessed. Fires from the bloody hip when he feels threatened. And he en't scared what he does. Feels he's . . . nobody can touch him.'

'Invulnerable.'

'Ar. Met that type a few times.'

Gomer, you *are that type*, Merrily thought dismally.

' "You're pushin' seventy, Gomer," Jumbo says, "and Roddy Lodge en't even forty. Don't be a bloody hero." '

'That was tonight?'

'In the Swan.'

'Look . . .' Merrily sensed his absolute certainty and turned to face him, an arm around the wheel. 'I accept that the guy's erratic, possibly a little unhinged. I realize you were right to tell the police, and I think you should tell them again tomorrow. *I'*ll tell them.' She turned the key in the ignition. 'Tomorrow, though. Let's just . . . go home now.'

She let out the clutch and the van lurched into the empty road. Gomer was silent for a while. Merrily considered the possibility that, in his state of desolation, he was simply demonizing Roddy Lodge. What little evidence there was still pointed at poor Nev.

'He knows they en't there, see,' Gomer said after a couple of minutes. 'These Pawsons. Knows they en't there 'cept weekends. Plus, he likely knowed we was coming to take out this Efflapure come the morning. Her said her was gonner tell him, right?'

'Sorry . . . what are you getting at?'

'Suppose he was plannin' to go for that tank hisself, mean-time?'

'Gomer, for . . . Why would he do that?'

'Keep his good name, ennit? Small county, vicar. Man like that couldn't live with folk knowin' Gomer Parry Plant Hire had come and took away his fancy tank on account he'd put it in the wrong place and it weren't needed anyway. Plus, also – I just figured this – we'd have one to look at, then, wouldn't we? We'd all know what a piece of ole junk it was. Suppose he was makin' sure we couldn't do that job at all, by torchin' the shed, destroyin' the gear? Listen, I en't sayin' he knowed Nev was in there. I en't sayin' that . . . yet.'

'Gomer, I know this has been a . . . an unimaginably awful thing to happen, but is that even vaguely—?'

'Meanwhile he comes for the Efflapure hisself under cover of dark, just to be sure. Knowing he got the place to hisself . . .'

'Is that entirely rational?'

'He en't a rational man, vicar. If he's done the job tonight, if he's been and took the Efflapure, that's evidence.'

'Possibly. If the Pawsons stick to their story.'

'Don't matter if they don't, vicar, we got it on tape on the machine.'

'Yes. I suppose you have.' Merrily drove slowly into Eardisley, the first village on the black-and-white tourist trail which ended up eventually in Ledwardine. At night – all dark oak, whitewash and shadows – the village shed centuries and the car-dealer's showroom right in the centre looked surreal.

'Seventeen, mabbe eighteen,' Gomer said. 'No more'n twenty.'

'What?'

'Miles.'

Merrily sighed. 'To this Pawson place, right?'

'No traffic in Hereford, mind. Say half an hour, max?'

'And what are we going to do if we find out he *has* taken the tank?'

'Vicar, we'll know.' The two moons were clear and sharp in Gomer's glasses. 'We'll bloody *know*.'

7

Legs Off Spiders

So this was what they called The Hour of the Wolf. Something like that.

The dark night of the soul. The time of being transfixed by this acute, piercing awareness of the total pointlessness of everything – and of an utter, mindless, universal cruelty.

Jane had lain awake for nearly an hour, with Ethel the black cat on the bed beside her and real life hanging over her like this huge, leaden pendulum swinging slowly from side to side in the darkness.

You might as well just lie here for ever because, if you sat up at the wrong time, the lead weight – which you were never going to see coming – would suddenly smash you down again with sickening force.

This was what happened. This was the great, almighty secret of everything.

The moon – the once-beloved moon – made fitful appearances amid smoky cloud in the attic window, turning the coloured squares between the timber framing of the Mondrian walls into variations of grey. Everything was variations of grey.

Jane felt suddenly almost breathless with horror . . . with the thought that this – where her life was now – could actually be as good as it was ever going to get. Felt aglow inside with this bitter rage – the understanding that, as you got older and your body got weaker, the lead weight would smash you harder and more frequently until you couldn't get up any more.

The way it was hammering Gomer Parry, who was one of the kindest, most actually decent people Jane had ever known, like a grandad to her now.

Because Gomer was getting *old*, and *old* people got ill and they got mugged – some universal law setting them up for this, the law that said: *it's always going to get worse.* It was as if she'd never fully realized this painfully simple fact of life.

Made her mad as hell at Mum, this smart, still-attractive woman devoting most of her creative essence to the totally pointless adoration of something which, if it existed at all, existed only to *treat us like shit!*

Jane sprang up in bed, switching on the wall light, plucking the pay-as-you-talk from the bedside beanbag. She leaned back against the headboard, switching on the phone, punching out Eirion's mobile number. OK, totally uncivilized time to ring anybody, especially the guy you were supposed to be in love in, but he'd have switched off his phone by now, so it wouldn't matter; she'd just dump something into his voice-mail. Had to say something about this, and couldn't call Mum without sounding like the little girl all alone in the big, dark vicarage.

'Hello, Jane,' Eirion said.

Oh sh—! She nearly stabbed the *no* button. 'Jesus, Irene, I am so *sorry* – I don't know what I'm doing. Like, why isn't your phone switched off? It's nearly one a.m.' She reached up in a panic and snapped off the light, as though he could somehow see her with her hair all over the place and her eyes all puffy. 'How did you know it was me?'

'Because,' Eirion said patiently, 'of the solemn pact we made that we would always leave our phones switched on at night, so that if one of us was in crisis and needed to talk . . .'

Jane swallowed. 'Oh.'

'We remember now, do we?'

'I didn't think we meant it.'

'Obviously one of us didn't.'

She started to cry. 'I'm sorry, Irene. I'm truly sorry. I'm the worst kind of bitch that ever—'

'What's wrong? You been listening to that Eels album again?'

'It doesn't matter,' Jane said. 'It was very stupid of me. I'll call you tomorrow.'

'Jane . . .' Eirion's soft Welsh voice sounded like it was weighted with all the sorrow of his ancestors. 'If you hang up on me now, I may have to steal my stepmother's BMW again and drive thirty miles to quench my overwhelming desire to strangle you very slowly.'

'All right.' Jane sniffed hard. 'You asked for this, right? Big question: am I the only person of my age ever to realize that God, if God exists, is in fact some enormous, moronic, cosmic . . . *infant* who just, like, *sits* there, pulling the legs off spiders?'

Eirion thought about it for some time.

'Probably not,' he said.

Jane said, 'Is there a longer answer?'

'There undoubtedly has to be a longer answer, *cariad*, and probably a good reason why that concept is theologically unsound. Just don't ask me what it is without giving me some kind of notice.'

'And you're *really* proposing to go to university next year?'

'But not to read theology.'

'Theology's shit, anyway. I speak from insider knowledge.'

'Jane, just tell me what's wrong, could you do that? What's happened?'

'How do you know something's happened?'

'Because you didn't ask me if I was naked.'

'Right,' Jane said.

'That was a joke.'

'I know.'

'I'm not, anyway.'

'Tonight, I don't think I even care,' Jane said.

And she told him why she was alone in the vicarage at one a.m.

It evidently knocked him back. He didn't seem to know how to react. He knew Gomer; she couldn't remember if he'd met Nev. 'Shit,' he said. 'Oh bloody hell, that's . . . The poor guy. Shit.'

'Like, consider, OK? Nev. Consider that this guy was just put here – this human being was created – to be a digger driver . . . to live in the same valley all his life . . . to become over-weight . . . to have a very bad marriage, to . . . to get humiliated, get drunk . . . and then get fucking *burned to death*. That's it! I mean, that's *it*, Irene – The Nev Parry Story. The whole incarnation! What was *that* about? What was it supposed to teach him? How is it going to help refine his immortal soul? And like don't give me any of that Welsh-chapel bollocks about redemption through endless suffering.'

'I don't know,' Eirion said soberly. 'Maybe it's not something we're permitted to understand.'

'Yeah, great. Either that, or it's all complete crap. How often do you think of that? I find I'm thinking it a lot now: no God, only chaos.'

'You're an emergent atheist suddenly? What happened to paganism?'

'Yeah,' Jane said. 'Paganism. What *did* happen to paganism? You want the truth? Sometimes I'm inclined to think modern paganism's purely and simply about having fun – a reaction to the grey, studied bloody misery of Christianity. Dressing up, casting spells, cobbling together phoney rituals that *sound* heavy and significant, and kidding yourself you have like *exclusive access* to some arcane inner knowledge, which . . . I mean, somehow, it all just like . . . dissolves in the face of real life, the fucking savagery of it.' Jane rubbed a wet eye with the heel of her palm. She felt cold and barren, nothing left to cling to except . . . 'I wish you were here, Irene.'

'Well, me too, obviously. I'm coming over tomorrow anyway . . . later today, would that be? Knight's Frome? The session?'

'Oh yeah.' Lol had finally fixed it with Prof Levin for Eirion, the all-time rock-obsessive, to sit in on a recording session. 'I don't even know about *that* now. I don't know how things are going to turn out. Life just comes at you, doesn't it, like an axe? I was just thinking – *again* – Is Mum Living a Lie? It often comes back to that.'

'Why don't you have a proper talk to her?'

'There's never time. If it's not trivial parish crap it's Deliverance stuff. And how valid is that, really? I used to worry that she was in genuine spiritual danger from the *unseen world* . . . But how much crap is that? How often does the bloody unseen world destroy your—'

'Jane, is this the time to talk about this stuff? I don't think so.'

'*Au contraire*, Irene, it's the time when you can see the reality of it in all its stark . . . reality.'

'What about your psychic experiences? You were always going on about that stuff.'

'I think . . . I think we fool ourselves half the time. We desperately want there to be something else, and our subconscious minds, our brains, help us out. Comfort chemicals.' For a moment she was shocked at the hard, croaky sound of her own voice. 'And she . . . like Mum always says, when everything else fails, you just have to believe in love.' Jane stared into the darkness. 'I don't know whether that's a smart answer or just a smart get-out.'

She was thinking, *What if love's also a lie? What if there's only sex, to take your mind off the shit for a few minutes?*

'I'd better go,' she said.

'Mabbe this was a mistake,' Gomer said as they followed the A49, a couple of miles out of Hereford, hitting the open countryside again south of Belmont. 'You needs your sleep, vicar, all these buggers in the parish trying to stab you in the back.'

'Parish politics, I'm afraid,' Merrily murmured, 'are what people do when life isn't happening to them.'

'I gotter be up early, too, mind,' Gomer said. 'See about hiring some machines for a week or two. Got a mini-digger at the bungalow, but he en't gonner handle much.'

She slowed. 'Oh, *Gomer.*'

'Got clients. They en't gonner wait around.'

'Gomer, that's not – excuse me – entirely sane.'

'Nev would want it.' He sounded like he was somewhere else: Planet Plant Hire. 'Twenty-four-hour service, see.'

Merrily flicked him a sideways glance. 'If you even attempt to work this week, I'm going to have you sectioned.'

'Wouldn't work, girl. Buggers'd only put me in the care of the community, then you'd get me back.' He paused. 'You knows me by now, vicar – I don't get back to work, it'll all come down on me.'

She was silent. It was true. If he didn't keep on, in the face of everything, he'd turn into some kind of elderly person, and not the most contented kind. This was why they were here now, heading towards Ross-on-Wye through the squally night. Nothing to do with obtaining evidence, because there wasn't going to be any. This was about Gomer Parry never giving in.

'Right.' He was on the edge of his seat. 'Not far now, vicar. We oughter stop some way off, pull off the road like we broke down. Don't wanner look conspicuous, see.'

The traffic was mainly long-distance container stuff, widely separated. Merrily settled in behind a tall van with a sign on the back that read *How's my driving?*, with a phone number. If there'd been one on the back of Gomer's van tonight, the line would be jammed.

'OK, slow down now . . . by yere.' He tapped the wheel, and she took the van over the kerb and onto the grass verge, braking hard when high bushes loomed, skidding on a mud path. 'That's all right, girl. Shove him tight into them bushes. I'll get out your side.'

Merrily switched off the lights and the engine, and climbed out onto the wet verge, looking around. She ought to have known where this was, but it was different at night: a stretch of tarmac, no houses visible. On the other side, the moon revealed what looked like endless fields, just a few tiny lights in the far distance. On the nearside, a ragged line of unbarbered bushes followed the road around a left-hand bend maybe a hundred yards ahead.

Gomer joined her. 'Got the——?'

'Torch, yes. Where's the house?'

'Just around that next bend.' Gomer looked back along the verge, pointing. 'See that wood – he runs along the back.' But he made no move to go that way, as if he'd finally accepted the futility of all this, realized he'd clutched at the idea of Roddy Lodge as saboteur simply because he couldn't face going home to an empty house, a cold bed and an answering machine with Nev's voice on it.

'I expect you'd be able to tell straight away if by any chance Lodge *had* moved this thing,' Merrily said.

'Sure to,' Gomer said dully.

'Let's do it, then.' She moved along the verge, the hem of her alb getting soaked in the long grass. 'If anybody sees us, we can say the van broke down and we're trying to find a phone.'

When they rounded the bend, the road began to dip and the house was below them, a block of shadow. It was no more than twenty feet back from the road and looked even closer because of its comparative isolation. Living here, you'd hear the traffic all night, a restless lullaby.

'Entrance is just past the house itself, up a little drive,' Gomer whispered. 'All the land's the other side, see.'

'And that's where the . . . thing is?'

'The Hefflapure.' He stopped and looked back at her, shaking his head as if he was just waking up. 'Bloody daft, this, ennit?'

'Something you had to do, that's all,' Merrily said.

'Naw, just an ole man lookin' for a . . . what's the word?'

Scapegoat? 'Can't think,' Merrily said. 'Look, tonight we . . . you've seen what no relative should ever have to see. Maybe . . . I dunno . . . maybe we both needed to drive around a bit.'

'Ar.' Gomer stood at the edge of the A49, squeezing his fingers together. He seemed to have left his ciggy tin in the van. Merrily pulled out her Silk Cut, offered him one. Gomer shook his head.

'People thought he must be called Neville. Used to get letters addressed to Mr Neville Parry.'

'I thought that, too. What *was* he called?'

'Nevin. Seaside place in North Wales, where his folks used to go on their holidays. Likely he was conceived there.'

Merrily smiled, and they both stepped back onto the grass as a high-sided touring coach swished past towards Ross, probably empty except for the driver. Its passenger windows, only feebly lit, were reflected, fragmented, in the leaded upper windows of the Pawson house.

But its dipped headlights set up more of a glare in Gomer's glasses. And in the dusty back windscreen of the big digger in the drive.

All the breath came out of Gomer in a rush and Merrily actually went cold with shock.

The digger sat there silently, unoccupied, its shovel half-raised in front.

'It's him,' Gomer said drably, after a moment. 'Lodge. He's bloody well yere.'

8

Nil Odour

After a moment, Merrily felt calmer. When she'd first seen the JCB in the drive it had been like the instant when a dream turned malignant, when your subconscious mind presented you, unexpectedly, with an image so loaded with menace, within the logic of the dream, that it jerked you awake for reasons of mental self-preservation. And then you thought, surprised at yourself, *For heaven's sake, it was just a truck.*

'Gomer,' she said, 'let's just . . . let's think about this.'

But Gomer was already off – the way he'd reacted back at the depot when he'd realized the savage truth behind Cliff Morgan's gentle probing about Nev's whereabouts. Only now he had a real, solid target; he was a man with something to prove, something tangible within his grasp. Before she could think to stop him, he was in through the gateway, urgently pushing back shrubs and squeezing around the side of the digger and under its wide front shovel.

Which was as far as he got, because that was when the nightmare came out of remission.

Merrily must have seen it first – a movement from the blackness between the drive and the house, and it made her jump, but she didn't cry out because it could have been a cat or an owl. And then she saw Gomer come skating backwards, bumping along the side of the digger, bushes ripping at his jacket.

'Gomer!' He crashed back into a timber gatepost. She rushed to him. He was still on his feet but wheezing. 'Gomer, Christ, are you—'

And then there was another man's voice uncoiling from the shadows.

'You want some more? You want some more, matey, you come right back now, look, and touch my digger again.'

Merrily gripped Gomer's arm, steadying him. 'He hit you?'

'Pushed me, was all. Caught me off guard, ennit? Can you . . . can you find my glasses, vicar? Somewhere just yere.'

Merrily crouched, fingers scrabbling in the gravel, but her gaze was fixed all the time on the narrow alley between the digger and the shrubs at the edge of the drive, made wider by Gomer's hurtling body. She found she was screwing up her eyes, expecting some sudden harsh light to hit them, but there was none. She could see the uneven roof-line of the house and the moving white dot of a plane between clouds.

She was about to switch on their own torch, then changed her mind because . . .

Because, oh Jesus, because maybe it was better kept as a weapon. She tightened her grip on the rubber stem of the torch, still patting the gravel with her other hand, while trying to rationalize this, trying to think of any possible explanation other than that Gomer's crazy theory about Roddy Lodge had been, for heaven's sake, dead right.

The only other explanations involved coincidence. One coincidence too many.

In the gravel, she touched smoothness and a wire earpiece and, in the same moment, saw a man standing at the end of the drive, between the tailgate and the house, moonlight glinting on the creases of his jacket: leather. He stood in silence, not moving, then he called out.

'What you at over there?'

Merrily stood up, thrusting Gomer's glasses into his hands. 'OK, that's it. This is where we leave. We've seen the digger, we know he's here. Let's go.'

'Can't do that, vicar.' Gomer pushed his glasses on, calmly curling the wires around his ears. 'Can't just walk off now.'

'We can call the police.'

'No good. Buggers en't gonner believe us. Anyway, time they gets yere, if they comes at all, he'll be long gone. We got this bastard cold right yere, now . . . two of us . . . witnesses.'

'Gomer—'

'Chicken, then, is it?' the man enquired, no hint of fear in the voice, although the words were spoken rapidly. 'You boys chickenshit?'

Merrily whispered, 'Let it go. Let's just go back to the van. You're right, we're witnesses. It's all we need. I promise you, Gomer, I'll back you up all the way, but we need to—'

Gomer straightened up, bawled out, 'You wanner know who I am, is it?'

'*No!*' Merrily dragged on his arm. Gomer didn't move, felt as firmly rooted as the gatepost. She let go with a sound she realized was a sob, as he started to shout.

'*WHO AM I?* GOMER PARRY PLANT HIRE! THAT'S WHO I AM, YOU MURDERING BASTARD!'

Silence. Merrily closed her eyes, squeezing the torch with both hands. *Please, God, get us out of this.* She could hear another lorry grinding round the bend in the A49 and considered running out into the road, waving her arms to flag down the driver.

'Well, well, well,' the man said.

Gomer stepped away from Merrily. Stood there with his arms by his side. Little soldier, little gunfighter. Merrily shook her head. *No.*

'Lodge!'

'Who says?'

'What you done with that JCB, Lodge?'

'En't your business.' The voice higher now, like a fox barking in the night.

'It's that bloody tank, ennit? You took him out.'

Pause. The lorry rumbled away on the road to Ross.

'What tank's that, then, Mr Gomer Parry?'

'The bloody Hefflapure.'

'Oh, you heard o' that, then?' Pause. 'Thought they was still digging cesspits where you come from. Carryin' it out in buckets.'

Gomer took a breath. There might be method in this madness, but Merrily didn't think so. A duel: plant-hire rules? And then she thought, *What if he isn't on his own? How could he move that thing without help? What if he's keeping us talking while someone else . . . ?*

She whirled round. The entrance gaped.

'You better 'ave a good explanation of where you was tonight, Lodge,' Gomer said. 'You better've got some good witnesses.'

A moment's silence.

'What you on about, little man?'

'You know bloody—'

''Cause I don't reckon you knows what the fuck you're talkin' about any more, Mr Gomer Parry. I don't reckon you knows nothin' 'bout nothin, ole man. Well bloody past it. Clingin' on by your bloody old arthriticky fingertips. Oughter've packed in while you was ahead, look, but you couldn't let go . . . else you was just doin' it to keep away from your ole woman.'

'You bas—'

'You don't bloody know—' Then Roddy Lodge just erupted. '*Shit!* You don't know shit!' Laughter like flames in the night. 'This yere tank, he en't no business o' yours. This is my digger, *my* fuckin' tank. I put him in, I took him out. No business o' yours. Never was your business. You en't *got* no business, boy. You en't got business worth shit, every fucker knows that, knows *I*'m Number One now, look, I got fuckin' respect for miles round yere . . . done tanks for all the nobs all over the Three Counties and down into Wales. I done Prince Charles's fuckin' sewage over at Highgrove!'

Gomer shook. 'You lyin' bloody *toad*!'

'I done Madonna's fuckin' sewage up in the Cotswolds! I done Sting's shit, down in Wiltshire!'

In other circumstances, Merrily thought, this could have been funny – surreal, anyway. 'Gomer,' she whispered urgently, 'listen to me, you were right, he's not rational. Let's get the hell out.'

'You go fetch the van then, girl. I'll keep him—'

'You bloody well won't! You can come with me now.'

'Who's that with you, Gomer? Darren Booth?' Merrily could see Roddy Lodge's silhouette, almost full-length now, in the alley between the JCB and the hedge. Bizarrely, Lodge seemed to be bouncing on his toes. 'Come on out, then, Darren – take you both on. Come on out . . . come on, boys!'

He sprang into the middle of the drive and started shouting again – voice high and rapid and streaked with outrage. 'Tried

to pinch my business. Tried to blacken my good name. Tellin'
porky pies about me! Come on, boys. Take you both . . . Her
din't believe you, look. Her knows what I give her was good.
Knows I'm Number fuckin' One, and don't you ever forget it,
Mr Gomer fuckin' Chickenshit—' Roddy Lodge broke off,
looked up, squinting. 'En't Darren, is it?'

Gomer said nothing.

'If it en't Darren, who is it? I bet it's only that fuckin' fat
mental-defective you got workin' for you.'

Merrily could almost see herself, as if in a film, slow-motion,
making a lunge for Gomer and Gomer not being there – Gomer
moving away from her, along the side of the JCB, thin branches
whipping behind him, until he and Roddy Lodge were facing
each other in the open.

'You murdering bastard!'

No, no, no . . . Merrily started edging around the other side
of the digger. It was a tighter squeeze and it brought her up
against the half-raised shovel, about six feet wide, with a piece
of tarpaulin hanging over the rim. *Please God* . . .

'Meaning what?' Roddy Lodge said, and she could see his
lean body and then his face: concave, with a jutting, pointed
jaw, pointed nose, eyes that slanted slightly. A puppet kind of
face, she thought.

And he was tense now; this was clear even in vague moonlight.
A sheen of sweat on his face. He'd run out of banter and
mockery. He was nervous.

Because he did it, she thought. He *did* it. She could hardly
breathe. Roddy Lodge and Gomer were standing only feet apart,
on a paved forecourt in front of the house. If Lodge made a
move on Gomer, took one step, she would have to go for him
with the torch.

She started to tremble.

'You set fire to my yard,' Gomer said.

'Never!'

'You set light to my place tonight, boy. And my nephew, he
was in there. I dunno whether you knowed that, but it don't
matter . . . he still bloody died.'

Roddy Lodge stood there, taking this in. She couldn't make out his expression. She raised the torch, ready to run out.

'And that's murder,' Gomer said.

Roddy Lodge didn't move but something did – maybe a cloud, because now his face was washed by pallid light, and she could see he was smiling. It was this big, loose smile, causing his jaw to drop, as though all the tension in him was evaporating in the moonlight.

Lodge said easily, 'You know what, Parry? You're fuckin' mad, you are. You're fuckin' out of it.'

'It was murder,' Gomer said.

'Whatever you say, matey.' Lodge's voice was quieter now.

'You en't denying it. You en't even—'

'I en't even talkin' to you n'more, ole man. You're senile. Fuck off home, I would, while you can still walk.'

Lodge began to move towards Gomer, not hurrying but not delaying either, and whatever he could see now in Gomer's face, it was making the smile on his own grow bigger and whiter. The torch felt sweaty in Merrily's hand as she squeezed past the digger, along the rim of its front shovel, trying to transfer the flashlight to her other hand . . . feeling it slip out of her grasp and down into the shovel. She expected a clang, but it landed on something soft: the tarpaulin. She leaned over, reaching down into the metal maw, grabbed for the torch, stumbled, clutching at the tarpaulin, dragging some of it back, releasing a curling, piercing, pungent sweet aroma . . . and her scream.

And she watched Roddy spinning round with all the inevitability of slow motion.

'Who's that? *Who is it?*'

Merrily pushed herself away from the shovel and staggered out into the forecourt, shaking hard, feeling sick.

Roddy Lodge walked towards her across the moon-stroked flagstones. Her stomach was turning over.

He wore a grey leather jacket, tight leather jeans and cowboy boots, everything covered with drying red mud.

'A *woman*?' His voice rose to a note of wonderment.

'You leave her alone!'

Merrily saw Gomer Parry about five yards away, both arms down by his side, fists tight, glasses opaque. Gomer's voice was weaker now, could have been coming from half a mile away. She was willing him not to move, and all the time her mind was scrabbling for purchase on a sheer cliff-face of solid ice. *It can't be.*

When Roddy Lodge came up to her, the first thing she noticed was his aftershave. He must have put it on with a paste brush. She almost retched.

'Nice one, too, en't you?' Roddy was examining her, as if she was something that had just been delivered to his door. '*Very* nice. What you doing with the likes of this little toe-rag, my darlin'?'

The aftershave was so pungent it made her think of Nil Odour, the fluid undertakers used in coffins – the stuff the nurses at the General had kept under the bed of Denzil Joy, whose stench still sometimes soaked through her sleep.

Flash image: the half-cooked corpse of Nevin Parry. She felt faint with nausea.

Can't be. *Can't be. Not again.*

Automatically, her mind was erecting a segment of St Patrick's Breastplate:

> *I bind unto myself the Name*
> *The strong Name of the Trinity* . . .

'I'm very sorry about this,' Merrily said calmly. 'I'm really sorry, Mr Lodge.'

He had his head on one side, peering down at her. His eyes were aglow. He had a luminous white smile. She sensed a lot of energy there and even some humour. She sensed him wanting to touch her. She didn't move away. Her coat had come open over her chest. She was expecting him to become aware of her dog collar, then realized she'd taken it off in the van.

She took a breath. 'Mr Lodge, my name's Merrily . . . The Reverend Merrily Watkins. I'm Gomer's parish priest. I've been with him all night, since we first heard about the fire.' She paused. 'Mr Lodge, I'm sure you can imagine what kind of effect all this has had on Gomer. His nephew dead, everything destroyed.'

'Why's he reckon it was me?' Roddy Lodge said.

'Look . . .' Her voice felt warm and soothing, full of pulpit-projection. 'That's what I've been trying to tell him. The police . . . the police said Nev had been drinking heavily, and they think he probably started the fire himself, accidentally.'

She didn't look at Gomer, but she could feel it setting around him: a shabby concrete overcoat of bafflement and betrayal. She lowered her voice.

'He's an old man, Mr Lodge. He's lost everything. When he wanted me to drive him here, I . . . I didn't know anything about this . . . whatever history there is between you and him. I just assumed this place . . . that it held some memories for him and Nev, or something. I don't know what he's got against you or why it's come up now, but I'm really sorry.'

'Turned his mind, is it?' Roddy said.

'I'm sure he'll come through this, with help. I'm just . . . I mean, I hope you're not going to go to the police or anything. I promise you I'll talk to him.'

'Come and talk to *me*, you want, sweetheart.' Roddy grinned. It was a wide engaging grin, but separate from his eyes, which seemed to have their own staccato light, like the sparks from her Zippo. 'Vicar, eh? I goes and talks to our vicar sometimes. Nice feller.' He unzipped a breast pocket of his leather jacket. 'En't as sexy as you, though. I reckon he's a bit scared of me, tell the truth.' He laughed, a high barking. 'I scared him, I did. I scared the ole vicar.'

'Did you?'

'Told him 'bout all the things I seen in the night. Spooky!'

'Sounds . . . interesting.'

'Well, then . . .' Merrily didn't move as Roddy pulled out a card and came right up to her. 'You come and talk to me any time you want. Any time. And anything you want doing, I'm your man. Special rates for the Church, look.'

He inspected her face, as though he was committing it, feature by feature, to memory.

'Thanks.' She took the card. 'I'd like that.'

'Yeah,' Roddy said. 'You would indeed, my darlin'.'

Merrily walked away without once looking back, Gomer following behind like a beaten old dog. She didn't look at him, either.

She walked along the side of the big yellow digger without glancing at it or breathing in, walked out of the gateway and along the verge of the A49, with the long grass wet and cold around her ankles, sensing that Roddy Lodge was watching them and so not hurrying, not giving in to the urge to run, to the pushing in her chest. She walked around the bend in the road to where the van was almost embedded in the hedgerow. She unlocked the van and opened the door wide, so that Gomer could climb across to the passenger seat, where he sat in silence, sagging, as if all the life-energy had been vacuum-pumped out of him. She got into the van and turned the key in the ignition and for a moment was afraid it wasn't going to start, but the engine caught on the second turn and she waited until there were no headlights in view before carefully reversing the van out onto the road. She drove for a mile or so in the direction of Ross before pulling off the road into the car park of a darkened pub. She switched off the engine but left the headlights on, illuminating a hanging sign featuring a rabbit or a hare, with a fluffy tail, seen from behind.

Merrily needed light. She needed to see anything coming. She tossed her head back over the peeling vinyl of the driving seat and let the breath out of her mouth, and when it came out it was an enormous sob, her body slumping into shudders.

'Vicar?'

She held the wheel as if she was never going to let it go. 'Couldn't you smell it?'

He didn't reply. He didn't understand.

Merrily pulled herself up and found her phone. She couldn't remember the number of Hereford Police. She'd have to ring 999 and see if they could put her through to anyone in CID.

'I stum— stumbled, Gomer. Grabbed hold of this tarpaulin in the shovel of the digger, and it came away.' She switched on the phone and turned to look at him. 'I know . . . I know the smell now, you see. From when we found Barbara Buckingham. You remember. No mistaking it ever again, is there?'

Gomer lurched to the edge of his seat. 'In the *shovel*?'

'Thought I was hallucinating at first. Thought it was the shock . . . you know, of seeing Nev and . . . But it wasn't the same. This one was putrid. State of decay.'

Merrily stabbed 9 three times. Later she would have to call Jane and explain why she might not be home until dawn, or later.

Part Two

His intelligence was born in the fields and woods on the very edge of Gloucestershire and Herefordshire, honed in the thickets of the countryside, nurtured in a world where it was sometimes safer to kill a man than to kill a hare.

Geoffrey Wansell *An Evil Love*

9

Phobia

The woman in Lol's bed smiled sleepily. An arm came out, a long, warm forefinger touching his lips as he bent down.

'Before you say a word,' she said, 'I will tell you right now, from the bottom of ma heart, that it was very, very good.' Looking into his eyes now and slithering up in the rumpled bed like a mermaid breaking surface. 'And also right. Right for this moment. What I so much needed. OK?'

Lol sighed.

'*OK*, Laurence?' She took away her finger but stilled him with her gaze, even though one eye was lost under this tumble of black hair with the long, pale streak, like a vein of silver in onyx.

'Ah, well, *you* were good.' Lol straightened up 'You were wonderful. Me . . .' He shrugged, spread his hands, did all this stuff that he was afraid was going to look deliberately self-deprecating. Uncomfortable now, he looked away, out of the left-hand window, where the mid-morning sky over Knight's Frome was grey and shiny with unshed rain. It made the window seem like a square of tin plate in the wall of freshly plastered rubble-stone.

'Aye, all right . . .' She swung her legs out of bed. 'If you push me, I'll concede that "good" was maybe just faintly inap-propriate. But "right" was . . . right. See, I was with this young guy before – doesnae matter who, these kids're ten a penny, believe me: slick, cool, deft . . . and empty, you know? Awful proficient, sure, but proficiency isnae even halfway there, especially when it's like *received* technique – out of Jansch, out of Thompson, John Fahey, whoever. In addition, I was getting well fed up with him trying to get into ma knickers.'

Like Merrily, she wore a long T-shirt in bed – this one worn thin from many washings; the faded figure on it with the top hat seemed, at one time, to have been Bugs Bunny.

'Like I should be grateful to him for being fifteen years younger, you know?' Moira said. 'Jesus, the arrogance of these guys.'

She stretched and the T-shirt rode up and, through the thin cotton, Lol saw her nipples over the rabbit ears. He backed up, embarrassed, catching the edge of the tea tray, which rattled.

'Like I'm some hag,' Moira said. She was sitting on the edge of the bed, her hair almost reaching the duvet. She started rearranging the things on the tray. 'This is entirely wonderful, Laurence, but faintly ridiculous. Why not just leave me a kettle?'

'Prof's orders,' Lol said.

He'd awoken her with a call to her mobile, as arranged, at eight, and then carried the tray rapidly along two hundred yards of mud track before the teapot could cool, and then up fourteen stone steps to the granary. There'd be a small kitchen here eventually; meanwhile, Prof had said he wanted Moira Cairns looked after in the old-fashioned way. This apparently was something to do with memories of Moira bringing morning tea and toast to *his* room when they were recording, way back.

'Ach,' said Moira when Lol went on to remind her of this, 'that was just to make sure the auld bastard didnae take anything stronger.' She poured tea, steam rising. 'Tell me, how's he doing now, in that particular area?'

'Carries this cappuccino machine around with him like a teddy bear. I don't think there's ever been anything stronger in the house.'

Moira nodded approvingly, sugaring her tea. Lol suspected she was sitting on a whole stack of horror stories about Prof's drinking days.

'And now you're here as well, keeping an eye on him. Good arrangement, on the whole?'

Lol hesitated. He'd been here for several months now, since abandoning plans to become a psychotherapist; since Prof Levin had persuaded him to work on the long-awaited solo album that was not, in Lol's view, long-awaited by as many people as Prof seemed to imagine. But now the album was virtually finished and Lol didn't think he was doing enough around the studio to justify his de luxe accommodation. It *was* a good arrangement, certainly. Altogether too good.

'Apart, that is, from when characters like me come down to strut our prima donna stuff and pinch your lovely wee apartment,' Moira said. 'Where are you sleeping yourself, meantime?'

'Oh . . . in the loft over the end of the studio. I slept there most of the summer anyway. It's fine.'

'It's no' summer now, though. There'll be no heating in there, will there, once the studio's off?'

'It's fine, honestly.'

Moira smiled, crow's feet developing, but it didn't matter at all; this woman would be sexy at seventy. 'This wee place, though, I have to say, is . . . totally magical. All those steps – like a tower house. You can stand at the window at night . . . the lights of Malvern in the distance. Would that be the town itself? Great Malvern?'

'West Malvern. I think.'

'Best not to know for sure,' Moira said. 'All distant lights at night should be the lights of fairyland. There to inspire us, but just out of reach.' She looked at him over the rim of her cup. 'Makes you uneasy, living here?'

'Just a bit.' Her level of perception was increasingly scary. 'Why?'

'Too perfect, I suppose. Paradise syndrome?'

The granary was on the edge of a field sloping down towards the Boswells' place and well separated from the stable block housing the recording studio. Prof Levin had managed to buy it, along with adjacent outbuildings and two acres of land, when parts of the surrounding Lake estate had been sold off at the end of the summer.

'But then,' Moira said, 'to a lot of people, this'd just be a high-level hovel in the middle of a muddy field, inconvenient to get to and too small to do anything decent with. It's a personalized concept, paradise.'

'Well . . . yeah . . .' When Prof had suggested that he might like to move in here, Lol had suspected, although nothing had been said, that Prof was also thinking about Merrily, with whom Lol must never be seen.

'I *would* say you'd become like a son to Prof,' Moira said, 'but possibly that would be overstating it just a tad. You're somebody he feels he has to help because he knows you're never gonnae help yourself. Like, if the whole ideology of this place is the Prof devoting the glorious sunset of his career to assisting – pardon me – the underdogs, like you, out of the money raised from the fat cats like *me* . . .' She threw up her hands. 'Whoops! Did that sound like charity?'

'I've no illusions, Moira,' Lol said. 'It *is* charity.'

'Unless, of course –' she raised a forefinger '– he gets it all back on the album.'

'Y–e–s.'

'Although we all know that unless you're immensely famous already, it's bugger-all use making an album if you're no' gonnae tour it.'

'Ah . . .' He should've seen *this* coming.

'Whereas a good tour's almost guaranteed to put an album into profit.'

Lol sighed.

'But, of course, we both know the Prof has no interest whatsoever in payback. Only, the way I see it, this is gonnae nag away at you, until you have to really do something about the whole . . . what? Allergy? Phobia?'

Lol went to look out of the window, over the Frome Valley. Across the meadow, he could see the Boswells' beloved donkey, Stanley, browsing his paddock, taking it all for granted, like he was only collecting a little of what was due to his species after centuries of toil and maltreatment.

'Obviously,' Moira said, 'when you've been out of it a long time, it's *bloody* hard – especially on your own.'

'Nearly twenty years. I was just a kid.'

'Good long time for the fear to feed. Which is what fear does. Like I've got these ten dates provisionally fixed for the winter, and that's gonnae start off being an ordeal, no question, even after two and a bit years.'

Lol turned back into the white room, where Moira Cairns

was sipping her tea. His feeling was that the word 'ordeal' would not, in Moira's thesaurus, carry any significant cross-reference to playing live in front of an audience.

'OK, listen now. Laurence . . .' She was watching him over her cup. 'Bottom line: *if* this proposed tour goes ahead, how would *you* feel about being part of that?'

Lol went hot, then cold.

'Aye, I know. All right, sunshine, don't panic.' Moira put down the cup and stood up, this beautiful, scary mature woman in faded Bugs Bunny nightwear. 'Stay right there. I have to take a pee. You stay right there and consider all your get-out lines. But also . . . remember how it was last night.'

This morning was actually the first time he'd been alone with her. Last night in the studio, Prof had been there the whole time and also Simon St John, who was the vicar of Knight's Frome and played bass and cello. Simon knew Moira Cairns from way back, when they were part of the same band, having its albums engineered, then produced, by Prof Levin. So this was in the way of a reunion, with Lol, the outsider, getting involved because he just happened to be here. Moira's new album would be the first major-league product of Knight's Frome Studio, where Prof wanted music to be made at leisure, songs laid down as and when, no pressure on anyone. Timeless.

Lol couldn't remember which of them had suggested they should try one of *his* songs – as if Moira didn't have enough of her own. The idea had just seemed to arise, and they'd wound up re-working his neo-traditional ballad about the changing face of the English village, 'The Baker's Lament'. At first Moira was singing, with Lol on guitar. And then – and he wasn't sure how this had come about, either – Lol had taken over the vocal, Simon St John threading cello through it, sinuous and low-lying like the River Frome, and Moira contriving this incredible harmony.

Prof had recorded both versions, and it had been, like Moira said, kind of . . . interesting. Not technically terrific, but there was *something* going on, something organic, something visceral.

Something a little wonderful. All those years since Hazey Jane folded, and Lol had felt like part of a band again.

Of course, it was just for amusement – a dream, a fantasy sequence. Who *wouldn't* imagine they sounded good, recording with Moira Cairns? Moira, who now lived in seclusion most of the year on the Isle of Skye, coming out to perform only rarely, leaving deep tracks strewn with legends. Moira who had been born half-gypsy in Glasgow. Who was said to be possessed of 'the sight'. A goddess of folk-rock. The vein of silver in the long black hair – how many pictures had he seen of that? Never before over a Loony Toons T-shirt, of course, but . . .

Why should she want to do this for someone she'd only known for a few hours? A favour to Prof? Laying all her hard-won credibility on the line as a favour to Prof? Last night it had seemed magical; now it was merely unreal.

'Tell you what I'm thinking,' she called from the bathroom. 'Maybe we should do the one gig, to begin with. Just to see how it goes, yeah?'

Lol sat down on the edge of the bed.

Moira said, 'Sorry, what was that? Couldnae hear with the taps on. See, what's happening, I'm booked to play somewhere called The Courtyard in Hereford in . . . I think it's a week on Wednesday. We could use that, for starters. As an experiment?'

Lol's heel clinked on something under the bed.

'Nothing formal, nothing on the posters – I mean, too late anyway. You just show up, drift in and out as you please. Then we toss in a couple of your own numbers, see how it feels.'

Lol already knew how it would feel. He could already sense his fingers sweating on the frets. With any more than three other people in the room, all the chords would crumble, he'd lose the tune, forget the words. And in any audience, there were always going to be two or three people who would remember . . .

He bent down. The item under the bed proved to be his kettle, its flex coiled up next to it. All that stuff about the morning-tea tradition never had made total sense – if Prof thought it was important to return old favours, why hadn't *he* brought the tray?

A set-up.

Moira Cairns came out of the bathroom, looking fresh and composed in a lime-green kimono.

'So,' she said, 'where do you wannae start?'

Well, naturally, Lol didn't want to start at all. Hadn't he done half a college course in psychotherapy, worked for a while with an analyst and counsellor in Hereford? He could deconstruct it all very efficiently for himself, thank you, even down to the implications of his Nick Drake fixation: Nick Drake had made three classic albums but was always afraid to perform in public. Consequently, perhaps, the albums had undersold, and Nick Drake, undervalued, had died of an overdose of antidepressants.

'But, Lol, the poor guy was *mentally ill*,' Moira pointed out. 'And you never were. You were just a victim of the system, with no support at all to fall back on when this . . . bastard bass-player very kindly gets you a conviction for having sex with a fifteen-year-old girl – to keep *himself* out of the shit – when you were – what, eighteen . . . nineteen?'

'Thereabouts.' She'd evidently been thoroughly briefed by Prof.

'An innocent, all alone – your parents having become these totally insane religious maniacs, who disown you . . .'

'The more Prof tells the story, the more insane my parents become.'

' . . . So you fall into the system: unnecessary residential psychiatric so-called *care* – i.e. drugged senseless by the fucking state.' Moira tossed back her hair – forked lightning in a night sky. 'No way *that*'d happen now, with no damn beds to spare for the real loonies. Laurence, why aren't you *angry*?'

Lol shrugged.

'One day,' Moira warned, 'your shoulders are just gonnae freeze *up*. Let me get this right: if you reappear on stage now – nearly two whole decades later – the whole audience isnae gonnae be thinking, "Ah, here's the awfully talented person from Hazey Jane, where the hell's *he* been all this time?" It's gonnae be like, "Hey, is that no' the big sex offender of 1982 or whenever?" You really think that?'

'*No*,' Lol said too quickly. 'Look . . .' He turned to her. 'I'm really grateful, Moira, and if I could do it I'd be – you know – I'd be incredibly proud. But we're talking albatross here. Like what you don't need around your neck.'

'Now, listen, I'm a vulnerable wee creature behind the shell.' She came and sat next to him on the side of the bed. 'I need compatible support. I don't need flash, I need sensitive and faintly flawed.'

'You need somebody who can get the chords right and won't just stand there in a pool of sweat.'

'Laurence . . .' She took him by the shoulders. 'You can do this. You *have* to do this. Where's your main income from?'

'This and that. Royalties.'

'From songs? From the old Hazey Jane albums? I wouldnae even like to ask how much *that* comes to. What's your girlfriend say about it?'

Lol tensed. 'Girlfriend?'

'The wee priest?' Moira said patiently. 'I bet even the wee priest earns more in a year than you do.'

'Who, er . . . who told you . . . ?'

'Prof told me. Simon told me. Now, see, *there*'s something – I mean, I shouldnae have to spell this out to an ex-loony who trained as a shrink, but that's something you did overcome. Rejected by the born-again parents, and now here y'are in a close personal relationship with an Anglican priest. Major psychological breakthrough, or what?'

Lol stared down at the bedside rug. 'They weren't supposed to say anything about that.' Which sounded a little pathetic.

'Who?'

'Prof . . . Simon.'

Moira blinked. 'But you're an item, right? You and the priest. You're "going out together".'

'Well, we . . .' Lol smiled ruefully. 'We stay in together. Sometimes.'

Moira stared at him.

'Or rather we just don't go out anywhere very public. She's . . . inevitably, like a lot of women priests, especially in a country parish, she's insecure about some things . . . attitudes. I don't want to make it any more difficult for her.'

It started to rain, a pattering on the east window.

'Lol, what year is this?'

'Yeah, I know, it sounds ridiculous. But when you consider that she also has this other . . . this other thing she does in the diocese.'

'Exorcist. Yeah, I know . . . they don't talk about it.'

'She still tends to attract publicity,' Lol said. 'I mean, there still aren't that many women priests in the UK, let alone women . . . Deliverance ministers. So if the press found out, even the local press . . .'

'Ah.' Moira contemplated this, supporting her chin with a hand, gnawing the side of a finger. 'Right. I think I get the picture. Crazy woman who pursues evil spirits for a living takes up with ex-loony singer with a conviction for a sex offence.'

'Not good, is it?'

Moira Cairns shook her head slowly. 'Jesus, Laurence, you don't go out of your way to make things easy for yourself, do you?'

Lol smiled his hopeless smile.

10

Caffeine

In the early afternoon, with wind-driven rain coming in hard from Wales and the last of the apples down on the vicarage lawn, the police arrived.

Actually, just one of them: DI Francis Bliss, of Hereford CID, which was a relief; it meant this was informal. DI Bliss sat at the kitchen table and drank coffee greedily. He was unshaven, been up all night, couldn't hide his excitement.

'Merrily, we've gorra name.'

'For the . . . ?'

'Dead person.'

'Oh.'

They had Merseyside in common, he and Merrily, if not synchronistically. She'd been a curate there, her first job in the clergy, her baptism of fire and acid, but good times, on the whole. By the time she'd arrived in Liverpool, Frannie Bliss – stocky, red-haired, raised a Catholic in Kirby – would already have left. It was unclear how he'd wound up in Hereford.

He folded his hands around his warm mug.

'Lynsey Davies. Local woman. Reported missing back in the middle of August by her partner – I say "partner" . . . *one* of her partners. The father of two of her kids, anyway, which he reckons gives him first claim.'

'Claim on what?'

'On any compensation that might be due to the dependants of a murder victim, I imagine. Everybody talks compensation now. You don't have a loss, you have an opening for gain.'

'Not a loving relationship, then.'

'With Lodge on the side?' Frannie Bliss sniffed. Merrily, feeling chilly even inside her oldest roll-neck woolly, carried her ashtray to the table and slumped down opposite him. It was a day for despairing of people. Bliss's excitement depressed her. But then, if everybody enjoyed their jobs that much, the sum of human happiness . . . She surrendered to confusion and lit a cigarette.

'When you say "local" . . . ?'

'Village called Underhowle. Backside of Ross-on-Wye, where it joins the Forest of Dean. I'd never been there before. Lodge has his depot on the outskirts, and a bungalow he's built next to it. Lynsey Davies lived in a council house in Ross. She was thirty-nine, had four kids by three different blokes, and was apparently Roddy's intermittent girlfriend. A fun-loving lady.'

'So she was . . . identifiable, then.'

Frannie smiled thinly. 'Ah . . . not strictly. The ex-partner, Paul Connell, reckons he doesn't mind having a quick glance, but I'm not sure how useful that would be. It does help a bit that the body was dumped in pea-gravel rather than soil, with this big tank thing on top, so it's not as badly eaten-up as you might expect after a couple of months underground. And the clothes tie in. We've sent for dental records, anyway.'

'Lodge actually took it . . . her out of the ground?'

'Dug down by the side of the tank, fished her out – probably manually. Dumped her in the shovel of the digger, tucked her in nicely.'

Merrily shuddered, recalling the mud drying on the front of Roddy Lodge's leather jacket, on his trousers.

'The, er, you know, the bodily fluids, they'd have gradually drained out through the gravel,' Bliss said. 'So although she was a big girl, the body wouldn't've weighed that much. Wouldn't've taken a great feat of strength for Roddy to roll her onto a couple of feed sacks and lift her out of the pit and into the shovel.'

Merrily thought of Roddy Lodge's pungent aftershave, wondering if he'd plastered it on to combat the smell. Didn't make too much sense; this was a man who installed foul drainage.

She and Gomer had seen the big digger go rumbling past while they were waiting for the police on the pub car park – the body presumably out in front, sunk into the raised-up shovel like an offering to the moon. Gomer had wanted to follow Lodge; Merrily had talked him out of it. Half an hour or so later, the police had cornered Roddy at his depot. The woman's body was still under the tarpaulin. Not much room for denial.

'How did she die?'

'The PM should be taking place as we speak.' Evidently, Frannie didn't want to say how she'd died. He finished his coffee. 'Can I go over a few points? According to your statement, you and Mr Parry went to this house because you had reason to think Roddy would be going there to retrieve this septic-tank unit. The, er . . .'

'Efflapure. But we didn't expect him to *be* there.'

'Right.' He lifted his cup. 'Don't suppose . . . ?'

'Sure.' She went to fetch the coffee pot, trying to recall what she'd said in her brief statement to a detective constable in Hereford in the early hours. 'I know it all sounds unlikely, Frannie, but you have to remember we were both pretty hyped-up last night. There was no way Gomer was going to go home and sleep. But we really didn't expect to find Lodge there.'

'Actually, Merrily, it all sounds far enough off the wall to be true, given the circumstances, even if I didn't know you well enough to think it unlikely in the extreme that you'd lie to the police.' He beamed at her. 'But in fact we've also spoken to Mrs Pawson in London, who confirms Lodge insisting that he should be the one who took the thing away. Which, of course, now makes perfect sense. Not a question of professional pride, as you assumed, but the fact that the bugger had a body buried underneath it, and he was panicking at the thought of it getting discovered by Gomer Parry. Makes a lorra sense, from Roddy's point of view.'

'It doesn't really make sense to me that he should bury a body under a septic tank.' Merrily poured Bliss more coffee and saw his wrist quiver; after a long night, he must be sizzling with caffeine. 'I mean, OK, he might not have expected it to be dug up again within weeks, but surely there was always going to be a chance that *some day* it was going to be re-excavated. They don't last a lifetime, do they?'

'They *can* last a lifetime, apparently. But yeh, I do see what you mean. But you've gorra remember we're not dealing with a fully rational person. A feller who drives through the night with a body held up in his bloody digger's shovel . . .'

'He did kill her, then? I mean, there's no suggestion that he might have been getting rid of a body for someone else?'

'An extension of his waste-disposal empire? He's arrogant and daft enough, but I don't see it, do you? My feeling is we'll have a confession before dark. I'm leaving him to stew for a few hours. I'm not hurrying.'

This was not Merrily's impression. She still wasn't quite sure why Bliss was here. She'd expected a visit at some stage, but not so early in the investigation, and it wasn't as if Ledwardine was on the Ross side of Hereford. This was a special trip.

'Will you be talking to Gomer again? Because Jane's round there at the moment. I don't particularly want . . .'

Jane was making Gomer's lunch. The kid had still been awake when Merrily had got in around 5.45 a.m. Neither of them had really slept after that.

'Er . . . yeah.' Frannie Bliss sounded doubtful. 'We *will* be talking to Mr Parry again at some stage, obviously. Though I've gorra tell yer it might be less easy than he thinks to prove that Roddy Lodge torched his yard.'

'And, besides, you've got something more important, now?'

Bliss looked pained. 'Don't put it like *that*. I know the lad's dead, and I'm not saying it *wasn't* down to Roddy. But while he's still dodging around Lynsey Davies, he's *flatly* denying the bloody fire. Says Parry's three sheets in the wind, gorra grudge, professional rivalry, all this kind of shite. Roddy is indeed very proud of his professional standing – among other things. Could be Forensics'll find traces of combustibles on his clobber, but meanwhile, all I'm saying is, let's get him sewn up on the easy one first, then see what else we can discuss with him. It's been a long night, Merrily.'

'What about DNA?'

'After a fire?'

'But you've charged him.'

'Er . . . no. No, I haven't. Not yet.'

'Oh?'

'I want it in the papers,' Bliss said. 'If he's charged, it's sub judice and the clamps go down. I want it splurged all over the papers, radio, TV, the lot, that we've found a woman's body under a new-fangled septic tank and that a thirty-five-year-old man is helping with inquiries. I want people to think about it and talk about it. Not just in the village. I want the name Efflapure in the public domain.'

'I'm sorry . . .' She poured another coffee for herself, maybe thinking it would attune her to Bliss's wavelength. 'Why?'

''Cause Roddy works over a wide area.'

'Yes.' *I done tanks for all the nobs all over the Three Counties and down into Wales. I done Prince Charles's fuckin' sewage over at Highgrove.*

'See, what I'm looking for, Merrily, is a full list of all the Efflapures or anything else he's put in. We've got his books, but we all know that, with a bloke like Roddy, they won't all be down on paper for the taxman. I want to know exactly where he's been.'

She nodded. She didn't really get this – too tired, maybe – but she nodded anyway.

'Merrily,' Bliss said. 'You're a woman.'

'Yeah, I still like to think so.' Suddenly, despite – or maybe because of – her fatigue and the sordid, sickening nature of the discussion, she felt a piercing need to be in Lol Robinson's bed in the white room in the granary. She looked away, knowing she was blushing.

'And a priest.' Bliss sat up in his chair, facing her with both hands flat on the table, his voice becoming Scouse-nasal. 'And you've been close to evil. Closer than most priests, I'd say, even if you've not been at it long. So I just want to ask you – off the record – about the kind of stuff that's not in your statement. I want to know how *you* felt about Roddy. As a priest. As a woman.'

She met his gaze. His eyes were bright with caffeine and candid ambition. She liked Bliss, actually – more than she liked his boss DCI Howe, who was apparently away on something called an SIO Module course. But she wasn't quite ready to say how she felt about Roddy Lodge.

You come and talk to me any time you want.

Thanks. I'd like that.

Yeah. You would indeed, my darlin'.

She said, 'You're leading the inquiry then, Frannie?'

'So far,' he said. 'But I may not have long before somebody takes over, you know how it goes.'

'So all that about being in no hurry . . .'

' . . . Was bollocks. Yeah. Truth is, Merrily, I'm chasing a feeling about this feller. I'm supposed to've gone home for a kip ages ago, but I've been driving round thinking about it.'

'Roddy?'

He nodded. 'What I reckon . . .' He took a breath and seemed to be swirling it around his cheeks before letting it out. 'I reckon there could be more of them. More Lynseys.'

The problem was, Jane realized, that nobody really understood Gomer. They looked at this weedy little old guy in the bottle glasses and they somehow failed to see the rebel warrior crunching down the border clay on his grunged-up caterpillars, swinging the arm of his JCB like some huge broadsword. They couldn't discern the *elemental* side of Gomer. Even Mum, who should have known better by now, had been like, *Keep an eye on him . . . make sure he takes it easy . . . don't let him overreact.*

They didn't understand. Overreaction was what kept Gomer fully alive.

He'd agreed finally to let Jane go to the chip shop, then he'd left half his lunch. All morning he'd kept phoning people, in a compulsive kind of way. '*No!*' he'd go. '*It don't matter what you've yeard, it en't over! Gimme a week, I'll be back to you. Gimme ten days, max!*'

But there was a dullness in his glasses.

'I've got my provisional licence now.' Jane wrapped the congealing chips in their newspaper and dumped them in Gomer's kitchen bin. 'I could work for you weekends. I mean JCBs . . . it's just a matter of experience and technique, right?'

'And an HGV licence,' Gomer said heavily.

'Oh. That, too, certainly. I knew that.'

She also knew that, in some curious way, he wouldn't feel free to mourn Nev until he'd secured the business. If he let it go, it would be a kind of betrayal. In the same way, the small, modern kitchen was amazingly clean and neat, everything shiny – the way Minnie had kept it, but not like a shrine, Jane thought. A shrine was static and frozen; in here you could still feel Minnie's busy spirit, and Gomer needed that. Like he always needed to know the big diggers were out there, oiled and ready to move the earth.

The kitchen window overlooked the orchard, out of which the buttressed church spire rose like a rocket on its launching pad. Starship Mum. Soon to be transmitting soft porn, if Uncle Ted got his way.

Everything was getting out of proportion.

Jane said, 'I suppose, if you could wipe off the jobs you've already got on the stocks, you could take some time to kind of reorganize things. Like, reduce the scale of the operation.'

Gomer looked up. 'Ar. Mabbe you put your finger on it there, Janey. Gotter deal with the commitments first, ennit? I en't given up hope. I know where I can rent a digger, and there's a coupler fellers I know would likely help me out, but they won't be in till tonight, see.'

'I suppose it's going to be an even smaller pool, now that this Roddy Lodge is going to be . . . whatever happens to him.'

Gomer's glasses, she would swear, darkened. Jane could've punched herself for bringing this up again. This whole Lodge thing was very weird and sick. When Mum had told her, she'd felt obliged to feign disappointment at missing the excitement, but in reality she was glad she hadn't been there. Awfully glad, too, that Mum had got herself and Gomer out of it, avoiding confrontation. Jane had learned that, in situations involving crime and death, only distance lent any kind of excitement. The fact that this Lodge, in all probability, had killed Fat Nev, who Jane had known – OK, not well, but she could picture him, could hear his voice, knew what a crappy life he'd had – made the guy repulsive, a monster.

But Gomer was different. Somehow, for Gomer, the discovery of the woman's body in the truck had been almost a frustrating development, an intrusion coming between him and the man who'd murdered his nephew and wrecked his business. Did

Gomer feel – maybe unconsciously – a certain resentment towards Mum for forcing him to take the easy way out, let the police handle it?

Unlikely, because Gomer's affection for Mum was almost a father–daughter thing.

But there was something.

'What are you doing this afternoon?' Frannie Bliss said.

'I . . . nothing vital.'

Lie down for half an hour, maybe. Go across to the church and say some prayers for Gomer and Nev. Phone Lol. Avoid Uncle Ted. Go back and talk to Gomer, see if there's any way to help him through this.

'Only, I'd like you to come and look at his place. At Underhowle. Take less than an hour to get there. You know me, Merrily, I don't have too much faith in psychologists and profilers, but I've still gorra sneaking regard for priests.' He gave a small smile. 'Of whichever side of the fence.'

'Frannie,' Merrily said, 'do you have any real concrete *reason* for suspecting he's done it more than once?'

'Just his attitude. And the fact that at least one other woman's gone missing from that area in the past year.'

'Oh.'

'He likes women.'

'It's not a crime.'

'I use the word "like" . . .'

'OK.' Merrily put out her cigarette. 'I'll tell you. He was heavily suggestive, I mean towards me. In an old-fashioned way, I suppose you'd have to say. I was standing a couple of yards away from a body he'd just exhumed and he was telling me I was . . . you know . . . It wasn't exactly sophisticated and it wasn't subtle: he actually used the word "sexy". Here we are in the grounds of an empty house, he's just been accused of murder by Gomer, and he's talking like we've just met up in a singles bar and we've both had a bit to drink.'

'Had he, do you think?'

'I wouldn't've thought so. His voice didn't seem to be slurred and I couldn't smell anything on him other than an awful lot of aftershave. He was still hyped-up, though.'

'In what way?'

She thought about it. 'At first, I thought he was nervous – Gomer had called him a murderer. However, as soon as he found out this was about the fire, he – as you said – kind of denied it. Laughed it off, anyway. That was about when I gave myself away – dropped the torch in the shovel, on the tarpaulin covering . . . Anyway, as soon as he saw I was a woman, maybe that was when he got cocky. He seemed quite relaxed, from then. *I* wasn't, of course. I'd smelled . . . the smell. I just wanted us to get the hell out of there before he pulled a gun or a knife or something.'

'Do you think he detected you were scared, and that was what made him so forward?'

'You mean, do I think he got off on that, a woman being blatantly nervous of him? Maybe. I don't know.'

'Where was Mr Parry at the time?'

'Mr Parry was standing there, gobsmacked at me selling him down the river. I really don't think . . . The impression I have, thinking back on it, was that Roddy had ceased to be aware of Gomer from the moment he became aware of me. He said, "a woman" – like, you know, "For *me*?" ' Merrily shook her head. 'I'm sorry, that sounds – even to me, that sounds like the kind of thing you say in hindsight, when you know you've been face to face with a . . .'

'It sounds about right, actually,' Bliss said. 'For instance, when the lads brought him in last night, he was rabbiting non-stop in the car, like they were his best mates. Like they were all on a coach coming back from an outing. He's there, jammed up between two burly uniforms, and at one point he's suggesting that if they ever fancy a one-nighter, with the trimmings, he can get them fixed up.'

'Trimmings?'

'I'll spare you the details.'

'Did he realize why they were arresting him?'

'Oh yeh. Merrily, you say in your statement he told you he'd been to talk to the local vicar?'

She nodded. 'That would be Jerome Banks. You spoken to him?'

'Would I need to?'

'Lodge claimed he scared the vicar. Told him about things he'd supposedly seen. "Spooky" was Lodge's word.'

'Didn't go into detail?'

'He seemed . . . I dunno . . . kind of proud of this – spooking the vicar. I said that sounded very interesting, and he said – in this heavily lecherous way – that I could go and talk to *him* any time I liked.'

'And you said?'

'I said that'd be nice, or something like that.'

'Ah.' Frannie Bliss rubbed his stubble-roughened jaw.

'What?'

'*Nice.* Yes. That's more or less what he said to us.'

'Huh?' She reached for the Zippo and the Silk Cut.

'Like I say, they couldn't shut the bugger up last night. And yet this morning, when we brought him out of his cell and into an interview room . . . he's a very different man. Withdrawn. Sort of hunched up into himself. Like he'd been drunk last night and now he's very badly hung-over. Didn't want to know us any more. Kept muttering, "*Not talking, not talking.*" Kept wanting to go back to his cell. See, that's a bit unusual. Normally they can't wait to get out. We tried all the usual things.'

'Good cop, bad cop.'

'We're a little more psychologically sophisticated nowadays, Merrily.'

'Since when?' She drew out a cigarette with her teeth.

'Anyway, it wasn't happening. We weren't getting anywhere. He didn't even ask for a solicitor. We offered him one, he said no. No to everything. No, no, no. Don't wanner talk, leave me alone. Sinking further back into himself, complaining of headaches. Well, all right, we'll have enough forensic by the end of the day to package him up, no problem. But I . . .' He looked into Merrily's eyes. 'I *know* there's a lot more to come out if we handle this right.'

'And you want to be the one to uncover it, before they send

Howe back from her course to take over.' Merrily eyed him along the length of her cigarette.

'Aw, please . . .'

'Sorry.'

'But eventually,' Bliss said, 'he just looks at me through his fingers and he says, "You get that little woman. I'll talk to that little . . . woman."'

'*What?*'

Bliss smiled a touch bashfully, not quite meeting her eyes.

'You took a bloody long time to get round to *that*,' Merrily said.

'Yeah. Sorry about that.'

'No, you're not.'

Bliss shuffled in his chair. 'Merrily, how *would* you feel about talking to him? Might save us all some time.'

Help you get it wrapped before they bring in some flash DCI from headquarters or summon Ms Howe back.

'By "talking to him" you mean either with you there or with a tape running.'

'Something like that. But I wouldn't like to have you going in there cold. That's why I want you to see his place. Get an idea of what kind of bloke we're dealing with. It won't take long.'

'Now?'

'Wouldn't mind.'

'Look, I know the Bishop and the Chief Constable have had drinkies together—'

'But you don't work for the police. Yeah, yeah. I don't want to cross any of your personal barriers. I just want a firmer idea of whether I'm talking to a sexual fantasist who got carried away one time, or to a real sexual predator – maybe somebody who started out degrading women and progressed to killing them. *Them* – plural.'

'And as well as whatever he might disclose to me, you probably want to watch how he reacts to me as a woman, right?'

'Well, you know, I hadn't actually thought of that.'

'Frannie, forget it.'

Bliss was silent for a moment. He waved away her smoke.

'You've disappointed me, Merrily. I thought what you did was all about stopping the spread of evil.'

'And suppose he's in some way innocent? Suppose you're getting carried away.'

'I can show you—'

'All right.' She put out her cigarette. She'd have to admit that the possibility of Lodge's innocence was remote. 'I'll talk to him, but I'll warn him first that under the circumstances there could be things I would feel obliged to pass on to the police. Then he has the option of telling me to push off.'

Bliss didn't look too unhappy about this.

'And no tape, no video.'

'Merrily . . .'

'Or I could put your idea to the Bishop. He'd need about two days to think about it, the old worrier.' She stood up. 'Frannie, are you even fit to drive?'

Bliss squeezed shut his eyes and opened them again.

'Wouldn't have any more coffee in that pot, by any chance?'

11

Just How Funny It Gets

They travelled down the long, misted valley, with steel skeletons striding ahead of them.

This was where Herefordshire and Gloucestershire lay back-to-back on a lumpy mattress of tiered fields rising into old woodland of browning broadleaved trees and conifers high on the hillsides. But the valley didn't look as if it belonged to either county as much as it belonged to the power industry.

'You can't believe they can still get away with this, can you?' Merrily said.

'Sorry?' Frannie Bliss, driving, was somewhere else.

'The pylons.' They looked seriously hostile, like an army of the dead, bristling with obsolete weaponry. 'I mean, would it be all *that* costly to run some of it underground?'

The joke was that there were so few homes in view that you could probably have electrified the lot with half a dozen wind-mills. Wreathed now in fog, the pylons were a primitive show of strength. Maybe one day they'd be industrial archaeology. Not yet.

Frannie Bliss glared at the countryside through the windscreen of his black Alfa, as though it was holding out on him. He was still a city cop at heart; you couldn't accost pedestrians the same in country lanes: *Where you off to, son? What's in the rucksack?*

They'd come in from the A40, the dual carriageway pumping heavy goods in and out of Newport and Cardiff and the West Country. Here, lorries lurched past the most voluptuous curves of the Wye Valley and that famous Ross-on-Wye skyline: the tall-steepled church crowning the town, above the river and the water-meadows and the mock-medieval sandstone walls. Dark wooded hills were the Ross backcloth, and those same hills were directly above them now, sunk into wet mist, a few miles beyond the town.

'No, I was just wondering,' Bliss said, 'how many sewerage systems Roddy's put in around here. Every farm needs one, doesn't it? Every cottage.'

Merrily saw where this was heading. 'You could start a terrible scare.'

Bliss nodded, didn't seem too concerned.

'You put this out in the media,' she warned, 'you get every-body for miles around wondering if they've got a dead body under their septic tank.'

In a pocket of her coat, she'd discovered the card that Roddy Lodge had given her last night.

Efflapure
R F Lodge
registered contractor
The Old Garage,
Underhowle,
Nr Ross-on-Wye.

It was in a plastic evidence bag now, locked in the boot of the Alfa. Frannie Bliss seemed close to becoming obsessive about Roddy Lodge.

'I wouldn't mind looking under, say, a few *selected* septics. Narrow it down a bit.' He smiled. 'We'll see, anyway. How's business? The Evil One doing much locally?'

'You'd know better than me.' He was changing the subject, but she could sense his anticipation and was unnerved by it.

He glanced at her. 'How's Lol?' He'd encountered Lol during the summer, over the hop-kiln tragedy and the problems sur-rounding Allan Henry, the developer. Oddly, Bliss and Lol had seemed to understand one another, but that didn't mean she could trust him with an update.

'We're still friends. And how's *your* private life, Inspector Bliss?'

'Not many private bits left.'

'What's that mean?'

He took a sudden right between a Scots pine and an untrimmed hedge. The car skidded on some mud, and Bliss narrowly avoided the hedge.

'Ah,' he said, 'just the usual police thing. Your married life suffers on account of the job, and then it gets so bloody messy at home the job becomes a refuge. Like that.'

'I'm sorry.'

'I don't *want* us to be over, but it's going down so fast now, I don't really know how to stop it. And before you say "Do you wanna talk about it, Frannie?" – no, thank you, not now. Maybe when this is finished.'

'I wonder how often you've said that. Maybe—'

'All right,' Bliss said, 'probe over. We're nearly there. Listen, when we get to the actual place, I'm not gonna force yer into a Durex suit, but try not to touch anything, eh?'

'We're just going to his house, aren't we? It's not as if it's a murder scene . . .' She registered his chilly half-smile. 'Oh.'

'We don't know for certain,' Bliss said. 'But he had to've done it somewhere. And we do know he brought women back here, and when you see inside the place . . . well, you'll probably *want* to wear a Durex suit.'

This was where Gloucestershire's Forest of Dean looked to be stealthily pinching bits of Herefordshire. The lane narrowed between wild saplings growing on the verges. And then, within fifty yards of a sign announcing *Underhowle*, but before any evidence of a community, they were there: a clearing and a short cindered track opening into a forecourt fronting a building of grey concrete – a classic garage from the 1950s, sectional temple to the motor car, with a white metal sign: R. F. LODGE. In front, the stumps of petrol pumps, behind one of the towering pylons that looked as though it had just walked down from the conifered hillside.

Either side of the garage with its high, twin entrances, shuttered now, stood newer concrete buildings. Frannie Bliss parked the Alfa between a police car and a white van on the forecourt, lowering his window as a uniformed constable came over.

'Sir, there's been a deputation of local people demanding to know what's going on here. DS Mumford didn't want to speak to them, so I just told them I wasn't authorized to make a statement, it'd be up to the SIO. Just to put you in the picture. I think they'll be back.'

'I do not doubt it, son. Andy's up at the house, is he?' Bliss turned to Merrily. 'I've had Andy going through Roddy's books, phoning his fantasy clients. *Is* he known at Highgrove, you reckon?'

'You're really building this up, aren't you?'

'Merrily, I'm a detective inspector who would like to be a detective *chief* inspector. I'm thirty-six years old, and I think I'm *worth* it.'

She grinned and stepped out into the peppery breeze. Bliss ushered her along a flagged pathway down the side of the garage, and there, within ten yards of the rear of the grey building, was the bungalow. It had been invisible from the front. Maybe just as well, as it wasn't pretty: multicoloured bricks assembled in no particular pattern, flat roof, no garden, no flower tubs, just a concrete surround and the tiled pit of a drained swimming pool near the back wall of the garage.

'And in summer you can float on your back and watch the sun sizzling through the power lines,' Merrily said.

'Apparently he got the land cheap. Built the bungalow himself, more or less.'

'You don't say.' Down in a parallel field she could see half of what looked like a stone chapel.

'Be worth quite a bit now. It's actually quite well built, according to Mumford who knows about these things.'

'Maybe it just lacks the feminine touch.'

Bliss glanced at her. 'How true that is,' he said.

Roddy Lodge's office was at the rear of the bungalow, to the right of the back door. Its walls were only half plastered, and its rectangular window looked into the brackeny hillside, through the steel bones of the pylon.

Merrily saw a filing cabinet and a metal desk with a bright red computer and a phone on it. Also, a bulky middle-aged man in a shapeless dark suit sitting in a vinyl-backed executive swivel chair. Bliss bent down to him, cocking his head on one side.

'So was the Prince cooperative, Andy? Was he as nice as he always seems on the telly?'

'Good afternoon, Reverend.' Mumford carefully folded up his mobile phone and placed it on the desk. 'Nice to see you again.'

'Hullo, Andy.' Merrily wondered, not for the first time, what kind of vocation this was turning out to be, when she seemed to encounter more coppers than priests.

Mumford looked at the mobile. 'Boss, I'm just waiting for a call back from Mrs Jilly Cooper's secretary. They do seem to remember being approached by Lodge sometime last year, but had no need of his services.'

'How wise,' Bliss said.

'And . . . Highgrove came back to me to confirm getting repeated letters and leaflets from him. I asked if they'd kept any, but apparently they didn't. I've also found a pile of press cuttings in the filing cabinet, mostly relating to famous people who've moved to this area . . . in fact, anywhere within a fifty- or sixty-mile radius.'

'What does that tell you,' Merrily wondered, 'apart from that he's enterprising?'

'And a terrible celebrity-stalker,' Bliss said.

'He's very upfront for a stalker.'

'He's certainly not efficient.' Mumford nodded at the scarlet computer, which had yellow speaker grilles and looked like a toy. 'At one time he seems to have tried doing his bills and stuff on that thing, but the last one I can find on the hard disk seems to be over a year old. He's all over the place after that, and the computer's gathering dust.'

'Other things on his mind, Andy?'

'Shows a lot of nerve, in a way,' Merrily said. 'I mean, a small operator making a direct approach to Prince Charles?'

'*And* Princess Anne at Gatcombe,' Mumford said. 'At least, she's down here on his list. When I phoned, I wasn't able to talk to anybody who might know about him, so I've arranged to call back in an hour or so. As for Sting's place – no answer at all. A couple of other people you won't've heard of, boss, seem to remember getting leaflets from Roddy as well as individual letters.'

'Yeah,' said Frannie Bliss, 'but have any of these nobs actually *hired* the bastard?'

Mumford shrugged.

Merrily said, 'This is like one of those old Ealing comedies.'

Bliss didn't smile. 'Right.' He opened the office door. 'Come with me, Merrily. I'll show you just how funny it gets.'

The focus of the living room was a big mahogany cocktail bar, brand new but well out of fashion. There were tall stools, optics, dozens of bottles and a neon sign: Roddy's Bar. The low seating was arranged around it: a couple of sloppy dark leather chairs and a sofa behind a long, glass-topped coffee table with copies of *Loaded* and *Front* on it.

'This is clearly a man who knows all the best discount warehouses,' Bliss said.

On one wall, a bullfight poster had Roddy's name added to the list of contenders. There was a Bang & Olufsen sound system with speakers on wall brackets, and a CD pyramid with one CD lying on top: *Ibiza Nights, Vol 2*. But the stereo was unplugged, as was the wide-screen TV, as if Roddy didn't use them much any more, didn't spend much time here.

'It's all very clean,' Merrily observed.

'He has a Mrs Wellings, from the village, comes in once a week. But she says this, and the kitchen and a couple of other rooms, are about as far as she's allowed to go.'

Bliss led her back into the passage. This was a plain corridor bungalow, doors to left and right, two of them still unpainted. It reinforced the feeling Merrily was getting of a man who moved around like a moth, never settling to anything for very long.

'How long has he lived here?'

'Built it about four years ago from money his old man left him. He's got two older brothers – like twenty years older. One's living in Oz, one has the family farm up the valley – both quite respectable, by all accounts. Roddy was a bit of a difficult boy, but not in the sense that he'd be known to us . . . and he wasn't.

I don't know the full circumstances, but you had a situation where the father bequeaths him a wodge of cash on the proviso that he uses it to set himself up in business. The brother up the valley says he seemed to have knuckled down to it.'

Bliss had stopped outside a door at the end of the passage with a conspicuous metal lock screwed to the outside. The lock was conspicuously broken.

'That's us. Most coppers are frustrated burglars.' He opened the door. 'After you. This is where you don't touch anything, but I don't suppose I'll need to emphasize that.'

It was dark inside, except for a shape like the screen of one of the old black and white TVs she remembered from when she was a little kid – when you had to fiddle with a switch labelled *horizontal hold* because all you could get were black, white and grey lines.

She blinked and realized it was only a window with Venetian blinds, their blades not quite fully closed. 'Oh, sorry,' Bliss said ingenuously, once she was fully inside the room. 'Lights. I forgot.'

Merrily was starting to feel annoyed. He'd been setting this up for her, so she'd be in the best viewing position to get the full effect when his hand crept around the door jamb and found the switch.

. . . and all the women came out of the shadows.

It didn't seem unusually disturbing at first. They were centrefolds mostly; you could even see the little holes and rips left by the staples. They were pasted on two white emulsioned walls. The other two walls were black or a very deep purple.

She hardly needed to screw up her eyes against the light. The only illumination came from shielded spotbulbs just above skirting-board level, and it was subdued, serving only to reveal the photos and deepen clefts between breasts and thighs.

Of which there were quite a lot. Could be as many as a hundred pictures? Merrily wondered. They were soft-porn poses, mostly, colour and black and white. A scattered few were harder core, a couple featuring women using vibrators. The weakness of the lights and the clouding shadows added the illusion of movement – *that* was disturbing, in an eerie way. The rest, Merrily decided, was just sad for a man twenty years out of his middle teens.

'Like some repressed schoolboy's fantasy den, isn't it?' Frannie Bliss stood in the bedroom doorway.

Merrily turned to glance at the bed, keeping her hands in her coat pockets. The bed was king-size, unmade. Black shiny sheets – well, of course. There was a thick smell.

'Makes you wonder how he ever got a woman to spend a night in here, doesn't it?' Bliss said.

'I don't think he'd get one for a second night.'

'Ah, well . . .' He came a little way into the room. 'The answer, of course, is that he's got another bedroom, along the passage. Red lights, pictures of Spanish dancers – nothing to offend, other than aesthetically, and I don't imagine there've been too many cultural exhanges in there. So if we assume that's where he takes the, er, young ladies, then this'll be where he . . . enjoys his own company.'

Merrily shuddered. She recalled the shadow of Roddy Lodge standing immediately over her in front of the Pawson house, the birthday-boy look on his trowel-shaped face. *A woman?* he'd said.

Like: *any* woman. Another one for the wall.

Bliss stood there, hands in his pockets. They both had their hands in their pockets. Bliss was watching her, waiting.

Merrily met his eyes.

'Er . . .' He cleared his throat. 'You're not getting it, are you?'

'Sorry . . . ?'

'Take a closer look, would you, Merrily?'

She didn't move. 'I don't see that—'

'There'll probably be some ladies you might not recognize – don't know them all meself. But the one just to the left of the door, for instance, is Kelly Emerson, who was found raped and murdered in Swindon last year. That was the picture the family gave the police for the crime posters. It was widely used in the papers at the time.'

'*What?*'

She followed his forefinger to a blurred black and white face, dark synthetic curls, big smile, naked body in shadow. She didn't understand; the newspapers had used a nude photograph of a missing woman? She moved in closer, realizing that there was something wrong here, something skewed. Saw that the face of Kelly Emerson was in grainy black and white, but the naked body was studio quality and, on closer inspection, was slightly too big for the face.

Merrily backed rapidly away, aware of breathing harder.

'Thing is, of course,' Bliss said, 'that he couldn't've done that one. There's a bloke doing life for Kelly. Feller from Bournemouth – they got him on DNA and then he pleaded guilty, no messing. It's beyond any question.'

'But . . .'

Lodge had pasted the cut-out face of a murdered woman onto the body of some anonymous pin-up from the *Sun*? Just another model . . . just another dead woman.

She made herself go back and examine both walls more closely. There were several faces she recognized now: celebrity murder victims, celebrity suicides. Also the most famous car-crash casualty of all time. All of them women, all of them now dead, their faces pasted onto cut-out nude bodies – tragic victims twisted, with scissors and paste and lighting, into profane pin-ups.

Merrily turned away from the wall. All the sensations of last night were coming back, from the feeling of grease and smoke in her hair at Gomer's burned-out depot, to the waves of aftershave, to the cloying perfume of decay under the tarpaulin.

'I don't understand,' she said.

'I think you do, Merrily,' Bliss said softly. 'You're looking at his inspiration. These are the ones he *wishes* he'd done. The ones he wishes he'd got to first.'

She stood in the dimness, staring no longer at the illuminated wall but into the very thin lines of grey and white between the blades of the Venetian blinds.

'They're all paste-ups?'

'Not all of them. I think some were just piccies he got off on. Part of the mix-'n'-match. I expected to find one of Lynsey, but she's not there. Maybe because she's not had her picture in the papers, yet. There'll be a reason. He . . .' Bliss paused. 'He might tell you what it is.'

It was as though he'd opened the door of a deep-freeze.

'I can't do it,' she said.

'That's your decision, Merrily. I can't force you to see him.'

'He doesn't want to talk to me. You know that. He just wants a woman in the room with him. Any woman. You *know* that.'

She remembered Roddy Lodge passing her his card, scrutinizing her as if taking a mental photograph, offering to tell her all the scary things he'd told the local vicar about what he'd seen in the night. She didn't like to think now about what he might have seen in the night, inside or outside his own head.

Thanks, she'd said. *I'd like that*.

Yeah. You would indeed, my darlin'.

Merrily pushed her fists hard into the pockets of Jane's duffel coat, determined not to shiver. 'You'd better tell me what you know,' she said to Bliss. 'How did he kill Lynsey Davies?'

He shrugged. 'Strangled her. The PM should confirm it. Roddy told the lads in the car he'd "throttled" her. He just hasn't said it for the tape yet. Probably not bare hands, we think something was used – possibly a belt.' He paused. 'You can probably understand now why I want to dig up a few more Efflapures.'

'Yes.' Bliss was probably right to want to dig up every Efflapure that Roddy Lodge had ever planted.

'I didn't want to say too much in advance. Open the blinds now, if you're feeling a bit oppressed.'

She tugged on the cord and grey daylight made the room look merely tawdry. The view, sliced horizontally by the blinds, was further slashed and diced by the great steel legs of the pylon at the edge of Roddy's garden.

'Would it offend the crime-scene people overmuch if I had a cigarette?' Merrily said.

12

Dark Lady

Eirion subjected Jane to this sideways perusal she didn't care for. They were heading out of Hereford on the darkening Ledbury road, bound for Knight's Frome.

'Like *what*?' Jane demanded. 'Go on, say it!'

They'd been dissecting her mother's love life to discover precisely why it was going nowhere. From the lofty plateau of a relationship that was actually *working* – OK, within the restrictive parameters of herself and Eirion being still at school and stuff like that – Jane figured this was legit, her duty even. After all, it had taken her over a year to engineer the Mum/Lol thing.

'*Jane* –' Eirion did this exaggerated sigh '– you didn't, though, did you?'

'What?'

'Engineer it. It was nothing to do with you. In fact, if you'd kept your nose out completely, it would probably actually have happened before it did.'

'Thanks!'

'Well, it's true. You can't leave anything alone.'

'You totally smug *fat git*!'

She glared out of the window at the newly stripped hop-frames around Perton. When Eirion had picked her up at five p.m., she'd noticed he'd put on a bit of weight, a big Welsh problem.

'It's because of all this driving to pick you up,' Eirion said. 'Maybe I should stay in and do sit-ups and weight training.'

'I'm sorry,' she said gruffly, not looking at him. 'I didn't mean fat . . . exactly.'

He didn't respond. They drove in silence for a mile or so. They were in Eirion's new old car, a little grey Peugeot with one of those *CYM* stickers identifying the driver as a resident of

Wales who'd taken the vehicle abroad, if only to England. In fact, usually only to England.

And everything – like *everything* – was irritating Jane tonight. Obviously, she loved to talk and theorize about Mum and Lol, but right now – she realized this, she wasn't stupid – it was also an escape from the aura of manic desperation surrounding Gomer. She wished there was something she could do for him, but even Eirion didn't have an HGV licence, probably wasn't old enough. Besides, it would take more than dealing with a backlog of digging contracts to put Gomer back together this time. The big pendulum had taken him down once too often this year. Anxiety began to inflate in her chest; she folded her arms over it.

'Anyway, it doesn't matter who engineered it if it was meant to happen, if it's the right thing for her – and for Lol, obviously – and it quite clearly is. But because of what she does she's got to be sure it's the right thing by . . . Him. Like He *deserves* that kind of deference. If He exists.'

'It's a big responsibility, being a priest,' Eirion said lamely.

'The truth is,' Jane said, 'they're both basically wimps. Neither of them had the confidence to commit. They were just kind of moving warily around one another, like cats.'

'That's not being wimpish, it's what you do when you're an adult,' Eirion said, the trite bastard. 'You've made a few mistakes before, and you don't want to jump into anything without being sure of the territory . . . especially when there's additional baggage.'

'You mean *me*?'

'No, you egomaniac – emotional baggage! History.'

'Well,' Jane said, 'it's not like they're *still* not making a complete bollocks of it – all this about everything having to be kept under wraps . . . which is like *totally* ridiculous.'

'It's not, totally, when you think about it.'

Jane leaned back against the passenger door. 'What's to think *about*? If you look at the Anglican Church as a whole, about half the priests are gay, right? And *they*'re not hiding their private life any more, are they? They're practically announcing it from the pulpit.'

'Dearly beloved brethren . . .' Eirion did this reedy voice. 'This morning, I have to impart to you all that the big black guy living with me at the vicarage is not really a Nigerian theological student, as originally announced in the parish magazine. In fact, he's my *special friend*.'

Jane fought back the grin. 'But I mean, with a gay vicar you've got an ordained minister who's having sex with one or more partners with no possibility of any of them ever becoming the vicar's wife, in the traditional sense, so why can't two heterosexuals—?'

'Because, right now,' Eirion said in his explaining-to-the-child tone, 'neither of them needs the *shit*. She's had more publicity than she ever wanted just lately. Plus, Lol's got a lot to work out, with this album and the chance of a comeback after, well, a very long time. Be bad enough for someone who hadn't had . . . the kind of problems he's had.'

'I'll tell you one thing, Irene, if Mum had walked away, he wouldn't've been able to finish that album. If you listen to the new songs, most of them are actually *about* her. Which has got to be just *the* most incredible turn-on, hasn't it? Like being the Dark Lady of the Sonnets.'

'Jane, with all respect and everything—'

'OK, hyper. But if *I* was his Muse . . .'

Eirion stopped for the traffic lights at Trumpet. 'You still fancy him, don't you?'

She stared at him, resentful again. He'd refused to let her drive, claiming the car wasn't insured for a learner. Which was bollocks, probably. The truth was he was afraid.

'But what this is really . . . Jane . . . ?'

'What?' she said sulkily.

'What this is really about is Moira Cairns, isn't it?'

'That's crap. Moira Cairns is really old.'

'And really beautiful and charismatic.'

'Moderately attractive, I believe. If you like that kind of thing and you can put up with the grating accent.'

'And – what – possibly *five* years older than your Mum?' His patronizing lilt was back. 'That's not *very* old, really, is it? And Moira and Lol have the same musical background. And Lol's going to be playing on her album. And she's doing one of his songs? And they're under the same roof, miles from anywhere, recording well into the night.'

'That is total, absolute, complete *bollocks*,' Jane said, furious.

It was getting dark now, and some of them were carrying torches or lamps. About a dozen people, men and women, with a few teenagers lurking on the fringes. From a distance, it looked like a group of very early carol-singers but, close up, Merrily could tell they weren't going to be bought off with mince pies.

A man came forward, his voice preceding him across the cindered forecourt of Roddy Lodge's garage.

'We'd like, if we may, to speak to the Senior Investigating Officer?'

Frannie Bliss turned to Merrily, raised an eyebrow and then walked out to them – a poised and dapper figure despite the loss of sleep and all the coffee. A pro, an operator.

'That would be me. DI Francis Bliss. How can I assist?'

'Well, I hope that, for a start, you can tell us exactly what's going on.' The man was half a head taller than Bliss. He wore jogging gear, luminous orange. He put out a hand. 'Fergus Young. Chair of the Underhowle Development Committee. Also head teacher at the school.'

He and Bliss shook hands, while Merrily stayed in the shadow of the concrete building, hoping on one level that all this wasn't going to take too long and on another – because of what lay ahead for her – that it would take half the night.

'Mr Young,' Bliss said. 'I'm happy to tell you what I can, but I'm afraid it's not going to be much.'

'Well, to begin with, if I may ask this, where is Mr Lodge?'

'Ah.' Bliss put his head on one side. 'Mr Lodge – to use a phrase which I only wish we'd been able to improve on over the years, but we somehow never have – is helping us with our inquiries.'

A woman shouted, 'Please don't patronize us. We know the kind of questions you people have been asking in the village.'

'Yeh, I'm sure you do.' Bliss peered cautiously into the assembly. 'The press aren't here, are they?'

'Of course not,' Fergus Young said. 'We're all local people, and we're here because we're quite naturally concerned about what appears to be intensive police activity around the community in which we've chosen to invest our lives. And if that sounds pompous I'm very sorry.'

It certainly didn't sound local. He was about Merrily's age, and had a bony, equine head with tough and springy dull gold hair. He looked like the kind of evangelical head teacher who did an hour's fell-running before morning assembly.

'Look,' he said, 'I can assure you that anything you say to us will be treated with sensitivity and discretion.'

Bliss looked pointedly at the teenagers.

'Or,' Fergus Young said, 'if you'd prefer to talk to just a few of us, in a less public place, I'm sure—'

'That might be a better idea, sir, yes.'

Young turned to the group to discuss it. Frannie Bliss moved away, hands in his trouser pockets. Merrily murmured, 'Shall I wait in the car?'

'Not unless you really want to. I might need back-up, with some of these plummy bastards.'

And so they all wound up walking, almost single file, into the village of Underhowle in the blustery dusk. The lane was slick with wet leaves. Nobody spoke much. Merrily knew that Bliss was working out how to turn this around, milk the villagers while telling them nothing they didn't already know and making it sound like he was taking them into his confidence. Walking a couple of yards behind the delegation, she had the feeling of being towed into something she was going to regret.

Underhowle: she didn't know what to expect. The village, though still in Herefordshire and close to the most expensive curves of the Wye Valley, was also on the fringe of the Forest of Dean, the less affluent part of rural Gloucestershire – former mining area, high unemployment, a fair bit of dereliction. It wasn't only the River Severn that separated the Forest from the Cotswolds, and it probably wasn't only the Wye separating Underhowle from the posher parts of South Herefordshire.

Bliss dropped back to take a call on his mobile. 'Yeh.' Then he listened for a while. 'So that bears out? Good, good . . .'

The trees dwindled, lights appeared.

'Lovely job. Ta very much, George.'

Bliss snapped his phone shut, dropped it into his jacket pocket and quietly punched his left palm with his right fist. Fergus Young glanced back at him sharply. Merrily wondered if Bliss had been given the post-mortem result, but he didn't enlighten her. She caught up with the others.

'Never seems to stop raining these days, does it?' she said to nobody in particular, reaching for her hood.

'Aspect of global warming,' a white-bearded man growled. 'We only have ourselves to blame.'

'I suppose so.'

There was a solitary street lamp at a staggered crossroads, a signpost pointing through the rain to Ross in the west, Lydbrook in the east. Ahead of them, Merrily saw sporadic cottages and modern houses edging warily up a stubbly hillside with the pylons marching behind. In the dusk, with few lights, it looked stark, like a big, sloping cemetery.

'We'll use the village hall, I think,' Fergus Young said.

Not what Merrily was expecting, given the bleakness of the village. Nor, after the abattoir ambience of Ledwardine parish hall, what she was used to.

It had evidently been a barn, left over from the days when the village centre had formed around old farms. Now it was the classiest kind of barn conversion: chairs with tapestry seats, tables of antique pine. Wall lights shone softly on unplastered rubble-stone, open beams and rafters.

A sandstone lintel, above a window in the end wall, had one word carved into it: ARICONIUM.

There was also a coffee bar. A dark, wiry guy with a shaven head went behind it, flicking switches. 'Gotta be espresso, I'm afraid. That all right for everyone? Inspector?' London accent.

'Lovely,' Frannie Bliss said. Merrily wondered how long before he succumbed to caffeine poisoning. She took a seat near the door, glad she was wearing civvies.

Most of the villagers, including all the kids, had dropped away at the entrance. Now there were only four locals in the hall: the shaven-headed guy, the man with the white beard, a weathered woman in her fifties wearing a tan riding jacket. And Fergus Young, lean and rangy and looking more relaxed in here, briskly unzipping his orange tracksuit top.

'I'll introduce everyone very quickly, OK? Ingrid Sollars, who runs our visitor centre; Chris Cody making the coffee – Chris is also on the Development Committee – and, er . . . Sam Hall.'

'*Not* on the Development Committee.' The bearded man was sitting on the edge of one of the tables. He had thin white hair dragged back into a ponytail, was maybe in his mid-sixties. Merrily had the feeling he'd invited himself to the party.

'And . . . I'm sorry.' Fergus Young turned to Frannie Bliss. 'Inspector . . . ?'

'Bliss.'

'Of course. And your colleague . . . Sergeant, is it?'

'One day maybe, if she keeps her nose clean.' Bliss smiled blandly at Merrily. 'This is DC Watkins.'

Merrily smiled back fractionally, saying nothing. Yeah, well, it probably made sense; the truth would only provoke questions they could do without right now.

She sat quietly, like a minion. In the civilized warmth, she was aware of her thoughts being sucked back into Roddy Lodge's necro-erotic grotto. This wasn't something she felt qualified to analyse; it needed a forensic psychiatrist more than a priest. In fact, specialist advice was essential before Bliss took this any further – although obtaining it would mean alerting his superiors to the possibility of something far more extensive, more labyrinthine, than a one-off domestic killing. Which was why he was counting on her to soften Lodge. And she wasn't going to be up to that, was she?

'And what's the Development Committee, exactly?' Bliss said.

There was laughter from Chris Cody with the shaven head, the youngest of them – probably mid-to-late twenties. He and Ingrid Sollars were laying out bright red cups and saucers on the bar top.

'It's what we're obliged to call ourselves to attract lots of terribly useful grants from various organizations,' Fergus Young explained. 'But it's all rather more casual than it sounds.'

'Brings results, however.' Merrily recognized the voice which had earlier accused Bliss of being patronizing. 'I was born here,' Ingrid Sollars said, 'and I can tell you this community has prospered more in the past five years than in the previous forty. We don't intend to let it slip back, and that's why we don't need any of the more unsavoury kind of publicity.'

'Man's only doing his job, Ingrid,' Sam Hall said mildly.

'Notoriety we can do without.'

'Lot of things we can do without.'

'Let's stick to the point, shall we?' Fergus Young glanced at Sam and then at Bliss, smiled and shook his head, as though implying this was a little local conflict, nothing to worry the police. Sam Hall wrapped his arms around his knees and stared at the ceiling. Chris Cody and Ingrid Sollars began to hand out coffees.

'Ta very much.' Bliss sipped contentedly, glancing from face to face. 'So, how well do we all know Mr Lodge?'

Ingrid Sollars frowned. 'Well enough not to say another word until you tell us what he's supposed to have done.' She had grey-brown hair pulled back into a tight bun.

'All right.' Bliss sat down and stretched out his legs. 'I can tell you this much, some of which you'll know already. We're investigating the suspicious death of a thirty-nine-year-old woman whose body was found on Mr Lodge's . . . property. It's now been confirmed by a pathologist that this woman was strangled.'

'Oh, shit.' Chris Cody sat down.

Sam Hall swung his trainered feet to the floor. 'You're saying you've charged Roddy with murder?'

'We've not charged him with anything yet.'

'But you're going to?'

'Would you advise me not to, sir?'

There was silence, except for noises from the coffee machine and rain on the window. It was quite dark outside now.

'Poor Roddy,' Fergus Young said.

Bliss tilted his head, inviting him to expand.

'I . . .' Young sighed. 'All right, I'm the local head teacher – at the primary school. If you'd told me that one of the kids had committed a murder, my reaction would be much the same. I'm not saying he's in any way retarded – well, maybe emotionally, and I'm not qualified to give an opinion on that. But the idea of Roddy Lodge as a murderer . . . it's just hard to—'

'This woman.' Ingrid Sollars was still on her feet. 'The dead woman. Who is she?'

'Sorry. Can't tell you that until she's been formally identified.'

'Is she local?'

'Depends what you mean by local. I'm sorry.'

'Because questions were being asked in the village about a woman who . . . who's been missing for some time.'

Bliss nodded. Merrily recalled his mention of another missing woman.

'Inspector Bliss, have you found the body of Melanie Pullman?' Ingrid Sollars stood in front of him, her back arched. 'Is Melanie Pullman dead?'

Bliss folded his arms. Merrily tried to catch his gaze; this wasn't fair.

'Did you know Miss Pullman?' Bliss asked.

'She worked weekends for me when I was running a riding school. Then she started going out with Roddy Lodge and I didn't see her so often.'

'Why did she break up with Roddy?'

'I assume because he took up with another woman.'

'Which nobody could understand,' Sam Hall said. 'Melanie was a nice girl and pretty, whereas the other woman looked, uh . . .' He glanced at Ingrid Sollars, smiled and shook his head.

'What?' Bliss asked.

'OK, good-looking, but older and . . . kind of a hard bitch, you want the truth.'

Sam Hall had a curious hybrid accent: the Gloucester roll you found east of Ross made more fluid by something transatlantic. Ingrid Sollars stared at him like he'd already said far too much.

'So who's the other woman?' Bliss said casually.

'Aw hell, Ingrid,' Sam Hall said, 'this is all gonna come out – why waste time? Name's Lynsey Davies, Inspector. When she's not in residence at Roddy's place, she lives over in Ross, which is where he picked up most of his, uh, companions.'

'So that's where we could expect to find Ms Davies at the moment, then, is it, sir?'

'I guess. Though there is another— OK!' Sam put up his hands to field Ingrid's glare. 'No gossip. I'll stick with the facts. Yeah, someplace in Ross. Personally, I haven't noticed her around the last couple weeks.' He raised an eyebrow at Bliss, then looked away to show he wasn't going to follow up on this.

Ingrid Sollars moved towards a chair, then turned back to Bliss. 'When Melanie Pullman disappeared, some of us thought you – the police – ought to have looked harder. But you abandoned her.'

'I don't think "abandoned" is quite the right word,' Bliss said. 'But, yeh, there are hundreds of adult missing persons, and not that many police. We have to prioritize and, unless we think someone's in immediate danger, we can't always devote the resources we'd like to. However . . . I *can* say I'd be very surprised if this turned out to be Miss Pullman's body. And not only because it's about two years since she disappeared.'

'Oh.' Ingrid Sollars sat down, expressionless. 'Thank you.'

'Nonetheless,' Bliss said thoughtfully, 'since you mention it, in the light of what's happened, the circumstances of Melanie's disappearance might warrant another look, do you think?'

'Oh, now just a minute.' Fergus Young sat up. 'This situation's fraught enough—'

'I'm just asking the question, Mr Young. How long after breaking up with Roddy Lodge did Miss Pullman disappear? Is it possible she disappeared *before* breaking up with Roddy? If you see what I mean.'

Sam Hall said, 'I'd say not. But around this time Roddy Lodge's love life would've been a little hard to chart. Boy seems to have gone through what you might call a delayed adolescence – like he'd discovered sex for the first time in his thirties. I guess you'd say no woman was safe. Although by *safe*, that's not to say . . .'

Fergus Young nodded regretfully. 'In a way Sam's right, I suppose that's what I meant earlier about Roddy being a big kid. His overtures to women were always so obvious, so unsophisticated – so immature, really – that we perhaps didn't appreciate how often he . . . you know.'

'Stop it!' Ingrid Sollars shouted. 'You've no grounds, neither of you . . .'

Fergus looked embarrassed. 'I'm sorry. It's true that most of us haven't been here long enough to give you a reliable opinion.' He looked at Ms Sollars. 'You were born here, of course.'

'And brought up not to gossip, Mr Young.'

'Well, I was born here, too.' Sam Hall lowered himself into a chair opposite Bliss. 'And I think this is a situation where the famous Forest caution can do more harm than good. I know the Lodge family reasonably well. Solid, traditional farmers, made a good living, looked after their money, regulars at the Baptist Church before it closed.'

'And Roddy was the baby, right?' Bliss said.

Sam Hall nodded. Merrily noticed he was drinking not coffee but spring water from a bottle. 'Mother dead, so it was an all-male household: Harry Lodge and the three sons, of which Roddy was the youngest by almost a quarter-century. Harry never remarried, and whatever happened, he tended to accept it as the will of God. Personally, I don't know too much about Roddy's life when he was growing up, being as I was away for some years, but I guess it was kinda . . . constrained?'

He stopped and glanced at Ingrid, who presumably *had* been here during those years, but she wouldn't be drawn and looked away.

'Don't give up on us, Mr Hall,' Bliss said.

Sam shrugged. 'Well . . . when I came back from the States, Harry Lodge had just died and left Roddy the money to start a business, give himself a direction in life. To everyone's surprise – not least Roddy's, I guess – it took off, and . . . and so did Roddy. After this confined, God-fearing life on the family farm, where earnings tended to be conserved, were certainly never flaunted, he suddenly had more money than he knew what to do with. I guess it went straight to his head.'

'There's this little sports car in the garage, along with the diggers,' Bliss said.

'Yeah, a red one. And some pretty expensive weekend wear in

his wardrobe, I'd guess. Sure, with his flashy car and a place of his own, he found he'd become suddenly attractive to a certain kind of woman. I guess he was getting to think he could have just about any woman he wanted – or a good proportion, anyway. Lynsey Davies didn't seem to mind – least, she stuck around. Maybe she liked the sports car.'

'And were the other women around, too, at the same time?'

'Not in Underhowle. But I have friends in Ross. In some of the pubs there, Roddy was felt to be a nuisance, always trying to pick up girls.'

'Sometimes succeeding?'

'Aw hell, more than sometimes. Rebuffs bounced off him. If there's such a thing as what the Americans call a *retard* – only with a mental age of sixteen – then that's what I guess you're looking at here.'

'Nicely put, sir,' said Frannie Bliss. Merrily expected follow-up questions, tracing the directions Roddy's new-found liberation might have taken him, but Bliss stood up. 'Well, thank you all, very much. I think we've managed to exchange some useful information there. If you can think of anything else, I'll leave a couple of cards on the bar here. Ring me.'

Outside, Bliss said to Merrily, 'Next time I talk to those buggers, it'll be individually. Like, the woman can obviously tell us a lot more, but she's not gonna do it in front of the rest of the Underhowle Development Committee.'

'What's that *about*? What are they developing?'

'Everything. Place has been going down the pan for years. Used to have three pubs, post office, bakery, all that. Used to be plenty of jobs in the Forest of Dean – mining and . . . forestry, obviously. Now, even farming's in trouble, and a place this scrappy's never going to make the tourist trail. All they had left was the school, and they had a hell of a battle to keep that going. That guy Fergus got a big campaign going, now he's a local hero.'

They walked back along the lane. The rain had stopped again, but the wind was up, rattling like a flock of pigeons in the trees on either side.

'And the other little bloke – Cody – the one who doesn't say much, he's the big industrialist. Builds computers.'

'Here?'

'Got a little factory. Doing very well, comparatively. Not exactly Bill Gates yet. More of a Bill Catflap – somebody called him that.'

Merrily laughed into the wind. Bliss looked at her. 'They don't pay you much, do they, the Church?'

'What makes you think that?'

'The knackered old Volvo. That coat. I always thought maybe you got extra for being an exorcist.'

'No, just the privilege of having only one parish, instead of about six, like the bloke who covers this patch.' Merrily looked down at her coat. 'Don't worry about me, I'll have saved enough for a new one from the Oxfam shop before winter sets in.'

Bliss smiled, his mind already moving off somewhere else – she could almost see it racing ahead of them down the windy lane, a striker needing a swift score before somebody blew the whistle. She tried to intercept.

'You learn anything back there, about Roddy Lodge and Lynsey Davies?'

'Just threw up more questions. If he was suddenly getting his leg over half the girlies in Ross, why the older woman?'

'Thanks.'

'You know what I mean.'

'What's *more* curious, I would've thought,' Merrily said, 'is why – if he's doing so well with real live women – why the wall full of dead pin-ups?'

Ahead of them, she could see lights in the garage complex, where Andy Mumford would be working stolidly on, alone in the bungalow with Roddy's gallery. She didn't want to see that again and was worried that Bliss was going to ask her to.

'And what's Ariconium, Frannie?'

'Eh?'

'The word "Ariconium" was inscribed on a stone in the hall.'

'I don't know. I've seen a few mentions of it around the village. Listen, are you up for this now? Roddy? You can ask him about the dead ladies.'

Merrily shivered. 'Frannie, it's a police station, not a wine bar. He's going to be on his guard. He isn't going to tell me anything that he wouldn't tell you. I really can't see that it—'

'Merrily . . .' He stopped at the edge of the garage forecourt, by the police tape. 'Let me be the judge, eh?'

'That's one of the things I'm worried about,' Merrily said.

13

The Tower

The Cairns woman was sitting alone in the glass-sided recording booth, cradling this curved-backed Ovation guitar. She wore this long, dark blue dress, and the white streak in her tumbled hair was like a silk ribbon that had come undone.

From up in the darkness of the gallery, about ten feet above the half-lit studio floor, she looked . . . yeah, OK, impossibly romantic. Made you want to puke. Jane, in her tight little woollen top, directed a resentful glare at Eirion – besotted, the bastard – as the goddess Moira put on her headphones, and began adjusting the tuning on the Ovation.

On the other side of Jane, in the tiny gallery, was Lol, who wasn't playing on this track; it was going to be a traditional folk song, stripped down. Jane was relieved to see how Lol kept looking away from the lovely Moira to where Prof Levin was hovering over his mixing board like a bald eagle.

Earlier, while Eirion had been drooling around the Cairns woman, she'd told Lol and Prof all about Gomer and the hateful pendulum of fate, and the impossible fix the poor little guy was in. And the dilemma: should he even be going back into a really back-breaking job, working alone, at his age? But what would become of him, mentally and emotionally, if he didn't?

Prof Levin, who was not that much younger than Gomer, had said that if this plant-hire thing was what the man did, age was a meaningless consideration.

But he would say that, wouldn't he, here in his cosy studio?

Later, Jane had privately conveyed to Lol as much as she knew about the even more grisly sequel to the fire, involving this Roddy Lodge – stuff she hadn't even passed on to Eirion because Mum had told her not to. But there were going to be no secrets from Lol, right? Nothing to make him feel insecure in the relationship, and therefore open to—

A low-level fingered riff started up on the guitar, in the drum-tight ambience, and then the voice came in: a voice that was low and heavy with dark magic and loaded with this beckoning sexuality.

Bitch.

Jane snatched a glance at Lol, noticing that he was looking less than relaxed, maybe wondering – and with reason – why Mum herself hadn't phoned to explain why she hadn't been able to see him just lately. He was wearing one of his sweatshirts with the Roswell alien face on the chest and his hair was nearly long enough again for the old ponytail. He was sitting very still. There was more Jane wanted to say but you weren't allowed even to whisper up here, or the wrath of Prof would come down on everyone, and she couldn't do that to Eirion, for whom this place was a bloody temple.

Other people: tact and consideration, walking on eggshells. Life was getting like some fragile little comedy of manners.

Jane sighed and leaned back in her canvas chair and listened to the song: predictable tragic-ballad stuff about a lady who waited in her tower room, watching every day at the window for her unsuitable suitor – and secret lover – to return from the wars. The way you did. Eirion was nodding, hands on his knees, so impressionable. She glanced at Lol. He was biting his lower lip, the way Mum would when something worrying was taking shape.

In a traditional narrative ballad, there were no wasted words and no sentiment. Long years passed and the hair of the Lady in the Tower was starting to go grey. Her father was bringing would-be suitors to her door, but of course she wasn't interested and refused even to see them. Jane thought of Penelope, Queen of Ithaca, waiting for Odysseus to return from Troy.

> 'As the seasons turned she moaned and cried
> To the moon and the sinking sun.
> And the flowers grew and the flowers died.
> How long can a war go on?'

And then suddenly, in this moment of, like, startling *telepathy*, Jane began to hear what she was sure Lol must be hearing: the awful subtext of the song. The realization just flew over her, like a ghostly barn owl, and she was sure she must actually have flinched.

The song was a mirror image of Lol's own situation. The tower was the granary on the edge of Prof's land, and the person in the tower was Lol himself – the Lol who would wait for long hours . . . days . . . weeks for Mum to come to him . . . *she* having to come to *him*, because of the covert nature of their affair. And it was *she* who was out there, following a vocation that, for two thousand years, had been the exclusive preserve of men . . . and working in its darkest places.

It was Mum who was away at the war.

Moira's voice had grown thin with despair. This was a voice that killed the cliché of the form, invoking not so much beery folk clubs as the smoky jazz cellars of another era. A voice laden with doomed love.

Jane thought, in horror, *It has to change, doesn't it? It can't go on.* She knew that Lol considered his music trivial next to Mum's spiritual work. He probably felt as confined and helpless, as furious and . . . impotent, as he once had in periods between medication. Like, outside of a recording booth, he had no reality. It would never occur to him, the way it occurred to Jane, that Mum – and the Church, too – might just be wallowing in self-deception. For Lol, it wouldn't be the validity of what Mum was doing that mattered as much as her having the nerve to go out and do it.

One bright morning, the lady in the song is looking out from her tower and sees a lone horseman, and her heart takes a great leap. At this point Moira's voice rose about an octave, and Jane saw Prof's bald head nodding in satisfaction.

She didn't actually know how the song was going to end, but she knew a bit about traditional music, and she recognized the fearful shrillness of false hope, as Moira Cairns sang:

> *'It was the springtime of the year*
> *And the sun was in the sky,*

*But the messenger climbed down from his horse
And night was in his eyes.'*

Right. So next time her lover appeared in the tower, it would be as a ghostly apparition. It was always as a ghost. *Last night he came to me . . . my dead love came in . . .*

When the next verse didn't come, Jane looked down and saw that the Cairns woman's fingers had fallen away from the strings. She stood for a moment, as if she'd forgotten the words, and then Jane heard her call across the studio, 'Listen Prof, can we leave this one for tonight, huh?'

Prof said something that Jane didn't hear. Eirion, clutching the wooden railing at the edge of the narrow gallery, exhaled a word that might have been '*Awesome.*'

'Aye,' Moira replied to Prof, 'goose over ma grave. Let's move on.'

DI Frannie Bliss, at the wheel again, said, 'If you ask me, those people, those villagers – the real locals, not the white settlers – *they* bloody know. They know at gut level that he's done it before. They've more or less given us another name: Melanie Pullman.'

'You're still naturally suspicious of country people, aren't you, Frannie?' Merrily said. 'You don't understand them, so they scare you a bit.'

'Balls.' Bliss drove past the pub with the hare on the sign where, only last night, Merrily and Gomer had huddled over a mobile, waiting for Roddy to drive past with his . . . cargo. 'No . . . all right, they *do* scare me. They have a different morality. It's a fact, is it not, that country people kill, without too much thought. Farmers, hunting types – they don't even question it.'

'It's still a big step to hunting *people.*' She pushed her cold hands into the opposite sleeves of her coat, Chinese style. The car heater wasn't doing anything for her. Basically, she didn't want to go to Hereford Police Station to absorb confidences from a killer; she wanted to go home.

'I don't know,' Bliss said. 'And unless Lodge opens up to you tonight, we'll be fighting for every scrap of the picture. And that's why I want to get into lifting some more septic tanks. Tomorrow, soon as it's light, if I can.'

'On your own? You're going to sign out the West Mercia police shovel?'

'Ah, well . . .' Bliss speeded up the wipers. 'As it happens, you've put your finger on a minor logistical problem there, Merrily. I want to lift a couple of Efflapures, right? Now, I could get onto headquarters, obtain the necessary chitties and have a nice, professional JCB team out here . . . accompanied by a bunch of nice Regional Crime Squad boys with a detective superintendent in green wellies. And it's bye-bye, Francis, thanks for all your help.'

'Modern policing,' Merrily said. 'You can't get around it.'

'But think what that would cost . . . and suppose I'm wrong? Also, they'd make a mess of a lorra nice gardens, specially with all this rain we've been having. So what *I*'m saying . . . how much better, how much more discreet, how much less likely to cause a panic, if we have a small operation conducted by a feller who really knows his Efflapures.'

'It's an argument, I suppose.'

'Good man, your Mr Parry,' Bliss said. 'A very able contractor, everybody says that.'

Merrily rose up against her seat belt. 'For*get* it!'

'Listen, it makes a lorra sense – feller who can whip 'em out, put 'em back, no mess. Might even make a better job of it.'

'But Gomer's got a personal axe to grind on Roddy Lodge!'

'Which is why I thought he might be happy to do it.'

'Frannie, you are so *irresponsible*.'

'Aw, Merrily, what's he gonna do? Plant evidence? Bring his own bodies?' Bliss drove placidly through the scattered lights of the village of Much Birch. 'I'm assuming not *all* Gomer's plant was destroyed. I mean, he'll be able to put his hands on a digger of sorts?'

'I'm not even going to answer that.'

'You just did,' Bliss said. 'Thank you, Reverend.'

She scowled. 'I can't help feeling that something here's swallowing us up. Me and Gomer.'

'Let's not be melodramatic, Merrily.'

'Maybe it's just you,' she said, 'and your voracious ambition.'

Bliss laughed. Presently they crested a hill, and there was the city of Hereford laid out before them like an illuminated pinball table.

Post-session, they were all – except for Lol – crammed into the scruffy kitchen behind the studio, where Prof Levin had his cappuccino machine going. Pinned to the wall over the sink was the proposed cover for Lol's album. He was shown in black and white in an empty field, wearing his Roswell alien sweatshirt. Someone had made him take off his glasses, so that he looked totally disorientated, which was quite a smart move actually, in Jane's view. The album title was stamped diagonally across the photo in stencilled, packing-case lettering.

ALIEN

Which was cool. It was a very cool cover altogether. Like Lol had been taken away and brought back but not to the place he'd been taken from. It wouldn't have his name on the front, so that the punters would have to take it out of the rack to find out who it was by.

She asked Prof Levin, 'Is it actually going to happen for him this time, do you think?'

'Jane, what can I say? It's a strange and lovely album. It needs word of mouth.'

'People say I've got an awfully big mouth.'

'Well, there you go.'

'And Eirion's very good at manipulating the Net.'

'It all helps.' Prof Levin wore an oversized *King of the Hill* T-shirt. His off-white beard was freshly trimmed. He was The Man, Eirion said.

Right now, Eirion was chatting up The Woman, having done his innocent, nervous approach, all pink-cheeked and lovable, the smarmy git, asssuring her he had all her albums. For heaven's sake, he was too *young* to have all of Moira Cairns's albums. Lol, meanwhile, had disappeared.

'So what's on your mind, Jane?' Prof said.

'Oh, I . . . Well, I was just thinking that it would be like seriously useful if Lol was to become mega very soon. I mean, not for the money or the fame, as *such*.'

Prof Levin inclined his head, over-conveying curiosity. Behind him, the cappuccino machine was making impatient noises. 'Give me a moment, darling, and I'll be with you,' Prof said to the machine.

Jane said, 'Like, if he was so big, so famous . . . well, we all know it wouldn't go to his head because . . . because it just wouldn't.'

'I agree totally.'

'I mean, if he was famous enough that people would be like, hey, can it really be true that *Lol Robinson* is going out with some little woman vicar? Does that make sense?'

Prof Levin considered. 'Some.'

'See, it's not as if *she* thinks she's any kind of big deal, but *he* does. He thinks she's spiritually over his head – like too good for him, I suppose, literally. When in fact he's probably been to places we can't even imagine. Mixing with really mad people on a level that even most psychiatrists never reach.'

Prof said gently, 'I think perhaps she understands that, Jane. But maybe they have one or two things to work out before they consider going public.'

'I still think it'd be useful if he was out there . . . up there, recognized, you know? I think he thinks that, too, though he'd never—'

'Give me a break!' Prof Levin spread his hands. 'I *agree*.'

'So is there anything else we can do?'

Prof shook his head. 'I think what we do, Jane, just for the moment, is nothing. I think we butt out and let what happens happen.'

Jane saw him lift his gaze across the room towards the Cairns woman. She heard Eirion asking the Scottish siren something about a man who played the Pennine Pipes, whatever *they* were. Moira was smiling politely, but her attention was on the doorway – Lol coming in.

'So where's your mother now, Jane?' Prof Levin said.

'She's, er, working, I think.'

Coming down from the gallery, Jane had said to Lol, '*I'm
sure Mum was going to call you tonight. She's just been kind of . . .
overburdened.*' Lol had merely nodded and then gone outside
on his own into the night, the alien, *Oh God.*

Prof called to Lol, 'Jane was just telling me she thinks you
should get out more.'

'No, I didn't.' Jane felt the blush coming, turned her head
away.

She heard Lol saying, 'I wouldn't argue.' He came over. 'Prof,
would it be feasible for you to spare me for the odd day? I've
kind of . . . I've just agreed to maybe take on this kind of part-
time job.'

'Job?' Prof said mildly. 'What kind of job?'

'Manual.' Lol looked down at his guitarist's fingers. 'I'll wear
gloves, obviously.'

'Sure, whatever.' Prof turned to attend to his cappuccino
machine, casually assembling mugs. 'Manual is fine. Maybe you
could also do bingo calling at night, to help destroy your voice.'

Lol explained to Jane, 'I called Gomer. I haven't got an HGV
licence or anything, but I can do the hand-digging and things.'

Jane blinked. '*What?*'

'Just to clear the backlog. Keep the business going until he
can get things reorganized.'

'You're . . .' Jane stared at him in dismay. He was sweating
lightly, his hair roughed up. 'You're going to work with like . . .
shit?'

Of all the people she'd thought might be able to step in and
help Gomer – even considering Eirion, for heaven's sake. Jane
felt herself going deeply red. Humiliated. Conspired against.

The Cairns woman tossed back her lovely hair and started to
laugh her croaky Glaswegian laugh. 'Aye,' she said, 'the thera-
peutic power of shit – that's been overlooked for years.'

On the other hand, it would at least get Lol away from this
bitch.

Pulling into the car park at Hereford Police Station, Bliss said,
'I'm not even going to *attempt* to compromise you. This is
down to your own conscience, Merrily. No tapes, no video, no

tricks, no water glasses up against the door. Just let him talk, and then you can tell me as much or as little as you want to.'

When Merrily got out of the car, her legs felt as unsupportive as they had last night when she was taking her first steps into the ruins of Gomer's yard. Bliss joined her under the lighted entrance on the Gaol Street side.

'There'll be an alarm you can sound if he makes any kind of move. I'll show you all that. And we'll be directly outside.'

Merrily pushed a hand through her damp hair. 'Could I go to the loo, first?' Prayer for guidance. You forgot how many toilet cubicles had served as emergency chapels.

Please get me through this. They walked up a ramp to the modest entrance. Inside: utility seating under Crimestoppers posters. A man sitting in the window, briefcase by his feet.

A white-haired sergeant appeared and raised a hand to Bliss. 'Francis – a moment?'

'Two minutes, Douglas, and I'll be with you.' Bliss led Merrily through a door and then through a couple of offices, both unoccupied. 'You want the lavvy now?'

'Maybe you could show me the room where we're going to do it?'

'Sure. One of the interview rooms, I thought.' He smiled tightly. 'You want to bless it first or something?'

When she saw the interview room, she thought a blessing wouldn't be such a bad idea. Claustrophobic was too friendly a word. It was below ground level, a bunker almost opposite the cells, a windowless cube no more than nine feet square, with fluorescent lights and air-conditioning vents. The air felt like very old air, *re*-conditioned.

'Bloody hell,' Merrily said.

Bliss shrugged. 'It's not the flamin' Parkinson Show, Merrily. Now, do you want the bog or do you want to stay here and purify the place while I fetch Roddy?'

There were two chairs, one small table. A microphone for the tape was plumbed into one of the brown-fibred walls. Merrily sat down in one of the chairs and said glumly, 'Whatever you like.'

The white-haired sergeant was in the doorway. 'Francis . . .'

'Douglas, can't this *wait*?'

The sergeant said, 'When you came in, did you happen to notice a young man with a briefcase?'

'Does he *concern* me?'

'That,' the sergeant said, 'was Mr Lodge's solicitor.'

Bliss stared at him. 'Douglas, Mr Lodge hasn't gorra fuckin' solicitor. He *refused* a solicitor. You were *there*.'

'You go and explain that to this kid, then,' Douglas said.

The solicitor was on his feet, waiting for them. He wore black-framed Jarvis Cocker glasses under glossy dark hair streaked with gold. He looked all of twenty-four, but he had to be older to have qualified.

'*He*'s a new one.' Bliss peered through the glass.

'Office in Ross,' Douglas said. 'Ryan Nye. High-flyer.'

'He's hardly out the fuckin' nest.'

'I did try to warn you, Francis, but your phone was turned off.'

'Yeh.' Bliss walked out into the reception area. 'Mr Nye? DI Francis Bliss. How can I help?'

Ryan Nye smiled affably, if a little nervously, shaking hands. 'Mr Bliss, this isn't my usual sort of thing, so I hope you'll excuse my naivety, but I was rather hoping you could either charge my client or release him. He's not well, is he?'

'Not well in what way, exactly, sir?'

'I rather thought you'd have been informed. Headache, nausea, disorientation.'

'It can be a very disorientating experience, sir, getting arrested for murder. And I'm afraid I don't see him being charged tonight.'

'Then I really think he should see a doctor, or— Look, I'm trying to be helpful here . . . have you thought about a psychiatrist?'

Bliss folded his arms. 'Are you an expert on mental health, Mr Nye?'

'Of course I'm not. I'm trying to be helpful.'

'You have reason to think he might harm himself, sir?'

'His behaviour's erratic, that's all I'm saying.'

Bliss was silent for a moment. Then he said, 'As a matter of fact – and I don't know whether he's mentioned this to you, sir – he *has* asked to see a priest.'

'What – for the last rites?' Ryan Nye's face expressed pained disbelief. 'Look, Inspector, it's my impression that Mr Lodge doesn't want to see anybody at all, and *I* certainly wouldn't advise—'

'Would you like us to go and ask him again, sir?'

'No, I wouldn't, actually. He certainly didn't say anything to me about a priest. I really do think you should consider quite carefully what I've been saying. My client is *not a well man.*'

Outside, Bliss went off like an inexpensive firework, storming into the night then fizzling out, next to a lurid traffic car at the front of the station, looking like he wished he had the energy to put his fist through its windscreen. Or into the face of Roddy Lodge's solicitor, Mr Ryan Nye, spoiling his glossy, streaked coiffure, dislodging his Jarvis Cocker glasses.

'You know what *this* means?' He leaned against the traffic car. 'Means we've gorra leave the light on in Roddy's cell, have an officer peeping in at him all night. Also means I've gorra get onto the Stonebow unit at the hospital and drag a psychiatric nurse over here. And if anything happens to him I'm up the Swanee.'

Merrily said, 'You don't really *want* him to be mentally ill, do you?'

'He's *not* mentally ill. He's a crafty sod. Fuckin' Nora, where do these leeching bastards come from? Is this lad an ambulance chaser, or did somebody engage him on Roddy's behalf?'

'Frannie . . .' Merrily looked over a traffic queue to the new magistrates' court that the planners had allowed to eat up a useful car park. 'Be careful, OK?'

Merrily went home by taxi. She hung her coat over the post at the foot of the stairs and fed the cat. Alone in the vicarage, she felt edgy and unclean, and also guilty at being grateful to Roddy Lodge's flash young lawyer for sparing her an intimate session with a man who kept eroticized pictures of dead women on his bedroom walls.

It was nearly nine p.m. To get this out of the way, she rang the Reverend Jerome Banks, Rural Dean for Ross-on-Wye. She remembered him as a wiry man with an abrupt manner, an ex-Army officer who'd once served alongside James Bull-Davies at Brecon. If Roddy Lodge had been mentally unstable, he ought to have spotted the signs. She got his answering machine and left her name, would try again tomorrow.

She had a shower, washed her hair, thinking of Jane at Knight's Frome with Lol, wishing she was there. After putting on a clean alb, she still felt uncomfortable, a little clammy. She was pulling her black woollen shawl around her shoulders, ready to walk over to the church for some further cleansing, when the phone rang.

It was the Reverend Jerome Banks. 'Mad?' he said. 'Oh yes. Absolutely barking, I'd say.'

14

Recognizing Madness

Had someone followed her in?

If it was a footstep, it was a light one. It might be a cat. Sometimes cats came into the church, and once there'd been a badger. But badgers weren't stealthy; they clattered and rummaged.

Merrily was sitting in the old choirmaster's oaken chair with her hands on her knees, a single small candle lit on the altar fifteen feet away, a draught from somewhere bending the flame, making shadows swirl and dip and rise to the night-dulled stained-glass window at the top of the chancel.

Ledwardine Church was locked soon after dark, nowadays, unless a service or a meeting was scheduled. She'd let herself in through the side entrance, which at least had a key you didn't need both hands to turn. Against all advice, she hadn't locked the door behind her. It was fundamentally important to feel she had protection in here, inside this great medieval night-dormant engine, or else what was the point?

Probably hadn't been a footstep at all. After a day like this, the world seemed riddled with tunnels of obsession. For a cold moment, Merrily held before her an image of the frozen smiles of all the dead women on Roddy Lodge's bedroom walls as they writhed in other women's bodies, and then she let it fade, whispering The Lord's Prayer. Apart from having to give evidence at the inquest on Lynsey Davies, her role in this particular police investigation was probably over.

And yet – shifting restlessly in the choirmaster's chair – how *could* it be over when she was still attached via Gomer, who would never back off until Lodge had been convicted for Nev? Plus, here was Frannie Bliss about to exploit Gomer in the interests of keeping the case in his pocket: bad, selfish policing, and he knew it. Maverick cops were for the movies, and Frannie was on a narrowing tightrope. Meanwhile, Roddy Lodge . . .

'Barking, of course,' the Reverend Jerome Banks had said at once. 'A complete fantasist. Wanted to tell me about the ghosts he'd been seeing all over the place. Well, isn't as if you and I haven't met lots of people like this, all the clergy do . . . They seek us out, expecting tea and cakes and a sympathetic ear that also happens to be entirely uncritical. Hardly dangerous, in the normal . . . I mean, not even to themselves, not in the normal course of things. Well, hardly going to spew out all this to the detective chappie, was I? What was I supposed to say? Boy didn't seem deranged in a psychotic sense. I had absolutely no reason at all to suspect he might ever do what he's done – well, of course I hadn't.'

'So you just offered him a sympathetic ear.'

'No, I said that was what these people *expected*. Personally, I've never been one to play the jolly old dim-witted vicar. That's what's got the Church into its present enfeebled condition, if you ask me. Public starts to think we're all half-baked. And this chap was getting on my nerves, to be quite honest. Bumptious? Full of himself? Never seen the like. I wasn't entirely sure, to tell you the truth, if he wasn't taking the piss.'

'You said he came specifically to tell you about the ghosts he said he was seeing?'

'Look . . .' Jerome Banks had made an exasperated rumbling noise. 'He was asking me how his property could possibly be *haunted*. How this could happen when it wasn't an old house? Just built it himself – so how could it be haunted? I said had he put the pipes in properly? Had he had the wiring checked by experts?'

'He was hearing strange noises, you mean? Lights were going on and off, that kind of—?'

'I don't know. That's what usually happens, isn't it? Look, Mrs Watkins, I'm not awfully ashamed to admit I've never really been into that kind of malarkey. Don't know how you people manage to keep a straight face half the time. And anyway, this was rather before your time, so the only alternative would've been to refer him to your predecessor, old Dobbs – who was *completely* bloody barking, in my view . . . well, in everybody's view, really. So I was rather relieved when Lodge reared up aghast, said no, he didn't want any of *that*, thank you very much.'

'Any of what?'

'You know . . . prayers for the Unquiet Dead.'

'Then why did he come to see you? His family was Baptist, anyway, surely?'

'No idea at all. Never met the chap before.'

'So *did* he say what kind of . . . manifestation . . . he'd been experiencing?'

'Oh, it was probably all washing over me by then. I didn't take detailed notes. You know as well as I do that we could spend all our time listening to all kinds of complete nonsense, but when you've got half a dozen parishes to organize you have to adjust your patience-level accordingly.'

'When exactly *was* this?'

'Probably in my diary somewhere but, off the cuff, two years ago? Three?'

She hadn't pushed him any further, but she guessed there was quite a lot he wasn't saying.

Not her business, anyway. Merrily let her head roll, shoulder to shoulder, with tiny cracklings like the beginnings of fire in kindling. Her woollen shawl was a distraction; she let it slip over the back of the chair and began to relax her body, starting with her toes – tightening muscles, letting go. Warmth would come.

For a while, she'd resisted Eastern-influenced meditation – the awakening of the *chakras* – as vaguely unChristian and also *very* Jane. But the demands of Deliverance, especially, had brought out a need for experience on a deeper level, a need to find moments of *knowing*. There were still too many times when she was appalled at her own weakness and ignorance, the frailty of her faith – a woman of straw. OK, humility was crucial, but so was a small, hot core of certainty. Some kind of retreat might have helped restore her inner balance, but there'd never been time for that – hadn't even been time for a holiday. This job was smothering her; it was everywhere, like fog.

Lose thoughts. Concentrate on the breathing. It had taken her some time to realize that this was not about breathing consciously but becoming conscious of your breathing, simple things like that.

Gradually, the fabric of the church faded: the stonework, the stained glass, the rood-screen with its carved apples, the pulpit where she tried to preach while hating the word 'preach' with all its connotations, the entrance to the Bull Chapel with its eerily sleepless effigy. After a time, the church ceased to be its furniture, its artefacts. Now came the space, the atmosphere, the charged air – *this* was the church.

Her spine straightened from what she hadn't realized had been a slump; there was a warmth in her chest, her breathing was deepening. There was a moment when the warmth aroused an underlying pleasure that was close to sexual; she had a glimpse of Lol and let it go at once . . . you just let it go, without guilt or self-recrimination. You let the breath become the Spirit and the Spirit filled you, pouring down to the stomach, with that strange, active relaxation of the solar plexus – separation, breath of God . . . *God breathes me* – and, at some stage, entered prayer.

Thack.

Merrily's eyelids sprang back. The building seemed to shudder, as though the pews, the pulpit, the stone tombs had been brutally hurled back into place.

She knew at once what it was, knew every little noise this church made after hours.

The latch. When you were used to it, you could let the iron latch on the side door slip silently back into place. When you weren't, the latch came down hard: *thack*.

Someone had been in here with her for a while, and then gone out.

Or wanted her to think they'd gone out.

The draught had died; the candle flame was placid now, making a nest of light on the altar. Merrily rose quietly, stood under the rood-screen and listened intently for more than a minute, staring down the central aisle.

Rat eyes in the dark? Anyway, she refused to be intimidated. If they'd gone, they'd gone. If they hadn't, she was safer up here, close to the altar. She hadn't finished, anyway. She knelt in the centre of the chancel and prayed for Gomer. And for Roddy Lodge. And for Frannie Bliss, who confused police work with poker, his cards up against his shirt-front, always raising the stakes.

She waited for two or three minutes before coming to her feet, bowing her head, gathering her shawl from the back of the choirmaster's chair and going to the altar to snuff out the candle.

She listened again. There was nothing to be heard inside, not even the skittering of mice. Only the wind from outside. The row of high, plain, diamond-paned windows was opaque – no moon to light her way down the aisle. She always thought she could find her way blindfold around this church, but twice she collided with the ends of pews. Nerves.

At the bottom of the aisle, Merrily walked into something that should not have been there and fell hard onto the stone flags.

The original plan had been to return to the studio, to carry on working until midnight. But after Jane and Eirion had left, Moira had said she was tired, so Prof had suggested they wind up.

Soon after this, Gomer had phoned, the familiar old buzz under his voice.

'How you fixed for ten o'clock, boy?'

'*Tomorrow?*' The mobile had halted Lol at the door, Maglite in hand, about to guide Moira back along the track to the granary. He'd been thinking maybe he'd have a week or so – at least until after Nev's funeral – to get himself a little fitter before Gomer summoned him to make a fool of himself laying field drainage under the sardonic gaze of some Radnor Valley sheep farmer.

'Police, it is, see. Can't say too much on the phone, but anything that'll help bury that bastard, I'll do it, they knows that.'

'We're working for the *police*?'

'Can't say too much. Ten o'clock, boy?'

'Early night for you, too, then,' Moira said when he folded

up the phone. 'Hand me the torch, Laurence, I can see m'self back.'

'You'll need someone to run for help if you get attacked,' Lol said.

Moira rolled her eyes, taking down her black cloak from one of the hooks inside the stable door. The cloak was well worn, he noticed, and its hem was frayed. She walked outside and waited for him. The night was dry now and the wind seemed to have pulled back into the west, leaving a thin breeze.

They followed the pool of torchlight along the track, between two old oaks, avoiding the puddles.

Moira said, 'Jane's mother, your . . . friend – how'd she come to be doing that job?'

'You don't believe in a calling?'

'No, becoming a priest, I can understand *that* part. In other circumstances I might've gone that way, too, who can say? I was meaning the exorcism side of it. I don't know how many women priests would be doing that job, but I'd guess not many.'

'No. How it happened was, a year or two ago she was faced with something she couldn't explain, a . . . well, a haunting. And the Church wasn't helpful, and she made some comments at a particular conference about the lack of any kind of real advice for the clergy on the paranormal. And there was a guy there who was about to become the new bishop of Hereford, and he had this old-style exorcist he wanted to get rid of.'

'He tossed her in there cold?'

'There was a training course.'

'Oh right, a *training course*. So that's all right, then.'

He looked at Moira, her cloak billowing a little as if it was responding to her annoyance.

She said, 'Were there no' some . . . aspects of herself she needed to resolve, perhaps? Just that I've talked to a couple of exorcists over the years, and they both got into this particular ministry to try and understand certain experiences or abilities they'd discovered they possessed – precognition . . . clairvoyance . . . mediumship.'

'Common ground there for you?'

'Oh, aye, it's all been pretty much normal with me since I

was a wee girl. Hereditary – from ma mother.' She stopped, pulling the cloak around her. 'I suppose what always bothered me most was not that I was sensing stuff that just seemed to go flying past other people, but *why*? Why me, y' know? What was I supposed to do with it? Was there some wider purpose, or was it just there to give me a hard time – penance from another life or some shit like that? I just wondered if this was how it was with your friend – if she had personal stuff to come to terms with.'

Lol shook his head. 'She wouldn't claim to be psychic. She realizes she was brought in because she was a woman, youngish, personable . . . new image. That's it, really. And she's trying really hard to live up to it.'

'Jesus.' Moira ducked as more trees locked branches overhead. 'These guys have some things to answer for, don't they just? The administrators, the politicians, the power people with their meaningless degrees and their cheesy Tony Blair smiles, who think finding their sensitive side is learning how to change nappies and slice the fucking quiche. They never appoint people they believe can actually *do* anything, in case they do it too well. Just the ones they're pretty sure they can control.'

'He's gone now, anyway.' Lol stopped at an old footbridge over the narrow River Frome, which had seeped through the summer and now was racing with the rains of autumn. 'You think that, as a normal person, with no obvious special . . . attributes, she maybe shouldn't be doing what she's doing?'

Moira leaned against the bridge's damp wooden railing. 'It bother *you*, what she does?'

'Well, it's not really my place—'

'Oh, come *on*!'

'It's just that she was doing it before we—'

'Does it *scare* you?'

'Maybe not as much as it should.' He pointed the Maglite vertically so that it made a white cone in the air. 'I don't know.'

'Or maybe you're more afraid of what's in here –' Moira pointed to the side of her head '– than what just *might* be out there.' She levered herself away from the rail. 'Well, more often than not, in my experience, Laurence, they are one and the same. Seems to me . . .' She crossed the footbridge. 'Ach, this is none of my—'

'No, go on.'

A single light gleamed ahead of them. She'd taken his advice and left a light on in the granary, so that when they came out the other side of the trees they could see it in the middle distance.

'It would be lovely,' Moira said, 'to think that the Holy Church confers protection. But I cannae help thinking that the awful mess that is modern Anglicanism is now becoming so far removed from the source that being an Anglican exorcist—'

'Deliverance Consultant.'

'Maybe it's a wee bit like going into an unknown tropical jungle without your injections, carrying a road map of the Home Counties. *Deliverance Consultant*. Jesus, the weak-kneed bastards can't even say what they mean.'

Lol stopped on the bridge. Beneath it, the swollen Frome foamed and spat; it wasn't the river he thought he knew.

From the far bank, Moira said, 'So I was lunching today with your not-invariably-amiable local clergyman, the Reverend Simon St John. A serious psychic, dogged all his life by premonitions, apparitions, all the bloody itions you can name. Still thinking of it as a kind of sickness, and the Church of England as his sanatorium. Guy who'll run a mile from the unexplained.'

Lol joined her on the bank, uneasy. The torch beam showed the frayed hem of Moira's cloak trailing in the mud; she didn't seem concerned.

'Simon and I were discussing your problem – the need to keep up appearances. In truth, we couldnae see you at the heart of village life – in your alien sweatshirt, handing round the vol-au-vents at the vicarage garden party, then stepping up on the podium with the Boswell guitar to perform a couple of angsty numbers for the parishioners. Simon said if it was him in Merrily's shoes they could all go eat their lace curtains. But then, he's a guy.'

The kind of guy, Lol reflected, who never worried about appearances and got away with it. Merrily tended not to get away with anything.

'In the end, though, we couldnae come up with an easy

answer, although Simon said it'd be a terrible shame if you didnae come through, the two of you. Not least, he said, *because* of what she's doing . . . this lonely path, full of doubt and soul-searching and wondering whether you're going clean out of your mind. She needs somebody around her who's up to recognizing madness.'

'Thanks.'

'As for the wee girl . . .'

'Jane?'

They came to the granary, the light from the window outlining the steps. 'Some problem there, Laurence, my impression. Not a happy kid. I may be wrong; I don't think so.'

Merrily limped into the vicarage, dragging the black sack after her – an ordinary Herefordshire Council medium-quality plastic bin liner. Under the security light over the church porch, she'd taken one look inside and then closed the top quickly, spinning the sack round and round.

She shut the front door and stood with her back to it, panting. She felt as if something was making circles of madness around her. She didn't know whether to call the police tonight or . . .

Tomorrow. She'd call them tomorrow. She needed to sleep on this. Needed to sleep full stop.

Except Jane wasn't back yet. She was late – she'd expected to be home by eleven, because Eirion would then have to head back to Abergavenny, and it was already twenty past. OK, not *over*-late; maybe she should wait ten minutes before ringing Lol at the studio to see what time they'd left.

She left the bin sack in the hall, went into the kitchen and found the Germolene, pulling up her alb to expose the kind of cut knees that Jane was always bringing home as a kid. Rubbed some on, couldn't be bothered with plasters. She went to put the kettle on, lit a cigarette and stood for a few moments staring through the open door at the print of Holman Hunt's *Light of the World*, the house-warming gift from Uncle Ted. A tired and disillusioned middle-aged Jesus doing this sorrowful simper: *I'll hold up the lamp but I don't really expect any of you to follow.*

She thought, *Sod it*, went into the hall and brought back the sack that someone had left at the bottom of the aisle. Someone who had entered the church while she was praying, left the bin liner and crept away, leaving her to fall over it. Afterwards, she'd sat there on the stone flags, which also served as memorials, feeling the lumps in the sack, thinking of Roddy Lodge and dead bodies.

Now she emptied the contents onto the kitchen table. She stared at the heap again and tried to laugh. This was beyond insane.

Merrily sat down at the table, picked up one bundle, pulled off the rubber band and counted out the notes slowly and meticulously: £2,000 in fifties. There must be forty or fifty similar bundles. On the top of one there was a printed note on a quarter-folded sheet of A4 copier paper:

> For maintenance of the Church at Ledwardine without the need for commercial enterprise. A donation.

She heard a car pull up outside, a door slam, Eirion's familiar parting tap on the horn. She swept the bundles into the bin liner. Rapid footsteps on the path, then Jane's key jiggling around in the lock. As she pulled the bag into the scullery, the phone began to ring.

'How did it go?' Huw Owen said.

'Huh? Sorry, Huw, I . . .'

'The meeting, lass. The mobile-phone mast?'

'Oh.' God, was that *this* year? 'Sorry, quite a lot's happened since then. No, Ted didn't raise it in the end. However . . .' Merrily pulled out the chair, slumped into it, stretched out her sore legs and suddenly felt like talking.

Not about the bundled money; she wasn't up to discussing that, not until she'd puzzled out a few things. She told him instead about Roddy Lodge, from Gomer's fire and the death of Nev to the discovery of the body on the truck, from the visit to Lodge's bungalow to the interview-room session that didn't happen. It took about twenty-five minutes. After half a day with manic Frannie and the shock of the bin bag, laying out the Lodge affair for the stoical Huw was almost relaxing.

'Underhowle, eh?' he said.

'Not a place I'd ever been to before.'

'Dobbs went,' Huw said.

'Sorry?'

'The late Tommy Dobbs, your esteemed predecessor. He were in Underhowle a few years ago.'

'Not at the invitation of the rural dean he wasn't, unless I've been misled.'

'Who's the RD?'

'Banks.'

'Happen before his time. Five, six years ago? Summat like that. Haunting job, sort of. Reason I remember it, Dobbs did summat he'd never been known to do before.' ·

'Mmm?'

'He rang me for advice. In the normal way, his consultative procedure would begin and end with God.'

'Flattering.' Merrily was thinking this couldn't involve Lodge's bungalow because it wasn't even built then. 'Were you able to assist?'

'I, er . . . no. He were right in this instance – not our usual thing. Alleged case of what I'm afraid you'd have to call "alien abduction".'

'Yes, that would've fazed him.'

' "Mr Owen," he says – always one for formality, was Dobbs – "Humanoid entities in silver suits: what does this convey to you, Mr Owen?" 'Course Dobbs didn't have a telly. Bugger-all use referring him to *Star Trek*.'

'This was in Underhowle? Someone in Underhowle was claiming to have had a close encounter?'

'Several, as I recall. Several encounters, not several people. Only one person – young woman, late teens. I believe Dobbs did a report on it, for the record, to cover himself. Sent me a copy. I could probably find it for you, but I expect Sophie'll have it on the files up at the Cathedral, if you're interested. Dobbs found it disturbing because he didn't think the girl was lying or mentally ill, but he still couldn't do owt with it. I've heard of alleged alien cases where blessings or minor exorcisms *have* helped, mind. Which makes you wonder if there isn't a spiritual dimension to some of these so-called close encounters. Not this time, though.'

Merrily yawned. 'OK, perhaps I'll have a glance at the records. You never know, do you? You wouldn't remember the name of the girl – for the file reference?'

'Aye, vaguely. Summat like yours. Melissa? No, Melanie. Pullford. Melanie Pullford.'

Merrily stiffened. 'Couldn't have been Pull*man*?'

'It's possible.'

'Because if she's been abducted by aliens again, this time they forgot to bring her back. Been missing two years. Bliss thinks Lodge might have killed her. You have any thoughts on *that*?'

'Aye – tell the bugger.'

'If it was confidential, between the girl and Deliverance, that might not be entirely ethical.'

'Tell him anyroad. I don't like coincidence. He won't *do* owt, mind. He's a copper. If even the likes of *us* are suspicious of alien abduction . . .'

On the whole, not the best thing to say late at night to Merrily, who always felt responsible, especially if nobody else did. *Sometimes your most appealing quality,* Jane had said once. *But most of the time your worst fault.*

She sighed and made a note on the sermon pad to call Sophie, first thing.

And then Gomer phoned and told her what he was doing in the morning, he and Lol.

Merrily went anxiously to bed that night, and anxiously to sleep. Had anxious dreams.

Part Three

It is important to acknowledge common experiences that emerge in all world cultures and religions when we are living in an ever-shrinking global village. All cultures, including our own, acknowledge the existence of spirits at levels beyond the human. We call them angels.

Matthew Fox and Rupert Sheldrake
The Physics of Angels

15

Holes

It had to be. *Had* to be. But now, on the steps of Chapel House, Merrily was sandbagged by second thoughts. How did you do this? How did you go about accusing someone of giving you eighty grand?

'*Tell me*,' Jenny Box had said the other night on the square, '*have you asked God? For the money? Have you asked God?*'

It was a very old house, as old as the vicarage but better kept. A narrow, cobbled alley now separated it from the timber-framed row that began with The Black Swan.

She'd always thought it was called Chapel House because it was across the street from the former Zionist chapel, now selling antique furniture. Obviously, the house was centuries older than the chapel, but she'd imagined it being renamed around the turn of last century, when Nonconformism was hot.

Beginning to feel conspicuous, Merrily lifted the knocker, let it fall and heard a long echo from inside the house. With any luck, Jenny Box would be out. This was a bad move. She wasn't ready. Yet how could she not have come?

After breakfast, Jane had casually told her what she already knew – that Lol had elected to become an unskilled labourer for Gomer. And they'd stared at one another for a moment, Jane displaying hostility, like this was Merrily's fault, while Merrily wondered if the kid could possibly know the worst of it – what it was likely to involve.

Evidently not. At about nine, Eirion had picked her up, and they'd said they were heading back into Wales for the day. If they'd secretly been going to join Gomer and Lol in the search for decaying bodies under waste tanks, Jane might have thrown up a smokescreen but Eirion wouldn't.

When they'd gone, she'd tried to ring Lol, twice. No answer.

Why did he still find it so hard to accept that someone might want him to *be* there? Spooked by the way the Lodge affair was starting to surround them all like a blanket of smog, she'd pulled the plastic sack from under the desk in the scullery, emptying it out again to make sure she hadn't dreamed its contents and carefully counting it *all* this time.

Eighty thousand pounds exactly, for the church.

Right. OK. She'd knotted the neck of the sack and called the Deliverance office in Hereford, got the answering machine – Sophie must be down at the Palace with the bishop. Merrily had left a message asking if they happened to have the Melanie Pullman file and, if so, could Sophie e-mail it.

It had been then, stowing the bin sack under the desk, that she'd realized she'd finally run out of reasons for putting off a confrontation with Mrs Box.

Inevitably, the old oak door of Chapel House opened – not bumping and scraping like the front door of the vicarage, but gliding – and here *was* Mrs Box, carefully made-up. Or rather, made-down: her hair was brushed and shining and her face wore pale foundation, but no lipstick, no eyeshadow. She was wearing a simple black dress with a loose cord around the waist.

'Why, Merrily.' Smiling her gracious smile, this silky-voiced, willowy woman, the ex-model who would always make you feel graceless and untidy. 'You couldn't've timed it better. I was just off to my morning prayers. Now we can go together.'

'Oh.' *She was waiting for me. She knew I'd come.*

Merrily turned to descend the steps, thinking they'd be off to the church. But Jenny Box had already slipped back into the dimness of the old house.

'Well, come on, then, Merrily. I've been dying to show this to someone who'd really understand.'

Gomer was standing up in the mini-JCB, leaning forward like a horseman on stirrups, to witness the uncovering. 'Easy now, boy. Don't you scratch him.'

As most of the tank had been buried and seemed to be coated with tough rubber, it was hard to imagine how a few scratches would matter. But this was Gomer's show, Gomer's world.

Lol eased up, using the tip of the spade like a trowel, teasing away shards of clay. This was how they'd unearthed the first Efflapure, a big rubber ball full of human waste – slow and careful, as though it was likely to explode like a giant landmine in a welter of shrapnel and shit. You couldn't pull it out without emptying it first, and they hadn't got a convenient tanker, so it was a question of digging down to it, getting underneath, and Lol was waist-deep in the hole, his jeans soaked through because he'd said no to plastic trousers.

Outside the hole, it was already late morning, but the sun was like a soft-boiled egg. Across the long field beyond the garden fence there were still woolly rolls of mist on the hill above Underhowle – Howle Hill this would be, hanging a literal name on a village that Lol had never heard of until today.

He didn't know this area, and he'd never been to the Forest of Dean, which Andy Mumford said began the other side of the hill. He didn't know it, and yet he was already inside it, feeling its juices, smelling its smell. Everything here was earthy and pungent, but it was also, thankfully, kind of unreal: Middle-earth. Gomerland.

Mumford was standing well clear, saving his suit from mud-spurts. As if he'd picked up Lol's thoughts on some mental police wavelength, he whispered loudly into the hole, 'You see anything or smell anything apart from God's earth, Mr Robinson, you come out of there quick, and we summon the white people.'

Meaning the forensic people – white coveralls. Until then, it would be just the three of them: two seasoned professionals and a wimpy little singer with muscles like sponge cake, guitar fingers delving in mud and slime. Gomerland. Maybe inches away from meddling with the dead.

Which would then be Merrilyland.

'Smell?' Mr Sandford, whose garden this was, had been peering in, quite intrigued, but now he jumped back, alarmed. '*Smell?*' Here it came, the first shower of outrage. 'I thought this was just a formality. That's what Inspector Bliss told us on the phone. He said it was just—'

'Yes, sir, I'm sure that's right,' Mumford said.

'No, you're not! You think there's –' the colour was flaking from Mr Sandford's smooth face '– a *dead flaming body* down there!'

'*Mike?*' Here came the blonde wife tottering in unsuitable sandals at the edge of their bungalow's colonial-style verandah. 'Mike, oh, for God's sake . . .' Glossy lips retracting in revulsion. 'It *is* this Melanie Pullman, isn't it? They're looking for Melanie Pullman's body. Oh please, *not here*!'

'You got some information you haven't told us about?' Sandford was waving his wife away and backing off from the hole like it might widen and swallow him. He was about Lol's age, wearing sweats and trainers: suburban weekend-wear in an area of well-patched tweeds, overalls and waterproofs. He'd told them he'd taken half a day off work for this.

'Please calm down, sir,' Mumford said in his stolid, farmerly way. 'We don't *know* anything. Like I said, this is just one of a number of installations we'll be checking out in the course of the day.'

In fact six, Lol had been told, in an area roughly bounded by the towns of Ross, Ledbury and Coleford. This was the first – recently installed and less than half a country mile from Underhowle where this Roddy Lodge lived. From Gomer, Lol had learned a lot about Lodge: liar, conman, incompetent installer of overpriced drainage systems. The man who murdered Nev. Also a woman.

They were here to look for number three; why deny it?

'Don't expect this, do you?' Mr Sandford had returned nervously to the edge of the hole. His wife had gone back into the house; she'd be calming herself by phoning friends, Lol thought. This was how panic spread. The next house they arrived at, discretion would no longer be an option.

'No,' Lol said, 'you don't.'

'Move out the bloody city to find a place where your kids can walk home from school in safety, and just when you finally think you've . . .' Mr Sandford nodded at the exposed tank. 'How long before you know?'

Lol shook his head. The pit Gomer had excavated on two sides of the Efflapure was wide enough now for him to move around the tank. He reversed the spade, holding it two-handed just above the blade, and began to scrape soil from the curved, rubbery casing, his arms already stiffening under sleeves of drying mud.

'You've got a job locally?' he asked Mr Sandford – talking only to cover his own nerves, because if there was something dead down here, he was likely to be getting very close to it. He was aware of a dark bib of sweat spreading over the front of his T-shirt.

'Computers,' Mr Sandford said.

'Oh?' Lol took a careful sniff at the earth: decay, yes – but vegetable, surely nothing more than that. Gomer had said grimly, '*You'll know, boy, when you finds it*.' Like he was certain they were going to.

'You're not local?' Mr Sandford said.

'No, not very.' Lol began to prod tentatively at the pea-gravel around the bottom of the tank.

'In which case, you wouldn't know this is Silicon Valley in the making.'

'You've got a factory?'

'Not me personally. Chris Cody's the genius. Saved the whole village from a slow death. Seventeen new jobs this year, if you include part-time employment for cleaners and so on. That's big-time here. And it's just the start.'

'What, software manuf—?' Lol recoiled as his spade found something in the gravel. Black. Could be a shoe. He looked up at Gomer.

'The lot.' Sandford hadn't noticed it. 'We make computers. Right now, the big thing's computers for kids.'

It was a pipe, just a thick, black pipe.

'I thought . . .' Lol collected some breath, unsure if this was relief because, of all the bits you might uncover first, a shoe would probably be the least distressing. 'I thought kids could use anything. Eight-year-old hackers getting into the White House and . . . all that.'

'Nah, *little* kids, this is. Simple computers for four-year-olds, three-year-olds, two or younger. With games they can under-stand. By the time they get to school they're computer-literate and most of 'em can read and write. Puts 'em a couple of years ahead of other kids. Fantastic. Might look run-down and primitive round here, but this place is the future, and that's why—'

'All right.' Gomer jumped down from the digger, tossing his ciggy into the mud. 'I'll come in there now, boy.'

'You sure, Gomer?' Lol was already out of the pit, a shiver up his back.

'But you do *not* expect this,' Mr Sandford said, watching the Efflapure, as if they were excavating Hell itself in his half-acre garden.

'Careful now.' Jenny Box pulled back the rug in her oak-panelled hall, revealing the hatch in the crooked wooden floor.

'Chapel House . . .' Merrily said. 'You mean . . . ?'

'Even the estate agents didn't try to make anything of it,' Mrs Box said. 'They thought 'twas just a little cellar – a "wine cellar" they called it – which they thought would sound more appealing to the kind of people they were expecting to buy the house.' She pulled back a bolt and slipped slender fingers under a black cast-iron ring. 'This hatch is Victorian, I'm guessing, and they'd have made a feature of it, but for most of last century it'd have been nothing but a storage space.'

The hatch came up easily. Jenny Box laid it down flat. She depressed a switch in the oak panelling. Stone steps were softly lit from below.

'After you, Reverend,' Mrs Box said.

Merrily put a toe on the first step. She was still wary of enclosed and windowless spaces after a harrowing night last Candlemas, in a private mausoleum in Radnorshire. Maybe she always would be.

'There used to be a rail,' Mrs Box said, 'but it'd fallen off and I didn't replace it. 'Twas always my feeling that, going down there, a certain sense of danger would be not inappropriate. Sometimes, if I'm feeling a little daring, I'll go down in the dark and light a candle.'

'You should be a *bit* careful,' Merrily said. 'What if you fell and got trapped?'

'Tssk,' Jenny Box said scornfully.

Merrily went down the steps, which curved. She was wondering: some kind of priest's hole? Was the house old enough for that? As she came to the bottom step, she glanced back over her shoulder, trepidation lightly brushing her, as if the hatch might come crashing down, the bolt thrown, sealing her underground with . . . what?

There was an absurd moment of relief when she saw Jenny Box following her. She went forward, ducking – not something she had to do very often, even in the oldest cottages, but here the curved ceiling was, at its highest, only an inch or so above her head.

Mrs Box laughed lightly. 'Kneeling room only, for most people today. I guess people were all a lot shorter when this was built.'

A round lantern, with an electric bulb, hung close to the wall, and Merrily saw she was in a short, narrow passage, its walls recently replastered and painted white. A smell. Incense? She didn't move. She felt cold down here, despite still wearing her coat – the short woollen one, newish; she hadn't wanted to look too poor this morning.

She wants me to know . . . is that possible?

'Go on.' Jenny Box was behind her, not quite touching her. 'Go through.'

The passage opened out into a small white room lit by a second lantern and given focus by a low wooden altar. The atmosphere was suddenly so pervasive that, if she hadn't been so unsettled, it might have brought Merrily instinctively to her knees.

'I didn't know this even existed.'

She'd been expecting something contrived, something fabricated, something faintly naff. But there were places where you could be brought in blindfold and you'd still be instantly aware of the energy of prayer.

The altar was of dark oak, its top a good four inches thick. It had on it a small golden cloth, a heavy gilt cross on a stand and two thick yellow candles in trays. Before it, a gold-coloured rug lay on the flagged floor and the ceiling was painted gold, like a chantry. There was an oak settle against the back wall. An incense-burner hung from what looked like a meat-hook in a corner and behind the altar was a tall picture involving a misty white figure with a down-pointing arm extending to form what could be a sword.

From a small alcove in the stone wall to their left, Jenny Box took down a box of cook's matches, and moved to the altar.

'When I contacted the previous owners . . . well, no, not them because they were only here two minutes, but the daughter of the people who'd owned Chapel House for about a half-century before that, she said they always knew there was something "funny" about this cellar, and in fact local people used to say it was haunted. The daughter said her parents just used it as storage space, for junk. They didn't know its history – nobody seems to, but I don't think that matters.'

'No.'

'I mean, I could tell straight off that there was *something*. I had it cleaned out completely, did most of it myself. Scrubbed for hours at the floor – the first time I'd scrubbed a floor in many, many years. It seemed like . . . an important thing to do. Like washing the feet of . . .' She broke off and smiled almost bashfully. 'It had obviously even been used as a coal cellar at one time. The walls were pretty filthy. So I started to scrub away at them, too. And that was when the cross appeared.'

Merrily looked around.

'Oh, it's not there now.' Jenny Box struck a match. 'It disappeared again, I'm afraid. There I was, scrubbing at the wall one day, and the plaster came off, and it left the exact, perfect shape of a cross, but when I came back the next morning all the rest of the plaster had fallen off. It wasn't for anyone else, you see.' Her faced tilted; she sought out Merrily's eyes. 'It was to show *me*,' she said. 'You know?'

Merrily said nothing. This was no place for scepticism. Although it was still cold, there seemed to be no intrusive air down here, and when Mrs Box lit the candles their flames rose elegantly and brought the painting behind the altar to flickering life. She saw a stormy sky over a church steeple and, parting the thunderclouds, the figure of white smoke with what was now clearly a naked sword.

'It's not exact,' Jenny Box said. 'A friend of mine did it in London. She's a fashion designer, so I suppose the whole thing's a bit glib and glossy, but she did her best with what I outlined to her.'

'An angel?'

'Well, someone said it must be the archangel Uriel, the one with the flaming sword, and perhaps there is something in that. I wish I could've painted it myself, but I've never been very good that way. 'Twas all I could do to paint the walls.'

It was hard to imagine Jenny Box sweating in overalls, collecting those unavoidable emulsion spots on her delicate skin.

'Well, I couldn't let anyone else in. Not after I realized what it had been before. I couldn't have vulgar fellers smoking and swearing down here, now could I?'

Jenny Box smiled down at Merrily, arms by her sides, her black dress simple and monastic, except for the way its velvet cord hung loose just above her hips. In this moment, Merrily was entirely sure that this woman *had* left the money, unpretentiously in the black plastic bin sack. And in the next moment, she recognized the church steeple in the painting. And the wooded hills behind it.

'It's . . .'

'Oh, *that* part's exact,' Mrs Box said. 'I gave her a fine set of postcards to work from.'

Merrily took a good hard look at the picture. It was about two feet by four, in a plain, matt-white wooden frame. The paint was probably acrylic, and it looked surreal now, like a Magritte – the church hard-edged, an almost-photographic image, no brush strokes either in the clouds. Airbrush, probably – very professional. She turned to ask a simple question: *What does it signify?*

Jenny Box had gone to sit on the oak settle, her hands folded primly on her lap, her face lambent like some Rembrandt saint.

Merrily saw that the question wasn't going to be needed.

Three tanks raised, and still nothing. Relief for the Sandfords and two other householders, frustration for Mumford. They'd moved almost in a circle around Underhowle but had never gone into the village itself. The last Efflapure had fallen back suddenly into its pit, and Lol had twisted his ankle hurling himself out of the way.

'One more,' Mumford said, 'and then likely we'll call it a day.' Like *he*'d been doing the digging.

At the last place, there'd been a bunch of curious villagers and this pitiful middle-aged couple from Monmouth whose nineteen-year-old daughter had been missing for five months. A relative in Ross had told them about a man being arrested and the police digging for bodies.

Anything, they said, was better than not knowing.

It was heartbreaking. And probably unnecessary, Lol thought. He was aching all over by then. Earlier, he'd listened to Mumford talking to Bliss on the phone, arranging for the couple to meet him.

'When do you decide this isn't working?' Lol asked Mumford as they were unloading the gear for the fourth time. No point in appealing to Gomer, for whom this was personal.

'Isn't for me to decide,' Mumford said. 'Likely, the boss'll turn up in person at some point.'

They were on the gravel forecourt of a tall Victorian stone house with an 'Old Rectory' nameplate on the gate. A woman of about twenty-five with short fair hair and an eyebrow ring was standing watching, hands on her narrow hips. After a while, she sashayed over to Lol.

'You don't *really* think Roddy's a mass murderer, do you?'

'Don't actually know the bloke,' Lol said.

'He's just a little weird.'

'Is he?'

'You people, if somebody's weird they're automatically some raging psychopath, right?'

'I'm not a copper,' Lol said. '*He*'s the copper.'

She looked over at Andy Mumford and rolled her eyes. 'For*get* it.'

Mumford went to meet a man coming out of the house. 'Mr Crewe?'

'*Connor*-Crewe. Piers. How's it going, Inspector?'

Big guy – well, overweight, certainly. Fiftyish, with luxuriant grey-speckled hair and a wide, easy smile. He wore a denim shirt overhanging baggy corduroy trousers.

'Sergeant, sir,' Mumford said, in the resigned way that told you sergeant was as high as he was going and even that had been unexpected. 'That's Mr Parry over there. He's a professional drainage contractor, he won't take long, and he'll leave your ground without a blemish.'

'I'm sure that's true.' Mr Connor-Crewe beamed, his big, round face like the friendly planet in a space picture book Lol had owned as a kid. 'Just as sure as I am that you're all wasting your time here. Not that it's my place to offer an opinion.'

'At this stage, sir,' Mumford said, a very slight eye-movement conveying what Lol judged to be intense interest, 'we're open to anyone's opinion. Did you know Mr Lodge?'

'Well, obviously he installed this set-up for me, and it's worked efficiently enough so far.'

Gomer sniffed in contempt.

'And he had an assistant, like your man here,' Mr Connor-Crewe said, 'and they were both very civil, very obliging.'

Which must have saved Mumford a question. At each of the other places, he'd asked if there'd been anyone helping Roddy Lodge. In each case it had been someone different, and, no, they hadn't been there all the time. Mumford had said Lodge was known to use cheap, casual labour, usually pulling someone from what he said was a bottomless local pool of fit blokes claiming sickness benefit.

'Or, rather, *not* like your man,' Mr Connor-Crewe said. 'In this case, the assistant was the – I believe *late* – Lynsey Davies.'

The young woman stared at him. 'You never told me she was helping.'

'Aha,' said Connor-Crewe. 'Lots of things I haven't told *you*, my sweet.'

'Shit, Piers,' she said. 'He might have dumped her here.'

'He certainly might have *killed* her here, the way they were carrying on – violent arguments one minute, practically shagging in the mud the next.'

Mumford got out his notebook. 'Right,' he said, 'let's have a proper chat, shall we, sir? In the house.'

At first, Lol had thought she must be Connor-Crewe's daughter. Evidently not. She stayed outside with him and Gomer, after Mumford and his notebook had followed Connor-Crewe into the Old Rectory, watching them mark out a circle around the Efflapure, which was sunk into a paddock behind the house.

'That was a shock, mind,' she said. 'Lynsey.' She looked out across the paddock and another couple of fields to the tops of some houses: Underhowle. 'We all knew Lynsey, in Ross. Everybody's saying she was a slag. Which is . . . yeah, I suppose, dropping babies everywhere, but that's not the whole story. She was smart.'

'Who's looking after them babbies now?' Gomer said, as Lol uncovered the top of the globular tank.

She shrugged. 'Who's always looked after them? Grannies, ex-boyfriends, ex-boyfriends' mums. Having kids never held Lynsey back. Ace at palming them off on people. "Can you just mind him for a hour?" And then she don't come back for six weeks. You had to admire it, in a way. She had this fierce determination to experience everything she could get out of life. Used to buy these heavy books from Piers's shop, which was how I got talking to her. I mean, she wasn't stupid. When she wasn't around any more we just figured she'd gone off with some bloke – could be anywhere. You just . . . couldn't imagine her being dead, that's all.'

'If her wasn't stupid –' Gomer slid an oily tow-rope under one of the thick rubberized loops on top of the tank '– how come her wound up with Lodge?'

'Dunno. Probably because he had a fair bit of money – like a *lot* of money compared to Lynsey's usual men – and a fast car. She did *use* people. Let's be honest, she was good at men.'

'You said Lodge was weird.' Lol stepped back from the tank, started to cut into the turf around it with his spade. He was wondering how deeply involved in all this Merrily might have become, because of Bliss.

'Yeah, well, he is. You talk to people round here, they'll tell you like . . . how he works at night, that kind of thing.'

'Ar?' Gomer came over. He got out his tobacco tin. There

was one cigarette already rolled in there, and he offered it to the girl.

'Cheers.' She stuck it in her mouth; Gomer lit it for her.

'Works a lot at night then, do he?'

'It's what people say. Bound to get all blown up now, so like suddenly he's become like this vampire.' She took a long, needy drag and let the smoke out. 'Piers and me were in the pub last night, in Underhowle. Nobody was talking about anything else, obviously, but the place was divided between the people who couldn't believe he'd done a murder and the ones who'd always known he was a psycho. Like when he did Mike Sandford's sewerage Lorna was uptight 'cause he was out there most of the night. They could see him prowling under the full moon, digging.'

'That's it for weird?' Lol said. 'He works nights?'

'Well, you know, mood changes. Up in the clouds one day – drinks-are-on-me, chasing all the women. Next day he's slinking around like he don't want to know you or anybody.'

'Like manic depression?' Lol said.

'Oh, *sorry.*' She peered closely at him. 'I didn't realize you were a psychologist.'

Lol smiled sadly.

'*Sure* you're not a copper? I mean, you don't *look* like a copper, but you don't look like . . . whatever *he* is, either.'

'No?' Lol was disappointed; he hadn't been this muddied-up in years. Not physically.

'I do like to suss people – as a writer. Short stories, plays. Poetry, when I'm moved. Dennis Potter was going to look at my TV play – he lived in Ross, you know? But then he snuffed it.'

'And your . . . has a bookshop?'

'Piers? Yeah, in Ross. Second-hand, antiquarian. I work there couple of days a week, more in summer. Piers phoned me, said I might want to come up this afternoon – as a writer – because you were digging for bodies. He's thoughtful like that.' Something caught her eye. 'Oh, look, the poor police can't get a signal.'

Lol turned and saw Mumford had come out of the house, was backing away, staring at his mobile held at arm's length. He ended up next to Gomer's truck, the phone now tight to his ear.

'Ariconium,' the young woman said. 'Last defensive outpost against the techno-invasion.' She came right up to Lol. She wore a black fleece, the zip pushed halfway down apparently by the pressure of her breasts. 'I'm Cola French.'

'Gosh.' Lol didn't move. 'Really?'

'All names are real. What's yours?'

'Lol.'

'There you go.'

'What's Ariconium?' Lol said.

'Roman town. On the old iron road between Glevum and Blestium – that's Gloucester and Monmouth to you. The historians say it was down the valley, where Weston-under-Penyard is now, but Piers reckons most of it was where Underhowle is now. It's his new buzz-thing. Piers gets obsessions, then there's no stopping him.'

Mumford came over. 'Leave that a moment, boys.'

'Woooh!' said Cola French. 'Something came up. Go, go, go!'

Mumford ignored her, jerked his chins towards the house. Lol and Gomer trudged after him to the edge of the paddock, Cola French watching them from behind her writer's knowing smile.

'Let's just quietly pack up the gear,' Mumford said. 'We're on standby to meet Mr Bliss.'

'Oh we are, are we?' Gomer said.

'Bear with us, Gomer,' Mumford said tiredly.

'Been bearin' with you all morning, boy, and we en't found a bloody thing. Your gaffer wants to check his information 'fore he gets carried away, ennit?'

'My gaffer,' Mumford said, 'says that Roddy's finally talking.'

'Ar? Talked about what he done to Nev yet, has he?'

'I don't know, Gomer.'

'They ever tell you *anything*, Andy boy?'

Mumford, maybe sensing mutiny, said, 'All right. This goes no further.'

Gomer looked scornful.

'Looks like he's coughed on three,' Mumford said. 'Lynsey, Melanie Pullman and the girl from Monmouth, Rochelle Bowen.'

Lol turned away. The sky was shabby and sunless now, and only the line of pylons gleamed.

'Soon as he decides to remember where they're buried,' Mumford said, 'they're bringing him out to show us. That good enough for you?'

Gomer clapped his hands together, producing a sharp echo from the direction of conifer-clad Howle Hill.

16

The Glory

'When I first came here,' Mrs Box said, 'I'd spent the whole day looking for somewhere to live. An agent had sent me the particulars of a place in the country out past Hereford that was far too big and had all this land – what was I supposed to do with seven and a half acres, buy myself a tractor? Besides, the local church was ugly and the minister was a disinterested auld devil.'

'I won't ask which one it was.' Merrily stood with her back to the candlelit altar and the long painting.

'Doesn't matter, I can see that now.' Jenny Box was demure on the oak settle, hands forming a cross on her knees. 'But at the time – and for other reasons, too – I was very deeply depressed. And the countryside was flat and unwelcoming and I felt lonely and unwanted and . . . unnecessary, you know? I'd spent a holiday here once, with my husband when things were good with us, and I loved it and I'd built up my hopes of finding somewhere . . . but now 'twas all wrong. I didn't feel I belonged, or was *ever* going to belong. I was starting to question the whole idea of moving out here. And the clouds were gathering, and I just got into the car and drove in any direction, I didn't care.'

Merrily asked hesitantly, 'Your marriage had—'

'Broken up? No. Oh no. And still hasn't, though he goes his own way, and has his women like he always did. Well, that's fine, I don't have a problem with *that* any more. No, I just decided I wanted a place in the country and he was in no position, quite frankly, to object. I mean, he comes down sometimes, from London, at weekends, to discuss business matters – you'll have seen him, no doubt, though not in church – but if he looks like staying for more than one night I'll go and stay in London for a few days. The marriage, you might say, is winding down slowly.'

Merrily recalled the gist of her words from the other night:

'*The business I was in, the things I was doing for money and self-gratification, all that's repellent to me now. I came here to cleanse myself.*' A reference, it had seemed, to her modelling days, her brief career in daytime TV. Was there more to it, though?

'But you'd still be business partners,' Merrily said.

'Would you happen to've been in one of the Vestalia stores lately, Merrily? Cheltenham? Cardiff?'

'Er, no. I don't seem to get out of the county too often.'

'Ah well, there's one supposed to be opening in Hereford in a few months' time, and that's what you might call a bone of contention. I don't like the name much any more – 'twas from my sad New Age days, I was one for the goddesses then. Well, it's too late now to change that, but I want the Hereford store to reflect a more robust spirituality.'

Merrily recalled what she could: the concept of Vestalia was about introducing spirituality into the home, from sacred candles and ornamental crystals to very expensive hearths like pagan altars. 'You mean . . . ?'

'A Christianization. I've been looking at Hereford Cathedral – at the ornamental chantries in particular. But we'll have a High Church feel, with censers and things. I'm going to London next week to talk to some designers. I want a store which is going to reflect the true magic, if I can use that word, of Christianity. The angelic.'

'And your husband . . .'

'Hates and deplores it. Thinks it's going to destroy us. Well, the hell with him, I'm the one with the ideas. Gareth has the contacts and the business acumen. Gareth it was who persuaded countless Londoners to install wood-stoves, to burn scented sacred apple logs brought up from the country at enormous prices. Would've been cheaper for some people to chop up their furniture and feed it to the flames.' Mrs Box laughed coldly. 'I don't even want to discuss that man, thank you very much, in this holy place.'

She stood up and glided to the door and reached up and put out the lamp, so that the sacred cell was lit only from the altar, and then she went back to her seat, in shadow now.

'Anyway . . . 'twas springtime,' she said.

'I'm sorry?' Merrily stepped to one side so she wasn't blocking the candelight.

'This day I found myself driving out towards Leominster. I'm leaving the main roads behind, soon as I can, looking for somewhere to get out and walk and think. 'Twas spring, and the leaves were half out, and some blossom on the trees, which were all startling white against a sky that was deep and mauve-coloured and loaded with rain that it wasn't about to part with until it was good and ready. I parked up close to a footpath sign, and I climbed over a stile and here I am on the top of a hill overlooking what proved to be this very village.'

'I think I know which place.' Merrily recalled a certain after-noon walking with the late Miss Lucy Devenish, proprietor of Ledwardine Lore, who had known everything there was to know about the history of the village and made informed guesses about the rest.

'Of course you do,' Jenny Box said. 'And you'll know how it overlooks the orchards, with the spire poking out through all the apple blossom. So very white, the blossom was, this day, under that heavy, heavy purple sky. And here's me just kneeling there on the grass, and praying and weeping, and weeping and praying . . . You know how it comes over you?'

'I . . .' Merrily looked down at the flagstones. 'Yes.'

A movement: Jenny Box sliding gracefully to the end of the settle.

'Sit with me.'

Merrily hesitated and then came to sit on the oak seat, opposite the altar and the picture of the church and the figure of light in the sky. There was some other movement, almost imperceptible, a small quiver, a flutter in the close air. Jenny Box gazed directly at the altar. When she began to speak, Merrily felt something like the breeze under Jenny's voice.

'I found myself praying to the Highest to be relieved of all that useless so-called spiritual debris. Praying with this absolutely overwhelming intensity – but the intensity wasn't from me, y' understand. It wasn't that half-phoney, feverish passion I'd known before; it was something *out there* that came around me and enveloped me. Something I was powerless to resist, to give you the auld cliché.'

Merrily nodded.

'You understand that, Merrily? You understand what it is I'm talking about here?'

'Yes,' Merrily said and relaxed for a moment into common ground and memories of blue and gold. Yes, this did happen.

'Of course you do,' Jenny Box said. 'See, I'd always thought myself to be a deeply spiritual person. But 'twas a poor spirituality, if I had but known it – Tarot cards and magical crystals and all the shiny paraphernalia of the Devil. Paganism slithering in round the back, like a door-to-door salesman with a suitcase full of glittery trash.'

Merrily, whose attitude towards paganism had become less black and white lately, said nothing.

'But I was drawn to it all, in the beginning, you see, because of its leanings to the feminine, its exaltation of *womankind*. Let no one say, Merrily, that it isn't men that've brought the world to the state it's in. Let no one *dare* to tell me that – me that was hurled away from the Catholic Church when I was barely out of my teens, soiled with the sick hypocrisy of men.'

Ah. 'Is this men in general?' Merrily said. 'Or . . .'

'Or more specifically, our parish priest, Father Colm Meachin.' The words coming out in a rapid, breathy monotone. 'The saintly Father Colm, with his stately manners and his high-flown rhetoric and his political friends, and his thin, white hands all over a quiet girl, Niamh Fagan, who was my friend. But that . . . Ah, you see, it's too perfect, that's the real problem.'

'Sorry?'

'Too neat and hard, it seems to me now, and it doesn't capture the glory of it all. The picture, Merrily – doesn't capture the quite *explosive* glory of the moment, and I never really expected it to, but I thought the moment should be commemorated here nonetheless.'

Merrily moistened dry lips.

'The moment?'

*

The unsettling thing was that Merrily was sure she could remember the exact day, last April or May . . . a ferocious electric storm heralding rain that had been almost equatorial. A Sunday. Tourists in the village hurrying into the church porch. Jane bored because Eirion had the flu and she'd been stuck indoors all weekend.

'A flash of lightning, Merrily! A flash so wild and bright I had to shut my eyes against it. And when I opened them, the whole of the sky was as black as a peatbog, and then –' the soft voice putting a thrill in the still air of the underground chapel '– came the tiny light, right at the centre, in the very darkest part of the storm.'

The church steeple in the painting was, without any doubt, Ledwardine's, shooting out of crowded apple trees, with the wooded hills behind it and the stormy sky above, charcoal clouds delicately parted as if by the point of the sword, and the light oozing through in violet-magnesium bubbles.

'The little light's growing larger before my eyes, until it's like a ball, or an egg shape, like some UFO thing. But I knew from the first that it would be more than that, more glorious.'

Merrily looked at the white figure, the sword-bearer: not Michael nor Gabriel but, apparently, Uriel, a peripheral archangel. Uriel came from the Biblical fringe, the Apocrypha.

'As I stood there on that little hill –' Jenny Box stood up '– absolutely transfixed, there was a sudden –' she swung her arm '– *slash* of fork lightning, and the lightning itself became the sword. The sword *was* the lightning. You know? And I just shut my eyes, Merrily, and the rain came down, so very hard that I was soaked to the skin inside a minute. Soaked through, and laughing like a fool.'

Jenny Box's face shone with joy in the altar lights. She'd stolen the show, had been in charge from the beginning. There had been no way of putting *that* question – '*So was it you who brought a sack full of money into the church last night?*' – not now, not here in Jenny's private chapel, Jenny's holy space, in the light of the candles and Jenny's holy vision.

'So I drove down to the village, and by the time I got here, in less than ten minutes, it had almost stopped raining and the weakest of suns had come out. And here I am, walking around the village in a dream, burning inside with the white heat of pure joy. I'm walking around the square, looking up at the old buildings and just *revelling* in the atmosphere . . . not the quaintness – that's all rubbish – but this tenuous strand of sanctity that still threaded its way through the streets in spite of all this commercialism. I seemed to see the thread unravelling before me, and so I followed it and . . . you can guess the rest.'

'It led you here?'

'There was a FOR SALE sign. The only one in the whole village, as I remember.'

Merrily tried for a smile. 'These things happen.'

But they didn't really, did they? Not very often.

'They do. I know that now.' Mrs Box's face was flooded with happiness. But, at the same time, Merrily was recalling the sense of loneliness and *disturbance* which had blown like dry leaves around the woman in the square on the night of the fire.

'And I knocked on the door, and the people didn't want to show me around at all – "Oh, you've got to go through the agent," they said, but I insisted, I was very strong that day, and I felt the absolute rightness of it and I virtually made an offer there and then. I don't think for one minute they believed me – thought I was some stupid, doolally tourist woman, but it didn't matter. I left the house and the sun was shining, and I walked down to the church, and it was there – it was right there in the churchyard – that I was granted another small vision: the one that clinched it.'

Merrily was silent. Too many visions.

Mrs Jenny Box, née Jenny Driscoll, this former model, this former minor TV-person turned successful businesswoman, said, 'What I saw was . . . I saw *you*.'

Merrily looked down at her own hands, one squeezing the other.

'In your dog collar and your long white tunic. Walking out of the church, talking to some visitor-type people with their anoraks and their cameras. I saw *you* . . . *all in white*. And I felt I was in the centre . . . of the future.'

Merrily became aware that she was no longer the least bit cold. Too warm, if anything.

'Will we pray now?' Mrs Box said very softly. 'Will we pray together?'

By the time Merrily got back to the vicarage, she was disgusted with herself: woman of straw.

In the scullery, the computer took for ever to boot up. It was a reconditioned PC bought primarily to receive e-mails, mainly from Sophie, and it hadn't seemed too healthy for some weeks now.

There was one message highlighted, from 'deliverance', subject 'extraterrestrial', and she printed it out. Couldn't get her feet under the desk because of the bin sack, which she now had no damn choice but to take to Uncle Ted.

After those brief and nervous prayers, Mrs Box had been very gracious, giving Merrily tea, giving her fruit cake, in a white-walled, low-beamed parlour that was furnished almost frugally: two grey sofas, a low, Shaker-style table, no pictures on the walls. And Merrily, sitting in the middle of one of the sofas, on the crack between two cushions, had said, eventually, 'We've had . . . there's been a donation.'

Watching Jenny Box who knew it, arranging herself on one of the sofas, a bleached sunbeam stroking her hair.

'To the church,' Merrily said. 'A substantial donation.'

'Really?' Mrs Box smiling vaguely. 'That's really wonderful. I'm so glad.'

'It's a very large amount, in cash. So large that . . . I'm not sure I can keep it.'

'Oh? Why ever not?'

'Because a cash donation of that size is bound to be considered—'

'Miraculous?' said Mrs Box. 'An answer to a prayer? To a dilemma?'

'Suspicious. Because it's anonymous, and in cash.'

Jenny Box inclined her head to one side, appearing to consider the implications and then said, in that light, velvety voice of hers, 'Well, now, surely, if the donor didn't want to put his or her name on the bottom of a cheque, then it would not be in the spirit of the gift for you to institute inquiries and thus risk causing unwarranted embarrassment. Would it not be the thing to treat it as just the most lovely coincidence and perhaps even an indication from God that turning His House into a place of business was not the way ahead?'

Merrily nodded, smiling weakly. Had she really been expecting a confession? Under the surface vulnerability, Jenny Box was clever, a slick operator – and rich. But that didn't make it feel any more right. So much of this seemed wavery, blurred by an intermittent aura of flickering instability. '*I saw you . . . all in white. And I felt I was in the centre . . . of the future.*'

Had she been wearing the surplice that afternoon . . . the white alb? She didn't remember.

But, to Merrily's knowledge, no one throughout the recorded history of the village had ever claimed to have seen an angel lighting up the sky over Ledwardine Church.

Hard to say which was the most unlikely: that or aliens in Underhowle.

I'm sorry, Merrily, this took rather a long time to find, and as, like most of Canon Dobbs's files, it was handwritten, I'm afraid I had to type it out. I'm now back in the office, if you have any more queries.

Sophie.

How extraordinary! Not, I would have thought, Canon Dobbs's 'thing' at all.

The report itself, dated April 1997, was quite short.

Subject:
Miss Melanie Pullman, of 14 Goodrich Close, Underhowle, near Ross-on-Wye.

Source:
The Reverend Iain Ossler, temporary priest-in-charge, Ross Rural.

Nature of the problem:
Nocturnal disturbances of unknown origins.

The attending minister, Canon THB Dobbs, states:

I was asked to look into this most bemusing case by the Reverend Ossler who, having been consulted by the family of the subject, was unable to determine whether or not it fell within the purview of the Christian Ministry of Exorcism.

I found Miss Melanie Pullman to be a relatively articulate young woman of some eighteen years, an employee of Boots the Chemist in Ross-on-Wye, who had been left in a some-what confused and, I would say, debilitated condition, allegedly resulting from a series of 'experiences' at her home over a period of four to six months.

Merrily wondered what Melanie Pullman had made of Canon Dobbs with his eroded graveyard archangel's face and no discernible sense of humour. A man who had rejected the term 'Deliverance' and all attempts to introduce a series of guidelines for Anglican exorcists.

I interviewed Miss Pullman in the presence of her mother, Mrs Audrey Pullman, and her elder brother, Mr Terence Pullman. Throughout the interview, Miss Pullman complained of headaches and said she had been experiencing a number of physical symptoms, which the family general practitioner had diagnosed as a nervous condition, sub-sequently prescribing small amounts of Valium. The family dwelling is a former council house on an estate of similar homes and has no record of psychic disturbance, according to my inquiries with previous owners/tenants. Miss Pullman recounted a number of incidents, an example of which I quote here, from my notes.

'I awoke in the early hours of the morning to find that the television set in the corner of my bedroom had inexplicably activated itself. I am certain that I had switched it off, as usual, before falling asleep. However, there was neither picture nor sound, only a blinding white light on the screen which I could not look at for long.'

Inexplicably activated itself. Merrily wondered what terminology Melanie had actually used.

'This light eventually became dimmer and finally faded away. However, concurrent with this, I became aware that my bed itself was becoming bathed in an orange light which became increasingly bright.'

Miss Pullman then related a most confusing story of apparently being taken from her bed and losing consciousness and subsequently awakening in what she described as a 'spacecraft' of a spherical nature where she was laid upon a white metal table and subjected to an intimate physical examination by humanoid creatures, which she described as being thin and grey with unusually large heads and eyes like black mirrors. She claimed the examination concluded with one of the creatures having sexual intercourse with her. Asked if she would describe this experience as rape, Miss Pullman became embarrassed and said that she would not. Her mother later explained that, some days afterwards, Miss Pullman had been treated by her doctor for what was described as a vaginal infection.

Whilst my information is that reports of this type of alleged experience are not uncommon, particularly in the Unite States of America, it was my impression that Miss Pullman had indeed undergone some manner of hallucinatory or 'dream' experience. That is, I did not believe that she was 'making it up'.

The central question, however, remains: was demonic interference involved?

I have learned that some investigators of the phenomenon known as 'alien abduction' have proposed a correlation between this type of experience and folkloric tales of people who were 'taken by the fairies' as they slept, sometimes with similar suggestions of sexual interference, often resulting in the birth of a 'changeling' offspring. As Miss Pullman does not appear to have become pregnant, I would be inclined to rule out any involvement of so-called elemental forces!

My own tests, through prayer and meditation, failed to detect the presence of a demonic evil, but I remained concerned by Miss Pullman's physical conditions, which had led to her taking considerable time off work and, according to her mother 'moping about the house'. Accordingly, after blessing the premises, with the use of holy water, I had a short meeting with the general practitioner, Dr Ruck, whom I must say I found to be less than helpful. Dr Ruck stated that this was the second such case reported to him within a year, from the same housing development in Underhowle, and he considered it to be a 'fad' among young people, arising from certain popular films and television programmes. I asked the Pullman family to keep me informed about any future developments but have not heard from them since.

CANON T. H. B. DOBBS,
DIOCESAN EXORCIST,
HEREFORD.

Merrily was unexpectedly impressed by Canon Dobbs's general diligence and open-mindedness. OK, this hadn't, unfortunately, extended to women priests – and women exorcists in particular. But he *had* done his best with what, to him, must have been a perplexingly contemporary kind of haunting.

The idea of aliens as post-modern fairies was one she'd heard before. True, there was no suggestion of the demonic here, nothing for the Deliverance ministry to combat with traditional means. But who *did* you go to when you were convinced that something which you couldn't resist had arrived in the night and taken you away for experimentation?

Certainly not the police. If she showed this to Frannie Bliss, it would only put question marks over Melanie's mental state. As for the doctor: bloody Valium, the universal panacea.

Merrily recalled when Jane, approaching the peak of her New Age phase a year or two ago, had believed she was having *nature spirit* experiences in the orchards of Ledwardine.

And she was startled by a pang of nostalgia, realizing that she very much preferred that fey, impressionable kid to the hardbitten cynic who'd emerged around the approach to her daughter's seventeenth birthday. She wondered what Eirion thought of the new Jane.

She went back to the computer to e-mail her thanks to

Sophie . . . and discovered that she couldn't. The screen had frozen, but in a peculiar foggy way, and when she tried to restart the computer she found it wouldn't.

Bugger. Hard disk gone, or what? She'd have to ask Eirion who, she had to admit, was becoming an indispensable extension of this household.

Meanwhile, she rang the Cathedral gatehouse. 'Sophie, thanks for doing this.'

'Do we have another case in this particular village?' Sophie's voice, which had once seemed severe, now conveyed this inimitable mixture of calm and capability.

'Alien abduction? No, but Dobbs's *subject* has since disappeared, and the police are worried about her.'

'And you've been consulted?'

'In a roundabout kind of way. Has there been anything on the radio about the discovery of a woman's body early today, near Ross?'

'Oh,' said Sophie, '*that.*'

'No, this is not *her.* That's . . . another one.'

Oh well, at least this would delay having to take the sack to Ted. She told Sophie everything that had happened last night up to, but not including, the bin-sack incident, which was purely parish business.

It was like unloading stuff on your older sister.

'My God . . . what an appalling night for you,' Sophie said. 'Two of them. Two dead bodies.'

'Possibly both victims of the same man.'

'I hadn't heard about Mr Parry's fire. I'm so very sorry. He's a wonderful man – and a good friend to you. Do you really think this person was insane enough to start that fire?'

'Gomer's in no doubt. And there's definitely *something* wrong with Lodge. The bedroom wall was very . . . yuk. I mean, I can understand why Bliss is convinced Lodge has killed more women.'

'And you say Mr Parry's out there now, digging for more corpses?'

'With Lol.' Merrily fumbled a cigarette into her mouth.

'Is this entirely wise of Inspector Bliss?'

'Not in my view,' Merrily said. 'But who ever listens to me?'

Jenny Box, she thought. *Jenny Box listens.*

17

Expecting Confession

Made sense, see, Gomer told Lol, as the truck bumped down into the valley, under the big pylons. This place was on the edge of the Forest, and anything could happen in the Forest – full of old secrets never told. Perfect place for a killer to lurk undiscovered for years.

Unlike Radnor Forest, that area of crowded green hills forty miles west of here where Gomer had grown up, the Dean was the real thing. Trees: oaks, chestnuts, sycamores, conifers. Miles of the buggers, wall-to-wall – twenty-five thousand acres, sure to be. Royal hunting ground in the Middle Ages, therefore operating according to separate rules, its own code.

'What you gotter remember, Lol, boy . . .' Gomer's eyes shrank shrewdly behind his telescopic glasses. 'What you gotter remember 'bout the Forest is it's wedged up between these two big rivers, the Wye by yere, and the Severn in the east. And the Severn's real wide; the other side's like another country, so you're lookin' across at neighbours you likely en't never gonner talk to the whole of your life.'

'Sounds like West London,' Lol said.

'Point I'm makin', boy, if you wanner get the other side of that river, from yereabouts, you gotter drive miles and miles down to the big bridges in South Wales, else your only alternative's all the way up to the city of Gloucester and struggling through the terrible bloody traffic you gets there. Now . . . in between Gloucester and South Wales, see, you got the Forest. Like a big island full o' trees.'

Trees were already thickening on both sides of the road and the cab of the truck was blue with Gomer's smoke.

'And if the Forest folk couldn't easy get out, where do they go but *down*? Pits, see? Iron mines, it was, way back to Roman times, and coal mines. All closed down and covered over now, mostly, but the land's still riddled with bloody ole shafts. Mines and secrets, boy, that's the Forest. *Mines and secrets.*'

Despite the cold and the shuddering of the truck, Lol's body was sagging into sleep. He sat up, shaking himself like a dog. 'How come you know so much about it, Gomer?'

'Ar, well . . .' Gomer's voice went gruff. 'My first wife, God rest her, her family comed from Cinderford. Used to have to go over at Christmas, times like that. Never felt accepted, mind. Suspicious devils, her family. Close. Interbred.'

It was noticeable that Gomer had been talking more in the last five minutes than he had all day. He'd never mentioned his first wife before, not in Lol's hearing. This was Gomer galvanized, sensing the closeness of a climax.

Coughed on three: Lynsey, Melanie Pullman and the girl from Monmouth, Rochelle Bowen.

Rochelle was the daughter of the couple who'd caught up with them when they were excavating the third Efflapure, at a brick cottage outside Pontshill. She was nineteen, a trainee dental nurse, missing for five months. Lol had felt heartsick; seeing in the faces of the parents this withering combination of resignation and cold dread, making it all searingly real. He hoped they weren't going to be around when Bliss arrived with his prisoner.

Gomer slowed at a sign pointing to *Under Howle* – two words, as though the village had no identity separate from the hill. Lol couldn't see a village out of the truck windows, only close-growing trees with brown, frizzled leaves.

'This actually counts as the Forest, Gomer? So close to Ross?'

Gomer sucked on his ciggy. 'This, boy, counts as a place even the Forest folk don't know. Perfect hidey-hole for the likes of Lodge. Bastard goes out from yere, like them bloody ole raiders from centuries ago . . . cheatin', philanderin' . . . killin' . . . He coughed. 'Burnin'. Then crawls back to his lair, all snug.'

They came down into the village, which looked muddled and haphazard, houses floating in the early dusk like croutons in a brown soup. They passed the hulk of a church, entering a street with – surprisingly – several shops, their lights coming on. Down through a disjointed crossroads, back into the trees.

And then Lol saw, on his left, the first police car, the police tape and the tiered façade of the garage, like a concrete Lego garage from his childhood, with the pylon rearing behind it. Gomer turned in very slowly and deliberately, truck wheels grinding cinders.

'All snug,' he said.

Merrily punched in the numbers of Lol's phone.

'I'm sorry, the mobile you are calling is—'

She switched off again. It was so basic, Lol's phone, that it hadn't come with an answering service. In fact, he probably hadn't even taken it with him. She pictured him digging, willing but a little inept, in some muddy field, red-brown stains on the alien sweatshirt – her mind could still never find him without the alien sweatshirt. Once she'd insisted on bringing it home to mend a hole in the shoulder and had ended up sleeping with the faded item under her pillow: how sad was that? You wanted to be adult about these things, wanted to take it slowly, but your emotions operated at a different velocity: feelings on fast-track, playing the old Hazey Jane albums when you were alone in the car – his voice a little higher then, a little smoother; he'd been not much older than Jane at the time, and now nearly twenty years had passed and – *Oh God.*

Merrily lit a cigarette. Her hand was shaking. It didn't seem to take much to make her hands shake nowadays.

Jane had also talked about the folk-rock singer, Moira Cairns, on whom Eirion had seemed to have developed a crush, although the kid had emphasized in disgust that the singer was old enough to be his mother. Merrily recalled a Moira Cairns album with a sleeve picture of Cairns trailing a guitar along an empty beach. Something special then; how special was she now? Last night, Prof Levin, according to Jane, had thrown an oblique glance at the lovely Moira in her slinky frock and had said they should 'Let what happens happen.' Was this Jane winding her up? Jane, who wanted a situation where Lol actually moved into the vicarage with his guitars, which . . . which was really not possible, at the moment, was it? What would they say about her in the village (*whore!*), the diocese, the press. And, of course, Uncle Ted . . .

Merrily stared at the phone. *Uncle bloody Ted.*

No real reason for putting this off any longer. She called him. She called Uncle Ted Clowes and arranged to meet him in the church in ten minutes. She put out the cigarette, got back into her best coat and pulled out the sack full of cash, its origins still uncertain.

With the sun going right down, the wind getting up, and still no sign of the Hereford coppers arriving with Lodge, Gomer left young Lol Robinson rubbing his hands in the cold, tramped across the cinders and dragged miserable Andy Mumford over to one side, by the garage wall. Time to have this out.

'You said three, right, Andy boy? You reckoned he'd confessed to three.'

Andy Mumford looked over his shoulder. 'I never said anything at all, Gomer, you know that.'

'Three, that it? Just the three women?'

'I don't know what you mean.'

Behind Mumford, coppers were moving through the dusk, unloading tackle from a blue van.

'Don't you give me that ole wallop!' Gomer levelled a finger. He'd known this boy for years. Born to a big family over by Wigmore, and if ole Ma Mumford was yere, she'd have the truth out of the bastard. 'What about torchin' a certain plant-hire shed? What do he say about that, boy?'

Miserable Andy looking frazzled. Coming up to retirement, didn't need this. Well, too bloody bad! Gomer could feel the old fury coming to the boil. He'd worked all day for nothing much, seen his good friend young Lol Robinson reduced to a limp rag and now in all the excitement of Lodge shooting his mouth off, just the one serious crime gets very conveniently forgotten.

'Not sexy enough – that it, Andy? Not got no spectac'lar headlines in it? Unknown Welsh Border drunk gets hisself roasted?'

'Look, Gomer,' Andy said awkwardly, 'we've been cooperating

the best we can with Dyfed–Powys on this one, but it calls for a lot of forensic, and that's not easy to come by after a big fire. I don't know how much *you* know about DNA, but it doesn't survive that kind of blaze. Anyway, proving that someone else other than Nev was involved is not gonner be a simple matter, take it from me.'

'Ole wallop!' Gomer was ramming his glasses up tight to his eyes. 'In the ole days, they'd've bounced the bastard off the cell walls a few times till he told the truth.' He was thinking of Wynford Wiley, the Radnor Valley sergeant – never liked the bugger, but he knew how to get the facts out of the lowlife.

'Gomer –' Andy sounding pained '– Lodge has a very smart young lawyer, I'm told. Going about it the old-fashioned way is the best way of not getting a conviction on anything these days, take it from—'

'Ar, we all know what goes on nowadays – three-course dinner and tucked up with a hot-water bottle, all cosy. 'Spect he'd be getting a conjugal bloody visit if he hadn't done for all his girlfriends.'

Bad-taste thing to say and, fair play, Gomer was truly sorry for those girls and their families, but there'd been no woman in Nev's life at the end, and nobody was going to stand up for that boy if Gomer didn't do it now.

Headlights blasting through the trees brought Andy Mumford out of his slump.

'They're here. Gotter leave this now, Gomer.'

Two cars . . . three.

'Do one thing for me, Gomer.'

Gomer kept quiet.

'I'll admit I warned the boss about hiring you for this,' Andy said. 'But he was in a hurry, and I reckon he thought you'd have a bit more of an incentive than most digger-men.'

Boy had *that* right.

'But don't – just *don't* . . . When you see Lodge, don't say nothing, don't do nothing. Soon as we nail this psycho on the women, we'll talk about Nev, I promise. Just you keep in the background, meantime, and dig where you're told. Don't do nothing else, you understand me?'

'You knows me, boy.'

'Exactly,' Andy says grimly.

The first car's pulling up just a few yards from Gomer. It's not a police car. The boy Bliss gets out first. He stands there, hands in his pockets, waiting, as the second car fits itself in behind.

Three uniform coppers in this one. And Lodge, bent drainage operator and likely the biggest serial killer in these parts since bloody Fred West.

Gomer fired up a ciggy in the fading light and waited too.

Stepping warily into the gloom of the vestry, Merrily found that Uncle Ted had already moved the wardrobe into a corner and folded up the card table, and was now brushing the dust from his sleeves, obviously envisaging the gift shop.

'I thought the main counter about *here* . . . and perhaps a second display stand under the window?'

Merrily said, 'Perhaps if we brick up the window altogether, we could have an even bigger display stand.'

'Oh, I don't think so,' Ted said, 'because when you add up the cost of extra lighting . . .'

He dried up, realizing – lips twisted in annoyance – that his niece, the vicar, was taking the piss. His face went a deep and petulant red. 'I very much hope,' he said, 'that you aren't going to backtrack on this. We do need the income.'

Backtrack? She didn't recall ever agreeing. 'Well . . .' She carefully re-erected the card table in the middle of the small, drab room and placed the black bin sack on it. 'Maybe we can now afford to postpone the decision for a while.'

She was still dreading telling him about the money. Obviously, they'd have to put it out that there'd been an anonymous donation, without necessarily revealing how it had arrived. The gossip, anyway, would be considerable.

Ted frowned. 'I admit the mobile-phone mast would bring in a regular income, but . . .'

'You haven't mentioned that in a while.'

'No, I . . . to be honest, I've been a trifle perturbed by what I've been reading about possible health risks. Particularly to, ah, elderly people, it seems. Nothing proven, but it might be wise to, ah . . .'

'I see.'

'Sorry to toss a spanner in the works.' He stood with his back to the door, hands across his belly, the last man in Ledwardine habitually to wear a Paisley cravat down the front of his Viyella.

'No, that's . . . very public-spirited of you, Ted,' Merrily said. 'Listen, there's something I have to tell you. Something's happened.'

He peered at her. 'Why are you all dressed up?'

'Because I'm leaving for Barbados tonight,' Merrily said. 'I've come into money.'

She emptied the contents of the bin liner on to the table.

Ted picked up one of the bundles of notes and then moved rapidly to the door and flung on all the lights.

'Bloody *hell*!' he said.

Lol saw them bringing Lodge out, couldn't easily miss him. In direct contrast to the dark blue uniforms on either side, he was wearing orange overalls, probably police-issue while they ran tests on his clothes. His head hung, so you couldn't see his face, and his hands were cuffed in front of him. He let the two coppers move him around in the greying light, like a bendy doll.

A mist-blurred, listless moon was skulking in the trees. The wind brushed fallen leaves into heaps against the closed doors of Roddy's garage, and the police clustered in front. Nobody was doing much talking, but Lol was aware of an excitement he guessed they wouldn't want to show – you could hear it in the agitated jostling of the leaves and the tense, metallic thrumming in the overhead power lines.

There were about eight police visible, among them DI Frannie Bliss who Lol had met during the summer – a brief liaison founded on the need to pull Merrily out of a threatening situation. There'd been a degree of self-interest then, but you felt you could trust him, up to a point.

Surprisingly, Bliss came over.

'Knew the music industry was in a bad way, son, but not this bad.'

Lol nodded gloomily. 'We've got Robbie Williams round the back, unloading the truck.'

'Yeh, I thought it was.' Bliss was dressed for action in a nylon hiking jacket, jeans tucked into calf-high cowboy boots.

'You look happy, though.' Lol was wary: the police and their prisoner waiting around, the night closing in, and the DI sparing the time to acknowledge the hired labour.

'*Tentatively* happy.' Small teeth flashed briefly. 'You're looking a bit knackered yourself, Laurence.' Bliss pulled leather gloves from his jacket and put them on. 'I suppose it was the little Reverend got you into this. Relieving Mr Parry's burden, in his hour of sorrow.'

'Thought it might help him to have somebody to laugh at.'

'And how can we ever refuse her, eh? All right, son, listen . . .' Bliss led him to the edge of the police tape, voice lowered. 'Here's the situation: after what's been a difficult day, by and large, Mr Lodge has decided to cooperate. But this is –' he waggled his fingers '– funny stuff, you know? Gorra go a bit careful.' He nodded at the spade. 'Obviously you've mastered the complexities of that, more or less, but what I need to know is, can you, if necessary, operate this little digger of Gomer's?'

Lol took half a step back, stumbled.

'Hey, we're not talking heavy plant,' Bliss said. 'This is Tonka toy.'

Lol looked around. He couldn't see Gomer anywhere, but he could see Roddy Lodge, luminous in his overalls, with a policeman either side and another man, in plain clothes, joining them. A policewoman was handing out plastic cups of tea or coffee from a couple of flasks in the boot of a police car, including one for the prisoner – Roddy clasping the cup like a chalice between his cuffed hands. The reality outside the recording studio – more of it than Lol had counted on.

'I'm not saying we're gonna *need* the digger.' Bliss tapped the spade. 'This might well suffice. But if we do need to go a bit deeper, I don't want Mr Parry within quarrelling distance of Roddy Lodge. Better an inoffensive little *artiste* than a combustible old bugger with a grudge, this is my view.'

'And how would you feel,' Lol said, before he could think, 'if *your* nephew's murder was getting sidelined by a slippery copper on the make?'

Must have been even more tired than he'd figured.

Bliss merely frowned. 'Suspicious death. His nephew's *suspicious death*, Laurence. I apologize for calling you inoffensive.' He paused. 'Anyway, that's over the garden hedge – Dyfed-Powys's case. I'm not saying there won't be meaningful discussions with our Welsh colleagues when this present business gets sorted, but right now I want to build on what we *know* we've got. It's about seizing the moment. Now you run along and ask Mr Parry for the keys of his little digger.'

Lol didn't move. 'I thought you'd have real forensic people to do it, now you've got something positive.'

'Never fear – you happen to strike anything softish, I'll have vanloads of the buggers here before you can scrape the shit off your wellies. I've just gorra be quite sure our friend here isn't being disingenuous.'

'So where will this be? Where are we going?'

'Going? We're not going anywhere.' Bliss patted Lol on the shoulder and walked with the wind behind him across the crowded forecourt towards the cops guarding the prisoner. 'Right then, Roddy, my son, let's be having yer.'

Here? He'd buried one on his own property?

'DI Bliss!' The third man with Lodge stepped out, his hands going up protectively as the headlights of one of the police cars sprayed his dark suit. 'I just want to say, before you—'

Lol saw Bliss quiver. 'Mr Nye . . . we've had an independent doctor in to check him over, we've also had him looked at by an experienced psychiatric nurse, neither of whom thought he was seriously ill or unfit to travel. Now, will you let us get on with our job, please?'

The guy shook his head. He looked young, maybe not too sure of his ground. 'Inspector, I have to tell you that I'm far from confident that anything Mr Lodge might say under these circumstances can be considered admissible. I think—'

'I *know* what you think.' Bliss stood with his arms by his side, fists tight. 'And what *I* think is that Mr Lodge's mental state has no particular bearing on the situation at this stage. And I'm more interested right now in what he's got to show us, rather that what he *tells* us. And if any of this upsets him further, I'm terribly sorry, Mr Nye, but in comparison with the parents of Rochelle Bowen, with whom I spent a very distressing forty-five minutes this afternoon, my sympathies—'

'Mr Bliss, I repeat that my client is unwell, and I think you could at least – bearing in mind that Mr Lodge *hasn't* been charged and he is cooperating fully – remove the handcuffs.'

Bliss threw up his arms. 'All right, we'll take off the f— the handcuffs.' He moved close up to Mr Nye. 'I should, however, remind your client that if he at any stage makes a *personal decision* that his continued presence here is no longer entirely essential, I've got police officers posted at the front and the rear and every conceivable exit from these premises. Is that fully understood, Mr Nye?'

'We wouldn't expect otherwise, in the circumstances,' said Mr Nye. 'Thank you, Inspector.'

Bliss nodded. One of the uniformed policemen bent to remove Lodge's handcuffs.

'You *believe* that?'

Lol turned. Behind him, Gomer was furiously assembling a ciggy, the headlights turning his glasses opaque, like cross-slices of banana.

'You ask me, en't nothin' wrong with that piece of rubbish you couldn't bloody shake out of him.' He shoved the new ciggy in his mouth and closed the tin with a snap.

'Gomer—'

'You don't need to explain nothing, boy. Miserable Andy's spelled it out. Keep Parry out of it. Don't nobody mention Nev. You go with 'em. I'll stay yere.'

'It's nothing personal,' Lol said. 'Just Bliss covering himself against any comebacks in court. If they do find anything and it was you who dug it up, a man with a grudge . . .' He sighed; he didn't want to operate the digger, either, even if he could be sure he knew how to. 'Nobody's going anywhere, it seems. Looks like they want to dig here. Maybe we should tell them they can do it themselves.'

'Not with my bloody gear, they don't. I've lent tools to cops before.' Gomer pulled a single key on a chain from his overalls. 'So don't you let anybody else—'

'Hang on to it,' Lol said nervously. 'It may not come to that.'

They watched Roddy Lodge flexing his arms, rubbing his freed wrists. Lol saw his face properly for the first time, and it was the colour and the texture of paving stone. His eyes seemed sunken, but somehow gleaming back there, like glass, like cat's eyes in the road.

And then he started slowly shaking his head, a smile forming.

18

Up

Jane said, 'So you're saying Jenny Driscoll saw an angel.' She flinched slightly. 'An actual . . . with like, wings?'

Merrily stood up, went to switch on the earthenware reading lamp on the wide windowsill. It had been clear to her that if she was going to tell the kid about the money then a preliminary account of Mrs Box and the vision of the angel was probably unavoidable.

Besides, this had been, not too long ago, very much Jane's kind of thing. Up in the apartment, against the Mondrian walls, two bookcases still bulged with pastel-spined paperbacks about contacting nature spirits, working with the elements, finding secret pathways to enlightenment.

Which had bothered Merrily quite a bit at one time; less so now. If, occasionally, it bordered on neo-paganism, it was still spirituality. Better than agnosticism.

Certainly better than the possible onset of atheism.

'Let's say a startling brightness formed out of the veins of light on the edge of clouds,' Merrily said. 'Resembling in this case, it seems, the Archangel Uriel. This is the lesser-known one usually portrayed with a sword, pointing down. It was very dramatic, Mrs Box says.'

'And it was pointing at the steeple. Your steeple?'

'This would be . . . you remember the huge, spectacular storm one Sunday last spring? Where we were standing here at the window and the whole of the orchard was lit up white, like a snowstorm? Well, Mrs Box parked her car and walked up onto Cole Hill. She was in a . . . an emotional state.'

'Evidently,' Jane said.

Eirion had dropped her off around four before having to go home for his step-grandmother's eightieth birthday party. Now the day was closing down, the old Aga making its smug Aga noises without putting much heat into the kitchen. Merrily and Jane had mugs of tea for warmth.

The lamp laid a golden mist on the room. The kid had changed into white jeans and a sweater discarded by Merrily as terminally shapeless. It seemed to fit Jane better. She slid forward on her elbows, chin cupped in her hands, gazing into her mother's eyes, very candid and calmed by something awesome that Merrily was seeing more frequently: a level of understanding that murmured *adult*.

Merrily's hand tightened around her mug.

'OK, just reassure me,' Jane said, 'that you don't believe a word of this bollocks.'

The strengthening night-wind rattled the trees.

'*Bastard!*' Bliss was livid. He stormed over to where Lol and Gomer were standing, out of Lodge's earshot.

'Lawyer's got it right for once, boss.' Mumford was ambling behind like a pack pony. 'Bloke's mental.'

'Andy, he's mental when he *wants* to be.' Bliss moved up to the barrier tape, clutched it with both hands, failed to snap it. 'I'm buggered if I'm chauffeuring the crafty bastard back to his cell after this little works' outing. I'd rather dig the whole site up and make him watch. Put him back in the cuffs.'

'Look a bit peevish?' Mumford said.

'I'm a peevish person.'

'En't bein' helpful n'more, then,' Gomer said insouciantly through blue smoke.

'No, he en't.' Bliss stared out across the lane into the trees, hands rammed into the pockets of his green and cream hiking jacket. 'As you may have overheard, Mr Lodge appears to have had a lapse of memory and is now effectively saying he no longer recalls precisely why he brought us here.'

'Ar.' Gomer smiled through his ciggy. Relief seeped into Lol's aching body like warm alcohol. It looked like this could be over before it started.

'What's he *got* here, Andy?' Bliss said.

'Boss?'

'How much ground? Acreage. Roughly. What we looking at?'

'I'd reckon . . . say two and a bit acres, all told. That's including the yard and the bungalow and the triangular piece of land at the bottom with the pylon on it. Oh, and the other side of the main perimeter fence it seems Lodge owns a paddock, and then there's about one and a half acres surrounding what used to be the Underhowle Baptist chapel. Lodge used to own that, too, but he's now sold it to the Underhowle Development Committee.'

'Proper little property speculator,' Bliss said sourly. 'We been in there?'

'The chapel? Empty, boss. The Development Committee's turning it into a museum for all the Roman finds.'

'We'll still put it on the list for the Durex-suits.'

'He's just had money to spare and a good accountant,' Mumford said. 'Property always makes sense, even derelict property. I bought the field next to us, with an old cowshed.'

'Yeh, you would.' Bliss hacked the heel of a cowboy boot into the cinders. 'Wouldn't know where to start here on our own, would we? Take days to dig up this lot, and I haven't got days.' He turned his back to the tape, looked across at Roddy Lodge standing motionless in his orange overalls. 'I'm gonna look a right twat when this gets out.'

Lol noticed two kids hanging around at the far end of the tape, one apparently shielding the other who was bending over the tape – probably cutting himself a couple of feet of it as a souvenir.

Gomer cleared his throat, but Frannie Bliss didn't look at him. A policeman advanced on the two kids, who ran off up the lane towards the village. Then one turned and gave him the finger. It began to rain very lightly.

There was a sigh of resignation from Bliss. 'Yes, Mr Parry.'

''Course –' Gomer spat out the last millimetre of ciggy '– if I hadn't been discharged from my duties, told to take a back seat, like . . .'

Lol became aware of just how cold it had become, how thin his old army jacket was, and how much night there was stretching ahead.

'What you got in mind, Gomer?' Bliss said.

Lol just hoped that whatever it was wouldn't involve him or his frozen muscles.

Merrily said, 'So I emptied out the sack, and waited for it to happen. And, sure enough, he metamorphosed before my eyes. Out goes the churchwarden, in comes the lawyer.'

'Dr Jekyll and Mr—'

'No, this is Ted,' Merrily said. 'Mr Hyde and Mr even-Hyder.'

Jane grinned fractionally. Merrily poured more tea, glad to be off the subject of angels. She was bewildered by Jane's reaction to the report of a dramatic visionary experience on her own doorstep. Was this not the kid who had entered her middle teens with a fervent belief in fairies and the kind of elemental forces not covered by the Bible? There was a point where New Age philosophy and Christianity crossed over, and angels were it, and you didn't just abandon all that virtually overnight – not even Jane.

'So what did he *say*?' Jane demanded, clearly far more interested in the manifestation of the money, obviously annoyed that this was the first she'd heard about it, when both Uncle Ted and Jenny Box had been told.

'Oh . . . "Lock the church at once, Merrily!" ' Merrily threw up her arms. 'Pulls out his mobile, brings up the police number, which he appeared to have in his index. "OK," I say, "but I'm locking it from the outside, I've not got time to sit around here . . ." "No, no! You can't leave me on my own with all this money!" I said, "Ted, I've just dragged it all the way along the bloody cobbles, from the vicarage, on my own." '

'So where is it now?'

'Probably in his safe at home. I somehow can't see him surrendering eighty grand to the police for safe keeping. He'll give them the minimum legal leeway, just to make sure it doesn't match up with some robbery.'

'And assuming it doesn't?'

Merrily shrugged. 'Goes into the parish coffers. End of story, everybody happy. We just don't spend any for a while, to be on the safe side.'

'It's a lot of money, Mum,' Jane said soberly. 'Take a whole canteen of collection plates to accommodate that lot.'

'Mmm.' Merrily was remembering a row she'd had with Uncle Ted when she'd decided to abolish the time-honoured practice of sending round collection plates during the final hymn. *Let's not make an exhibition of it, Ted. They can put something in the box on the way out.* Ted had insisted this wouldn't work; people never shelled out unless they were publicly shamed into it. It even emerged that the old bugger had sometimes taken twenty-pound notes from parish funds, placing one on each plate prior to its circulation, setting an example.

'And Jenny Driscoll didn't come close to admitting it was her?' Jane said.

'Maybe I didn't push her hard enough, but . . . I suppose it's actually quite a considerate thing to do. If it had been a cheque with her name on it, we'd both have felt uncomfortable. Like she owned the place or . . . me.'

'Yeah, but secretly you *know* it's her. And she knows you know. And nobody else does – just you and her. That makes it altogether more subtle, don't you think?'

'Too subtle for me, flower.'

For a few moments neither of them spoke. The only sound was Ethel the cat at her bowl, crunching dried food.

'You know your problem, don't you?' Jane was carefully inspecting her nails. 'You're becoming unworldly.'

Merrily reared up. '*Me?*'

'Obvious side effect of Deliverance.' Jane put her hand down and met Merrily's stare across the table. 'Like, in the job, if you're exorcizing some house or something, it has to be that it's not *you* doing it, it's God. You're just the vehicle. If in doubt, butt out. God will find a way.'

'No.'

'Think about it,' Jane said. 'She's targeted you. All that bollocks about seeing an angel over *your* church. And then she bungs you eighty grand. She wants something. You're in the cross-hairs, vicar.'

Merrily took in the kid's serious face, the hair – darker now – pushed back behind her ears. A face she hadn't seen before? She felt a stirring of panic, very glad now that there were some aspects of that unnerving couple of hours in the incense air below Chapel House that she *hadn't* told Jane about.

She finally flared a little. 'Somehow, I just can't help being a little surprised at hearing the rational, not to say cynical argument from someone who used to stand on the lawn on nights of the full moon and solemnly utter ritual incantations.'

'I was a *kid* then!'

'It was last year!'

'Look . . .' Jane planted both palms flat on the table, leaning across. 'Doesn't this worry you in the *slightest*? She might look like a wilting snowdrop, but what you have here is an ex-TV person, a top businesswoman with shops all over the place who's probably never been known to do *anything* that wasn't for publicity . . .'

'The money's for the church, not me.'

'*Your* church.'

'What – you think I should take it back?'

Jane shook her head helplessly. 'I don't know. But I should be really, really careful, if I were you.'

Merrily said nothing. She was hearing Jenny Box from the square, the other night. '*It isn't over, you see . . . those things aren't over . . . those things have hardly begun.*' No, she didn't know what that meant either.

'Because, if you think God's going to see you right, protect you from whatever devious shit—'

'Jane—'

'Like he protected Gomer. Like he protected *Nev.*'

Merrily closed her eyes. Not tonight, *please*. 'All right.' She breathed in and out slowly. 'All right, I didn't do very well, did I? There were things I should have asked her that I didn't. Maybe I had a lot on my mind, with this . . . police thing. Which is probably all over now, anyway.'

'All over? Not for Gomer it isn't! Not for Lol either, who probably wouldn't have got involved at all if you—'

'What?'

Jane shrugged sulkily. 'Just something else you're letting slip away, isn't it?'

'Oh, for God's sake.' *This is not going to become a row.* 'I've tried to ring him several times.'

'Maybe you've got more problems than you know, Reverend. Maybe Uncle Ted's actually right –'

'I do not—'

'– when he says Deliverance is taking over your life. And he doesn't even know what it's done to your basic common sense.'

Merrily's lips tightened. Bloody teenagers. What a great shame it was that there wasn't some kind of hormone-reduction therapy.

'So how did you leave it with the Driscoll woman?' Jane said. 'Like, thanks for the cakes and see you in church?'

'She . . .' Merrily stared into her cooling tea. 'She asked me to do something for her. She wanted me to formally reconsecrate her private chapel. In the cellar.'

Jane's smile was three parts sneer. 'And?'

'No consecrations. But a blessing, yes. Probably.'

The kid's exhaled breath was like a slow puncture. The kitchen seemed bigger and felt colder.

'Well, what was I supposed to say, Jane? It's what I do!'

'And of course what you do is of major spiritual, like *cosmic* significance. Even though it's all f— *fantasy.* Whereas, us down here . . . I bet . . . I bet you don't even know about Lol's first gig in twenty years.'

'Lol?' Merrily whispered. '*Gig?*'

The rain fell steadily on the field at the back of the bungalow. Lol held the rubber-covered lambing lamp over a spot just off-centre, lighting up a circle of green and yellow. He could hardly flex his fingers any more. He thought that if he were to lie down now in the cold, wet grass, he'd probably be asleep within a few seconds.

'*Yere.*' Gomer bent down, pushing his fingers through the grass. 'Just about yere. Sure t'be.'

Where Gomer's hands were, you could see the soil level was lower, the grass a slightly different shade. Before locating this spot, Gomer had spent no more than twenty minutes scouring the site as if he was dowsing for water – sometimes pulling back bushes and brambles, getting Lol to shift piles of building rubble.

A circle of police was forming around them, as Gomer came triumphantly to his feet alongside Lol and the lamp.

''Bout last spring, I reckon, this was dug up. No later'n that. Try it, anyway, I would. You'll know soon enough.'

Bliss was sauntering up, looking less than impressed, when a howl of outrage exploded over the heads of the circle of cops.

'*You don't wanner take no notice of that ole fuck! He's well past it, he is! He don't know what he's—*'

In the choked silence, Lol was aware of the razory thrumming of the power lines.

Then a chuckle. One of the uniformed police fisted his palm in glee. Frannie Bliss, smiling in the lamplight like a freckled cherub, punched Gomer joyfully on the upper arm.

'Thank you, Roddy. Thank you, God.'

Laughter. You could feel the current passing around the circle.

Bliss beckoned the policewoman. 'Gomer, this merits a nice plastic cup of tea, which Tiffany here will provide for you, if I'm not being sexist there. And an Eccles cake?'

'Welsh cake, boss,' the policewoman said.

'Sorry, Tiff.' Bliss was still smiling as he handed Lol the spade. 'Take it slowly, son.'

Like he could take it any other way. Quite when he began to tremble, he wasn't sure. He was just suddenly aware of doing it. It could've been the cold, because it *was* cold, and it was wet and the earth was clammy. But he knew it wasn't that; he'd been cold and wet most of the day.

His head was full of rumbling: they'd brought two cars round the back, with their engines running and the headlights on full beam. He was caught in the lights, the star attraction, sweating under the scrutiny of a hyper-attentive audience – Lol Robinson on stage for the first time in nearly two decades, Lol Robinson performing live, digging up the dead.

He was directly under the power lines – heavy-gauge black strings on a fretboard of night cloud. The spade was about eighteen inches down now, raising a little hill of muddy soil and wedges of clay at the side of the hole. Lol's glasses had misted up and the spade was feeling sledgehammer-heavy, pulling him down, the way the old solid-body electric guitar had done once, on stage with Hazey Jane – Lol sagging under the responsibility, the knowledge that all he had to do was touch a string with a fingernail – the wrong string, the wrong note, the wrong chord – and there would be this hall-filling blast. A power he didn't want, the amplification of his inadequacy.

His head felt hot. The sweat on his face was like cream. Moira Cairns said smokily in his head, '*Let me get this right: if you reappear on stage now, the audience isnae gonnae be thinking, "Ah, here's the awfully talented person from Hazey Jane, where the hell's he been all this time?" It's gonnae be like, "Hey, is that no' the big sex offender of 1982 or whenever?"*'

Lol hated it here. The half-imagined zinging of the power lines was like the panting of old amps on stage, and like every chord he played, every spadeful he dumped on the heap at the side of the hole, they landed on it, pulling it apart, mauling it: blurred figures in boots and uniforms. Spotlit from several angles, Lol had the clear sensation of digging his own grave, like some prisoner of war, surrounded by uniforms, and he didn't even notice when the spade found something – something that was actually not *softish* – until Frannie Bliss, his Liverpool accent cranked up to distortion level, was bawling:

'*Stop! What's dis? What's dis, what's dis . . .?*'

A skull? A human skull caked in clay? Lol was out of there fast, gripping the spade with both hands.

'Leave it,' Bliss said, as if people were going to rush to the thing in the hole like it was a holy relic. He snatched a lamp and shone it down. 'Spade, Laurence.'

Bliss grabbed the spade from him and stood astride the hole. Handing the lamp to Mumford, he started to probe with a corner of the blade. Lol found himself next to the lawyer, Mr Nye, who turned away from him, like Lol had flakes of dead flesh on his arms.

'Hang on,' Bliss said. 'What the . . . ?' Lol saw something in the hole that was dull and grey and blistered with earth. Bliss said, 'Right. Fetch Roddy. Now.'

He got the spade under it and levered it half out.

It was not a skull.

'Suitcase, boss?' One of the police crouched down. The curved, shiny bit, Lol saw, was a metal corner-support.

'Too small.' Bliss looked down in disgust, like a kid on Christmas Day who didn't get the bike after all. 'Attaché case, more like. Feels like it's bloody empty. I said, *fetch Roddy!*'

Lol, thinking he was maybe the only person here who was relieved, walked away from the lights towards the shelter of the garage.

Hands in leather seized his left arm and spun him around. White flashlight speared his eyes. All around him, there was heavy movement in the mud, scuffling, panting. Torch beams were intersecting erratically in the rain.

When they let him go without an apology, he realized something had happened.

'Oh shit.' Panic scraping a young copper's voice. 'I can't bleeding believe this.'

The initial stampede had been constrained. Procedure now. They were fanning out, covering the ground, lamp and torch beams pooling.

Someone had gone into the bungalow and put on all its lights. The whole compound was lit up now, multiple shadows climbing the windowless back wall of the garage.

'Somebody,' Bliss said through his teeth, 'is going down for this.' The hoarsened edge to his voice suggesting that he was getting worried it was going to be him.

The hole in the grass lay abandoned. Someone had taken the case away. There was no stench of decaying flesh, but that didn't mean there wasn't a body down there, somewhere. Lol stayed away from the hole. Only Roddy Lodge could explain this, and he wasn't around. Roddy Lodge had taken a personal decision that his presence here was no longer essential. He'd just walked away into the darkness.

'Can't've got out of here,' Mumford kept saying. 'That's for certain. I know this place now, end to end, and if everybody's stayed in place, he cannot have got out. '

'You better be right, sunshine, for all our sakes.' Bliss turned to the lawyer, 'And if *you*—'

'He was ill.' Mr Nye had his arms folded and kept looking over his shoulder. Lol instinctively looked over his: how dangerous *was* Lodge? 'He was *ill*,' the lawyer insisted. 'There was no question at all that he was ill.'

'I'm not feeling too marvellous meself, pal, and if I thought for one minute that when you asked for those handcuffs to come off—'

'Don't be absurd!'

'This man —' Bliss's forefinger came out like a gun '– is a suspected *multiple murderer*. So don't you go anywhere, Mr Nye.'

'Is that a thr—?'

'And who the *fuck*,' Bliss roared out, staring past Mr Nye, 'let *these* bastards in?'

Maybe it was the kids driven away from the perimeter tape who'd spread the word. But it wasn't just kids this time. Lol thought of a football crowd filing through turnstiles. Only with lamps and torches.

'Jesus, it's a fuckin' *circus*!'

The group of people moving along the path on one side of the garage building was led by a tall woman in a long stockman's coat. A lone PC behind them spread his arms, helpless.

'Sorry, sir, they—'

'Get back to the entrance! *Now!*' Bliss walked up to the woman. 'Mrs Sollars, you should know better than this. We're not running a funfair here.'

'Then what *are* you running?' a man demanded. 'You've spent the whole day digging up people's gardens with abandon. I suppose you thought you were being discreet.' He looked down at two children. 'Miles . . . Ffion . . . home, please. I did ask you before.'

One of the kids said, 'Aw, Fergus!'

'Or there may have to be proportionately less time on-line for the whole of next week,' the man said calmly.

The woman said, 'If you'd had the common decency, Inspector, to keep the community informed—'

'Oh, pardon *me*,' Bliss snarled. 'I'll have a special flyer pushed through everybody's door next time. Look, I don't have time for this. You'd better go over and stand by that wall, all of you, and stay together, you understand me? Because if any of you gets in my way, I'm gonna do you for obstruction, and that's not—'

'You've mislaid him, haven't you?' a man with a white beard said. 'You don't have Roddy right now.'

'I'm telling you not to come any further. Stay together. And don't let anyone else in here. Can you do that? Can you do that for the sake of the *community*?' Bliss began to walk away.

The bearded man said, 'You don't look very far, do you?' He had a vaguely transatlantic accent. He wore a loose denim jacket and a plaid cap, and he had a canvas bag hanging from a shoulder strap. Also good night-vision, Lol figured; although he didn't have a torch, he was peering around into the dark areas.

Bliss continued for a couple of paces and then stopped.

Lol saw exactly where the bearded man was gazing.

Up.

19

On Angels

Jane had gone upstairs for a bath, leaving Merrily hunched by the sitting-room fire, feet in woolly socks, cardigan buttoned to the top, but still feeling cold. She pulled St Thomas Aquinas from the shelf: *Aquinas on Angels*. Intellectual exercise could sometimes deflate anxiety.

She opened the paperback, immediately shut it again, snatched up the cordless and tried Lol's phone. It was now over a week since she'd seen him, and, OK, it felt very much longer – really, what kind of relationship *was* this? To Jane, for whom two nights without a call from Eirion was cause for sleep-loss, it must look like a trial separation.

Merrily felt angry, frustrated, losing her grip – a marionette with its strings pulled in different directions by Jenny Box, Uncle Ted, Frannie Bliss and . . . *Jane*? Like, what had happened suddenly to turn the kid into the self-appointed voice of rationality in this household?

'*The phone you are calling is switched off . . .*'

Inevitably.

Nearly two hours into darkness, now. Were they still out there digging for Frannie's corpses on the windy fringe of the Forest? Merrily tapped in Gomer's home number, on the off chance that they were out of there.

'*This yere is Gomer Parry Plant Hire. We en't in, but that don't mean we en't available, so you be sure and leave your number.*'

Damn.

Merrily hit *end* and tossed the phone on the sofa. Slumping down with the book, she found St Thomas Aquinas no more accessible.

It is not necessary that the place where an angel is should

be spatially indivisible; it can be divisible or indivisible,
greater or less, according as the angel chooses, voluntarily,
to apply his power to a more or less extended body. And
the whole body, whatever it be, will be as one place to him.

She read the paragraph twice more. You could always rely on
Thomas to make you feel totally thick. Hard to imagine a mind
this colossal functioning within a society of bows and arrows,
boiling oil, trial by ordeal . . . but then, inside grey walls in the
thirteenth century, with no TV or radio or phones or kids, only
a solitary circle of candlelight, a trained intellect powered by
spiritual energy might well acquire laserlike focus.

In the dog grate, a mix of coal and apple logs burned with an
intensity that she could neither feel nor find in herself. To be a
serious student of Aquinas, theology was not enough. You also
needed to be Stephen Hawking.

An angel is in contact with a given place simply and solely
through his power there. Hence his movement from place
to place can be nothing but a succession of distinct power
contacts.

What she was hoping for was . . . OK, a *sign*. Like, sometimes,
you could open a book – it didn't have to be the Bible – to a
random page, and the solution would be there, as though at the
end of a shaft of light. The answer might not depend on a literal
interpretation of the text; it might be a certain metaphor which
sprang a diversion, lit some indirect path to an unexpected truth.
Jenny Box: what the hell does she want from me?
Jenny's angel: was *that* a metaphor, or what? A person coming
from New Age spirituality – from earth-powers, shamanism and
healing crystals – to Christianity would probably need some kind
of visionary incentive, real or imagined. Jenny Box would have to
find ample metaphysical justification for her move to an obscure
village in Herefordshire: Ledwardine as Glastonbury, Ledwardine as Lourdes. Just as Merrily herself often wondered if she'd
been washed up here for a *reason* – at college, she'd always seen
herself as an urban priest, firing faith in concrete alleys full of
vomit and discarded syringes.

She lay back on the sofa with the Aquinas paperback on her lap, closed her eyes and saw four possibilities:

1. Jenny Box had hallucinated the angel.
2. Jenny Box had invented the angel.
3. An optical illusion.
4. An angel.

Floodlit by a dozen small lamps, it looked like a gigantic headless metal puppet, with six arms rigidly outstretched – wires from its pendulous fingers, wires from its elbow joints.

If there was a formidable elemental force travelling those wires, the pylon itself looked dangerously unstable, Lol thought. And archaic. A skeletal survivor of the days when cars broke down every few weeks and a single computer filled a whole room.

This was your standard National Grid tower, the bearded man in denims had explained in his relaxed, tour-guide kind of way. He'd hung around with Lol when the adrenalin kicked into Frannie Bliss. There were over fifty pylons in this part of the valley, he said, and this was one of the big ones. It was carrying 400,000 volts.

And Roddy Lodge.

Lodge was about forty feet up, like a crawling insect, not far beneath the first pair of arms, at the end of which the live power-lines were coiled around insulators resembling hanging candles of knobbly green glass.

Lol heard Bliss telling someone to call for an ambulance and the fire brigade. He was standing about twenty feet from the pylon's splayed legs of reinforced steel, hands in the pockets of his hiking jacket, more controlled now that he could see his prisoner again – could see that the prisoner had nowhere to go.

Nowhere in this world.

Lol wiped his glasses on the sleeve of his jacket. It had stopped raining, but the wind was up. The wires were zinging in his head. Vicarious vertigo.

'You're not with the police, then,' the bearded man said.

Directly in front of them was the abandoned excavation, the spade still sticking out of it. From here they could see the whole of the pylon, maybe 150 feet tall, and the shape of Howle Hill behind it, a black thumbprint on the sky.

'I'm just one of the gravediggers,' Lol said.

'That mean I can actually talk to you without I get told to climb back on the school bus and leave it to the grown-ups?'

'Least the police don't have guns,' Lol said, hoping he was right about this.

'One of the reasons I came home, my friend. Protest about something in New Labour Britain, you don't get shot, you just get patronized. Name's Sam Hall, by the way.'

'Lol. Lol Robinson.' He saw that Sam Hall was older than he'd first appeared, well into his sixties, maybe beyond that – that backwoods-pioneer look grizzling over the years.

'Tough day, Lol?' Sam said mildly. As if they were unwinding at something not over-exciting, like crown-green bowling.

Before Lol could reply, a woman screamed. He saw Roddy Lodge gripping an overhead girder, swinging himself, apelike, into a steel V, finally wedging there. The orange overalls might have been designed to make him conspicuous in a pylon at night, like a warning beacon for aircraft.

'Aw, *Roddy*!' A small shrillness under Frannie Bliss's voice as he called up, 'Roddy, you daft bugger, where's this gonna get yer? Tell me that, eh?'

No answer.

'That's because he doesn't know,' Sam Hall said to Lol.

'Sorry?'

''Less, of course, he has an end in mind.'

Lol glanced sharply at him.

'Which would depend on whether he's done all they say he's done,' Sam Hall said.

'How much danger's he in?'

'Boy, we're all of us in danger from those monsters. I could name you three, maybe six people'd be alive today if they'd lived the other side of that hill. But Roddy . . . My guess would be that he's done this before. You'll notice somebody already cut through the barbed wire the power guys snag around the base to stop people climbing – and this is Roddy's land, so I'd say it was him. Evidently knew where to find the footholds. He's been up there before. Just look at the guy go . . .'

Roddy was moving again, pulling himself onto the first of the great arms, about sixty feet up now, lamp beams following him.

'For God's sake,' a woman shouted from behind them, 'can't anyone get him down?'

'Not possible, Ingrid,' Sam Hall said, although there was no way she could hear him. 'Not worth the candle,' he said to Lol. 'Tower's earthed, so anyone standing on it's earthed, too. Electricity will do anything to hitch a ride to the ground. What happens – he gets too close, it's gonna jump him, and I wouldn't like to be the person holding on to his feet when it does.'

'You know a lot about it.' Lol had his hands deep in his pockets, hunched against the shivering. 'Worked in the power industry?'

Sam Hall let out a big, echoing laugh that sounded a little shocking in this situation, like it was bouncing around the valley. 'Partner, what *I* do is I work *against* the power industry.'

Roddy Lodge had come fully to his feet. He was standing on the arm, a yard or so out from the shoulder, holding on to a diagonal steel bar with one hand. On the ground, the police-woman, Tiffany, and a male colleague were arranging a sheet of white plastic over the hole Lol had dug, weighting down the edges with bricks from a pile of building rubble.

'Fact is,' Sam Hall said, 'a bunch of fat cats here and over in the US would give just about anything in the whole world to have me up there, 'stead of that poor sucker.'

A gasp of wind hit Roddy and he swayed and lost his footing and slipped down between two girders and hung there, his feet dangling in space.

'Christ,' Lol whispered. Three police officers ran, amid screams, towards the pylon.

'Could be safer if he dropped now,' Sam Hall said. 'He doesn't hit metal on the way down, he *might* not die. All depends on what he wants out of this.'

*

'This is a little early for you, *cariad*,' Eirion said.

'How's the party?'

'*Yn Cymreig*. I'm having to watch my grammar.'

'The whole party's in Welsh?' Jane sat on the edge of her bed, wrapped in the big bath towel.

'My step-gran's discovered cultural correctness in her old age. And her heritage – distant cousin of Saunders Lewis, see.'

'You've lost me already.'

'Anyone who wants to speak English is finding it expedient to go outside,' Eirion said. 'Bit like having a fag out on the balcony.'

'Wow,' Jane said, 'another world. Is that where you are now?'

'I'm in the kitchen. But not, I have to tell you, because my Welsh isn't wholly fluent. Where are you?'

'My bedroom. Just got out of the bath. Goose bumps every-where.'

She heard Eirion moan faintly.

'We could have telephone sex, if you like,' Jane said. 'I'm letting the towel slip slowly down my breasts. There are tiny bubbles of moisture . . .'

'What is it you want?' Eirion said tightly.

'OK, I lied. I'm fully dressed. In fact, it's so cold in this house that I'm wearing my fleece and leg warmers.'

'Thank you.'

'Listen, how far are you from the nearest computer?'

'Decades,' Eirion said obliquely.

'Check someone out for me? On the Net? You remember Jenny Driscoll? All soft-voiced and drippy. Did these crappy daytime TV shows on fashion and decor and make-overs and stuff.'

'Like the ones I always watch to find my feminine side.'

'Irene, this is—'

'Yeah, I do know who you mean. Nice-looking.'

'You're really into old ladies, aren't you? There's a word for it.'

'And she lives in your village.'

'Who told you that?'

'You did.'

'Christ, was I ever that sad? Irene, listen, this sounds . . . this is going to sound very stupid. But this woman, this Driscoll – or Mrs Box, as she now calls herself – she's got her claws seriously into Mum.'

'Meaning what?'

'I can't tell you, but it comes out of some middle-aged religious obsession. Or maybe it's just attention seeking, or maybe she's just a lonely old bag, I wouldn't like to venture a hard opinion at this stage but, essentially, she's claiming – this is what she's told Mum, right? – that she's had a mystical experience. Involving an angel. In the sky, over the church – our church. Don't laugh. And she has a chapel in her house – this kind of shrine, under the floor, and she took Mum down there, and there was incense and candles and stuff. And of course Mum's reacting in a suitably spiritually correct fashion.'

'And you think *this* is another world,' Eirion said.

'It's not actually a joke. It's not actually funny, for at least one very bizarre reason that I'm not allowed to tell you about, so don't ask me. But I do not believe this woman has had any kind of . . . experience, and— Irene, are you still there?'

'Yeah. I . . . Jane, it's still happening isn't it? You're still . . .'

'Huh?'

'Your . . . This whole dark-night-of-the-soul thing. A few months ago, if anybody claimed to have seen an angel within fifty miles of Ledwardine, you'd have been so excited you'd be up all night with a video camera.'

'Yeah, well, I'm over it, all right? It was pitiful, and I'm finally over it. You can waste your life on that kind of shit.'

'I don't think you mean that, Jane.'

'How would you know what I mean?'

Eirion sighed. 'What do you want me to try and find out?'

'Anything. What happened to her marriage. Why she got out of TV. Any of the kind of scurrilous flotsam that gets washed up on the Net.'

'Surfing for shit?'

'Just help me, Eirion.'

Silence. *I called him Eirion,* Jane thought in dismay.

'You want any dirt I can find on Moira Cairns at the same time?' he said.

'That's not fair.'

'No,' he said. 'I'm sorry.'

Eirion didn't sound sorry. He sounded disappointed, somehow.

A crowd had gathered, the way crowds did. Suddenly it was just there.

Lol didn't know how many people lived around Underhowle, but at least seventy of them had to be here now. The ones who hadn't broken through the police tape must have come across the fields on the other side of the pylon, by the edge of the woods fringing Howle Hill. Perhaps forty people were standing within twenty feet of the tower, like they'd bought tickets. Not enough police here to move them on – like the police didn't have enough to think about.

Frannie Bliss was pacing around the base of the pylon, conspicuously uneasy now. Lol could make out people crouching with their camcorders. Bliss stood back, hands cupped around his mouth. A sudden white light shone all around him – someone had brought along one of those long-distance spotlamps.

'Roddy. Can you hear me, son? This is DI Bliss. Frannie Bliss.'

Roddy Lodge had pulled himself back on to the metal arm; he was braced against the tower's skeletal spine. Clouds had dropped away from the wafery moon, and the girders gleamed white like bone.

'Roddy, can you hear me?'

On the ground, Bliss was competing against the spectator buzz, but the voice from the pylon burst sharply in the air.

'NO!'

Like a hole punched in a paper bag, making its own hush.

'DON'T WANNER TALK TO NO MORE COPPERS!'

'Roddy . . .' Bliss bent backwards. 'Let's be sensible. You're about six feet from enough juice to light up half the county. Just let yourself come down, and take it very carefully. You got nowhere else to go. You know that, son.'

'THAT'S WHAT . . .' A surprise blast of wind. Gasps from the crowd as Lodge clutched at a steel diagonal, caught it and clung to it. 'THAT'S WHAT YOU RECKONS, IS IT, MR COPPER?'

'It's very dangerous, Roddy, that's all I'm saying. There's massive voltage up there, you know that.'

Silence.

'Roddy, if you—'

'NOT TO ME. EN'T NO DANGER TO ME, COPPER. I'M ELECTRIC ALREADY, LOOK!'

Frannie Bliss stared at the churned ground. Lol could feel him groping for viable words. High above him, washed by swirling lights, Roddy Lodge was glowing red like a pantomime demon – Lol willing him to give it up, come down from there, don't raise the stakes.

Roddy suddenly reeled back, one arm locked around the cross bar, the other thrown across his face. His feet seemed to skate on the metal.

'The light,' Sam Hall said. 'Light's affecting him. Plus the shit coming off of the power lines. He's gonna be disoriented by now. His balance'll go completely, can't they see that?' Angrily, he strode down the field towards Bliss. Two uniformed police came out of the dark from two sides, restraining him. Sam turned on one of them. '*Not me*, you asshole! Get across there and tell some of those stupid bastards to switch off their lights if they don't want to kill him. *Jesus!*'

'Why'n't you jump?' A sudden, strident male voice in the crowd. 'Why'n't you take a bloody running jump, Lodge?'

They do *want to kill him*, Lol thought, sickened. He was sweating and trembling with the cold but, at the same time, he was glad he was this side of the pylon, away from that crowd. It was an audience. Audiences wanted it all. He felt hollow inside, and his head was throbbing with fear for the man on the pylon, the performer in the spotlights. '*You reappear on stage now*,' Moira said softly in his ear, '*it's gonnae be like, "Hey, is that no' the big sex-offender?"*' When he turned away, teeth clenched, he could still see the shining red figure projected like a hologram, vibrating in charged air.

'Why'n't you go for a swing on the high wire, Roddy?' The

same man's voice. 'Save the tax-payers havin' to keep you the rest of your bloody useless life!'

A fragment of silence.

'*Shaddup!*' a woman shrieked. 'You en't lived here two minutes, it's no damn business of yours!'

Bliss was tramping back up the field. 'This is useless. How am I supposed to try and talk him down with these fuckin' hay-seeds—? Andy! Where's . . . ? *Right. Listen.* Get half a dozen uniforms, go across and get the lot of them out of there. It's gorra be private land. Tell them they're trespassing, they're obstructing the police, whatever you want. But the first one objects, you *nick him*!'

He tore past Lol, making for the cars.

Sam Hall was back, brushing himself down, straightening his denim jacket. 'This is not good.'

'No.'

'He looks down, all he sees now is row upon row of blinding lights. His head's gonna be close to exploding.'

The lamps aimed up into the pylon made a white gauze in the rain mist. Lol sensed an ambivalence in the crowd. *He's a murderer. He's murdered one of our own. At least one.* Yet Lodge himself was one of their own.

The lights went in and out of focus. Lol looked down.

He saw a tiny red glow tracking across the field.

'*Lodge!*'

The beams from the crowd swung down again, like they were voice-activated, and found – *Oh God* – found Gomer Parry, standing where Bliss had stood, his cap off, his white hair on end in the wind, like a hearth brush, a fresh roll-up in his teeth.

'Lodge . . . Gomer Parry Plant Hire! You yearin' me?

'*Gomer!*' Bliss went lurching back. '*No!*'

'Where was it you set that fire, boy? Where'd you go? Where was it you went Monday night?'

'YOU *KNOOOOOOOOW*!' A roar of pain.

Gomer snatched out his ciggy. 'Say it, boy! Say it again. Where'd you go exac'ly that night? Tell these folks.'

Silence. Beams intersecting like aircraft-spotting searchlights. Gomer waited, rocking back on his heels in the mud.

'I DONE IT!'

Gomer bounced. 'What? Where?'

'I BURNED HIM! *I . . . F – FRIED HIM.*' A shrill giggle, tremolo yelps. '*I FRIED THE FUCKING BASTARD IN HIS OWN FAT!*'

Bliss had hold of Gomer, was dragging him away. 'Christ's sake, what you trying to—?'

'YOU *KNOOOOOOOOOOOOOW!*'

'Tryin' to get at the bloody truth.' Gomer pulled away. 'Which is more'n you done. And I'm tellin' you, boy, it en't—'

'I . . . DONE . . .' Roddy Lodge was shambling slowly along the down-sloping arm of the pylon, arms outstretched like a tightrope artist, a man on a high diving board. Not too far above him now hung one of the insulators from the second tier, its power-hugging glass discs gleaming cold green. Candle of death. 'I DONE 'EM *ALL!*'

Bliss's head went back. His fists were clenched tight. Gomer just stood there and stared down at the ground. Both of them in shadow, all the lights trained on the pylon. Roddy stopped. Even from where Lol stood he could see Lodge was grinning.

'I DONE . . .' He shuffled, swayed. 'I DONE ALL THEM WOMEN! I DONE LYNSEY! I DONE . . . I DONE MEL! YOU YEARIN' ME? I DONE 'EM ALL! I DONE THAT WELSH GIRL! I DONE . . . I DONE MORE'N YOU KNOWS. 'CAUSE . . .'

Bliss stood there, ramming his fists into the sides of his thighs. Roddy reached up like he was trying to clasp the wind and the night.

''CAUSE I'M THE DEVIL! I'M SATAN! I'M THE BIGGEST FUCKIN' SERIAL KILLER EVER LIVED! *YOU HEAR ME?* I WAS GONNER DO FUCKIN' . . . FUCKIN' *MADONNA!*' 'CAUSE I'M NUMBER ONE, LOOK . . . *I'M NUMBER FUCKIN' ONE!*'

Silence fell like a canopy. Lol was suddenly and horrifically aware of something in the crowd that was less apprehension than a kind of active anticipation.

And yet he also actually heard someone beginning to weep, a hoarse, bubbling sound as the rain came down harder.

*

A distant siren – the ambulance or the fire brigade. Lol watched Gomer walking slowly away from the pylon, looking at the ground. The wind had reined itself in. There was a dense, waxy stillness to the air.

One of the police laughed uncertainly. 'Got the biggest witness list of all time there, boss. When he's in the dock—'

Lol heard Sam Hall saying very quietly, 'He won't be, will he?'

Gomer reached them, muttering.

'We digs holes, is what we do. En't no affair of ours now.' His voice was shaking. Lol had never heard Gomer's voice shaking before, not even with anger. 'En't up for no public execution. We just digs holes, ennit?'

He kept on walking, along the alley by the side of the garage. Lol followed him, holding his spade. At the end of the alley he looked back once and saw Roddy Lodge standing halfway down the arm of the tower, with his hands reaching up, as though other hands were up there in the night sky, waiting to catch him.

Lol didn't think he either saw or heard what happened next; maybe his mind edited the moment, a jump cut. All he was fully aware of was the lights going out in Roddy's bungalow.

20

Stadium Rock

They seemed to have awoken at about the same time, in the still hollow of the early hours. Merrily sensed him becoming aware, by touch, that *she* was actually here, in this strange bed, in this unknown timber-framed chamber that was strange to her, too – she'd never slept in here before, the air was different, the sounds in the walls.

And it was the first time they'd slept together with no sex.

Not that they'd slept together many times. Pathetically few, in fact, since they'd first done it in the summer.

Done it.

Here she was, thirty-seven years old, actually thinking of it with that old teenage delight in the forbidden. An adventure: two kids in a small, secret room in an ancient house with timbers that creaked and grumbled in the late-October night. It felt deliciously out of time, a place you thought you could never re-enter, soft and sticky and warm and illicit. And in the *vicarage* . . . where the vicar might come in and catch you *doing it* . . .

Doing it: more spontaneously thrilling than *making love*. That hint of . . .

Sin?

Shameful. Utterly. When she thought, *It's me . . . I'm the vicar*, she couldn't stop giggling and hid her shame under the duvet, because there really was nothing at all to laugh at tonight.

Jane had gone off to bed with a book half an hour before Gomer had arrived at the back door. The kid must already have fallen asleep – if she'd heard him, she'd have been straight down.

It was 11.15 p.m. Gomer had been looking very tired, his glasses half-clouded. In fact, more than tired: perturbed, unhappy. He didn't seem in the mood to talk.

He had with him some wreckage dressed in Lol's clothes.

'Boy en't in no fit state to drive home, vicar. Figured you might have a bed made up in one of the spare rooms. Being as how you've always been strong on the idea of sanctuary, see, for the weary.'

Yes, Merrily had agreed, that was a possibility. Lol had smiled lopsidedly. There was a smear of dried mud on his forehead. A pocket of his jacket was hanging off. He stood there among the fallen apples, looking like a refugee who'd crossed Eastern Europe on foot. She'd wanted to laugh, and to touch him.

Gomer said, 'And I figured you'd wanner know, anyway.'

Know?

Evidently, this had not turned out as expected. Looking at Gomer now was reopening narrow channels of anxiety. Merrily hadn't asked about anything, only offered him some tea and something to eat, which he'd declined, claiming that if he sat down, he wouldn't get up till morning.

She'd watched him tramping back to his truck, small and grey against the remaining lights of Ledwardine. There was only one other vehicle parked on the square. She'd gone back in and made some tea for Lol and left him to drink it while she slipped upstairs and quickly made up a bed – in the fifth bedroom, the small one at the back of the house, over the kitchen and therefore warmer than most of them. Also, well away from the stairs leading to Jane's attic.

'We'll talk in the morning,' Merrily had said.

Lol had wanted to tell her everything now, but she'd slipped away to run a bath for him. He was here, in her home. What else mattered?

A lot, but it would wait. While he was in the bathroom, she'd stolen most of his clothes and loaded them into the washing machine. When she came back upstairs nearly an hour later, dressed for bed, he was still wrapped in the towel, lying on his stomach on the single divan in the fifth bedroom.

She'd stood looking at him for quite a while, his compact body, his wet hair, before taking away the towel and covering him with the duvet. Then she'd set her alarm clock on the windowsill, knelt and prayed silently, and then slipped in next to him, putting out the light.

'So we . . . we went back,' Lol said. 'How could we not?'

They had their arms around one another, holding themselves together in the narrow bed in the darkness.

'Chaos. People screaming and pushing, as if they thought the whole area was in danger of becoming electrified. Couldn't get out of there fast enough.'

She was visualizing it, recalling the pylon standing over the bungalow in a whole valley polluted with pylons.

'Bliss went crazy. Had everybody thrown out, except Gomer and me – and that was only because he wanted to give Gomer a bollocking.' Lol stared into the dark. 'Gomer was right. It turned into a public execution.'

'He wasn't still . . . up there?'

'No, he fell off. When we got back to the field, he was lying at the foot of the pylon. Someone said he was still twitching, but I couldn't . . .'

'But *you* didn't actually see it happen?' Wanting him not to have. Detailed images lived for years in Lol's head. Today had left multiple bruises and scratches on his body and his face, and that was enough.

'I don't know.' His hand tightened around her upper arm, against the memory. 'It's all mixed up with what other people said they saw. There was a bang. A flash of light. He was all lit up for a moment, somebody said.'

Merrily was picturing Roddy Lodge's angular, jutting, puppet face jerking in spasms. She shuddered. Was this really where he'd wanted to end up, when he'd slipped quietly away from the police? She recalled him screaming at Gomer that night at the Pawson house: *Chicken, then, is it? You chickenshit?*

'When we saw him afterwards,' Lol said, 'I didn't know what to expect. Whether he'd be . . . burned to a crisp. But it doesn't . . . this guy told me it's like a microwave . . . cooks from the inside.'

'But was he *trying* to kill himself? Did he know what he was doing?'

She was feeling leaden inside now, with guilt and remorse, recalling that initial relief when she'd been spared a meeting with Roddy Lodge at Hereford Police Station – because of the intervention of his solicitor, who had insisted his client was mentally ill. Why had Lodge wanted to see her? What had he wanted to tell her that he was refusing, at least at that stage, to tell the police? And would it have made a difference?

Lol said, 'In the end, he was holding out his arms. Standing there, on the arm of the pylon, spotlit from all directions, and he's suddenly flinging out his arms. Bliss had been shouting up to him about the dangers. He shouted back that he was electric already. This was some minutes before he . . . before the electricity jumped into him. There was this guy there, called Sam, and he'd said that was what might happen. Whether the wind or the rain made a difference, I don't know, but he couldn't've touched anything. His fingers must've been at least a couple of feet from this . . . hanging thing, the insulator, hanging down from the second arm, above him.'

'This was just after he confessed?'

She felt his face move against her hair – Lol nodding.

'So Gomer . . .'

'Bliss obviously blamed Gomer for pushing Lodge to the brink. The confession . . . obviously that was what Bliss wanted, but not in public. The way it happened, it was like Lodge was – I don't know . . .'

'Stealing his glory,' Merrily said. 'Stealing the case right out of his hands and giving it to everybody. Stealing the whole judicial process. Roddy Lodge having the last laugh, hijacking Frannie's result. And Gomer . . .'

'Gomer wasn't laughing.'

'He'd got what he wanted. Roddy *did* confess to the fire. And Nev? What about Nev?'

'He said he . . . fried the fat bastard. So Gomer got *his* confession, too, finally. It was really odd. All the way back here, he said hardly a word. You'd expect some kind of cathartic reaction. But not a word. I think Gomer was seriously stunned.'

'You travelled all the way back in silence?' Merrily felt around on the oak-boarded floor for her cigarettes.

'No, he talked about this and that – the tanks and why we hadn't found any bodies underneath them. How that was one secret Lodge had taken to his grave. Which, of course, is another problem for Bliss. Nobody's going to tell him where to look now. He could dig up half the county and still not get close.'

'Lot of explaining ahead for Frannie, I'd imagine.' She thought about Bliss and his 'messy' home life and the Job – only the police gave it a capital J – becoming his refuge. It wasn't going to be much of one now. His superiors would want to know exactly how he came to mislay his prisoner, why he'd sat on the case, kept it to himself, hired the volatile Gomer Parry to dig up septic tanks installed by a man Gomer believed had murdered his nephew.

She wondered how much of a basis Bliss had really had for bringing Roddy Lodge out to Underhowle, how much Lodge had actually told him in the interview room. Evidently he'd admitted to several killings, but had he given any indication of *why*? Serial killers had become a species, their motives taken for granted. They were male predators, and that was it, jungle carnivores, bringing down young women like gazelles, to be pawed and raked at leisure.

Leave it. Merrily peered at the old luminous alarm clock in the window; she didn't want to oversleep and have Jane find them here in the morning . . . even though the kid would probably be delighted.

Hell, it *was* the morning. In three minutes' time it would be four a.m.

Lol said suddenly, 'I felt sorry for him.'

'Bliss?'

'Lodge.' His voice sounded distant, detached. His arm went slack around her. 'That's not right, is it? How can anybody feel sorry for a man who killed women?'

Merrily said, 'It's a . . . Christian thing.'

Trite.

'Empathy,' Lol said. 'I saw him up there, and I seemed to feel what he was feeling. Or it translated itself. It was like stadium rock. All the lights. Pink Floyd or something. Crazy.'

Or something. Merrily said, 'When's the gig?'

'Oh. Next week. Wednesday.'

'Why didn't you tell me?'

'I . . . In case . . .'

'You mean you're considering not doing it.'

'It's a Moira Cairns concert. That's all it says on the posters. Nobody would be the wiser.'

'I'm going to order some tickets.'

'Don't do that. I can get you some. She'll be worth seeing.'

She.

'I want to buy them,' she said, 'out of my meagre stipend.'

'Merrily—'

'Shush.'

They'd agreed that in the morning he would stay up here until Jane wasn't around, and then he'd slip quietly away through the orchard to pick up his car at Gomer's. No one would know. Merrily felt tearful.

'Why did you do it? Why did you offer to go with Gomer?'

'I like Gomer.'

She reached for his hand; it felt like half-set concrete. 'Feels like you won't be able to pick up a guitar for days.' She stiffened. 'Is that why? Is it?'

He kissed her naked shoulder. 'And I sensed people wanting him to die. I was sure I sensed people wanting to see him die.'

Lol sighed, as if this was something he needed to get out of himself. Merrily was about to say something when she realized he was asleep.

She kissed his forehead and wondered if he was dreaming about Roddy Lodge. Or Moira Cairns.

Part Four

I am glowing radioactive
We draw
Beams around the world

Super Furry Animals
Rings Around the World

21

Icon

It was during her sermon the following Sunday that Merrily realized it wasn't over – that Roddy Lodge, though dead, wasn't out of her life.

This morning, she'd awakened at five a.m., or thereabouts, after the return of that old recurring dream: the one where she suddenly discovered she was living in a house with three floors, after thinking there were only two. And on the third floor was something dreadful, and she knew that she'd have to go up there and face it alone.

She was moving very slowly up the second staircase, the fear of reaching the top intensified by the inability to turn back – in dreams, turning back never seemed to be an option – when the dark upper landing suddenly came into view, and then she *was* at the top, and the first strange door was just above her and beneath it was a thin grin of icy, violet light.

This was enough. Ejecting in terror from the dream, Merrily had rolled over, with an urgent need to be held. But the bed was wide and empty and outside the uncurtained window the boughs of old apple trees were creaking in the sour October wind.

Alone.

For two nights after Lol had gone, she'd gone back to the fifth bedroom, slept in the single bed they'd shared, before returning despondently to her own, bigger room. *Sad, huh?*

And puzzled and unhappy, because now she actually was living in an old house with three floors, and Jane was in possession of the attics. She thought she'd dealt with the third floor.

Here in church, there were more stairs she preferred to avoid: the polished wooden steps to the pulpit. She knew she should really be up there this morning: little woman, big congregation, even for October when they tended to increase because there were no lawns to mow and the kids had stopped demanding days out. Here, close to the front, sat Big Jim Prosser from the Eight-till-Late, which reduced its Sunday opening hours at the end of the tourist season. Here even was Kent Asprey, heart-throb, jogging GP, back with his wife after a midlife-crisis fling. A penitent Kent, with Mrs Asprey – one week only, probably.

Merrily put a tentative foot on the first pulpit step, then backed down again. What she'd been doing during the summer and early autumn, when congregations were smaller and cosier, was to sit on a hassock on the carpeted chancel steps, under the apple screen, and not preach but chat. Sometimes, a few members of the congregation would join in, and there was a sense of warmth and unity. She found it exciting, was never sure where it would lead. One Sunday it had spontaneously opened out, like a flower, into communal meditation.

It was hardly going to happen today. The congregation was like the bed: too big, too cold, too quiet. And swollen by too many comparative strangers whose presence could only be explained by curiosity over rumours of Merrily's links, through Gomer, with the Roddy Lodge sensation – an electric death still pulsing in Herefordshire like a snaking naked wire.

This was a small county; everybody knew somebody related to the Lodge family or the families of girls and women missing from home – one was from a farm near Staunton, just a few miles from Ledwardine – or at least someone who had con-sidered having an Efflapure system installed. Everyone had been exposed to radio and TV reports and centre-spreads with the same grisly sequence of pictures and tasteless variations on the *Daily Star*'s:

> *Villagers watch in horror as man boasts:*
> *'I'm the biggest serial killer ever', then is*
> *FRIED IN THE SKY*

Underhowle itself was reported to be in a grey state of communal shock. Nearly a hundred people, including children as young as five and six, had heard Roddy Lodge confess, then watched him die. Many were being treated and counselled for the trauma.

And the shock waves radiated outwards.

TRACKS OF THE BORDER BEAST.

On the third day, most of the headlines were variations of this one from the *Mail*. Where had Roddy Lodge been? Where might he have interred the bodies – *Is there a corpse under YOUR septic tank?* the *Mail* asked. The speculation now was that this was a false trail: cold-storing the body of Lynsey Davies in the pea-gravel under the Efflapure had been a one-off emergency measure – maybe Lodge had felt in danger of discovery at the time. Anyway, there would surely have been better options open to a killer with his own JCB.

So the other bodies could be anywhere.

All over Herefordshire and the Forest of Dean, this particularly was a live issue, and Merrily had felt obliged to address it, had assembled a sermon around the life and death of Roddy Lodge. Why did such people exist? Why had God created serial killers?

A difficult one. Why exactly?

It was certainly not a question voiced by the grateful papers, as the search for bodies went on, as police interviewed and re-interviewed the relatives of missing women and girls across five shires, as press and TV cameramen prowled Underhowle, reporters free to speculate now that the killer who had confessed so publicly was never going to face trial.

And the police, in this case, were . . . who exactly? No mention in the papers of Bliss. Or indeed of DCI Annie Howe. All the press briefings had been given by a Detective Superintendent Luke Fleming. Merrily had never heard of him – must have been from Headquarters. She noticed that there was nothing in any of the papers about Roddy's taste in bedroom decor. Given that he was dead, why not?

Every day she'd expected her own involvement in the discovery of Lynsey Davies to be disclosed by the police, but despite the local gossip – inadvertently fuelled by Gomer, she suspected, as he pursued the truth about the fire – nobody had approached her.

This morning, preparing for Holy Communion in the early

light, she'd decided to dump the Roddy Lodge sermon. It had seemed unnecessary, gratuitous.

Sermon B, then.

She didn't sit on the hassock, but she didn't go into the pulpit either; she stood at the side of the lectern.

'Erm . . .'

She felt obscurely nervous; she really needed notes for this one, but there was nowhere to conceal them. And because pews were filled further back than of late, she had to project more than she'd become accustomed to. Had to make like a preacher.

'If we . . . if we sit down and really think about it, I suspect most of us will remember an occasion when something's happened, very suddenly, to divert us from a certain course of action. Maybe a flat tyre that stopped you making a particular journey. And then, some time later, you find out that that journey might have led you into a far bigger crisis – a motorway pile-up, or some confrontation that you might not have been able to handle. And then you say – and how often have most of us said this . . . ?'

She leaned out, an arm around the stem of the lectern, found herself locking gazes for a second with James Bull-Davies, three pews from the front.

' . . . *Perhaps it was meant.*' She stepped back. 'That's a useful phrase, isn't it? Meant by whom? By God? And why should God single *us* out for salvation? Why should *we* be diverted from the pile-up that's going to kill or injure several other people?' Longish pause. 'For the Christian, there's . . . another option. Suppose we think about that phrase in the context of the possibility of there being –' she smiled faintly '– angels among us.'

Jenny Box was close to the front, to Merrily's right, washed in amber light from the circular stained-glass window in which a clutch of apples was pensively surveyed by several angels. Jenny Box, with her fine old-gold hair under a small white hat that was almost a skullcap, her eyes unblinking but also unfocused, as if gazing into the ether. Merrily wondered how Thomas Aquinas would have handled this.

'What do I mean by angels? To be quite honest, I'm not sure. Do I mean heavenly forces, agents of change? Powerful, invisible intelligences capable of assessing a situation, seeing the direction it's going, anticipating the consequences. And occasionally intervening, sometimes as a result of prayer, but often quite spontaneously. Or so it seems.'

Mrs Box was watching her now. Merrily avoided her gaze.

'We talk about governments being interventionist or non-interventionist – should they step in and overrule market forces or whatever? It's always a fine balance and, because governments don't have Godlike wisdom – or much wisdom at all, you might think sometimes – they often intervene over the wrong issues. But we have to assume that angels . . . that they *never* get it wrong.'

She hadn't had time to prepare this properly. She was opening a can of worms. Were angels messengers of God or *aspects* of God? To what extent were they independent? Was this the time to mention Ledwardine's own angel? Not the one with the sword allegedly witnessed spreading its radiance over the church in a thunderstorm but the anonymous one with the bin sack full of used fifties. That would take their minds off Roddy Lodge for a while.

Maybe not. Uncle Ted had whispered to her earlier, as they came into church, that he was still awaiting police clearance on the money. If he didn't hear anything this week he was damn well getting back onto them.

'The Bible doesn't go into too much detail about the nature of angels. They just *are*. Most of us, if we think about them at all, think of them in the context of particular episodes – usually involving halos and harps and a few gobsmacked shepherds. Or we might mention – with a shiver – something we like to call the Angel of Death, which . . .'

Merrily looked up at the stained-glass window with the apples. The angels there were solid and looked female, with their extravagant golden curls and small pursed lips.

' . . . which we always see as something horribly sinister rather than something gentle and understanding which exists to guide us through what, for most of us, is the only situation since birth in which we are one hundred per cent helpless.'

Jenny Box had lowered her gaze. Merrily thought of all the

hospital beds she'd sensed to be enfolded in dark, downy wings. *But then* – the thought pierced her like a thin blade – *what was the Angel of Death doing when the face of Lynsey Davies was turning blue under the savage pressure, her eyes bulging, her tongue—*

'I . . . As far as I know, I've never seen an angel. So I really can't tell you if they look like the ones in the windows over there – if they've got actual wings, or if they're light and vague, or as invisible as breath. I suspect that angels look . . . just like us.'

And how many others are dead? Nobody knows. And why? Nobody knows.

'Some people do claim to have actually seen them in times of crisis, some to have . . . sensed them.'

She swallowed. Lifted her eyes and her thoughts. Had *she* sensed them? At her shoulder during a Eucharist? Once, perhaps, on Christmas Day, in an aura of profound holiness, as the bells awoke the valley?

'Most of us, though, have only seen evidence of what appears to be a practical intelligence which comes out of nowhere to . . . *alter a situation*. Now that in itself – that's such an amazing concept, such a *Superman* thing, that it's easy to get carried away, to start looking for angels, looking for evidence of angelic intervention in everything, every little situation.'

She paused, looking around for Jane, who would occasionally slip in at the back, without making a thing about it. No sign of her today. No surprise.

'My own feeling, for what it's worth, is that angels are a layer of creation, an aspect of divinity, of which we should be aware. Or *more* aware. And if we ever have reason to think that an angel has intervened for us, then maybe we shouldn't just say "Oh, it was meant," we should spend some time thinking: *Why?* Why me? Why now?'

What Merrily was thinking right now was that all this sermon had told its listeners so far was that this vicar hadn't yet worked out where she stood on angels. Or, indeed, on Jenny Box, probably the parish church's biggest benefactor since the Bull family ran out of spare cash.

She looked into the congregation, perhaps for some guidance on how far to take this, and caught a movement from the bottom end of the nave: Frannie Bliss walking quietly through from the porch.

Frannie Bliss?

But, like several others, Bliss must have left before the after-service tea and coffee – either that or she'd imagined him. Jenny Box didn't stay, either, but then she never had; she probably considered the serving of refreshments to be misuse of a holy sanctuary. On this one, Merrily would always disagree; this was about giving and sharing and opening up, not taking people's money.

Sometimes, people would want to discuss aspects of the sermon, but not today. Nobody, it seemed, wanted to disclose a personal angelic encounter. Outside, after everyone had gone, only James Bull-Davies hung around in the churchyard.

It was a James kind of day: stiff, blustery. He angled over, hands behind his back, stared moodily at a windfall apple that had landed on a grave.

'This Box woman.'

Merrily drew her woollen cape over her surplice, tilted her head to one side, curious. Pulled prematurely from the Army on the death of his father, James had reluctantly shouldered what he perceived to be his family's burden of responsibility for the village. Lately, however – under the influence of Alison, no doubt – he seemed to have shrugged much of it off, coming to church alone, avoiding the traditional Bull pew, generally adopting a neutral stance on parish issues.

'Don't like to interfere, Mrs Watkins.' He cleared his throat. 'As you know.'

'How's Alison?'

'Fine.' He flicked a brittle wafer of lichen from the eighteenth-century headstone opposite the porch. 'Met the husband, have you?'

'Husband?'

James folded his arms, looked down at his shoes. He had on a checked shirt and a mud-coloured tie under the old tweed jacket he wore like battledress. 'Encountered the guy in the Swan, Friday evening. Up here for the weekend. Works in London.'

'I've never met him.'

'Worried man.' James gazed over Merrily's head towards the lych-gate. 'No one wants a wife playing away.'

Merrily blinked. She got a sudden flashback of James at the height of his crisis, drunk on the square, Alison trying to haul him into the Land Rover. *Mistress*, he'd called her. And then *whore*. Ownership. But Alison had been cool about all that.

'Another man?' Merrily said. '*Here?*'

'Good Lord, no.' James snorted. 'Gord, Mrs Watkins. *Gord!*'

'What?'

'Has its place, religion – the Church. Always accepted that, as you know. Part of the framework. More of these newcomers we can bring into the fold the better.'

'Absolutely.'

'Fanaticism, however . . . something else entirely.'

'Oh, I see. You mean God is the . . . the other man.' She smiled. Church, for James, was a local obligation, a necessary hour of faint tedium on a hard pew smelling of polish. Echoes of public school. James's school had had masters. When the idea of a woman priest-in-charge had been mooted for Ledwardine, he'd apparently been the first to object. She'd kind of thought that was in the past.

'Find this amusing, do you, vicar?'

'James,' she said, 'He's my boss.' He sniffed. 'Look,' she said. 'It's not awfully warm here. Do you want to come back to the vicarage? Sit down with a cup of tea and—'

'No . . .' He shook his head quickly. 'No time, sorry. I just . . . This is simply the gypsy's warning, all right? I'm strongly suggesting you keep that woman at arm's length, if you know what's good for you. Sorry . . . don't mean that to sound like a threat.'

'Of course not.'

'Simply that Box told me some things. Guy'd had a few drinks, so I'm treating most of it as confidential. However, presume you know she's been in psychiatric care?'

'No, I didn't know that.'

'Well, there you are.'

'But . . .' Merrily thought of Lol. 'We do try not to hold it against people. "Let the loonies come unto me," sayeth the Lord, "and I shall . . ." '

'Mrs Watkins,' James said wearily. 'I realize that taking the piss out of me has become a little hobby of yours, but—'

'What's he like?'

'What?'

'Mr Box.'

'Oh.' He considered. 'My height, perhaps an inch or two taller. A little older than her, but not appreciably. Keeps himself fit.' He avoided Merrily's eyes, inspecting the oak frame of the porch, as if the Bulls still paid for its maintenance.

'Yes,' she said, 'but what's he *like*?'

'Ex-journalist. Businessman now, handles her shops. Says he does all the work, she wanders round, tweaks a few things. Don't know these shops myself . . . *decor.*' Saying it like you'd say *blue movies.* 'Smoothish type.'

'Is he still here?'

'Wouldn't know. We were only introduced on Friday. Guy'd drifted into the Swan for a few drinks because he was a little tired of sitting there watching his wife reading her Bible and mouthing psalms.'

'He told you that?' Behind him, in the churchyard, Merrily saw a tiny tendril of smoke rising.

'Not in so many words. Conjecture. Look, vicar, I don't know the ins and outs of it. Never been anyone's idea of a marriage-guidance counsellor, thank Gord.'

'I suppose not.'

'But if Box is blaming anyone –' James dropped his hand from the oak '– then I'd say he's looking in your general direction. And that's a bit more than conjecture.'

'How do you mean?'

'Well, I . . . I . . .' James glared down towards the lych-gate, as though wishing he was out of it. 'Woman's got a bit of a crush on you, after all. Pretty common knowledge in the village.'

'*What?*'

'Ah . . . wrong word, as usual. Sorry. Still . . . big thing, women getting ordained. More underneath all that than any of us suspected. And you yourself – all this cross-waving, holy-water – I'm simply saying you've probably become a . . . what's the word?'

'If you mean role model—'

'Icon?'

'Bloody *hell*, James.'

'Wrong word too, is it? Shut your mouth, James.'

'Bloody hell.'

She was shocked, couldn't look at him. As they walked out under the lych-gate, she glanced back down the crooked alley of graves to where she'd seen the smoke. Gomer Parry was sitting in his usual spot on Minnie's grave, a roll-up in his mouth.

'Poor old Parry.' James had followed her gaze. 'Never bloody rains, eh? They buried his nephew yet?'

'Next week. After the opening of the inquest.'

'Bad show. Didn't notice him in church. Having problems with the old faith, you think?'

Merrily said nothing. Gomer always went to Minnie's grave when he had something to work out. Along with Minnie, he'd buried both their watches, with new batteries. Gomer's was one of the old kind which, despite the batteries, still ticked loudly. Sometimes, he'd said, he thought he could still hear it. Helped him think.

She watched the smoke rise from Gomer's ciggy, darkening the day, a signal of distress. Something was wrong. After he'd told Minnie, maybe he'd tell her.

When they reached the square, she said to James, 'You going to come and discuss this thing in private? Tell me what on earth people are saying?'

'I think not.' James sniffed the air. 'Never been a gossip. Anyway, told Alison I'd be back before one. I've said all I wanted to say. Question of watching your back, vicar. Watching your back.'

'Thank you.'

James merely nodded and walked away with long strides. Merrily looked around the square, as if there might be small knots of people pointing at her and muttering. Maybe the angel sermon hadn't been such a good idea. Maybe – if Jenny Box had told anyone else here about her vision – it was a very *bad* idea.

In fact, the square was empty except for Frannie Bliss leaning against one of the oak pillars of the little market hall, munching a Mars Bar.

Merrily sighed.

22

Aura of Old Hippy

Lol took the call just before one on the kitchen phone at Prof's. From the studio he could hear a playback of Moira's 'Lady of the Tower', veined now with the seamless cello of Simon St John. Just Moira's voice and Simon's cello: experimental.

On the phone, he heard, 'That you, boy? You know who this is?'

A warm voice, not quite American. Lol was momentarily baffled, before the voice threw up an image of the sepia sleeve of The Band's second album, all beards and back porch.

'Sam?'

'Lol, I hope you don't mind this intrusion. I got your number through talking to the cop . . . Bliss? Came over to see me a couple days back.'

'Has he calmed down now?'

'I guess you might say that,' Sam Hall said, 'though he doesn't strike me as a man who can handle calm too well. Anyhow, we had a talk, and it, uh . . . it all came out about you and what you did when you weren't up to your ass in mud.'

'That Bliss,' Lol said. 'So discreet, it's a wonder he never made the Special Branch.' Behind him, Simon's cello glided over the chasm left by Moira's voice after the verse where the messenger climbed down from his horse and the night was in his eyes.

'So in the afternoon I went on down to the village hall,' Sam said. 'They have a community computer room there, courtesy of Mr Cody, and I started to search the Web, and, hey, there you were, boy, all over the show – folks saying how come this guy is a footnote to so many other people's careers? Where'd he go? Folks all over the world – America, Australia – asking questions about Lol Robinson.'

'But you didn't just ring up to scare me.'

Sam laughed. 'Which, I concede, is the good side of the Web – people talking to each other, sharing enthusiasms. The payback, however, in phone lines, in power, that's bad, bad, *bad*. But even a dangerous crank and a madman such as myself has to compromise sometimes . . . which is how I wound up at Ross Records, and they didn't have the Hazey Jane albums, but they did have this collection by Norma Waterstone, with "The Baker's Lament". And . . . well, the up and down of it is, you're good, boy. You . . . are . . . good.'

Lol was confused. 'Thanks. That's kind of you, but—'

'I like how you write what are essentially new folk songs. "The Baker's Lament", that's a new song sounds like it's been around for ever till you really listen to the words, discover it's a new take on an old theme, and it packs a strong message about what is happening to the countryside. So, the upshot, I wound up *buying* this Norma Waterstone album.'

'Er . . . Waterson,' Lol said.

'Some voice, huh? Played it four times last night, used up all of my power ration. Listen, I'm gonna come to the point, Lol. You're a guy feels strongly about the destruction of the country. You know my take on all that – and the power lines. But you don't know it all. There is so . . . much . . . more.'

'Well, I'm sure—'

'And, listen, I don't mean worldwide, I mean here. I'm talking Underhowle, I'm talking Lodge and I'm talking Melanie Pullman. I talk about this the whole time, and nobody listens to me 'cause I'm this old crank, this lunatic with a chip. I'm the fool on the goddam hill, man, and nobody listens. Wanna cut me off now?'

'Go on,' Lol said.

'You wanna cut me off, you cut me off. Everybody cuts me off *sometime*. Anyhow, after the boy died the other night, I listened to all my neighbours walking home saying how it was all for the best, save the taxpayers having to keep him in jail for the rest of his miserable life, and I'm thinking, Hell, am I the only person in this whole village sees this as some kind of a tragedy? I'm always saying that – am I the only person in this whole valley knows what's happening to us all? Anyhow, this time I went home and I started to write myself a poem. Sat up the whole night to finish it – a two-candle poem. And when Bliss told me about you, I started thinking, hey, this is more than coincidence. This is *meant to be*.'

Not one of Lol's favourite phrases. *Meant to be* was a trap.

'I'm gonna ask you straight out,' Sam said, 'I like to be direct. If there's any way at all that you could find the time to turn this poem into a song – well, I don't have the money to pay you, but you could keep the song, if you liked the idea. And the cause is good. It's a world issue and a big one. It's what my life's been building towards.' Sam paused. 'You still there, boy? You hung up on me yet?'

When Eirion called, Jane was lying on her bed with Ethel the cat and a paperback. As soon as she heard his voice, she thrust the book under the pillow, as if he could see it down the line.

Eirion said, 'I'm afraid I have to tell you she seems genuine, Jane. There is like no dirt *at all* on Jenny Driscoll – not on the Net anyway, and I searched hard. In fact, what I've read I rather like.'

Jane thought that, with this unnatural thing he was developing for once-good-looking old ladies, his opinion was hardly to be trusted, but she didn't say anything.

'Do you want to know now?' Eirion said. 'Or shall I print some of it out and fax it over or something?'

'Can you give it to me potted? I'll stop you if anything sounds interesting.'

'OK.' Eirion cleared his throat and started to enunciate like it was the voice-over on a TV biog. 'She was born in County Wicklow into a respectable lower-middle-class family. Father was the manager of a small soft-drinks business. As a teenager, Jenny apparently got itchy feet and sent her picture to a model agency with an office in Dublin. It turned out she had the kind of looks that appealed at the time, and she wound up in London within a year. Someone said she "looked like a girl who bruised easily". Evidently a famous quote. This was the post-punk New

Romantic era, apparently. Terrible clothes, terrible music. And this element of sadomasochism.'

'Mum was there – I've seen the pictures. She was briefly into Goth.'

'Yes,' Eirion said thoughtfully, 'I know.'

'*Lewis* . . .' Jane gave it serious menace. 'Kill that fantasy *right now.*'

Eirion chuckled.

'OK, so New Romantic.' Jane knew some of this, but there might be something new.

'But romantic in a kind of *besmirched* way,' Eirion said. 'Because she looked so vulnerable, they were putting her into these Vivienne Westwood type of things, so that she came across like some kind of teenage streetwalker. Smudged lip gloss and mascara with dribbles, like she'd been crying. Tarnished before her time, you know? It was all a little bit pervy, I suspect.'

'I'm so glad you recognize it.'

'*She* seems to have recognized it, anyway,' Eirion said. 'She suddenly packed in modelling at the height of her career, washed off all the make-up and got a job in children's television, on the production side.'

'How saintly.'

'Where she was soon found to have an aptitude for presenting.'

'What do you know?'

'And kids liked her because she still had this faintly risqué reputation, so in no time she's presenting this cult teenage show – she was out of her teens by then, but she didn't look it. And she eventually became quite popular with parents and older people because there was obviously a genuinely nice person underneath. And, as she got older, she resurfaced, presenting these lifestyle kind of shows – this is the mid- to late nineties, when she was also offered a column on one of the papers – could've been the *Mail* or the *Express*, I forget, but that was how she met her husband, Gareth Box. A journalist.'

'Wrote the column for her?'

'Do you have to be disparaging *all* the time?' Eirion said. 'Box was an assistant editor in charge of features or something but, since she was making so much more money than him, he seems to have packed that in soon after they got married, to manage her career. Maybe she was being exploited.'

'Hmm,' Jane said sceptically.

'Anyway, this was when private TV production was really taking off, and Jenny and her husband came a long way very rapidly and started creating these home make-over type of programmes, with heavy emphasis on *feng shui* – there was a series for Channel Four which I remember seeing a couple of and it was actually pretty good. And that was when they set up this shop called Vestalia, which very rapidly became a chain and seems to be worth . . . well, a lot of money.'

'Never put a foot wrong, then.'

'But then she backed out of the spotlight.'

'Or she saw when the spotlight was about to move on. Or they were making so much money that she didn't need all that bullshit any more.'

'There *was* some speculation at this time that the marriage was cracking up,' Eirion said, 'although she was never linked with anyone else.'

'Staying together for the sake of the business?'

'I don't know, Jane. They were worth quite a lot by then, because Vestalia was into major cities, and also changing direction. One article I found, from the *Telegraph*, at the end of last year, was about how she was increasingly into personal development and meditation and spirituality, and *he* wasn't particularly, but he went along with it. And it was then that the shops started to really specialize in creating a spiritual home environment. They'd stopped using the phrase *feng shui*, though, because that was seen as a passing fad.'

'This is quite good, actually,' Jane said. 'We're getting closer.'

In fact, this was moving nicely in the direction of home chapels.

She slid the paperback book out from under the pillow. It was called *Working with Angels, Fairies and Nature Spirits*. About a year ago – OK, she would admit this – she'd been finding it seriously inspirational, entirely sensible in its evocation of a complex world with all these different layers of existence, all these forces and incorporeal intelligences you could call on to improve and focus your own life.

Now, however, as a more balanced person, she was simply consulting the book to establish where the Box woman was coming from. Obviously, it *helped* that not too long ago Jane herself had been just as loopy, but there was method in Jenny's particular madness; her so-called spiritual development always seemed to run parallel with an increase in material wealth.

The bottom line: this didn't sound like a woman who gave away eighty grand without some underlying purpose unconnected with her immortal soul.

'You actually did OK here, Irene.'

'How very kind,' Eirion said.

'No, really, I mean . . . thanks.'

Maybe she and Eirion, approaching this from different directions – his investigative skills, her background esoteric knowledge – could nail the duplicitous bitch to the wall before Mum got stitched up.

'What do you do now? How do you respond to this?' Prof Levin advanced on Lol across the studio floor. 'What you do now, Laurence, is *not* respond. That is, you decline . . . *rapido*. Because the one thing you, of all people, do not need at this stage is to get in with crazies. So what you do is you call him back and you put it very politely and very firmly. You don't ask any more questions, you resist all his attempts to make you read the lyric, and you never *ever* write a song or the merest line of a song that reflects this proposed theme in any way.'

'Except . . .' Lol backed up against the glass-sided recording booth, 'I kind of—'

'You then make sure to avoid having dealings of *any* kind with this person, ever again.'

'Only I kind of like him,' Lol said.

'Jesus.' Prof feigned an intention to put his foot through the golden weave fronting the Guild Acoustic amp. 'Of *course* you liked him. These people, they're oh so very nice and humble and they tell you you're Lennon and Dylan and Paul Simon all rolled into one, and they would consider it an honour to, in some small way, serve your art. Pah! Two years later, five, ten . . . whenever it seems like you're finally doing OK for yourself, along comes the exceedingly unfriendly letter from their lawyer.'

'He actually dealt with that,' Lol said. 'He said he was prepared to sign the whole thing over to me. Draw up whatever document you like, he said, and I'll sign it. He said this wasn't about money.'

'Laurence, everything, at some stage, is about money. However, this is your funeral.' Prof turned away, shaking his head, and mooched off towards the kitchen and his cappuccino machine. 'Make it a noisy one.'

When he'd gone, Moira Cairns leaned back against the outside wall of the recording booth. She wore very tight jeans and a black top, her hair loosely tied behind with a crimson ribbon.

'So,' she said, 'what *is* the great world issue this guy feels so strongly about?'

'Electricity,' Lol said. 'Pylons, dangers of.'

'Ah. So this would be a person you met at the, ah, execution.' Moira came to sit on the amp opposite. 'Tell me about it. Where's the guy coming from exactly?'

'Strong aura of old hippy,' Lol said. 'He's very proud that some elements in the US government and the power companies were glad to get him off their backs. He talks about extensive scientific research linking overhead power lines with everything from brain tumours to leukaemia clusters – research that is constantly ignored.'

'There'll be background. There always is.'

Lol told her that Sam Hall appeared to live in a remote cabin on Howle Hill, generating his own electricity with a windmill while putting pressure on the power companies if not exactly to accept responsibility for all the health damage then at least to run more cables underground in rural areas.

'He says he's a crank and a loony and proud of it, and he admits to propositioning anyone he thinks might be able to publicize the cause. He says that seeing Lodge dying up there traumatized him into action – again. I mean, if he was asking Bruce Springsteen or Sting to write a song about it . . .'

Moira put her head on one side. 'Perhaps he doesnae *know*

Sting and Springsteen. Listen, loony or not, I wouldnae quarrel with the sentiments – I hate those things. There has to be a better way.'

'Going round with Gomer, I got to see the whole valley. On environmental grounds alone, I'd *like* to help. Assuming he's on the level. I mean, we don't get to do much for anybody, do we, in this business? Not like some people.'

'Not like your wee friend the Reverend, huh?' Moira smiled.

Lol stared at her in dismay. People always said she was psychic; they didn't say she had the ability to uncover the hidden motives you hadn't even admitted to yourself.

'It's so charming, the way you blush,' Moira said. 'So few guys today can still do that. Laurence, it's perfectly fine for you to wannae be involved with the stuff in her life. Like I said the other night, a guy who understands the nature of madness . . .'

He let out a shallow, baffled sigh. 'There was something else. It was when I was standing there watching this man climbing up towards . . . eternity. Knowing how it was going to end. And getting a strong feeling of people *wanting* it to happen.'

'What, like the audience at the Colosseum or somewhere, willing the emperor to give the thumbs-down to the gladiator who came second?'

'I don't know. It was like there was something there to be . . . understood.'

'What did you arrange with this guy?'

'He said come and see him sometime. "Bring your lady," he said.'

'Will she go with you?'

'I . . . can't see her having time.'

'Tell you what.' Moira stood up. 'Suppose I were to tag along, check out this guy. I can be quite intuitive, you know? That wouldnae bother you, if I came along?'

'No, that would be—'

'Call him, then.'

'I can't call him. He doesn't have a phone. You leave a message for him at the village hall, and he calls you back. There are lots of things he doesn't have.'

'Interesting,' Moira said.

23

Nothing But the Night

'The wife,' Bliss said, 'Kirsty . . .' Shovelling a third sugar into his coffee, letting the spoon clang on the tabletop. 'Aw, it's dead difficult, Merrily, this *personal* shite.'

The first thing she'd noticed was that he hadn't shaved. This wasn't Frannie. Frannie was dapper, Frannie was tidy.

He drank some of the coffee, made a face.

'I mean, I've gorra say I never really wanted a wife. In some ways it was that simple.'

Merrily rolled her eyes.

'The police . . . It's like you either go at it firing on all four cylinders, day and night, or it's just a . . . just a job. Me, I never wanted just *work*. I'm like you, it had to be a vocation, a calling – and there was never gonna be a wife, not till I was pushing forty anyway, and I *certainly* never wanted kids.' There were tears in his eyes now. 'Needy little twats.'

'Have you had anything proper to eat, Frannie?' Merrily asked. He'd told her on the square that he'd give her an hour or so to get changed, get sorted – meaning get Jane out of the way, she guessed – and then he'd come and see her, if that was all right.

'Nothing for me, thanks.' He put up both hands. 'Kirsty . . . she used to make me take a flamin' yoghurt to work. She doesn't bother any more. I miss that.'

He looked out of the window towards the ragged apple trees. There was silence, not even the mouse-scratch of Jane listening behind the door to the hall. Perhaps, Merrily thought, she'd grown out of that and therefore really had gone up to her apartment after lunch. She'd be back at school tomorrow.

'So she's a local girl,' Merrily said. 'Kirsty.'

'Shit on her shoes soon as she could walk.' Bliss made a desolate face. 'All her family's sunk into these bloody dead-end farms, all within about ten miles – ma and pa and her old bloody gran and about six thousand aunties. Jesus, they look so *normal* when you first meet them, country girls. She worked in the fashion department at Chadd's. She was . . . very chic. So anyway, that's why I'm still out here, chasing sheep-shaggers. Before we got married, West Mercia was gonna be strictly short-term. I was looking towards – I dunno . . .'

'The Met?'

'Yeh, maybe the Met. Or even back to Merseyside, with a bit of rank to stand on. But Kirsty, she'd just die in a big city, just curl up and . . . I'm not kidding, I'm not exaggerating.'

'I know.'

'I hate that in her. It's not how wives are supposed to be, is it? She's supposed to want to follow me to the ends of . . . wherever.'

'Except that wherever *you* go, you've always got your family around you,' Merrily said. 'Because your family's coppers – the Job. And she knows that. And she knows that if she's stuck in some city suburb and all she has is you and you're not there half the time . . .'

'Very slick, Reverend. Very psychologically acute.'

'True, though?'

'Probably,' Bliss said.

'Tell me if this is not what you came for. I mean, you could always go to your long-suffering priest for five *Hail Marys* and a—'

'Yeh, all right, it's what I came for. Shuffling round the village square like a stray dog on a Sunday morning. It's finally come to this.'

Merrily poured herself some black tea. 'So you made a martyr of yourself. You put your career on the back shelf for love.'

'Tugging me forelock to fast-track floozies like Annie Howe. Grovelling on me knees to po-faced jobsworth gits like Fleming. Listen, I might not be university-educated, Merrily, but I was doing all right. I've had . . . approaches, you know? You get enough results, it's still possible to make your own fast track.'

'Until you fall off it.'

'Yeh.' Bliss looked at her. 'You fall off, you go down the

flamin' embankment so fast, you break both legs. So I've gorra simple choice: stay here and rot in an office or bugger off. What a waste. Either way, what a fuckin' *waste*.'

'OK.' Merrily reached for her cigarettes. 'Let's look at the facts. After what happened in Underhowle, this Luke Fleming comes over from Headquarters and decides that you mishandled the case from the start. If you hadn't kept it all to yourself, played all these wild cards, including Gomer, Roddy Lodge would be safely tucked up in his cell instead of on the slab.'

'I took a risk.' Bliss leaned on an elbow, hand cupped around his unshaven jaw. 'Several risks.'

'Even I could've told you that.'

'You did.'

'Mmm, well . . .'

When you thought about it, he was actually lucky his conduct hadn't been the subject of an internal inquiry. In fact, with an inquest pending, he wasn't out of the disciplinary shadows yet.

And yet Merrily couldn't help thinking that the last time she'd been aware of him bending the rules was when, last summer, he'd passed information to Lol that might well have prevented Annie Howe hanging her out to dry on a very public washing line. Did she still owe him? Did it matter, anyway?

'I mean, it could have been worse, Frannie.'

'Suspended. Bumped down to sergeant But that would've been a *public* admission that we fucked up. Still comes down to the fact that I've no future in West Mercia now, and the normal thing would be to go on the transfer list. And we know what that means.'

'Have you asked her?'

'Indirectly. We had a big row last night. Ended with me driving off and sleeping in the car. My fault . . . as usual. When the job's going well, I'm not there; when it's not, I'm there but I'm flamin' unbearable. I could stay on in Hereford, work me shifts, gradually mature into the mellow – but secretly bitter and twisted – old DI who lets the youngsters buy him pints and passes on his wisdom.'

'How would it be if I had a chat to Kirsty?'

'And let her know I've been telling yer all this? Look . . . I've gorra fair bit of leave owing, as you can imagine. It's been suggested that I take it now. Kirsty thought it might be a good idea if we left the kids with her ma and went away for a week to try and get ourselves sorted.'

That was a *very* good idea, Merrily thought.

'That was what the row was about,' Bliss said.

Merrily closed her eyes in despair. 'Oh, Frannie, you clown.'

'I can't leave it like this, Merrily. I've gorra *know.*'

'Know *what*, for heaven's sake?'

'If I was *right*!' Bliss leaned heavily on the table, spilling sugar, making his mug and spoon rattle. 'You know what they're saying now? You know what Fleming's saying? He's saying that what we're looking at with Roddy Lodge is a one-off, bog-standard, common-as-muck domestic. That he strangled his girlfriend during a drunken barney, figuring he could cover it up with no fuss, but when we pulled him, being the kind of cocky sod he was, he gets carried away with the big-killer image. That was Fleming's first assessment of the situation. In other words, he's saying Roddy Lodge, serial killer, was created by *me*.'

'Oh.'

'And then he talks to Roddy's GP, and then he consults Moffat, the forensic shrink who confirms that Roddy was exhibiting absolutely classic symptoms of advanced manic depression. You see where that's going?'

'It . . .' Merrily hesitated. Lol would know for sure, but she had a good idea, and it fitted all too well. 'They lie, don't they?' she said glumly. 'Manic-depressives lie on an industrial scale.'

'Exactly.' Bliss smiled icily. 'In the manic phase, they may tell extravagant lies, which can be very convincing because they half believe it themselves. If it isn't the truth, they believe it *ought* to be. In other words, they boast about things they haven't actually done.'

I done tanks for all the nobs all over the Three Counties and down into Wales. I done Prince Charles's fuckin' sewage over at Highgrove.

Bliss said, 'Fleming's pointing to one thing in particular that Roddy came out with when he was up the pylon. He said he was gonna kill Madonna – we have all this on tape, of course, thanks to some local smart-arse with a video camera. You yourself said he claimed to have done Madonna's drainage in the Cotswolds. And of course, Madonna doesn't even live in the Cotswolds – he got that wrong. Her place is down in bloody Somerset or somewhere. Roddy Lodge never got closer to Madonna than pictures in the *News of the World*.'

'But what about the other two? Melanie Pullman and the girl from Monmouth.'

'They're saying I offered those names to him and he went for them with his tongue out. They say my style of questioning was antiquated and inept, given that we've no proof that either of the women are even dead. To deal with it once and for all, Fleming's hired another firm with five diggers. They'd excavated about fifteen more Efflapures by yesterday.'

'Nothing?'

He didn't even answer. Merrily didn't know what to say. If Roddy Lodge in fact *hadn't* been a serial killer at all, if there *weren't* any more bodies buried, then that was surely the best possible outcome . . . except that Frannie would be seen as an ambitious but misguided detective who'd driven a man to his death – a man who, if hardly innocent, was certainly guilty on a far lesser scale than . . . *Oh hell.*

Bliss put his hands behind his head and stretched out his legs, talking flat-voiced to the ceiling.

'The last thing Fleming said, yesterday afternoon, was that if I'd suggested to Roddy that he'd killed Lord Lucan's nanny he'd have gone for that, too. He said I was dangerously naive. He said that in my craving for fame and glory, I was probably only slightly less manic than Lodge himself. He said the combustible combination of Lodge and me had created something it was gonna take West Mercia a long time to live down. He said – finally, he said that if he didn't see me again for the rest of his career he'd consider himself a very fortunate man.'

His hands fell away from his head and he slumped in his chair, his lips compressed into the kind of smile you put on to ward off weeping. He didn't need a Catholic priest; *this* was his confession. Merrily wondered if he'd told any of it to his wife; she feared not.

'Which I thought spelled it out very nicely,' he said after a while. 'Pastures new, Frannie, and don't expect a reference.'

She didn't even like to ask what Fleming was saying about the incineration, allegedly by Lodge, of Nevin Parry.

Bliss stood up and walked across to the window. 'Another option, of course, is for me to quit the Service altogether.'

'Frannie, this is just one man. He might move on himself.'

'Doesn't matter. Marked me card now. No, I'll do exactly as advised: take two weeks off. Use them as best I can.' He turned away from the window and came up to where she was sitting. She could smell dried sweat on him. She could smell anxiety and frustration, a toxic mix. 'I'm telling you he *did it*, Merrily. He did Melanie Pullman and he did Rochelle Bowen. And maybe some more. I could see it in his eyes, I could feel it in me chest. Somewhere, there are *bodies*.'

'Oh.' It was what she'd been afraid of. If the maverick loner cop was history, the suspended cop determined to clear his name was *movie* history. Anyway, Frannie's situation was, in a way, worse than suspension: his conduct would not be investigated, the investigation would simply continue without him. An investigation that was no more now than a tying-up of loose ends. Nobody was in danger; the beast was dead, and perhaps he hadn't been that much of a beast after all.

'I'm gonna find them, Merrily.'

'What – commandeer Gomer and Lol again?'

'I'd *pay* them.'

'Frannie, you're bonkers. You don't even have anything to go on, do you? You wouldn't know where to start.'

'Well, I would, actually,' Bliss said. 'If, for instance, we talk about the piccies on the walls—'

'Part of his fantasy. Despite all this chatting up in pubs, making a fool of himself when he was in his manic phases, he was actually afraid of real live women; he only felt truly safe with dead ones.'

'Aw, you're just—'

'I'm just saying what the shrink's going to say. I don't recall you had much to say about Lodge throwing his weight around in the police station. Subdued . . . uncommunicative . . . sick . . . didn't want to leave his cell. "Hunched up into himself" – I think that's what your phrase was at the time. The word *depressive* somehow springs to mind.'

'All right, then.' Bliss sat down again. 'Let's go back. Put yourself back in that bedroom for a minute. Look at the bed with the nasty black sheets. Sniff the air. Now look at the pictures in half-light from the low-wattage bulbs, so that they're not like pictures any more; they're actual shadowy women, right there in the room with you. Flickering about. Moving in the dark. And you know they're all dead.'

'But *he* didn't kill them.'

'Tell me you couldn't feel the evil in there, Merrily. Tell me you couldn't feel it. As a priest.'

'I don't . . . I don't know what I felt.'

'I know what *I* felt.'

'It still doesn't make too much sense, Frannie. You don't have any kind of scenario for Roddy Lodge as a mass murderer. You don't even know why and in what circumstances he killed Lynsey Davies, do you? What happens if you don't find anything to support the theory you don't yet have? What happens if you go blundering about and you don't find anything at all?'

'Merrily—'

'I seriously think you should follow Kirsty's suggestion and go on holiday somewhere quiet and uncomplicated with good food, nice views and room service, and spend a lot of time talking to one another. She's throwing you a lifeline, if you could only see it. At the end of the week, if you play your cards right, who knows how the situation might've changed? I mean, I'd be the first to miss your famous scowl around the place if you went back to Merseyside, but—'

'Merrily, I *do* have a scenario.'

'What?'

'Lol tell you about the attaché case? The one Gomer dug up just behind Roddy's bungalow before he went up the pylon like a monkey?'

'Possibly. I—'

'Stay there.' Bliss stood up. 'Don't go away.'

*

Bliss didn't have the actual case any more. The case had gone to the lab.

It had been so lightweight that they'd thought at first it was empty, he said. He didn't have the stained and crumpled newspaper cuttings that had subsequently been found inside, either, but he did have photocopies, and if she'd give him a minute he'd fetch them from his car on the square.

This just doesn't go away, she thought. *Why doesn't it go away?*

When he returned, she saw that the old briskness was back, his caffeine eyes burning through the fatigue.

'Whatever this is, should you be showing it to me?'

'Merrily, I shouldn't even've taken the copies away. Who gives a shit?'

He dropped the A4 buff envelope on the kitchen table and slid out a stack of papers. He spread them. Merrily recoiled.

Headlines snarling, headlines pleading, headlines shouting outrage, black on white, hard and contrasty and unremittingly ugly.

IN THE DEPTHS OF EVIL
THE PREDATORS
THEY GREW INTO MONSTERS
A LETHAL LUST

'I don't understand.' Even though they were only copies of copies of old newspapers, she didn't like to touch them. A low cloud of black-flecked smog was almost visible above the heap. Bliss fiddled about in the papers and brought out one with a font that looked, among the rest, almost comfortingly familiar: the *Hereford Times*.

INQUEST ON REMAINS FOUND IN FINGERPOST FIELD, MUCH MARCLE

'It's funny how many people mentioned it when we were in Underhowle,' Bliss said. 'We never thought. It's only about eight miles away, Marcle, as the crow flies. Nothing really, is it?'

'Sorry, I don't—'

'Much Marcle?'

'Frannie . . . ?'

Merrily froze up.

The table was whited out by ghastly flash-photo images: bodies under concrete in a cellar in Gloucester, police digging up red Herefordshire fields. A series of young women raped, tortured and butchered over a period of twenty years. Gloucester Council had demolished the house and talked of eradicating the name of Cromwell Street, but both Gloucester and the village of Much Marcle, in Herefordshire, would retain the memory of this man and his vicious wife for ever. An evil you couldn't see through because there was nothing on the other side but the night.

24

On the Sofa in Roddy's Bar

'How many?'

'Twelve, officially. Including his first wife and two daughters.'

'But probably more.'

'Oh, yeh,' Bliss said, 'could be a lot more. The estimates range from twenty to sixty. The little bastard kept careful count, I'm sure of that, even if he could never remember their names. Very efficient, in his way – this is what people don't realize. Most serial killers, they relish the reputation, the drama of it, the fancy names the papers give them: *The Night Stalker*, all this shite. They enjoy that sense of ritual. With him, that was no big deal at all. He just had an extremely skewed sense of right and wrong. He didn't relish *being* evil, because he couldn't *see* himself as evil. It wasn't a concept he understood. This is a man with a big part of him missing, and the space filled up with something black.'

'Yes.' Merrily was finding all this sickening, didn't see the point, wished they were still into marriage guidance.

Bliss had hung his jacket over a chair back. Now he was unfolding one of the cuttings, flattening it out.

'This is the important one. Not the article – the photo.'

The picture under the headline, though embellished with the smuts and smudges of hasty copying, had a feeling of formality. A flash photograph, carefully posed, of the two of them. Merrily was sure she must have seen it before.

Even if you didn't know who he was and what he'd done – what they'd both done – you would automatically have given him an identity: maybe the one-time randy paper boy grinning over his handlebars, grown now into the backstreet grease monkey who would guarantee to get your banger through its

MOT for twenty in hand or – *'Seeing it's you, my love'* – a tenner and a kiss.

Frederick West, in suit and shirt and tie, was leaning over the back of a sofa that had floral cushions. Behind him was a photo-mural of mountains and fir trees. Fred's hands were resting around the shoulders of the woman sitting on the sofa – plump, mumsie Rosemary, his wife. Fred looked like he'd rather be doing something else to her; Rose looked happy about that.

Two big smiles for the camera, four eyes alight with twisted love and shared memories of dead girls.

'Oh, it was an eye-opener for all of us, no denying that,' Bliss said. 'It shocked us out of our provincial complacency, Merrily. It actually shocked coppers.'

'Look, I . . .' She pushed the paper away; West wore a grin that could sear your dreams. 'Maybe I should've read more about it at the time, but I couldn't face it. When was it – ninety-five? I wasn't here then. And I still had . . . some other problems, personal.'

'I had nothing to do with him meself,' Bliss admitted. 'I'd not been down here long – still a DC when they were digging at Marcle. It was a couple of years later when I was in a pub with a sergeant from Gloucester, who once escorted West to a remand hearing, and this guy, he said that the worst thing of all, the very *worst* thing, was that you could actually get on well with him. One of the lads, good for a laugh. Of *course* you'd hire him to install your new bathroom – why not?'

'And leave him alone with your wife while you were at work?'

Bliss inhaled through clamped teeth. 'It's easy to go through all the pictures now and say, yeh, you can tell straight off he's an evil bastard. But if you didn't *know* . . . I mean, look at him – an imp, a troll. Where's the serious harm in him?'

Merrily chose not to look, for the moment. It hadn't even registered at the time that he was a Herefordshire man. He was always 'the Gloucester mass-murderer' because that was where he lived, operating as a self-employed builder out of a tall ter-raced house in Cromwell Street. The house where Fred had promoted Rose as a willing prostitute, watching her doing it with other men, especially black men. Where the Wests had rented out rooms to young people who didn't take too much luring into sex. And where the police had found most of the bodies of women and girls – buried in the garden or concreted into the cellar. Frederick West who lived for sex – and then killing became part of it. Fred West, the lust murderer, and Rose, his all-too-complicit wife.

But the killing had started long before Fred and Rose moved to Cromwell Street. It had started when he was a Herefordshire country boy, born and bred less than thirty miles from Ledwardine and only a ten-minute drive from Underhowle. This was where the police had gone next, after Cromwell Street, discovering that the roots of the evil lay deep in Hereford red soil – something Bliss now kept emphasizing.

'I remember when the lads came back from Marcle. After they found the first body in the Fingerpost field. Probably his first victim, Ann McFall – tied up and strangled, stabbed . . . butchered. *Here.*' His fingertips pressing into the pine top of the kitchen table. 'A feller who grew up among farms, worked for a slaughterhouse. In the country, where—'

'Where everybody killed, yeah. You keep saying that.'

'*And buried the bodies.* To West it was no different from disposing of a dead ewe. He cut them up for more efficient burial. Efficiency – that was the only ritual for Fred. An efficient workman. An efficient workman always *makes good* afterwards. Is it really such a big step? I mean, if you can kill and butcher an animal, you've got over the queasy part, haven't you? Only the morality of it left to deal with. And he didn't have any of that, anyway.'

'Frannie, can we just get to the point?' Merrily felt jittery, like a child who couldn't swim, standing on the edge of a frozen pond and watching a friend skating enthusiastically towards the centre. 'He's dead. He hanged himself in Winson Green prison while awaiting trial, and his wife's serving life for her part in the murders.' She pulled her cigarettes towards her. 'And Jane will be coming down for tea very soon and when she does I really would like not to be discussing this stuff. Get to the point.'

'You *know* the point. These selected articles were in an attaché case buried in what would have been Roddy Lodge's back garden, if he'd been of a horticultural bent.'

'And are *they* – Fleming, the SOCOs – entirely sure that Lodge was the one who buried them?'

Bliss sniffed. 'I don't know what *they* think. They're not telling me things any more. But *I*'m sure. And I'm asking meself, *Why?* Why did he bury them? Why didn't he just burn them if he wanted to get rid of them?'

'Was that all there was in the case – the cuttings?'

'No. This is it. This is the point. There was one other thing – one photo which, to my great sorrow, I didn't have time to copy.'

'Of?'

'So I can't show yer it. But you've already seen it, in a way. It's a happy snap of Roddy and Lynsey. In Roddy's Bar. You remember Roddy's Bar?'

'In his bungalow? Neon sign, optics, tall stools, leather suite, copies of *Loaded*.'

'The same. What this photo shows is Lynsey on the sofa in a nice red dress and Roddy in his suit and tie leaning over her from behind, like he's dying to start pawing. Got his back to the bullfight poster. Smiling for the camera. Geddit? Identical pose to the famous shot of Fred and Rose.'

'I may be starting to feel sick,' Merrily said.

'Well, hold on to it a bit longer.' Frannie Bliss went over to his jacket and dug an envelope from an inside pocket. 'Now then, I've gorra cutting of me own here. Andy Mumford put me on to this. Good memory, Andy.'

Bliss laid the paper in front of Merrily. It was from the *Daily Telegraph*, dated 5 December 1996.

LIFE FOR KILLER WHO COPIED THE WESTS

'Frannie . . .'

'No, read it first.'

It was the report of the trial at Cardiff Crown Court of a man from South Wales known as Black Dai because of his preference for black clothing. In 1996 he was thirty-two, a car thief who'd never had a proper job. He was obsessed with Fred and Rose West.

'Oh God.'

Bliss said nothing. He sat down again. The phone rang in the scullery; Merrily let the machine take it.

She read that the prosecution had told the court how Black Dai had suggested to his girlfriend that 'just like the Wests, they could travel the country, pick up girls, have sex with them and torture them'.

No. Merrily took out a cigarette then pushed it back into the packet.

The girlfriend had thought it was 'just fantasy on his part'. Until Black Dai abducted a young woman from a pub disco in Maesteg, Glamorgan, and subsequently drove her sixty miles to Herefordshire, where he beat her to death with a wheel brace and dumped her body in woodland at a place called Witches Fell, at Symonds Yat.

Symonds Yat: just a few miles outside Ross-on-Wye. Five miles from Underhowle.

Black Dai got put away for life.

'And I keep thinking what a great pity it was,' Frannie Bliss said, 'that we were prevented by a green young lawyer from letting you and Roddy have your little chat.'

'And what do you think he'd have told me that he didn't tell the entire population of Underhowle?'

'If he'd opened up to you, we might not even've needed to take him out to Underhowle, Merrily. I'm thinking of when Gloucester pulled West in, and he was leading them a bit of a dance, until a woman social worker was brought in to look after his welfare while on remand. Seems she looked a bit like Ann McFall, the first victim, his first love – the words "love" and "victim" tended to be synonymous in Fred's world – and pretty soon he was telling her everything. Out it came: possibly the full body count. No more ever found, but still . . .'

Merrily jerked upright. 'That's why you set me up for it?'

'No. Honestly, swear to God, I had no idea then. Never

even thought about West. And no, don't worry, you don't look remotely like Lynsey. She was twice as big as you, for a start.'

She had a flashback then to her one contact with Lynsey Davies, the nauseous blast of human decay from under a tarpaulin, a stench like a howl of pain and outrage. She pulled out the cigarette again.

'Lynsey, however,' Bliss said, 'did look more than a bit like Rose. Bit bigger maybe – taller. But buxom.'

Merrily lit the cigarette. 'You're saying that Roddy saw her as his Rose-figure. That he saw the two of them as . . .'

'Can't say there's no solid precedent for it, can you?'

'Yes, but when you look at all the women Fred West killed and the one he *didn't* kill . . .'

'That's because Rose was what she was.'

'His soulmate – if he had a soul.'

'And also found guilty of ten murders,' Bliss pointed out. 'And now in prison with a recommendation from the judge that she should never be released. Talk about star-crossed lovers – when you start to ask yourself what the chances are of two people that depraved finding each other within a small area of rural England . . .'

'Yes.' The aura of an almost alien abnormality lit the image of Fred and Rose, two people who'd formed into something that lived for physical gratification in its most twisted and degraded forms, mixing other lives at random into the bubbling sexual soup.

'Lynsey might've put it about over the years,' Bliss said, 'and she might not've been on the shortlist for the Mothercare Trophy. But my guess is that when she posed for that picture she wasn't aware of the true significance. So when she *did* become aware that she was posing as Rosemary West – well, how would you react?'

'You're saying he killed her because she found out and was threatening to shop him?'

'Probably. We don't know. We probably never will know.'

'Who took the picture?'

'Automatic exposure, I should think. There were two SLR cameras around the place, and a camcorder in the car. Lodge liked gadgets, just like Fred did. On the other hand, Roddy was different from Fred. He boasted more. Fred was talkative, but Roddy was loud. Yeh, it's possible he got somebody else to take the picture – flaunting it a bit.'

'Frannie, why did he go up that pylon?'

'There was nowhere else to go. We'd got men on all the possible exits, he knew that. Maybe he stupidly thought we wouldn't spot him up there in his orange overalls, and he could wait till we'd gone. He'd been up the pylon before, I reckon – somebody'd cut away the barbed wire they bind around the legs. Maybe he used to go up them as a kid. Like kids do – for a dare.'

'You don't think he *intended* to die?'

'No, I don't. I think he saw himself as invulnerable. Merrily, look, what I wanted to ask you . . . why do *you* think he buried all these West cuttings – together with the picture of him and Lynsey as Fred and Rose? If he was suddenly worried about them being found, why didn't he just set fire to the lot? He was good at fire, if we accept Gomer's viewpoint.'

'Well, he didn't get rid of the pictures of women in the bedroom, did he? What do Superintendent Fleming and his pet psychiatrist think?'

'We didn't exactly get around to discussing it.'

Merrily shook her head slowly. 'I don't know, Frannie. I mean, you've established that he did have some kind of West fantasy, although how far he took it none of us can say for certain. As you say, if he wanted to put all that behind him, burning would be a quicker and safer option. Sealing the picture, together with the news cuttings, in the case – making it absolutely clear, by the context, what that picture was meant to convey – seems more of a . . . an affirmation, I suppose.'

She found herself thinking of Gomer who, when Minnie had died, had buried both their watches, with new batteries, in her grave.

'Go on,' Bliss said.

'Like it's a way of binding them all together. Fred and Rose and Lynsey and Roddy.'

'Binding together how?'

'Sealed up together, underground. I don't know.'

'You see, he took us back there, leading us to think we were gonna find bodies. And there are no bodies buried there – only this little case, which Gomer found in the end, making Roddy bloody furious. And it was shortly after that that he did a runner.'

'Perhaps that case was more important to him than bodies.'

'He took us back to uncover something and then when we got there he changed his mind. What's that tell us?'

'Tells us he wasn't thinking straight, Frannie. Look, I . . .' Merrily didn't see how she could help Bliss any more. From where he was sitting, his future in the police service depended on proving that he'd been right from the beginning about Roddy Lodge. It depended on finding bodies.

Bliss stood up, put on his jacket. 'Well, thanks, Merrily. You're a pal.'

'I haven't done anything.' She followed him out into the hall, where the jaded Jesus stood with his lantern.

At the door, Frannie Bliss turned. 'Fred and Roddy. Two self-employed contractors, who pride themselves on being methodical, efficient in what they do . . .' Under the light, with those freckles, he looked like a schoolboy, and schoolboys would do anything. 'Somewhere, Merrily, there are *bodies*.'

Merrily shut the front door, went back into the kitchen, reached automatically for another cigarette, then tossed the packet down and went into the scullery office, where the light was flashing on the answering machine. She pressed *play.*

'*Oh, Merrily, I'm so sorry to bother you on a Sunday, but could you ring me at home? It's twenty past five. Thank you.*'

Sophie.

She rang back. 'Something I've forgotten, or something I don't yet know about?'

'You sound gloomy, Merrily.'

'Just trying to untangle some things, Soph. Sorry.'

There was a short silence, and then Sophie said, 'Merrily, I've been meaning to ask . . . Why don't you and Laurence Robinson come for supper one night?'

'Oh.' She knew, of course. Nothing had ever been said, but

Sophie had known maybe even before Merrily had known. 'That's . . . very kind of you.'

'I don't mean tonight or even this week. But sometime.'

This was Sophie reaffirming that it was OK. She was not a priest – as the Bishop's secretary, she didn't need to be – but Sophie lived for the Cathedral, and if you knew it was OK with Sophie there seemed no immediately obvious reason why it shouldn't be OK in the sight of God.

'Thank you,' Merrily said. 'Was that what you wanted?'

'Oh no. That would have waited until we met. This is rather more complicated. I understand you've been peripherally involved in the police investigation at Underhowle, of which we've all been reading.'

'Who told you about that?' She'd never thought to inform the Bishop; perhaps she ought to have.

'You spoke, I think, on the phone to the Reverend Jerome Banks. Who, in turn, spoke to the Bishop. In connection with the late Mr Lodge.'

'It wasn't an official approach.'

'He isn't *complaining*, Merrily. According to the Bishop, he seemed not ungrateful for your interest. From what I understand, Mr Lodge dead is considered no less of a problem in the parish than was Mr Lodge alive.'

'Mr Lodge wasn't considered a problem alive. Nobody knew about his hobby.'

'Well, they do now, and it's put the Reverend Banks into what he perceives as a rather difficult situation. Merrily, we do realize your involvement here had no connection with the Church and that it isn't your parish, obviously . . . but the Reverend Banks did have a suggestion to make which the Bishop has asked me to put to you, and that's what I'm doing.'

There was a movement at the door. Jane stood there, wiggling her fingers in a resigned *hello again* kind of way. Merrily smiled and did it back.

'In relation to Mr Lodge,' Sophie said, 'I have to ask you . . . how you would feel about burying him?'

25

The Plague Cross

The skyline had broken into a lushness of wooded hills and an elegant tiered town, the River Wye fronting it like a moat. In the late afternoon, a low, unexpected sun was burning across the dual carriageway, gilding the town and its tall steeple.

Moira looked enchanted, Lol thought, as though the pattern had been laid out especially for her, the sun's last curtain call timed for this moment. She wound down her side window.

'Has quite a soft air, actually. That would be the sandstone walls, I'd guess.'

Lol's geriatric Astra rattled down the side of a traffic island and then crossed a long bridge that became more like a causeway, with green parkland beside the river bank on the left, sandstone cliffs hanging over them on the right. There were no suburbs this end; you entered the town almost at its centre, expecting a fortified gateway. Instead, there was a single medieval-style round tower set into the red walls: Victorian Gothic, but it fitted.

Moira nodded approval. 'Somebody got this place right.'

Lol glanced at her. Often, she talked like she was reacting to a sixth sense she no longer questioned. Moira had something of the threshold about her.

According to Gomer Parry, the way the council had ballsed things up only disabled taxi-drivers could be guaranteed to get parked on the street in Ross. But this was Sunday and Lol found a space close to the top of the hill, before the first shops.

He locked the car. Moira was waiting for him, leaning on a wall, peering down towards the twisting river, pulling a black woollen wrap around her shoulders. It was that time, just before the street lights came on, when the autumn air was thickening and the church, no more than a couple of streets away, seemed less solid than it had from across the river, the steeple a sepia spectre.

'Where's he gonnae be, this guy?'

Lol almost said, Where do you *want* him to be? This woman seemed to persuade things to happen. When he'd rung the village hall at Underhowle to leave a message for Sam Hall, Sam himself had answered the phone as though he'd been waiting around for Lol's call. '*Sure, let's do this right now. But let's not do it here. Let's meet in town. Hour and a half, say?*'

'He said he'd find us in the churchyard.' Lol looked towards the steeple, along a narrow, uphill street where everything was Sunday-silent. There was no wind, and the dusk was forming like coppery smoke around them.

And Moira said, 'So you're definitely up for the gig, right?'

They walked up some steps to the churchyard, their footsteps echoing from the buildings of brick and stone on either side.

'So the offer's still, er . . .'

'Open, yeah.' Moira, who persuaded things to happen, took his arm, hugging it to her. 'What a difference a death makes, eh?'

Something like a pebble landed in Lol's gut.

'Directly under your feet,' Sam Hall said, 'are hundreds of dead people. Buried in their clothes – no shrouds, no coffins.'

Sam had found them at the edge of The Prospect, a plateau behind the church with a view of the river and, beyond it, twenty-five miles of darkening countryside rising to the slopes of the Black Mountains on the Welsh border.

He'd explained that there used to be a bishop's palace up here, a second home for the bishops of Hereford who, for centuries, had been the biggest landowners hereabouts. Now The Prospect was mainly public space, a high garden sloping down to the sandstone walls and the Royal Hotel.

Moira had looked around, tossing an end of her wrap over a shoulder. 'No sign of power lines.'

'Oh, they're around,' Sam had said. 'Come with me. I'd like to show you something.' Turning away abruptly and setting off back along the path with a seasoned walker's easy gait, a small knapsack hanging from his shoulder like just another crease in his plaid jacket. They went back into the churchyard under mature trees still heavy with dark foliage, where a straight path led from the church itself down towards the centre of the town.

Near the end of the path, opposite a shadowy street of houses and offices, was this stone cross on a hexagonal plinth with steps. Now Sam Hall had a foot on the lowest one.

'This is the Plague Cross. In 1637 the Great Plague took out more than three hundred people, putting Ross into quarantine. All the trading with the outside world was done down by the bridge, and they washed the money in the river. Even the church services here were suspended. And the dead . . .'

Lol glanced at Moira, who was standing very still, the white streak in her black hair gleaming in the last of the light as she watched Sam climb to the third step and put a hand up to the stem of the cross.

'The dead were buried in pits right here,' Sam said. 'At night. Buried, according to a local account, "in their wearing apparel". The bodies were brought up here on carts, and dumped . . . while the minister stood here, right where I'm standing now, and gave the last blessings by torchlight. Can you imagine that?'

Moira said nothing. Lol thought she probably could – in full colour, with agonized suppurating faces and the stench of disease. Suddenly, in the stillness, he saw it all too, was aware of people in a state of exhaustion, beyond despair, beyond pity, beyond both fear of death and expectation of life. The images were so dense and complete that it felt as though Moira was sending them to him.

'This is the same Great Plague that swept through London?' he asked.

'Only it came to Ross first. Prosperous-looking place, even then, but the streets were thick with filth and packs of rats. Most of the rich folk left town. But the minister stayed, to bless the sick and the dying.' Sam turned to Moira. 'You'd have heard of this man, maybe?'

'Me?'

'Name was the Reverend Price. At the height of the plague, the darkest hour, he had all the townsfolk that could make it to their feet join him in a procession – all walking with this desperate dignity through the town streets at five a.m. chanting a litany, a solemn appeal to the Lord for deliverance.'

A light came on in one of the houses across the street, making it seem darker in the churchyard.

'And his faith was rewarded. When the sun rose that day, it was said, the plague went on the run.' Sam Hall stepped down from the cross. 'And you're wondering why I'm showing you this, right? Well, see, a plague is how I think of it. The Great Plague of the Twenty-first Century. I have an engraving of this cross as the motif on my notepaper.'

'This new plague is about power lines?' Lol said.

'The power towers are the enemy we can see.' Sam stared up into the sepia sky. 'If we could see all the TV and satellite signals, all the radio waves serving mobile phones, police communications, cab fleets, air networks, the sky would be this kind of poisonous black the whole day long. If we could smell them like exhaust fumes, we'd all choke to death. But it's a whole lot more subtle than that. They zip unseen and unfelt through our atmosphere and through our bodies and our brains. They are the insidious wind that blows right through us all – through flesh and tissue, through bones.'

It sounded like a speech he'd made before. Sam was back on the path.

'You'll notice I came down off of the cross before I said all that. I'm no preacher, just a guy who seethes inside whenever he sees some twelve-year-old kid in the street, calling up her pal on a piece of pink plastic that burns brains.'

'Which is always gonnae be denied,' Moira murmured.

'Oh, sure. The bigger the investment, the stronger the denial. Like the electricity industry denied the report that came out of Bristol University a couple years ago linking overhead power lines to leukaemia, skin cancer, lung cancer – you name it.'

'A plague on all humanity, huh?'

'Sure. And we're all of us guilty to some extent, even me. I won permission for a windmill to generate clean power for my place up on Howle Hill. I don't have a phone, let alone a mobile. But if I want to get on the Web, I'll still go down the hall, use one of Cody's community computers. Act of plain hypocrisy, with the guy hell-bent on turning Underhowle into the hot spot to end all hot spots.'

'Hot spots?' Lol said.

' "Hot spot" is the term for a dangerous configuration of transmitters, pylons, what-have-you which renders an area . . . let's say difficult to reside in. Cody's computer plant came to the area on account of a development grant and a derelict site going for peanuts, and now they want to . . . but you know all this.'

'I'm a stranger,' Moira said. 'I don't know any of it.'

Sam Hall looked hard at her in the dimness. Moira folded her arms in her wrap.

'We have a complex situation,' Sam said. 'The small industries which once built up Underhowle into a community with three, four pubs, a bunch of shops and its own school went to the wall long ago. By the mid-nineties, the shops had all gone out of business, the school was threatened with closure, and the village wasn't pretty enough to attract the cottage-hunters from London – specially with these damn pylons like watchtowers around Belsen and Auschwitz.'

It was almost night now and growing cold. Somewhere at the back of his mind Lol could hear Prof Levin saying, *The one thing you, of all people, do not need at this stage is to get in with crazies.*

'Biggest disease in Underhowle, when I came back from the States, was apathy,' Sam Hall said. 'I didn't mind. I just wanted a place I could afford and where I'd be left alone to be a crank and a pain-in-the-ass idealist, sustain my fantasy that we could live without the goddam mains services run by fat cats who'd watch us die one by one, to stave off wasting-disease of the wallet.'

Lol wondered if Sam saw himself as the new Reverend Price, who'd chosen to live and fight in the plague hot spot.

'At first, I was as pleased as anyone,' Sam said, 'when, like the recipient of a touch of magic, Underhowle began to undergo a small revival.'

Two things happened, almost simultaneously, he told them. Two new elements of growth that fed one another, two men with compatible dreams. Fergus Young, a teacher with real vision, took over a dying primary school, down to fourteen pupils. And Chris Cody, this computer whizz, brought in enough employees with young families to fill it up again.

'I like Fergus. He's evangelical, like me. Gave up a lot for that school – even his marriage, in the end. Hell, I even like Chris. Fergus knows how to inspire kids, he was getting incredible results very quickly, but I guess it was the computer input that revolutionized everything.'

'They provided computers for the school?' Lol recalled the Efflapure owner, Mike Sandford, telling him about the children's computers they were manufacturing – for four-year-olds, three-year-olds, two . . . younger.

'They *donated* computers,' Sam Hall said. 'Not only to the school, but to every household in the catchment area with a small kid. Time the kid reaches school, it's computer-literate, with all the educational benefits that brings. Plus most of them could read and write by age five or earlier. So between them, at this run-down school in a run-down village, Fergus and Chris have already created a generation of very smart kids.'

Lol recalled Mike Sandford again: *Might look run-down, but this place is the future.*

'This been publicized?' Moira wondered.

'In all the right journals. Result: Cody's kiddie computers are starting to sell, internationally – so yet more jobs. Parents squeezing themselves into the catchment area to get their kids into Fergus's school. Property prices rising. Place still isn't pretty, but it's changing fast – two shops reopened in the past year, one by Cody, as a retail software outlet, but the other sells food. And we have a hairdresser, we have the refurbishment of the village hall as a sophisticated community centre. And – you know – so far, so good. We were all getting along together fine on the Underhowle Development Committee. Till we fell out.'

Sam said that although he'd been less enthused than some by the idea of Underhowle becoming a blueprint for rural regrowth, he'd kept quiet about the aspects that worried him. Until the demands for better communications began bringing results. Until the growing complaints about the poor mobile-phone signals in the valley and the bad quality of TV reception began to have enough relevance for the fat cats who ran the networks to act on them.

When the Development Committee had voted to express its approval of a plan for a new and powerful mobile-phone transmitter on the side of Howle Hill, along with a TV booster less than half a mile away, Sam had quit the committee in an atmosphere of serious acrimony. Now the booster was up and shooting signals at Underhowle, the new phone mast only awaiting the green light from the council. And no groundswell of opposition to get in the way. Only Sam, the crank, the fruitcake.

'I expected support from the newcomers, but hell, with the village taking off the way it is, they're scared to be seen as blocking progress. In most cases, their jobs depend on it. But it's . . . with the number of goddam power lines we already got intersecting here, it's my absolutely unswerving belief we're in for one *hell* of a hot spot. Health problems – and *mental* health problems – on a scale you can't imagine. Signs are there. I can give you a long list of people who died prematurely – people living too close to 140,000 volts. When that damn mast goes up, it's gonna be electric soup. But . . . I got no proof and no back-up.'

Lol was thinking Sam was going to need more than a rally and protest song to raise any. He didn't know what to say.

Sam said, 'Sure, I have friends *outside* – links with Green organizations. But Green activists, they tend to be gentle people. They don't have maybe the blind *rage* needed to tackle what is one enormous ecological problem and – I would venture to suggest, Reverend – a spiritual one.'

Moira said, 'Huh?'

'I can explain this aspect, if you'll give me some time. If we can meet this week, perhaps, I can explain it in detail. But, essentially, our local minister, Reverend Banks, is a man with – and, as someone who's at least half a Christian, I make no apology for this – a man with a small, closed mind, who refuses to absorb or even to consider—'

'Mr Hall, I wouldnae doubt that he is, but if I could—'

'I realize your position's bound to be sensitive, where another clergyperson's concerned. But there are some things I need to get aligned in my own mind, and I could use some advice from someone . . . such as yourself.'

He stood at the foot of the Plague Cross, shoulders slumped, sagging a little, looking more like his age. He unshouldered his knapsack, as if it had suddenly become too much of a burden, and laid it on the bottom step.

'Sam,' Lol said gently, 'I think . . .'

Lol drove around the island and back onto the A40, from which the town of Ross glittered in the early night, like a birthday cake, across three lanes of traffic and the river. He drew a fold of paper from his jacket pocket.

'Gave me this just as we were walking back into town. I guess it's the poem. The song. He took it out of his bag almost like an afterthought, just before we went our separate ways.' He handed the paper across to Moira. 'Sorry, the interior light doesn't work, but there's a torch in the glove compartment.'

'I suppose I ought to feel flattered,' Moira said. 'This could be the first time in ma whole life I was ever mistaken for a good and devout person.'

There was only one way this misunderstanding could have come about: Sam had talked to Frannie Bliss, and Bliss had disclosed Lol's close friendship with the diocesan exorcist for Hereford. Lol had introduced Moira to Sam only by her first name. Moira – Merrily? It was an honest mistake.

'I don't think he's crazy,' Lol said. 'But he certainly seems less stable than he did the other night. Or maybe it's me who's more stable than I was then.'

'Well . . .' He heard the snap of the torch switch. 'I don't think he's crazy either, but he sure is no poet.'

'Not good?'

'It's like he just scribbled it down, off the top of his head, before he came out.'

'Maybe he did.'

'Aye.'

In the darkness of the car, Lol was aware of Moira's scent; it made him think of deserted sand dunes in the Hebrides. Or maybe that wasn't the scent at all. Her voice came back, low.

'He doesnae want you at all, Laurence. Or your talents. It was a wee ploy and not a very convincing one. He wants your friend. He wants an exorcist. It's why he asked you to bring your lady.'

'Yes.'

'If you'd been alone, I guess he'd've sounded you out about an introduction. When he thought *I* was her, he went for it: "an ecological problem, but also a spiritual one". But when he found out I wasnae exactly ordained, the spiritual part stayed under his woolly hat. I guess he'll find your wee reverend some other way.'

Lol said, 'What if he's a *little* crazy?'

'Ach, Laurence, we're all of us a little crazy.'

'And the Plague Cross?'

'Well . . . there's a sickness there, all right,' Moira said.

'Still?'

She was quiet for a moment. 'He's scared of something, and he's no' sure exactly what.'

Lol was puzzled. 'He *is* sure, isn't he?'

'He knows what he can see – the pylons and the TV masts and those sinister mobile-phone masts with the bits sticking out. But he cannae see electricity and he cannae see evil.'

Lol said after a while, 'Is this a warning?'

'Oh, Laurence,' Moira said, 'if it was all as simple and direct as, like, *Don't get on any planes on the 18th*. What do I say to you here? I'm standing by the Plague Cross and this guy's talking about people buried without coffins, and then I start thinking about you and your friend digging for dead people, and I get this rather loathsome curling sensation down in ma gut – *which* I believe I managed to conceal rather well. *I* don't know what that means, do I?'

'What should I say to Merrily?'

She let him drive in silence for a while.

'Aye well,' she said, 'that's a difficult one.'

*

That night Lol called Merrily on the mobile, from his loft.

'Mmm,' she said, 'I met Sam Hall when I was in Underhowle with Frannie Bliss. He didn't go out of his way to speak to me then. On the other hand, Bliss had introduced me as a DC. Which nobody seemed to question at the time.'

'Maybe assuming there must have been a change in the height regulations,' Lol said.

'Ho ho. So am I supposed to go and see him?'

'Why would you need to? I was just warning you he might try and get in touch. So you'd know what it was about, vaguely, if he did. And if I could just—'

Merrily said, 'Only, I've been asked to bury Roddy Lodge, you see.'

'Bury him?'

'Not dig the hole – conduct the funeral.'

'Why?'

'It's a Christian tradition. But if you mean *why me*, it's because a large number of people in Underhowle are saying, *We* don't want this murderer in *our* churchyard, and the local minister's got cold feet from sitting on the fence. And I'm like your Mr Hall. An established fruitcake.'

Lol said, 'Do you have to do it?'

'I don't *have* to.' A pause. 'What's wrong?'

'Nothing.'

Lol imagined her at her desk, shoes off, toes curled under the electric fire. He felt that, whatever she was getting into, she should not be left in there alone.

26

Black Sheep Kind of Thing

He'd come down from the hill on his quad bike as soon as his wife had reached him on the mobile. 'I can't discuss this,' she'd said miserably when she saw the dog collar. 'You'll have to speak to Mr Lodge.' And went on talking about the rain and how much of it there was these days, until he was pulling off his wellies at the kitchen door.

Out of the plain, square kitchen windows, all Merrily could see was damp fog, greenish like mucus.

Mr Lodge: this defined him now. His father was dead, and he was the eldest brother. This was his farmhouse, brown-washed and hunched into the foggy hillside, and this was his name: Mr Lodge, the last one in the valley.

They looked at one another. By the frosted fluorescent tube on the kitchen ceiling, Merrily saw a fawn-haired man in a working farmer's green nylon overalls, edging quietly towards sixty, lean and wary as a dog fox. *He* saw something that evidently worried him.

He coughed. 'I'm sorry I, er, I didn't expect you'd be a woman.'

Well now, wouldn't she be running a wealthier parish, if she had a pound for every time someone had said that?

'I'll make some tea,' Mrs Lodge mumbled.

'Yes.' He nodded at Merrily. 'Well . . . thank you. Thank you for coming.' He indicated a wooden chair with arms and a car cushion on it, near the Rayburn. 'You have that one. In the warm.'

'Thank you.' She took off Jane's duffel coat and hung it around the back of the chair. She was wearing the black jumper-and-skirt outfit and her fleece-lined boots. He looked away.

'Tony Lodge,' he said reluctantly.

'Merrily Watkins. I'm . . . afraid I only heard about this last night. From the Bishop.'

'Ah.' He sat himself on a hard chair at the edge of the gate-legged table, leaving about seven feet of flagged floor between them. He sat with his cap on his knees. 'So you en't spoken to Mr Banks.'

'Not about this, no. I'll probably be seeing him later.'

'If you're lucky.'

She smiled, easing her chair to one side so that Mrs Lodge could put the kettle on the Rayburn, which Mrs Lodge accomplished without looking at her.

'Not, er . . . not that I'm a churchgoing man any more,' Tony Lodge said. 'My parents were chapel, and I was raised to that. When the chapel went out of use my father, he started going to the church instead, because at least the church was still here, even if the services were few and far between. He wouldn't go to Ross to worship. And he wouldn't go to Ross to be buried. And that's what this is about.'

Merrily said, 'I gather there's a long-standing agreement with the Church, on burials.'

'Never been any other way, look. They reckon the chapel here was near as old as the church, and there's only one graveyard in Underhowle – that's up at the church, where the land's better drained, more suitable for burial. And that's where we goes, the Lodges.' He paused. 'That's where my brother's to go. Friday, we thought, if that's all right for you. Funeral director's Lomas of Coleford.'

'Your father . . .'

'Would not be happy if the sons were not around him and my mother. You understand that.'

'Of course. Erm . . .'

Mr Lodge raised bony brown hands in a warding-off gesture. 'No,' he said calmly. 'I don't want to talk about what he's done. My duty to my father, as eldest son, is to see my brother buried at Underhowle – *not* cremated. I would like there to be a proper service. If Mr Banks wants to throw in his hand with the newcomers, that's his business.'

Merrily didn't say anything. She might have known it would be something like this.

'There was a deputation here last night,' Mr Lodge said. 'How much you know about that, I en't sure.'

'Deputation?' All Sophie had told her was that the Rev. Banks had said the Lodges were not members of his congregation, whereas the family of the missing Melanie Pullman was, and therefore he would prefer it if an outside minister could handle Roddy's funeral. It wasn't an unusual procedure in cases like this.

'Local people,' Tony Lodge said, 'and some not so local. Wanting me to have my brother cremated. Said it would be better for his ashes just to be scattered in the churchyard, that a grave would become a . . . "tourist attraction". Not the sort they wanted for Underhowle. The *new* Underhowle.' Bitterness tainting his tone now. 'Not the image they wanted for the new Underhowle.'

'I see.'

'I doubt you do.' Mr Lodge almost smiled. 'I doubt you do, Reverend, but I don't suppose that matters.'

'I *have* met some of the people in the village: Mr Young, the headmaster. And . . . Ingrid Sollars?'

'Mrs Sollars. Yes, I was surprised she was part of it, but there you are. They all have their own concerns. Things aren't simple like they used to be. In the old days, you accepted responsibility for your village, in good times and bad. And the people there, good and bad. You kept together. Now it's all about what you looks like to outsiders.'

'True, I suppose.' She was mainly worried about how she'd justify this to Gomer: leading prayers for the everlasting soul of the man he believed had murdered his nephew, incinerated his depot and his machinery, taken a pickaxe to the foundations of his life. She'd tried to reach him last night: no answer.

'You'll be wanting some personal information about my brother,' Tony Lodge said. 'I've written out a list – date of birth, where he went to school, that sort of detail.'

'Well, actually, what . . .' What Merrily wanted most was a cigarette. 'What I normally do is have a chat with the relatives of the person who's died so that, at the service, I can talk about them, as people. We don't bury bodies, we bury people. If you see what I mean.'

She wondered if he did. There were few signs in this drab, functional farmhouse of real sorrow, only of resignation: perhaps an attitude branded into farmers by BSE and foot-and-mouth and endless forms from the Ministry of Agriculture, now called DEFRA – which Jane said stood for Destroying Every Farm-Reared Animal.

'Look . . .' Mr Lodge was facing her, although she could tell his eyes weren't focused on hers as much as on the space between them. 'I don't want no fuss. I don't want things said about him that weren't true, just for appearances. I don't really want anything said about him at all. Just like it done quickly and with dignity. Isn't as if there's going to be much of an audience anyway.'

Merrily sighed. 'I'm afraid you might find there's rather more of one than you think. There'll almost certainly be police and . . . reporters. Possibly even television – I wouldn't like to say.'

He stood up. He said, without raising his voice, 'He was cursed from the first, that boy.'

The kettle came to the boil behind Merrily and began to shriek, as if demanding she should leave. She stood up, too. 'Look, if you want to have a think about it, I'll leave you my number, or I can ring you. We'll also have to discuss the choice of hymns, that kind of . . . Oh, and one other thing – Roddy. Roddy's . . . body. Where do you—?'

'I don't know all the details yet of how they release him. There's already been a post-mortem. They reckons the inquest is being held tomorrow.'

'Well . . . opened,' Merrily said. 'All they'll have is a short hearing at which the coroner will take formal evidence of identification – which means that the body can be released for burial – and then it's adjourned, usually for several weeks.'

'So the worst is to come.'

How could she deny that?

Mrs Lodge almost brushed past her to reach the kettle on the Rayburn. Close up, Merrily registered that she was quite a few years younger than her husband, although the age gap was fogged by colourless, wispy hair and an absence of make-up – somewhere along the line, she'd lost the need or the will to be noticed.

Merrily pulled her coat from the back of the chair; they both knew that she wouldn't be staying for tea. 'Meanwhile, if there's, you know, anything at all I can do . . .'

'You will conduct the service, then?'

'Of course. If that's what you want. I'll talk to Mr Banks, see when's best for everyone.'

He nodded once. 'And beyond that,' he said, 'I wouldn't do anything, if I were you. Let's get him in the ground, and there's an end to it.'

A bleak statement in bleak surroundings on a bleak day. She wondered if, in the end, he hadn't been jealous of his manic young brother, travelling the countryside and apparently making a lot of money while he, the inheritor of the farm, stayed and rotted in it. Was that how it was? On the way here, she'd felt she ought to explain the circumstances of her own brief meeting with Roddy Lodge; now she didn't think it would change anything, would probably not help at all.

At the door, she said, 'What I meant was . . . if there's anything I could do to help the two of you cope with this.'

'Oh, we'll survive.' He smiled crookedly. 'In this job, most of us gave up looking to God for any help a *long* time ago. If it's the same God that helps the continentals to reject our beef, where's the point?'

Not the time, either, for theological debate. Merrily saw that Mrs Lodge was standing over the Belfast sink, staring into in, unmoving.

'I, erm . . . I have to call and see Mr Hall. Sam Hall? I was told his house is somewhere near here.'

'Aye, carry on up the track and you'll see his windmill. It's a bit mucky up there, but you'll get through. Friend of yours, Mr Hall?'

'I've not really met him. As such.'

'Nice enough man,' said Mr Lodge. 'Used to be local, then he emigrated to America and come back a bit cranky.'

'Oh?'

'Takes my dogs for a run. Loves dogs, he says, but he won't have one himself 'cause he reckons there's too many dogs around for no particular reason. That kind of cranky.'

'Ah. Right. Look, I . . .' Feeling, if anything, more hopelessly inadequate than was usual on these occasions. 'I just want to say I'm very, very sorry for what's happened.'

'Thank you. But you don't *know* what's happened, do you?' Tony Lodge presented her with his summary of Roddy's life, scribbled in felt pen on half a sheet of lined notepaper. 'None of us do. And likely that's best for everyone.'

Spectral in the fog, the windmill rose like a huge, petrified sunflower out of a clearing on a small escarpment, a plateau on the edge of the hill. It looked alien and probably always would, Merrily thought. The house was about thirty yards away, behind a wall around four feet high and the winter remains of vegetable patches.

Pulling on woollen gloves, she left the Volvo at the top of the track, before it narrowed into a footpath and curved past the house towards what she guessed would be the summit of the hill – could only guess because it was smothered by the fog, whitish here like a blank stage backcloth.

Despite the murk, she could see no lights in the house. But then, from what Lol had said, this place would never be well lit. It was a brick-built bungalow, square and compact, with small windows, dense as Gomer's glasses, and a solar panel like a blister in the roof. There was no smoke from the chimney.

The wooden front gate was unlocked, and Merrily went through, along a path between veg beds, to the front door inside its wooden porch. She couldn't see a bell or a knocker and ending up banging on the panels with a gloved fist. No answer. She went back outside.

Electricity and radiation, Lol had listed. *Pylons, power lines, TV and mobile-phone transmitters. The twenty-first-century plague. Hot spots and the death road.* 'And something else it was clear he wasn't going to tell me or Moira.'

Me or Moira. Moira and me. Why did this nag? They were all supposed to be adults. But it had got into her dreams last night. In the last dream, she'd suddenly realized – with the dramatic intensity that only dreams could bestow – that Lol Robinson was in the music business . . . where everybody slept with everybody else. Awakening anxious and cold – again. Of course, she knew he wasn't like that – quite the opposite in some ways, after what had happened to him all those years ago. But he was insecure about his abilities and perhaps this mature, experienced Moira Cairns was giving him the reassurance that only another musician could.

Oh God. The fog swirled around her like hostile floss.

Merrily heard footsteps on the track, then a slurring in the mud, the sounds somewhere inside the white fog. She stayed inside the garden wall, hands cold inside her coat pockets and the gloves.

The engine was running to support the heater, doing its best, but this was an old car and the heater took a while to get going, the car warming up very gradually like an old man rubbing his hands and massaging his joints.

The Volvo was backed onto the grass beside the footpath, out of sight, if not earshot, of Sam Hall's eco-house. On the passenger side, Mrs Lodge was bulked out by a US Army parka, far too big for her. She'd started talking outside on the track, her voice high and querulous and revealing the remains of a South Wales accent. '*He's not heartless,*' she'd cried. '*I didn't want you to leave thinking he's heartless.*'

Merrily said, 'Mrs Lodge, this is one of the hardest situations anyone has to go through. When it's not of your making but you're dragged into it and you don't know where your loyalties are supposed to lie.'

'Cherry,' Mrs Lodge said. 'My name's Cherry. Like the fruit, not Mrs Blair.'

The run up the track had reddened her cheeks, as if to underline the point. She told Merrily she'd known Sam Hall wasn't at home, had seen him walk past, towards the village, over an hour ago, and when her husband had climbed back on his quad bike and gone back to finish his fencing in the top field, she'd grabbed her chance to say what she couldn't say in front of him.

'Not that we're not close.' She stared through the windscreen into the fog. 'Not that we haven't *been* close, I should say. The bad things that happen on a farm – even the money problems – are things you can discuss. This—' She sniffed and dragged out a clutch of tissues to wipe her nose. 'This is beyond everything.'

Merrily said, 'Do you mind if I smoke . . . if I were to open the window an inch or two?'

'Of course.' Cherry almost smiled, seeming grateful for this sign of human weakness. Merrily lit a Silk Cut.

'He's changed, of course,' Cherry said. 'He doesn't *think* he's turning into his father, because the old man was always so religious, but he is.' She put away the tissue and turned in her seat to face Merrily. 'Still, there are worse things. Lord knows what Roddy was turning into. All in all, I can't help thinking, God help us, that it's as well it ended the way it did. If we could say it *had* ended. If we're ever going to be able to say that.'

'Were you there?'

'No. Neither of us was there. I remember I went out to fill the coal scuttle about teatime and I thought I could hear something from down the hill, but I thought it was just kids. It was about ten o'clock before the police even came and told us he was dead. We didn't know what to do. Nobody else came. We didn't know everybody had seen him . . . electrocuted. We just . . . Tony and me, we just sat there and talked about it until the early hours. But then the next day he didn't want to know, and that's how it's been since. That's how the old man would've been. And then it was in the papers and on the telly – the videos people'd taken. Our neighbours, so-called.'

'How long've you been married?'

Wanting to take her away from those images. The car, swaddled in fog, was warming up inside now and Cherry was talking freely. It emerged that she and Tony had met through a dating agency for farmers. Born in Newport, where her parents had a shoe shop, she'd always dreamed of life on a farm. They'd been married twenty years, since she was twenty-seven, and had two sons, both now working in Cardiff and loving it. If Tony Lodge left them the farm, it would only be sold off. He had a decision to make and fairly soon. He didn't need *this* on top of it all, his wife said.

And when they'd turned up at the door last night, the villagers, the *new* villagers, telling him he ought to do the decent community thing and have Roddy tidily cremated . . .

'I don't think I'm quite understanding this,' Merrily said. 'All this talk of the "new" Underhowle. Would this be something to do with the Development Committee?'

'They don't even like to call it Underhowle any more. "Oh, it's a nowhere sort of name," one of them said once, when they had a public meeting about it. "A neither here-nor-there name".'

'Meeting about what?'

'Ariconium. That's what they call the project. Ariconium was an old Roman town that was supposed to be further down the valley towards Weston, but Mr Crewe, who bought the Old Rectory, he reckons it was more this way, and he found a little statue of a Roman god and they all got excited, and that's how it started, really. I can't see it myself – I mean, there's nothing there. It's not like as if there were walls and ruins, things you can walk round. It's just marks in the ground.'

'I saw a stone plaque thing in the village hall, with the word Ariconium carved into it.'

'They wanted to put it on the signs at the entrance to the village, but some historical organization objected because they said it wasn't proved, but they're fighting that. They're setting up a museum of things people've found and maps and audio-visual stuff – in the old chapel. They've had a grant from the Lottery, lots of things like that.'

' "They"?'

'Well, Mr Crewe and Mr Young at the school and the chap who has the computer factory. People like that. Seem to be more of them every day. But they've done a lot for the village, kind of thing, put a lot of people in work, so everybody's going along with it. And they make it all sound so exciting for the future – more tourism, more jobs. They're planning this big launch next Easter, with leaflets and articles in the papers and television and that. The last thing they want is for the village to be associated with a mass murderer. Oh, dear God, no, not *now*.'

'Pretty tactless, however, coming to your husband, so soon afterwards.'

'Had to come in good time for the funeral. They were nice enough about it, I suppose. Said they'd help keep it discreet. Keep the press away. How it was in everybody's interests to develop an upmarket tourist economy kind of thing and until that was established we had to be conscious of our public profile.'

Merrily shook her head at the crassness of it. 'Not, even in normal circumstances, the best thing to say to a traditional farmer.'

Cherry Lodge managed a smile. 'That's true.' She was actually quite pretty; there had probably been a time, before the reality of it all started to wear her down, when Tony Lodge hadn't been able to believe his luck. 'All tourism means to my husband is people tramping across his land, leaving gates open. That's what he's doing up there now – repairing fences, tightening the barbed wire. Battening down the hatches.'

'That's not good, is it?' Merrily said carefully, and collected another grateful look.

'Like he's accepted that we're supposed to be hermits now, for the rest of our lives. Not show our faces down there 'cause we're going to be tarred with it for ever.' A glimmering of tears. 'And this family's been here longer than any of them. Longer than *any* of them.' She leaned forward in the seat. 'You know what *I*'d like to do – sell our story to the papers. We had the reporters here, loads of them, and Tony was ready to get his gun out to them. But I'd like to get them back, tell everybody what he was really like, how weird he *really* was – that'd teach—' She blinked. 'I keep forgetting you're a vicar. I don't get to talk to many women. You must think—'

'No. Not at all.' Merrily focused rapidly, glad that Jane's duffel was still toggled over the dog collar. 'What would you tell them, Cherry? What would you tell them about Roddy? Weird how?'

'Oh . . .' Cherry looked uncomfortable again. *Too eager. Blown it.* 'All sorts of things. Tony used to talk about him a lot at one time – all the things he couldn't understand. There's always somebody in a family you talk about, isn't there? Somebody you always despair of. Always, "Oh what's he gone and done now?" Black sheep kind of thing.'

'What kind of things *did* he do?'

Cherry's hazel eyes flickered. 'You've put me on the spot now. I'm not sure I should—'

'It's OK.' Merrily nodded quickly, pushing her cigarette into the ashtray. 'I'm sorry, I shouldn't've asked.'

'Anyway, I've taken up too much of your time already. I've got the lunch to make and everything. Not that he'll eat much.'

'I'll take you back down.' Merrily let out the clutch, biting her lip. *How to play this* . . . 'Look, you can take up as much of my time as you want, whenever you want. Any time you feel this is getting on top of you and you want to talk.'

She backed into some bushes in the fog – more scratches – before managing a clumsy three-point turn, dragging the Volvo back onto the track, crawling down the hill in second gear, foot on the brake, headlights on, until the farmhouse imprinted itself drably on the clogged air. Cherry was silent the whole way, and when Merrily pulled up, she made no move to open the door.

'You're not an ordinary priest, are you?'

'Well, most of them are bigger . . .'

'Mr Banks, it was, who told Tony. About what you do.'

'Well, whatever Mr Banks said, I don't think it's anything to do with why I was asked to take over the funeral.'

'Isn't it?'

'If it is, nobody's told me.'

Cherry stared out of the window. 'You on e-mail, are you?'

'Yes. Well, no . . . actually the computer's crashed at home, but you can reach me at the office in Hereford.'

'Write down the address for me, can you? Don't look so surprised, I'm not a peasant, I've been doing the accounts on an IBM computer for four years now. Listen, if I write all this out for you and send it, no one will see it? You promise me that?'

'Except possibly my secretary. Who's also the Bishop's secretary. Who you could trust like your mother. But—'

'I don't know what good it's going to do – except I think we should've told the police and Tony wouldn't do that. It was when the police told us about all these pictures on his wall, and they asked could we throw any light on it, and Tony said no, we couldn't. And afterwards he was going, "What difference is it going to make now, anyway – except everybody thinking, *Oh they're all like that, all the Lodges*. Mental. Sick." '

Merrily's throat was dry. The fog seemed, if anything, thicker now; it felt like when you were a kid burrowing under the bedclothes with a pencil flashlight. Cherry opened the car door, got out and then leaned back in.

'It torments me. I keep thinking, maybe we should have tried to get him to see a psychiatrist, we might've saved those girls. I mean, he went to his doctor, with the headaches, and *he* didn't spot anything.'

'Whatever it was, I think a lot of people failed to react to it,' Merrily said. She was thinking of the Rev. Jerome Banks. She was thinking of her own wimpish relief at being denied access to Roddy Lodge at Hereford police headquarters.

Cherry said, 'This is going to sound stupid, but what it comes down to is Roddy and dead people. From an early age, this thing about the dead.' She leaned on the door frame, looking around, listening perhaps for the putter of the quad bike. 'Maybe I'm making too much of it.'

27

Lamp

The school bus was actually starting up when Jane looked out of the window and saw Eirion standing there by his car, in his school uniform, in the fog. And her heart pulsed the way it used to when he drove all the way from the Cathedral School in Hereford because he just like *had* to see her. Serious turn-on.

And today he'd come all this way in terrible driving conditions.

But when she scrambled down from the bus, dragging her flight bag full of books, she saw that he wasn't smiling. From the beginning, the most amazing thing about Eirion had been his smile, and when it wasn't there he looked pasty, a bit jowly, even. These days, anyway. Especially through the fog.

In the old days – March, April – arriving at her school, he'd say, '*I was just passing.*' Both of them knowing that this wasn't a place anyone in their right mind 'just passed'. So it was a catchphrase nowadays, and they'd be touching one another before the car's doors were properly shut. But tonight . . .

'I just needed to see you.' Eirion making it obvious by his tone that today it wasn't *that* kind of need. 'You want a lift home?'

When she got into the new old car, the sky was going dark. It always seemed to be going dark, Jane thought. Life was one long dusk. Eirion just started the engine and when they were through the gates, he said, 'Jane, do you think we need to talk?'

Like, how many crappy soaps did you hear *that* line in, in the course of an average week? Or you would if you watched them. Jane tried to think of a corresponding cliché, couldn't come up with one.

'What about?' she said finally.

'Well . . . you.'

He took the back lanes to Ledwardine, prolonging the journey like he used to when they weren't quite going out together but he was hoping. It could take for ever today, with these conditions. The fog had never really cleared from this morning; they'd had the lights on in the school all day. And what a long and tedious day it had been. In Eng Lit, she'd collected a couple of dagger-glances from Mrs Costello whom she liked really but, *come on*, wasn't life just a little too short for flatulent prats like Salman Rushdie?

'I, er, checked out the insurance,' Eirion said. 'It's probably OK for you to drive this car, after all. I mean . . . when it's a better day than this.'

'Yeah,' she said. 'A better day.'

A better day. A bright new beginning. '*You're so young*,' people said. '*What I wouldn't do if I was your age again.*' When what they really meant was that when *they* were young the idea of a bright new beginning for the world didn't seem quite so laughable.

In the summer, after she and Eirion had made love for the first time (the first time for both of them, with anybody, it later emerged) it was incredible, like climbing a mountain, and it was all there at your feet: the whole of life a glowing patchwork of endless, glistening greenery.

Jane scowled. *Didn't 'make love'. Had sex.*

And that was it. Done it now. Done it a bunch of times and, sure, sometimes – before and during and after – it felt as though she was very much in love and didn't want there to be anyone else ever . . .

In which case, this was *really* it? Seventeen now, an adult. Now what?

And why? Why bother? It was all going to end in tears, anyway.

'I've been wondering what's made you so negative lately,' Eirion said.

'Oh, really.'

'And whether there was any way I could help.'

The car heater panted. The dipped headlights excavated shallow trenches in the grey-brownness. It was a situation that, at one time, might have seemed cosily mysterious. As distinct from totally dismal.

'Because if I can't,' Eirion said. 'You know . . .'

'What?'

'I don't know.'

'Well, if *you* don't know . . .' After a while, Jane stopped noticing the limited views – atmosphere was just a psychological condition, right? She found she was gripping folds of her skirt. What was *happening* to her? She didn't even want to drive. What was the point? Be gridlock everywhere within about ten years.

'It's like you just want to wreck things,' Eirion said. 'If things aren't working exactly as you'd planned them, you don't want to wait.'

'Life's short. Very short for some people.' Thinking of Layla Riddock, who hadn't even made it out of school when the big pendulum did it in one blow. Thinking of Nev. Thinking of their day out in mid-Wales, when Eirion had taken her to see this particular standing stone, and it had somehow just looked like . . . a stone. And Eirion had been dismayed because she wasn't going like, '*Hey, wow, can't you feel that earth energy?*'

Jane felt her eyes filling up as the car bumped around a bit. She thought at first he'd just gone over the kerb in the fog, but it was deliberate. He was fully in control. The car stopped, and he switched off the engine. Jane looked out and saw wet grass.

'Where are we?' Turning to him, wanting for a moment just to see his old smile in the dimness and then fall into his arms and everything would be all right.

For a while, anyway.

So where does it begin, this clinical depression? At what stage do they prescribe the pills? She pulled her bag onto her lap, folding her hands on top of it: self-contained, untouchable. Inside, along with the books, was her Walkman with the Nick Drake compilation CD – Nick Drake, who died of an overdose of antidepressants. It could all be really funny. Except it wasn't.

Eirion scrubbed at the windscreen with his hand. 'You can't even see it.'

'What?'

'The steeple at Ledwardine. We're on Cole Hill.'

'What are we doing here?'

'I don't know, really.' He sank back in his seat. 'This is where she saw it, isn't it? Where Jenny Driscoll saw the angel. Or didn't . . . as you decided.'

'So?' She stared at him. If she was getting an inkling of what this was all about, she wasn't inclined to allow the idea to develop.

'Doesn't matter, anyway.' He stopped rubbing. 'It's too foggy.'

'I don't understand.'

'I think you do.' He swallowed. 'It's like I said before – a few months ago this whole thing would've been just so exciting to you that we'd've been up here every night on some kind of angel hunt.'

'No, we wouldn't. That would be stupid.'

'Yeah,' Eirion said. 'It probably would be, now. But the thing is . . . it would also have been fun. I would've liked it. Flask of hot soup and the . . . you know, the need to keep warm.'

'Oh, right,' Jane said, laying on the scorn. 'This is about *sex*.'

'*No!*' Almost a scream. 'That's not what—'

'Think about it very carefully,' Jane said sadly. 'Underneath it all, it would be about sex.'

Eirion drew in a tight breath. 'So we're into Freud now, is it?' Stirrings of anger bringing out the Welshness in his voice.

'I really wouldn't know about that,' Jane said. 'I think I'm probably just coming to my senses.'

He exploded then. 'This is your *senses*? It seems to me that you're *losing* your fucking senses. All . . . all six of them.'

Jane said, without thinking much about it, 'Can you take me home?' The windscreen was opaque with fog and condensation; it was already going cold inside the car.

'Is this it?' Eirion said. 'Is this it for us?' Talking in this dramatized way to provoke from her an outraged denial.

'I don't know,' she said. 'Maybe like the angel will float down and spread this healing radiance all around us and we'll feel really cool.'

It was hard to see his face in what light was left, but she could feel the extreme shock coming off him. It was like being in one of those cold patches that Mum was supposed to look for in haunted houses. And though she'd caused it, Jane felt detached from it – and that wasn't right, was it? That was kind of . . . cruel.

'Listen,' Eirion said urgently. 'We all get like this sometimes. You read about executive stress and mid-life crisis, but I think those people've just forgotten what it was like when they were in their teens and there were like whole big areas of their lives they couldn't control.'

'What?'

'They don't remember how bad it could be sometimes. When you can't cont—'

'You really don't understand, do you?' She looked at him with pity. 'I've realized that *nobody*'s in control. Nobody and nothing. All this information going round and round the world on the Internet and stuff, and it's all bullshit and everybody's got a website that tells you nothing you want to know, and all the politicians are like . . . And Mum . . . Mum knows these guys know sod-all really and are never going to get us anywhere, and the hospitals and everything are always going to be totally crap, but she can live with it, because she's managed to con herself into thinking that way above all this ridiculous mess there's this all-knowing, benevolent *thing*.'

'Oh Jane—'

'And meanwhile she and Lol are coming apart before it ever came together. And he'll shag the Cairns woman, if he hasn't already, because at least she's there for him. At least she's *there*. And Mum will just spend the rest of her life humouring fruit-cakes like Jenny Driscoll. And poor old Gomer will start sitting in front of daytime telly – day after mindless day of soaps and Kilroy – not even seeing it after a bit, and falling asleep, until one blessed day he doesn't wake up.'

Silence.

'It's a phase,' Eirion said feebly at last. 'It'll pass, Jane.'

She jerked in her seat. '*I don't* want *it to pass, you cretin! This is reality!*'

She started to cry, and wound down the window to let the fog come in like a damp facecloth.

'I'll take you home, then,' Eirion said emptily.

*

Merrily had come home via Hereford, calling in at Tesco to pick up a sandwich and then at the hospital to see a couple of parishioners in the geriatric ward – Miss Tyler and Mrs Mackay, once neighbours in the village and now they didn't even recognize one another on the ward. But they recognized Merrily, or seemed to, and Mrs Mackay wanted her to pray with her and, at the end of it, Merrily added her own silent prayer that something could be done about geriatric wards. Even the word itself had become demeaning and contemptuous, and when you said it aloud it made a sound like a creaking wheelchair.

Back home, she found a parcel – a brown Jiffy bag – in the porch and dumped it on the hall table when she heard the phone ringing. She exchanged grimaces with the lamp-bearing Christ and went through to the scullery to answer it.

'You sound a bit down, lass.'

'Oh. Hullo, Huw.'

'You find that stuff about the girl?'

'Yeah. I was trying to think if it could be relevant, in any way, to her disappearance.'

'Depends if it were still going on.'

'Getting abducted by aliens becomes a regular thing?'

'*Sometimes* the experience is repeated. Sometimes it even seems to be site-specific.'

'You mean the *house* is haunted, rather than the individual? That rather argues against aliens, doesn't it? More like geological conditions – fault lines, underground springs. Any atmospheric conditions that might promote hallucinations. Nothing to do with rehabilitation of the displaced dead. No requirement for social services of the soul.' Merrily sat down, still wearing her coat. 'Huw, I've got to bury Roddy Lodge.'

'So I heard.'

'*Did* you?' Amazing how much gossip drifted up the Brecon Beacons. 'And would you have any advice on that? For instance, there's a body of local opinion doesn't want him in the churchyard.'

'That bother you?'

'I feel OK about it. He's entitled to a Christian burial.

However, bearing in mind that I've never buried a murderer before . . .'

'Aye.' A pause for consideration. 'Complications are possible. A lot of psychic fallout drifting round a murder. As for *several* murders . . .'

'Not proved. He's still an innocent man in the eyes of the law.'

'And that can make it even more complex. Unfinished business, lass.'

'This is what you rang about, isn't it?'

Huw was silent for quite a while. Long enough for Merrily to tuck the phone under her chin while she shed her coat.

'I had a call from young Francis,' Huw said. 'The detective.'

'Bliss? You had a call from *Bliss*?'

'Catholic, am I right?'

'Ten a penny in Liverpool.'

'And a bit . . . not exactly *unstable*. Would "volatile" be a better word?'

'Let's say "impetuous". What's this about, Huw?'

'Lad's been out and about, asking a lot of questions in certain areas. Bee in his bonnet. Bees buzz.'

'Certain areas?'

'Specifically, the West case.'

'Why would he phone you about that?' She was cautious now.

'I, er . . . I were a consultant on that inquiry.'

'You never mentioned *that* before.'

'Couple of us were brought in after talk of the Wests being involved with a satanic cult.'

'I wasn't aware of that.'

'Talk by West himself, mostly. Some of it was allegedly said in discussions he had with his prison carer, while he was on remand. Could've been bullshit. Anyroad, during the police investigation, a number of us were asked if we knew of anything, any groups operating around Gloucester or the Forest of Dean. Satanist, sadist, anything deviant. One suggestion was that Fred West were supplying this group with virgins. Abducting women, taking them to some farm for ritual abuse, subsequent murder. 'Course, he lied a lot. Probably just a latent attempt to shift some blame was how the coppers saw it, but they didn't want to take any chances.'

'And were you able to help?'

'Well, we couldn't supply a string of addresses of satanic temples, if that's what they expecting. But there *was* evidence of hard magic in 25 Cromwell Street itself. One of the victims – young lass of seventeen – was into occultism and blood-ritual, linked to bondage, S-and-M. Whether they believed in it or not, the Wests were only too happy to join in. Lass ended up tied by her ankles to a beam in the cellar, hanging upside down like a side of meat.'

Huw's tone of voice had altered, gone flat. The level of emotion in his voice was often an inverse reflection of his actual commitment. Merrily recalled one of her fellow students on the Deliverance course saying, '*Funny chap, old Huw. Been through the mill. Wears his scar tissue like a badge.*' This had been unfair. He didn't. He might slope around in baggy jeans and trainers with holes in them, looking ravaged – but only ravaged like the lead guitarist of some old blues band you vaguely remembered from your childhood. And he rarely talked about the mills he'd been through, dark or satanic.

'Anyroad, Bliss reckons there's a link between Lodge and West that his esteemed colleagues are not taking seriously enough.'

'He told you about the attaché case and the pictures?'

'Asked me if I could see any ritual angle.'

'Asked me, too. *Could* you?'

'Told him I couldn't see either of them buggers being bright enough for that kind of stuff. However, we can't rule out a link, can we? West got around the Forest of Dean a lot. Him and Lodge were both two-bit contractors.'

'Hold on . . .' Merrily's hand tightened round the phone. 'I don't think even Frannie Bliss is going that far. He told me about a man from South Wales who had a sick fascination with the Wests and killed a girl on the edge of the Forest in '96. Bliss was thinking along those lines – West as role model. He didn't see a *personal* connection, for heaven's sake.'

'Merrily, what I'm saying is this: you've got one woman dead, and the coppers are looking at the possibility that Lodge killed her either because she wouldn't go along with his horrific West fantasies *or* she found out what he'd done to the others. *What he'd done to the others*. See? What *did* he do to the others?'

'Nobody yet knows whether there *are* others.'

'Aye. And happen that's why the police aren't publicizing it about those pictures and the cuttings. Because once you throw down the name *West*, it's no longer an ordinary murder investigation. No longer, God forbid, even an ordinary *sex*-murder inquiry. It's kidnap . . . torture . . . mutilation. It's the unspeakable. It's saying to the parents of every missing girl within a fifty-mile radius or more: you've read about West and what he did. Well, we're not trying to worry you or anything but . . .'

'Huw,' she said, 'he's dead. Lodge is dead and West is dead.'

'Merrily, West told this woman in Winson Green that he'd done another twenty. He also said there were other people involved. Now, there must be a lot of folk with missing relatives who can't help wondering, whenever they wake up in the night. And in that area of West Gloucestershire and the Herefordshire border and the Forest, it's all a *bit* close. Still raw. If any link with West came out, then you really would have a problem with that funeral.'

'Yeah.' She sagged a little in her chair. 'I hadn't really thought about that.'

'Keep it to yourself,' Huw said, 'and pray that Francis does the same.' He paused. '*The lamp of the wicked shall be put out.*'

'Sorry?'

'Book of Proverbs.'

'I know. What's the relevance?'

'I don't know if Lodge had any connection, real or imagined, with West,' Huw said. 'All I know is that nowt reignites faster than the lamp of the wicked.'

Jane let herself in and put on the hall light, which lit up *The Light of the World*. She stared into His lined face: so benign, so sad and world-weary, so . . .

. . . So *holier than thou*.

She experienced this shockingly powerful urge to pull down the picture and smash it to pieces on the flagstones. *This* was how the Church had been keeping bums on pews for two millennia. *He died for you. You owe Him.*

Guilt. Original guilt.

They gave you pictures like this to underline it: you owe Christ, you owe Uncle Ted, you owe the parish and the smug bloody Church that pays you peanuts. *Bastards!*

Jane's face was stiff with drying tears. The kitchen door was open, the light was on, and from the other side of the room she could hear Mum on the phone in the scullery, living the lie. She closed the kitchen door quietly, and went upstairs to her apartment in the attic, where she and Eirion had first . . . had sex. She dropped her bag on the floor and threw herself on the bed under the Mondrian walls, and sobbed in rage and incomprehension. It used to be so wonderful up here, so exclusive. It had never felt so lonely, so empty.

What's happening to you? Are you like some kind of freak that you can't just talk about blokes and bands and DVDs, like your mindless little friends at school?

Not that she actually had any friends. Not really. She got on with everybody OK, on a superficial level, but there was nobody to really *talk* to, no real-life friends. The one who might have been, Layla Riddock, was gone. Leaving only Eirion, who was intelligent and thoughtful and only a little overweight, and who she'd just . . .

. . . Just abused. For no real reason . . . other than that he probably *did* understand. And of course she'd known that he didn't just want sex, he wanted love, which she couldn't give him.

And now it's over. You just ended it, like on a whim because . . . maybe because he was getting too close; he was blocking your horizon . . . the horizon beyond which is nothing. Nothing at all.

No heaven; you could only make a temporary heaven, out of money or sex or drugs. She'd never done drugs. Had opportunities, inevitably – Es, whizz, spliff, all that – but she'd resisted it. Felt slightly contemptuous of kids who spent all their spare cash on chemicals, because there were other ways to get there, weren't there? Meditation, ritual dance, spiritual exercises. Other ways of *actually being there*.

Or not. Maybe there was nowhere to go but deeper into your own delusions.

Jane turned the pillow over to the dry side.

Merrily remembered the parcel she'd left on the hall table, and went to fetch it. She was suspicious of parcels now. The Jiffy bag wasn't light, and it bulged. Suppose it contained another few thousand pounds in used fifties.

She took it into the scullery and pulled it open under the Anglepoise.

There were three paperback books inside, all scuffed and with split spines: *An Evil Love. Happy Like Murderers. She Must Have Known.*

There was a note on yellow paper attached to one of the books with a paperclip.

EVERYTHING YOU EVER WANTED TO KNOW
ABOUT THE WESTS AND A LOT YOU'LL WISH YOU
DIDN'T. JUST IN CASE YOU WERE INTERESTED.
LET ME HAVE THEM BACK SOMETIME.
F.

'Well, thanks, Frannie.' Merrily put the books back in the bag. 'Just what I bloody needed.'

She switched off the lamp and sat there in the blood red of the old electric fire and wondered where all this was going.

28

Bloody Angels

Jane said, 'What are you doing sitting here in the dark?'

Silhouetted in the doorway, with the creamy kitchen behind her, she looked so slight and vulnerable that Merrily wanted to rush over and hold her. The way you did sometimes, even in normal circumstances.

As if she'd sensed it and didn't want it, Jane backed off into the kitchen.

'Sorry.' Merrily felt a cool wave of dismay. 'Sorry, flower. I was on the phone, and the light just faded on me. What's the time?'

'Twenty to six.'

Merrily got up. 'Things have been a bit . . . Maybe we could put some music on later?' Code for a deep and meaningful chat.

'Whatever.'

'You OK?'

'Yeah.' The light, throwaway kind of *yeah*, carrying many times its weight of meaning. And now the damn phone was going again. Merrily glanced back to make sure she hadn't switched off the machine by mistake.

'Better get it,' Jane said quickly. 'Might be important.'

Merrily hesitated, and Jane turned away. Merrily sighed, went back and picked up. 'Ledwardine Vic—'

'Mrs Watkins!' Cheery, booming male voice. 'George Lomas, Lomas and Sons, Coleford. We haven't done business before, but we're burying a certain gentleman – if that's the correct term in this instance – for Mr Tony Lodge and your good self.'

'Ah, right. Erm . . . hullo.'

'You have Friday, I believe.'

'As I understand it.'

'And, unfortunately, Mrs Watkins, I have to tell you, as *quite a number of people* now understand it. Mr Lodge had hoped to keep it discreet by using ourselves, rather than one of the firms in Ross, but it seems someone's let the cat out of the bag, and I had a phone call this afternoon from the local press.'

'Oh dear.'

'Quite. *Not* what we want, under the circumstances. However, I've spoken to the parties concerned, including the Reverend Banks, and we have an alternative proposal to put to you, if it can be accommodated into your schedule. And that is Wednesday – the day after tomorrow. We're suggesting late afternoon – *very* late afternoon.'

'You mean under cover of darkness?'

'I think it makes sense, Mrs Watkins. It *had* been arranged that Mr Lodge's coffin should spend at least one night in the church prior to burial, so no one will be surprised to see a hearse arrive. We propose – and Mr Tony Lodge is somewhat reluctantly in agreement – that the funeral should be carried out as soon as possible. We expect there to be no more than five mourners.'

'A clandestine funeral?'

'That wouldn't exactly be my choice of word but, under the circumstances . . . well, Mr Banks is certainly in agreement. It means that Mr Lodge will be safely interred before anyone can . . . cause problems.'

'You've been warned of problems?'

'Not if it's dealt with on Wednesday evening and arrangements remain confidential. Could we say five-thirty?'

'Well . . .' There really wasn't an alternative, was there? 'OK.'

'Splendid,' said Mr Lomas.

When she put down the phone, it rang again, under her hand. 'Damn.' Merrily picked up. 'Led—'

Sophie said, 'I was just doing my final check on the e-mail, and there's one you might just want to know about before the morning. Cherry Lodge?'

'*Already*? How long is it?'

'Quite long. Merrily, I've already mailed it, but I thought I'd tell you in case you weren't going to check your e-mails again until the morning.'

'Fine. Thanks. Oh, sh— the computer's gone down. It's not

working. I was going to ring up someone tomorrow. Oh God, look, under the circumstances I think I'd better come in and collect it.'

'I could drive it over there if you're tired. You sound tired.'

'No, that's ridiculous, I'll come in. How's the fog?'

'Patchy. I'll wait for you.'

'No need.'

'I'll *wait*.'

'OK, give me just over half an hour.'

When she'd put the phone down, Merrily went into the kitchen and found Jane at the farthest window, where the light was dim, looking out at dark nothings in the garden. The kid didn't turn round.

'Off to HQ, then.'

'Sorry. Something I need to pick up.' Merrily saw that Jane's hair was flattened on one side, as if she'd been lying on it. 'Erm . . . why don't you come, too? We could call for some chips on the way back.'

'I've got homework to wrap. Anyway, it always takes you longer than you think it's going to, once you're up there closeted with Auntie Sophie.'

'No, I'll be as quick as I can, honest. But if you want to get something to eat, meanwhile . . . or I could—'

Jane said, 'Just go, Mum, huh?'

Desperately cuddling Ethel, Jane had thought about it for a long time, and it was her fault. No question, she was the guilty party.

So she would call him.

A mature decision. You didn't – because of your own weakness, your own inadequacy – just walk away like this from someone who was not only your first lover but also your best friend. Who you'd lain with and laughed about things with together. Who had virtually nicked his stepmother's car last summer to drive you home from Wales on a whim. Who, also last summer, had been – face it – *hurt* for you, and almost very badly, in fact almost—

Jane clutched the edge of the refectory table with both hands, squeezing hard until she, too, was hurting. Ethel watched her, big-eyed, from the stone flags.

She should be able to understand why she was feeling like this, continually juggling rage and despair. Like, she'd read *The Catcher in the Rye*, about the kid in the 1950s making the shattering discovery that all adults were hypocrites. But this wasn't the 1950s and she wasn't a kid any more, and she'd known for years that all adults were *total* fucking hypocrites.

OK, maybe except for Lol. And Gomer. And Mum, who did her best.

And anyway, all these were people in the process of getting damaged.

Jane let go of the table, walked into Mum's office, and snapped on the light. It was actually quite calm and plain in here. No awful Victorian Bible scenes. Just a blue-framed print of a painting by Paul Klee, which Huw Owen had once given Mum: irregular coloured rooftops under a white moon. On the wall above the desk, there was just one smallish cross, in oak. A paperback New Testament and a prayer book lay on the desk. There was a single bookcase in which the standard theological tomes were being gradually displaced by the kind of books that Jane herself used to borrow: paranormal stuff.

The Deliverance Ministry. My mother, the exorcist.

An Anglican shaman, a Christian witch doctor. Paid peanuts to humour fruitcakes.

Could be worse; she might actually have finished her university course and become a lawyer, like Dad, like Uncle Ted. Jane forced a grin, picked up the phone, tapped out a mobile number more familiar than their own. He'd be home now, in the grim family fortress outside Abergavenny.

Irene, what can I say? I don't deserve you. I don't deserve to live. Could he bear to hear that again?

Ominous silence. No ring.

Vodaphone robot: '*The Vodaphone you are calling has been turned off . . .*'

And nothing about voice-mail. *No, please . . .* Jane felt like she was about to start hyperventilating. He'd even disabled his voice-mail.

Oh Christ, I didn't mean it. Slamming down the phone, staggering back into the kitchen. *I didn't mean any of it. You know I didn't, you utter bastard!*

Drawing in a breath like a long, thin hacksaw blade. Once too often – she'd abused him once too often.

Jane wrapped her arms around herself.

It was over. It really *was* over.

She stood there, not moving, as though she was set in marble, an angel on a grave. Stood there for well over a minute before moving numbly to the sink, half-filling a glass with water and drinking it, watching Ethel disappearing purposefully through the cat door.

She went back to the table and pulled out the chair where Mum normally sat, removing a book from the seat before sitting down. This house was like a nunnery; even the book was by St Thomas Aquinas, Mum's place marked with an envelope at a page with – she opened it – some stuff about . . . angels, of course. Bloody angels.

Messengers of God. Jane shook her head slowly in contempt, then lowered it into her arms on the table top. This was what Mum had once admitted to doing when all else failed, when she didn't know where to turn. With a cringing curtsy to primitive superstition, she would actually open the Bible or some other holy tome at random, seeking divine inspiration from the first thing she read. God, the weight of sadness in a gesture like *that*.

And wasn't it ironic that, after years of mocking Jane's own passing fascination with nature spirits and angels, Mum should get finally get round to investigating the subject because a mad-woman had given the church a hefty bung? Wasn't it also typical that she'd turned to a medieval theologian rather than simply ask her own daughter, who had read more books on angelic forces . . .

Jane lifted her head slowly, then shook it, smiling what she guessed was a smile of near-insanity but really, what the *hell*?

Maybe it worked. A sign from God. Angelic inspiration. She looked at the clock: five to seven. Be a least a couple of hours before Mum got back.

She got to her feet and went through to the hall. Didn't, for once, feel the need to take down *The Light of the World* and smash it onto the flags, didn't even give it a glance as she pulled her blue fleece jacket from the peg, shrugging it on as she opened the front door, Mum's voice bleating in her head from when they'd had the row about Jenny Driscoll.

Maybe I didn't push her hard enough.

Well, of course she didn't. She wasn't intellectually equipped for it. The truth was that Mum simply didn't have the knowledge. Everything she knew about angels came from the Bible or the works of guys like Aquinas, whereas Jenny Box-née-Driscoll was coming directly from the New Age, where angelic energies corresponded with the *deva*s, the high-level faerie entities supervising whole areas of life . . . where angels were considered to be an ecological fact, not a religious device.

OK, it was all sad crap, but it was crap she *knew about*. Nobody in – well, OK, certainly nobody in this village was better equipped to get the truth out of Driscoll.

The fog wasn't bad now, actually. Jane zipped up her fleece, plunged her hands in the pockets and set off down the drive, towards the square and Chapel House. It would have been good to discuss this first with Eirion, but she was on her own again now, had to find her own way, make her own decisions.

29

Seeing Marilyn

Deliverance
From: cherry lodge <cherry.lodge@agritel.co.uk>
To: deliverance@spiritec.co.uk

'Has her own separate e-mail address,' Merrily noted. 'But I'd be a bit concerned about mailing her back, all the same.'

'I wouldn't worry – the husband probably never even goes near the computer,' Sophie said. 'Some older farmers are uncomfortable with them. Their farm's a private world, a domain, and they don't like the thought of anything having access – whether it's through a public footpath or the Internet. Electronic intrusion is as big a threat as a Ministry man with a clipboard.'

Lately, Sophie had been letting her white hair grow; in the subdued light it looked unexpectedly dense and dramatic above the grey cashmere and pearls. She was perched elegantly on a corner of the desk, her back to the window, conveying no hurry to be away. Sophie Hill: a woman who lived close to and *for* the Cathedral. Who didn't, therefore, keep 'hours'.

There'd been tea waiting for Merrily in the Bishop's Palace gatehouse, and chocolate biscuits. Jane's 'Auntie Sophie' jibe had not been entirely misplaced. It *was* a bit like going to your auntie's when you were a kid. A guilty pleasure now, especially with Jane at home nursing her private angst.

'Have you read this?' Merrily asked. Below the Cathedral gatehouse, the lights of Broad Street were still fuzzy with fog.

'Merrily, it's why I called you.'

'So what do you think?'

'Well, obviously my first thought was that they should have told the police.'

'*I* can't.'

'No, of course not – not without consulting her first. But then, when you think about it, how interested would the police be anyway? What difference would it make, now he's dead?'

> *We've been feeling isolated, like outsiders now in our village, even though Tony's family has been here for generations. We're the nearest farm to the village, but we don't feel involved any more or especially wanted, and since all this came up it's got much worse. Some people we've known for years have been very kind, but they don't run things here any more. That's why we didn't want to talk about it to the police or anyone, it could only have made things worse than they are.*

'She's very fluent, Sophie. Getting things off her chest.'

Sophie nodded. 'E-mail can be a liberating experience, as I'm sure you know. One can say things it would be difficult, if not impossible, to say in a two-way conversation on the phone. While the problem with letters is that not only are they more formal but one is inclined to read them back an hour or so later and think, *I can't send that*, and tear them up. But with an e-mail . . .'

'You pour it all out and you've pressed *send* before you can change your mind.'

'For people – especially for women – in remote situations, it's become a refuge, a confessional . . . a lifeline. Particularly women who can't discuss some things with their husbands. She probably gets into chat rooms as well. Therapy. Company.'

Merrily, sitting at Sophie's desk, looked up, head on one side. 'I've often wondered, never asked . . . but are you in The Samaritans?'

Sophie smiled briefly and looked away. It was obvious now, when you considered. And she'd be very good at it.

'Also, one can write and transmit an e-mail while one's other half is still in the house, without the danger of being overheard. Without even having to sneak it into the post. I suppose it's become, for many people, the nearest thing to thinking aloud. Or crying aloud.'

'Yes.' Merrily thought of Cherry Lodge and her IBM and her

spreadsheets. Tony Lodge slumped in front of the TV, and his wife ostensibly at work on the accounts in another room, dealing with DEFRA forms on the Net, in the night when it was cheaper . . . while secretly entering the bigger world, the limitless virtual world.

Merrily started to go through the printout for a second time, pencil-marking key paragraphs.

The police took me and my husband to Roddy's bungalow, and we were both shocked because we'd not been there much. They didn't mix, Tony and his brother, him being so much younger, and we'd certainly never been in the bedrooms before. Well, I was not as shocked as Tony because I thought, well, he was just a lad, even though he was thirty-five, and him being single and everything it didn't shock me that much. I mean the black sheets and everything. We all knew how much he'd changed since he went on his own, how much more confident he was, perhaps through being in business. But then when we saw the pictures of women Tony squeezed my arm to say nothing, and when they asked us if we knew he collected pictures like that, all of famous women who were dead now, with nude bodies of page three girls pasted onto them, Tony said it didn't make any sense to him at all, and he was just disgusted and he hoped it wasn't going to be talked about publicly or told to the papers because things were bad enough.

'I saw those pictures when I went to the bungalow with Frannie Bliss. He was hoping I might be able to throw some light on it, but it was as much a mystery to me. I mean, without knowing the full background I'd never have been able to come up with anything as bizarre as this.'

His father was very religious and he wouldn't even think about it and so obviously it wasn't to be talked about in the house, but there's no doubt in my mind it comes back to the death of Roddy's mother when he was so young. She was well over 40 when she had him, and never very fit, always ailing, they never thought she'd make old bones. Well she was dead before the baby was 3 years old. It was all so unexpected, and it must have taken a toll on her.

You'd have thought he'd feel resentment towards Roddy, the old man, because of that, instead of him being his favourite, but he was very religious, he always saw Roddy as a gift from God for which there was a price to pay and that was the loss of his wife. I never understood the logic of that, but Roddy was always special. If anyone was resentful I suppose I would have to say it was Tony and his brother Geoff who had lost the mother they knew and loved and got Roddy instead.

'Merrily, what do you suppose she means by that?' Sophie fingered the phrase *gift from God*. 'All right, it was unexpected, a fluke – but is she actually saying that he believed his ailing wife had been preserved by God just long enough to give birth to this . . . ?'

'Monster?' Merrily shuddered.

The farm was doing quite well in those days and the old man was able to employ a woman to look after the child in the daytime and stay over when he wasn't well, but they never became substitute mothers, because they never stayed in the job long enough. It was a male household with a bit of help with the meals and the cleaning and childcare on top of that.

My husband has told me how Roddy was always asking about his mother, what she looked like and so on, and one day Marilyn Monroe was on the telly and the old man laughed and said That's what she looked like and although there must have been pictures of his mother around the house Roddy seemed to get fixated on this idea and he started collecting pictures of Marilyn Monroe to put up in his bedroom. When one of his brothers said something about it, Roddy said it was all right because she was dead. And then he'd find other pictures of women he liked the look of and if they were dead he'd say he'd have them for his mother and he'd put them up too and he seemed to find comfort in it so nobody thought anything of it.

'You heard of anything like that before?' Merrily asked. 'Be interesting to talk to one of the nannies, wouldn't it?'

'Perhaps the police already have.' Sophie picked up the electric kettle to refill it. 'Reinventing his mother: not some worthy but possibly rather dowdy middle-aged farmer's wife in some fairly dour farmhouse, but in fact something world-shakingly beautiful, with glittery dresses and glossy lips.'

'Making a goddess of her.'

'A sex goddess,' Sophie said quietly.

'That came later,' Merrily said. 'Let's do the child-psychology stuff first. A boy with no mother, an all-male household. He's quite lonely at home; his brothers are grown men with work to do; his father's well into middle age and strict in all kinds of ways. It's an altogether rigid regime. So here's a child desperately in need of a mother's love, jealous of all the other kids he sees being taken to school by their mums.'

'What you would call a projection, then?' Sophie offered.

'Or a simple invention? Some kids have imaginary friends, Roddy has an imaginary mum. But is he looking for maternal love or a situation where he feels, to some extent, in control – the way he doesn't, normally, in that house? The dead don't push him around. He doesn't feel quite so small and insignificant with the dead.'

'Quite touching, in a child.' Sophie took the kettle into the adjacent washroom. 'But it can only get unhealthy, can't it, as he approaches the dread years of puberty and all his burgeoning urges become fixated upon . . . well, I think we can both see where this is going. It's very hard to understand why they allowed it.'

'Household of working men. If it kept him quiet at night . . .'

Sophie's voice came thinly from the washroom, over the rattle of water on metal. 'Not if the rest is true.'

Roddy was always seeing people who were not there, so he said. He didn't seem to be afraid of them. At first it seemed like just his imagination, but when they heard him talking to them in his bedroom at night, the dead, well, this was a very stiff God-fearing house and talk of ghosts and spirits was thought of as sinful in the extreme! Roddy got into a lot of trouble with his father. Of course, in most homes today they would have him to a psychiatrist but there was still a stigma attached to that kind of thing then even though it doesn't seem so very long ago to me.

When he was older it seemed to stop. But Tony reckoned it was only that he stopped talking about it. They never said anything to the old man, knowing it would distress him, but it was definitely going on well into Roddy's teens. Tony said you could still hear him talking and giggling in his room in the dead of night and you would swear, listening to it, that he was not alone in there. He said he and Geoff tried to laugh it off but there was something frightening about it too and they just tried to put it out of their minds and not hear it and get on with their lives. He said it was because they didn't want to worry their father but I am not sure this was a good attitude to take, especially now obviously. I am also sure that Tony himself saw or heard more than he will talk about to me or anyone but there's farmers for you. Head in the sand!

'*Was* he psychic? Is that what we're looking at, Sophie?'

Sophie sat down opposite Merrily, with her back to the window and the lights of Broad Street, reached for a pencil and her shorthand pad. 'What do you know that would reinforce that theory?'

'Not much. Told me he'd been to see the vicar and scared him. After talking to Jerome Banks myself, I'd say the scaring bit was wishful thinking, but Banks did admit Roddy had been to see him – claiming his bungalow was haunted. The usual poltergeist effects were mentioned, but that was probably Banks being dismissive. So either Roddy was genuinely experiencing something or he wanted to give people the impression he was. And this is in a *new* bungalow, don't forget. No history apart from his own.'

Sophie lifted an eyebrow. 'He brought Marilyn and the others with him?'

When Tony and I were married we lived in a bungalow in the village so that he could carry on running the farm with

Geoff. Roddy was about fifteen then and I never saw that much of him. He didn't want anything to do with the farm except driving the tractor, so he had a few other jobs including training as a mechanic at a garage in Ross but he didn't stick that of course, he never stuck at anything for long. The old man said he was sure Roddy was going to make something of himself one day although none of us could see it. Then Geoff went to Australia with his family and the old man died soon after. Tony got the farm and there was money for Geoff and Roddy with the proviso he spent it on setting himself up in a decent business which Tony was to approve and oversee in the early stages. Quite a few local farms etc said they would offer him work if he got himself a digger and a bulldozer and the parish council said he could dig graves, so that was how it started, although we never imagined it was going to take off like it did. I think that was because of getting into septic tanks. He never looked back, especially after he got that contract as representative for Efflapure. How he managed that we'll never know.

I think Tony was also relieved when he started going out with girls. Or rather Melanie Pullman who was his first real girlfriend, they were going out together for quite some time, over a year, but then they broke up and then she disappeared and he started going out with that Lynsey.

'Now that's interesting, don't you think, Sophie?'

'The fact that both he and the Pullman girl were having odd experiences?'

'I wonder why they split up.'

'People do, Merrily – especially a first relationship. Men have one sexual liaison, and it gives them confidence to go out looking for something new.'

Merrily recalled Sam Hall in the community centre. *Boy seems to have gone through what you might call a delayed adolescence – as if he'd discovered sex for the first time in his thirties. No woman was safe.*

'So, how do we follow him into the next stage? Which is killing living women.'

'I'm not sure that's somewhere I want to follow him,' Sophie said. 'And I'm not sure you need to either. I'll just make the tea.'

Merrily marked one more paragraph.

I should also say it came as no surprise to either of us, the way he died. He was always one for the pylons, according to Tony. He had long legs and was always good at climbing. When he was about ten he had a good hiding off his father for going up the one in the field behind the farm, almost right to the top. He wasn't afraid. He never seemed to be afraid of anything, Tony said, so it came as no surprise at all how he went.

Was that part of his world of the dead? Climbing to another level of – what? But that whole area was an electric valley. Always part of his world. Who knew what connections he might have made?

Merrily read the last sheet again.

I have never had any kind of experience in this house so I must assume that when Roddy went from here it all stopped. Well, it stopped here anyway, and that was all that mattered to Tony, I am afraid to say. Head in the sand until it's too late! Isn't it always the case? I'm telling you all this, Mrs Watkins, and I haven't told anybody else and I hope that as a Church minister you will respect this. None of us could possibly have known, could we, what was going on inside him. We couldn't. Tony says that if we could just get him buried and do our duty by his father then we can try and settle down but I don't know. I think Tony is getting very depressed about it and I think sometimes that it would be the best thing for everyone if we were to sell up and move from here. But we can't do that yet because who would want to buy a farm where a mass murderer was raised?

Sophie came back with the teapot and went to the window. 'Fog's clearing.'

'Glad you think so,' Merrily said.

30

Light and Sparks

Before Jane was even across the square, she knew precisely how she was going to play it: deceit against deceit. Lies, illusion . . . *front*.

Despite the fog, the square was collecting its nightly quota of upmarket 4X4s: well-off couples coming in to dine – on a Monday night, for heaven's sake – at the Black Swan and the restaurant that used to be Cassidy's Country Kitchen. The Monday diners were mostly the youthfully retired with up to half a century to kill before death. The Swan, mistily lit up, had become more like a bistro than a village pub and pretty soon Ledwardine would be more like a theme park than a village, with its shops full of repro, its resident celebs – and, of course, its state-of-the-art, postmodern, designer vicar with the sexy sideline in soul-retrieval. *Poor as a church mouse, but you wouldn't kick her out of* your *vestry, haw, haw.*

Unfair. *Bitch.* Jane straightened her back and siphoned in a slow breath. You had to channel your anger or it would all come back at you; she'd learned that much, at least, from her New Age years.

The lights of the Swan dimmed behind her in what remained of the fog, as the pub's façade sobered up into a couple of timber-framed terraced houses. Then there was an alleyway with a wrought-iron lantern over it, which looked pretty old but probably wasn't. It was unlit. On the other side of it – narrow and bent, with one gable leaning outwards like a man in a pointed hat inspecting his shoes – was Chapel House.

The house was the real thing. As for its owner . . . *Hello, I'm Jenny Driscoll and this afternoon I'll be looking at ways you can turn your living room into a true sanctuary . . . a place where you*

*can really be yourself . . . and yet also be taken out of yourself.
What do I mean? Let's go inside and find out . . .*

Yeah, right, let's do that.

Three steps led from the pavement up to the front door. Jane
stood at the bottom, clutching the cold handrail. It was quite
dark here, away from the fake gaslamps on the square. There
was a glow in one of the downstairs windows but the bottom
of the window was too far above the road for her to tell where
the light was coming from or if there was anyone in that room.

Cold feet, now, of course. Something like this was always 'the
obvious thing to do' until it actually came to it. Like, would she
even *be* here if Eirion had left his phone switched on, if he'd
answered it? If it hadn't been *over*.

Well, probably not. But that was not what had happened and
this, in the event, was where the obvious path had led. Probably,
it was meant. A confrontation waiting to happen.

Jane paused, with a hand on the knocker. All right. Stop.
Consider. This was her last chance to backtrack home and think
this through properly, for it might not, in fact, be such a good
idea. And if it failed, and the Driscoll woman hung the whole
thing on Mum, it could get seriously dicey – believe it.

Clear footsteps behind the door, then. Oh God, she'd been
seen from inside. So much for the element of surprise. Jane
swallowed fog, coughed. *Mrs Box, look, I hope you don't mind
me just arriving like this, but I'd really like to talk to you about
angels. We might be able to help each other.*

Aw, she could wing this. As it were. She unzipped her fleece
halfway, thinking of Jenny Driscoll at seventeen: *Terrible clothes,
terrible music. And this element of sadomasochism.* Thank you,
Irene. Goodnight.

Oh, shit, run!

Too late. None of the tugging and creaking you got at home;
the door opened like it was greased. But not to reveal Jenny
Box. A man stood there.

There was a hum in the studio, and Prof Levin was trying to
track it down, lying underneath the mixing board, scrabbling

about. Concerned about all the electricity under there, Lol offered to switch off at the master.

Prof's howl came out boxy. 'You crazy? How would I find it then? Why don't you take a walk, Laurence? I can't concentrate.'

Lol said thoughtfully, 'Prof, you've spent whole decades in this kind of atmosphere. Has it . . . you know, affected you at all?'

'Huh?'

'All the electricity.'

Prof's bald head came up, glowing with sweat. 'It's an electric world. What's your problem?'

'Just, is there too much of it? Are we killing ourselves?'

'Nah,' Prof said scornfully. 'Our bodies adjust. One day we'll become electric beings. Just light and sparks.' He crawled out from under the mixing board. 'This is about the mad guy wanted you to do his song, right? Moira told me. The guy who now wants urgently to meet the Reverend to discuss who-knows-what.'

Lol had driven up to Ledbury to collect supplies from Tesco and got back to find Merrily had left a message with Prof: she'd tried to see Sam Hall but he wasn't there. She'd call Lol here again, early this evening. She hadn't. *He*'d called: answering machine. Then Gomer had called, asking if he was free tomorrow.

Prof stood up and laid his electrical screwdriver on the board. 'You ever know Mephisto Jones?'

'Mephisto Jones, the session guitarist?'

'No, Mephisto Jones, the road sweeper, Mephisto Jones, the systems analyst. Jesus.'

'He doesn't seem to have been around for a while.'

'Plays acoustic now. That's all he plays. Acoustic.'

'Well,' Lol said, 'if he's happy . . .'

'Happy? He's fucking wrecked! Case, I suspect, of what your man's talking about. Mephisto takes his headaches to the doctor, is referred to a neurologist. The neurologist invites him to have a brain scan. Mephisto says, "What, you wanna kill me now?" Brain scan – that's how much they know about it, these neurologists. A brain scan involves the use of a massive electro-magnetic field.'

'Mephisto Jones was damaged by electricity? I always thought it was the drink.'

'Drink would've been easier. And when *I* say that . . . No, this came out of nowhere, out of the ether. Headaches, weakness, pain in the joints, fingers swollen. Started with he couldn't work in the studio, so he'd go home, lie on the sofa with a bottle of Jameson's and the TV on. And feel even worse. It was a while before he put it all together that this was the TV, not the drink. By then, he couldn't even listen to a Walkman. Mobile phones . . . goes without saying. He told me he felt so ill some nights, he couldn't stay in the house, so he used to go and sit in the car – in the cold, because if he switched on the engine to power the heater . . .'

'He became *allergic* to electricity?'

Prof tilted his hands. 'Some people it just happens to. Like anything else, some people are more sensitive to it than others. Most doctors still don't even accept it as a valid condition. Most doctors are arseholes: give you a choice of nerve tablets . . . red ones or blue ones. In the end, Mephisto found this international support group for electro-allergics or whatever the hell it is they're called.'

'So where is he now?'

'Somewhere in Ireland, with no power to speak of and a bunch of acoustic guitars. Living on old royalties and looking fearfully out the window in case someone should decide to drag his valley into the last century. They'd have a lot to talk about, Mephisto Jones and your madman. If Mephisto's in a mood to answer the phone.' Prof picked up his screwdriver. 'Not a mobile, needless to say. Now will you leave me to my wires?'

'That's very interesting. Thank you, Prof.'

But Prof had already vanished, like a badger into its set. Lol went through to the kitchen and out through the stable door, trying to think what use a priest might be in this kind of situation.

Tendrils of fog were still ghosting the trees along the banks of the hidden River Frome, but the rooftops were clear. It was cold out here, colder than he'd expected. Presently, his own song came drifting out, as Prof tested the system. These Burt Bacharach kind of chords he couldn't put names to, sounding better with distance.

> *'Remember this one? The day is dwindling*
> *Down in Badger's Wood, collecting kindling*
> *Smudgy eyes, moonrise . . .*
> *Golden.'*

Warm images. The toes curling by the electric fire.

The rather loathsome curling sensation in Moira's gut. This bothered him. He'd heard too many shivery stories about Moira's premonitions.

In fact, Lol shivered and was about to go back into the kitchen, out of the cold, when headlights lit the bushes along the track from the road.

The car came very slowly, mud sucking at its tyres, as the song went into its second short verse. At the end of it, streaked with cello, the chord change registered as bitter and paranoid in the dense air.

> *'The camera lies*
> *She might vaporize . . .'*

The headlights splashed Lol's eyes. The car stopped, the lights went down. He heard the driver's door opening, feet on gravel, and then the door closing very lightly and carefully to make the most minimal of clinks. A visitor sensitive to studio hours.

Lol walked out and saw that it was young Eirion, on his own.

On the drive home, the fog was patchy. The road would be clear for up to a mile and then a sepia canopy would fall silently around the Volvo's windows, muffling. Inside the car, a grey passenger was nestling beside Merrily all the way from Hereford to Ledwardine: anxiety.

Dead people. We're talking about dead people.

For much of his life, Roddy Lodge seemed to have found solace in the dead, and now he was among them. Gone. Nobody could be damaged by him any more. Except, perhaps, his family.

And the community? Really?

On the way out, Sophie had regretfully handed her another e-mail, received by the Bishop's office late this afternoon from the secretary of the Underhowle/Ariconium Development Committee asking for a meeting with Mrs Watkins. She could hardly say no.

But the anxiety came from something more amorphous. She was starting to feel spiritually darkened by the shadow thrown by Roddy Lodge and its merger with the even more monstrous shade of Fred West, a connection now strengthened by Huw Owen.

Skirting the square, slowing at the entrance to the churchyard, Merrily could see a light in the vicarage through the trees.

And then, to one side, another light – a tiny one, ruby splinters under the lych-gate. A light she knew of old – its level above the ground, the speed it moved, like the landing light on a small boat: Gomer Parry following his ciggy to Minnie's grave.

Merrily braked hard. *Right*.

Pulling the car half under the lych-gate and sliding out. The cold was a shock, made her gasp. She left the car door hanging open and ran through the gate into the churchyard, spotting Gomer where the path forked by the first apple trees. He didn't turn round. He knew who this was, was mumbling his response before she caught up with him.

' . . . En't your problem, vicar.'

How many times had he said that to her? She moved alongside him, walking on the wet and freezing grass. 'Cold and nasty night, Gomer. Catch your death.'

'That time o' year, ennit.'

It was like she was interrupting some interior dialogue. The way Lol had described him on their night ride back from Under-howle. Like he *wanted* to catch his death.

'Listen,' she said, 'I'm going home to cook something for Jane and me. It'll be pretty basic, but we'll be most insulted if you don't join us.'

'Vicar, this en't an issue you can sort out.' Gomer kept on walking, the give-away ciggy cupped in his hand.

'All right.' She moved in front of him, crooked old grave-stones, damp and shiny, on either side. 'Who told you?'

'Ar?'

'About me conducting the funeral at Underhowle. For Roddy Lodge.'

She felt his attention hardening, as if he was only now becoming fully aware of her presence. It was almost as if she could see his glasses lighting up.

'*You*'re plantin' Lodge?'

The night air around them was unexpectedly pale, as though the village lights had soaked into the fog and been carried out here. Branches of the old apple trees poked out like arthritic hands.

Bugger. He hadn't known, then.

'*You*'re doing Lodge's funeral?'

'Must seem like a betrayal to you.'

Gomer laughed, without much humour. 'Can't none of us get away from it, can we?'

'That's how it seems.'

'Like it was bloody well meant.'

'Sorry?'

'Ar,' he said. 'You and me both, vicar.'

She didn't understand, pushed both hands far into the corners of the pockets of Jane's duffel.

'Think we got it all worked out, see,' Gomer turned and started walking back between the graves towards the lych-gate. 'Feelings get the better of you, ennit? Go shootin' your ole mouth off, 'fore you knows . . .'

Merrily followed him, saying nothing, new frost crackling under her shoes.

'Had to fix up Nev's funeral, see,' Gomer said. 'That's why I en't been around much.'

'Is everything . . . OK?'

'Rector of Presteigne's got it in hand. We'll likely have Nev's . . . Nev back next week. Anyway, been talkin' to other folk, while I was over there. Folk like Cliff Morgan.'

'The police sergeant?'

'Told me what I already knowed, vicar.'

'They've finally linked him to the fire? Lodge?'

There was the sound of a woman's laughter from the square: people entering the Black Swan. Gomer stopped under the lych-gate.

'Nev started the fire.' He stared out towards the square. 'Accident, like they thought. Found bits of an ole Primus stove. Boy was likely frying bloody sausages, pissed out of his head. Always used to say he didn't like eating at home n'more. So that's it. Lodge is in the clear – for what it's worth to him now.'

'When did you learn all this?'

Gomer looked down at the cobbles. ''Bout five seconds before the bugger went up the pylon, if you want the truth.'

'*What?*'

He sighed. 'En't got much of an appetite these days, vicar, but I wouldn't mind a cup o' tea.'

Lol cleared a space in the clutter of the kitchen area and gave Eirion a cappuccino from Prof's machine. Eirion was looking upset – shoulders hunched, eyes downcast: the demeanour of the dumped.

'I didn't know where else to come. You know what she's like – this . . . loose cannon.' Gone eight p.m., and he was still wearing his school uniform.

'You've got to drive back to Abergavenny tonight in this fog?'

'It's clearing. And they know where I am. You don't mind, do you, Lol? I just—'

'Eirion, look . . .' Lol climbed onto a stool at the breakfast bar, which was still made up mainly of old packing cases. 'Look, maybe the main problem is that the last thing she ever wants to think is that she's at all like her mum, you know?'

Eirion smiled faintly. 'A religious maniac?'

'Bad enough if your dad's a vicar. But your mother? So . . . What's she going to do by way of rebellion? Obvious. She's going to be a practising pagan, secretly joining a women's mystical group meeting over a health-food café in Hereford, Next thing, she's out in the vicarage garden bonding with the full moon.'

Eirion smiled.

'And then suddenly Merrily's realizing – as if she didn't really already know – that not all pagans are sacrificing animals and deflowering virgins on the altar. She's even made friends with a *witch*, for heaven's sake. And so from Jane's point of view, some of that essential inter-generational friction that you need, as a teenager, to grow up with a positive sense of yourself is not there any more. Her mum's no longer shocked and appalled.' Lol spread his hands, the way Prof would do. 'Too easy, this stuff. I should've stuck with the psychology course.'

Eirion grinned.

'So which way does she go next?' Lol said. 'Satanism?'

'You're right,' Eirion said. 'It's denial, isn't it? It's not real atheism at all. It's just spiritual denial.'

'See? You don't need me at all.'

Eirion gratefully drank some coffee.

'What you've got,' Lol said, 'is a reluctant – and therefore unhappy – atheist. We're oversimplifying here, because she's still towing a lot of emotional luggage, including her dad, all of that. And, like you say, bad things happening to people close to her – like Gomer – giving her ammunition to use against Merrily's faith. Lots of triggers.'

'Including me, I expect.' Eirion looked up, slightly red. 'It's pretty clear I've been a serious disappointment in . . . certain areas. Implying I'd been putting it about a lot, with the band and everything, the way you do. I'm probably totally crap in bed and she's thinking, Christ, is this *it*?'

Lol tried not to smile. 'Often it's the ones who *don't* think they're crap that . . .' There was history he could have gone into, but the boy needed to get home tonight.

'And then there's this Jenny Driscoll situation,' Eirion said. 'The woman behind the Vestalia stores? Jenny Driscoll's discovering Christianity and she's supposed to have seen an angel over Ledwardine Church. And Jane's seriously contemptuous of her and all she stands for. Of course, she'd've given *anything* to have had that kind of experience herself . . . So a lot of resentment, lot of anger. Inflamed by all this about her mum not having a normal life – giving everything up for God. Who doesn't exist anyway, and if he does he's a complete shit. You know?'

Lol leaned on his elbows on the breakfast bar. 'She was laying all this on you, day after day?'

'I wouldn't mind that if I thought there was anything I could do.' Eirion looked at Lol, then looked away.

'But you think there's something *I* can do.'

'Well, it's just that Jane thinks you're . . . I'm sorry, Lol . . . she thinks you and Moira . . .' Eirion hesitated, biting his lower lip. 'Are perhaps having sex,' he said mournfully. 'Together. Like musicians do. With the erotic charge of playing together.'

Lol sprang off the stool.

'Not that she's *blaming* you. She blames her mother, for neglecting the relationship. Putting God first, as usual, when God's only going to stab her in the back, if He exists, because He's a shit, right?'

'She said any of this to Merrily?'

'I don't know. She was so happy about you and her mother finally getting together. She thought *she*'d brought you together. I mean, it's obvious she really loves her mum, despite all the rows they have. Maybe the only person she does truly love. I mean I . . . I was thinking, isn't it just maybe a lot more simple to think that maybe she's found somebody else?' Eirion shook his head. 'Look at me – you'd think we were married or something, wouldn't you? I mean, there's bound to be someone else at some point, isn't there? It's what happens. Childhood sweethearts, twin souls – that's pathetic, isn't it?'

'Eirion . . .' Jesus, Jane thought Lol and Moira Cairns were having sex. 'Would it be OK if I talked to Merrily about this?'

'Well, I would hate it if she thought I was hoping she'd, you know, intercede on my behalf, but . . .' Eirion sat there, wearing his school uniform, his puppy fat, his dismal expression. 'It's just that Jane . . . Suddenly all she sees is darkness, doom, nothing amazing out there any more. Mrs Watkins has been a bit busy lately. Maybe she hasn't noticed how bad it's been getting.'

'Look, I'm helping Gomer again tomorrow,' Lol said. 'Maybe I can call in the vicarage.'

'I'm really sorry.' Eirion pushed fingers through his hair and stood up. 'Lol . . . look, man, I might be overreacting, all right?'

Lol looked at him, shaking his head. 'This is *Jane*, Eirion.'

'Yes,' Eirion agreed miserably.

The man had said, 'She can't be long, I suppose. Do you want to come in and wait?' And at first Jane had been completely wrong-footed; this was hardly the kind of issue she could raise in front of both of them together, especially if their marriage was more or less on the rocks. And then she'd thought, *On the other hand* . . .

And had felt suddenly clever and strong, in a thinking-on-your-feet kind of way. In a *let's use this situation* kind of way.

'Yeah, OK,' Jane had said coolly. 'I suppose I could hang on for a few minutes.' Following him into the dark-panelled hall and then into . . . wow . . .

'I feel quite embarrassed about bringing anyone in here,' he'd murmured. 'I'm afraid my wife's tastes have become a little minimalist.'

Minimalist. At once, Jane had liked the way he didn't talk down to her. Then she learned that this was how he was: serious, saying what he meant.

Just two areas of light: the smoky greenish night in leaded windows and the glowing, crumbly fire built on the hearth – just enough to bring out this oaky feeling of age and strength. No TV or stereo on view, or anything modern or new; and the room was heavy with the oldest aroma in Herefordshire, the rich, sweet scent of apple wood.

In fact, she ought to be in two minds about all this really because, although it felt like the old Ledwardine, this was actually the *new* Ledwardine. Most ordinary people didn't have the money for this sympathetic, sparing kind of conservation; they just lived *around* the past, with exposed wires along the beams and a Parkray in the inglenook.

Still, Jane had felt immediately at home. Enclosed. He'd taken her fleece to hang up. 'Sorry about the temperature, but my wife absolutely refuses to have central heating in here. It would damage what she calls the monastic purity.'

'It's fine. It's quite warm.'

'It's not *terribly* fine when you have to keep the damn fire going all the time,' Gareth Box had said, sounding tired at the very thought of it, but with this sort of attractive ashiness in his voice. 'When I'm here, I tend to build it up and keep it in all night, which I suppose is wasteful nowadays.'

'Maybe "nowadays" isn't what this house is about,' Jane said smoothly. 'You have to give it what it needs.'

'Really.'

'I suppose you don't get to spend as much time here as you'd like.'

'I think I probably do,' he said, 'actually. This is my wife's house. She chose it, restored it. With her instinctive taste.'

Yes, Jane thought now, observing him over her glass, *she at least has taste. Nothing minimalist about* you, *Mr Box*.

The two Tudor-looking chairs were facing one another, either side of the fire, and were actually more comfortable than they looked, and when you sat down you felt kind of *transported back*. Especially with a glass of wine in your hand – red, full-bodied, naturally.

And especially when you were served by Gareth Box because – call this corny but, with his collarless white shirt and black jeans, his longish hair and his heavy, wide moustache – there really was something of the cavalier about him. Sitting down opposite Jane, pouring himself a glass of this serious wine and standing the bottle on the fairly rudimentary oak table by the side of his chair, he looked far more suited to this house than the insubstantial Jenny Driscoll ever could.

A weary cavalier, though, perhaps depleted by civil war.

'I'm sorry.' He held an arm towards the fire to see his watch; there was no clock in the room. 'She really should've been back by now. Seems to have very little awareness of the passage of time these days.'

Jane felt his gaze on her, like a touch.

'Look . . . Jane . . . There isn't anything *I* can help you with, is there? I feel awful now, wasting your time.'

Wasting my *time? Oh, I really don't think so.*

31

Good Worker

Gomer finally took off his cap and sat down at the refectory table. He seemed to have lost weight, the way he had just after Minnie died. His glasses were dulled.

Merrily glanced into the scullery, with Ethel floating around her shins. No sign of Jane anywhere. 'Gone up to her apartment, I expect. Can I at least do you some toast?'

'Tea'll be fine, vicar.'

'See how you feel afterwards.' She moved around switching lamps on, then went to put the kettle on, quite glad that the kid wasn't around. She didn't want Gomer inhibited.

'Oughter've told the cops straight away. But he was already mad as hell at me, that boy. And it was all confused, some folk near-hysterical. Bloody pandemonium.'

'I can imagine.'

As soon as they'd left the church grounds, he'd emptied it all out for her, no flam, no excuses. He'd been mad as hell that night, see – likely with himself. Couldn't hold himself back, even in public.

She remembered the location, under the pylon, could conjure the scene from what Lol had told her: the cops trying to conceal their panic at having lost a murderer. Local people all over the place, smudging the picture as Roddy Lodge went weaving between the flashlight beams, fast and lithe on his own territory, used to moving by night, covering a lot of ground very quickly. Easily avoiding the police, because they'd be watching all the possible exits, certainly not the pylon at the far end, fully enclosed and no way out but up.

Only Gomer, who was outside the action, having left Lol to do the spadework, had seen him go. Catching up with his enemy at the foot of the pylon. Seizing his chance, keeping his voice low.

'*You told 'em yet, boy?*'

'*You mad ole fuck!*' Gomer asking the vicar to pardon his French, but that was what Lodge had called him: *Mad ole fuck.*

At the time, he'd been edging Lodge back towards the giant girdery legs of the pylon, telling him, '*You're goin' down anyway. Why'n't you just tell 'em the bloody truth 'bout what you done to my depot? What you done to Nev. Tell the truth, boy, just once in your nasty, lyin', cheatin' little bloody life.*'

Lodge's eyes swivelling all over the place, Lodge in his bright orange overalls. But it was dark here, no coppers anywhere near, just Gomer standing his ground.

'*Fuckin' kill you, ole man, you don't get out my way.*'

Gomer not moving. Merrily could imagine all the scattered lights in the field gathering in his glasses as he raised himself up to his full five feet four, glaring up into Lodge's concave face.

'*Oh aye? What you gonner kill me with? Got a can o' petrol on you, is it, sonny?*'

Half a second for it to get through, and then Lodge had come for him, come at Gomer, rage going through his whole body – you could feel the electricity of it, Gomer would swear. And in the shock of it he'd backed away, giving just enough ground for Lodge to straighten out an arm, his open hand going flat into Gomer's face, ramming the glasses tight into Gomer's eyes, into his nose. And then Lodge had hissed out the typically crowing, boastful sentences that proved he'd had nothing whatsoever to do with the death of Nevin Parry.

'*'Course I done it, you ole fuck. Been over to fuckin' Ledwardine loads o' times, look. Got clients all over that village – rich bastards. Hadn't planned to torch your place, but I'd got a coupler minutes spare that night.*'

Then a final contemptuous push, leaving Gomer on his back in the mud, and then Lodge was off and away – up the pylon, though Gomer didn't know that at the time, as he heaved himself to his feet, straightening his specs, winded, unsteady. But perhaps it had been his brain that was most battered, by what he'd heard.

No wonder he'd been so quiet for days, hanging round Minnie's grave.

Merrily put the kettle on the stove and came to sit down opposite him. She was remembering Lol's graphic description of the exchange between Roddy Lodge up in the pylon and Gomer on the ground – Lol recalling Gomer's opening challenge as completely as if it was the first line of one of his own songs.

Where was it you set that fire, boy? Where'd you go? Where was it you went Monday night?

'You just couldn't believe it, could you?' she said.

'Couldn't be sure I'd yeard it right,' Gomer said. 'Well, I *was* sure, see, but then I'm thinking mabbe he was – 'scuse me, vicar – pissing up my leg, so to speak.'

'I don't think he was ever that clever, do you?'

No. Lodge had surmised that, because Gomer lived in Ledwardine, that was also where his depot was. Aggressively admitting to something he hadn't done just to get the little guy out of his way, and simultaneously proving his innocence. And how had Gomer reacted? He'd straightened his glasses and gone to the pylon to seek confirmation.

'You were trying to get him to say it again, just to be sure, in your own mind. Or maybe to catch him out.'

'Ar.' Gomer took off his glasses, rubbed them on his sleeve. 'Silly bugger. Gutted, see. How could I get it that wrong? Ever since, been asking meself, asking Min at the grave if it was me killed him. Hounded an innocent man to his death.'

'Well: A – *you* didn't force him up the pylon, and B – he *wasn't* innocent at all, was he?'

'Innocent till proved guilty.' Gomer rammed both hands through his wild, white hair. '*Rock-solid sure*, I was, that he'd started that fire.'

'Which he admitted again on the pylon.'

'Ar, along with how he was gonner do . . . wossername?'

'Madonna. I know. Who doesn't even live in the area.'

'Load of ole wallop! All bloody lies. Couldn't trust a thing he said. He was in Ross that night, from early on – Cliff Morgan told me that. They got witnesses seen him in two pubs in Ross.'

'But think about it this way . . . If you hadn't had good reason to suspect Lodge, we'd never have gone over there and found what we found, and Lynsey Davies would've been quietly reburied somewhere more discreet. God moves in myst—'

'I *tried* to tell him. Tried to tell that boy, Bliss, when he's draggin' me away.'

'Perhaps that wasn't really the best time, Gomer.'

'Still oughter've told him afterwards, though, ennit? Likely they'd have talked him down off there, see, if I hadn't been standing at the bottom givin' the bugger stick. Worst of it is, they en't never gonner know the full truth now, is it? *Never.*' He looked across at Merrily, then lowered his gaze. 'And now I've dumped it all on you, vicar. Didn't wanner do that.'

Merrily patted his hand. 'It's what I'm here for, as we vicars like to say.'

'You gonner tell him?' He looked apprehensive, but she knew that whatever she wanted he'd go with it; he nearly always did – a channel for God's opinion, wasn't she? Which made offering Gomer advice so much more of a responsibility.

'I don't somehow think it's going to arise. You . . . haven't heard from him again, have you? In connection with more digging?'

Gomer shook his head. No time for that in the last couple of days, anyway. He'd been tidying up a few small jobs, things he could do without hauling young Lol out. Need the boy tomorrow, mind, to install a new tank for Mrs Pawson, now the cops had finished messing up her garden. Her'd been in London, and who could blame her, with no working drainage and knowing what had lain underneath the Efflapure?

The two phones began to ring simultaneously, in the kitchen and the scullery. When the answering machine kicked in, the message was fully audible through the open scullery door.

'Merrily, I need to talk to you . . . *urgently*, so call me soon as you get back, eh? Or if you're there now, will you *please* pick up the phone?'

'Oh God,' she said. 'Coincidences, eh? Give me a minute, Gomer.'

*

'Jesus, Merrily, you took your flaming time.'

'God's work, Francis.'

'Yeh, listen, I'll keep it short. The shit's just hit the fan. One of the people Andy Mumford spoke to in Much Marcle – on my behalf, on the subject of our late friend West – decided there could be a few quid in it and phoned some bloody hack.'

'Oh *no* . . .'

'Who of course gets onto our press lady at Hereford for an official quote. And the upshot is, to head off any really *wild* speculation, Fleming's been forced to put out a statement on the West angle. And he's fuming, naturally. And Andy's on the carpet. And I'm lying *very* low. So if anybody contacts you, you haven't spoken to me in yonks.'

'Why should anyone phone me?'

'You didn't see the local TV news? They had this story about the Rector of Underhowle backing out of Roddy's funeral due to protests by people who don't want him lying shoulder to shoulder with their God-fearing ancestors. Then it was mentioned that you'd be standing in.'

'I was *named*?'

'I'm afraid so, Merrily. So if you're talking to anybody there, or here or anywhere, I did *not* take you into Roddy's lair, you know *nothing* about any pictures on walls, et cetera, et cetera.'

'You're saying you want me to lie for you?'

'If you would, please,' Bliss said. 'Er, you got the package?'

'Yes, thanks very much. It'll make a change from the Bible.'

'Seriously,' Bliss said, 'I should give them a glance. There *is* a connection with West, gorra be. Huw Owen knows that, as you—'

'*What?*'

'Sorry, Merrily?'

'Right, let's sort this. Why did you *really* phone Huw Owen? And how does Huw Owen *know* there's a connection between Roddy Lodge and Fred West?'

'Well, he doesn't *know*,' Bliss said awkwardly. 'I mean, none of us *know*.'

'It's all right,' Merrily said tightly. 'I'll ask him myself.'

*

'Fred bloody West,' Gomer said. 'Now why don't that surprise me?'

Merrily had left the scullery door open; he could hardly have avoided overhearing. Hardly mattered now, if it was all coming out in the press.

She sat down. 'You remember the case you found for them, behind the bungalow? It contained a pile of press cuttings on the West case. Things like that.'

'Always givin' you all this ole wallop 'bout what he done and who he done it with,' Gomer mused. 'Showin' you photos of his missus's . . . of his missus.' He looked beyond Merrily towards the dark window in the back wall. 'Just the same as Lodge – lies, lies and more bloody lies. You never thought much of it, see . . . and then the truth turns out to be . . . a sight worse. Sight more worse than you could ever imagine anybody *could* be. Least of all some cocky little builder, love nest in the back of his bloody van . . . always showing you photos.'

Gomer took out his ciggy tin and extracted one he'd rolled earlier. Merrily stared at him.

'You *knew* West?'

Gomer wrinkled his nose in distaste. 'Wouldn't say I *knowed* him, thank the Lord – though you might've thought you did after 'bout half an hour, the way he went on. Givin' it *that*' – making rabbiting motions with fingers and thumb – 'the whole time. Bugger could've yattered for Hereford. 'Bout . . . private things, mostly, and you can only take so much of that kind o' chat.' He lit his ciggy. 'Good worker, mind, couldn't fault him on that. Always looked after his tools.'

'You said photos?'

'Ones I saw was just pictures of his wife with no clothes on. But this feller I worked with once said West'd offered him, you know, bit of a session with the missus. Free, like.'

'I've heard that.'

'And later they reckoned there was these video tapes doing the rounds. Never come across 'em meself, mind.'

'Porno videos?'

'Worse.' Gomer looked down at the table.

'How do you mean?'

'Ar, well . . .' Gomer coughed.

'Oh God,' Merrily said.

Quite when it became clear that Gareth Box was actually interested in Jane *as a woman*, she was not sure, but it must have been fairly soon after he first called her 'Jane', as if he really knew her. As if they'd known one another quite some time.

She supposed at first that it was simply a journalist's thing, assuming this easy familiarity – although he hadn't been an actual reporter for a long time, she guessed. If Eirion had got it right, he'd already become some sort of executive editor when he'd met Jenny Driscoll.

It was just the way he said 'Jane'. Hearing her name in his deep, world-weary voice. There was a kind of *charge* under it. Also an intensity in the way he looked at her. He was a very intense person.

And that *wasn't* stupid. And she'd only had one glass of wine. Well, OK, he'd topped it up, so say two, but definitely not much more than that; it wasn't as if she'd been here very long. And anyway Jane could usually hold her drink, no problem, except for cider. Just have to be a bit careful she didn't say too much, too soon.

'My, er, my . . . ex-boyfriend . . . wants to be a journalist.'

'Could do worse,' Gareth said. 'Opens lots of doors.'

'Well, at your level, I suppose. Not round here.'

He shrugged. 'I started not all that far from here, actually. Worked for a news agency. It doesn't matter where you start, if you're good enough, if you can spot opportunities.'

'Yeah.' She supposed Jenny Box must have seemed like a good one at the time, if you could put up with her obsessive behaviour. 'Er, you haven't actually met my mother, have you?'

Gareth Box sighed. 'I certainly *feel* as though I have. My wife talks about your mother quite a lot.' The way he kept saying *my wife*, Jane thought, conveyed a definite detachment. 'I tend to hear about all her problems, though it's hardly *my* business.' He smiled wryly. 'How *are* things between her and . . . er . . . ?'

'Lol.'

'Yes, of course.'

'Oh, well . . .' Wow, the old girl really *was* getting in with Jenny Box. 'Complicated, you know, unsatisfactory. But like . . . what's new?'

And he poured her a bit more wine and they chatted about Lol for a while, and a few other things. He was very easy to talk to. He concentrated on what you were saying, made meaningful observations, seemed concerned, treated you like a person, a woman. Yes, that was the point: from the first, he'd treated her like an equal. Only Lol had ever really done this before. Even with Gomer, who was never patronizing, it was still always 'young Jane'. So this felt good, she wouldn't deny that.

'So like . . . how do you feel about the angel thing?'

A pause. 'More to the point –' he leaned back in his chair, tossing one long leg across the other, tilting it so that an ankle lay easily on a thigh '– how do *you* feel about it, Jane?'

'Well, I . . .' Jane drew breath and went for it. 'Frankly, I'm inclined to think it's kind of bollocks.'

Gareth didn't laugh. He just nodded, a lock of dark hair falling over his forehead. Jane felt obliged to qualify *bollocks* immediately and talked about angels and the kind of people who professed to see them. Talking too fast, maybe. He didn't interrupt. She felt hot now, edged her chair away from the fire.

'I mean, there's a history of sightings like this, in certain places, mainly abroad – although most of them sound like mass hallucination. But obviously there's no history of it here . . . not over Ledwardine Church.' She forced a laugh. 'The problem is, the business my mother's in, you can't just knock something like that on the head. Not easily, can you?'

'No,' he said. 'I imagine not.'

'And it's hard for her, you know?'

Gareth Box nodded. 'So *you* thought you'd come over and . . . knock it on the head.'

She squirmed a little. 'I just wanted to know what was really happening . . . what's really behind it.' Best not to mention the money at this stage. 'I don't like to see her getting taken for a ride.'

He was silent. *Shit, I've gone too far.*

A log collapsed in the hearth. Jane jumped. Gareth Box didn't move.

'I'm sorry,' she said. 'I don't mean to be offensive or anything.'

He met her gaze, although his own eyes were just shadows. Kept on looking at her steadily, as though he was trying to make up his mind about her. Intense. A little shiver went up her spine. Deliciously.

Then he said, very quietly, 'What if I was to tell you – in absolute confidence – that she's done this kind of thing before?'

She jumped again. *Oh my God.* Didn't know what to say.

'Look,' he said, 'all this is pretty painful for me, as you can imagine. No man likes to think his wife's . . .' He looked away. 'How old are you, Jane?'

'Old enough.'

He smiled. 'I wouldn't doubt it. Jane, can I rely on your absolute discretion?'

'Yes . . . absolutely.' She was aware that her voice had shrunk. She found she'd come to the edge of the chair. She saw that two logs had enmeshed, forming a red, ashy heart. The applewood scent filled her head.

'This is a village.' Gareth Box uncrossed his legs and sat forward with his hands pressed together between his knees, which seemed uncharacteristically hunched and defensive. 'Whatever's happening needs to be handled with a certain tact.'

'I'm used to that,' Jane said. 'It goes with the territory.'

He nodded. 'Look, I don't know very much about your mother . . . but I think we both have to accept that, in Jenny's eyes, there's only one angel in Ledwardine.'

The log fell apart.

Christ.

Standing under the porch light, Merrily watched Gomer walking away down the drive, feeling relieved when he turned right at the bottom, heading towards his home and not the churchyard, not Minnie's grave.

What a small county this was. Gomer had met Fred West when they were both involved in the renovation of some farm buildings at a small equestrian centre near Ross. Gomer and Nev had been putting in drainage, and Fred had been rebuilding walls and installing the electrics. His van seemed to have been furnished in the back for sex, which he talked about all the time. For all these women he seemed to run into who were begging for it.

Merrily had asked Gomer if West might have had any contact, in the course of his work, with Roddy Lodge. Gomer, who knew a lot of people in the service industries, had said he couldn't be sure about Lodge but more men – and women, of course – had been associated with West than were ever likely to admit it.

Merrily closed the front door, locked it and barred it top and bottom.

She went to the bottom of the stairs. '*Flower!*'

No reply. It was after nine-thirty now; the kid had probably made herself something to eat earlier, although there were no signs of it in the kitchen. Merrily switched on the grill to warm it up, just in case. Then she went into the scullery, sat down with a sigh and the first of the three books about the West case. On the back it said,

How and why an evil psychopath was able to ensnare so many in a web of unseeing complicity.

Horrific, but there was no avoiding it any longer. Perhaps she should know. Everybody else in the county seemed to. It was part of the underside of Hereford history. Fred West still crouched like a spider in a corner of so many lives.

Even Gomer's.

The videos he'd mentioned – the ones he'd only heard of, after the West murders had become public knowledge – were snuff videos. It was said that Fred had rigged up cameras and shot videos of himself doing what he'd done to girls and young women.

Gomer had wondered if maybe Roddy Lodge had somehow got hold of a copy.

The phone rang. Merrily looked at it, didn't feel like speaking to anyone else tonight and let it go on ringing until the machine picked it up.

This is Ledwardine Vicarage. Sorry we're not around, but please leave a message after the bleep.

Bleep.

Then, '*Bitch!*'

Merrily put the book down.

It was muffled – one of those tissues-over-the-phone voices. '*Bitch, if you do that funeral on Friday, you're gonna regret it. You stay at home on Friday, you understand? You bitch.*'

Jane let herself in very quietly by the side door and padded up the stairs to the attic, collapsing on her bed under the Mondrian walls.

This was killing her, and there was nobody to ring. Nobody at all.

She lay there, numbed by this shattering hyper-awareness, listening to parts of the past clunking into place like the pieces of one of those really obvious wooden jigsaws aimed at very small children.

Or the ratchets on some crude medieval engine of torture, squeezing your brain.

Dad.

Poor dead Dad. *Why exactly* did he go off with Karen, his secretary with whom he'd died in a ball of blazing metal on the M5? Jane remembered seeing Karen a couple of times in Dad's office, and she wasn't exactly to die for, was she? Maybe a bit younger than Mum but not as pretty. So what exactly was there *missing* from his marriage that drove Dad into Karen's arms, Karen's bed?

And why had Mum, instead of working to save her marriage, thrown herself into the arms of 'God'?

Consider: it was a known fact that a huge percentage of male clergy were gay. OK, so maybe no figures had emerged on women priests yet, but looking at pictures of some of them in the papers you could soon draw your own conclusions.

Jane sat up. Opposite the bed, the longest Mondrian wall, with its garish red and yellow and blue emulsion, looked like a bad idea clumsily executed. She wished she was lying on Gareth

Box's hearthrug in the red glow of the apple-log fire. *Please, Gareth, show me I'm normal.*

Eventually, she got ready for bed. Sleep? No chance. And what was she supposed to say tomorrow over the breakfast table?

What was she supposed to say the next time she saw Lol?

Or maybe he *knew*. Oh yeah, it would certainly explain all that, wouldn't it? All that keeping-up-appearances shit, Mum and Lol not being able to see one another very often. It was never a question of the relationship going stagnant – because it had never happened, had it? It was another lie.

Jane began beating her forehead into the pillow. *Lies, lies, lies, lies, lies . . .*

Part Five

The areas called the temporal lobes, which are the most electrically unstable brain areas, create a feeling called a sense of presence when they are irradiated by an electronic signal. This is where a person has an overwhelming feeling that someone is in the room with them and they are being watched . . .

Albert Budden
Allergies and Aliens: The Visitation Experience
– an environmental health issue

Other murderers claim they are being visited by the spirits of the people they have murdered. They see apparitions. They hear voices. With him it was bricks and mortar. The changes in temperature and acoustics in remembered spaces . . . Hallucinating himself back to his house.

Gordon Burn
Happy Like Murderers

Fred*erick* . . . no diminutives for *that* man.

Martin Amis, BBC Radio Wales

32

Ariconium

The doors of Roddy Lodge's garage were painted dark green. Somebody had been at one of them with chalk. The message read:

Put him down a cesspit
where he belongs

Merrily pulled into the verge just short of the village and took off her dog collar. No point in asking for confrontation on the street, though she might put it back on before meeting the Development Committee at ten.

When she went into the Post Office and Stores to buy some cigarettes and a paper, the fat man behind the counter asked if she was a reporter.

'Pity,' he said. 'We want all the publicity we can get. We ain't rolling over for this one, no way.'

London accent. Who did he mean by 'we'?

She glanced at the paper rack. The story hadn't made the front pages of the tabloids, but she glimpsed the name Fred West in a single-column headline halfway down the *Daily Telegraph*. She took the paper to the counter and said casually, 'Why *are* people so worked up about this man being buried here? He's local, isn't he, whatever he's done.'

'So was Melanie Pullman,' the fat man explained.

'And how would *you* feel –' a fiftyish woman in a yellow PVC jacket detached herself from a carousel of tights '– if your sister was lying under some cold field you didn't even know where, and a man who called himself Satan gets a Christian burial?' Birmingham accent this time: how would *yow* feel?

'No way,' the fat man said. '*No way.* They should get him cremated on the quiet. Do what they like wiv the ashes, long as nobody knows. You got a situation where this place is finally getting on its feet at long last. Do we want connecting wiv a sicko? *No* way.'

'You only got to look at this female priest.' The woman was looking at Merrily without recognition. 'We all know what *that*'s about. That's the woman who got herself made exorcist. Making a big thing out of it. Anything to make a name for yourself these days. Publicity mad.'

Merrily nodded. 'So I've heard.' She folded up the *Telegraph*.

On her way out, she heard the man say, 'Exorcist? What's that about, then?'

'Making sure he don't come back, Richard.'

'Dump him somewhere else, and it ain't a bloody problem!'

Laughter. *Put him down a cesspit. Shove the fame-hungry bimbo priest in after him. Bitch.*

But these two were both incomers. There had to be *some* sympathy for Tony Lodge and Cherry among indigenous villagers. Must be people here who'd known Roddy for years, drunk in the pubs with Roddy, been to school with Roddy, played on the hillside with him, nursed him as a baby – this poor kid with no mother in a house full of taciturn men. The poor kid who turned into a murderer. Who tomorrow gets buried – darkly, quietly, before his time.

You didn't have to be here long to understand why the undertakers wanted to switch dates.

Merrily took the newspaper back to the car on the main street of Underhowle: exposed at last in fog-free, rain-free daylight. She'd left the Volvo where the road shuffled uphill by the primary school and the new village hall that had once been a barn. The school was utility Victorian Gothic; she hadn't even noticed it in the dark when she'd walked up with Bliss and the locals, but now there were lights on inside and the windows were lurid with finger-painting and the severity of the main building was mocked by the yellow panels of a mobile classroom in the yard.

It was coming up to 9.15. There might just be time, before

the meeting with the Development Committee, to check out the church and the Lodge family graves. *Lay him to rest before anyone sees. Bury him with dignity, if you must, but essentially with speed, because . . .*

Oh God – Lol's gig! It was Lol's gig tomorrow night. There'd just be time to get home, get changed, get up to Hereford . . .

She leaned against the car. Behind the school, the village was crumbling down the hillside, in all the dull multicolours of broken dog biscuits. Close to the centre was the rusty-brown bell tower of the church and the green areas between graves; on the outskirts the blue smoked-glass roof lights of the computer factory fitted into the gap between two small housing estates: one in pink brick, one rendered a drab, sub-Cotswold ochre.

And bestriding all, like the watchtowers of a concentration camp against the forest and the sky, the lines of pylons.

One of them a killer. Why should anyone worry about a single stone marking the spot where Roddy's body lay when you had only to look up to see the massive instrument of his execution, the real Lodge Memorial, sculpted in grey steel?

It stood defiant, gleeful as a guillotine. But right now nobody else seemed to be looking up. The initial trauma was over and the community was functioning again – happening on the ground in the unforced way it never seemed to in perfect, pickled Ledwardine. Underhowle in motion: vehicles drawing up and moving off, from Land Rovers to a vintage American car with tail fins, people slipping in and out of the few shops with shouts of greeting, hands raised. Soft lights coming on in a unisex hairdressers' called Head Office.

'*Finally getting on its feet.*' How many ways had she heard that expressed? '*Prospered more in the past five years than in the previous forty. And they make it all sound so exciting for the future.*'

Well, good luck to them. Merrily got into the Volvo, opened out the paper on the passenger seat and found that the story was straightforward and more restrained than she'd expected.

FRED WEST LINK IN BORDER MURDER INQUIRY

by Eric Birchall
Crime Correspondent

THE SELF-CONFESSED 'serial killer' Roderick Lodge, who was electrocuted after climbing a pylon to escape from police, had an obsession with the mass-murderer Fred West, detectives said last night.

An extensive collection of news cuttings about the West killings has been found hidden at Lodge's Herefordshire home, along with what West Mercia CID describes as 'substantial evidence that he saw Fred West as a role model'.

West, 53, hanged himself in his cell in 1995, while awaiting trial for the murder of twelve young women and girls, many of whom were found buried in the cellar and garden of his house at 25 Cromwell Street, Gloucester – 15 miles from Lodge's home in the village of Underhowle, near Ross-on-Wye.

Lodge's only confirmed victim, Lynsey Davies, a 39-year-old mother of four, was buried under one of the septic tanks he installed over a wide area of Herefordshire, Gloucestershire and Monmouthshire. But police have not ruled out the possibility that he may have murdered at least two other women.

'Without bodies, we can't establish how much of this was sick fantasy,' said Det. Ch. Supt. Luke Fleming, who is leading the inquiry.

'Lodge operated over a very wide area, using heavy plant equipment. We've been able to trace many of his recent customers but it's clear that not all of them were recorded in his accounts, and we'd like to talk to anyone who has employed him in the last five years or so.

'I would stress that this man was a known fantasist, with possible psychiatric problems, and the last thing we want is to create any kind of unnecessary panic.

'Lynsey Davies was Lodge's girl-friend and it is quite possible that what we are looking at is a one-off domestic murder by an inadequate who liked to identify himself with the most notorious mass murderer of recent years, who happened to have lived and committed his murders in a neighbouring area.'

Meanwhile, a row has broken out in Underhowle village, where many residents are objecting to Lodge being buried in the local churchyard.

They say his grave would become 'a sick tourist attraction', especially if more bodies are unearthed.

The local rector, the Rev. Jerome Banks, has declined to conduct the funeral service. The Diocese of Hereford said a priest from outside the area would be taking it over.

Taking it over. Oh yes, in the capable hands of the Deliverance Consultant what could possibly go wrong? Merrily leaned back in the driving seat, wearily closing her eyes and glimpsing Jane at her most sullen at the breakfast table this morning before leaving for school with hardly a word, and Merrily too droopy with insufficient sleep to make a thing of it.

A tapping on the window made her jerk back, crumpling the *Daily Telegraph* against the wheel.

The face sideways at the glass was a long face, with a wide mouth, springy yellow hair.

Fergus Young, head teacher and chair of the Development Committee.

Merrily wound down the window.

'Tough night, detective constable?' Fergus Young said.

What Merrily noticed first was all the red computers, pushing out everywhere, like the heads of wild poppies. She was wondering where she'd seen one before and then realized.

'Roddy Lodge's office. Roddy Lodge had one of these.'

'No surprise in that,' Fergus Young said in his deep, easy voice. 'Most households in the village have one now. Not only small children use them but also elderly people who'd never imagined they could operate a computer. And, yes, people like Roddy, I suppose, for the same reason.'

He showed her into his office, a little friendlier now, his long, bony features more relaxed. When she'd felt forced to re-identify herself, he'd closed up, visibly pondering the earlier deception – why had Bliss had introduced her as a colleague? Fergus didn't get the joke, and why should he?

But, OK, if she was already being widely condemned as some self-publicizing clerical bimbo, she was going to sit this one out, very quietly.

There were two more computers in the headmaster's high-ceilinged office, another red one and a more conventional model. It was central goverment's declared aim, Fergus had told her, to provide one computer for every secondary school student in Britain. The primary kids here had two each, one at school, one at home.

There was a knock on the door and a boy of about eight stuck his head round it. 'Would you and your visitor like some coffee, Fergus?'

'Thanks, Barney, I think we probably would. And if you see Chris and Piers Connor-Crewe, send them through, would you, mate?'

The kid nodded, vanished. Merrily raised an eyebrow. 'First-name terms?'

'It kind of phased itself in.' Fergus motioned Merrily to a green leather sofa under the window and settled himself on the arm at the other end. He was wearing jeans and a yellow tracksuit top. 'Some of them were getting so enthusiastic I realized they were beginning to see us as friends.'

'And is that, erm, *good* for discipline?'

Fergus tossed his stallion head. 'Surprisingly so. After a while you find that most of the actual disciplining of antisocial elements is handled by their peers. They're inclined to take a harder line with disruptive behaviour than the staff ever would. Disruptive behaviour being anything that gets between them and what they're trying to achieve.'

'You mean between them and having fun.'

'Well, sure, having fun is how they see it at first. But by the time they get to nine or ten, it's serious. I mean, we're not regarded as teachers, we're advisers . . . enablers. They want to know something, we're here to help them. It's simply a question of awakening that desire to learn, and that usually happens before they start school. If we put a computer into every home as soon as a child can walk, then another child, a bit older, shows the youngster how to operate it. And by the time they're four, they can't wait to get here to meet the people they've already seen on screen.'

'Blimey,' Merrily said. 'How do you afford it?'

'Chris – Chris Cody? – he's been very good, starting us off. Which, of course, is paying off for him now, in orders from all over the country. Word of mouth so far, and I've got a book on the Underhowle experience coming out next year so it's likely to rocket. I've also been on the scrounge. Part of a school-director's job, nowadays, is to go out and involve the local community, and then the wider community . . . and also discover where the grants are.'

'It all sounds . . . Utopian.' And it did. The school at Ledwardine had just quietly closed because it was too small to survive. There hadn't been much resistance; Ledwardine had an ageing population, and it was starting to show.

'Look,' Fergus said, 'there are problems, of course there are. We've got a hell of a social mix here, from families where a book's something you use to balance the table legs to the offspring of downshifting high-flyers who came here for the air quality. Sometimes I'm beating my head against a wall and saying, *Why the hell did I start all this*? But I have to tell you there are far, *far* more of those fist-in-the-air moments.'

His face burned with fervour. It was difficult, in here, not to feel the heat of progress, a community on the turn. Merrily wondered why she hadn't read about this anywhere – possibly because Underhowle was on the extreme fringe of the circulation areas of most of the local papers, the *Hereford Times*, the *Ross Gazette*, *The Forester*. The way it was moving, it would soon be national press and TV.

'Occasionally,' Fergus said, 'we'll get some sniffy education officer coming over from Hereford, trying to put a wire in the cogs. If you've managed it without them, they hate you. But we've reached the stage where we don't need those pygmies. Five years ago, they were ready to close the school down through lack of numbers. Now, if they tried to mess with us, we could go it alone, and they know it. Look there.' Fergus pointed at a tray full of letters held down by a classical statuette on a plinth. 'I actually get applications now from people in the cities prepared to move here just to get their kids into this school. I could probably fill it twice over . . . but I don't want people like that. I want a proportion of those kids whose own parents can barely read. I want the *mix*.'

'Except in the graveyard?' Merrily said. It just slipped out.

A pause, Fergus frowning.

Then he grinned. 'OK.' He stood up, went over to his desk and switched on the red Cody computer. 'Take a look at this.' There was a tap on the door. 'Yes, come in.'

It was the kid, Barney, with a tray of coffee things, and two men. Shouldn't Barney be in class? Maybe the class system had become outdated here.

'Perfectly timed,' Fergus said. As if they hadn't met before, he introduced Merrily to Chris Cody, the dark, shaven-headed twenty-something who'd made coffee for them at the village hall. Then he presented a bulky, cheerful-looking older man in a baggy cream suit. 'And this is Piers – the scholar and gentleman who gave us *this*.'

They all turned to look at the computer which, Merrily noticed, had booted up in less than half the time it took hers and Jane's. Kids liked *instant*. Fergus zapped an icon. A blue sky shimmered. A word formed out of white cloud, hardening up slowly.

ARICONIUM

The screen began to cloud again, around the word. 'You heard about this, Merrily?' Fergus asked, and she had the sensation of being drawn into the screen and what it represented, absorbed into this all-pervading enthusiasm.

'Heard a *bit* about it. It's a Roman town originally thought to be further down the valley, but new finds apparently have indicated it was actually . . . here?'

'Bugger-all to see on the ground, unfortunately,' Piers said, 'although we think an excavation would be illuminating – and one day, not too far in the future, we're going to have the money for it. Might persuade the Channel Four *Time Team* lot to start us off – that's how we usually work . . . or Fergus does.'

'The point *about* Ariconium,' Fergus said, 'is that it was as wealthy and successful – as *unified* – as this area's ever been.'

On the screen a picture of Underhowle village had faded up – an overview, seen, presumably, from Howle Hill, with most of the pylons below the eye-line. There was a dull sky, duller than today's, but it began slowly to lighten and the random scree of Underhowle's architecture faded into a regular pattern of simpler buildings of stone and wood and a straight road along the valley.

Merrily said, 'This is a vision of the future?'

'You've got it, m'dear.' Piers nodded, beaming. He had a football head, a loose-lipped smile. 'Wealth. Growth.'

'Out of iron in those days,' Fergus said. 'The Silures – the local Iron Age Celtic tribe – had it first. You can still see the sites of old iron workings and, of course, the hill forts above here and on Chase Hill above Ross, and into the Forest. Then the Romans crushed the Silures and Ariconium arose on the back of the iron industry, on the main road to Glevum – Gloucester – and Monmouth in the west.'

'Iron was smelted here, big time,' Piers said. 'Big business. Plenty of work.'

Fergus levelled a forefinger at the screen. 'I want the next generation to identify with *that*. Not with twentieth-century decay.'

'We're building this website to chronicle the project,' Chris Cody said in his quiet cockney accent. 'And the school's actively involved, along wiv the Development Committee' – he bowed his head to the other two men – 'in creating a visitor centre in the old Baptist chapel. There'll be displays of the latest finds, plus reconstructions, models, computer enhancements.'

A menu had appeared. Fergus clicked on *finds*, and the screen filled up with a section of what looked like mosaic floor.

'We're expecting confirmation of a Lottery grant any day now. And then we'll make a start. Building a tourist industry for the first time. New life, new blood, more jobs. There's a fantastic surge of energy going through this place which you must have been able to feel.'

It certainly looked as if it was flowing through Fergus. He hit the mouse with the heel of a hand, bringing up shards of pottery, some coins, then turned to Merrily on the sofa. All three of them standing over her now, defying her to deny the energy.

'Yes,' she said. 'I can see what you're trying to do. It's . . . exciting.'

'Yes, it is,' Piers Connor-Crewe said. 'It's *bloody* exciting. However, we had a taste, at the weekend, of a different kind of tourism.'

Fergus nodded grimly. He clicked on an icon bringing up the Ariconium homepage, clicked again and then the screen went blank. 'I was about to get to that when you guys arrived.'

*

Of course, the point was that getting any kind of tourism here was a coup. Not only was Underhowle not a pretty place but it had the misfortune to be surrounded by places that *were*: riverside Ross and Symonds Yat, Goodrich with its medieval castle, Weston-under-Penyard with its hilltop Norman church. Underhowle wasn't in the Wye Valley and it wasn't, strictly speaking, in the Forest of Dean. There would be people over in Ledwardine who'd suggest Underhowle should be grateful for whatever it could get.

'They've been coming down from Gloucester,' Fergus Young said. 'Over from Hereford. Up from South Wales, even. Unbelievable. Scores of them. Clogging the lane, parking on all the verges.'

'Standing there like the morons they are,' said Piers Connor-Crewe, 'and just staring at the pylon, or taking photographs of their ghastly children with it in the background. Some of them *brought sandwiches*. Can you believe that? I mean, have you seen today's papers?' Piers turned to Chris Cody. 'They're linking Lodge with West now. *West!* Christ. What was that one . . . *Spawn of Satan?*'

'*Devil's Disciple.*' Chris was smiling sadly, probably at the outdated excesses of the non-virtual world. 'In the *Sun*. Or was it *Demon Seed?*'

'Just doesn't go away, does it?' Piers said. 'After all these years, that loathsome little man is still a household name. He's won his place in the Black Pantheon now – the most famous murderer . . . God forbid, probably the most famous *man* – to come out of Herefordshire. And now Roddy Lodge. How many has Roddy killed? Could be years before they find them all. And the difference is that Gloucester Council was able to *remove* 25 Cromwell Street. They turned the site into a walkway so nobody can tell any more where the house was. And, as far as I know, there's no physical memory of Frederick West in Much Marcle either – I believe they scattered his ashes in the churchyard there, and that was it. Blown away. Gone.'

'About half the children at this school were watching when Roddy Lodge died,' Fergus said. 'Listening to him screaming out all that filth. We've talked about it with them, we've analysed it, we've had individual counselling where necessary. So the children will forget, of course they will – *if* they're allowed to. We all realize we're never going to get rid of the pylon, but we can make sure the tourist trail ends there. Merrily, I beg of you, if you have any influence at all over the Lodges, persuade them to have him decently cremated, and let's all try to forget he ever existed.'

Chris Cody said, 'I don't really have a personal angle on this, but a few of our people – down the factory – are saying they got relatives in that churchyard and they don't like to fink of them lying in the same, you know, soil, as Roddy Lodge.'

'It's a point,' Fergus Young said. 'Would you want Lodge buried side by side with members of your immediate family? No, it's all right, I know what you're obliged to say.'

Piers Connor-Crewe folded his arms. 'But if it comes to the crunch, the Church itself can say no – you obviously realize that.'

'But the Bishop *hasn't* said no,' Merrily told him. 'I suspect he takes the line that if we were to refuse to bury sinners, it might just contravene one of the basic tenets of Christianity. As well as leaving us with the problem of where exactly to draw the line, you know?'

Connor-Crewe looked pained. 'I understand that, but I think we're—'

'And let's not forget that Lodge hadn't actually been convicted of anything.'

'Neither had West,' Fergus said, 'but that didn't prevent some forceful opposition in Much Marcle. Which I believe succeeded.'

'In fact, I also think I'm right in saying Lodge hadn't even been charged.'

'Look,' Connor-Crewe said, 'what you're dealing with here – that is, *us* – is the polite form of protest. I can assure you that some of the locals would be more inclined towards what we might call direct action.'

'As in . . . what?'

'Well, if there *is* a grave, it could well get vandalized,' Fergus said. 'And I have to tell you we're not only talking about relatives. I'm told there are friends of Melanie Pullman already making dark threats. And it seems to me, without laying it on too heavily, that this is as good a reason as any to tell the Lodge family it really can't be done.'

'All right . . .' Merrily got to her feet. She'd faced hysteria, she'd faced tears and rage; there was nothing worse than reason. 'Maybe they haven't thought about the vandalism aspect. I'll put it to them. But you have to understand there's family history here. Tony Lodge feels an obligation to his father.'

'Whereas *we* merely have an obligation to the future,' Fergus Young said.

'*You have voice-mail,*' the mobile told her when she switched it on.

Merrily put the phone on the dash, sitting for a while, gazing through the windscreen at Underhowle: late-autumnal, yet throbbing with the spring of its future. *Education, education, education,* Tony Blair or somebody had once said, when asked about New Labour's priorities for a new Britain. She wondered what it would be like to have Underhowle as your parish: a kindergarten rather than a retirement home. Couldn't see anything progressive in it for the Church, not short-term anyway. Not with the narrow and cynical Jerome Banks in place.

'It's out, then,' Huw Owen's voice grated from the mailbank. 'Bliss – self-seeking little bastard. Lass, I'm coming over tonight. Don't go anywhere.'

She flung her head back over the top of the seat, where the headrest had come off. *Bloody men with their bloody agendas.* She closed her eyes.

When she opened them, another shadow had fallen across the side window.

'I'm gonna take a chance on this,' Sam Hall said when she wearily wound it down. 'I think you have to be Merrily Watkins.'

33

Empty Heart

It was all here, from the Norwegian cast-iron wood-burning stove – no glass, therefore no friendly flames to watch – to the two solar panels in the roof. Even the radio was clockwork, but there was a small, traditional stereo. His one vice, he said.

Otherwise, showpiece good-life. But how good was it really? It was a dark room, this big living area; the windows were triple-glazed and small. One of them, in a wall insulated with several hundred tightly packed books, offered a view down the hillside, picking up a line of pylons.

The wrong view, it seemed to Merrily.

'I know . . . you're asking yourself *why*,' Sam said. 'Why, if I want to live like this, don't I do it on some Hebridean island, or in the empty heart of Wales?'

'I did wonder that, but then I thought I'd come up with an answer. Which was: because he needs to keep reminding himself of something?'

'You must've been a great loss to the cops, Mrs Watkins.' Silent laughter in the dimness. 'That goddam Bliss could've saved us all a heap of time and trouble if he hadn't tried to pass you off as a detective.'

'Why did he come to talk to you again?'

'Usual stuff. He saw Ingrid, too. What did we know about Lodge? Did we know of any other girls Roddy went out with? Any guys he hung around with? I doubt if I was able to help him.'

'But you think you can help *me*?'

'Maybe we can help each other.' Sam got down on his knees, opened up the stove and fed it a log that looked to have been sawn to size. 'OK, I'm gonna condense this – I'd rather have derision any day than pity. Yeah, you're right, of course. I lost my only kid to leukaemia in the States and, yeah, we lived directly under power lines and, sure, I became fanatical about the whole issue, drank too much, destroyed my marriage. And now I'm back in England and I'm still angry and I figure this is still a small enough country to make an impact. And yeah, you're sorry for my loss – thank you – so that's all *that* dealt with. How much did Lol tell you?'

'He told me what you'd said about hot spots and the symbolism of the plague cross. And he said there was a spiritual side to it that he thought you weren't inclined to discuss with him.'

'The spiritual side, yeah. I guess he and I caught more than a hint of all that the night Roddy died. When we met in Ross, Lol had this other lady with him who I thought was gonna be you, and it threw me when she turned out to be another singer, so I kind of clammed up.'

'Moira Cairns,' Merrily said neutrally.

'I think I was supposed to have heard of her. I guess I was away too long.'

'The spiritual side . . . ?' Merrily prompted.

'Sure. I tried to talk to the Reverend Banks one time, but if you've ever had anything to do with that guy . . .'

Merrily nodded. Sam Hall, bulked out with an Icelandic sweater, waved her to a big, overstuffed armchair and put himself into another. He'd untied his ponytail and salty hair framed his bearded face.

'When I was a kid we lived for a while in the village. My dad was a friend of old man Lodge and I was a few years older than Tony Lodge, and Roddy was just a small kid when I left for the States. So I knew the family well enough to recognize the changes when I came back.'

'What did you do out there?'

'Oh, I was a film cameraman for some years – industrial, nothing glamorous, no movies. Then I got into some stills work for the underground press, who paid peanuts in the early days, though it improved when magazines like *Rolling Stone* took off. And that got me into radical politics – I was kind of an old hippy even when hippies were young. Which was fun. I wound up in this commune with my wife on the edge of the Nevada

Desert – under power lines, as it happened. And then our daughter, Delawney, got sick and died and it all got serious. I guess I . . . became a little crazy for a while – paranoid. Became convinced the power industry had a contract out on me – hell, maybe they did, those bastards. When the wife walked out on me, I decided it was time to make plans to come back to the green and pleasant land.'

'Only to find the power industry had beaten you to it?'

'Yeah, and what was worse –' Sam walked over to the window and looked down the valley '– the village had come out to meet the pylons. They must've been some distance away at first, with only the Baptist Chapel and the old garage up close. But then they built the council estate, with some houses right under the damn cables. Nobody gave a shit in those days, and of course some developers and local authorities still don't. I was so mad when I saw that. It ignited all the old rage, and I thought, this time, *this time*, I'm really gonna *do* something about it.' He turned around. 'Hell, Mrs Watkins, this wasn't gonna be about me, I was gonna give you the science.'

'I'm not that good at science.'

'And I found out one thing about the British media – you only get one chance. They come and they do one serious story on you and after that you either succeed or you become a joke. I became a joke very quickly. The Fool on the Hill – that's my sig tune. By the time I had something worth saying, nobody was hearing me.'

'And that was?'

'Roddy Lodge, of course. And Melanie Pullman. Fellow sufferers, but it was Melanie I was most concerned about – maybe a mistake.'

'Sufferers from what?'

'Let me start at the beginning – which isn't too long ago. Not quite three years. Just around the time my honeymoon with the media was coming to an end. The day Melanie Pullman told me about the lights in the night.'

Gomer climbed down from the digger. It was not yet lunchtime.

'Done?' Lol was surprised: it was already over and he could

still walk? In fact, the ground frost, the wintry friction in the air, had put an edge on his senses.

'At a quarter of the bloody Efflapure price,' Gomer said, 'and no fancy dials to check. Now, if you go up the house, get her to flush every toilet they got – upstairs, downstairs, en suite, the lot. Wanner make sure it's coming through proper, see.'

Gomer beamed; he knew it would. On the way here, he'd talked about his mistake concerning Lodge and the fire and how the vicar had helped him get that into perspective. Gomer seemed very relieved this morning, like a Jack Russell unleashed.

Walking up the leaf-matted lawn, past the Gomer Parry Plant Hire truck, Lol saw smoke coming from one of the chimneys of what was a nice old stone house built at a time when nothing heavier than a horse would be moving along whatever had pre-dated the A49. Through a front window, as he passed, he saw Mrs Pawson hunched close to a wood-burner in the inglenook. She rose quickly, had the front door open before he reached it.

'Is it finished?' She looked pinched and starved.

'Gomer thinks so. He'd like you to flush all the loos. Could I . . . help?'

She hesitated. 'All right.' A bit snappy. 'The downstairs one's just there, off the hall. I'll do upstairs.'

He flushed the downstairs cloakroom toilet and went back outside to wait for her. He noticed the front door had two new locks, big-city style. When she came down, she was wearing a thick green woollen jacket and still looked shivery.

He smiled. 'It should be fine. Anyway. Gomer won't leave until it's all perfect.'

'Oh . . .' Mrs Pawson shook her head absently, as if he'd said something unnecessarily technical. 'I just want it to be working, that's all. Then I can get out of here.'

'For good?'

'What do you think?' She looked at Lol as though she wouldn't expect someone like him really to understand. 'Look, if you need me for anything, I'm booked into the Royal in Ross for tonight, to see estate agents. Then I'm going back to London. Mr Parry has my address, for the bill.'

'You feel personally unsettled by all this?'

She'd turned away, as if to go back into the house. She turned back. 'What do you mean by that?'

'Well, he's dead. And she . . .' It wasn't as if she was murdered here, was what he meant.

Mrs Pawson looked away from him, along the drive towards the road. 'There was a morning paper in the hotel lounge, which I was silly enough to pick up. They now think he had a sick fascination with Frederick West, they don't know how many other women he killed, and his neighbours don't want him to be buried at their church. Is it *so* hard to see why this house is blighted for me?'

Gomer had talked about West on the way here, telling Lol about what had been in the attaché case they'd dug up at the back of the bungalow.

Mrs Pawson looked at Lol. 'Did you *know* Lodge?'

'Only by . . . by sight.'

'He was a nightmare,' she said. 'A nightmare person.' She was holding the lapels of her jacket together across her throat. 'And so was the woman.'

'She was with him, when . . . ?'

Mrs Pawson didn't reply and started to walk away then, but he sensed a very real distress that didn't seem to fit in with the kind of woman she was. And afterwards he talked to Gomer about this, and Gomer agreed.

Sam reached over his shoulder and pulled a loose-leaf binder from a shelf behind him. 'I'm not gonna make you read this, I just want you to know it exists. It's the report of a six-year study out of Bristol University, linking power lines to a bunch of different cancers, depression and an estimated sixty suicides a year.'

'I didn't know about the suicides,' Merrily said. 'But I've heard about the other health scares.'

'It's estimated that the deaths caused by power lines equate with the number of fatalities on the road. But, as only one in fifty of the population lives under power lines, that makes the risk fifty times as big. We're talking heavy shit here, Reverend, and it's no surprise that governments and the power industry try to rubbish it.'

'I understand that, but . . .'

'But where do you come in? I'm getting there. Let's look at what's more or less proven. Magnetic fields reduce the body's production of melatonin, which is manufactured by the pineal gland at night and regulates mood. People living under power lines suffer insomnia – sleep deprivation. And because of the reduced melatonin levels, people living under power lines are prone to depression. Sure, you'll find wonderfully cheerful, fit characters who spent their whole lives under 140,000 volts – some folk produce more melatonin than others. However, those with a tendency to depression may find they become *very* depressed. And those already very depressed may become suicidal.'

'And people suffering from *manic* depression . . . ?'

'May become more manic and more depressed. Loosely, whatever you got there's a strong possibility that electromagnetism will intensify it. And a certain number of people are gonna develop a chronic condition that we called electro-hypersensitivity – EH. That's where the whole body becomes allergic to electricity. So you see, the risks from power lines are many and varied . . . and *more* varied than any of us could've imagined.'

He replaced the loose-leaf folder on the shelf, placed his hands on his knees and looked down, gathering his argument.

'When I was living near the Nevada Desert, in the eighties, the alternative lifestyle was getting jaded – too many bad drugs, too much paranoia. The spark had gone out. Around the time my daughter got sick, one of the guys in the commune started rambling about saucers coming in the night, landing in the desert. Humanoids in silver suits who came and took him out of his bed and messed him around. Ten years earlier, we'd have been like: Hey, cool, let's all light candles, get out there and welcome the mothership, man! In the eighties, however, we were suspecting he might be a little crazy.'

'A lot of it about – alien-abduction stories.'

'Sure. Those were paranoid times, the Reagan years. Was it aliens, or was it the government?'

'So when did you hear about Melanie Pullman's experience?' Merrily asked.

'Aha!' He leaned forward. 'Who told you about that?'

'Her family called in my predecessor, suspecting their house might be haunted. We actually have files.'

'And you've seen the file?'

'Yes.' She told him about the red or orange light bathing the bed, Melanie's belief that she was taken away by grey creatures with big eyes like mirrors and subjected to an examination that ended with one of them having sexual intercourse with her. 'Which she seems to have found not entirely unpleasant.'

'Good,' Sam Hall said. 'I mean, that's right. That's what she told me.'

'When was this?'

'Year or so after she saw the priest, I'd guess. She told me he'd said some prayers and threw a little holy water around but that it didn't help much, long term.'

'So it happened again.'

'Twice. Not precisely the same, but similar enough as makes no difference.'

'This was widely known around the village?'

'Hell, no. Nobody wants to be thought crazy. No, it came out when I ran into Melanie one day leaving the doctor's surgery – Ruck, you know him? Asshole of the old school. Anyway, the kid looked like shit, and the point is, I knew where she lived, and I'd heard she hadn't been well.'

'She lived on the former council estate.'

'Yeah, but whereabouts? Right in the arc of the turning circle at the end of Goodrich Close is where. The damn pylon – next one along to the one where Roddy Lodge died – is almost in the back garden. The lines are directly overhead. Plus you're in line with the TV booster across the valley and . . . I won't go on, but this is close to the centre of the hot spot defined by Lodge's garage and the old Baptist Chapel.'

'So you think . . .' Merrily was getting an idea of where this was going. She remembered Canon Dobbs's conclusion that Melanie Pullman had undergone a genuine hallucinatory or dream experience, had not been making it up. 'You think that the effects of, for instance, sleep loss caused by electromagnetism might have been causing her to hallucinate. Like your friend under the power lines in the Nevada Desert?'

'Which, at the time, we attributed to far too many drugs over the years. But let me say first of all, this is not only me. There's been considerable research – OK, fringe research, but that's how it usually starts – which demonstrates a correlation between both alien-visitation experiences and some plain old-fashioned hauntings, and the presence of high-voltage overhead lines, usually in conjunction with other radiation from TV transmitters, mobile-phone masts, sub-stations . . . I could find you scores of examples.'

'Well, sure . . . but how is it explained?'

'The effect of electromagnetic fields on the brain . . . on specific areas of the brain – irradiation of the temporal lobes, for instance, can promote a sensation of what you might call "presence". Of not being alone. Stimulation of the septum area of the brain can produce intense sexual sensations, which explains—'

'Except that, in Melanie's case, there was also, if I recall, a vaginal infection?'

'Mrs Watkins . . .' Sam spread his hands. 'I wouldn't claim to be any kind of authority on women's clinical conditions. However, the growth on the body of various fungal bacteria, of the candida type, can, I assure you, be accelerated by exposure to a significant degree of electromagnetism. You are free to check this out with whatever scientific or medical sources you may have access to.'

'Can I have a cigarette?'

'Depends what kind of lighter you have . . . No, I'm kidding, help yourself. If tobacco was all we had to worry about, I'd be a happier man. Look, Mrs Watkins, this kind of stuff is not helpful to me or my cause, which is why I've never made an issue of it. Tell the Great British Public they could be in for leukaemia or a brain tumour and you've got their full attention. Warn them of possible encounters with alien beings or a ghost in the bedroom, they heave a big sigh of relief, say: "Phew, so it can't be true about the cancer either." Believe me, I do not need this shit. I beg your pardon if that seems to be demeaning your profession – it wasn't intended that way.'

'Don't worry about it. What happened with Melanie?'

'She worked at a chemist's, in Ross, and I met her for lunch one day and it all came out. For instance, for some time she'd been finding it impossible to watch TV and was going up to her room – which made it worse, of course. Her room was at the rear of the house, backing onto the pylon, wires zooming immediately overhead. She couldn't sleep and . . . you know the rest. Also, by this time, she was becoming allergic to her place of work – all those huge bright lights in the drugstore. I advised her to start looking for another job . . . someplace darker, at least.'

'And was she involved with Roddy Lodge at this time?'

'She'd been with Roddy 'bout a year. See, this was before Roddy's big change. He hadn't been long in his own place, and I imagine she was his first real girlfriend. It was a case of like attracting like. Although he was maybe ten years older than she was, they'd both had experiences they couldn't explain – stuff they couldn't even discuss with most other people. It must've been kind of a relief to both of them when they found out they weren't alone.'

'Roddy being under the same power lines . . .'

'Well, let's not forget he'd been around power lines all his life – got some big ones going over the farm. But when he moved, he was right in the heart of the hot spot. Whatever was happening to him before must've been intensified hugely once he was in that bungalow.'

'Did they know this? Had they put two and two together?'

'I don't believe they had. People often don't. Roddy, for instance, was convinced there was something wrong with his eyes. Took to wearing dark glasses and working at night when he could. And I'm sure that relieved the symptoms to an extent. No, I told Melanie what I knew and referred her to an alternative practitioner in Hereford who wasn't as blind to all this as the medical profession seems to be. I don't think she managed to persuade Roddy to go, too, because things were becoming complicated by then. Am I making the remotest kind of sense to you, Mrs Watkins?'

'I rather think you are.'

'You're making connections.'

'Too many.'

'Anything you want confirmation of, I have whole shelves of reports . . .'

'I just want to think about this. How much have you told Bliss?'

'Hell, none of it. Guy's a cop. He's gonna believe Lodge's behaviour was conditioned by electromagnetic radiation? Does he care? He just wants to know where the other bodies are buried.'

'And were you able to help him on that?'

'No.' Sam stood up and walked back to the window with the view down Howle Hill towards the pylons and Underhowle. 'Do I think Melanie Pullman's dead? Maybe . . . but maybe not. There was every reason for her just to get the hell out of here and not look back. See, she was coming to see me quite often those last few months – reporting her progress. She'd taken a vacation with some relations up in Shropshire, well away from power lines. Done some walking up there. Cut out the Valium, of course. When she came back home, she switched bedrooms to a smaller room at the front of the house, not directly under the cables. Gave in her notice at the drugstore. She was feeling a little better – even just knowing about it makes you feel a different person. But electro-allergy goes deep. It takes a long time to get it out of your system, if you're lucky enough to be able to do that totally. There's good reason to think she just upped and left Underhowle, knowing there was no future for her, healthwise, in this place.'

'Leaving all her possessions, all her clothes?'

'Maybe she went someplace else and felt so good she just didn't come back. Maybe she met somebody. People do this kind of thing with far less reason than she had.'

'What about Roddy?'

'I think she tried to help him, I really do. I just don't think he wanted to know. Besides, he had a new girlfriend by then. He had Lynsey. And he was changing – boy was he *changing*.'

'Would you mind if I told Bliss about this?'

He shrugged. 'Long as there's no comeback on me.'

'I think I can guarantee that.' Merrily stood up. 'So that's what you meant when you told Lol about a spiritual aspect to all this.'

'Uh . . .' Sam turned his back on the view, plucked at his Icelandic sweater. 'I guess I still hope it is. I'm not sure. I have a friend – you met Ingrid Sollars?'

'At the hall.'

'Sure you did. Well, Ingrid and I are very close friends, but we don't always agree. And there's stuff happening here . . .' Sam shook his head. 'I dunno . . .'

'What stuff?'

'Could I go fetch Ingrid?'

Merrily looked at her watch. 'I have to go and see Cherry Lodge, and then I've got to get back for someone. Can I call you? Tonight, maybe?'

'Sure.' Sam followed her to the door. 'This has become a weird place, Mrs Watkins. And more than a little sick.'

Parked outside the Lodge farm, Merrily called Bliss from the car and left a message on his voice-mail. Cherry Lodge, in her army parka, was coming round the side of the house, carrying a paper sack of mixed corn.

'Been and seen them, have you, Reverend?' She put down the corn sack. Freed from fog, the farmhouse behind her looked less stable, with rubble-stone showing through holes in the rendering. Less fortified.

'I'll come straight to the point,' Merrily said. 'Has anybody threatened you?'

Cherry Lodge managed a tired smile. Merrily decided not to tell her about her own anonymous caller.

'Just I was told that people – friends of Melanie Pullman – had threatened to damage Roddy's grave, if . . . if there was one.'

'There's brave of them.' Cherry pulled the sack of corn up against the wall. 'Do you want a cup of tea?'

'No, thanks, I've got to get back. Erm . . . the other argument is that it'll be an unpleasant sort of attraction to the wrong kind of tourists. But the committee said that to you, didn't they?'

'The wrong kind of tourists. Oh yes, we had that.'

'Cherry, in your e-mail, you said how much Roddy had changed when he went to live on his own. You said he'd become more confident. Did he change in any other way? I mean, for instance, he went around all the time in dark glasses . . . people saying he was a bit of a poser. But could there have been another reason? For instance, Sam Hall thinks—'

'Sam thinks a lot of things and some of them sound sensible and some sound like rubbish and I don't think he knows the difference. What does it matter now? Roddy killed a woman – only one woman, as far as we know, despite all this West rubbish – and then he killed himself. And if he was *going* to kill a woman – and don't go quoting me – then he couldn't have chosen a better one. Slut. Gold-digger. She kept coming back. He'd try and get away from her, go out with other women, but she kept coming back. Maybe, God forbid, he couldn't get rid of her any other way.'

'Look,' Merrily said. 'I'll *have* to ask you one more time, because I don't really know how deep the feelings are down there, but you *do* still want to go ahead with burial? You won't opt for cremation, perhaps a plaque in the church?'

'Mrs Watkins . . .' Cherry's face wore BSE and foot-and-mouth and stupid EU regulations in layers of dried-out anxiety; what did she care about petty village vigilantes with a manufactured crisis? 'If anyone vandalizes the grave, it's up to the police to deal with it. Anyone threatens us, *we'll* deal with it.'

'And you're . . . happy about tomorrow, rather than Friday.'

'We're not happy about any of it,' Cherry Lodge said. 'But if it's what we have to do to keep it quiet, it's what we'll do.'

'What about flowers and things? You got all that arranged?'

'Flowers for Roddy? I don't think so.'

Merrily nodded. 'You know my number.'

'Don't take too much notice of Sam,' Cherry said. 'And don't try and find excuses for Roddy – it's not worth it now.'

'Don't you want to know the truth?'

'I don't think we ever will know. Perhaps some of it's beyond knowing.'

'You mean the ghosts? The dead women?'

'I won't talk about that again. It needed to be said, that's all. It was hanging over me. Hanging over the family and never talked about. I just thought that, now he's gone, someone out-side should know. Just to . . . take it off us.'

Merrily nodded. There was more than one level of exorcism.

But she no longer thought it was beyond knowing.

When she was on the A49, the other side of Ross, the mobile bleeped and she pulled the Volvo into the kerb. It was Bliss, and she told him what she wanted.

34

EH

RECORD OF INTERVIEW

Person interviewed: *RODERICK LODGE*

Place of interview: *HEREFORD HQ*

Time commenced: *10.30 a.m.*   Time concluded: *11.23 a.m.*

Duration of interview: *53 mins*   Tape reference no.:   *HHQ 3869/1*

Interviewing Officer(s): *DI BLISS, DS MUMFORD*

Other persons present: *NONE*

Merrily had phoned Frannie Bliss to ask if he had a copy of the actual tapes, but transcripts was the best he could do. He'd arrived at the vicarage as the day was fading, in hiking jacket, jeans and a terrible mood.

'This better be worth it, that's all. Coming, as it does, on a day I just want to be . . . *over*.'

'Caffeine?'

'Intravenous, if you have it, please, Merrily.' He hooked out a dining chair with his foot, collapsed into it.

'I've only seen the *Telegraph* so far,' she said.

'How I wish I could say the flamin' same.'

She poured coffee for him and sat down opposite. She'd changed into jeans and a black, cowl-neck sweater. 'I thought you *wanted* it to come out about West.'

'Not like *this*.' Screwing up his eyes as if he'd been hit in the face. 'When I had some evidence. When I could go in and say, right, dig there, lads. I *agreed* it was the best thing to sit on it, meanwhile not to panic parents, husbands . . .'

What had happened was that Bliss had asked Andy Mumford to keep his ear to the ground, and one of Andy Mumford's contacts in Much Marcle, birthplace of Fred West, had told him that Roddy Lodge had been seen there a couple of months ago with a woman answering Lynsey's description. Mumford had gone over there, in his own time, and talked to a few people, testing out an idea of Bliss's that Lodge might have disposed of a body in the area of Fred's old burial ground – some kind of homage. It was one of the blokes Mumford talked to in the pub who'd gone to the press.

'He'd had some money in the past for background stuff on the West family – in these difficult times, farmers are encouraged to diversify. Well, I couldn't let Andy take the shit for that. Had to phone Fleming, tell him it was me behind it.'

'Honourable of you.'

'Yeh. What the Japanese call the honourable way out.'

'And how did Fleming react?'

'Dunno, Merrily. I was on the mobile and the signal was weak, you know?'

'You got cut off.'

'Question of postponing the inevitable. I'm stuffed, anyway.' Bliss tapped the interview forms. 'What's this about?'

She got up and brought over the lamp from the window ledge. 'You probably won't like it.'

'*Now* you tell me.'

'You remember you once asked me if there could be a spiritual aspect?'

Bliss said, 'I now know all about West's claims that he was involved with a black magic sect, supplying them with virgins. That *was* investigated. Normally, you'd treat that kind of crap with a big pinch of salt, but this was a guy for whom no muck-heap was too smelly. Compared with some of the things Fred did to women, black magic was cucumber sarnies on the terrace.'

'I may disagree there, but that's not what I meant. I think you said you talked to his GP?'

'Dr Ruck. Didn't speak to him meself, but I gather he wasn't the kind to come the old patient-confidentiality. He thought

Roddy was neurotic, possibly depressive, and prone to hyp-ochondria.'

'What, forever coming to him with headaches and various pains?'

'That kind of thing.'

'Maybe the sort of symptoms he was exhibiting in the inter-view room?'

'What *is* this, Merrily?'

She was skimming through the first transcript, an interview laid out like a radio play.

> DI BLISS: *Roddy, a dead woman, now identified as Lynsey Davies, was found in a truck registered to you and being driven by you. How do you explain this?*
>
> DEFENDANT: *What you saying?*
>
> DI BLISS: *It's a simple question, Roddy. Why was Lynsey Davies's body on your truck? A body that was decaying, having been in the ground for some time.*
>
> DEF: *She was cold down there, look.*
>
> DI BLISS: *I see.*
>
> DEF: *Told me she was cold, so I went and fetched her out.*
>
> DI BLISS: *How do you mean she told you, Roddy?*
>
> DEF: *She come to me.*
>
> DI BLISS: *I'm sorry?*
>
> DEF: *Come to me in the night, look. They comes to me in the night and I'm cold too. Hard and cold.*
>
> DI BLISS: *Hang on, let me get this right – you're saying this was after she was dead? No – for the tape, please, Roddy, don't just nod or shake your head. You mean after she was dead.*
>
> DEF: *Yes.*
>
> DI BLISS: *After you killed her.*

DEF: Trying to trap me now, ain't you, copper?

DI BLISS: I'm being absolutely straight with you, Roddy. You were found with the dead body of Lynsey Davies. Somebody killed her, and as you seem to have buried her and dug her up again, you will agree that it's reasonable to suppose you also had something to do with her death. How well did you know Lynsey Davies?

DEF: Her said I was Satan. Give it her hard and cold like Satan.

DI BLISS: Was Lynsey Davies your girlfriend?

DEF: I ain't feeling good. Got a headache.

DI BLISS: Can I get you a glass of water?

DEF: Got a headache. Can't think proper.

DI BLISS: Roddy, you've seen a doctor, and he's pronounced you well enough to be interviewed.

DEF: Can't think. It's bloody shitty in here.

DI BLISS: This is not productive, Roddy. I asked you if you wanted a solicitor, and you said no, giving me the strong impression you were prepared to answer my questions. Now why aren't you doing that, Roddy? What's up with you, son?

DEF. Can't think in here.

'I'm sure you said that, once or twice, he appeared to black out – to faint,' Merrily said.

'He put his head down on the table, yes. He gave the appearance of having lost consciousness. He gave the *appearance* of it.'

'Frannie, if this was the same interview room you took me into, it was below ground level and lit by a fluorescent tube. It had electric air-conditioning. It had a tape machine. Also a video camera. An awful lot of electricity for a very small room – even *I* found it unhealthy in there.'

'Well, you know,' Bliss said, 'we'd naturally prefer to chat to prisoners in the police conservatory, to a background of gentle fountains and aromatherapy candles, but the uncouth ruffians *are* apt to throw up, break things and wee on the walls.'

'Humour me some more, Francis. How would the interview room compare to, say, Roddy's cell, which I think he kept asking to be taken back to. How much power was there in the cell?'

'Just the one ceiling light. But—'

'You ever heard of EH, Frannie?' She rose up. 'And *don't* tell me it's a hospital show on Channel Four.'

'No. I haven't heard of it.'

'Electrical Hypersensitivity. An allergy affecting people surrounded by electronic gadgetry or living in close proximity to high-voltage power lines and a confluence of transmitted signals, such as from mobile-phone masts, TV transmitters, satellite—'

'Merrily—'

'Probably only a very small percentage of people are affected to any marked degree. But in some cases we're talking about a serious, chronic condition. You might find, for instance, if you looked into it, that Roddy Lodge was unusually sensitive to electric light and wore sunglasses even at night-time. You might find he was unable to wear nylon overalls because of the static or whatever. And we already know about his mood swings – miserable and withdrawn and then, *I'm Number One, I'm Satan, I'm the best drainage man in the known universe, the biggest serial killer . . .*'

Bliss smiled. 'So this is your personal diagnosis. Roddy was suffering from a condition that appears to have gone entirely undetected by various doctors and psychiatrists, but may be identified by priests.'

Merrily sighed. 'I realize it's something not universally accepted.'

'Now tell me something I *hadn't* already surmised.' Bliss leaned back, locking his fingers behind his head. 'Like what other bullshit Mr Sam Hall filled you up with.'

Jane put her head around the door then. Merrily hadn't heard her come in from school. A long talk was way overdue.

'Hullo, flower. You want some coffee?'

'No, thanks. Sorry, didn't know you were busy.'

'You can come in if you want, Jane,' Bliss said. 'This is nothing *I*'d be terribly afraid of a little child hearing.'

'It's OK,' Jane said, with world-weary indifference. 'I try not to be seen hanging out with the Filth. People might think I'm a snout.' Her head vanished and they heard her going upstairs.

'I love that kid,' Bliss said. 'She's just like you, only more so.'

'Thanks.'

'Look, don't get me wrong. I even quite like Mr Hall, the old shit-stirrer, and I think his intentions are good. I even think there's probably a lot to what he says, about the profusion of overhead power lines arguably causing ill health. I just think that kind of wild speculation, at this stage of the game, about a man who isn't ever gonna be able to confirm it, is a totally pointless exercise.'

'It does explain a lot of things, though, doesn't it? It might even make sense to Mr Nye, the lawyer, who was convinced his client was in poor health.'

'So tell him! I'm sure he'd absolutely love to spend an hour or so, at no fee whatsoever, discussing his dead client's medical mythology.'

'It also explains why Roddy blacked out – which is common-place, apparently.'

'Who says?'

'Frannie, look, I had already *heard* of this. But it's something Hall's been researching for years, here and in America. I find it convincing, or at least worth investigating, but that's neither here nor there. I'm not out to try to prove or disprove it, I'm just saying it answers – very plausibly – a lot of questions.'

'No, it *doesn't*, Merrily, it just—'

'And it also explains why Roddy Lodge confessed to every putative murder you could lay on him.'

'Aw, come *on*!'

'EH is an acute condition. It can apparently become entirely unbearable. He'd have confessed to strangling his own granny to get out of that interview room.'

'Whose side are you *on* at all?'

'He'd offer to show you as many bodies as you wanted just

to get you to take him out of there. All the people he *hadn't murdered*.'

'All right.' Bliss finished off his coffee and laid down the mug. 'Let's look at this. He wanted us to take him out of the horrible, electronically charged interview room, back to his nice country home under the big pylon – which he then proceeded to *climb*.' He gave her a big smile. 'Go on, you take it from there.'

Merrily didn't say anything. She'd put the same point to Sam Hall. He'd said that in his experience no two cases of EH were exactly the same. He said allergics were often mysteriously drawn to the allergen in its most obvious form. He said a certain frequency of the electromagnetic field might prove particularly addictive to a particular person. He said this all needed much more research, but it was one explanation of why Roddy had climbed that pylon, just like he'd done repeatedly as a boy.

'Did you know that Melanie Pullman was a fellow sufferer?'

Bliss's eyes narrowed.

'With side effects. You interested?'

'Go on,' he said.

She told him about the side effects. She brought out the transcript of Canon Dobbs's report. Bliss read it slowly. He looked up and didn't smile.

'This is getting very silly, Merrily, even by your standards. Now we learn she was taken by aliens. Could even be the same aliens that strangled Lynsey and buried her under the tank.'

She carried on, in the face of it all. 'I also gather Roddy Lodge had been having inexplicable experiences for most of his life, and that his condition worsened when he moved to the bungalow, where electromagnetic radiation levels were far stronger. It seems likely their relationship – him and Melanie – grew out of mutual support.'

Frannie Bliss gritted his teeth, making a hissing noise. 'So they were both bonkers. What does that tell us? Does it explain why he might have killed her?'

'You're sorry you got me into this, now, aren't you?'

'I just don't understand why you suddenly care so much,' he said.

'Because I'm burying him, and too many funerals today are

superficial and meaningless and don't manage to lay anything to rest – we talk to relatives and we gather up a handful of anecdotes about the deceased and reel them off, then it's on with the soil and bring on the next one. I just think we owe it to them to try to understand what their lives were about. God, didn't *that* sound pompous?'

In the dregs of the daylight, she saw a shadow shambling past the big kitchen window. Not many people came round the back, not even Lol. This was someone who liked to move softly, like God's secret agent. Someone who even used spy-type euphemisms for the negative numina of his trade: *volatiles, insomniacs, hitch-hikers* . . . Bliss had his back to the window and hadn't seen the shadow.

She stood up. 'So . . . how are things at home, Frannie?'

'Crap, thank you,' Bliss said.

'Huw's here.'

'*Owen?* He stood up quickly. 'Shit. Is there another door out of here?'

35

Sackcloth

She'd never seen Huw like this before. He was white with anger, and he was wagging a forefinger under Frannie Bliss's nose.

' . . . Always feet first. Bloody great copper's boots. No matter how long you're in the CID, you never lose them copper's boots!'

The finger trembling in the lamplight.

'Huw . . .' Bliss was out of his chair again, and they were nearly head-to-head across the table. 'It's *my* career going down the bloody toilet, pal!'

Not the most well-chosen response, all things considered.

'Oh aye.' Huw's expression was . . . not priestly. 'Never a thought for the parents of all them dead and missing girls, lying awake night after bloody night wondering precisely what were done to their kids and how many times. Waking up in the dark, heads full of cellars and concrete. Dreams full of blood and filth and sobbing and wondering how long it went on before they died. How much of it they took before they wound up naked and dead under some . . . some bloody septic tank.'

'For starters,' Bliss said through his teeth, 'Lynsey Davies wasn't in fact found naked.'

'You *wanted* a national scare. Big, high-profile case to play with.'

'But not *now*, for Christ's sake! Will you just let me—?'

'Will you both, for God's sake, shut up?' Merrily said quietly. 'You're scaring the cat.' She came and sat down at the far end of the long table, away from both of them. 'And me.'

'Aye,' Huw said, looking at her at last, as if realizing where he was. 'I'm sorry.'

And she was shocked at the sight of him, at how much someone could change in six months or so. He was wearing his clerical shirt, the dog collar parchmented with age, under a patched tweed jacket. The effect was decrepit rather than casual. His long hair was dry and salted with dandruff, and there were lines she didn't remember down each cheek, deep as sewn-up knife wounds. He was breathing hard.

'Papers came same day for once. *West, West, West*. They all want him to be another West.'

'And what do *you* want?' Frannie Bliss's face was maroon under the freckles. 'We let it lie? We let the missing stay missing, the bodies stay buried?'

Huw had shut his eyes, was digging his knuckles into the table top. He stayed like that for several seconds before breathing out and opening his eyes, pulling out a rueful smile like an old handkerchief.

'Hello, lass.'

'Hello, Huw.'

'That woman,' Huw said to Bliss, as if the last few minutes had somehow been wiped. 'Lynsey. Were there any bits of her missing?'

'Bits?' Bliss sat down again.

'Bones. Fingers, toes.'

'Like Fred did to them?'

'Aye.'

'What are you talking about?' Merrily said.

'All of the West victims,' Bliss told her, 'had several bones missing. Mostly fingers and toes, but sometimes shoulder bones. Like he was keeping souvenirs.'

'Another of the reasons the Gloucester coppers suspected occult belief,' Huw said. 'A sense of ritual about it – always took the same bones.'

'I've been reading as fast as I can,' Merrily said. 'I just haven't got to this bit.'

'Came to a lot of bones – well over a hundred. None of them have ever been found.' Bliss turned to Huw. 'No, Roddy didn't go that far. Not with Lynsey. But then, she wasn't your *regular* victim, was she?'

'There *were* no regular victims, wi' West.' Huw's voice was as flat as hardboard again. 'Mostly they just ended up dead because there was nowhere else for them to go.'

Merrily winced.

'What I mean is,' Frannie Bliss said, 'Roddy probably killed Lynsey because she found out about him – what he'd been up to. Not just as a result of getting his rocks off.'

'West killed his own daughter, Heather, because she said she were leaving the happy home,' Huw said. 'Lost patience with her.' He turned to Merrily. 'Do you remember Donna Furlowe?'

'No. Who was she?'

Huw mopped up some spilled coffee with his sleeve, possibly to hide the fact that he wasn't replying. What the hell was the matter with him?

'I'll leave you to explain, Huw,' Bliss said. 'And then Merrily can tell you about this wonderful pseudo-scientific theory which argues that, far from being a psychotic serial killer, Lodge was actually a victim of his environment. Should comfort a lot of people.'

Huw looked up at Merrily. That old wolfhound look.

'I'm going home now,' Bliss said, 'to try and get used to spending more time with me family, who hate me nearly as much as me colleagues.'

Merrily had put the lamp back on the windowsill. It was all a little mellower in the room now. Huw was drinking tea, dunking chocolate digestive biscuits in it. His voice was softer.

'A twenty-first-century plague village, eh? Would it worry *you* to live there?'

'Actually,' Merrily said, 'I was only thinking earlier how much more exciting Underhowle was – more progressive, more *alive* than Ledwardine. But I suppose everything has its drawbacks. I mean, you can go on telling yourself it's all overheated rubbish, but every time somebody dies prematurely after living for five years under high-voltage power lines you immediately forget about all the people who spent half a lifetime underneath and made it to ninety-six.'

'And the apparitions? The hallucinations? The little grey men with big eyes?'

'Used to be that electrical gadgets were affected by aliens. Now they're saying electricity *creates* the aliens.'

'I can buy it,' Huw said. 'I can also accept that electrical stimulation of the temporal lobes, whether it's by a roomful of computers or whatever, simulates the sense of "presence" you get in a haunted house. But it's not the whole story. It's just another one of the rational explanations we have to be aware of. Another mine in the minefield.'

Merrily sat back, relieved. She might have guessed he'd know about it all: he subscribed to dozens of scientific and esoteric journals; his library filled four rooms of his rectory.

'Superficially, it's a fast-changing world, Merrily.' He brushed crumbs from his shirt-front. 'Your feller's right: we're surrounding ourselves wi' transmitters and receivers. We've got CCTV in every town centre, scores of techno-industries competing to sell us bits of tat that do some meaningless trick the only point of which is that the last bit of tat *couldn't* do it. And nobody really wants to tell us what it's all doing to our brains, else that's another industry gone to the wall. Oh aye, I'm perfectly willing to believe that a certain configuration of signals and electromagnetic fields in a small area is likely to set up a . . . what was it?'

'Hot spot.'

'However, once you start spreading these stories, the centuries drop away and you get into an essentially medieval situation. We're every bit as impressionable as folk were then. This gets around, there'll be five times as many people think they've got a brain tumour when it's only a headache. Five times as many kids who *think* they've got company at night when it's only a bad dream or headlights on the window pane. And if the rector's as unapproachable as you say, who else do they go to with their fears?'

'So why . . .' She hesitated. 'Why have you come, Huw?'

He dunked his biscuit. 'Merrily, if you think I know what I'm doing, you're wrong. If you think I'm a balanced, laid-back old bugger, wi' a steady finger on the pulse, you're wrong again. You don't know owt about me, really.'

'So tell me.'

'Bag of nerves? Bubbling cauldron of hatred and regrets? Oh aye. I reckon I've had a hatred of God, sometimes, as strong as anybody alive.'

'And Donna Furlowe?' Merrily said. 'Who is she?'

Silence.

'You remembered the name,' Huw said.

'Only from when you said it earlier. Who is she?'

'She isn't,' Huw said. 'Any more.'

And Jane, listening at the door, crept away. Thrown by that sentence. '*I reckon I've had a hatred of God, sometimes, as strong as anybody alive.*'

The things the clergy said sometimes, usually only to other clergy. She didn't know Huw Owen very well, suspected nobody did, really. She'd still been a kid when Mum had first met him, last year. Oh yeah, still a kid last year: she understood that now.

Jane went up to her apartment and sat on the bed. Probably Mum would be shouting up for her soon. *Flower, I'm really sorry about this, but how would feel about going to the chippy?* Always chips these days, since she'd got bogged down with this thing at Underhowle. And now Huw Owen was involved, which meant it was serious – something Huw didn't think a woman could handle, because he was from Yorkshire.

And sometimes he hated God. And when Yorkshiremen said *hated*, there were no two ways about it. If God existed, it must be rough to have nobody who really liked you, nobody who actually trusted you not to shaft them in the end. Jane looked up at the ceiling, and she began to giggle with sheer, sour despair.

You poor, all-powerful, sad git.

'I knew her mother, you see,' Huw said.

Merrily sat down. Huw was looking down at his fingers on the table. He'd pushed his mug away, and then the biscuits.

'Her mother lived in Brecon. Julia. A white settler in Mid-Wales. She were everything I didn't like. Well-off. Widow of a bloke who ran a company that did up old country properties and flogged 'em off to folk like themselves – rich and rootless, desirous of a slice of countryside, a view they could own. Julia had a lovely farmhouse, down towards Bwlch, and she worshipped at Brecon Cathedral.'

Merrily suspected Huw was a socialist of the old, forgotten kind; his contempt for the former Bishop of Hereford, Mick Hunter, and Hunter's New Labour friends was memorable. He leaned back. The lamplight made his skin look like sacking.

'I went into the cathedral one afternoon. August '93, this'd be. Funny, really – I hadn't intended to go in at all. I were going for groceries at Kwiksave, only the pay-and-display were full – height of summer, hordes of tourists. I weren't up for carrying a bloody great box about half a mile, so I decided to come back later. Parked up by the cathedral. Popped in, the way you do. Or, in my case, the way you don't, not often. And there was this woman near the back, very quietly in tears.' He looked across at Merrily. 'Some of 'em, they make a big deal out of it – *you* know that. They want a sympathetic priest to come over: *There, there, what's the problem?* This one was quite the opposite: private tears. You wouldn't notice, unless you were a bloke on his own, thinking, *What the bloody hell have I come in here for?*'

It was true. A cathedral was the last place you'd expect to find Huw – he might run into a bishop.

'I left her alone. How she wanted it, you could tell. Stayed well away, said nowt, walked out.'

Merrily was picturing Brecon Cathedral: dusky pink stone on the shaded edge of town, near what was left of the castle. Unlike most cathedrals, it was a very quiet place, usually.

'Anyroad, I sat on the grass, outside. Very warm day. Birdsong. Very near fell asleep. Didn't notice her until she were coming past, not looking at me, like I were some owd vagrant. I opened me eyes, and before I could think about it, I just said, "Tell me to sod off, lass, if you like . . ."'

Merrily was shaking her head. Who could resist that one? It was no big surprise to learn that, about fifteen minutes later, Huw and Julia Furlowe had been having afternoon tea together in a café in The Watton.

Her daughter was missing, this was it. Her only child, Donna, had just finished her final year at Christ College, Brecon, and was due to go up to Oxford in October. Meanwhile, she'd had a summer holiday job at a country hotel in the Cotswolds, up near Stroud. Although this was over two hours from home, and Donna had to stay there, it was a good arrangement because the proprietors of the hotel were family friends who would keep an eye on her. She was eighteen but, to be honest, her mother admitted, in some ways immature.

And now she was missing. She'd gone shopping in Cheltenham, getting a lift with the cook, arranging to meet him at a car park at four-thirty p.m. But when the cook came to collect his car, ten minutes later than arranged, she wasn't there. When she didn't show up after an hour, the cook called the hotel to find out if she'd made her own way back. When nobody had heard from her by nine that night, they first called Julia and then they called the police.

Three weeks now, and nothing. No sightings. Well, Cheltenham in August, what could you expect? Besides, missing eighteen-year-old girls, it wasn't all that unusual. Not in the summertime. Try not to worry *too* much, they said.

But Julia knew that something must have happened. They were close, she and Donna, always had been, especially since Tim had died, so suddenly – never any suspicion that there was anything wrong with his heart; he'd still been playing rugby at forty-eight.

Couldn't Donna have fallen in love – whirlwind holiday romance, gone off with him, the way young girls did? Absolutely out of the question. Was it possible Donna might have been unhappy about going to Oxford, felt unable to confide this to her mother? No, no, *no*. How could she be so sure? Because they were *close*. Truly, truly close.

The *Brecon and Radnor Express* had carried the story; Huw must have missed it. Julia Furlowe went to the Cathedral every day, to pray; Huw wouldn't have known, hadn't been near the place in weeks.

Middle of the following week, he'd driven Julia down to Stroud and Cheltenham and they'd done the rounds with colour photographs. *Have you seen this girl?* You wouldn't forget, if you had – lovely girl, soft ash-blonde hair.

Like her mother: Julia Furlowe, forty-nine, a widow for six years, one daughter, missing. A soft-spoken southerner, exiled in Wales. Alone now in a luxury farmhouse with a view down the Usk, where she painted local views in watercolour and gouache, very accomplished, and sold them in the local craft shops.

'And I held back,' Huw said. 'As you would in a situation like that. Held back a long time. Longer than *she* were inclined to. Separate rooms, the first three trips. By the fourth, it seemed ridiculous. We'd prayed together every night, always went to the nearest church and prayed together. Knelt together and prayed to God, for Donna to be all right.'

Merrily met Huw's eyes; his face was pale and roughened in the feeble light: sackcloth and ashes.

'We never lived together. I'd spend a couple of nights at her place at Bwlch, either side of Sunday. What a strange bloody time that were. Love and sadness. Love and anxiety. Love and stress, love and desperation. We used to tell each other how it would be when Donna turned up. Happen wi' a babby – Julia were ready for that . . . that would've been just fine. I used to think, I wonder what she's like when she's really smiling . . . smiling from the heart, without reservation?'

They spent Christmas together. Christmas 1993, the first Christmas there'd been no Donna. Christmas morning, Julia came to Huw's church, up in the Beacons. The locals knew by now, knew who she was but said nowt. A farmer's wife said she was glad for them, glad for Huw – a minister up here, all alone, it had never seemed right. Julia had cried a lot, that night.

The next day, she started a painting, of the snow on Pen-y-fan and then abandoned it, saying she had to get home – what if Donna had come back? What if she was coming back for New Year? Donna always loved New Year, more than Christmas as she'd got older.

Donna didn't come back for New Year.

It was sometime towards the end of February when Huw went over to Julia's place, picking up her paper, as usual, at the shop in Bwlch, tossing it down on the long coffee table in the vast stone sitting room.

And Julia had glanced at it and then picked it up and – he'd never forget this as long as he bloody lived – Julia had held the paper at arm's length, feeling in the pocket of her denim frock for her reading glasses.

And she'd said, almost vaguely, she'd said:

'That's *Fred*.'

A long moment, because Huw had read the story by then and thought nothing of it except his usual tired disgust, and Julia hadn't the faintest idea what it was about, she'd just seen the picture. Some nights, even now, Huw would lie in bed, hearing her voice on the north-east wind from Pen-y-fan: *That's Fred . . . that's Fred . . . that's Fred . . .*

'He'd worked a couple of times for her husband,' Huw said. 'Years before – before they'd come to Wales. When Donna was a little girl. When they were living at Highnam, near Gloucester. You never forgot Fred – such a cheerful little man, and a hell of a good worker. Nowt he wouldn't turn his hand to, Fred. And always a smile for you. Always a smile for a lady. And a big grin for little Donna.'

Huw's eyes were like glass. 'Oh dear God,' Merrily said.

'That were early days – the first bodies had been found at 25 Cromwell Street: Fred's daughter Heather and two other girls, Shirley and Alison. Within a week or so, he's confessed to nine more murders, and the whole bloody nation's agog. By April they're exploring two fields on the border of Much Marcle and Kempley. Digging up his first wife, Rena. Two months later, Ann McFall in Fingerpost Field.'

'You went to the police . . .'

'Oh aye. Like the relatives of every other missing girl within a hundred miles of Gloucester. And when it come out that Fred had worked for Tim Furlowe, that he knew Tim's family . . . See, all these girls – they weren't random kidnaps, he knew 'em all, before. Even Lucy Partington, the undergraduate, who seemed like a random snatch off the street, there's evidence he knew her slightly, way back. "*It's me? Don't you recognize me – worked for your dad?*"'

'But if Donna was just a child . . .?'

'The feeling was it happened the other way round. Donna

bumps into him in the street, in Cheltenham. He was always in Cheltenham. Well, not a face you ever forgot, West. Do anything for you.'

A soundtrack was playing in Merrily's head. Traffic and the bustle and chatter of a summer pavement and . . . '*Oh, gosh, it's Fred! I bet you don't remember me. Donna Furlowe?*' ''*Course I do, Donna, well, well, well . . . Give you a lift somewhere? The ole van's just round the corner.*'

Huw leaned his head forwards, digging his fingers into the skin of his forehead. When he looked up, there were red marks.

'That was when the police asked me if I knew of any satanic groups. I didn't, so I went round all the local Deliverance priests. Took some leave from the parish. Stayed in Gloucester for over a month, me and Julia. No more bodies, but they always expected to find more. But I think it was Lucy Partington did it for Julia. Not like the others – an intelligent, cultured girl. Found in Cromwell Street, with tape around the skull, bits of rope. Evidence of— You don't want to hear this, lass, I don't want to tell you.'

'She was Martin Amis's cousin, wasn't she? The novelist.'

'Aye. Cultured lass. Artistic. Sensitive. So the cops are saying now to West, what about Donna Furlowe? Where did you bury Donna Furlowe? He denies it. He always denied it. Just like he denied murdering Ann McFall – buried her, but he didn't kill her. He loved her, she was his angel – just let *him* bloody find out who killed her, that's all . . . He lied, you see, Merrily, he lied all along. And all the time, I'm saying to Julia, *It's coincidence. Coincidence, that's all, let's go home.* She wouldn't.'

'I wouldn't, either, if it had been . . .' Merrily swallowed. She found she was holding a hand to the neck of her black woollen jumper. She wanted to get up and make more tea, but she couldn't move.

'We did leave in the end,' Huw said. 'We had to. I had to go back to the parish, and the Deliverance courses were about to get started. But it were never same after that. I'd go over to Bwlch every other day. Stay the odd night. She'd keep saying, "I can't settle, Shep, I can't settle." Always called me Shep.

Said I reminded her of a border collie, always ready, always on watch.'

'Yes.'

Another Christmas. A couple of dozen half-finished paintings. Then a week later, New Year's Day 1995, Fred West, awaiting trial for a dozen murders, constructed a rope out of shirts – always a practical man – and hanged himself in his cell at Winson Green. Having told his carer he'd killed a lot more girls. As many as twenty more girls. No names.

'It were summer again before we knew it. This was when Julia told me about the medium in Brecon. I'd asked her to marry me by then, she said let's leave it a year, see how things are. And that she'd been to a bloody medium.'

'It's understandable. Kind of situation that sends most people to mediums.'

'*I* know that, lass. And all I could do was beg her not to. You know the shite that comes through at these bloody sessions . . . not to be trusted, mediums, not ever. We had a row. I didn't see her for a week. I went back, crawling, beginning of August 1995, and stayed the night, and when we got up the next morning there was a call from a copper in Gloucester to say they'd found a female body, butchered, in field near Lydbrook, in the Forest of Dean.'

Merrily tried to say something, couldn't. She hadn't known, hadn't recognized the name.

'We saw some of the clothes. She were still wearing clothes, but there were thick brown parcel-tape round the lower part of the skull.'

'Huw . . .'

'And bones missing. Finger bones and foot bones.'

Merrily's nails pierced her palms.

'See, we'd read it all by then. Hundreds of pages already in the papers, books being written, Rose coming up for trial on ten murder charges. She must've known . . . Oh aye, we all knew by then exactly what Fred West did to his victims, him and Rose. We knew all the details. Fred abusing his children and watching Rose with other men, through a hole in the door. Taking in girls, at first, who were up for it – *they* thought, but not the things Fred and Rose did, nobody were up for that. Then girls who weren't up for it, Fred and Rose getting off on the fear.'

And she heard him at Frannie Bliss across the table: *cellars and concrete . . . dreams full of blood and filth and sobbing.*

'Can I tell you what it were like for Julia, then, Merrily? Can I start to tell you?'

'No need.'

''Course not. She started painting again, within days. Painting Donna, from photographs. But very pale. Paintings you could see the white paper through, like she was trying to clean off the child's body. I tried to get her to come to the cathedral. She wouldn't. But she was still going to the medium. What could I say about that? I couldn't bring her comfort, the Church couldn't do owt.'

Huw was feeling in an inside pocket of his tweed jacket, bringing out what looked like an old tobacco pouch of yellow plastic. He unwrapped it and took out a small piece of folded paper. Thick paper, quality notepaper. He unfolded it and passed it across the table to Merrily. She took it to the lamp.

I'll keep it short, Shep.

I'm so, so sorry about this. But I do believe there is somewhere else – you showed me that, you know you did – and that Donna needs me there now. She so needs someone to comfort her, I feel this very strongly. I'm so very sorry, because I love you so much, Shep, you know I do, and it's only thinking of you and sensing your arms around me that's going to give me the last bit of strength I need for this, so please don't take your arms away and please, please forgive me, and please go on praying for us. I'm so SORRY.

Merrily stood there by the lamp, holding the paper, feeling its texture, the weight of it. Paper made to last. She was thinking of all those times she'd wondered if there had ever been a woman in Huw's life.

When he started to speak again, she couldn't look at him.

'It were me found her. I think that was what she wanted. Thought I were strong. Owd Shep. Seen it all. She'd left the farmhouse doors unlocked. Lovely balmy summer's evening, and an overdose of sleeping tablets.'

'Huw, I . . .' Blinking back the tears; that wouldn't help.

'God?' His voice was down on the flagstones. 'I went into me own church that night and screamed obscenities at God for the best part of an hour. Close as I've ever been to chucking it in. They say it makes your faith stronger in the end, and happen they're right, but you can't *possibly* know that at the time. It's not a time when faith makes any kind of bloody sense.'

'No.'

She had to put the paper down. Wondering if he'd brought it tonight specially to show her, or if he carried it with him all the time, in his inside pocket next to his heart, the suicide note of a woman he'd never really had and perhaps was already losing when she died.

36

Dying of Guilt

'And you know the joke?' Huw said.

'There's a joke?'

With the lights of Hereford city centre clustered in the rear-view mirror, Merrily headed left by the Belmont roundabout, finding the Ross road. They were going to make a surprise call on the Reverend Jerome Banks. Huw's idea. Huw sat placidly in the passenger seat, wearing his donkey jacket, hands clasped on his knees, no seat belt on. *Wears his scar tissue like a badge.* No, not like a badge at all. Like scar tissue, the kind that was never less than inflamed. She was glad she no longer had to look into his stricken eyes.

'The joke, Merrily, was that it's possible Donna wasn't down to West after all. 'The bones – aye *that* matched. Otherwise, a few differences. The Home Office pathologist were the first to question it. He knew the West style by then, see.'

'What kind of differences?'

'Well, there were nowt wrong with the hole. West used to bury them in holes that were deeper than they were wide. They weren't *graves*, they were holes. Practical. Like you'd have for dead sheep.' Huw's voice was as flat as the road ahead. 'Nobody had ever just stumbled on one of Fred's bodies. He'd cut them up, then bury them neatly. Efficient butchery, economical disposal.'

'Thank you, I've read about that.'

'And Donna *had* been cut up, but with no great skill. The head ... hacked off, the legs broken. The hands, too. One foot mutilated, bones removed. But not Fred's way, was how the pathologist saw it. Too rough, he figured, therefore too frenzied.'

But after Donna had been in the ground for the best part of

two years, Huw said, there was no strong forensic evidence either way – not much more than the pathologist's feeling that this wasn't down to Fred.

'You can bet most of the coppers *wanted* it to be him, mind. You don't want more than one of these buggers, do you? Not on the same patch. So whatever investigation there was must've been cursory, wi' over seventy per cent of the team convinced the case was already solved. Always somebody to say, Oh, happen Fred were in a hurry this time, not his usual self . . . especially under the circumstances.'

'Circumstances?' Down the Callow pitch now, and off into the country, reminding her of that night with Gomer, when it all began, experiencing again that feeling of being *drawn in*.

'He'd just had a rather difficult year, Merrily. One of his kids had told a schoolfriend about the domestic arrangements at 25 Cromwell Street, and Fred had found himself in Gloucester court facing charges of tampering with a daughter. Three counts of rape, one of buggery. Rose next to him, accused of cruelty and complicity. Police and social services walking all over the beloved home, kids taken into care. So then Fred has to discuss his married life in detail with the coppers – '*My wife and I, we leads a very full sex life.*' Nudge bloody nudge.'

'They got off, though, didn't they?'

'Aye. So near and yet so far. In the end, the victim wouldn't give evidence. Nobody would. Nobody wanted to break up the happy home. So they got off, the pair of 'em – embracing in the dock, picture of bloody innocence.'

But the police had been inside number 25, seen all the signs – the sex aids, the pornographic home-videos. And, while the other children were in care, the social workers had heard the family jokes about Heather, who was missing (run off with a lesbian, Fred said), being buried under the patio. It was the beginning of the end. Within nine months they'd arrested him for the murder of Heather, buried more or less where she was said to be buried. Not a very good joke any more.

So did Fred realize the clock was ticking? Was he determined to get a last one in before the bells went off? Or did he just happen to run into Donna in Cheltenham and couldn't resist?

Or did somebody else kill her?

'You think Donna might've been killed by Roddy Lodge, don't you? That was what you told Bliss. And it's no wonder Frannie's excited. Because if this *was* down to Lodge, it proves that we're not just looking at another copycat,' Merrily said.

'No.'

'Because, while it might not have been a perfect match, it was still very close to West's *modus operandi*, including the bones. And when poor Donna was buried, two years before the arrest and all the publicity, the only way anyone could possibly have known about West's *modus operandi* would have been by *actually knowing West*.'

'There we are, then,' Huw said placidly.

So Huw had come to take over, AGENDA written now in neon capitals between the lines on his forehead. Huw was running a crusade on behalf of *the parents of all them dead and missing girls, lying awake night after night wondering precisely what were done to their kids and how many times*.

Or just for one parent, one girl.

Or just – God forbid – for his own redemption.

Now Huw wanted to talk to the Reverend Jerome Banks, to whom Roddy Lodge had gone with his haunted-bungalow stories and been turned away. Why? And why had Banks offloaded the funeral so fast? Why had he *really* done that? Huw wanted answers. Huw Owen, with his wolfhound hair and his slow-burn stare.

Scary.

Before they left, Merrily had gone up to the apartment, with the chip money in one hand – Jane, at seventeen, was becoming what in Liverpool they used to call a latchkey kid. This couldn't go on.

'Flower, Huw and I have . . . someone to see.'

'Wow,' Jane said in her most bored tone. 'Really?'

'Shouldn't take long, but—'

'Yeah, yeah, chips'll be fine.'

'Unless you want to come along? We could call somewhere for a meal afterwards.'

Jane had turned down the stereo and stared at Merrily, with that awful twisted little smile. 'Let me get this right. You're offering me a night out with a couple of vicars talking shop. Discussing like *God's Work.*' The kid had sighed, shaking her head in slow motion. 'Merrily, if you only *knew* how distressingly patronizing that sounded.'

'You used to be quite interested in . . . aspects of the job.'

'Interests change,' Jane said. 'Or maybe we get people wrong. Like, for quite a while, I thought my mother had a normal interest in men.'

'Now what does *that* mean?'

Jane had shrugged.

They passed a pub on the Ross road called, with an awful irony, The Axe and Cleaver.

'If there ever is evidence that Lodge killed Donna,' Merrily said, 'what could that mean? It would seem to me to suggest there really might have been a group of them.'

'Aye. The cult that Fred talked about, and everybody thought he were just trying to spread the blame. However, when all's said and done, if Roddy Lodge killed Donna he didn't kill Julia. Fred killed Julia.'

'You mean just the thought of . . . ?'

'The thought of Fred and Rose and what they'd done to the others. The images of his hands on Donna. Julia was an artist. She couldn't live with the images.'

'I'm so sorry, Huw.'

'Been dreaming about her again, Merrily. Julia and her white portraits of Donna. Keep seeing the white portraits. I've got one at home. I don't think she's at peace. I don't think either of them are at peace.'

'No.'

'And West's still killing,' Huw said. 'He always has been. You read about his grown-up children attempting suicide. And a man called Terry Crick: in January 1996, he attached a hose to his car exhaust and killed himself with carbon monoxide . . . couldn't live with the thought that he might've stopped it. They were mates, you see, back in the late sixties – young Terry, bit of a hippy then, and genial young Fred. Do anything for you, Fred. Showed Terry his abortion tools once. Very proud of his abortion tools, was Fred. Loved to tell women that if they ever needed help that way, he was their man. Terry thought it were a joke.'

'Huw—'

'Until, years later, when he read about the case and remembered staying with the Wests when they were in a caravan near Cheltenham, hearing Fred and Rose giggling in bed . . . became convinced he must've heard future murders being conceived. Didn't go to the police until it were too late. Couldn't go on living with the thought that he might've prevented something. People have been dying of guilt, Merrily. I doubt it'd've made any difference at all if Terry Crick had told the cops about Fred West waving his abortion tools around. Just having a laugh, Fred would've said. Mucky owd tools like that, who'd believe it . . . ? Why've you stopped?'

Merrily wrenched up the handbrake and switched off the engine. 'I was trying to tell you – Banks's rectory is up that lane on the left, I think. You still want to go?'

'Of course I still want to go. Be some guilt there, I reckon, don't you? Let's go and help Mr Banks get it off his chest.'

They were parked with two wheels on the verge, at the side of the A49, the old Volvo shaded by high bushes still heavy with sodden leaves. Merrily said quietly, 'One more time – what are you doing here, Huw?'

Never before, in all the hours she'd spent with him, had she felt the quiver of instability that was now so real it was almost shaking the car.

'Covering me back,' he said. 'Put it like that if you want. Call it selfishness. Call it me not wanting to take any guilt to *my* grave if more lives get lost.'

'Why should more get lost?'

Huw leaned back against the passenger door. 'If there's a group of people out there *still*, and they're taking lives or harming folk in any way, it's a police matter. If there's a spiritual evil, it's ours. Accepted?'

'I suppose so.'

'I don't know anything about Lodge – yet. But I know a lot about West. A man driven by lust. An uneducated man who arranged his life around the constant need for sexual pleasure. No moral values, no sense of remorse. Not a hint of basic *decency*. A man who watched through holes in doors, who had sex with his own kids because they were *there*. In his house. *His* house. The house he'd converted with his own tools. A man who loved nobody, yet loved *things*. Tools, gadgets. A man who *possessed*.'

'Huw—' Merrily wound down the window. She wanted both fresh air and a cigarette.

'And what's changed, Merrily? He might've gone, physically, but how many people have died *since*?'

'Because the lamp of the wicked must be put out.' Cold air on her face. 'That's why you're here. You've come with a view to snuffing out his lamp, haven't you?'

'Start the car,' Huw said roughly. 'Let's go and see this bugger Banks.'

Dressed for dinner, in a dark wool jacket over a white blouse, her features sharp with suspicion, Mrs Pawson was scanning the reception area at the Royal Hotel for whoever had put out the call.

Lol stood up and walked over to her. He didn't have the smallest idea how he was going to handle this but, on the night before his first gig in nearly two decades, fear was relative.

'What do *you* want?' Mrs Pawson's voice was hard and brittle as dried nail varnish. She was flicking glances to either side of him, probably to see if there was anyone around she could call on if he attacked her.

'Have you . . . ?' Lol looked around too, saw two elderly women, nobody else. 'Could you spare a few minutes?'

Mrs Pawson didn't move. 'What's this about?'

'It's about Lodge,' Lol admitted. 'I've not been able to stop thinking about what you said this morning, and I'm sorry, but I think there was more you *weren't* saying.'

'And are you, in fact, something to do with the police?'

Though aware that Mrs Pawson's general experience of the

drainage trade would not predispose her to be generous or open, he still shook his head.

'In that case,' she said, 'I do *not* want to speak to you. That man caused enough damage. I don't want to discuss him. You'd better go.'

Lol nodded and had half turned away, to leave, when he suddenly turned back. He'd thought about this a lot after returning to the studio, rehearsing a couple of songs in a desultory kind of way, finding that even at the eleventh hour his heart wasn't in it. Mrs Pawson had been perhaps the last person to have any business dealings with Lodge, and she was a woman on her own and something was *not right*.

'You mentioned another woman,' he said. 'When you said Roddy Lodge was a nightmare person, I didn't think you were talking about getting conned over a septic tank. And then you mentioned a woman.'

And then he told her that he'd been there when Lodge had died, standing underneath that pylon. And that something like this didn't just go away. He told her he didn't normally work with Gomer Parry and was just helping out because Gomer had had a lot of trouble that he didn't imagine Mrs Pawson even knew about as it hadn't exactly been national news. And then he told her he and Gomer were both friends of the church minister who'd landed the job of burying Lodge.

He shook his shoulders helplessly and told her what a small county it was. He apologized to her again.

Mrs Pawson looked him in the eyes. 'You don't give up, do you?'

'Usually, yes,' he said, 'to be honest.'

'What's your name?'

'Robinson. Laurence Robinson. If you don't want to talk to me, what about Merrily Watkins?'

'The priest?'

'I could probably arrange that. Maybe I could bring her here.'

She stared at him. 'Why do you think I'd want to talk to a priest?'

'I was thinking maybe a woman. The woman who found the body in the shovel of Lodge's digger after he . . .'

It was this that seemed to do it.

Jerome Banks's study had Ordnance Survey maps on the walls, with coloured drawing pins marking his churches. It was next to the living room and you could hear the sound of the TV through the wall. His wife was sitting in there. He'd told her not to bother with refreshment; this wouldn't take long.

Jerome was irritated by their visit and was making no effort to conceal it.

'My day off,' he said. 'Always take every second Tuesday off, everyone knows that.'

The wrong attitude to take with Huw, tonight.

'Creature of habit, eh?'

'Something wrong with that? I've always found people like to know where they are with their clergy.'

'No mysteries,' Huw said.

None here, Merrily thought. The rectory was a modern house on the edge of a small estate of neo-Georgian detached homes west of Ross. There was a cold street lamp outside the study window. Only one hardwood chair in front of the desk, and he'd made Merrily sit in it, and she felt very small but aware that this probably wasn't going to be her showdown.

Jerome Banks surveyed Huw, both of them standing up. They were about the same height, but Banks held himself straighter. Military backbone. His checked shirt was crisply ironed, and you could have sliced bread with the creases of his trousers. 'We met before?' He had stiff, sandy hair and a nose with a small red bump on the tip, like a bell push.

'Can't see it, somehow,' Huw said.

'No. If you're who I think you are, I agree it's unlikely. And if you've come about what I think you've come about, I doubt there's much I can say to assist you.'

'What would that be?'

'You tell me, Mr Owen.'

'Well, like a lot of people, including the police, I'm becoming a little concerned about events in and around the village of Underhowle. And in my experience it's always best to have a chat with the lad on the ground. We don't stick our noses in much these days, the clergy, but there's not much we don't at least hear about.'

'Some of us stick our noses in further than others,' Banks said.

'Agreed. How long have you got before retirement, Jerome?'

Banks coloured. 'Obviously, Owen, I've heard about you and your little *Deliverance* empire. Your incantations and your Thermos flasks of holy water, your new medievalism. And, yes, you're quite right. I *don't* have long before retirement – eighteen months at the most – and I don't intend to spend any of that time kow-towing to the charismatics and the damn *happy-clappies*!'

Merrily smiled.

Huw scowled. 'I don't clap much, pal. And I'm not happy.'

'What do you *want*?'

'I want to know about a few of the incidents that've been brought to your notice but which you haven't felt inclined to do owt about, being as how you're not into *new medievalism*.'

Merrily sat still and said nothing. She just wouldn't have dared . . .

'I don't even know what you're talking about,' Banks said, but he'd left too long a pause. 'If you think I've been "got at" over the Lodge funeral, I can show you two dozen letters and a small petition, all of them urging me not to bury Lodge at Underhowle, and no letters at all in support.'

'Urging?' Merrily said. 'No threats, then? *I've* had a threat.' Huw looked at her. 'Had an anonymous phone call warning me to stay at home on Friday.'

'You never said owt about that,' Huw said. 'You told the police?'

'As the funeral's now tomorrow, I didn't think it really applied.'

'If anyone had threatened *me*,' Banks said, 'I should have made a point of personally digging the grave.'

'Why did you suggest Merrily for the job?'

Banks waited a couple of seconds. '*Did* I suggest her?'

'Somebody did.'

'Perhaps because her name had already been mentioned in connection with Lodge?'

Huw nodded, letting the silence hang until Merrily began to feel uncomfortable.

'Look,' Banks said, 'I'm aware that there's a particular local activist in the Underhowle area with a chip on his shoulder about high-voltage power lines and pylons being detrimental to health and possibly causing some people to have . . . odd experiences. I don't necessarily subscribe to any of that and if I did, I should be obliged to conclude that it wasn't a matter at all for the Church – not even your particular outpost.'

'Aha,' Huw said.

'You've had reports of odd experiences?' Merrily said.

'As you know, people often say things they have difficulty justifying.' Banks was gazing over Merrily's head at his own and Huw's reflections in the window. 'Often because they want rehousing. A better house. Think we're all idiots.'

'This is hauntings?' Huw asked.

'As there are usually also physical symptoms, I've tended to refer people to the doctor.'

'He cure them?'

'I've no idea. I have heard of some people going to so-called alternative practitioners in Ross and Hereford. The very people to deal with their alternative problems. It's nothing to do with religion.'

'And that's what you said to Lodge, eh?'

The tip of Banks's nose went white. 'How bloody *dare* you—'

'Look!' Merrily stood up. She was getting tired of breaking up Huw's fights. 'Mr Banks, you might not think much of what we do – or try to do – but if there's a remote possibility that it helps people to cope, we'll just . . . we'll muddle on, if you don't mind. If I told you what this was really about, you probably wouldn't thank me. And call me overzealous, but I kind of like to know exactly who I'm burying. Isn't that the most important thing we ever do for someone?'

'Are you trying to tell me my job?'

'Not your job any more,' Huw said. 'You unloaded it. Be interesting to know why.'

'You *know* why – matter of local politics.'

'So you ignored all the other complaints of psychic intrusion for purely political reasons, and not wanting to encourage happy-clappy hysteria.'

'You bastard.'

Huw beamed. 'That's the first perceptive deduction you've made all night, pal.'

'Look,' Merrily said, 'we all appreciate that we – the clergy – come from different directions . . . which is healthy. And we're not trying to cause trouble, Mr Banks. We'd just like to be able to work out what we're dealing with. A bit of background – in confidence – would help.'

She watched Banks contemplating this, working out where he stood.

'All right,' he said. 'And this *is* political. One complaint concerned the old Baptist chapel.'

'The one more or less adjacent to Lodge's garage.'

'Disused. Previously used as a bottling plant for spring water, which failed. Now being converted into a museum, or some sort of visitor centre. But still a Baptist chapel in my eyes, and I *don't* intrude on other denominations.'

'You were told the place was haunted?'

'I was told of disturbances, but some looked to me to be of distinctly human origin. For instance, the firm working on the conversion had complained of equipment going missing. Nothing supernatural *there*. Probably find the items in various garages in Goodrich Close.'

'And that was it?'

'Oh, the usual: noises, smells. I suggested they had the drains examined for blockages. Suggested they . . .' Banks smirked ' . . . hired Lodge to look into it. In fact, I believe he owned the chapel at one time. Came with the garage. All part of the bottling enterprise, which I gather failed because of impurities in the spring water.'

'And did they hire him?' Merrily asked.

'I don't know. The Development Committee had obtained some sort of grant to buy the property from Lodge. I . . . don't really know. I do know that one building firm apparently refused to work there after a while. You'd have to ask Mrs Sollars about that; she's supposed to be in charge there.'

'Erm . . . When we spoke on the phone a few nights ago, you said Roddy Lodge came to you with a problem, the details of which you seemed to have difficulty remembering.'

'He was—'

'Barking, you said. Lodge told you he was seeing images of women in his new bungalow. Which I understand from relatives was nothing very new for him. When he was a child, he seems to have created projections of his dead mother – or mother-substitutes. Comfort projections. Maybe you or I wouldn't have been able to see them, but it was all very real to him. And when he moved into the bungalow, the images – hallucinations, whatever – obviously intensified, whether through environmental effects, or . . . Anyway, they seem to have acquired a different . . . status. And this was what he told you about, wasn't it?'

Banks turned away, stood thinking. Then he went to sit behind his desk. There was a regimental photo on it: Banks and fellow officers either side of an armoured car.

'It disgusted me,' he said. 'And after half a lifetime in the Army, as you can imagine, I'm not easily disgusted.'

'He told you about having sexual fantasies involving women who were now dead.'

'Yes.'

'How long ago was this?'

'About two years ago.'

'Did he just show up and ask to talk to you?'

'No, he . . . I don't know whether I should be telling you this, but he was more or less referred to me. By his GP. Dr Ruck.'

'This is the same man *you* refer people to when they complain of nocturnal apparitions or whatever?'

'He'd gone to Allan Ruck with general complaints of debilitation, headaches, muscle pains. And then he'd starting talking about all this psychic malarkey. I believe Allan eventually sent him to a brain specialist, but of course they couldn't find anything. After that he could only suggest a psychiatrist. Lodge reacted somewhat aggressively to this. Ruck said, then why don't you go and see the rector?'

'Palming him off.'

'If you like.'

'Did nobody even consider the possibility of anomalous electrical—?'

'And give that maniac Hall more ammunition? Anyway, how could it possibly explain the sexual fantasies?'

Huw said, 'Electrical stimulation, if I've got this right, of the septum area of the brain.'

'I think what we're suggesting,' Merrily said, 'is that if someone like Roddy Lodge, who already has a well-established fantasy life, moves into what's become known as an electromagnetic hot spot, then the foundation – the template – for sexual fantasies of a very real and intense kind is already laid. Perhaps it all became just a bit *too* intense. Too intense to be pleasurable, in the conventional sense. And coupled with the debilitating physical effects of electro-hypersensitivity . . . Well, no wonder he went to his doctor.'

The mobile shuddered in her coat pocket. She thought, *Jane*.

'Tell me,' Banks said, 'what basic proof do you have of any of this, Mrs Watkins?'

'None at all. When do people like us ever have proof?' She pulled out the phone. 'Excuse me.'

She went to stand in the doorway, remembering Banks telling her on the phone that he'd actually offered 'prayers for the Unquiet Dead' but Roddy Lodge had rejected the idea. *Bumptious? Full of himself? Never seen the like, I wasn't entirely sure, to tell you the truth, if he wasn't taking the piss*. It suggested that, while Roddy would have been very glad to lose the side effects, he really didn't want to part with his ghosts, which was perhaps why he'd resisted Melanie Pullman's efforts to get him to talk to Sam Hall.

'This is Merrily,' she said into the phone.

'Where are you?'

'Lol! I'm out near Ross.'

'That's brilliant. You—'

'I'll call you back, OK? Five minutes.'

'So what advice did you give Roddy Lodge, Jerome?' Huw said. 'What did you recommend for his little problem? Cold showers?'

Banks looked down at his desk. Waited his customary two seconds before replying.

'I believe I told him to – in the modern parlance – get a life.'

Huw smiled.

Banks didn't. He looked at each of them in turn, as if to make sure they understood the significance of what he was about to say.

'I suggested to Lodge that instead of following his solitary . . . pursuits, he might consider making the acquaintance of real girls.' Bringing his fist down on the desktop. '*Real girls!*' The fist coming down twice, like a mallet. '*Now* do you see?'

37

Long Old Nights

Jane heard the voice from the kitchen and grinned with relief, saw herself floating in slo-mo across the room and into the scullery towards the answering machine and the phone, the light entering her eyes like turning up a dimmer switch, and then . . .

Then *what?*

'Er, this is actually quite important,' Eirion said, 'so I'm going to hang on for about half a minute while you decide if you can possibly spare some time to speak to me.'

Jane didn't move. Had to admit that what she was missing most right now was having someone she could open up to – someone she could lay her deepest, most secret fears on. Someone who knew exactly where she was coming from. And who was not her mother.

It was just that she'd been trying to avoid considering the name Eirion in this context – even though there was no one else.

Eirion said, 'Basically, it relates to a website I found concerning the Archangel Uriel.'

Naturally, he was uncomfortable too, after what had passed between them. He needed a pretext.

'It's something I thought you ought to know about. I mean, I don't know much about this stuff, and I believe it's very much on the iffy side of the scriptures, and with people who do websites you get a lot of cranks and fanatics – but the site gives a list of people throughout history who it reckons have become vehicles for Uriel. Especially women. And the thing is, you seem to be one of them.'

'*Me?*' Jane said.

And simultaneously realized the truth. This wasn't for her at all. The bastard was addressing *Mum*.

Jane felt cold, like marble. Wasn't exactly the first time they'd conspired, was it?

The doorbell went. Meanwhile, the treacherous git was still waiting for someone to pick up the phone; she could hear his breathing in the speaker. Panting – overweight.

Jane straightened up, raised a stiffened forefinger at the answering machine and went to answer the door. Hoping it was Uncle Ted or someone else who she could take down with her, whose night she could ruin.

In the hall, she was about to give the finger to the The Light of the World, when she met the eyes of the guy with the lamp – saw how old he looked, noticed his crown of thorns, felt that it must actually hurt in a nagging, chronic kind of way – and didn't give him the finger after all. It would've been gratuitous. She was *not* gratuitous.

The bell went again. Jane turned on the porch light and opened the front door.

Jenny Driscoll stood there, in a shiny waxed jacket with a white scarf half over her head, Virgin Mary-style.

Merrily felt in the driver's-door pocket and brought out her pectoral cross. She slipped the chain over her head, under the cowl of her sweater.

'I can't believe we *did* that.'

'Did what, lass?'

'Good priest–bad priest.' Her initial sense of triumph felt wrong now. She started up the car and pulled away from Jerome Banks's executive rectory.

'Aye,' Huw said, 'one so seldom gets an opportunity for such finesse.'

'Huw, we practically bludgeoned the truth out of the poor sod!'

'Doesn't matter how we did it – where's it got us, apart from a hint on the Baptist chapel? Not far. Confirms what you already knew: Lodge were a sick bugger, on a number of levels. But Banks's professed sense of guilt – that's half-arsed. Who's going to believe Lodge got launched into a life of rape and murder by a man-to-man chat with the rector? I'm disappointed. I expected summat better than this.'

'You can see why he wouldn't want it broadcast, though.' She braked at the poorly lit T-junction with the A49. 'And why he didn't want to conduct the funeral.'

'If it were me, I'd feel bloody well obliged to conduct it.' Huw sank back and stretched out his legs.

Merrily fumbled a Silk Cut from the packet. 'Could you pass me the lighter from the dash, or can I use your halo?'

'Cheeky besom.' He found the lighter and lit her cigarette. 'This woman we're going to see, this is the woman whose septic tank . . . ?'

' . . . Started it all.' The tiered skyline of Ross appeared, part-floodlit, across the dual carriageway and the Wye: the Hereford-shire Riviera. Behind it was Howle Hill, the Forest, the dark country. 'And as we don't want to scare her, you can stay in the car.'

Mrs Jenny Box, née Driscoll said, 'You're not expecting her back soon at all, are you, Jane?'

'Well, she said she—'

'Thought not.'

Driscoll sat with her white scarf around her shoulders and the cup of weak tea Jane had made in front of her on the refectory table.

Not quite the soft touch that Jane had expected.

In fact, knowing the woman's background, why had she expected a soft touch at all – Driscoll having come over from Ireland, worked with the hard cookies of the fashion world, the flash cynics in television. Having been married, for years, to Gareth Box.

Jane sat across the table, uncomfortable. Why hadn't she just told the woman that Mum was out and offered to pass on a message? Instead of thinking this could be heaven-sent and saying what Gareth Box had said: *she can't be long, I suppose. Do you want to come in and wait?* Getting her into the house, just the two of them, a cosy chat. This woman: Mum's . . . lover?

Would-be! Would-be lover!

Oh Christ, get me out of this.

'So, is there something you wanted to say to me, Jane?'

This soft-spoken, soft-eyed, soft-skinned woman, sitting with her soft hands, one over the other, on her lap. This very feminine woman. Very feminine, like Mum. Wasn't one of them supposed to be kind of . . . butch?

Something she wanted to say? She said the first thing that came into her head. 'The Archangel Uriel.'

'And what about her?' Jenny Box asked gently.

'*Her?*'

'Of the four principal archangels, Uriel is the only one sometimes perceived as female. In works of art mainly.'

'Oh.'

'You don't know too much theology, do you, Jane?'

'I know quite a lot about angels, actually. But that's not proper theology anyway. The Bible doesn't have very much to say about angels. And certainly not Uriel, who only shows up in the book of Esdras, in the Apocrypha – which is like a bit iffy.'

'The Bible's been censored more times than you or I will ever know,' said Jenny Box. 'Uriel's the Divine Fire, an energy of light and summer. Of warmth. And so can only be female. Which, I suppose, was one reason she was pushed out of the picture for so long.'

Jane found she was clasping and unclasping her hands under the table. She pulled them apart. 'So like this would be the Uriel you're supposed to have . . . over the church?'

'She told you about that?' No expression. Not bothered.

'She tells me everything. We're very close. She . . .' Jane hesitated. *Sod it.* 'She told me about the money, too.'

'Ah yes,' Jenny Box said, 'the money. Doesn't everybody always get so excited about money?'

'I mean, like . . . *was* it you who brought it?'

Mrs Box raised a faint eyebrow. 'An anonymous gift is an anonymous gift, Jane. 'Twas always my feeling that *all* donations to the Church ought to be anonymous. Nobody can buy admission to Heaven, can they now?'

'You're pretty slick, really, aren't you?' Jane said.

Jenny Box laughed. 'Years around TV. So hard to shed. All right, where's your mother, really?'

Jane shrugged awkwardly. 'Ross, I think.'

'Underhowle?'

'Maybe.'

'I hoped to speak to her about that. I read all the papers. I've been up in London and I read all the papers on the train coming back. That's more important than she could know – maybe what her whole life's been leading up to, you know?' She smiled at Jane. 'Yes, I'm sure you do.'

'No.' Jane felt a slow seepage of anger. 'No, I *don't* know, actually.'

'Oh? I thought you said she told you everything.'

'But not as much as she tells you, evidently.'

The eyebrow went up again, like a goldfish flicking its tail.

'You never really saw an angel at all, did you, Mrs Box?' Jane said. Because at this stage of the game there was really nowhere else to go.

Mrs Pawson's arms were down by her sides, stiff. Lol saw the knuckles tighten on her small, white fists. Oddly, he found he was starting to like her. She didn't seem neurotic, she was really quite strong. She probably would have got along quite well in the country, in normal circumstances.

They were waiting in a carpeted, cream-walled passageway, people passing them on the way to dinner.

'Mr Robinson, I'm not usually a wilting violet, and if I thought this might have helped someone I would have told the police. I would have made a full statement. But, as you said, he's dead. Lodge is dead, and . . . *oh* . . .'

They'd both seen the discreet glint of the cross at the entrance to the passage, and Lol's heart did what it always did when he saw Merrily for the first time, after . . .

He said, 'I'll go, shall I? Leave you to it.'

Mrs Pawson looked embarrassed. 'No, don't. This is becoming surreal.'

Merrily smiled, held out a hand. 'I'm Merrily.'

A man and a woman had come out of a room to the right,

and Mrs Pawson looked in through the door. 'This is empty now. Let's go in here.'

They followed her in, Lol shut the door behind them. It was a residents' lounge, narrow, with pink and gold Regency-striped sofas and the same extensive view as the one from The Prospect.

'How is this really going to help anyone?' Lisa Pawson said.

Merrily walked to the window. 'Wonderful view.' There was a floodlit terrace and, in the middle distance, the lights of the traffic on the bypass. She turned to Mrs Pawson. 'I get the feeling we've both had slightly disturbing experiences with Roddy Lodge. I'm supposed to be conducting his funeral, and I suspect there's quite a lot that needs to be laid to rest.'

Mrs Pawson was holding her blouse together at the neck, as if it had suddenly gone cold in the room. 'I was teaching in comprehensive schools for fifteen years, and I've seen some very distasteful things. But this . . . I still don't see how it would help *you* to know about it?'

Merrily sat down on one of the sofas, near the window. 'If you had a missing relative – a daughter, a sister – wouldn't you want to know whether there'd been another Fred West at work?'

'I mean, in some places,' Jane said, 'there are *legends* of angels being seen. Like in the local folklore. And apparitions of the Virgin and all that. But, I mean . . . Ledwardine? Do me a favour.'

Immediately regretting the scorn, but it was too late now.

'You don't believe people see angels, Jane?' Jenny Box said.

'Depends what you mean by angels.'

'Oh, I think we all know what we mean by angels.'

'I think I know what *you* mean.'

'I'm entirely sure of what I mean. *And* what I saw.'

'What I think is that you just saw Mum. You were looking for somewhere to live – like, that bit was probably true. You were looking for somewhere to live and to like . . . entertain yourself. Out of sight of the media and all the London gossips. And then you saw Mum.'

'Eventually, yes.'

'And you fancied her,' Jane said.

Jenny Box didn't move, but her eyes flickered. Jane was suddenly so choked up with horror at what she'd said, mixed with rage and hurt at the possibility of it being true, that she could hardly get her breath.

'That's something like blasphemy, Jane.'

Jane stood up. 'It's true, though, isn't it? You've got, like, everything – brilliant house, successful business, gorgeous husband – and you have to come here and mess with people's lives. There's nothing angelic in any of this. *Divine fire?* Like, the way I see it, there's only one kind of divine fire as far as you're concerned.'

Jenny Box was out of her chair now. She was very pale. Her white scarf had slipped to the flags.

Jane was in tears. It didn't matter; she'd said it. It was out. Her eyes were wet. She wiped her sleeve across them and saw Jenny Box picking up her white scarf. Then the older woman was standing at the open kitchen door, with the table and ten feet of stone flags between them.

Jenny Box said, 'When did you see my husband?'

'How do you know . . . ?'

'He's back in London now. We have the same houses, but we don't live together. Did he come here?'

'No.'

'Which means you went to him.' Jenny Box stood in the doorway, and when she spoke all that fey lilt had been punched out of her voice. 'And did he touch you, Jane? As well as defaming me the best he could, did he touch you?'

'*What?*'

'Did you let him near you?'

Jane felt her mouth going out of shape.

'It's all right,' Jenny Box said calmly. 'I won't distress you further. I'm going now.'

Jane came round the table, her fists clenched. When she reached the hall, Jenny Box had the front door open and was standing next to the Holman Hunt picture, half under the porch light but blocking it, so that it looked for a moment as if she was actually lit by the lantern that Christ was carrying in the picture. Her face was as white as a communion wafer. And she was muttering 'Oh, dear God, dear God,' and pulling her scarf over her head.

'It was as if they wanted me to know,' Mrs Pawson said. 'From the first.'

'They *both* came to install it?' Lol asked.

'It was quite a warm autumn day. She – the woman, Lynsey – was wearing a skimpy black top with nothing underneath it. Even when they were unloading the appliance from the truck, they kept touching one another all the time.'

'What was *she* like?' Merrily said.

'Quite a big woman. Not much over medium height, but big bones. She had black, frizzy hair, dark eyes. She wasn't *particularly* good-looking, but she had a sexiness about her, I suppose you'd have to call it. A sexiness that was not so much sultry as *glowering*. The way she moved – prowled – even when she was working, hauling these plastic pipes and equipment and . . . She hardly ever smiled – that was something that struck me – and when she did it wasn't a very big smile, and . . . sly isn't quite the word. It was as if she knew something you didn't.'

Lol noticed that Mrs Pawson kept glancing at one of the table lamps as if to make sure it was still on.

'I made the mistake of asking them in when they first arrived. They . . . their glances were everywhere. Looking at the furniture – which was fairly sparse at the time – not exactly admiring things, but *noting* them. As if they were checking if there was anything valuable. Then he asked if he could go to the lavatory, and I directed him to the downstairs washroom, but then I could hear him walking about in the bedroom overhead. Meanwhile, she started looking among the books, and she pulled one from the shelf, and she said, "John Donne – he was a sexy bugger, wasn't he?" and gave me that half-smile. And then Lodge came back down, still smelling of that dreadful aftershave, and before they went back out, he stared at me in . . . I suppose a rather blatant way, and he asked me how I was getting on. Whether I was lonely without my husband. "*Long nights*," he said. "*Long old nights, eh?*" '

Mrs Pawson squeezed her arms together and began to rock slightly. Lol didn't think she was aware of it.

'At lunchtime, they would . . . They had a van – which she drove, because he'd brought the digger – and it was parked at the back of the house with the rear doors facing the kitchen. At lunchtime, they went into the back of the van, supposedly to eat their sandwiches, but it became obvious very quickly what they were actually doing. There was a single mattress in there. No attempt to hide it, no attempt at all to keep it quiet. In fact, they seemed to be making as much noise as they could. As if they were oblivious of everything else, like rutting animals. The van was actually creaking on its springs.'

Mrs Pawson stopped and looked at them, perhaps to make sure that they didn't consider this was perfectly reasonable behaviour during a lunchtime break.

'How many days did the work take?' Lol asked. 'The installation?'

'Two. I'm sure it could have been done in one, but they seemed in no hurry – about anything.'

'Evidently,' Merrily said.

'Naturally, but now I was regretting I'd ever hired him.'

'Did you say anything to them?'

'What was I supposed to say, without sounding middle-class and sanctimonious and . . . like a townie? Like some sort of buttoned-up townie who didn't understanding country . . . spontaneity.'

'What, you wondered if perhaps this was how all healthy young rural workers . . . ?'

'It's not funny.'

'No, it's not,' Merrily said. 'Especially when you were on your own. It's insulting, and it's threatening.'

'Anyway, on the second day, they left the back doors of the van wide open, and I assumed they really were eating their sandwiches this time, and I went out to ask . . . I *steeled* myself to go out and ask if they wanted a cup of tea. And they were both sitting there in the back of the van, naked. Well, *she* was, almost . . . she had her top off and her jeans unzipped. He was stripped to the waist, his belt undone.'

Merrily closed her eyes, shaking her head.

'I screamed, I'm afraid. One tries to be cool in this sort of situation, but . . . Then Lodge laughed. He said what a hot day it was. Just cooling off, he said. I said something like, You'll have to excuse me, and then *she* said, in this very low, throaty voice, "*Why don't you join us? Why don't you join us, love? Do you good.*" '

Mrs Pawson started to cough, brought a hand to her mouth. Lol asked, 'Can I get you a drink? Some coffee?'

'No, thank you, I'll be going in to dinner soon. If I can face it. So I said, very coldly, "How long will you be before you've finished?" I could smell the awful aftershave, and I was feeling sick. And she said, *As long as you want . . . as long as you can stand it.* And Lodge said, *Longer* . . . And he laughed. And I ran back to the house and locked the door and stood over the phone for quite a long time, wondering if I should call the police . . . if what they were doing – or what they'd *said* – constituted any kind of offence.'

'They never came out of the van?' Lol said.

'No, not at this time. It could have been said that they were demonstrating nothing more than what you might call a lamentable lack of common courtesy. But there was – I really can't tell you – an indescribable menace around them both. A quite palpable sense of something . . . predatory. I know people will say this is all with hindsight.'

'What did you do?' Merrily asked.

'I didn't know what to do then. I didn't go out again. After a while, they came out of the van and simply finished the job, replacing all the soil. They didn't come back to the house. I felt I *should* have gone to the police or somebody. But it would be my word against theirs. A townie, an incomer. And of course I absolutely dared not tell my husband. He never wanted that house, never really wanted to move to the country. Kept talking about, you know, living among . . . sheep-shaggers. I wasn't going to give him the satisfaction. The next day, I just had the locks changed – and doubled.'

'Did you see them again?'

Mrs Pawson laughed harshly. 'I went back to London that

weekend to spend some time with our child, Gus. We have a nanny, who I'd hoped to persuade to come down here with us, so that I could continue my work – I do some proof-reading for an educational publisher – but she has a boyfriend in London, and it . . . Anyway, I came back on my own the following week, to meet the surveyor we'd hired, Mr Booth – who would subsequently point out the problem with the Efflapure and point me in the direction of Mr Parry. I was finding it hard to sleep, and I remember getting up in the night to go to the bathroom and get a drink, I . . .' She closed her eyes for a moment, took a breath through her mouth. 'I'm sorry, but this is absolutely the first time I've talked about this to anyone.'

'Take your time,' Merrily said.

'The bathroom overlooks the side of the house, where the Efflapure had been installed. And when I looked down – it was about half past midnight, and a bright night, with the moon almost full – she was standing there. The woman. Standing on the lawn under one of the apple trees. Just standing there, quite relaxed, with her legs apart and her arms folded, dressed much as she had been the first time I saw her. Looking up at me with that same smile that said, *I know things you don't.*'

'What did you do?'

'I was terribly afraid. I thought at first, Oh my God, they're *both* here. They've come to rob me or . . . or worse. I got dressed in the dark, very quickly. I found the mobile phone and I keyed in 999, so that I'd just have to press the button, and then I ran into the front bedroom and looked out of the window. Went all around the upstairs, peering through windows, but there was no sign of the van or the truck or . . . anything. Or anyone. And when I went back to the bathroom, she . . . wasn't there any more.'

Merrily said softly, almost casually, 'When *exactly* was this? Do you remember?'

'It must have been at least a week after I'd seen them. I remember there was a bill for the job – for the Efflapure – waiting behind the door when I returned from London.'

Lol looked at Merrily and saw her bite her lip.

The door of the lounge opened suddenly, and Mrs Pawson's whole body jerked.

A man in a dark suit said cheerfully, 'Are you all right in there? Anything I can get you?'

'Fine,' Mrs Pawson said. 'Everything's . . . fine.'

38

Bit Player in a Fantasy

The Royal Hotel was tucked into the side of the Ross churchyard, and they went up into it, then followed the path down towards the Plague Cross. The cross was edged with cold moonlight.

Lol said, 'You didn't really push her on dates.'

'No point. I think we both knew what we might have been talking about,' Merrily said. 'If she knew for a fact that Lynsey Davies was dead by then, how would *that* help her to sleep? I slipped her a card on the way out, whispered I could maybe help if anything happened again.'

'I don't think she wants to go down that road. She just wants out.'

'No wonder she's staying in the hotel. I'm not sure I'd want to be in that house on my own, even now.'

Lol looked up at the Plague Cross. The cross itself was quite small, like a fist on the end of an upthrust arm, representing the triumph of mere survival.

'The picture that's coming over of Lynsey Davies is not really the image of a victim, is it?'

'Nothing I've heard about her so far makes her *terribly* endearing,' Merrily said. 'Dumps her kids, probably breaks up Roddy's relationship with someone who might have helped him and tries to lure an already nervous woman into three-in-a-van sex.'

'Do you want to know more about her? Would that help?'

There was no one else in the churchyard. The street-front opposite – now mainly offices – was hushed, but the air around them was vibrant with the sharp spores of frost.

'Lol, why aren't you rehearsing? Why aren't you getting an early night before the gig?'

'Because I'd start thinking it was important. And if I start thinking it's important, I'm . . . Anyway, there's someone here, in Ross, who knew Lynsey well – someone Gomer and I met on the tank dig. If you wanted to come with me, we could maybe—'

'I can't. I've left Huw Owen in The Man of Ross, trying to find a pint and a pasty. We're going over to Underhowle. He's decided he wants to be involved, which is not, frankly, as reassuring as you might think.' She looked up at the cross. 'So this is Sam's symbol.'

'*The insidious wind which blows through skin and tissue and bones.*'

'He said that?'

'It's the only good line in his song, and even that sounds more than a bit reminiscent of Dylan's "Idiot Wind".'

'Electromagnetic waves,' Merrily said, 'radio waves . . . ghost waves . . . alien waves . . . soft porn blowing through the church steeple. It's a wonder *any* of us can breathe.'

'Prof says we're mutating into it. One day we'll become electric beings, just light and sparks. That's a better line, maybe I'll use that instead.'

Merrily said, 'Huw wonders if there's the remains of some satanic cult still out there. I wouldn't know what to do about it if there was. It's not even against the law any more.'

'Killing people is.'

'And the known killers are dead, so the police aren't interested.'

'No. Listen . . .' Lol turned away from the cross. 'There's no good time to say this, but I don't imagine there'll be a better one.'

He saw her stiffen.

He said, 'When I was here with Moira, something happened.'

Merrily said sharply, 'No. Maybe this *isn't* a good time.'

'If I don't talk about it now . . .' She didn't look at him. 'Sam Hall was telling us about how the bodies were buried, without coffins, all that . . . and later Moira said she'd experienced what she described as a loathsome, curling sensation in her gut. She

talked in an oblique way about evil. She—' Lol shrugged.
'That's it.'

Merrily looked at him and he thought she almost smiled.
'That's it? That's what you had to tell me?'

'I know how you feel about clairvoyance. Just thought I ought
to tell you about *this*. Even if you scoffed. But if you do accept
this sort of thing, you might think she was getting it not so
much from the cross and this situation as from . . . Sam.'

'Lol—'

'I'm worried about this, that's all. Underhowle, Lodge, West.
Worried about you. Sorry. Also, Eirion came to see me last night.
On his own.'

'Oh God,' Merrily said. 'They've split up, haven't they?'

'She told you?'

'Didn't need to. I like Eirion a lot – the kind of guy she needs
to meet in ten years' time. At Jane's age I suppose you need to
split up a few times.'

'He may even be prepared to wait. He . . .' Lol breathed out.
'He also said Jane thinks I'm sleeping with Moira Cairns.'

'Did he?'

'The way we musicians do. When we're not shooting heroin
into our arms.'

'I've heard that, too.'

'About Moira?'

'*And* the heroin, but I think that's exaggerated in your case.
Look . . . we're OK, aren't we?'

Lol nodded. He kissed her slowly, both hands in her hair. 'I
hope.' And then they walked down, towards the not-very-bright
lights of the town.

Jane snatched her fleece from the peg and ran out of the front
door, catching up with Jenny Box on the edge of the square.

'I'm sorry . . .'

Jenny Box turned. Her scarf fell away. Her red-gold hair shone
under one of the fake gaslamps.

'Mrs Box, I'm really sorry, OK? I should not have said that
stuff.'

'Jane—'

'It's not my place to be judgemental. I'm immature for my age and I'm probably becoming right-wing and moralistic and—'

'Jane,' Jenny Box said, 'if you want to continue the conversation, fine.'

'Do you want to . . . come back to the vicarage?'

Jenny Box looked around the square. 'I think I'd rather walk, if you don't mind. Sitting there facing each other across a table, that can be a little fraught. Besides, there's less opportunity for me to try and seduce you out here on the street.'

'I'm sorry,' Jane said, eyes still full of tears. 'I don't know what to believe any more. About anything.'

Merrily took the Walford road out of Ross, turning left when the headlight beams penetrated the tight steel compound that was the base of the first big pylon in the great chain.

'I've never come into the Forest of Dean from this end,' Huw said. 'Always come down from Gloucester before.'

'It's strange. Like a frontier.' She drove slowly along the narrow valley road, the full beams occasionally finding one of the pylons gripping the hillside like the skeletons of steel-clawed eagles. 'The Forest's a different country. You assume it must have different laws, and you wonder if you might be breaking one of them without knowing it.'

'You feel insecure?'

'Bit.'

She'd told him about Lisa Pawson's unnerving encounter with Roddy Lodge and Lynsey Davies, expecting him to make some reference, as Frannie Bliss might have done, to the couple behaving like Fred and Rose West. But he'd said nothing. She hadn't told him about the postscript; she wanted to ask Bliss if they'd been able to ascertain roughly when Lynsey had died.

Merrily said, 'I'm still not sure what we're going for . . . what you're chasing – peace-of-mind, redemption . . . or some kind of revenge.'

Huw did his small throaty laugh – a smoker's laugh, which was odd in somebody who didn't smoke. He didn't reply. What a strange, unfocused job this was: no framework for measuring success. Not like Frannie Bliss, walking away with a conviction, a *result*. Most times, you just came away confused.

The headlights picked up the base of the lone Scots pine at the right turning for Underhowle. There'd be a big sign here next summer, perhaps: *The Ariconium Centre*.

'I went over to Much Marcle once,' Huw said, 'one fine afternoon – October '95, some weeks after Julia's death. I went into the church – a white feeling inside, lots of marble, nothing there. Nothing for me, anyroad. And then I went and sat inside the hollow yew tree, in the churchyard, where I *know* he must have sat, because everybody has. Happen that were the problem: every bugger had sat there at some time or other. It was all smudged.'

'You were looking for anything that might be left of West?'

'So I got back in the car and I drove up on the Kempley road, to the Fingerpost Field and the Letterbox Field, up near where the bugger lived. Where he buried two bodies – happen more, but two's all they found. County boundary goes through there, and he knew exactly where it was and he buried 'em both on the Gloucester side because, when it come down to it, he never really liked Much Marcle, on account of everybody knows your business in a village. He liked the anonymity of the city. So he planted 'em on the Gloucester side, so they could look down on Marcle and nobody in Marcle'd ever know.'

'How do you know that?'

'I know *him*,' Huw said, and under the flat ridge of his voice there was a kind of horror, like the bodies under the floor in Cromwell Street. 'When the cops took him back to Marcle, he said he could see ghosts in the fields. Said they came to him in his cell: Rena, his first wife and Ann McFall – Anna, he called her. Said he saw their ghosts, but later he took it back, said he'd made that up.'

'And you,' Merrily said softly. 'Did *you* see any ghosts?'

Huw sniffed. 'Stood at the top of Fingerpost Field, thought what a lovely place it were, with the view down to Marcle church and across the valley to Ridge Hill. I had a . . . a rite in me pocket. In a notebook. A procedure . . . a formal . . .'

Merrily slowed right down. 'An exorcism?'

'Didn't give it a title.'

'For Fred West?'

'Happen.'

'But you can't . . . can you?' Roddy Lodge's garage was on the right, across its cindered forecourt. She'd been planning to point it out to Huw, and the message chalked on the door – *Put him down a cesspit where he belongs* – but this was more important and she drove past. 'You can't exorcize Fred West. Because, however much evil there was, you can't . . .'

Can't exorcise a ghost, she was going to say. You could only exorcize a demonic presence. Anything that had once been human – an unquiet spirit – could only be directed back to its maker.

She shut up; it was, after all, Huw who'd taught her this stuff.

'Sometimes . . .' He leaned forward, scrubbing at the condensation on the windscreen. 'Sometimes I think in the modern Church you can make it up as you go along. What's this, Merrily? What are all these lights? Who the bloody hell are all *these* buggers?'

Merrily leaned on the brakes.

But they were already surrounded.

Lol's pub crawl ended at an inn down by the River Wye, with a beer garden extending to the dark water's edge. This was where he finally found the girl who had said her name was Cola French.

Down the far end of the bar was a group of people of varying ages but a shared self-conscious and slightly dated eccentricity. There was a woman of late middle age in a purple bolero and black lipstick, a bald guy in an elaborately torn biker jacket and bangles, and a small, round man with a long crimson beard who was doing the talking until Cola French, grinning, poked him in the chest. 'Jaz, you're a lying old bastard!'

'And you are a whore,' Jaz said mildly, and Cola cracked up laughing.

Then she saw Lol standing near the doorway – Lol, who didn't drink much, never knew where to put himself and sometimes found the friendly English pub the loneliest place in the world.

'Hey!' Cola said. 'Shit!'

Her hair was a dazzling white tonight with tiny gold stars in it. She wore the same black fleece top she'd had on the other day at the Old Rectory. It was not yet eight p.m. and she seemed to be moderately drunk: Cola French, the writer and occasional bookshop assistant whose TV play would have been perused by the great Dennis Potter himself, if he hadn't snuffed it.

She unstitched herself from the Bohemian tapestry at the bottom of the bar, weaved right up to Lol and peered into his eyes.

'This guy who was in, I dunno, some pub, said there was a bloke looking for me. Tell me it was *you*.'

'Could've been,' admitted Lol, whose quest had taken him to four other bars in Ross – soft drinks and suspicious looks that said, *If you only want a small orange juice and you're on your own, what are you* really *doing here, mate?*

'Which is like . . . serendi— serendipitous,' Cola said. 'Because you know what? *I . . . know who you are.*'

She prodded Lol once in the chest, making a big gesture of it and then stepping away like she'd identified him from a wanted poster. She bent forward, with a hand on each thigh, and began to sing softly:

'And it's always on the sunny days you feel you can't go on.
On rainy days, it rains on everyone.
And I'm running for the subway and I'm hiding under trees
On fine days like these.'

'Hey!' someone shouted. 'If it was karaoke night, it'd say so on the bloody door!'

Cola said. 'I grew up with that song. My older sister had the album. *Hazey Jane Two*, right?' She leaned right up to Lol again, shared with him some warm brandy breath. '*Right?*'

'Who told you?' He was thrown. This did not happen. Nobody had ever recognized him. It was all too long ago. The bar was suddenly twice as full, and everybody was looking at him, and his body began to quiver with the need to run and keep on running.

'Ah!' Cola tapped the side of her nose with a forefinger. She took his arm and turned to the woman in the purple bolero. 'Deirdre, if I do *not* shag this guy tonight, then all life is meaningless, right?'

It all happened so quickly, like a night raid, the first banner screaming *WE DON'T WANT HIM!*, then someone spotting the dog collar on Huw, a whoop going up, a dozen lamp beams clashing in the air like random fireworks.

And then figures were running at the car, some with placards brandished like shields, others pointing the poles outwards like battle stakes – Merrily hitting the brakes when the windscreen was filled with a white board demanding KEEP SATAN OUT! – and faces bloated with self-righteousness.

She looked around vainly for anyone she might recognize, couldn't spot a Sam Hall or a Fergus Young or a Piers Connor-Crewe or even the fat man from the newsagent's who didn't want his adopted village connected with a sicko.

BURN HIM! appeared in Huw's side window, and there was the blast of a hunting horn, sinister in the night, a baying for blood. If it hadn't been for the TV crew she'd have locked all the doors. She certainly wouldn't have wound down her window except for the young woman in the red jacket, with the furry-covered boom mike.

'Amanda Patel, BBC *Midlands Today*. Is it Mrs Watkins? Could we have a word?'

The light on top of the camera was full in Merrily's eyes. She was on her own; Huw had slipped out of the car without a word and moved away. Huw who had never been known to give an interview, not even to the *Church Times*.

'Could you give me a minute to find out what's happening?' She'd managed to drive as far as the community centre before the crush of bodies had forced her to stop. There must be a couple of hundred people here: men, women, kids.

'OK, look,' Amanda Patel said, 'we'll come back to you in about five. If you want to listen to what some of these people have to say and then respond to it, is that OK? It'll be for the half-ten bulletin, and breakfast.'

Merrily nodded. No dog collar, frayed old duffel coat. She

didn't want to do an interview at all, and the Bishop wouldn't be happy, but it would look worse if she backed out and all they had was pictures of the Volvo surrounded, and her and Huw blinking in the lights, bemused, inneffectual clergy.

The camera light swept from her face to illuminate a placard opposite.

Roddy's body – OUT!

Amanda Patel was setting up a tall, rangy-looking guy in a fur-trimmed leather jacket. 'OK, Nick, if you just stand . . . yeah, that's fine. OK, George? Right.' A giggle, then into TV-tone. 'Nick Longton, you're the councillor for this area, why are *you* backing this protest?'

'Well, let me say first of all that I'm very proud to represent this village on the Herefordshire Council – an example of the wonders that can be achieved when we all work together, the people and the local authority . . .'

Merrily recalled Fergus Young this morning saying that five years ago the council had been ready to shut down the school.

' . . . And I don't want to see this place becoming notable for the wrong reasons.' Nick Longton's accent was not local. 'I also have enormous sympathy for the relatives of people already buried in the churchyard who don't want to have to walk past the grave of a serial murderer.'

'But surely,' Amanda Patel said, over muted applause, 'Roddy Lodge, in the eyes of the law, is an innocent man because, however damning things may seem—'

'Amanda, we know he killed one woman, and dozens of the people here tonight heard him confess to killing at least two more. It may be weeks, months, even years before more bodies are found, and this is going to hang over everyone – particularly the family of Melanie Pullman, whom Lodge named as one of his victims – and it would be disgraceful if they had to keep walking past his name on a gravestone, with some pious Rest in Peace carving on it. What kind of peace will his victims be resting in?'

'But he's a local man. Isn't *his* family entitled to have him buried here?'

'In my view and the views of my constituents, a murderer

forfeits that kind of right,' Nick said. 'We don't want that man's body here.'

Amanda Patel nodded, and the camera light went out. Merrily was thinking how pompous councillors had become, talking of their 'constituents', having their own 'cabinet'. She felt annoyed. Stared at the flickering faces, saw duplicity, hypocrisy . . . and the funfair factor. How many of these so-called protesters were *really* angry or distressed at the thought of having a murderer in the churchyard? How many of them wouldn't be secretly thrilled by the vicarious notoriety?

Merrily saw Huw beckoning to her from the village hall entrance, turned to him and spread her hands, helpless. And then the light was back on her, and up came the boom mike in its fluffy wind-muff, like an inquisitive woolly puppet, deceptively friendly.

'Merrily Watkins,' Amanda Patel said, 'you're the priest sent in by the Church to conduct the funeral service for Roddy Lodge, after the local minister refused. Do you feel entirely happy about what you're doing?'

'Nobody could really feel happy in this situation, but everyone, in my view, is entitled to a Christian burial. I feel deeply sorry for people whose missing relatives were named by Mr Lodge, but even if he's guilty – which, as you said earlier, he is *not*, in the eyes of the law – he should be properly laid to rest.'

'Don't you think it would be better if he was simply cremated?'

'That's not a decision for me.'

'It's no secret, Mrs Watkins, that you're also the Diocesan Deliverance Consultant – the Hereford exorcist. Roddy Lodge referred to himself as Satan. Does that have any bearing on why you were selected for this job?'

'Erm . . .' Well, BBC News didn't believe in the supernatural, and certainly not in connection with a hard news story. 'No,' Merrily said. 'None at all.'

Amanda Patel nodded. 'Mrs Watkins, these residents – now supported, as you can see, by dozens of people from surrounding villages – say they're going to keep up a permanent watch, and any hearse attempting to bring Roddy Lodge's body into

Underhowle will be stopped. Even the regular gravedigger's saying he'll be refusing to dig a grave for Lodge. How do you feel about that?'

Merrily said, 'I think you'll find that any interference with the free flow of traffic is probably a matter for the police, not for me. However, grave-digging *is* a matter for the Church, and I'm sure something will be sorted out.'

'So *you*'re saying you're prepared to go ahead with this funeral no matter what happens.'

'Like if somebody puts a bomb under the church?'

Amanda Patel smiled in resignation and signalled to the cameraman to stop recording. The light went out. 'Cheers,' Amanda said.

People had started chattering again. She heard a woman say, 'Of course, half of them are lesbians . . .' as some of the pro- testers set up a chant: '*Roddy's body OUT, Roddy's body OUT*'.

It was unlikely, especially with the TV here, that this demo was spontaneous. But who would have planned it? Perhaps the media-wise Development Committee. Merrily stood in the lane, feeling furious. A bit player in a fantasy – several fantasies col- liding like the torch beams, like short-lived fireworks, brief explosions in the common-sense night.

'Merrily . . .' A hand under her elbow.

She turned. Huw was standing under one of the globular lamps outside the village hall.

'Let's get out of here, Huw.'

'Merrily,' Huw said. 'This is . . .'

There was a woman with him: flaking waxed jacket, pen- etrating brown eyes in a faintly familiar, wind-tanned face.

Huw said, 'Ingrid's going to show us the new tourist centre.'

'Huw, I just—'

'The Baptist chapel? You remember Jerome telling us about the Baptist chapel? A place of considerable historic significance. Well worth a visit. Besides . . .' Huw nodded at an elderly woman in a long purple mac advancing from the crowd. 'You might not want to hang around here.'

'*You!*' The elderly woman pointed at Merrily. 'I've said it before and I'll say it again: you're the begining of the end, you are, women priests! Only a woman so-called priest would bury the damned!'

'Don't get involved, lass,' Huw murmured.

Amidst the half-manufactured excitement, the chants of *Roddy's body OUT*, there was an eye-of-the-storm stillness around him, conveying an awareness of being exactly where he needed to be.

39

Good at Men

'I'm writing a new play,' Cola French said from the bed, 'about a woman I'd be, you know, really scared of being. You know what I mean? A woman whose appetites are so . . . *extreme* that . . . wow, it's apocalyptic. See, we think of these larger-than-life people as being like, you know, big movie stars and rock idols. But that's so totally wrong. In reality those guys are all dead lazy and boring and too vain to realize it.'

She didn't seem very drunk any more, now she was back home in this well-organized bedsit, with a computer and printer and bookshelves with so many books that they were stacked horizontally, and a view over a car park to the tall steeple of St Mary's.

'I don't include *you* among the boring rock stars, of course,' she told Lol. 'You are *very* interesting. You're among the exalted ranks of the Disappeared – kind of Syd Barrett.' She raised herself, propped her head up with an elbow. 'He's actually older than my dad, the great Syd Barrett. You can't be anywhere near that old. I'm like . . . amazed how young you look. I'm even more amazed that you were wandering the streets, the night before your big comeback gig – looking for *me*.'

'Gig?' Lol said.

'Aw, come *on*! I've known about that gig for days. It's even on the Net.'

'It can't be.'

'Lol . . . Lol . . . honey . . . you've got a serious cult-base out there, didn't you know that? God, look at your face! You *didn't* know, did you?' Cola scrambled up and sat on the side of the bed. 'The copper it was, told me who you were. Mumford, who came back to see Piers. So . . . OK, there's this website, right? Devoted to the Dead and the Disappeared – Morrison, Barrett,

Drake, Edwards, et cetera – and you, as it happens. And so I e-mailed them. I said, I have just seen the real Lol Robinson and he was working for this little guy who installs septic tanks. And some dickbrain e-mails back and says, You're talking crap because Lol Robinson's on at the Courtyard, Hereford, on Wednesday night as support to Moira Cairns, so there! You can't win. *I* can't, anyway. Even bloody Dennis Potter dies on me.'

'This woman's Lynsey Davies, isn't it?' Lol said.

'Huh?'

'The woman with extreme appetites. The woman you'd be scared of being.'

'Hmm.' Cola's eyes narrowed. 'What makes you say that?'

Lol shrugged. He was sitting on a plastic pouffe at the foot of the bed, his back to a chest of drawers supporting a lamp made out of an ouzo bottle. The lamp had a red bulb and made the room look like an intelligent brothel.

'The point I was trying to make,' Cola said, 'is that it usually isn't the famous people who become the most extreme members of the human race, it's the people with something to rise above. That's what the play's about. This woman who comes out of a council estate in the Forest, does surprisingly well at school even though she don't give a toss, then drops out of college and goes on the game. Just because she's bored. Does the booze and the drugs and then goes on the game, at the age of about seventeen or eighteen.'

'In Ross?'

Cola exploded with laughter. '*Ross?* And make actual money at it? Listen, I know some of these women – they're lucky if they can turn over a hundred a night in *Hereford*. Hey . . .' She blinked. '*You* didn't go with Lynsey ever, did you, at some time?'

Lol shook his head.

'That's not supposed to be insulting, by the way,' Cola said, 'because that woman could *pull*, you know? Where'd I put my cigs?'

Lol spotted them on the computer table with a book of matches. He went over and collected them for her.

'Ta,' Cola said. 'Well, that's something.'

'A lot of people around here went with her?'

'That a serious question?'

Lol recalled her saying, when they were digging up Piers Connor-Crewe's Efflapure, *Let's be honest, she was good at men.* He went back to sit on the plastic pouffe. 'It's just I remember you saying, when we were at the Rectory, that Lynsey Davies had this fierce determination to grab everything from life.'

'Did I?'

'I'm kind of a writer too, Cola. Despite "Sunny Days". I remember these lines.'

Cola grinned and yawned and stretched. 'Yeah, all right, the play's about her. She's the protagonist. Lynsey. She wanted to grab things from life that maybe you aren't supposed to, and she scares the shit out of me, still. But you got to write about what scares you, otherwise it's all meaningless, right?'

'Why does she scare you still?' Lol asked.

'Do I have to? Couldn't we just have sex?'

'Please don't give me a hard time,' Lol said. 'I have a feeling this is somehow very important.'

She lit up. 'Why?'

'Because of the reason I can't have sex with you.'

'A woman, right?' Rueful smile through the smoke. 'What else? Well, I'm glad for you. I read the stuff on the website and I'm glad for you, OK?' Cola rolled off the bed, leaned across him to the chest of drawers, brought out a wine case from behind the ouzo lamp. 'But this is gonna fuck up your night's sleep even more, sunshine, believe me.'

It had the feel, Merrily thought, of some desperate ballroom in the Depression, where, although it was semi-derelict, people still came to dance against the darkness.

'How old?' Huw asked.

'About 1740, originally, but it was completely refurbished early last century, which, I expect, is why it avoided being listed.' Ingrid Sollars offered a smile to Huw; it was thin but it was a smile. In the twenty minutes or so while Merrily had been with the TV people, he appeared to have sought out and charmed the formidable Sollars, so spiky and unhelpful to Frannie Bliss.

'So 1740, that'd be . . . what?' Huw said. 'A century or so after they broke away from the C of E?'

'They were a new and radical movement in those days, Mr Owen, and this was one of the earliest chapels. Nearly as old as the one at Ryeford, down the valley. I expect you're surrounded by the things in your part of Wales.'

'Not like this,' Huw said.

It was *big*. Bigger than most village churches in this area. Coming in through the door – Victorian Gothic, like the school, so not the original one – there had been that numinous vacuum waft you always got when a small door opened into a disused auditorium. And then what Merrily always thought of as the slightly soured stench of spent spirituality.

Ingrid Sollars said, 'Since it was abandoned as a place of worship in the 1970s, it's seen service as a warehouse, a kind of sports hall and finally a water-bottling plant – another local enterprise that bit the dust.'

Huw said, 'Water from . . . ?'

'There's a spring virtually underneath.'

'*Is* there?'

'Not a terribly reliable one, unfortunately.' Mrs Sollars's weathered face seemed more open than Merrily remembered; her dusty bun of hair less tight. 'No one was surprised when the business failed, because things generally did, you see. That's the story of Underhowle – a short wave of industry, then a long, slow, bloodless decline. We are – we *were* – hoping for a stronger foundation this time. Industry supported by education.'

'So you're the historian here, Ingrid,' Huw said. 'The curator.'

'I ran a small tourist initiative here years ago, when my husband was alive, had a few hundred leaflets printed. We had trekking ponies at the riding school then, making us probably the only tourist enterprise in the village. They . . . Well, I suppose the committee keep me on in recognition of that pioneering initiative – and as the token local.'

'And how do you feel about them turning this place into a museum?'

'I'm in *charge* of the project,' she said, as though this effectively prevented her from commenting. 'I'm the keyholder.'

'So?'

She didn't blink. 'And I suppose I *must* be unhappy about it, in some way, or I wouldn't have let you in.'

Merrily took a proper look around. The chapel walls had been replastered, and an old gallery was being rebuilt, presumably for museum exhibits. But the altar was long gone, and the pulpit, of course. There were large areas of shadow, resistant to the naked bulbs hanging from the ceiling on frayed black flex. The bulbs, twelve of them, were probably high-wattage, but you could see all their filaments inside the straining veins of light.

'Unhappy?' Huw prompted.

Mrs Sollars didn't expand, clearly wasn't going to without some more effort on their part. It would be a matter of asking the right questions.

'The Lodge family worshipped here,' Merrily said. 'And I think it was once actually owned by Roddy Lodge?'

'Both the chapel and the garage were owned by the bottling company, and the whole lot was sold off when they went bankrupt. At the time, as I recall, Roddy Lodge had his bequest, which I believe was quite substantial – his father had sold the land on which the council estate was built – and he bought it for a silly price and then sold *this* building to the Underhowle Development Fund last year.'

'Not short of money, are they?' Merrily said.

'They're clever at attracting grants. And Christopher Cody puts funding into it as some sort of tax hedge. The Fund is administered by his solicitor, Ryan Nye.'

'Who was also Roddy's lawyer.'

'I didn't know that,' Ingrid Sollars said, 'but this is a small world. The same fingers in many pies.' She paused. 'As you'll have gathered, I'm rather proprietorial about this village. My father was the last . . . squire – I guess you'd call it that – and he lost most of his money through unwise investment, and my family moved away. I was the only one who chose to stay. Found it hard to separate from my roots, you might say.'

Ingrid Sollars was very slim, and Merrily thought of a small, tough thorn tree on a hillside, bending with the wind.

'My ambition was to see some stability here in my lifetime,'

Ingrid said. 'I thought, perhaps foolishly, that this might at last be in sight, but it seems it only takes one disaster . . .'

Merrily said tentatively, 'This protest . . .'

'Crass. Stupid. The whole thing's entirely out of hand and likely to draw even more unwelcome attention to something that should have been allowed to die quietly. But we live in times of gracelessness and excess.'

There was silence, echoes absorbed by the dust sheets on the flagstoned floor and others draped from the gallery like the frayed and mournful curtains in a dying theatre.

'I suppose Jerome phoned you,' Huw said. 'Told you we'd been to see him.'

'Mr Banks said that you were attached to what he called, rather disparagingly, the Spook Squad and that he'd informed you about reports of an atmosphere here.'

'That his word or yours?'

Ingrid Sollars hesitated. 'Mine.'

Atmosphere, Merrily thought. *Yes*. And it was very cold. Her body acknowledged it; she shivered inside the duffel coat.

Huw didn't seem aware of the atmosphere. He was walking around slowly, looking down, shards of old plaster cracking under his shoes. 'So this is where some of the Roman stuff was discovered.'

'Notably a statuette of what we think is Diana,' Ingrid Sollars said. 'It was found by Piers Connor-Crewe about a year ago. And some pottery. And the usual coins.'

'More here than other places?'

'That's what Connor-Crewe always says. Not that he's as much of an expert as he likes to think. But bookshop owners are often like that, don't you find?'

Merrily said to Huw, 'You're thinking this was possibly the site of a Roman temple, aren't you? Because of the spring.'

'Aye. If not also pre-Roman.'

'That's also what Connor-Crewe thinks. I suspect he'd quite like to knock this building down just to find out for sure.'

'It makes a certain sense, Ingrid.' Huw said. 'Folks think churches were no longer being built on ancient sacred sites after medieval times. All the mystics and the visionaries involved in

Nonconformism tend to get overlooked, because of the puritan element.'

Merrily shivered again. She didn't like this place with its hanging shadows and straining bulbs.

Huw turned to Ingrid. 'Was it you who went to Banks originally?'

'Could hardly go over his head. I attend his services.'

'And he said what?'

'Suggested it might be better if I consulted a Baptist minister, in Ross.'

'Nice get-out. But you wouldn't do that, would you?'

'I was hardly going to bring in an outsider.'

'When *was* this, lass?'

'Five months ago, something like that. When the conversion work started for the museum. When the first grant came through. When the builders started asking me if it was haunted.'

'Because?'

'Footsteps when there was nobody there. Laughter – sniggers, they said. And items disappearing – tools. Although the doors were locked each night and there were no signs of breaking and entering.'

'And you said?'

'I said, quite truthfully, that I had no knowledge of the former Baptist chapel being haunted. And then there was the accident.'

'Ah.'

'One of the builders was working near the ceiling – up there, I think, in that top corner, knocking away damp plaster – when he claimed the hammer was snatched out of his hand. He was so shocked that he reeled away, dislodging his own ladder and falling to the ground. Broke a hip.'

Huw looked up. 'Bloody lucky it weren't his neck.'

'After the first phase,' Mrs Sollars said, 'the firm told us they couldn't fit Phase Two into their schedules for at least a year. In other words, they were pulling out.'

Merrily asked her, 'What did the Development Committee have to say about that?'

'Not the kind of publicity we need. Get another firm.'

'Think back,' Huw said. 'It was converted into a bottling plant – when?'

'Oh, quite recently. It didn't take long for businesses to crash in Underhowle. Early nineties?'

'Any trouble then?'

'If there was, I didn't hear about it.'

Merrily said, 'The power lines go right over here, don't they? Did they follow the same route then?'

'I don't think anything's changed,' Mrs Sollars said. 'But I get all that from Sam.'

'Good old Mr Hall,' Huw said, and she glanced at him sharply.

'I don't have to *share* his obsession, Mr Owen, but I respect his right to have one.'

'I *see*.' Huw smiled. 'So you've got new builders in now.'

'Starting on Phase Two in a couple of weeks.'

'You felt anything in here yourself?'

'I don't come in alone unless I really have to.'

'And if you do . . .'

'There's an atmosphere, I'll go that far. You have a feeling of . . . being observed.'

'In what way?'

She didn't look at him directly. 'Sam says that's a symptom of electrical hypersensitivity, but I certainly haven't exhibited any of the others. I live, like him, on the hill, well away from the power lines.'

'So what do you think it is, lass?'

'I don't know. But it's not a *good* thing.'

'Would you like us to say some prayers?'

'Whatever you think might help.'

Huw said, 'But there's summat else, isn't there, Ingrid?'

The wine case was sealed along the top with brown parcel tape. Cola set it down on the hessian rug by the computer table under the window, slipped a fingernail under the tape and slit it open.

'I want free tickets for your gig for this.'

'They'll be on the door,' Lol said. If he didn't make it, at least she'd enjoy Moira.

'Nah, I didn't mean that,' Cola said. 'I don't want anything.'

'They'll still be on the door.'

They knelt together on the rug. Cola lifted the box's cardboard flaps. 'So you were actually there when Roddy went to the angels. I wasn't. I waste all that time watching you not finding a body under Piers's tank and then I miss the big one. Some writer. OK, here they are.' She took out some books, trying to hide the first one, but he saw it. It was a children's Bible with Noah's Ark on the front.

'Scary,' Lol said.

'That's mine. I'm embarrassed.' She held the children's Bible to her chest.

The second book was a thick black paperback, but its spine was white with fishbone creases: Aleister Crowley's *Magick*. Then a hardback: *The Secret Rituals of the OTO*, by Karl Wurtz. Cola let this one fall open to show Lol some scribblings, in black biro, in the margins. There were two more books on Kundalini serpent power and sex magic. 'You know about this stuff?'

'A little.' Lol noticed that since she'd opened the box, all the bounce had gone from her voice, like a rubber ball rolling away.

'Sex magic – you use the build-up to an orgasm to channel and focus energy for a particular purpose and then . . . boom. I mean, I've only been a little way along that road, but it *is* scary. You just have to look at some of the people who went in for it. Aleister Crowley? I mean that guy was a total shit, he was a *professional* shit. But she's like – this is Lynsey – "Oh Crowley, he was a pioneer, he knew about real freedom, he didn't give a fart for anybody. *Do what thou wilt shall be the whole of the law.* Brilliant!" She actually wrote it out – *Do what thou wilt*, et cetera – in big Gothic letters, had it as a kind of frieze over her bed.'

'The OTO was the magical society founded on all that – is that right?'

'*Ordo Templi Orientis*, something like that. Yeah, still going, I think. Lynsey studied everything she could find, and she got quite a few people into it.'

'Not the OTO?'

'Nah, she wasn't *in* anything. But she was *into* everything, if you see what I mean. Into pushing out boundaries – sexual boundaries. Overcoming your inhibitions and breaking through to, like, real enlightenment. Overcoming pain, humiliation and . . . well, revulsion sometimes.' She paused, looking at him almost shyly. 'Coprophagia – you know what that is?'

'It's, er, an old album by The Who, isn't it?'

Cola grinned.

'Not really, was she?' Lol said.

'Don't ask.' She gathered the books into a pile. 'See, I was always having to keep stuff like this for her since the day she had a row with this guy Paul, who she was living with, and he burned some of her books. She said she didn't mind when they had fights – I mean actual *fights*, black-eye, split-up stuff – but she drew the line at him messing with her stuff. She had two kids, I think it was, with Paul. Big guy, Jamaican, smoked dope on an industrial scale. If you'd told me Paul had done for her, in a barney, I wouldn't't've been that surprised. His ma has the kids now, which is just as well.'

'If she was still with this Paul,' Lol said, 'where did Roddy Lodge come in?'

'The word "with" is relative.' Cola dipped back into the wine case and brought out a cardboard folder. 'I feel better for this, really. I still had this stuff when she died, and I thought, do I take it to the cops or what? But I couldn't think how it was gonna help anybody and . . . you know . . .'

'You had this idea for a play.'

'See . . . you understand. Another creative person. I still haven't decided whether to do Lynsey herself – kind of documentary – or have a character based on her. You'd have to tone it down, either way. People wouldn't believe the – you know – the appetite.'

'You said, good at men . . .'

'You ever seen her? Look . . .' She opened the folder and slid out a photograph but kept most of it covered up so that Lol could just see the top half of a woman with frizzy black hair and deep-set eyes. 'I'm not a man, but *I* could feel it sometimes, you know?'

'How well did you know her?'

'From the pubs. And of course from the shop. From Piers.'

'Piers was . . .?'

'Oh *yeah*! Payment for books was how it started. Piers likes to *interface* with his customers, says a bookseller should be like a good doctor or a herbalist – give you advice, supply you with what you need to cure your . . . mineral deficiencies.' Cola tried half-heartedly to wink and her eyebrow ring dipped. 'It's a bigger shop than it looks. Some punters get to go up into the attic or down into the basement, if you see what I mean.'

'Sorry, I'm naive,' Lol said. 'You mean for books or . . .'

'Yeah, books. Books, too. Mainly books. Heavy books, heavier than this stuff. The other activities, it's The Old Rectory mostly.'

'He also does –' Lol tapped the books '– this stuff?'

'Sex magic? Mostly he just does sex, but he's up for most things. Nice enough guy, in a lot of ways, Piers. Easy-going, and he doesn't ask for too much in some departments, if you want the truth. You could actually feel sorry for him with Lynsey, 'cause Lynsey asked for a *lot*. And didn't always ask. You know?'

Lol said, 'You have mixed feelings about having these books around, don't you?'

'Aw, I just . . . you know, I didn't like to think where they'd been, and when we knew she'd died I packed them up. I mean there's a lot of stuff in there, a lot of notes she made. I like to think I'll get round to unscrambling it all one day. But not yet. It's too soon. And . . .' She put down the children's Bible. 'This was . . . I just felt I wanted something like a barrier, you know? It was all I could get in a hurry. Bought it from the second-hand stall on Ross market. Religion and innocence. Put it on the top and sealed the box.'

'Let's put them away,' Lol said.

'I was gonna show you this.' Cola held up the photo again, uncovering all of it this time. 'See, Lynsey used to talk about this a lot. There was a time in her life when she said she was like on this big high the whole time, had the most fun you could ever have, the most freedom. She'd've been about seventeen.'

In the colour photo, Lynsey Davies was sitting on the grass beside a van. There was a man sitting next to her. Lynsey wore jeans. The jeans were partly unzipped. The man had a hand inside the jeans, the zip around his wrist. The man was quite a bit older than Lynsey. He had curly hair and a yellowy butcher's boy grin for the camera. A 'look what I've got' grin.

'Oh my God,' Lol said.

Cola said, 'You don't want to stay the night, do you?' and her voice was quite small now. 'No. You've got a girlfriend. I'm sorry.'

'I'm sorry, too.'

'You actually don't know the half of it,' Cola said. 'Do you *want* to know the rest?'

'I know someone who might.'

'Yeah,' Cola said and thought for a while. She looked, momentarily, very young and uncertain. 'Perhaps this is best.' She handed him another book, a white one without a dustjacket. 'You better take this. I mean take it away. I've read it. Some of it. I don't want to read it again.'

It was a fat, page-a-day diary. On the front, was inscribed in black, by hand: *The Magickal Diary of Lynsey D*

'It doesn't follow the dates or anything; she just wrote in it when she had something to say. I never gave it you, if anybody asks. I don't think I want it back.' She packed up the box and put the children's Bible on top before closing the flaps. She looked up at him. 'Your girlfriend – she's a priest, isn't she?'

Lol nodded.

'Mumford told me,' Cola said. 'The copper.'

'That's why you got these out, isn't it?' Lol said.

Cola nodded. 'Tell you what, why don't you take the lot? She'll know what do with them.' She tried for a wry smile, which soon faded. 'I'll hang on to the kids' Bible.'

40

Big Shoes

The air in Ledwardine was damp and chilly, and Jane told Jenny Box that she felt old, felt like she'd been alive for ever and knew everything the world had to tell her, and it all came to nothing. All you needed to know was that everybody had a banal personal agenda and, after a short-lived glow, everything faded into grey disillusion and the realization that anybody – *anybody* – given the circumstances, would shaft you, to attain something really trivial. And, as there was no God to intervene on behalf of justice and balance, you just went through life trying to avoid getting shafted. And that was it – you *went through life*. That was it. Nothing. Nothing but *going through life*.

As soon as it was out, gasped into the misty village night, Jane couldn't believe she'd said it. Especially to Jenny Box, this superficial, pseudo-spiritual business person, this daytime-TV phoney. She felt like one of the stupid punters on Jerry Springer or Kilroy or *Livetime*, coughing up great gouts of angst like phlegm for people to say, *Oh how disgusting, thank God I'm not like that*.

But Jenny Box didn't react as expected. *Didn't* say this was a stupid attitude for someone so young, at the dawn of everything, on the threshold of the great adventure, and all that crap.

'It *can* be a bad time,' Jenny said. 'When I was your age, most of the time I was in a state of confusion and terror. I'd shut myself in my room – whichever anonymous room it happened to be – and I'd shiver and cry and take pills sometimes. And then, at some strategic point, a kind man would come along and he'd go, *There, there, I'll look after you, you're with me now, and everything's going to be all right*.'

'This was when you were modelling?' They were standing just

under the fat oak pillars of the market hall, which inhabited the cobbles like some giant, fossilized crustacean.

'I left home after an unhappy experience with the priest, Father Colm. I told your mother it was a friend of mine he'd had his auld hands all over, but I don't suppose she was fooled.'

'Oh.' Mum hadn't mentioned this.

'The awesome injustice of it was that, although they never talked about it and they still don't, my family and the whole damn community held *me* responsible for the downfall of a Good Man.'

That figured, thinking back to what Eirion had gleaned from the Net: Jenny Driscoll brought up in a rigid, rural Catholic community, and then 'escaping' into the heartless, soulless media world of a foreign country. *Looked like a girl who bruised easily.*

Jenny said, 'Modelling. Yes, you can model for passing fashions or you can model for old, old perversions. Oh, I was a model, all right. I was styled for abuse.'

Jane looked at the pale face under the white scarf, lustred by the haloes of the fake gaslamps. *Romantic in a besmirched way.*

'Some women *are*, you know – quite literally. This was the heartless eighties, and I became the image that fuelled the fantasies of thousands of men of a certain sort. A woman with the frailty of a child doll. Turn her upside down and listen to her cry – *mama, mama* – and then make it better. And they *do* make it better for a while. But when you stop crying, it isn't long before they start to miss it, and they have to make you cry again and again. And they don't realize the crying mechanism's all worn out, and that's how the doll gets broken. Does this shock you at all, Jane?'

'Well, I . . .'

'Ah, but you're a modern girl. You've heard it all before.'

'Maybe I just haven't thought about it,' Jane admitted. 'Not really. Like, you're bombarded from all sides with statistics and reports and people opening their hearts, and there's just so much of it that it all becomes a mush. You don't really hear it any more.'

'No. Well, the thing I'm trying to explain – the time's come when I have to explain it – is how I came to . . . fancy your

426

mother. I didn't think I'd be explaining it to you, but no matter, you're the one that's here.'

'Oh,' Jane said, with a tightening of the gut.

They walked through the deserted night-time village, through the centuries from cobbles to tarmac, down Church Street where Lucy Devenish, the folklorist, had lived in a black and white cottage and inspired Jane in all kinds of ways before dying. And then down towards the modern bungalow where Gomer Parry lived, alone now since Minnie had died, alone at work without Nev and without even Gwynneth and Muriel, the diggers.

Ledwardine itself remained unhurt by any of it, an organism, as Mum liked to call it, with the joins between the ancient and the new glossed over in black and white paint, and the warm lamps in the windows melting their bits of night. In many ways, it was the ultimate place to live. A nest.

But that wasn't why Jenny Box had come. That was, like she'd told Mum, because of the angel. And also, it seemed, exactly as Gareth Box had said, because of the angel that was *Mum.* And yet it all sounded different, as Jenny Box talked about men and women and the Church.

' . . . All the men who directed the religions of the world, waged the holy wars – leaving the women at home because the women weren't strong enough to fight or strident enough to preach. Well, thank God for that, because during the time they were left behind, with only the small, domestic things to exercise their minds, women were learning to look inwards. To journey inside themselves and reach the ocean of the spirit.'

Jane struggled with this. It wasn't feminism as she knew it.

'We find the strength inside ourselves,' Jenny said, 'and that's the only *true* strength. All the rest is violence.'

She'd fled the Church because it had been dominated, for her, by male violence, and she'd taken refuge in the New Age – all those hazy places Jane had been – because it was all basically Goddess-dominated. And that was how Vestalia had come about.

'We mind the hearth, is what we do, the altar of the home. It's *men*, you see, who despoiled the old, simple churches, so you have areas like the Bull Chapel in the parish church here, with the tombs of brutal men and their effigies reflecting material wealth and power. I'd surely take a jackhammer to that auld divil now and throw the pieces in the river.'

'Yes,' said Jane, who'd often felt the same about the sandstone effigy in the Bull Chapel, with its eyes fully open and its arrogant little smile.

But, while bemoaning the way it had been dragged into the male world of warfare and brutality, Jenny had come to miss the Church, the weight of it, the tradition, the sometimes pure beauty of it. And then something happened to beckon her back.

'One day, I was in North Wales, alone. I'd had . . . well, call it nervous exhaustion, and I'd been lent a cottage, to disappear there for a while. And this day I'd walked for hours on my own, trying to cool my head, and it started raining, and I came upon this wee church, not far from the sea, and it was open, and so I went in to shelter. 'Twas very plain – no stained glass, no statues, no tombs, no carvings. The simplicity, that was a big statement in itself, a huge statement. And for me it was as if I was coming home again, you know? I was enfolded by it. I think your mother would understand.'

'She's been there. Well, not *there*, but like . . . somewhere similar.'

Yeah, a similar church, on a similarly desperate day, bringing away with her what she'd talked of as the vision of blue and gold, the lamplit path – less a calling than a beckoning whisper at a time of personal crisis, and the one aspect of Mum's religion that Jane had always understood.

But had Mum told Jenny Box about the experience? And had Jenny Box now absorbed it into her own mythology? Uncertainty seized Jane again. Was she being used in some way? She glanced at Mrs Box, walking with her head down, hands in the pockets of her brown, rain-bubbled Barbour, talking about why, when she came back, it was not to the Church of Rome but to the Anglican Church that she'd been taught, as a child, to despise.

'You see, the strange thing was, the day I went into that little Celtic church – though I didn't know this until afterwards – that was the very day the Synod, or whoever it was, voted to permit the ordination of women. So here was I, feeling the call back to Christianity . . . and here was God meeting me halfway.'

Jane stopped in the street. 'You mean you joined the Anglican Church because it had accepted women as priests?'

Jenny smiled at last. 'And wasn't *that* the most significant development since Christ himself was on earth?'

There was a stage, Jenny Box told Jane, when she'd even wondered about becoming a nun, but didn't think she could handle the discipline. And no, she didn't really see herself becoming a priest. Too much of a private person. But when her marriage went the way of all her other relationships – she didn't elaborate, perhaps she didn't need to – and she was looking for a permanent bolt-hole, it was natural to seek out somewhere with a woman priest who looked like staying.

The questions started hammering inside Jane. 'No, listen,' Jenny Box snapped, 'I know it sounds like I was stalking her, but it isn't like that. I needed to know this was the *right* place. The right home. The right *hearth*.'

'What are you saying?' A car came around the corner from Old Barn Lane, sending up spray from the gutter, and some of it hit Jane in the face like spit. 'What did you *do*?'

'I just did my research, was all. If we're taking on a new manager for one of the shops, I like to know where they're coming from, whether they fit in with the ideology of the business.'

'You had her *checked out*?'

'There's . . . an agency we use in London.'

'Like . . .' Jane wiped her face with the sleeve of her fleece. 'You don't mean a private investigator?'

'Obviously, the agency we use doesn't work out here, but they subcontracted it to a local man. Don't look at me like that, Jane; I needed a priest, I've *always* needed a priest, someone who could guide me on my journey into the great ocean of the spirit. Maybe join me there. Don't *look* at me like that! It's not sexual and I'm not mad, all right?'

Jane felt suddenly light-headed. 'Not sexual?'

'Holy God, girl!' Jenny Box flinched, and her features

appeared suddenly blurred and oblique, as though she'd been struck. 'Does *everything* have to be sexual? I'm on the run from all that. My husband is greedy, violent . . . and worse.'

'Gareth?'

'Yes, the charming Gareth, who likes young girls, gets off on the vulnerable, who only married me because when I was thirty-five there was still something about me that looked eighteen, but let's not go into *that*. Oh, he has a very considerable charm, does Gareth, and a wonderfully plausible manner, and it worked on me for a *long* time – I'm not easy for the charm, but he was good at it, and I thought he wasn't like the others, but . . . You see, it took God to show me what I was doing – *letting* them bully me, Jane. Hadn't I always been attracting the kind of men who loved to bully women? And me turning it to my advantage, *I* thought – figuring I could get my own way in the end by letting them dominate me. Which is all fine and well until the day you say no, just the once, and then it starts to get ugly. Christ, does *it* get ugly. So if you ask me what I wanted from your mother . . . I wanted a friend, was all, a friend to go with me on the spiritual journey.'

Oh God. Jane looked away, across the street.

'And the things Humphries found out, the private eye . . . all he told me, Jane, were *good* things – how she helped sort out that trouble in the village over the play, the things she'd done as an exorcist . . . I'd never even heard of a woman exorcist before, a woman appointed to deal with the Devil himself – well, this was stepping into the *big shoes*. And how she stopped this charismatic priest who was abusing women. And then helping the mentally ill guy – that kind of thing.'

Jane looked up. 'Mentally ill guy?'

'Robinson?'

'Oh. Right.'

'And when I saw her, what kind of a person she was – so unassuming – I knew she was someone I wanted to help. I swear to God it's no more complex than that. So whatever Gareth told you . . .'

And Jenny began talking of this recent discord over the business, Vestalia, how Gareth Box had opposed her attempts to introduce a Christian dimension to try and reflect in a domestic setting the spiritual simplicity she'd discovered in that tiny seaside church in North Wales – Gareth saying this was commercial suicide. At the same time knowing his hands were tied, because *she* was both the creative force and the figurehead. And now the inevitable split was looming, and Gareth was accusing her of being brainwashed by the Church, by this woman priest.

'He found out about the money,' Jenny said.

'Money?' It didn't strike Jane at first.

'The *money*. In the sack. Well, he was salting away what *he* could, knowing he didn't have long before the golden goose flew the pen, shifting what money he could get his hands on, investing in other companies. So I thought . . . why not? And here was Merrily in a situation where male priorities were attempting to influence her better judgement, penetrating the sanctuary. And he found out. And then *he* wanted to know about Merrily, this woman priest who'd bewitched me. So when you arrived at his door, the bastard must've thought 'twas his birthday . . . in all kinds of ways.'

'He didn't touch me,' Jane said quickly.

'Would've happened Jane, if not the next time you met, then the time after that. The older he gets, the younger *they* get.' Jenny Box tightened her white scarf around her head and neck. 'Another destroyer. Starting off, I suppose, trying to get information out of you – anything he could use against me, to blackmail me or humiliate me. And then he'd release the poison. Like a serpent. And then, he'd bide his time, and he—'

'She'll give it back, you know.' Jane didn't want to hear this. 'The money. She won't keep it now.'

'She'll keep it,' Jenny said.

'*No*. Maybe you don't know her as well as you think you do.'

'I know *him*, Jane. I know him better than I ever . . . dreaded I would. I know where he came from. We'd better be getting back, it's starting to rain again.'

Jane followed her, in a fog of self-dismay vaguely lit by a kind of tentative elation – a rare feeling when she'd been so very wrong about so much. She found she was almost relishing the cold rain on her face, a cleansing . . . she needed that. She felt – although she wasn't sure the feeling was going to last – that she needed, in some way, to start again.

At the square, Jenny Box pointed at a long blue and white car parked in the line of vehicles directly opposite the Black Swan. 'There you are, see, that's my man. Humphries.'

'That's *his* car? But I've seen it loads of times . . .'

Jenny Box said, rather sadly, 'When he realized who I was, he became most assiduous in his inquiries, perhaps anticipating regular work in the future. Came up with a lot of stuff I hadn't asked for. Some of which was useful. Told me things about you, for instance.'

'Me?' Jane didn't know whether to feel outraged or flattered.

'About your dalliance in the various spiritual byways. The man seems like a buffoon, but he's surprisingly good at what he does. Garrulous. Asks questions without you realizing they're being asked.'

'Is he as obvious as his car?'

'Twice as obvious. He . . . I wanted to know about Under-howle, all right? When I read about Lodge, and when I heard on the radio news that Merrily was involved, I asked Humphries to find out what he could from his contacts. On an impulse, I paid him to go to Underhowle.'

God, what it must be like to have unlimited money. 'Did you tell Mum what you were doing?'

Jenny Box shook her head.

'I don't think she'd be too happy about that,' Jane said, 'do you?'

'Well, that's what I was coming to see her about. Things he uncovered. Things I should've known. I've been more stupid than I can say. Do you know at all when she'll be back?'

'Could be anytime. She's with Huw Owen. He's a bit bonkers, to be honest. They could be there all night.'

'Jane, listen . . . I hope I've convinced you – because I've embarrassed the hell out of myself – that I only want to help her.'

'Well, yeah, but . . .' Jane felt awkward. 'It's just . . . the website? Uriel?'

'Yes, I sent your mother's name to be put on the Uriel website. For people to pray for her. The Uriel website's an international site for promoting women's spirituality, nothing at all sinister. I put her name on the site because it attracts a weight of prayer from all over the world, and that's what she's going to need, believe me. It's a deep-embedded evil she's confronting, and she needs the angels at her shoulder.' Jenny Box stood on the edge of the square. The blur was gone. Certainty shimmered around her now. 'So would you tell her to come and see me, please? Before Friday. Before she buries that man. Believe me, there're things she very much needs to know.'

'Sure, but—'

'I wasn't kidding before. Whatever kind of lunatic you think I am, I don't care. This is an awful satanic thing, and it's close to us all.'

'Well, can't you—?'

'No, Jane, you've pushed me too far as it is. I won't have this going out second-hand.'

Jane nodded soberly. 'OK, I'll . . . tell her to call you in the morning.'

'Thank you, Jane.'

'I'm sorry, OK?'

'There's nothing to be sorry about. Goodnight now. God bless you.'

'Thanks.' Jane turned away to walk home, past the forecourt by the entrance to the church, and saw the steeple rising from the middle of the ragged apple trees.

And then she turned back and called out, '*Did* you see it? Did you really see an angel?'

Jenny Box stopped, her white scarf slipping back. 'Jane, it doesn't *matter* what I saw. It was a personal experience. A confirmation. It's nothing to do with anyone else. I'm not claiming to be Bernadette. I don't *care* whether anyone believes me.'

'You don't understand what I'm asking, do you?'

Jenny came up to her. They were alone in front of the lych-gate. Jane felt suddenly forlorn.

Jenny reached out and took both Jane's hands in her own. Jenny's hands were cold.

'Yes,' she said. 'I saw it, Jane. And she was beautiful.'

41

A Rainy Night in Underhowle

Huw concluded, '*In the name of the Father and of the Son and of the Holy Spirit, we pray that this building might be free from all powers of darkness, spirits of evil. Defend from harm, Lord, all who enter and leave through this door . . .*'

The words dissipated, Merrily thought, like the smoke of a single cigarette. This was Huw going through the motions – never leave a possibly disturbed place unblessed.

Ingrid Sollars put all the hanging bulbs out of their misery before locking the Victorian oak door with one of the keys on a jailer's ring. She pulled at the iron handle. 'Sometimes it's come open in the night.'

'How do you mean?' Merrily looked at Ingrid: scratched waxed jacket, practical slacks: a woman who looked like she could shoe horses and change oil filters. 'How could that happen?'

'It just has. I'm the one who usually locks it. I don't make mistakes.'

Huw leaned an elbow on the small window ledge. 'Still happening?'

'Not for some months, but I still check.'

'Rogue energy, happen?'

'I beg your pardon?'

'A church or chapel this size is an amplifier for energy, and when a place has been used for worship, it accumulates. When you take away the prayer, where's it go? If it's left derelict, the energy might turn negative. If the worship's replaced by something antisocial or irreligious, it *definitely* will.'

Merrily stared at him. Did he actually *believe* that?

'A spring-water bottling plant?' Ingrid Sollars said sceptically.

'Hmm.' Huw inclined his head. 'Would you happen to know who the people are who ran this enterprise, Ingrid?'

'I do know them,' Ingrid said guardedly. 'They're running a similar operation in the Usk Valley. Is it important?'

'Think you could get them on the phone tonight?'

'I could try.' She opened the modern porch door. Outside it was raining. In the distance, Merrily could still hear a chant of *Roddy's Body OUT.* It was irregular now and punctuated with laughter.

'If you could do that,' Huw said to Ingrid, 'happen you could find out the name of the contractor who did the conversion.'

Merrily said, 'What—?'

'Meanwhile,' Huw said, 'there's the other thing. Come on, now, Ingrid, you've been on the brink of telling us.'

Ingrid sighed. 'Actually, Mr Owen, I've been hoping the person concerned would come over herself. I did ask her.'

'People get coy sometimes, lass. Who is it?'

Ingrid hesitated. 'A girl. Schoolgirl.'

'Parents know?'

'I think so.'

'Where's the problem, then? Not like we're the police, is it?'

Merrily thought she'd rather face the police than Huw in this mood.

The mother wore a purple fleece top, crushed-velvet trousers, green-tinted hair and a gold nose-stud on a chain.

'They were just having a bit of fun together,' she said. 'You're only young once, aren't you?'

You didn't realize how much things had changed, Merrily thought, until you heard that from a parent. The attitude seemed to be that they were going to do it anyway, so why erect barriers? She thought about Jane and Eirion. Perhaps the most you could ask for was that your kids should wait until the age of consent and that there should then be a degree of emotional commitment.

Merrily wanted to get home. She felt cold and anxious.

Huw was clearly in no hurry. 'So you found the door open?' he said to the girl. He and Merrily were sharing a red leather sofa in the front room of number 27 Goodrich Close, where the central heating could have sustained tropical lizards. *Who*

Wants To Be a Millionaire? was on TV; nobody had turned that down either.

'I didn't want to go in, right?' Zoe Franklin said. 'But Martin had been to the pub, and he was feeling brave.'

Zoe was a serious-minded girl, according to Ingrid Sollars. Doing A-level maths and sciences in Ross. University material. Not an *imaginative* girl – that was what Merrily thought Ingrid had been trying to convey. Zoe's long-time boyfriend had been Martin Brinkley, two or three years older, a junior bank clerk and a good lad, generally.

'If they wanted to keep people out, why didn't they just lock it?' Mrs Franklin demanded. She'd told them that Zoe's dad and Zoe's brother, Curtis, had gone on the Roddy Lodge demo. Pub, more likely, Mrs Franklin said.

Ingrid had said that Zoe's mother wouldn't have minded much if Zoe had stuck with Martin Brinkley, got herself pregnant and forgot about all this university rubbish, because that was likely to cost them, wasn't it? Ingrid said Zoe's parents were what you would have regarded as typical Underhowle parents. Typical, at least, of the pre-Fergus era.

'What had you heard about the place, Zoe?' Huw asked.

'I thought it was all stupid.' Zoe wore jeans and a T-shirt and an anxious expression. 'It's just one of those stories that goes around the school. It was supposed to be haunted and they said that when the ghost was there the door would be open. So if you tried the door – that's the old oak door inside the porch – and it opened for you, you could go in and . . . *something* would be waiting there.'

'And what had people seen?'

'Nothing, really. They just said you could feel it watching you.'

'What did *you* feel?'

'Martin, I'll bet!' Mrs Franklin said and rocked with laughter.

'You wanner make us a cup of tea, mam?' Zoe said patiently. 'I'm here as your responsible adult!'

'Jesus,' Zoe said, 'that was when the police had Curtis in. This is the Church, for Christ's sake! Please?'

Mrs Franklin stalked out and Zoe grabbed the remote and switched off the TV.

'They wanted to sue the Development Committee because I had bruises. They thought they could make some money out of it. That's why I didn't say anything, except to Mrs Sollars. They didn't believe the other stuff, anyway. Thought I was making it up. My parents can't believe anybody actually tells the truth. Like, I *was* going to come and see you tonight, but I didn't want any of *them* to know.'

'The protesters?' Merrily could stand the heat no longer and shrugged off her coat.

'It's all stupid,' Zoe said. 'It's Mr and Mrs Lodge who are going to suffer. What've they ever done to anybody?'

It had been raining, and Zoe didn't fancy going on the back of Martin's motorbike in that kind of weather, thanks very much, and while they were thinking about what to do they'd gone into the chapel porch to shelter for a bit, and Martin had grinned and said, 'I wonder if it's open tonight.'

It was one of those myths that took hold: modern folklore, almost always passed on by children. Martin Brinkley had heard it from his younger brother, who said he'd heard it from a boy who'd gone in with his girlfriend and she'd been so frightened she'd *let him do it*.

Zoe had said 'Don't be stupid' and 'Let's go' and things like that, but Martin had already had a pint in the pub with his mates and he was, you know, a bit skittish. He'd tried the door and . . . would you believe it? Hey!

Martin had gone in.

'Don't be stupid,' Zoe had shouted from the porch.

Silence. Martin hadn't come out.

'Don't be so *bloody* stupid!' Zoe had cried.

And had taken a step inside – and, *bang*, the door had slammed behind her, and Zoe had screamed and Martin's arms had come around her: *Don't be scared, I'm here.* And she'd had to laugh, and then they'd started kissing and, you know . . .

Well, the door *was* open, look, and it wasn't as if there was anything they could damage in there; the place was already gutted. But it was dry and cleaner than Zoe would have expected, and it wasn't that cold and where else was there to go on a rainy night in Underhowle? So they'd fetched a rug from the box on Martin's bike. Though, actually, the truth was that Zoe hadn't liked it in there from the first, but what could she say without looking like a wimp?

'Why exactly didn't you like it, lass?'

'It was . . . as if the walls had eyes, you know? As if they were bulging inwards to make sure they didn't miss anything. You could, like, feel it, even though you couldn't see much, just the light in the windows. Now I know that sounds stupid, but at one point, because I was so convinced someone was watching us, I made Martin put all the lights on, even though people might see them from outside.'

'If it was me, I'd've been *hoping* people would see,' Merrily said.

'Yeah.' Zoe smiled gratefully. 'Actually, it was worse, somehow, with the lights on, because of all the shadows which made it seem like the walls really *were* swelling.' She moved her hands in and out, like an accordionist. 'You felt there was something there – *inside* there, with us – that *wanted* the lights on. So it could see us. So we put them out again.'

'You didn't actually see anything, though?' Merrily asked.

'No.'

'What about the temperature? Did you feel it was especially cold? Colder in some areas than others, say?'

'Maybe. I don't know, really, it was all cold. I didn't want to stop there *at all*, but Martin's putting his arms round me, and he'd rolled up these dust sheets, which were fairly clean, and . . . Oh, I don't have to talk about this stuff, do I?'

'Of course not. We'd just like to know when anything happened that you . . . weren't expecting.'

'Yeah, well, I wouldn't let him go any further, anyway. I said no, that's it, I've had enough, this is stupid, and I got up to go. I remember getting up, and then . . .' Zoe closed her eyes for a moment and, in the botanical-garden heat, Merrily actually saw goose bumps appear on the girl's arms. 'I was just thrown back, really roughly. Back on to the dust sheets – that's when I got the bruises, yeah? And I wasn't afraid then, so much as – you know – startled and angry. I'm like, Geddoff, you dull bugger!'

Merrily said, 'Did you – when you were thrown back – feel anybody actually *touch* you?'

'Yeah, I . . . I think so. But I didn't really have time to, because I couldn't breathe, you know? I was choking. There was suddenly this awful pressure on my throat.'

'What kind of pressure, Zoe?' Huw said. 'What did you actually feel?'

Zoe rubbed her arms. 'I couldn't exactly say it was hands. I couldn't say it *felt* like hands. But I *thought* of hands. I thought of these rough – what's the word? – callused, kind of hands. And *dirty*. And what I heard – this was the very worst moment, I can tell you – I actually heard Martin's voice. He was going, like, "What's up with you? What you doing?" And his voice was like a long way away. I mean, what – five, six metres? And I'm trying to shout, scream . . . and all I could make were these little rattly noises, like snorting. And I was . . . absolutely . . . bloody terrified.'

'I bet,' Merrily said.

'I thought I was gonner die. I thought I was gonner die there and then. You believe me?'

'Yes.'

'You're, like, a vicar, too, yeah?'

'Mmm.'

'And I'll tell you something else. Martin, he en't got hands like that. He works in a bank.' Zoe nodded towards the door, lowered her voice. '*They* still don't believe me. Not really. Sometimes I think I dreamed it. You know, that we fell asleep in there or something. But I can't have. I wasn't comfortable in there, you know, not from the start.'

'What happened in the end, Zoe?' Merrily asked.

'Martin put the lights on and there was nothing there.'

'How far were you from the lights?'

''Bout four metres.'

'Could you still feel the pressure as he was putting the lights on?'

'When the lights went on, I could breathe. It wasn't Martin. It definitely wasn't Martin. And there was nobody else in there, I swear to God.'

'Did you have any marks on your neck, Zoe?' Huw asked.

'No. Well, redness maybe. But no bruises like you'd expect. Listen, can you tell me what happened? I've heard some of this stuff Mr Hall talks about, and I'm doing physics at A level, so . . . I mean, I've been trying to tell myself this was all caused by electromagnetism and radio waves on my brain. That maybe, like he says, there *is* some problem caused by like intersection of electrics from the power lines and signals from the TV booster and the mobile-phone transmitters . . .'

Merrily looked at Huw.

'Aye,' he said, 'it's possible.'

'Then what are *you* doing here?' Zoe said.

An old Land Rover was parked outside the house; its lights flashed once and a rear door opened for them.

Ingrid Sollars was at the wheel, Sam Hall next to her. 'If this was daylight,' he said, 'you'd see the goddam pylon right at the back of the house, and you'd see the TV booster across the valley. The existing mobile-phone transmitter's in the wood across there, and the big new one—'

Ingrid switched on the engine, creating foundry sounds. 'This is the Reverend Owen, Sam, and I really don't think he believes this begins and ends with electricity.'

'More sick people on this estate than you could otherwise account for – how d'ya do, Reverend Owen? – and Melanie Pullman lived right over there, end of the turning circle.'

The turning circle was jammed with cars, so Ingrid Sollars had to reverse off the estate. She drove them back into the centre of the village, where a few people still hung around and the placard saying KEEP SATAN OUT! was propped against a lamp-post.

Sam leaned over the back of his seat. 'Ingrid, of course, would actually prefer this whole thing to be down to Satan.'

Ingrid pulled in behind Merrily's Volvo. 'What he means is that Ingrid would prefer it *not* to have been caused by something the removal of which would damage the progress of this village out of the Dark Ages. We need communications, and we need all those computers, and we need the power to make them work. At the moment, a child as bright as Zoe Franklin is the exception in her age group. In ten years' time she'll be the norm.'

'It's the main source of argument between us,' Sam said. 'I don't believe this *is* progress if it's gonna kill off half the people and give the rest waking nightmares.'

'That's a ridiculous exaggeration.'

'Sure it is – at present.'

Huw said, 'You talk to the spring-water people, Ingrid?'

Ingrid switched off the engine. It subsided with noises like the collapsing of metal plates. 'Yes, I did. I said the Development Committee had limited funds and would very much like to know the name of the contractors they employed in the original conversion.'

'And?'

'They said they didn't have a phone number but they were pretty sure this particular contractor was . . . no longer available.'

'I bet they they couldn't remember his name, either.'

Ingrid said, 'What do you propose to do about this, Mr Owen?'

'I intend to discuss it with my colleague here, who I hope will allow me to be involved in tomorrow's funeral.'

'*Tomorrow?*'

'Don't spread it around, eh?'

'You're a bastard, Huw.' Merrily realized she was driving too fast and her foot stabbed the brake. The rain had stopped, but the night clouds hung low and sombre as the lights of Ross began to flower around them.

'Me mam never tried to hide it,' Huw said placidly.

'For a start, you *knew* what Zoe was going to tell us.'

'Ingrid told me about it while you were messing with the TV people. She didn't give me the name then, though.'

'But you had to make the kid go through it again.'

'Cathartic, lass. Anyroad, I wanted *you* to hear it. You might not've believed me. A few tools disappearing and a bloke punched off a ladder doesn't amount to much. I wanted you to feel that sense of being watched. And the rest of it.'

'It doesn't prove anything.'

'Nothing's ever proven.'

Merrily drove slowly through the medieval centre of Ross, behind the ancient sandstone market house, the church rising on her left, roofs glistening.

'You even knew who the contractor was.'

'The good Mumford and his contacts,' Huw said. 'Ear to the ground, that lad. A respectable spring-water firm would hardly like it broadcast. Nobody wants to be known as having employed him, having been to the pub with him a time or two, and certainly not—'

'You wasted Ingrid's time.'

'I wanted her to hear it, and I wanted you to hear it from her.'

'Because you didn't want me to think it was all down to you.'

Huw said nothing.

'Which it is, of course.'

'Who else cared enough?' Huw said.

Consider, Huw said.

Consider Cromwell Street, Gloucester: a street full of flats and bedsits and therefore young people in need of cheap accommodation, coming and going, moving out and moving in. And the top rooms in number twenty-five were the cheapest of the lot. Police had actually traced about a hundred and fifty former tenants, some of whom had paid no more than a fiver a week.

So it was a haven for itinerant kids, some of whom might otherwise be sleeping in cardboard boxes in shop doorways. Some actually said it was the happiest, *safest* time of their adult lives, being in Cromwell Street, being part of Fred and Rose's big family, with all that this involved. Looked back on it with real nostalgia.

Strange. And yet not so strange.

Because it was an *organism*, was 25 Cromwell Street, Huw said, and Fred loved it for that. It was end-of-terrace, tall and narrow – three storeys, plus cellars, plus attics – built like a person. And Fred knew all its private parts: where the wires went, where the pipes went.

He liked to feel the presence of the bodies in there, bodies live and dead. Bodies became part of the fabric of that place, said Huw, who had studied it all in nauseating depth. Bodies, not people, because Fred basically was not interested in *people*, only their bodies.

25 Cromwell Street: a bargain flophouse, a free brothel and a burial chamber, and Fred loved it. Loved messing with it, altering this and that, contriving, bodging. He turned one room into a primitive cocktail bar – the Black Magic Bar, they called it, with optics on the bottles and a big mural of a Caribbean beachscape. It was the first real house he'd ever owned; got it for seven grand, but it needed renovation; it needed a builder, needed *him*. And he'd keep working on it whenever he had the time: extending it, building new bits, fabricating this, concreting that. Building *himself* into that house. Putting his consciousness into it.

Such as it was.

Fred's consciousness was basement stuff, Huw said. Fred thought about sex all the time, talked about sex most of the time he was awake.

And if the walls in 25 Cromwell Street all had eyes, they were Fred's eyes. Eyes and ears: microphones and speakers, video cameras, so Fred could absorb the sights and sounds of sex – squeals of ecstasy upstairs, sobs of fear and despair in the cellars, the dungeons. 25 Cromwell Street throbbed with it. The house that Fred built, full of Fred's porno pictures, Fred's porno videos, Fred's tools. And the dead.

'And they knocked it down,' Huw said. 'That were all they could think of to do with it afterwards. There *was* talk of having a memorial garden, for the victims, but nobody wanted to be reminded what had happened there.'

So the council had knocked it down and built a walkway, with street lamps, so that nobody would know it had even been there. So you could walk past where it had been, walk over it, as a short cut to the centre of Gloucester. They'd turned it into another small extension to the old Roman street plan that still lay at the heart of the city – one of the best-preserved Roman street patterns anywhere in Britain. Glevum, the Roman name for Gloucester, meant *place of light*.

The darkest corner of the place of light: gone. But where had *Fred* gone? The man who was so attached to the flesh and to gadgets and tools and working with his hands; the man with no morals, no sensitivity, no spark of spirituality.

A one-man definition of the term 'earthbound'.

Where was Fred? The man who remained unconvicted, who had cheated justice, who was said to have sat in his cell, between interrogations, and dreamed of Cromwell Street.

Where was whatever remained of Fred?

'This is crazy,' Merrily said.

'Is it? You know about Lodge. You've been in his bungalow. You've seen his facsimile of the Black Magic Bar. You've seen the buried cuttings and the photo of him and Lynsey Davies on the sofa, posing like Fred and Rose. All *I* know is, lass, there were too much holding him to Cromwell Street and they took it away. First, they took his kids away, then they took the dead away. And they took him away, and he couldn't cope with that. And then, when he was dead and burned and sprinkled over Much Marcle, they took the house itself away . . . his creation.'

'Huw . . .' Merrily was finding it hard to breathe. 'This is a notorious killer of the lowest kind who—'

'I don't believe you can lay a man like that so easily to any kind of rest. I expected traces—'

'– Who, in the end, avoided the processes of the law—'

'I expected traces in the fields at Marcle, but I should've realized – he didn't like it there because it was a village and everybody knew your business. He liked to watch, not *be* watched.'

'– And now nobody can get at him,' Merrily said. 'All the relatives of the dead denied justice. All the relatives of the missing who'll never know for sure . . . never.'

'No,' Huw said.

'And nobody can get at him. Except . . .' She was gripping the wheel tightly with both hands. ' . . . Except, perhaps, for you, and I wonder what the Christian Deliverance Study Group would think of whatever you have in mind.'

Huw didn't reply. Merrily drove slowly over Wilton Bridge towards the bypass, and the moon edged out for a moment and glimmered in the Wye.

42

Vampires

*The van pulls up in the Tesco car park, where it backs on to the
bus station, just the other side of the little wall, and Jane sees him
getting out and she has to smile.*

*Coming towards her, pointing with his stubby right forefinger,
a loose semi-grin on his face, plastic carrier bag hanging from his
left hand. He's actually not bad-looking in the right light, for
his age, in this gypsyish sort of way. In this earthy sort of way,
which you'd probably call 'coarse' if you were snobby and middle-
class and buttoned-up, which Jane definitely is not.*

'Well, well,' he says, 'I thought it was you!'

*Jane's been waiting for her bus to Ledwardine, and it's late and
there's nobody else waiting in the North Hereford queue, and in
fact she was beginning to wonder if she'd missed it. Bugger. Going
to be late, so she needs to ring Mum, but she's left the mobile at
home again, and if she goes off to phone and the bus comes, she'll
be stuffed.*

'How you doing, then, girl?'

'I'm OK, Fred. You?'

*'Busy. Up to the eyes, as usual, look, but that en't no bad thing.'
Looking her up and down, with the old saucy wink. 'You've grown,
en't you? How old you now?'*

'Seventeen.' Jane rolls her eyes. 'Over the hill.'

*He smirks in delight. 'Well, don't seem no time at all, do it,
since we done your bathroom, took out the ole shower? Had a good
laugh then, di'n't we? How's your ma? Still doin' the ole . . . ?'
Miming the dog collar like it's got a ball and chain attached.*

*'Well . . . She's probably OK now, at this moment,' Jane says
doubtfully. 'But she'll be mad as hell if it turns out I've missed this
bus and she's late for her communion class.'*

'Missed your bus, is it? Bugger.'

'It's OK, there'll be another three in about two hours.'

'Well now, hang on . . .' He purses his lips, thinking. *Just you hang on a mo, Jane . . . Ledwardine, ennit? I'm off up to wossername . . . Weobley, look. So how far's that from Ledwardine? No distance, is it, if we goes back along the ole Brecon road – no time at all. Hey, listen, I got Rose in the van, too. You en't met Rose, did you?'*

Jane's actually curious to know what Fred's wife's like, the way he went on about her, this great big bundle of fun, always ready for a laugh, day or night, know what I mean?

But in the van, when Jane gets in – it's actually quite decent of him to do this; she knows what he's like, always on the go, always another job lined up, do anything for anybody – Rose doesn't seem like that at all. Bit frumpy, actually. Got this kind of high, whiny voice. Still, she seems friendly enough, in her way. Just not as instantly outgoing as Fred, as is often the case with wives of really extrovert guys.

Fred's leaning across, apologizing to Rose. *'Now I know you won't mind, my love, not really, but we gotter drop Jane off in Ledwardine. Take us n'more'n five minutes out of our way, I promise. You all right in the back there, Jane? If you moves them tools, in the black bag, there's an ole mattress, be more comfortable for you. That's it.'*

The van rattling out of Hereford now and into the country up towards Stretton Sugwas, Rose taking the occasional glance back at Jane, to make sure she's OK in the back. There's a strong smell of oil in here, and sweat. A working van. Jane remembers the problem with Fred is he's always working so hard he doesn't get that much time for baths, as he was the first to admit when he was putting in their new shower at the vicarage. *'Oughter 'ave a quick one now, Jane – test him out, look. You wanner get in there with me, scrub me back?'* he'd said. Little grin and a wink to show he didn't really mean it. Totally faithful to Rose, is Fred – not that he don't get a few offers, mind. Beggin' for it, some of these housewives, have you up the ole stairs in no time at all, you don't watch it.

'So how's wossername, the Welsh boy, Irene?' Calling back over his shoulder as he drives. *You still goin' with him? You know what*

they says about the Welsh? That true, Jane, you found out yet? I bet you bloody 'ave, girl, I seen the look in your eyes. You all right back there? Sorry about the state. Tell you what, I'll move that ole ...'

The van stops.

Jane notices he's pulled off the road and driven through an open field gate and, looking between the front seats, through the windscreen, she can see that there's a thick hedge now between the van and the road, and she's thinking, Why are we ...? What's he stopping for? They haven't been on the road five minutes. Then the rear doors creak open and Fred climbs in with her. He's wearing his old overalls; the smell of sweat is very strong now.

He's holding a roll of wide, brown tape that he's pulled from the tool bag.

He isn't smiling any more. He's got this intent look on his face, like when he was sizing up the bathroom wall, working things out. There are little points of light so far back in his bulblike eyes, it's as if they're actually shining from somewhere inside his brain.

'What are you ...?' An amazed fear shoots up through Jane's body.

And with that first lilt of it in her voice, she sees that something has happened. The little lights have filled up Fred's eyes, making them glow as if they're veined with filaments, and his teeth are bared. The whole atmosphere in the van has changed, become charged, Fred and Rose connecting now like jump leads on a battery, sparks bouncing between them.

Then this great big bunched fist, knuckles like ball-bearings, thrusts up like a greased piston on a machine and smacks Jane thunderously in the mouth. She can feel the blow echoing in her skull.

Then there's this kind of time-lapse and the next thing she's on her back tasting salty blood, smelling this overwhelming sweat smell – Fred on top of her taping her wrists together, his lips drawn back, teeth set in concentration, breath coming in efficient little spurts.

And then, satisfied with his wrist-taping, he's saying,

'You di'n't 'ave no dad to show you what's what, did you, Jane? Me and Rose gonner help you out now, look. Be thankin' us, you

*will, you and that Welsh boy, wossername, Irene. Show you what's
what, where the bits goes, you little smart bitch . . .'*

Merrily spasmed and jerked up in bed. The light was still on,
and *Happy like Murderers* was spread spine-up on the duvet.

It was ten past two in the morning, and the experience had
been so shatteringly vivid that she had to get out of bed and go
rushing up to Jane's apartment, to stand panting in the doorway,
listening to the kid's breathing.

Afterwards, at the top of the stairs, she felt so faint that she
had to go down on her knees, head in her hands. Her hair was
matted, her skin felt like latex, and she'd have to have a shower,
even if it sent the pipes into a strangled symphony.

Under the water, she relived the unspeakable, through the
split consciousness in the dream that had been scripted by her
reading – the absolute insanity of reading that stuff until sleep
had blurred the filth.

In the dream, part of her had been Jane, and yet *she* was there,
too, invisible and helpless, as Jane's mum.

Knowing what Jane could not know – knowing what was
going to happen. What *had* happened, over and over again: Fred
and Rose feeding off fear.

Sexual vampires.

Merrily thought about the mothers of the known victims, all
the stricken mothers who *had* to read about it, *had* to know,
had to *be* there with their daughters, at least once, in the greasy,
blood-smelling, semen-smelling darkness.

In Fred and Rose's cellar, which was not there any more.

A one-man definition of the term 'earthbound'.

Was it conceivable that whatever had been inside Fred, whatever had ignited the bilious filaments of evil in those eyes, could
be passed on, could jump – the way the electricity had jumped
into Roddy Lodge from live coils around the insulators on the
pylon – into someone receptive?

And *was* it – as some deeply troubled part of Huw might *need*
it to be – something beyond the human?

*

Wearing a clean white T-shirt under her towelling robe, Merrily crept up the stairs to check on Jane again.

The kid had seemed to be genuinely asleep when she and Huw had arrived back at the vicarage just after midnight. Behind the front door, they'd found a brown paper bag containing a white, hardbacked notebook labelled *The Magickal Diary of Lynsey Davies*, and a note from Lol that said: *It's all here. You don't even need to read between the lines.*

When she'd shown Huw to his room, he'd taken the diary with him. She wondered what *his* nightmares had been like.

As she stood looking down at Jane she thought the kid's eyes opened briefly. But then they closed again and she turned over onto her side, and Merrily slipped out.

She stopped by the top landing window with its view through the trees to the village square and the all-night lantern on the front of the Black Swan. And then she knelt, in her long white T-shirt, and prayed for guidance, slow and intense, from far inside herself, inside her heart-centre, in the emotional silences back there.

Part Six

Countless repetitive murderers have said that they felt they were in the grip of something foreign, that 'something strange came over them' which they could not resist at the time of the offences . . . 'I don't know what got into me.' Priests do know, of course . . .

Brian Masters
She Must Have Known

A hundred years from now, we will look back at pylons as relics of the mid-20th century. It probably won't happen in five or ten years, but eventually a new generation will come along, change things and wonder why we did nothing.

Denis Henshaw
Professor of Physics, Bristol University

43

Fun Palace

It was down at the bottom of Ross town centre, among a cluster of antique shops, and still hard to find. It had a door with no glass and one narrow window with no actual books in it, just a small sign on a greying card.

Piers Connor-Crewe
Bookseller

Frannie Bliss found the discretion interesting. 'Porn. Gorra be. How else is he gonna make any kind of a living?'

'Word of mouth,' Merrily said. 'The Internet. You can turn over a week's income on about four books, if you know what you're doing – so I'm told.'

'We're not talking John Grisham here, are we?' Bliss pushed at the door; it didn't give.

'Try the bell, Frannie.'

'Hard porn – mark my words.' Bliss pressed a black button in the white door. 'I've been summoned, by the way.'

'Fleming?' Merrily looked up the hill towards the Market House, where clouds were massing like bonfire smoke. It was not yet eleven a.m.

'It was only a matter of time. He knew I was still around – well, obviously. Wants to see me in Hereford at four this afternoon, which is ominous – anything heavy, you say it late afternoon. Limits the victim's options. He thinks, Aw, sod it, I'll go and get pissed instead. I'm guessing formal suspension this time.'

'What sort of case have they got for that?'

'He's been heard to say, "If Bliss wants to be a private eye, I'm not going to hold him back any longer." And he'll have stuff going way back. I never claimed to be the divisional Mr Popular.'

'What does Kirsty say?'

'Kirsty left last night, Merrily. Back to the farm. With the kids.'

'Frannie, no . . .'

The door opened. A woman of maybe twenty-six stood there. 'Sorry, we're a bit behind this morning.' She had short hair bleached white and a silver ring in her left eyebrow.

Bliss smiled bleakly at her. 'Mr Connor-Crewe in, is he?' Like he hadn't phoned first, to make sure of it.

'He's unpacking some books upstairs, if you want to hang around for a couple of minutes . . . You trade?'

'Collector,' Bliss said. '*Beano* annuals, mainly.'

'Yeah?'

Bliss flashed his card. 'DI Bliss, West Mercia.'

'Oh, right.' She seemed unsurprised. 'Go through, officer.'

'Ta.'

They went in, Merrily holding the plastic carrier bag with Hereford Cathedral on it. The window had been deceptive; the building was narrow but deep, a darkening tunnel of shelves. Arrowed signs indicated two other floors. The woman stood at the bottom of some narrow wooden stairs.

'Hey . . . you know Mumford?'

'So this is where he gets his first editions.'

She grinned. 'I'll tell Piers. So it's DI . . . ?'

'Bliss. And, er . . .'

'Merrily Watkins,' Merrily said, thinking, *Cola French*?

The white-haired woman stopped on the second step, turned with a hand on the rail and inspected her. Merrily wore her best coat over the black cowl-neck sweater, the cross concealed. 'Yeah,' the woman said sadly. 'Oh well.' And carried on upstairs, leaving Bliss peering curiously at Merrily.

'If you go straight down, you'll find an alcove on your left, with some chairs,' Cola French called back. 'Criminal History's right at the bottom. But, er . . . Theology's in the cellar.'

'Bound to have read them all, anyway,' Merrily said.

*

What bothered Merrily most was that she hadn't seen Jane, not to speak to. She'd overslept, and it had been nearly nine a.m. when she'd staggered into the kitchen to find a note on the table.

Mum, I've gone.

Just in case you're vaguely interested, it's Lol's gig tonight at the Courtyard. So I've taken a change of clothes with me and I'll carry on to Hereford on the school bus. If you don't make it there later I'll just have to thumb a lift back or something, so don't let it interfere with your spiritual schedule or anything.

J.

And Jenny Box called. She'd like to talk to you. You should.

'She wouldn't actually thumb a lift, of course,' Merrily had said later to Huw. 'This is just a gentle dig.'

'With a bayonet,' Huw said.

'No, for Jane, this *is* a gentle dig.'

Huw had refused to eat breakfast or to drink tea. He'd drunk one glass of water. Was this a fast, purification, in anticipation of . . . what?

Merrily had eaten half a slice of toast and felt guilty. Then she'd gone into the scullery and looked up the number for Ingrid Sollars. She had in front of her Lol's note, which said, *The PCC mentioned in the diary is Piers Connor-Crewe. If you feel you have to go and see him, please don't go on your own.* This morning, Lol had phoned, filling in some gaps, bless him.

The phone at Ingrid's place had been picked up by Sam Hall, which didn't surprise her a lot. Merrily had asked Sam some straight questions about his former colleague on the Underhowle Development Committee.

Before leaving the vicarage, she'd left a message on Prof's answering machine asking if Lol, or even Prof himself, could keep an eye open for Jane tonight. Left a similar message on their own machine for the kid to pick up if she rang in. Just in case this situation proved more complex.

As now seemed likely.

*

Piers Connor-Crewe, plump and moon-faced and cheerful, wore his baggy cream suit over a denim shirt with a frayed collar. One of those men, Merrily thought, who might greet you in pyjamas, always confident that you'd be blinded by the aura of his personality, his intellect.

'Merrily Watkins, how nice. And back in your role as consultant to the Herefordshire Constabulary.'

Bliss stood up. 'DI Francis Bliss. We haven't met.'

'No, indeed – I'm afraid I was working late the night you encountered the Committee.'

Connor-Crewe went to sit behind the desk, which filled half of this dimly lit airspace between bookshelves. He motioned Bliss and Merrily to a couple of battered smokers' chairs. The alcove seemed to serve as his office. There was a phone on the desk, a vintage, crane-necked electric lamp and a large book on Roman pottery.

'Well now,' he said, 'if this is about what I think it's about, let me first apologize that the police were *not* informed about last night's demonstration. However –' he opened his hands '– neither was the Committee. Seems to have been entirely impromptu – grass-roots protest – therefore, any damage is—'

'Not why we're here,' said Bliss. 'We've come to ask your advice about a book. Whether you think it's authentic, that kind of thing.'

Piers Connor-Crewe inclined his big head to one side and raised an eyebrow. Bliss turned to Merrily, who placed her Hereford Cathedral carrier bag on the desk and extracted the white book: *The Magickal Diary of Lynsey D.*

Piers leaned over and looked at it but didn't touch it. 'And where did you acquire this, Inspector Bliss?'

'Pick it up if you like, sir.'

'Oh, dear me, no. One never knows about journals like this.'

Bliss turned to Merrily. 'What's he mean by that, Mrs Watkins?'

'I think he means there might be some sort of protective curse around it.'

'Like King Tut's tomb.'

'That sort of thing.'

'No problem, then, for a man like me with bugger-all left to lose.' Bliss opened the book, turned it round to face Connor-Crewe, pulled the lamp over, switched it on and directed its cuplike shade at the page. The light illuminated one of the pages of complex-looking tables and correspondences, all meticulously drawn in different-coloured inks.

'What's this about, sir? What are all these funny little squiggly things?'

Connor-Crewe coughed. 'Those would be sigils, inspector. What one might call condensed spells. Configurations of particular desires, alphabetically and numerically reduced to their basics for, ah, intensity of focus.'

'Spells.'

'This is what might be described as someone's magical wish-list.'

'Would you be able to decode it yourself, sir?'

'Possibly, to an extent. Given time.'

'You're an expert on the occult, then?'

'In a largely academic way. There's a very significant international trade in old books on ceremonial magic and ritual. Something no antiquarian dealer can afford to ignore.'

'You handle a lot of them?'

'It probably accounts for up to twenty per cent of my trade. Perhaps even more.'

'But you didn't want to handle this one.'

Connor-Crew smiled. 'When I said that, I was being a little ironic. The so-called magical diary—'

'Because you knew where this one had been?'

'The *magical diary* is a very personal and private document, often considered to be a magical tool in itself.'

'I see.'

'I'm not sure you do, inspector, but I don't suppose it matters, in a strictly forensic sense.'

'So you've never seen this before?'

'Occasionally one appears on the market but in the case of this one I can safely say . . . no.'

'But you did know its owner.'

'Oh? Did I?'

'My information is that she was a regular customer who even helped out here sometimes. In one way or another.'

Connor-Crewe flipped the book shut and glanced at the cover. 'Ah. Of course.'

Bliss smiled like a wintry sun. 'You remember.'

'Poor woman,' said Connor-Crewe.

'What exactly was your relationship with the late Lynsey Davies?'

'Bookseller and customer.'

'Sleep with many of your customers, sir?'

Connor-Crewe sighed. 'Some.'

Merrily blinked.

'Inspector, a bookseller is not like other retailers. A *good* bookseller will very quickly develop an intimacy with his regular clients, based on his feeding of their intellectual desires. And if it should progress *beyond* that level, well . . . if there's an element of misconduct that might apply in the case of, say, a doctor and patient, then I'm afraid I'm not aware of anything similar concerning the book trade.'

'You're a slippery bastard, aren't you, sir?' Bliss said.

Connor-Crewe frowned.

Bliss said, 'Lynsey sometimes lived with you at The Old Rectory, is that correct?'

'Occasionally *stayed* with me would be more correct. Overnight.'

'Quite a formidable woman?'

'That's fair comment.'

'Been around.'

'I wouldn't doubt it.'

Bliss tapped the book. 'Who taught who about this stuff?'

Connor-Crewe thought about it. 'When she first came to me for magical literature, I would say her knowledge was, at best, rudimentary. But she had the persistence and, it would seem, the time to devote to the subject. After a year or two, I would say that her knowledge – certainly her practical ability – far outweighed mine.'

'Practical ability,' Merrily said. 'Mmm.'

Connor-Crewe smiled at her, with indulgence. 'We may be

getting into areas, Merrily, that you, as a Christian, would find repugnant. Let me remind you, however, that magic is an entirely legal discipline that functions these days all over the free world, largely unhampered by the secrecy that stifled it for centuries. Yes, I have practised magic. It's a wonderful mental exercise. It expands the being.'

Bliss turned to Merrily. 'That's put you in your place, vicar.'

'It's no big secret, inspector. There are even a number of further-education seminars on ritual magic at various colleges.'

'But what you're saying,' Merrily said, 'is that, while you have an extensive theoretical knowledge of esoteric practices, Lynsey Davies was what you might call a natural.'

Connor-Crewe looked pained. 'She was a strong-willed woman who was able to summon, to an enviable degree, the kind of concentration required for the visualization exercises that are crucial to the successful practice of magic.'

'By successful,' Bliss said, 'you mean actually making things happen.'

'I would say, rather, helping to move events towards the most satisfactory conclusion.'

Frannie Bliss nodded doubtfully. 'But to go back to my earlier question – where did she get it from? Did she suddenly show up at your shop and say, "Here, Piers, I fancy a go at that – you gorra couple of basic primers on the shelf?" '

'Now look . . .' Connor-Crewe leaned back, arms folded across his chest. His normally generous mouth had shrunk into an expression of petulance. 'I've been patient with you, Inspector Bliss, but I think that, before I answer any more of these questions, I have a right to ask you what this is all about.'

'Mr Crewe, I thought this was understood. I'm investigating a murder.'

'Whose?'

'You tell me,' Bliss said. 'Maybe there are some I don't know about.'

Lol had been aware of Prof Levin watching him for some minutes.

'You're beginning to worry me,' Prof said.

Lol put the electric tuner back in its case. The Washburn was now in tune with the Boswell. He'd keep tuning them through the day.

'It's the fear,' Prof said.

Lol had run through three songs in the studio – 'The River Frome Song', 'Kivernoll' and the acidic rocker 'Heavy Medication Day'. He figured that was going to be enough. This, after all, was a Moira Cairns concert. He thought the songs, which nobody would ever have heard before, had sounded acceptable – just.

'Where's the fear?' Prof demanded. 'What have you done with the fucking fear?'

Lol looked up. He was alone on the studio floor. Prof was up behind the mixing board. Moira had gone into Ledbury to buy some things and bring back some lunch for them. Lol had been running through the songs and, at the same time, wondering what correlation there might be between magic and the side effects of electricity experienced by people like Mephisto Jones and Roddy Lodge.

'This will do you no good, Laurence.'

'What won't?'

'Popping pills so far in advance. I was hoping you might make it without them. But eight, nine hours before you go on . . . believe me, this is not professional.'

Lol contemplated the ceiling.

'Then what's the matter with you?' Prof came down to the studio floor. He was wearing his *King of the Hill* T-shirt with a cardigan over the top. 'It's twenty years, give or take, since you last did this. You were a boy then, now you're a man approaching middle age. My advice – and I've seen this before, with other people, although not in such an extreme situation as yours – is to do the screaming now – but not so hard you damage your voice. Because, if you bottle it up until just before you go on, you're gonna balls this big time . . . throw it all away . . . pouf! Hey, you listening to me?'

Lol said, 'Prof . . . Mephisto Jones . . . You think he'd mind if I phoned him?'

*

Frannie Bliss said, 'I don't know much about sex magic, but I do know that Lynsey had quite a reputation locally as a bit of a goer. Which might explain what attracted her to this particular discipline, as distinct from, say, Transcendental Meditation or the Jehovah's Witnesses.'

'Stupid and simplistic assumption,' Connor-Crewe said.

Bliss nodded. 'Do you know much about Lynsey's early life? Did you know, for instance, that she went to college in Gloucester and then dropped out after less than six months and became a prostitute in the city?'

'I do a certain amount of business in Gloucester,' Connor-Crewe said. 'Not that kind.'

'Not a *career* prostitute, as such,' Bliss said. 'But she needed money and somewhere dry to sleep and eventually, like many other hard-up young folk in Gloucester in the 1970s and 1980s, she found this dead convenient place not far from the centre. Cheapest in the city, it was said.'

Merrily was aware of movement behind the shelves: either there were mice, or Cola French was listening.

'Specializing in accommodation for . . . shall we say, liberal-minded young things,' Bliss said. 'The Gloucester fun palace. Perfect refuge for a big girl who liked trampling on taboos.'

'Inspector, what *are* you—?'

'We don't know how *long* she was living there, but she seems to have fitted into the domestic arrangements all too well. Really took to it, you know? The atmosphere of tolerance.'

Merrily said, 'You could form meaningful friendships there, with one another and also with the proprietors. If you didn't like the idea of that, you probably left quite soon, or—'

'Or you stayed until someone dug you out,' Bliss said. 'Sorry, uncalled for. But if you don't know what we're talking about now, you must've been so stuck into the old books that you never read a single newspaper in the mid-1990s.'

Connor-Crewe's football face darkened. 'If you're telling me that Lynsey Davies spent some time at 25 Cromwell Street—'

'No,' Bliss said, 'I'm asking if you *knew* she'd been at 25 Cromwell Street.'

'The answer to that is no.'

'Of course,' Bliss said, 'the vast majority of people could've had absolutely no idea how far it went with Fred and Rose. But we do know that one or two of the residents, over the years, had a strong interest in various occult practices of a kind probably *not* demonstrated at most colleges of further education. So it seems not unlikely that it was there that Lynsey was first introduced to the concept of sexual magic.'

'*If* she was there.'

'Take it from me,' Bliss said. 'Or take it from this.' He stabbed the diary with a thumb.

'Inspector Bliss . . .' Connor-Crewe's smile was like elastic, overstretched. 'I wouldn't take *anything* from that account. My experience of magical diaries is that they contain a considerable amount of fantasy. Often less a record of what actually happened than a rather faulty memoir of what the diarist would *like* to have happened. And I *have* to say—'

'You'd have to be a strange kind of person, sir, to fantasize that you'd been to Cromwell Street and had a sexual relationship with the mass murderer Frederick West.'

'I have to say that I do not see what possible bearing any of this could have on the presumed murder of Melanie Pullman.'

'Did I mention Miss Pullman, sir?'

'No, but—'

'So stop trying to change the subject. You see, my information is that, for Lynsey Davies, the period at Cromwell Street was the most exciting time of her life. A lot of youngsters said something similar. Must've been a terrible comedown when she had to leave.'

'Then why did she?'

'Well, I'm only guessing here,' Bliss said, 'but I'd imagine that, at some stage, Lynsey saw the writing on the wall. Not Fred's writing – Rose's. Rose had lesbian tendencies and girls were often shared. Rose was a bully, and this was Rose's house. In Lynsey, you've gorra big girl with a forceful personality – not the kind to be used as a plaything. Fred and Rose . . . I think it's fair to say that, under different circumstances, it could just as easily have been Fred and Lynsey. Maybe there just wasn't room for *two* big, insatiable women.'

Piers Connor-Crewe listened without uttering a word, as if his interest was academic. Piers was useful, Sam Hall had said on the phone, because he had extensive marketing know-how, having been in publishing, and of course he knew a great deal about ancient and Roman history. In the background Merrily had heard Ingrid saying brusquely, 'Man fancies himself as Nero, if you ask me.'

'So there we are, sir,' Bliss said. 'For Lynsey, the end of a golden era. The most excitement she'd ever had. And now she's got to go back to the boring old Forest of Dean.'

'As I understood it,' Connor-Crewe said, 'she had a relationship with a man, and at least one child.'

'Which she seems to have rehomed, like with kittens – she was very good at that, apparently. Then she came to work in Ross – as a barmaid, I think – where she pursued her interest in the dark arts, acquiring some books from *this* little treasure house and usually paying, I'm told, in kind.'

Connor-Crewe's eyes flared. 'That's—'

'Irrelevant. The point is you had a relationship with her, founded on a mutual interest in the occult, whether commercial or private, and she spent time at your old rectory, full of bedrooms . . . which, in a strange kind of way, must've rekindled a few happy memories for Lynsey, perhaps sparked a few ideas.'

Connor-Crewe's hand came down hard on the desk. 'That is an utterly outrageous—'

'Piece of gossip in the village of Underhowle,' said Bliss. 'Mr Connor-Crewe and his house parties and all those young guests.'

'I think I ought to telephone my solicitor, don't you?'

'The ubiquitous Mr Nye, sir? Who is perhaps not *quite* as young as he looks, and probably likes a good party himself.'

'And is doubtless well acquainted with the law relating to slander.'

Bliss looked blank. 'What did I say?'

'I think you accused me of allowing Lynsey Davies to use my home to recreate whatever filth took place twenty years ago in Cromwell Street.'

'I think that's your dirty mind at work, sir, but if you say so . . . Anyway, Ms Davies soon became interested in another property.'

Bliss flicked over a couple of pages in the *magical diary*. In between the impenetrable esoteric formulae, the text was an uneven record of what Lynsey considered to be significant episodes in her 'spiritual development'. These entries, at least, were very clear – hand-printed and phrased in a schoolgirlish mixture of the colloquial, the portentous and the breathless prose of the romantic pulp novel.

We have been bound together by the stars and I knew we would meet again and so it has come to pass! Saw him in Ross yesterday, after ten years, and it turns out he's working locally, and he took me to see the Place, which he says he has already become attached to. I was immediately picking up a powerful energy there and feel certain it's on the sight of pagan Roman worship with blood sacrifice. We could do really incredible stuff there; the two of us, to reawaken the power. It is just mindblowing how things work out just when you need a buzz in your life.

'Who's she talking about here, Mr Crewe?'

'Once again, why would I know?'

'Because if she was in Underhowle I think you'd have known about it. And what she was doing. I take it you know which building she's referring to.'

'I can only guess the Baptist chapel.'

'Where I understand you yourself have discovered Roman remains. Was it you who told Lynsey it was the site of an ancient Roman temple?'

'I may have done. It's an interest of mine.'

'And was it an interest of hers?'

'She was interested in anywhere she thought might have been used for ancient and mysterious rituals. She was . . . romantic, in that way.'

Merrily thought about Jane, who would also have been fascinated. *Would* have, once. She said, 'Lynsey seems to have been very excited by the idea that the site was used for blood sacrifices. Did you tell her that?'

'I doubt it. I told you, my interest is largely academic. It may have been, say, a Mithraic temple, but nothing's been found there to suggest that. So why would I have told her something for which there was no archaeological evidence?'

'You might just have enjoyed getting her excited,' Bliss said mildly, and Connor-Crewe came out of his chair.

'I . . . have . . . taken . . . *enough* of this mélange of ill-informed speculation and cheap innuendo!' He gripped the desk, leaning across. 'So *you* . . . can either get to the point or get out.'

Frannie Bliss didn't move. 'Imagine how Lynsey feels . . . when she finds that this ancient site of pagan rites and blood sacrifice is currently the workplace of her favourite builder, sex maniac, amateur abortionist and . . . who knows what else she knew about him? Anyway, the man who'd given her the times of her life ten years earlier . . . and this time no wife around. Just the two of them.'

Connor-Crewe sat down, with his arms folded, gazing beyond Bliss at the walls of books. 'I know nothing about this.'

Bliss said, 'The indications in the diary are that the atmosphere of the place sparked something off between them. See, this was a woman fascinated with the high priest of sex magic, the late Aleister Crowley, self-styled Great Beast of the 1920s or whenever it was, who . . .' He faltered. ' . . . Who Merrily knows more about than me.'

Especially after last night's lengthy examination of the diary with Huw; Crowley was another guy you could learn too much about. Merrily sighed.

'He and West were both obsessed with deviant sex,' she said. 'The difference is that Crowley was an intellectual who had consciously *made* himself into what he was – embracing the dark. Whereas West, like Lynsey, was a natural. A man with absolutely no moral sense. A man who didn't even recognize what *was* taboo. As long as . . . he got off on it, it was all right.'

'Didn't philosophize about it, just did it,' Bliss added. 'And it was West, we have to assume, who enabled Lynsey to, to—'

'Free her dark side,' Merrily said.

'Exactly. Filthy mind, filthy hands, perverse and insatiable,' said Bliss. 'And here he was again, ten years on, working on his

own in this magical place, obviously with the keys to the premises. And now here's Lynsey in there with him. Don't tell me
you didn't know about that, Piers.'

'I swear . . .' Connor-Crewe was pale now, but it might simply
have been outrage. 'I swear to God I did not know that man
had even *been* in Underhowle. And I did *not* know about him
and Lynsey.'

'What sort of people came to your parties, Piers?'

'Certainly nobody like *him*.'

'So you don't know what went on in the chapel while it was
being converted into a bottling plant?'

'As I've already stated.'

'When the water venture failed, the chapel was sold to Roddy
Lodge. And then Lynsey started "going out" with Roddy, while
still giving her address as the home of Paul Connell, father of
two of her children. And while maintaining a friendship with
you, and even working here sometimes.'

'She was easily bored. Enjoyed variety.'

'Why do you think she became interested in Roddy Lodge?'

'Presumably because he was quite well off. How should I
know? She'd often latch on to men.'

'Oh, Piers, *please*. She was initially interested in Lodge because
he was the new owner of the chapel which was now more
important than ever to her – after whatever she and Fred did
there.'

'All right,' Connor-Crewe said, as if suddenly weary. 'She did
ask me if I knew Lodge and whether he had anything in mind
for the building. I understood he'd simply bought it as part of
the deal for the old garage.'

Bliss was silent, thinking.

Merrily said, 'Whose idea was it to buy the chapel from Lodge
and turn it into a museum?'

'We . . . we all thought it was a good idea, but I imagine it
was Cody who said why don't we buy it? Both he and Lodge
were enjoying their wealth, the ability to buy and sell. And as
Cody's solicitor was now representing the Development Committee, it made it—'

Bliss looked up. 'Mr Nye?'

'It simplified things,' Connor-Crewe said.

'Something here stinks like the inside of an Efflapure,' Bliss said. 'But we'll let that go for the present. What were Roddy and Lynsey doing in the chapel?'

'I wouldn't know that. I never went in there. I did ask Lodge's permission once to do some minor excavation of the area immediately around the chapel. This was after I'd made some small finds – coins and things – in nearby fields.'

'And was Roddy accommodating?'

'He even lent me his small digger to put in a couple of trenches.'

'Did you find anything?'

'I found the statue of Diana, as we like to call it. Eight inches long, headless, not terribly well preserved, but what it tells us about the site is significant.'

'Right.' Abruptly, Bliss stood up. 'Thank you very much, sir – for the moment.'

Merrily could almost feel the heat coming off Bliss as he stood on the edge of the raised area around the Market House in the heart of Ross, with traffic edging past down the hill and the rain starting. He was stabbing at his mobile as if it was a detonator.

'Frannie,' she said, 'why don't you just tell Fleming? If you're right, he'll see it as a selfless gesture from someone he thought wasn't capable of one. But if you're wrong, and he finds out . . .'

He stared at her like she'd suggested that he throw himself under a truck. He put the phone to his ear and waited for nearly half a minute before snapping it shut in irritation.

'Yeh, yeh, I'm dog meat. I'm already dog meat. Now, where's Gomer, Merrily? Where can I try? Does he have a mobile?'

Merrily sighed. 'He could be on his way to Underhowle. As the local gravedigger was refusing to dig one for Lodge, I thought I'd better make provision. He's meeting Huw over there about . . . now-ish.'

The tip of Bliss's tongue crept to a corner of his mouth.

'You little beauty, Merrily.'

'So what happened with Kirsty?'

'First things first,' Bliss said coldly.

44

Void

'Now we're *moving*,' Frannie Bliss said.

In fact, Gomer was the only one of them moving – walking slowly, head down, across the acre of land that ran parallel to the paddock behind Roddy Lodge's bungalow. Like he was dowsing, but without the divining rod: plant-hire instinct.

Merrily and Bliss were standing up against a rotting five-bar gate, snatching lunch from a bag of vegetable pasties she'd bought from a health-food shop in Ross. The rain had stopped, but the wind was rising. The sky was sepia and flecked with shrivelled leaves. It was 1.25 p.m. The stone chapel stood in front of them, like a beached hulk, against the light.

In front of the chapel stood Gomer's truck with the mini-JCB on the back. Piers Connor-Crewe had grudgingly given them permission to excavate here – no real choice, with Bliss in this mood – yet had elected not to join them.

'Which I find *very* odd,' Merrily said when Bliss mentioned it in passing.

'Smug public-school twat.' Bliss finished his pasty in a small, triumphant cloud of crumbs. 'Probably gone to alert Mr Nye.'

'Think about it,' Merrily said. 'If you were any kind of serious student of archaeology and the police were coming to dig up your prime site, if you couldn't stop it you'd at least want to watch, wouldn't you? So you could jump in the trench and check out anything that looked interesting in the way of archaeology, prevent anything being despoiled. Wouldn't you?'

Bliss watched Gomer bending down, patting the grass. 'So?'

'So why isn't he here? Did you hear him once asking you to be very careful with that digger?'

'Maybe he assumes he's exhausted the site.'

'Well, yeah, that's one possibility.' She looked over at the back fences of the houses in Goodrich Close, about two hundred yards away, the village sloping up behind them to the parish church, which was actually only a couple of fields away. 'The other is that he couldn't care less because there never *was* a site.'

'Not quite following you,' Bliss said.

'I think Merrily's implying an element of fabrication, lad.'

Huw Owen drank spring water from a small plastic bottle. He hadn't eaten. Merrily felt guilty about this, although Huw had insisted *she* should eat.

'The site of Ariconium was always said to be at Weston-under-Penyard, right?' She pointed down the valley. 'I mean, they haven't found all that much there, either, but that was where the evidence always pointed. Now, when I was talking to Sam Hall this morning, he said Piers was not popular in Weston. Which Piers would always laugh about – saying Weston was a pretty place that had never deserved Ariconium anyway. Under-howle, however . . .'

'He *faked* it?' Bliss stood away from the gate. 'How would that be possible? What about all the bits of pottery, the statue, the—?'

'Bits of Roman pottery and mosaic are not that hard to come by. Lots of them about, and not too expensive. Piers does anti-quarian books and he's surrounded by antique dealers. Not too much of a problem to pick up a few odds and ends, then either pretend to have found them or bury them for someone else to find. Not much of a problem convincing people, either, when everybody local *wants* to believe.'

'Had *me* going,' Huw admitted. 'I were quite ready to believe the chapel's on the site of a Roman temple, complete with spring. And of course it *might* be.'

'Exactly,' Merrily said. 'It might be. Even if they had an archaeological dig there that found nothing, that still wouldn't disprove it.'

'Let me get this right,' Bliss said. 'You're suggesting the whole Ariconium thing's a scam, to give Underhowle historic status? The Roman town never was underneath here?'

'I think Sam Hall suspects it. Ingrid Sollars, too, obviously, and she knows about local history. But if we're only talking a couple of miles, and if it isn't harming anyone, and it helps put Underhowle back on the tourist map . . .'

'All down to Connor-Crewe?'

'One of his academic jokes. A few finds, a lot of informed conjecture. And they'll have their visitor centre with audio-visuals and maps and computer-generated mock-ups put together by *real* experts at Cody's. All very state-of-the-art. Are they even breaking any laws?'

'Not if you ignore obtaining large sums of money, in the form of substantial grants, by deception,' Bliss said. 'Might have some difficulty proving it. But, when all this is over, we can try really, really hard.'

'I could be totally wrong.'

'The fact that it's even occurred to you – a little priest who tries to think well of us all – might suggest otherwise.' Bliss looked across at the village, scattered down the hill like the crumbs on his shirt. 'These obscure little places do attract them, don't they? Connor-Crewe a liar, Cody with form . . .'

Merrily blinked. 'Form?'

'It's not exactly in his brochures – and *I* didn't, of course, tell you this – but he did a little time. Detention centre, as a teenager. Street crime in London. Car theft, mainly, finally earning him nine months in a grown-up prison.'

'Bloody hell,' Merrily said.

'Which, of course, was where he learned about computers. Discovered a wondrous natural aptitude. Came out directly into software, making more out of it than crime ever paid. And then, when he got into the hardware too, it was probably expedient to move to somewhere he wasn't known. He'd got relatives in the Forest, and so . . . Yeh, Andy Mumford, it was, stumbled on that one. One day, if he gets *really* big, it'll be part of the Cody legend. But not yet.'

'Ah, well . . .' Huw's smile was sour. 'For every sinner who repents and becomes a millionaire . . .'

'The morality's skewed,' Merrily said, 'but it's a flawed world. Look at what Cody's done for Underhowle in terms of jobs and morale and education.'

Huw nodded at the hillside, where the mobile-phone transmitter poked out of its clearing. 'And health.'

'A *very* flawed world,' Merrily acknowledged sadly.

Huw turned his face into the rising wind and gazed down the valley, where the Roman road had led from Ariconium to Glevum, the city of light, the way marked now by electricity pylons. *And spirits*, Merrily thought uneasily. She could almost see the cracks opening in the façade of Underhowle, in the soil and the tarmac, like ruptured graves on Judgement Day.

Gomer came over. 'Right then, folks. Three places I can see there's been a bit o' digging. Nothing recent, mind.'

'How not recent?' Bliss asked.

'Not since summer. Can't say n'more'n that. So . . . I got two hours for you, boy.' He turned to Merrily. 'That all right with you, vicar? I been up the churchyard with Mr Owen yere. Lodge plot's out on the edge where it joins the field and the ground's soft. Reckon I can do the grave by hand – less noise, ennit?'

'If you're sure.'

'*He*'s sure,' Bliss confirmed. 'Right.' He dug into a pocket of his hiking jacket and presented Merrily with his mobile. 'If you wouldn't mind holding on to that for me. I've asked Mumford to try and get me some more background on Lynsey Davies, since she's now centre-stage, so to speak. So if he calls I'll take it. If it's any bastard from headquarters, you don't even know where I am.' He clapped Gomer on the back. 'Let's do it, son. We're looking for a body, female. Maybe more than one.'

'And what are *you* looking for, Huw?' Merrily screwed up the bag that had held the pasties and stuck it in her pocket. She wished all this was over: the digging, the exposure, the secret funeral.

'Looking for an end, lass.'

She realized she didn't want to know what he meant.

Frannie Bliss was helping Gomer bring down the mini-digger, a grown-up yellow Tonka Toy with caterpillar tracks. Here was Gomer starting to work again, resilient, his demons dealt with – not entirely satisfactorily, but no longer burning inside his head. But Frannie was like a failing footballer at the start of a winter game: jumpy, rubbing his hands. Dangerous.

Merrily said, 'What happens now?'

'All down to you.' Huw looked her in the eyes – an old wolfhound, trusting.

Deceptively trusting. She was fairly sure now that Huw must have had a hand in setting her up for the Lodge funeral. A quiet call to the Bishop, a favour called in. Huw, by virtue of what he did – a responsibility that few would shoulder – could quietly pull ropes that made bells ring in cathedrals. Huw had unfinished business, and he was looking for a way in, and she was it: the female Deliverance minister, the vulnerable one who relied on guidance.

'Family wants a small funeral,' Huw said. 'Quickie. No hymns, no eulogies. Everybody'd like that. You could give 'em their quickie and walk away. Let Underhowle get on with its bright, clean future full of new jobs and computer literacy.'

'I *could* do that. What *should* I do?'

'Modern world, lass,' he went on, as though he hadn't heard her. 'And not even your parish. It's Jerome's – good old turn-a-blind-eye-for-tomorrow-we-retire-to-the-seaside Jerome. You're just the hired help, the dishrag.'

'Yes. Thanks. Now, what do you think I should do?'

'I'd think about the full requiem.'

She stared at him. 'A *requiem eucharist* . . . for Roddy Lodge? Are you serious?' This was not the Roman Catholic Church, not even High Anglican. 'We don't *do* requiems in this area, except for the seriously devout, and . . .'

Huw regarded her solemnly. The yellow digger trundled slowly past, Gomer in the saddle, Bliss walking in front like he had Gomer on a rein.

' . . . The unquiet dead,' Merrily said. 'Ah, yes.'

'The *insomniacs*,' Huw agreed.

'Huw, this is an actual funeral. At night.'

'Exactly,' Huw said. 'Things need to be laid to rest. Anyroad, if these lads find a body, the whole place'll be alight by then.'

'I don't know.' In Deliverance, a requiem eucharist was

employed to unite a disturbed, earthbound spirit with God. 'Who are we talking about? Roddy . . . Lynsey? Or . . . ?'

'Or the whole village, if you like. And the evil that's come into it.'

'For most people,' Merrily said, 'nothing's come into this village but progress. Therefore, good.'

'And what do you think?'

'I don't know.' She gripped the top bar of the gate with both hands. It was greasy with lichen. 'You're like Sam and his death road. You're following a black trail all the way from Gloucester, and I don't know how valid that is. I don't know if it exists. You always told us to question everything – question, question, question. So now I'm questioning you. Like, how objective is this?'

In her coat pocket, a phone began to buzz. She pulled out two: her own and Frannie's.

Hers.

'Mrs Watkins?' Female, young-sounding. 'My name's Libby Porterhouse, from the *Mail on Sunday.* I know you're rather busy at the moment, but I wonder if we could have a chat.'

Not what she needed, but if there was one thing you learned about dealing with the press it was never to say *no comment.* Express interest, surprise, ask some questions of your own, but never let them think you had any reason to be unhelpful.

'Well, I'll tell you what I can,' Merrily said, 'but I'm not sure I'm the best person. I'm just the hired help on this one.'

'Ah, we may be talking at cross purposes,' Libby Porterhouse said. 'I know you're involved with this serial killer funeral row in the Wye Valley, but this is something entirely different. I'm with Features, and I'm doing quite an extensive piece on Jenny Driscoll.'

'What about her?'

'I understand she's a friend of yours.'

'We live in the same village.'

'And that she's given you a large sum of money. I'd like to ask you about that and a few other things, get your side of the story.'

'Story?'

'How long have you known Jenny Driscoll?'

Merrily said, 'It's just that I'm standing in a muddy field, with some people . . .'

'Well, if you tell me when it's best to call you back. I really don't want to keep hassling you, and I truly think, when you know about this, that it's something you'll want to comment on. For your own sake.'

Oh *God*. 'Can we leave it till tomorrow? If you're not carrying the piece until Sunday . . .'

'What about tonight?'

'OK, I'll see what I can do,' Merrily said.

Remembering the note from Jane but not Jenny Box's number, Merrily rang Directory Inquiries and asked for Box, Ledwardine. It turned out, as expected, to be ex-directory. Damn. Nothing else she could do from here.

'Problem?' Huw said.

'Parochial.' She rang Uncle Ted's number. What the hell kind of story had the *Mail* got? She remembered James Bull-Davies: *Woman's got a bit of a crush on you, after all. Pretty common knowledge.*

No answer at Ted's. She shut down the phone and stood staring across the scrubby field to where Gomer was shovelling out his first shallow trench, Bliss walking alongside now, peering down. The chapel, behind them, was black and formless.

'Ring the brother, eh?' Huw said close to her ear. 'Tell him you think a requiem would be best for all concerned and, as nobody's going to know, time's no longer of the essence.'

'Huw,' she said, 'did you set me up for this funeral?'

'Banks genuinely didn't want to do it.'

'I realize that.'

'Merrily,' Huw said, 'you've not been at it long but, of all of them, you're the one I trust most. You don't make assumptions and you never just go through the motions. And you're never too sure of yourself, never afraid to say when you don't understand.'

'I don't understand,' Merrily said.

Huw looked away. 'I've said enough. Don't want to influence you.'

'I'm already influenced. I think you and Frannie are letting personal issues block your objectivity. Personal grief, in your case.'

'Sometimes you have to follow your heart.'

'You never said that before. That's the opposite to what you told us on the course.' She stood in front of him, her back to the digger. 'You *never* said that before!'

'Happen I never knew it.'

'Christ, Huw . . .' Her shoes were sinking into the mud. 'You *cannot exorcize him*! Even if you think he's here. Even if you think he's in that chapel, you cannot do it. Because, no matter what kind of pond life he was, he was *of this earth*.'

'What if there were summat else?'

'There was *nothing* else.' She thought of the missing builders' tools, the callused hands around Zoe Franklin's neck, the walking definition of the term *earthbound*, the lamp of the wicked and the hunger of the dead. 'It was soiled lust of the worst kind – a depraved appetite that could only be sated, in the end, by causing extreme, mortal fear.'

'And what happens when the body's gone and only the appetite remains in a black void? What *is* that? And what happens when there are human beings out here, amongst us, who actually *aspire* to the black void? People who are, by whatever means, prepared – eager – to call it into themselves?'

Merrily closed her eyes. She felt the cold mass of the old Baptist chapel very close behind her, almost as if she was carrying it on her back. She could hear the digger coming towards her, and then the shuffling, metallic scraping of the blade in the earth.

'At least do the requiem,' Huw said.

She nodded and brought out her phone.

45

Execution

There was a low rumbling: the wind on ill-fitting leaded windows.

'*In the name of the Father and of the Son and of the Holy Spirit. Amen.*'

No need to raise the voice above normal, not for a congregation of nine, including the two undertakers and the corpse.

Under lights that were dusty orbs, yellow going on brown, Merrily walked over to Roddy Lodge's coffin.

'*I'm convinced that neither death, nor life, nor angels, nor rules, nor things present, nor things to come, nor powers, nor height, nor depth, nor anything else in all creation will be able to separate us from the love of God in Jesus Christ our Lord.*'

It had been well after dusk when a white van had been driven to the church door. George Lomas, cheerfully overweight, with rimless glasses, and his son, Stephen, stocky and hedgehog-haired, had slipped Roddy inside like contraband.

Only ninety minutes later than planned.

'*No disrespect, but it seemed like the best way,*' Mr Lomas had whispered to Merrily, shaking hands in the porch. '*I panicked a bit after that demo last night. Didn't want no scratches on the hearse, so I phoned the Lodges, suggested we put the whole thing back until everybody's home from work, watching telly. Didn't nobody tell you?*'

'I'm afraid not,' Merrily had said coldly to Mr Lomas, whose bill might reasonably be expected to reflect the unorthodox hours.

Lol's concert! She could have wept.

From the glass wall beside the stairs you could see most of the city glowing just below you, and you wanted to walk out into it, like some glistening sea.

'Maybe I'll go out for some air,' Lol said.

Prof leaped up and put his back against the door of the Green Room. 'You'll stay where you are, you paranoid bastard!'

'It's OK,' Lol said. 'Loads of time.' He wasn't due to go on until halfway through the gig. *And then only if it feels right,* Moira had said.

As if it ever could.

The Courtyard, all glass and Lego, was set at right angles to the road, in the city's recreational quarter, opposite Hereford United's Edgar Street ground. Lol had driven himself there in the Astra, Prof driving tight behind him the whole way to make sure he didn't take a detour via Birmingham, Manchester, Cardiff . . .

When he'd driven into the car park, the lights in the glass front were scary, making it seem very public, like a bus station. Within a couple of hours he was supposed to be standing alone on a stage inside that glass palace with the lights burning down on him, only a guitar to protect him and a crowd four times the size of the one which had watched Roddy Lodge die. Screaming encouragement: *Why'n't you jump?*

Moira had the dressing room immediately behind the stage and Lol was changing here in the Green Room, with a wash-basin and a kettle, the Washburn guitar, the Boswell guitar and Prof Levin hopping about like a surrogate nervous system.

'Why you got to keep messing with that mobile? Just switch it off. If he calls now, you'll have to say you'll get back to him in the morning.'

Lol had left two messages for Mephisto Jones. Maybe Mephisto was sick, struck down with an electric migraine. Then, half an hour ago, Merrily had rung, upset, close to tears. She wasn't going to make it in time. Probably wasn't going to make it at all. He was almost relieved, and he told her that, and she said, '*If you run away, now . . . don't you dare run away . . .*'

He'd gone down to the booking office to leave a message there: when a Jane Watkins arrived to pick up her ticket, tell her to wait for Lol Robinson afterwards. Then he'd changed into black jeans and a fresh alien sweatshirt with no holes in it, remembering how King Charles I had worn an extra shirt for his execution so that at least he wouldn't be trembling with the cold. Sitting on a stool in the Green Room, Lol had a terrible feeling now: ominous.

'What's wrong?'

Moira had drifted in, the beautiful folk-rock goddess in her long dress of midnight blue, low-cut. A silver pendant was trickling like water between her breasts, as though it was part of the same stream that began in her long dark hair.

'Talk him through this, Moira,' Prof said. 'I have to go check things in the booth.'

Lol smiled uncertainly at Moira. 'So you'll do half a dozen songs ending with "Tower", and then I kind of creep on and we do "Baker's Lament".'

'Then you play for as long as you feel happy about, and I'll come back as and when. Piece of cake, Laurence.'

'Piece of cake,' he said and felt that flicker of separation, putting him minutely out of synch, and for a moment he was watching himself looking at the beautiful woman in midnight blue and silver, knowing now for certain that it wasn't going to happen for him, that this was her concert and hers alone and nothing else was going to happen.

'Oh, it *will* happen,' Moira said, and he didn't even wonder how she'd plucked that thought from his mind, because he might actually have said it while he was out of synch. Anything could have happened; his head was full of storm clouds.

A possibly important thought came to him, then wafted past like a pale moth, and he put his head in his hands for a moment to try and catch it. But it had gone, and he heard Moira saying, 'Who the hell are you?'

Cola French was standing in the doorway, the golden stars in her hair and a small black hat with a feather.

'How'd you get in?' Moira growled.

'Friends,' Cola said. 'And lies. I tell a lot of lies.' She looked past Moira at Lol. 'I lied before, Lol – I lied when I said I wasn't involved.'

Lol was on his feet. Then his phone buzzed.

'Lynsey and Piers and Roddy and the whole bit,' Cola said. 'But when I heard the copper with Piers, and your . . . lady, this morning at the shop, I'm thinking, I can't sit on this shit any more.'

'Aye, well, you can sit on it a wee bit longer, hen,' Moira said. And as Lol watched her shepherding Cola French into the passage, he heard in the phone, 'It's Jones here. That Lol Robinson?'

Another voice, one of the Courtyard staff, said, 'Ten minutes, Moira.'

'*We meet in the name of Jesus Christ, who died and was raised to the glory of God the Father. Grace and mercy be with you.*'

There was a muffled gonging from one of the cooling radiators. Under those opaque glass globes, it looked as cold inside here as it was starting to feel.

No warmth for those who would mourn a murderer.

It was a boxy place, the Church of St Peter, Underhowle, so regular and heavy with dark wood that it might have been a Victorian magistrates' court. A Jerome Banks kind of church. Merrily, wearing her monastic white alb, was not comfortable here.

'*We . . . we've come here to remember before God our brother Roddy, to commend him to God, our merciful redeemer and our . . . judge. To commit his body to be buried. And to comfort one another.*'

There were two rows of pews – to her right the Lodges, on the left Ingrid Sollars and Sam Hall. Ingrid wore a brown shawl over her ravaged wax jacket. Sam's silver ponytail was tied with a thin, black ribbon.

The light-pine coffin rested on a bier like a hostess trolley. Lomas and son sat two rows down, behind the Lodges, inflating the congregation by twenty-five per cent.

'*Almighty God, you judge us with infinite mercy and justice . . . and love everything you have made. In your mercy, turn the darkness of death into the dawn of new life . . .*'

Alone at the bottom of the nave, hunched like a night-watchman, was Huw. He'd phoned Banks himself, to arrange for the sacrament. Merrily didn't trust him. The word AGENDA hung in the air above him, in mystic neon.

' . . . *And the sorrow of parting into the joy of heaven; through our saviour, Jesus Christ.*'

Meanwhile, Gomer was out there, working by hurricane lamp at the bottom of the churchyard. Tony Lodge had shown them the spot, to the left of his parents' grave, about ten feet from the boundary hedge, a line of laurels screening it from the rest of the churchyard. Seeing the spot had made Merrily wonder why anyone had thought it worth objecting; this would be a grave you'd need a map to find.

It was fortunate, in a way, that the funeral had been delayed because Gomer had also made a late start.

This was due to his stoical digging around the Baptist chapel uncovering nothing but stones.

At 4.30, Frannie Bliss, pale and sweating, had still been refusing to give up, raging against the dying of the light, '*Try here . . . Try back there. It's gorra be here, or it all falls down.*' And then, in agony, '*Don't let me down, Gomer!*' Until Gomer, exasperated, had snatched out his ciggy: '*I'm tellin' you, boy, you blew it. There en't nothin' buried yere but clay.*'

At 4.55, Fleming's secretary had rung, wondering where Bliss was. Merrily saying, '*Isn't he there already? I hope he's not had an accident,*' like she was Mrs Bliss, poor woman. By then Frannie – so convinced earlier that he'd be making the triumphant call that would bring Fleming and his team down here, with a small army of SOCOs and the Home office pathologist – had been close to tears. He'd said he might come up the church later; Merrily hoped he wouldn't. Rage and despair were not helpful at a funeral.

The reflection of the cold globe above it wobbled now in the steel plate on the coffin. Merrily imagined Roddy Lodge lying there in the merciful darkness, sealed away from a hostile world of electric lights, televisions, mobile phones, radiation.

The schedule for *Common Worship* suggested this was the most suitable time for the first hymn. Hymns were useful; they gave you a break, time to gather your thoughts for the next stage, which was your 'tribute' to the deceased.

For which she wasn't ready. There were some things still to work out. It was important to at least *approach* the truth.

But there would be no hymns tonight. There was no organist. She imagined seven strained voices raised in stilted intimacy under the dismal hanging lamps.

No hymns.

She was grateful, at first, when the side door opened and Gomer slipped in. He didn't come any further, just stood by the entrance, still carrying his hurricane lamp, and when she raised a questioning eyebrow at him, wild, white light flared in his glasses: *warning, warning, warning*.

'Would you . . . excuse me . . . one moment.' Merrily moved down past the coffin and followed Gomer into the porch, closing the doors against the wind. Gomer coughed.

'This yere grave, vicar. Problem with him. En't entirely vacant.'

'Oh.' This sometimes happened. A graveyard was crowded underground; there was slippage. It *would* happen tonight. 'How far down is the other coffin?'

Gomer said. 'That's the point, ennit? This one don't have no coffin.'

'Put it out of your head, all right?' Moira picked up the Boswell guitar by its neck and handed it to Lol. 'I told the girl you'd talk to her afterwards. She'll find you. Now let's get this stuff on stage.'

Mephisto Jones had said he'd been out all day helping a friend to do some fencing on his farm. Then he'd called in for a beer on his way home. He said he was feeling good at the moment; on nights like this, feeling stronger, he wondered if it wasn't time to come back to England, give it another try. Yeah, he remembered Prof, of course he remembered Prof.

Lol had made himself sit down and ask some questions about the symptoms of electrical hypersensitivity, telling Mephisto about Roddy Lodge's death on the pylon. At one point, Prof had looked in, his bald head shining with sweat, shaking both fists.

'*He'd be well out of it*,' Mephisto had said. '*Wouldn't know who he was any more.*'

'*He said he was Satan*,' Lol had recalled.

'*Makes sense*,' Mephisto had said. '*I used to think I was the walking dead, but you know what they said about Satan . . .*'

Now Lol and Moira carried the guitars down the passage, under muted lights, and out onto the stage, where black curtains concealed the auditorium. Sounds of mass movement out there. This wasn't a big theatre, but it still felt like standing on a cliff-top overhanging a vast city.

They put the guitars on stands: the curved-backed Boswell, the Washburn and Moira's thin-backed Martin. There were voice microphones and guitar mikes at waist level.

'Check the tuning,' Moira instructed, and Lol went through the motions while she fingered a couple of chords on the Martin, provoking a whoop from beyond the curtain. She put the guitar down, placed both hands on his shoulders, gripping hard, and hissed, 'She's no gonnae go away. She'll find you. But you have to do this first, OK?'

A young guy in a black sweater appeared. 'Whenever you're ready.'

'Thanks.' Moira nodded. Rustling, chatter, laughter from behind the curtains. An audience. Hundreds of people anticipating an experience. 'Will your wee priest have made it?'

He shook his head. 'She's been delayed.'

I lied when I said I wasn't involved . . . Lynsey and Piers and Roddy and the whole bit. What were the implications here? What could he do about it tonight? Moira would play for maybe forty-five minutes, then he'd shamble on, do his forgettable best, shuffle off. An hour lost, maybe more.

On the other hand, if he were to shuffle off now . . . ? It wasn't as if he'd be letting Moira down – probably the reverse; appearing with sub-standard support didn't help anyone's reputation. And he certainly wouldn't be letting the audience down. But how easy would it be to find Cola French and then get out of the theatre?

They came to the black curtains at the back of the stage. The main curtains had opened now, and he could see the audience in the steep theatre, could see that it was almost full, that all the boxes set into the walls on either side seemed to have been taken.

The house lights went down. The chat sank as sweetly as the ambient noise being lowered in the mix of a live recording. The mike stands and the guitars stood in pools of golden light, and you could almost hear the steel strings vibrating in the air.

Silence like a gasp. Four hundred people out there. Anticipation.

Then Moira said, 'OK, off you go.'

He spun in shock, and she stepped behind him to cut off his retreat, and the curtains either side of her were execution black.

'I thought, with you needing to get away, you could go on first after all,' Moira said.

Lol's lungs made like a vacuum pump.

Moira pushed him hard. 'Just get the fuck out there, eh, Robinson?'

46

Mephisto's Blues

Gomer had left an earthen step inside the grave, and he went down onto it, but he held the hurricane lamp away so that Merrily couldn't see.

'En't terrible attractive, vicar,' Gomer admitted.

'Doesn't matter.' She stood on the slippery rim of the grave and leaned over, the wind pulling at the hood of her alb and rattling the laurel bushes. The church crouched above them with its stubby bell-tower, and the lights from inside were dull and unhelpful.

The smell was mainly of freshly turned earth and clay, but it was still the smell of mortality. Her foot dislodged a cob of soil, and she stumbled.

'Careful, vicar.'

'I'm OK. Go on . . . let's have a look.'

She drew a breath. Gomer flattened himself against the side of the grave and lifted the lamp so that it lit up the interior of the grave like an intimate cellar.

'Deep,' Gomer said. 'Cold earth – preserves 'em better, see.'

Merrily looked down into an absence of eyes. Decay was a corrosive face pack. In its nest of clay-caked hair, the face was like a child's crude cardboard mask, the emptiness of it all emphasized by the mouth, the way the jaw had fallen open on one side into a last crooked plea.

And all of it made heartbreaking by the rags of what looked like a red sweatshirt and an uncovered hand with its dull glimmer of rings. She had to be fully six feet down. Some gravediggers today didn't go that deep. She could have ended up with a coffin on top and never have been found.

Merrily stepped back, making the sign of the cross.

'There was this.' Gomer climbed out. He held up the lamp

and opened out his other hand. 'Cleaned him up a bit, vicar, so's you can see.'

She saw an angel.

An angel on a chain.

'If he was still round the neck, see, I'd've left him on, but he was lying on top, he was. Loose. Like somebody'd put him in after the body.'

The angel was no more than an inch and a half long, with wings spread and hands crossed over its lower abdomen, which protruded as though it was pregnant. In fact, there was something curved there, like a small locket or a cameo.

'Any idea what he is, vicar?'

She felt a sadness as sharp as pain. 'Think I just might.'

'Valuable?'

'It was to someone,' Merrily said.

Lol felt like he was dying, his recent past laid out before him in a mosaic of faces.

He stood there, frozen, gazing into purgatory, a warm-coloured vault with boxes set into the sides like the balconies of apartment blocks or the doors in an advent calendar.

The house lights had come up again, because somebody thought he wasn't ready – some technical problem, maybe – and now he could see the individual faces in the mosaic.

He saw, in one of the boxes, Al and Sally Boswell – Al in his Romany waistcoat and his diklo, Sally in that long white dress with the embroidery around the bosom, the dress that was so much a part of her personal history. The two of them sitting in their box, gypsy aristocracy, as if this was a ceremonial occasion for them. Al, who'd given Lol the Boswell guitar, had come to Hereford to see it abused.

The Boswell guitar was behind Lol, on its stand. He had the Washburn hanging from his shoulder; it felt unresponsive, like a shovel.

He saw Alison Kinnersley, this woman who'd originally gone with him to Ledwardine and then left him for the squire, James Bull-Davies, and his farm and his horses. '*Bad for you*,' Lucy Devenish had told him sternly. '*Wrong type of woman entirely.*'

James was there, too, in a tie. '*A male-menopausal stooge*,' said Lucy Devenish, '*who's known only two kinds of women – garrison-town whores and county-set heifers.*'

Lol's hands felt numb as he stared into the huge, cavernous silence and all the people stared back at him with a tremulous fascination – that apprehension-turning-to-anticipation which had been so palpably apparent when Roddy Lodge was high in the pylon, reaching out to the insulator, the killing candle.

Lol saw Jane, close to the front. Jane Watkins who one day, before he knew her mother, had come into the cluttered folklore emporium, Ledwardine Lore, when he was minding the shop for Lucy.

What the hell was his first song supposed to be? *Oh God*. The amplified silence boomed in his head. How long had he been standing here like this? How long before they started the slow handclap? How long before someone pulled the curtain? What was he supposed to *do*?

Directly opposite him was the glass-fronted control booth where Prof Levin sat. Prof was standing up, very still, his hands theatrically over his eyes, like this was some Greek tragedy.

Then Lol saw Eirion, on the far left, probably the only person in that audience not staring back at him, because he was looking at Jane, who *was* looking at Lol, hands clasped, face taut with anxiety. '*Suddenly all she sees is darkness, doom, nothing . . . nothing amazing out there any more.*'

There was an unexpected prickling in the corners of Lol's eyes. He hadn't mentioned the gig to the Boswells, wouldn't have dared – it must have been Prof. But who had told Alison and Bull-Davies? And surely that was . . . who could possibly have told *Sophie Hill* . . . who was sitting with a man who must be her husband, very near the back, presumably in case the sound level proved insufferable.

'Hey, man, where you been?' A lone male voice curling out of the third row.

Nervous laughter from somewhere. The sweat in Lol's hands felt like cold honey.

He whispered into the mike, 'Away.'

The whisper was as crisp as an iceberg lettuce, and huge; how sound systems had improved.

'When you reckon you'll be back, then?' the guy in the third row said.

'Well, I don't really know,' Lol said. 'It depends on . . .'

. . . remembering what the first song is.

And then suddenly he did, his fingers finding the riff. Into the mike, he said,

> *'Tuesday on Victoria ward*
> *We always hated Tuesdays.'*

And he must have sung it, kind of, because the lights went down and some applause bubbled up.

The last face Lol saw before the whole audience went into deep shadow was Jane's. She was slumping in her seat with her head thrown back, and he could almost hear the whoosh of breath coming out of her, as he did the number.

Did the number!

Leaning on the guitar, now, as he went into the chorus.

> *'Someone has to pay*
> *Now Dr Gascoigne's on his way*
> *And it's another . . .*
> *HEAVY MEDICATION DAY.'*

Wondering, for the first time, whether it might have been wiser to change Dr Gascoigne's name.

Nah. Stuff you, Dr Gascoigne, you cold-eyed sadist.

Lol discovered he was smiling. The people out there, the *unknown* faces, must have thought it was part of his act, faking disorientation. Only a real professional could do that and get away with it. Lol felt he was floating, and when the song was over, someone at the back started shouting, ' "Sunny Days"!' and there were ragged handclaps in support.

Well, he wasn't going to do that trite crap, not in a million years.

Definitely not.

When he reached the chorus, he was staggered at the number of people singing along.

'And it's always on the sunny days you feel you can't go on
On rainy days it rains on everyone
But I'm running for the subway and I'm hiding under trees
On fine days like . . .'

'Yes.' Sam Hall held the angel under the brass-shaded pulpit light. 'It's what's known as a bio-electric shield pendant.'

'That's what I thought,' Merrily said. 'Jane – my kid – was looking for one. I just couldn't remember what it was called.'

The two of them were up in the pulpit, voices lowered. The service had been suspended. What else could she do? There was no way this coffin was going in that grave. A grave that, before the night was out, would be surrounded by what Bliss called the Durex suits.

'In here –' Sam put a finger on the cameo part that had made the angel look pregnant '– we have a bunch of crystals – quartz, maybe some malachite – that are supposed to interact with the body's own energy field to deflect electromagnetic radiation. Often worn by people who work with computers.'

'And . . . have you seen one before? In Underhowle?'

'Yep.'

'So, when you said Melanie Pullman was getting nothing but Valium from Dr Ruck, and you suggested she should consult an alternative practitioner in Hereford about her EH, was this . . . ?'

'This was one of the items they got for Mel. Told her to wear it day and night. For a short while, she was a familiar figure in the village, with the angel around her neck. In fact, you can ask Bliss about this, but I think, when she went missing, the description the police put out suggested that she might well be wearing it.' Sam gave the angel back to Merrily. 'Where did this come from, Reverend?'

'Excuse me, Mrs Watkins.' Down in the nave, Mr Lomas was tentatively on his feet. 'I don't like to interrupt, look . . .'

Merrily flashed a warning glance at Sam, and went down to talk to the undertaker. Taking Mr Lomas over to the door where Gomer was waiting, telling him there'd been an unforeseen problem with the grave, that it wasn't empty. Mr Lomas nodded, not entirely surprised; he'd been here before.

'What do you want to do, then, Mrs Watkins? I don't suppose it's a problem easily dealt with until tomorrow. Which might cause another problem here.' Mr Lomas nodded at the coffin. 'You want us to take him back? Or you could lock him in here for the night, and we'll be back tomorrow.'

Tony Lodge came over. He'd overheard. 'Can't be nobody else in that plot, Reverend, it was a field twenty years ago. Our field. That's how we got the family plot extended – we gave the field to the Church.'

'Sloping graveyard, ennit?' Gomer said knowledgeably. He'd replaced half the soil over the remains, for concealment. 'Slippage, see. Likely there was coffins under that field when you was still ploughing him.'

'God, God, *God*.' Cherry Lodge was out of her pew. 'Is this bloody nightmare *never* going to end?'

'Don't you worry, Mrs Lodge,' George Lomas said. 'We'll get this sorted in the morning, *no* problem. We'll sort out another plot, but you can't do that by torchlight.' He looked at Merrily. 'Leave him here, then, is it?'

Merrily looked at Tony Lodge, who looked non-committal. 'I suppose so. Yeah . . . OK. Thank you, Mr Lomas.'

And so the Lomases left. And then there were seven, with Gomer. Seven and a corpse. Merrily looked at the four mourners, all of them on their feet, faces waxy under the sour-cream lights. 'I don't really know what to do now.'

She was aware of Huw Owen moving quietly up the aisle. Sam Hall said, 'You can tell us about the body. That'd be a start.'

She nodded. 'Well . . . it's a woman, as you've gathered. And it isn't in a coffin.'

'Oh God almighty,' Cherry Lodge said.

'Roddy . . .' Merrily hesitated. 'Roddy dug graves for the church sometimes, didn't he?'

'They always had a regular gravedigger,' Tony Lodge said, 'but when the ground was difficult or they hit rocks, they'd call the boy in with his digger.'

Ingrid Sollars came over to inspect the bio-electric angel. She took it out of Merrily's hands, held it tenderly in her own. 'It *is* Melanie, then?'

Merrily nodded. 'Looks like it, I'm afraid. Who are her nearest relatives?'

'Her parents moved six months ago, into Ross. There's an aunt over at Ryford. Was this still around her neck?'

'It was lying on her chest. Whoever buried her evidently put it there. You can see the chain's broken.' *Did it snap when she was being strangled?*

'Well, that's the end of it, far as I'm concerned.' Tony Lodge looked at the coffin with contempt, then down at his feet. 'Let him be cremated. Empty his bloody ashes in the gutter.'

Huw Owen said quietly, 'You can do what you like after the requiem. But finish it now, before you leave him in here for the night. Before the place is swarming wi' coppers.' He looked at Merrily. 'Take it from me, lass, you mustn't do half a job on this.'

Her heart sank. He was right. She turned to Gomer. 'Do me one last favour? Frannie Bliss is probably down in one of the pubs. If you could give us, say, twenty minutes and then go and find him, put him in the picture, and . . .'

Make his night.

Gomer nodded, opened one of the double doors and stopped. There was a group of people packed into the porch. Seven or eight of them.

Merrily closed her eyes. Maybe they would go away.

'This is so utterly contemptible,' Fergus Young said. 'Who would have thought the Church would lie and cheat and *conspire*?'

Lol didn't know if it was any good, but he'd done it. As his eyes adjusted, he could again see Jane in the front row, and he was convinced at one point that she was crying – during the song he'd written about her mother when the longing was becoming acute.

*'Did you suffocate your feelings
As you redefined your goals
And vowed to undertake the cure of souls?'*

It was somewhere between this song and the next that he caught the mothlike thought that had glided past him in the Green Room, and he held it fluttering in his mind along with something Mephisto Jones had said: *'What happened, I was getting blackouts more frequently, and they're not ordinary blackouts – you come round and you're out of synch, don't know where you are or what you've done.'*

It was like a song already: 'Mephisto's Blues'. The idea rocked him so hard that he muffed the tidy bit of Elizabethan fingerstyle at the end of 'Cure'. A signal that it was time to go.

'Thank you,' Lol said, bemused. 'I mean . . . you know . . . thanks for having me.' He nodded to the audience, turned and left.

They were stamping furiously by the time he reached the wing of the stage. Stamping for Moira, probably.

Moira was hugging him. '*Back.*'

'What?'

'One more.'

'I've got to *go*, Moira. I'm so grateful to you for this, but—'

'Yeah, yeah, now get back out there. This is how it's done – don't you remember anything? And you forgot "Kivernoll".'

He shook his head. His whole life had changed, but tonight that wasn't very important. He had to find Cola French.

'It's organized,' Moira said. 'One more, then you can go.'

Something else hit him. 'I need to collect Jane.' Dismay. 'She's got no way of getting home.'

'*I*'ll see to Jane, God help me.'

Moira turned him round and pushed him hard in the small of the back '*Go!*'

When Lol went back, it was like he'd won the war. He picked up the Boswell, of which he was unworthy. 'Right,' he told them. 'Local-knowledge time.' The Boswell eased her curvy back into his stomach. He did the unsurprising A-minor fingerstyle intro. Exorcizing Alison Kinnersley.

'Under mountains of winter
Where the river of gold defines the valley
Something delicate splintered there . . .'

He glanced over to where Alison sat with James Bull-Davies, but couldn't make either of them out. This was a song that had come out of the Alison period, towards the end, when James was making his move. Lol and Alison had driven up to the Black Mountains on the Welsh border and there'd been an outburst and crying and, somehow, a reconciliation as they were motoring back down into the Golden Valley, and Lol had seen a name on a sign in a nowhere kind of place, with flat fields and a roadside barn-conversion in progress, and the place was called Kivernoll.

Approaching the chorus, he heard a rustling behind him, and Moira was there, a graceful ghost in midnight blue, and the response to this from the audience was like a wall of heat.

'In Kerry's Gate the tears abated,
Cockyard found her smiling,
From Abbey Dore to Allensmore
By Kiverno—'

And then Moira's voice was lifting the line from under him: '*—oh . . . oll.*' Dropping away, leaving Lol to sing, unaccompanied,

'We were on a roll . . .'

He knew that she was introducing magic to an undistinguished little song and that this was approaching the best he would ever achieve, and when it was over, he just shouted into the mike, 'Moira Cairns!' and ducked out.

It *was* over this time, and Moira was mouthing *Good luck* and Lol was out of there, leaving the guitars on stage. Down the stairs and into the huge glassed area, all lit up. A bar to one side, a bunch of people in there. He needed to get into the auditorium, find—

'Cannot *wait* for the album.' Cola French had come up behind him. 'Give me a lift home?'

She'd evidently been waiting for him; Moira had organized her. She followed him out into the blustery night to where the battered Astra was parked, the way he always left it, close to an entrance, vaguely pointing outwards.

'*This* . . . is yours?'

'It's quite safe.'

'Jesus.'

Lol was fitting his car key into the door when a man said, 'Lol Robinson?' The night blared white, three times. He was blinded. He stumbled against the car. 'Sorry about that, mate,' the man said. 'Thanks a lot. All the best.'

Cola said, 'Does this mean we're an item?'

Lol stared after the photographer, fifty yards away by now, walking fast. He thought he could rule out the *Hereford Times*.

It couldn't even be mistaken identity; the guy had known his name.

They got into the Astra; he drove to the roundabout and then over Greyfriars Bridge, on to the Ross road.

Cola said, 'I'm not even called Cola French, it's just the name I write under. But if your name was Tracey Gilbert, how would *you* play it?'

'You said you'd lied when you said you weren't involved.' Lol drove south from the city. Not too many suburbs this side; you were soon out of the street lights. 'What did you mean?'

'She's pretty,' Cola said, stepping over the question. 'She's not what I imagined.'

'No. What did you mean? Not involved in what?'

'All right. That copper, the Liverpool guy, he asked Piers what kind of people went to his parties. Like, what kind of people would do sex magic? Like he thought it was all black robes and manacles and blood sacrifice. Well, yeah, some of that. Though you don't realize when you start. You think it's just games. Risky games, but still games.'

'And you were involved in that?'

'It was like, how can you be a writer if you haven't lived? At first. And then you think, do I really want to be that kind of writer? And that's when you know it's bad. I don't mean bad, I mean evil. There's a difference, isn't there? I mean I've been *bad* lots of times, but I don't think I've ever been evil. Because that's a thing in itself, isn't it? A commitment. No going back.'

'So when did you get out?'

'When I knew where it was coming from, of course. I mean . . . shit.'

'Cromwell Street.'

'I read about it. I went and got the books.'

'From Piers?'

'You're joking.' She was hunched up in the seat as though she was very cold. 'See, he did a lot of stuff nobody could explain. He'd travelled a bit, been to sea, mixed with all kinds of weirdos. Picked up stuff he maybe didn't understand.'

'West?' Lol put the heater on; sometimes it worked.

'Yeah. He had all these weird ideas that were maybe just an excuse for kinky sex. There was all this stuff where he was trying to like mix his sperm with the sperm of these other guys who were giving it to Rose. I won't go into details, but it was like he was planning to create some kind of super-race situation. Genetic experiments. Well, you don't have to be a bloody biologist to know what kind of bollocks that is. I mean, it's a joke, right? In the scientific sense. Where did he *get* it from? Where did he get those ideas?'

Lol said, 'You mean it only makes sense at all from an occult viewpoint.'

'Something like that.'

'And Lynsey?'

'Yeah,' Cola said, 'I think you could say something made a sick kind of sense to Lynsey.'

47

Requiem

Merrily was sure she heard this: 'You were warned.'

From one of the men in the porch. Just like that. *You were warned*. Some urban lout with a degree in computer science introducing pseudo-gangland into rural village life. She didn't recognize his face, couldn't even see it properly, but she thought she recognized the voice from the phone, muffled under a handkerchief.

'If one of you was the threatening caller,' she said tiredly, 'I took your advice. You said if we held the funeral on Friday I'd regret it. This is Wednesday.'

'At night?' Piers Connor-Crewe said. 'You're actually holding a clandestine funeral . . . at night?'

'Hold on – *threats*?' Fergus Young's sharpened voice raised a silence. He turned to his companions. 'What does she mean?' He turned to Merrily. 'We'd just concluded a meeting at the Village Hall with the MP – to discuss aspects of possible Government funding, when we saw lights in the church. Are you saying you've been *physically* threatened?'

As well as Connor-Crewe and Chris Cody, Merrily recognized the fat man from the Post Office and Stores, who had said, '*We ain't rolling over for this one, no way.*' She didn't know any of the others.

'It was just the one call,' she said. 'It doesn't matter. I'm not making a thing about it.'

'It *does* matter.' Fergus's long face hardened. He wore a dark suit and a tie tonight. 'We don't descend to that level. We're not *thugs*. Does anybody here know who was responsible for that? Richard?'

'Not me, Fergus,' the Post Office man said. 'But I know a lot of people were upset when Lodge got tied in with Fred West.'

Fergus, already taller than the rest of them, seemed to rise up further, his chin jutting. 'Well, *I* would like very much to know who was prepared to risk tarnishing this community's reputation. We are civilized people, we are *educated* people. We do *not* issue anonymous threats to members of the clergy or anyone else.'

Bizarre. It was the first time Merrily had seen him behaving like an old-fashioned headmaster. He treated the kids at school as equals, but seemed about to threaten these adults with mass detention unless the culprit confessed.

She was worried. If it emerged now that Melanie Pullman's body had been found, the entire village would be up here within ten minutes. Melanie left to rot in the soil while her murderer lay here in state, the subject of a requiem eucharist, no less. How did *that* look?

Huw Owen met her gaze and looked thoughtful for a moment. Then he smiled, stepped to the doors and, just when she thought he was going to slam them in Fergus's face, flung both of them open like the church was a bingo hall.

'Gents. Huw Owen, my name. The Church, in its old-fashioned way, didn't feel it were appropriate for a lady minister to conduct the funeral service for a murderer. Not on her own, in such a *hostile* community. I'm back-up.'

'Look, I apologize,' Fergus said tightly. 'However, this remains a betrayal of our—'

'Please!' Huw lifted his hands. 'Let me explain. All we've got here is a simple memorial service. Something the Diocese feels is essential to clear the atmosphere surrounding a chain of events going back . . . oh, quite a long way.'

He stepped back into the nave. Richard, from the shop, saw the coffin. 'Bloody hell, he *is* here.'

Huw went to stand by the coffin and put a hand on it, almost affectionately. 'First, I should tell you that, without wanting to appear to bow to any kind of pressure – particularly the kind of drunken behaviour we observed the other night – Mr Lodge here has now said he'd be quite happy for this lad to be consigned to the flames.'

Cherry Lodge looked up at her husband, as if afraid he was

going either to deny it or change his mind. But Tony Lodge said nothing.

Fergus looked at both the Lodges and smiled stiffly. 'We all know Underhowle's emerging from half a century of hardship. All we want is for it to be known as a decent and progressive place. Not some sinister haunt of darkness and perversity, famous for its murderer. I'm sorry if that sounds blunt.'

'Blunt's my language, lad,' Huw assured him. 'Let's all be blunt. Now, we're here as Christians, and all *we* want is to send this lad to his maker – not, as you seem to be insinuating, in a furtive way, but along a path lit by truth and honesty. He's avoided earthly justice, but that's not the end of it as far as we're concerned, as you can imagine.'

Merrily thought, *God, he's good.*

Huw stepped away from the coffin, rubbing his nose.

'We didn't want a circus, and we didn't want the press lads here. And we honestly didn't think it were likely that any of you would want to join us. However, seeing as you *are* here . . .'

There was some shuffling. Richard mumbled something about having to get home for a phone call at ten, and he started backing towards the door. Some of the others hadn't even bothered to come in.

Ingrid Sollars said, 'Personally, I think it would be very appropriate if the members of the Development Committee – as representatives of the future of Underhowle – were to assist Mr Owen and Mrs Watkins and the Lodge family to draw a line under this whole miserable episode.'

There was silence. Huw waited, smiling his placid, benign-priest smile.

'Very well,' Fergus said. 'Why not? Thank you. Let's *end* this discord.'

'Wonderful!' Huw went over to the doors. 'We have any more committee members?'

Chris Cody came in, looking uncomfortable. He wore a dark brown overcoat that almost reached the stone flags, a leather cap that he pulled off. Connor-Crewe, still in his cream suit, shambled in after him, scowling. Merrily noticed Gomer slipping out.

Huw pulled the doors to and rubbed his hands.

'Bit parky in here, but that'll sharpen our senses, won't it? Take a pew. Where were we up to, Merrily?'

'Well, we . . .' Merrily stood under the pulpit as Cody and Connor-Crewe went to sit in the pew behind Ingrid Sollars and Sam Hall, and Fergus sat alone behind the Lodges. 'As you can see, this is rather an unusual service. With so few of us, we decided to dispense with the hymns, but we'll be taking communion later. Perhaps Huw could . . .'

. . . Get me out of this again.

'Aye.' Huw took up a position across the chancel arch, to the left of the coffin. 'Happen we should explain what we're at to God, eh? Let's start with a prayer.'

Cherry Lodge was the first to kneel, Connor-Crewe the last. Connor-Crewe kept his eyes open, which Merrily knew because she didn't close hers either – nerves. She was aware that at some point Huw had switched off the lamps at the bottom of the nave, so that this small but significant congregation was pooled in light, while the shadows behind suggested there were others back there in the darkness.

Huw began softly: 'Lord, we come here tonight in all humility, with a full awareness of our own ignorance. We come here on behalf of certain sad, unquiet spirits on either side of the Divide. We come . . . to seek healing.' He paused, then his voice roughened. 'But we realize that, before there can be healing, there must be knowledge of the condition. Secrets must be laid open. There must be truth. Help us to find that truth. Hold up your lantern for us. Throw its light into the blackest, dingiest corners of human experience, where only the lamp of the wicked flickers with its bilious flame. Help us. Through Jesus Christ, amen.'

There was a hollow hush. They were all watching Huw, even Piers Connor-Crewe.

But Huw was looking at Merrily.

'Your show, lass. I believe you were about to address the subject of our friend here. Roddy.'

Cairns was nauseatingly wonderful, of course. Eirion was right, Eirion was always right about these things, and one day she would tell him. But anxiety brought Jane out before the end, slipping up the aisle during the climactic applause for something epic called 'The Comb Song', and standing at the back, examining the entire audience, row by row, left to right.

Mum was not there.

Check again. Her gaze tracked sytematically along the backs of heads, right to left this time. *Definitely* not there.

It was nearly 9.30 p.m. At first it had been anger: *nobody* should have missed Lol's totally mesmerizing, electrifying comeback, least of all the woman purporting to be in love with him. It was just a complete, total *insult*.

But in the electric brightness of the foyer, she admitted that Mum was not like that, never had been. Mum always felt responsible.

Emotions cocktailed inside Jane, making her feel slightly queasy. She could hear the music, Cairns's voice all smoky-smooth. She thought she'd spotted Eirion in there, worshipping. Maybe she could crawl down the aisle, throw herself at his trainers.

She went to the entrance and pulled out her mobile. Sometimes, Mum would leave a message for her on the answering machine. She put in the number.

'*Hello, this is Ledwardine Vicarage . . .*' She keyed the code, waited, heard several bleeps.

'*Merrily, this is Ted . . .*' Didn't even listen to that one. '*Flower, this is me . . .*' Right.

'*. . . Look, I'm really, really sorry I missed you this morning. No excuses apart from being completely knackered, and if this all goes as badly as I suspect it's going to . . . and, God forbid, I don't make it tonight, I've told Lol, so please look out for Lol afterwards, OK? I'm sorry.*'

Yeah. She hung on in case Mum had called back with an update.

Bleep.

'*Merrily, it's Jennifer Box. It's . . . I don't know what time it is, it's dark. Please help me. He's defiled the chapel, he's defiling everything. He's the evil you are fighting. And, dear God, he's coming back.*'

Merrily stood there, behind the lectern with her prayer book on it. The lectern, which stood to the left of the pulpit, was a dark mahogany stand with a brass eagle, wings spread to hold the heaviest old Bible. Apart from in the oldest churches, the lecterns – like this one – were always too high for her.

She was very aware of the grave-dirt on the hem of her alb.

Earlier, before Gomer had come in with his lamp, she'd planned to address the subject of Roddy's afflictions, the multiple pressures on him, of which perhaps no one here was fully aware. Hoping that, by the end of it, she'd at least have planted the seeds of understanding and something would come of it. One day.

It was different now. The atmosphere was charging up. Soon, arc lights would be burning in the churchyard, tapes would go up, police would guard the site until dawn. Then statements would be taken; they'd all be making statements in the search for a kind of truth that perhaps wouldn't be the truth at all. And there would certainly be no sympathy for Roddy Lodge.

She became aware that she was clutching Melanie's angel, very tightly, in her right hand. It felt almost hot.

Truth. Directness. Simplicity.

'I . . .' Because of the height of the lectern, she was almost speaking into her prayer book. 'I met Roddy Lodge just the once. I was with my friend Gomer, who was convinced Roddy had started a fire that killed his nephew. Roddy was manic, dancing about as if he was on strings. He was talking a lot of rubbish about all the famous people he'd installed drainage for. All lies. While there, on his trailer, not ten yards away, lay the decomposing body of Lynsey Davies.'

Merrily looked up, registering the surprise on the faces of people who, at every funeral they'd hitherto attended, had listened to all the bad stuff being swept under the pews.

'Gomer was wrong, as it turned out. Roddy Lodge didn't start the fire; he was nowhere near there that night. But Roddy had a reputation – as a liar, a crook. And Gomer – and there isn't a nicer, more well-meaning bloke in my village – had demonized him. The way that, first *this* village, and then maybe the whole country has done since. Demonization – a lot of it about. A monster.' She tapped the coffin lid. 'There's a monster in here. What do we do about him?'

She stared at them, helpless.

'I thought I wouldn't have anything to do with Roddy Lodge ever again. But then another friend, a detective from Hereford, said Roddy remembered me from that night and wanted to speak to me. Well, that never happened, in the end – he'd acquired a solicitor, who didn't want him to speak to me or anybody else, and yet allowed him to make a very wide-ranging confession. I gather a few of you know him – Mr Nye? Ryan Nye?'

She looked at Chris Cody. He'd taken off his leather cap. His once-shaven head had grown into a tight, light-brown bristle.

'Yeah, we . . . we figured Lodge ought to have a brief.' He looked a lot younger, somehow: a street kid, the tearaway who'd discovered a massively lucrative talent. 'We'd used Ryan when we was buying the chapel off of Roddy. We put work his way when we can.'

'*You* sent him to represent Roddy?'

'We . . . yeah. We figured he needed a brief.'

Merrily nodded. 'Mr Nye stopped me talking to Roddy, and I was glad. We're trying to build a spirit of honesty here, so, yes – shamefully – I was glad I didn't have to talk to a monster. I knew he *was* a monster, because I'd seen his bedroom, plastered with pictures of famous women, all dead, with parts of nude pin-ups added. Obscene, degrading, sick. A monster – my mate, the detective, wanted to dig up every Efflapure in the county, fully expecting bodies underneath some of them, and I'm thinking, yes, it's possible.'

She wondered where Frannie Bliss was now. How he'd react when Gomer told him about Melanie. The sensible thing would be to call Headquarters, which meant she and Huw didn't have much time. And with a eucharist to organize . . .

'And then the next night, Roddy wanted to come home, so they brought him back. He'd confessed to three murders – all the murders that my friend, the detective, had put it to him that he'd done. Why was he so keen to confess, to come back here and show the police where he'd buried the bodies? Had Mr Nye told him it was for the best? Why would Mr Nye tell him that?'

She looked at Chris Cody, who looked perturbed.

'Well, Mr Nye isn't here, so we can't get any enlightenment there. But there *was* another good reason why Roddy Lodge found Hereford Police Headquarters – with its mass of equipment, its radio transmitters and especially its almost subterranean interview rooms – an unbearable place to be. Because Roddy had become electrically hypersensitive. He had to get out of there and he didn't care what it took.'

Merrily moved out in front of the lectern, feeling more confident.

'But there *was* more to it than electrical pollution; there had to be.'

She talked about Roddy's childhood, his isolation in an all-male household, his manufacture of a series of mother substitutes, the peculiar comfort he found in the realm of the dead – nothing essentially morbid in it, a way of coping, a world he felt he could control.

'Can we say he was psychic? Can we say he actually began to see the dead? Had he developed what some people like to call mediumistic faculties? Sam would say he was simply the victim of hallucinations, caused by the effects of force fields on the brain. All I know is that it was something he was allowed to grow up with, something that was never discussed.'

She didn't look at Tony Lodge; this wasn't an inquisition. Tony Lodge didn't say anything.

'We do know that Roddy was becoming disturbed by his condition, because he went to see the doctor. Who, like most GPs, seems to have believed in neither psychic powers nor EH. And who referred him to the Rector. Who gave him some advice which was . . . well meant.'

Ingrid Sollars made a small, contemptuous noise.

'In fact, there seems to have been only one person with whom Roddy Lodge was able to discuss his condition. And that was Melanie Pullman, a girl who was also experiencing problems of an apparently psychic nature . . . which Sam believes to have been a result of living *very* close to power lines and other signals.

I've had access to some background on Melanie Pullman. On balance, the evidence of some electrical stimulation of parts of the brain does seem, in her case, to be the most persuasive explanation. But Melanie's not . . . here to discuss it.'

Merrily heard the muffled clunk of the door latch and saw figures moving in the shadows. Gomer. And Frannie Bliss. Nobody else.

'My feeling is that Melanie was good for Roddy. The evidence is that they had a close relationship. She was probably his first real girlfriend. There was nobody else in Roddy's life at that time – as far as I can tell.'

'It's true.' Cherry Lodge was leaning over the prayer-book shelf. Her face was flushed. 'He was never any kind of a ladies' man. He wasn't smooth and he wasn't that bright, if you want the truth. Never a girlfriend when he was young – Tony'll tell you. *Tell them.*'

Tony grunted. 'Embarrassed him, women did, when he was at home. Afterwards, he embarrassed *us*, all the tales. And the sports car. Nobody in our family ever had a sports car.'

'What changed?' Merrily said. 'What made him . . . in a woman we call it promiscuous, but in a man it's "a bit of a lad". I mean, when he was with Melanie he wasn't like that, was he?'

'She was a nice girl,' Tony said. 'Quiet. Nice-looking – I never knew what she saw in him.'

'A soulmate, perhaps?'

'Then why did he . . . ?' He turned his face away.

Merrily said quickly, 'Sam Hall found out about Melanie and tried to help her – with some success, I think. And Melanie, in turn, tried to help Roddy. Maybe she encouraged him to go to the same alternative practitioner who'd given her a device to wear around her neck to ward off electromagnetism. But Roddy didn't want to know. I wonder why not?'

Frannie Bliss slid into a pew halfway down the nave, where the shadows began. 'I think we both know that, don't we, Merrily?'

She nodded as the other heads turned. 'What's happening, Frannie?'

'Nothing special,' Bliss said coolly. 'Thought I'd see how

things've changed in the so-called Church of England before I made any kind of move.'

Merrily saw Piers Connor-Crewe bounce a disdainful glance from Bliss to her. 'You two lovers or something? I think we should be told.'

'Uncalled for, Piers,' Fergus Young snapped.

'Fergus, I'm so *tired* of these shallow, nit-picking people. Why do we even *care* about the mental state of the waste of space in that box? As for this bloody little woman trying to find a new role for the ailing Church in some sort of spiritual-criminal profiling . . .'

Merrily said, 'What did Lynsey Davies say about Roddy Lodge, Piers? Did *she* think he was a waste of space? I suspect not.'

'Get off my back, Mrs Watkins.'

'I think Lynsey found him *extremely* interesting. Because of what he was – i.e. someone apparently in day-to-day contact with the dead . . . of whom *he had no fear whatsoever*. And because he was the owner of Underhowle Baptist chapel. Which for her had become a kind of shrine.'

She looked at Huw, but he didn't react. The angel was almost burning in her hand.

'There was a problem, of course: Roddy had a steady girl-friend, with whom he had a lot in common. And Melanie, who seems to have suffered for years from EH, was suddenly – thanks to Sam – discovering a possible cause. And a possible solution.'

She looked at Sam, guessing that she was reaching a con-clusion he'd come to several minutes ago. He left his pew and went to stand in the aisle, slowly punching a fist into a palm.

'She was trying to persuade Roddy to go to the same alterna-tive practitioner, to understand what she was now convinced was the real nature of the problem. Maybe she would've succeeded. Maybe she'd have helped him, if . . .' She opened her hand and let the angel dangle on its broken chain. '*If . . .*'

'If Lynsey Davies hadn't killed her first,' Sam said.

Merrily looked down at her prayer book. 'Or persuaded some-one else to do it?'

48

The Make-over

'Ah yes,' Moira Cairns said, like she'd just remembered something vaguely distasteful. 'Hi, Jane.'

'I don't understand.' Jane stepped away from the box office, dismayed. 'This woman says Lol's gone.'

Cairns was looking smaller and somehow younger in jeans and this big Hebridean sweater, her hair tied up, the make-up washed off.

'Aye,' she said. 'He had to leave.'

Leave? The big star gone off with some major international promoter, some record company exec. Goodbye to the old life. Hello hotel rooms, hello groupies.

Jane bit her lip, feeling isolated among the crowd in the foyer, probably the only one of them who was here alone and now would leave alone. Come to support Lol, and he'd triumphed and gone. She'd twice called Mum's mobile to tell her about that call from Jenny Box, if she didn't already know about it. Nothing – switched off.

'I said *I'd* run you home,' Cairns said, autographing the sleeve of an old vinyl album some sad git had brought along. 'Sorry about the shaky bit,' she said to the sad git. 'Must be ma age.'

'You look younger than ever,' the sad git said, going off, and Cairns blew him a kiss.

Jane looked down at the poisoned blade of betrayal. '*What?*'

'Give me five minutes, OK?' Cairns said.

Jane said tightly. 'I can get a bus.'

Of course, there was no late bus to Ledwardine midweek, and she caught herself making swift glances to either side. Maybe Eirion? He must still be around. He couldn't *really* have dumped her. Just because she'd come on like somebody spoiled and bitchy. He wasn't like that. He loved her.

Or what she used to be. He'd loved what she *used to be*. Eirion would have come here to see Lol and Moira, no reason to seek out Jane. It was *over*.

'Or I can get a taxi. I've got enough money.'

Moira pulled a bunch of keys from her jeans and tossed them at Jane. 'Grey BMW, right down by the bottom entrance. I'll be there in about five minutes. I just have to see Prof, OK?'

And she turned and walked off, the smug bitch, leaving Jane standing there, holding the keys.

Jane spun away, with a semi-sob, and walked out of the building into the squally air, gulping it in. Looked up in despair at the night over Hereford, saw a faded cluster of stars, small holes in worn denim. Gas balls in a barren universe.

None of them wanted to know her now, not Eirion, not even Lol. She was spoiled and peevish and stupid; she was *negative*. She'd grown up a negative person in a negative world, this floating cyst of dying matter about which everything was known. A world that had peaked some time ago, and all scientists were doing about it was shrinking it more rapidly, while finding ways of keeping you alive longer so that you could go on and on being crapped on.

Halfway across the car park, seeing a couple of guys in their twenties watching her, she caught herself actually starting to think of the several individuals who would be twisted with guilt for the rest of their lives when she was found raped and murdered behind one of the warehouses off the Holmer Road or just killed, in a cursory way by some heroin addict, for her mobile.

In the end, she just found Moira's BMW and let herself in and locked the doors to keep out the junkies and the rapists. Then she made another fruitless attempt to call Mum and tell her about Jenny Driscoll, who had been so anxious to see her before the funeral on Friday, possibly because of something this guy Humphries had turned up in Underhowle. But the funeral had happened. It was all over. Mum should be home now.

Should be home.

Jane rang home, and listened to all the messages again, ending with '*Dear God, he's coming back.*'

Like Gareth Box was some kind of rapist/slasher.

Poor Driscoll. She wasn't crass and superficial, just damaged. And likeable, really, another emotional refugee, although it was still hard to know how much of what she said you could seriously believe. The angel stuff: *'I'm not claiming to be Bernadette. I don't care whether anyone believes me.'* And then: *'I saw it, Jane. And she was beautiful.'* Was that the final confirmation that Mum *was* the angel?

Yet nothing sexual – could you believe that? You certainly believed it when she said it last night; you grabbed it gratefully, squeezed it to your bosom: *Oh thank you, thank you.* But now? How did you feel about Jenny Driscoll, with hindsight?

Jane said, *'Oh God.'*

God who did not exist, who just served now as an all-purpose expression for dismay, confusion, exasperation, contempt – and fear.

By now, any semblance of a service had evaporated. There were eleven people and a corpse under the ice-cream lights, and no reason for anyone to be here any more, not even the corpse.

Yet nobody was trying to leave.

Merrily saw Frannie Bliss placing himself next to the church door, needing to contain everybody while he worked it all out, examining the cards in his hand, rearranging them, wondering which ones to throw away.

It was like this: if Lynsey Davies *had* killed Melanie Pullman, it threw up a new and plausible motive for Roddy to have killed Lynsey, a – God forbid – *normal* motive.

Arguably, a hot-blooded killing: Lodge had discovered that this warped and dangerous woman had murdered his girlfriend. The kind of killing, then, for which – had he lived to appear in court – he might well have ended up with no more than a couple of years in prison.

If Lynsey Davies was the only one he'd done. *If* the serial killing was something happening only in the dark mind of Lynsey Davies.

Did you confess just to get it over, to get the police off your back, the heat from your brain? Merrily put her hands either side of the pine coffin, just where Roddy's head would be, cooled at last. She saw him scaling that pylon, gripping the steel skeleton of his personal tormentor, swinging up into the rigid, spindly arms of Kali the Destroyer, with the killer candles in her fingers.

Sam Hall was at the foot of the coffin, and their gazes met: *what now?* She didn't know. If Roddy was going to the crematorium, there didn't even need to be a funeral.

From over by the door, Frannie Bliss called, 'Do we want to take this further? I don't think I'm in any position to demand that everybody stays, but if I phone my boss – which is what I ought to do – I can guarantee a long night for some of us.'

Piers Connor-Crewe's big, pale body twitched. 'Are you going to tell us exactly what you've found?'

'*Found*, Mr Crewe?'

Sam Hall said, 'Merrily, you just raised the possibility that Lynsey Davies had someone else kill Melanie. You want to explain that?'

'Well . . .' She moved away from the coffin. 'I think if we look at what we know about Lynsey . . .'

'I know a bit more now, in fact,' Bliss said. 'Andy Mumford finally called. It's not much, but it might make you think.' He moved away from the door, resting a foot on a pew seat, hands on his knee. 'Some of it we knew, but there's no harm in going over it again. Lynsey – like Roddy, actually – grew up in a Noncomformist household on the edge of the forest – Drybrook or Lydbrook, one of those places. Her old feller was a coalman – one of the blokes who carted the sacks about, rather than ran the yard – and he was also the caretaker at his chapel. There were four kids, and Lynsey was the eldest. And the old man used to make them go twice on a Sunday to chapel. Strict. Very strict.'

'He still alive?' Sam asked.

'No, neither parent, but Mumford talked to a sister, who hadn't seen Lynsey in years but did remember things like how she was once suspended from school for bullying. And how much she hated the chapel.'

'Figures,' Sam said.

'Actually, it wasn't that simple,' Bliss said. 'Funny, these are things you'd never bother going into when somebody's just "the victim". Even less important when you're just *a* victim – one of several. When we say she "hated the chapel", we mean the organization, the religion. The actual building – this stark old place with the Dr Phibes harmonium – she bloody loved that. Used to pinch her old man's keys and go in with her mates at night, playing.'

Merrily said, 'Presumably, you don't mean the harmonium.'

Bliss did his acid smile. 'I think the games got more adventurous the older she became. And then one day – the sister's not sure what happened, it being a serious scandal at the time and a great embarrassment for the family – one day traces of these activities were found by the cleaner. As a result of which, Mr Davies lost his position as part-time caretaker. And he was not a happy man. And he held Lynsey responsible.'

Mumford wasn't sure what Mr Davies did to Lynsey, but there was certainly a long period of fear and loathing in that household, Bliss said. The sister had told Mumford they didn't. see much of Lynsey once she got into her middle teens. But there was a teacher who thought she was an intelligent girl with prospects and suggested she'd be better away from home, persuading the parents to let her go to this commercial college in Gloucester – possibly even arranging a grant.

'Either way, Mr Davies was probably glad to see her go,' Bliss said. 'And I think some of us know the rest. So there you have it: an intelligent girl raised in a strict household starts to rebel against it from quite a tender age. Though tender's not the word for Lynsey, is it? The suspension for bullying, the hints of early sexual adventures . . . all hinting at the bad things to come.'

'And the use of religious premises in a sexual context?' Merrily said.

'Dead right. And we're all looking at you, Mr Crewe. 'Cause of all the people here, we're thinking, nobody knew Lynsey as well as Mr Crewe.'

Connor-Crewe didn't look back at him. 'I've told you all I know.'

'You said you didn't know about Lynsey being at Cromwell Street. I wonder if that's true.'

'If you want to accuse me of anything—'

Huw Owen said, '*As* Francis has raised the issue of Cromwell Street, I think we can all agree that his original theory of Lodge as a West obsessive has been turned on its head. It was Lynsey who was obsessed.'

Bliss shrugged.

'Thank you, lad.' Huw went to stand at the lectern. 'Nobody likes to think of anybody, especially a woman, becoming so corrupted inside as to find inspiration and energy in a situation as foul as that. But we have to face it. Just as we had to face the fact that the number of lives *destroyed* by twenty years of carnage in Cromwell Street far exceeded the number of lives *lost*. Which itself may be a lot bigger than the list read out at the trial of Rosemary West.'

'I'm sorry . . .' Fergus Young looked like a man who'd been containing himself for as long as he reasonably could. 'I don't see the relevance of this. It's frankly obscene. There's no proven link between Underhowle and anything connected with West, and I really don't think we should manufacture one. Lodge and Davies are both dead . . . gone . . . *finished*.'

'No, lad. Nowt's finished. If you don't see the living darkness at the heart of this—'

'*Living darkness!*' Fergus stood up, his hair springing. 'That is *such* nonsense! That's *defamatory* nonsense.'

Huw held tight to the wings of the brass eagle. 'See, I don't usually talk like this to lay folk. It doesn't help. But I'm looking at a woman who was drawing energy from a black hole, a place from which all kindness, tenderness, pity and moral awareness had been sucked out. Drawing *energy* from that. Can you understand?'

Merrily said softly, 'I think we should look at what she was creating. With Melanie out of the way, she'd begun to reorganize Roddy's life. Perhaps starting with something fairly innocent like setting up his sitting room as Roddy's Bar – like the one at Cromwell Street. And then redecorating his bedroom.'

Cherry Lodge whispered, '*Yes.*'

'There were two bedrooms in that bungalow – the one Roddy set up for himself, which was a bit old-fashioned. And the one I think Lynsey created for him, with black sheets and eroticized pictures of beautiful women who also happened to be dead. Reflecting the connection he was perhaps already making between sex and death, but . . . brutalizing it, I suppose. Like she was trying to turn him into . . . somebody else.'

Fergus said, 'Somebody *else*?'

'Work it out, lad,' Huw Owen told him.

'It's preposterous!'

'She also revamped his social calendar,' Merrily said. 'Poor Jerome Banks thinks he was the one who encouraged Roddy to go out and find some real girls. In fact, Lynsey was building up his confidence . . . and also turning him into a predator. Like people train hawks.'

She looked up at the sound of Piers Connor-Crewe edging out of his pew, making for the door. 'I've heard enough.'

Bliss stood in his path. 'I don't think so, Piers.'

'Are you actually attempting to *detain* me?'

'I have some questions.'

'Up your arse with them, inspector. I've had quite enough of you for one day.'

'It's just that I've been wondering: if Lynsey – or somebody else, other than Lodge – killed Melanie Pullman, who buried her? I've just recalled you saying this morning that Roddy lent you his digger, to put in some trenches near the chapel. Only, I was watching my good friend Mr Parry today. You could take a digger – as I presume Roddy often did – from his garage to this churchyard, along the path through the fields, in . . . what? Ten minutes? Bit longer at night?'

'You're insane.'

'It's just a thought, Piers. Neither you nor Lynsey would want Melanie buried near the Baptist chapel, if there was ever any chance of a real archaeological dig. Nowhere safer for a body than a graveyard. And who'd be next in there – Tony Lodge? Well, not in the near future, we all trust and hope. And anyway, as soon as they saw bone down there, it'd be, whoops . . . that's another one slid down the hill, better move on a couple of yards.'

'Unless they found this.' Merrily held up the angel. 'Bit of a give-away. Was to us, anyway.'

The angel shone with a coppery light, brighter somehow than the lighting globes.

'Yeh, that's odd,' Bliss said. 'I can't explain why they didn't take that off her, dispose of it.'

A discreet cough from Gomer. 'Likely di'n't see him, ennit? If her weared him under her clothes, next to the skin, like, mabbe he wouldn't be visible. At night, if they was in a hurry. But then the clothes starts to rot . . . up he comes.'

Thank you, Gomer.

He knew as well as she did that it couldn't have happened like that, because the fabric of the clothes had not rotted. The angel shone from Merrily's hand and burned with a soft heat. A witness. Perhaps it had found its own way to the surface.

'What do you think, Piers?' Bliss asked.

'What *should* I think? I have no proof you've found anything at all.'

Bliss said steadily, 'You planted her, pal. Let's start with that, see where it gets us.'

'You *dare* to accuse me of that – in front of all these witnesses?'

'I'm feeling lucky.' Bliss opened the door into the porch. 'Go on, if you want. You go home and have a couple of glasses of your favourite fifteen-year-old malt and a good night's sleep. Or maybe you'd prefer to lie awake all night and think about it, work out your story.'

Bliss was winging it, Merrily thought. He wouldn't even have seen what was in the grave.

'Or perhaps, if you want to be less public about it, you could drop in at police Headquarters tomorrow.' Bliss held open the door and froze. He took a cautious step back, then relaxed, smiling thinly. 'Ah, Mr Laurence Robinson, as I live and breathe.'

Merrily almost ran down the aisle. Lol stood in the doorway, smiled bashfully at her, the way he always did when she was in uniform. But the slanting alien eyes were watching sardonically from the region of his chest. Merrily stopped.

'If you've come to collect the little woman, she may be a while yet.' Bliss let Lol in and closed the door.

'Who the hell's this?' Connor-Crewe was looking limp with unease now.

Lol said nothing. He went to stand with Gomer in a shadowed spot under a stone plaque commemorating *Ald. Joseph Albert Persham: 1894–1966.*

'If you drop in at Headquarters,' Bliss said to Connor-Crewe, 'we can fingerprint you, take a little DNA swab . . . and that should put you in the clear.'

'You don't frighten me in the least,' Connor-Crewe said. 'You're an ambitious little bastard, but of limited intelligence.'

'He don't *need* intelligence.' Chris Cody was leaning wearily against a pew-end, rubbing his face and then looking over his fingers at Connor-Crewe. 'And for what it's worth, he frightens *me*. You got no idea, have you, Piers? You don't know what these animals are like, mate.'

Merrily's hand closed around the angel. She was staring, like everyone else, at this slightly built man in an oversized overcoat, who could buy and sell all of them and the church around them. Cody shook his head like he was sick of the whole thing.

'It's a murder inquiry now. They lose all sense of proportion on a murder, 'specially if it's a woman or a kid. They'll lie, they'll plant evidence, they'll have you on a fucking sandwich, mate. You're this upper-class bastard who's been to fucking Oxford. They love nailing a nob.'

'Chris, what on earth are you . . . ?' Connor-Crewe was sweating.

'You go out there,' Cody said, 'you'll find another twenty coppers lined up like bleeding dominoes. I'm telling you, soon as I knew they had the body, I'm like, you know, this is it, we been set up. We walked into it.'

Merrily exchanged glances with Frannie Bliss. The tip of an angel wing was piercing her palm and she felt almost faint. But Bliss was deadpan, entirely relaxed, as if he'd been expecting this and wondered why it had taken them so long. But he hadn't; inside, he'd be as shaken as she was. She looked around for Huw and found him sitting on the chancel step, leaning forward with his hands in prayer position between his knees, not looking at anyone, listening.

Bliss said, 'Who killed Melanie, Mr Cody?'

Cody looked at Piers Connor-Crewe and shrugged.

'Lynsey, of course,' he said. 'Oh yeah – and Fred West.'

Moira Cairns drove quite slowly out of Hereford, her face lightly tanned by the dashlight. Hands low down on the wheel, relaxed. Like they had been all night. Like she was totally unaware of the tension in Jane.

'He was awfully good.'

'Yes.'

'Like, I was scared out ma mind when he first went out there but, Jesus, once he was into it, it was like this was the second week of his long-awaited world tour. And I guess the reason for that was he had something bigger on his mind.'

'Mmm.'

A long pause as Cairns let this huge lorry come growling past. For Christ's *sake*.

'And you're thinking Lol and I are making out, yeah?'

'Sorry?'

'Well, I'm sorry, too, if that's way off,' Cairns said, 'but I couldnae think of a better reason for you behaving the whole time like a wee pain in the arse, you know?'

'It's the way I am,' Jane said. 'I *am* a pain in the arse.' And then, as Cairns slowed right down for the Whitecross round-about, she said, '*Are* you?'

'Er . . . no. We're not.'

'Oh.'

'Where's Eirion, Jane?'

'Dumped me.'

'For being a pain in the arse?'

'Something like that.'

'Uh huh.' Moira Cairns drove in silence for maybe half a mile. The road was quiet, too. Then she said, 'But when life's such a bitch, and the world's this big kidney stone floating in a universe of liquid manure, where's the point in *not* being a pain in the arse?'

Jane turned her head and looked directly at Cairns. Neither of them was smiling.

Jane moistened her lips. 'Have you been speaking to Eirion?'

'Not since the night the both of you were there, at Prof's. And Eirion was doing most of the talking then. Why?'

'Just . . . wondered.'

They hit the countryside, and she turned away to look out at the empty fields opening up on the left, all the way to the Black Mountains.

'Tell me something, Jane. Does it make it worse when your mother's a priest of God?'

'How do you mean?'

'Well, she's up in the pulpit, telling a dwindling audience about the Kingdom of Heaven, and you're thinking, what's *this* shite?'

'I wouldn't say that to her.'

'Or at least no more than twice a week.'

'That's not exactly—'

'But, hell, if it's what you *think* . . . ?'

Jane said, anguished, 'It's not what I *used* to think.'

'But in those days you'd had no real experience of life, right?'

Jane slumped. It was like all her thoughts and fears had been laid out in this smorgasbord situation, and the Cairns woman was collecting a slice of this, a segment of that on a plate, and poking them with her fork, but not actually eating anything.

'Next right,' she said. And as they made the turn, at the sign pointing to Weobley, she rallied, hit back with the big one. 'Do *you* believe in God?'

They must have driven for nearly a mile before the reply came. They were passing through a wooded stretch, no visible sky, the headlights on full.

'Doesnae mean I have to like the bastard.'

'What?'

'God – whatever he/she is – if it thinks you can take it, it's likely to give you a hard time. You want a nice life, the best way is to turn up for the weddings and funerals and don't even think about any of it the rest of the time.'

'But that—'

'Or, of course, the other way is, whenever some shit comes at you, you say, Ah, well, it's the Will of God. *That* works. That saves a *lot* of heartache.'

'So your philosophy is what?'

'You just heard it.'

'I don't think I believe you.'

'But once in a while I forget, and I stick my head out the trench, then *slam* . . . two black eyes, chipped teeth, nosebleed.'

'And when people say you're psychic . . . ?'

'Aw now, Jane, *you* know what a pile of crap *that* is.'

Jane said, 'Can't you go any faster?'

'Probably. Would there be a good reason to?'

'I don't know,' Jane said.

'You could try telling me.'

Chris Cody looked over at Connor-Crewe. 'There's no *point* now, mate.' He folded his arms, his back braced against the pew-end, and addressed Bliss. 'One night, Piers asked me round, and there was four of us, Piers and me and Lynsey and this woman who worked for Piers down the shop, and – after some stuff – Lynsey says, "What would you like most in the world? Apart from this?" And she pulls up her . . . Anyway, that's how it started.'

'The magic.' Bliss smiled.

'I dunno what I was expecting – black robes and upside-down crosses, maybe, but it was nothing like that. Well, candles . . . bit of atmosphere. And a circle. Bit of mumbo-jumbo, but nuffing you couldn't live with. The others had done it before, but Lynsey said that wasn't a problem. She said outsiders could bring in new energy.'

'Lynsey was in charge.'

'Oh yeah. Piers was – I'm sorry, mate – like a bloody schoolgirl when Lynsey was there. Sometimes you felt she'd got more testosterone than any of us. Anyway, we were pretty small-time at the factory then – struggling, you know? And there was this contract I was after, to run a system for this new stationery manufacturer over at Tewkesbury, and Lynsey asks me to describe the place and talk about it, and then refine what I want into this like single image.'

'Image?' Huw said from the chancel steps.

'I'm not telling you what it was, 'cause I'm superstitious. Wasn't then, but I am now. The four of us had to fink about the image and then we sat in a circle, naked, almost touching, but not quite, and then—'

'For God's sake,' Connor-Crewe snapped, 'they can imagine the rest.'

'And you got the contract,' Merrily said.

'Oh yeah. First of many that year. Before I went home, Lynsey told me some fings I could like . . . practise. Fings I could do . . .' He grinned uncomfortably. 'You know, on me own. To build up . . . the visualization skills in connection wiv . . . Anyway, the next time I went – no, the time after that – Roddy Lodge was there. I didn't know who he was, but there was a hell of a . . . I mean it was incredible. Powerful, you know? It was like you'd taken somefing. Acid or somefing. At one stage, I could've sworn there was other people wiv us. Big black figures. Weird.'

'This was still at The Old Rectory?'

'Nah, this was in the chapel. The old Baptist chapel. I didn't like it at first in there, it was a bit cold. I'm like, what's the point of this? Then I found out.' Chris Cody shook his head. 'Roddy and that chapel – crazy. Energy, you know? You come out, you felt you could do anyfing.'

'Was Roddy on his own?' Bliss asked. 'No Melanie?'

'Nah. I didn't know about Melanie then, but a few months later we goes along to the chapel – I mean, I'm well into it by then. I had a few qualms now and then, but bloody hell . . . Anyway, I get there, and Roddy's on his way over, and there's this girl like clinging to his legs and that, screaming at him – like does he want to destroy himself, don't he realize what he's getting into? And she's crying and screaming and he's trying to ignore it and he's pulling away, but in the end she's making so much of a scene he has to go back wiv her, and he don't come in that night at all. And you could really tell the difference wivout him there. Somefing missing, you know? I can't put this into words, but . . . somefing definitely missing.'

Merrily glanced at the coffin and caught Ingrid Sollars's look.

Ingrid was sitting straight-backed on the edge of her pew, as if she was on horseback.

'There was a couple of other times Roddy didn't show,' Chris Cody said, 'and we knew she was getting to him, wearing him down. One night we couldn't get in – she'd been up and locked the chapel. Which was becoming our place by then – essential. We all knew it was moving now, like big time, and we was scared of losing the momentum. One day, Piers says why don't we buy it off of him?'

'With your money, of course,' Bliss said.

'Yeah, well, I'd got a bit by then. And this was important. Like, it was all tied in – wivout what we had going there wouldn't *be* no money. The energy we was generating, you know? I mean, I know what it must sound like coming out wiv all this in church and everything, but . . . it didn't feel bad. It didn't feel *bad*. Not then.'

Bliss said, 'And you thought it might be better, given his domestic problems, if the chapel wasn't owned by Roddy Lodge.'

'Wasn't as if it was worth much, and I felt it was putting something back. So we got Nye to arrange it. And the Development Committee was up and running, and we put in for grants, turn it into a museum. 'Course we'd still use it. Lynsey said that'd be cool, surrounded by all these ancient ritual artefacts and that.'

Bliss looked across at Ingrid Sollars. 'Did you know about this?'

'No, she didn't,' Cody said. 'Nor did Fergus. And I bloody wish I never had, now.'

'Why?' Bliss asked innocently. 'You were doing all right.'

'Look, I'd probably *still*'ve been doing all right. I realize that now, but Lynsey was charismatic. She could make you believe anyfing, especially when it was all so . . . intoxicating. Like, it was around this time that Roddy gets the contract with Efflapure. Never looked back. Lynsey magicked it. Truth was, Lynsey knew this guy who was a director of Efflapure, and she rigged it – probably blackmailing the guy over something, knowing Lynsey.

I found out later, but Roddy never knew. He fought she'd magicked it for him. Magicked it. Bleedin' hell.'

'Aye,' Huw said. 'That's how it works. They operate outside the rules. All the rules. Sex, drugs, blackmail. You can never work out where it begins. Or quite where the evil seeps in.'

'So you fixed up to buy the chapel,' Bliss said.

'Yeah. I'd just do fings on a whim then. I was flying, man.'

'What was Roddy's relationship with Lynsey around this time?' Merrily asked.

'Oh . . . like he was hypnotized. It was pretty much like you said. She was giving him the make-over.'

'And Melanie?'

'She went away for a few weeks. She was ill and she went away, and Lynsey just moved in. Wiv Roddy. And she had him. I mean really had him in her hand. And then this complete make-over. We didn't know what was happening then, but I never seen a bloke change so fast. And then Melanie's back. Looking really well, you know? Fresh. I mean, she was a nice girl. And, like the vicar said, she was on at Roddy to get treatment. We didn't know what that was about, but Lynsey did, and that's when fings started happening . . . like very fast. We – me and Piers – we get summoned to the Baptist chapel.'

'By Lynsey?'

'Yeah. When you was summoned, you went, mate. You didn't get her angry, you couldn't predict what she was gonna . . . So we went. It was one afternoon, and Roddy was out on a job for Efflapure, and Lynsey's there alone, except for this big thick plastic sack. Lynsey and a sack. Like she's just collected the rubbish for the tip. Never forget that fucking sack, tied up with orange baler twine. She opens it up, so we can see in. Jesus.'

'Melanie?' Bliss said.

Cody rubbed his eyes. 'Worst fing I've ever seen.'

'How?' Bliss said.

'Strangled. Froat was all black, you know? Tongue out. Stiff. Rigor mortis. And the fucking smell. And Lynsey's shouting at us. "Come on . . . move yourselves. Get this out." And I knew if we didn't help her . . . I mean you didn't know which way she'd go. She wasn't *safe*.'

Merrily came closer and realized he was rubbing his eyes because he was crying. Cody looked at her.

'She said she done it for Fred West. She said Fred West had been wiv us from the start, when we was . . . doing the business, the rituals. Fred fucking West. Over our shoulders. She said he—'

Huw Owen spoke over Merrily's shoulder.

'Liked to watch?'

49

Apocryphal

As they filed down the hill into the half-lit street, Sam Hall said, 'Maybe we oughta be chanting a litany. Like, in the darkest hour of the plague, when the minister led a procession through Ross?'

Huw, who was leading them, rounded on him. 'It's not a school outing. Best if we don't even talk.'

He was afraid of shattering the spell, Merrily thought. Dissolving the horror before its time. To keep this little ragbag congregation, he needed them all to accept the continued reality of the evil, needed to keep the lamp of the wicked held aloft, lest anyone should start to see this as no more than a sordid tale of small-town ambition and sexual games gone catastrophically wrong.

She was still holding Melanie's angel like a talisman, apprehensive. He might know what he was doing, but was he the right person to be doing it? Oh yes, they'd been in the wrong place, Huw had known that from the beginning. *Lodge? Leave him be, lass. Who's he harming now? We'll do the chapel.*

Huw scenting the enemy.

Lol walked beside Merrily. She sensed a calm around him, which meant the concert had either been a big success or a monumental failure. He'd whispered that Moira was taking care of Jane. Moira? Jane and *Moira*?

A police car slid past towards the church. Cody and Connor-Crewe had already been taken to Hereford in separate cars. Bliss had not arrested either of them, simply asking, with a certain savage courtesy, if they'd care to discuss it in more depth.

What would the charges be? Accessories to the concealment of a murder? Cody said he and Piers had taken the body through the fields in the early hours, on a trailer pulled by a quad bike. Maybe they could simply have shopped Lynsey, Cody said, and still saved their business lives – all they'd done was participate in what would be known as 'sex orgies'. No big deal, these days, even out here in the sticks.

Merrily suspected that Lynsey had had more on them than they would ever disclose.

Bliss had seen them into the cars. Then he'd made a short call and cut the connection and waited. Within three minutes the phone had buzzed. Bliss had listened with a foxy little smile, and then said, 'No real need for you to turn out at this hour, boss.' Then, cutting the connection again, he'd said ruefully, 'Fleming'll be here in just over an hour.'

Gomer had stayed behind with Bliss, to show the Durex suits where to dig.

As she walked towards the crossroads, with the old duffel coat over her alb, Merrily was still hearing: *Done it for Fred West . . . wiv us from the start.*

Fred West, several years dead, who liked to watch. It was all that Huw had needed.

They were passing the school now. Fergus Young held up his long head, his hair high in the wind, and didn't give it a single sideways glance.

How much had *he* known? He must have known *something*.

At the bottom of the hill, past the steel-shuttered Post Office and Stores and the Head Office unisex hair salon, Cherry Lodge waited for Merrily and whispered, 'We won't come with you, if that's all right.'

'Nobody could expect you to.'

'I feel somehow empty inside now,' Cherry said. 'Do you know what I mean? These were the very people who came to our door, asking us to see some sense, not damage the community.'

Merrily squeezed Cherry's arm. 'At least you know now why they were so keen to prevent Roddy going into that grave.'

It didn't take much to spark a protest, not with people like Richard, the newsagent, around – a word here, a word there, a suggestion that the value of your property might be damaged.

'And if you want to arrange something at Hereford Crematorium, soon as you like, I'd be happy to do it properly.'

'Thank you,' Cherry said. 'We might sleep tonight. Even-tually.'

Merrily raised a hand as the Lodges walked away, following their lamp up the narrow lane to their bleak farm on the hill above the place that was, or wasn't, Ariconium.

What would happen to all that now: the plans, the reconstruc-tions, the suspect artefacts and the audio-visuals?

Underhowle . . . where nothing succeeded for long.

By the grimy gleam of the last street lamp, she saw the face of Ingrid Sollars and wondered about all the things Ingrid must have chosen not to see for the sake of progress. And yet, in this light, you might have thought Ingrid's expression was actually one of relief.

But then, Ingrid couldn't know what Huw had in mind, as he brought out a stubby torch to lead the rest of them past the darkened community hall and out of the village towards Roddy Lodge's garage and the track to the old Baptist chapel.

No wonder he didn't want to talk to anyone.

Jane saw Jenny Box as soon as they came into the square at Ledwardine.

It was just on closing time at the Black Swan, and some people were leaving, urged into their vehicles by an irritable wind.

Jane saw James Bull-Davies and Alison Kinnersley, who she was sure she'd spotted at the Courtyard – could have got a lift back with *them* if she'd realized in time. She saw Jim Prosser from the Eight-till-Late, and she saw her appalling ex-school-mates, Dean Walls and Danny Gittoes, going into the Swan in the hope of a last pint.

And then, between the rainy haloes around the fake gaslamps, she saw Jenny moving across the square – not from the pub, but from the other side, from the direction of her home, Chapel House. Jenny Box, with her scarf over her head like the Virgin Mary and that flickering, flinching blur passing across her face, as she paused on the edge of the cobbles as if looking for a light in the vicarage, before turning back.

'Moira, stop!'

Moira braked. 'What's wrong?'

'It's her. Jenny Driscoll.'

'Where?'

'Just going . . . the woman with the white scarf over her head.'

'Uh huh,' Moira said.

'She doesn't know this car. Did you see?'

'What?'

'The look on her face. That look she has – as if her expression's out of synch with her feelings.'

Moira pulled up on the edge of the square, where you weren't supposed to park. In the last fifteen minutes, Jane had just kept talking, without thinking, like someone did when they were drunk: talking about Jenny Box and the angel, which seemed to have brought everything to a crisis. Telling Moira Cairns what she'd never told anyone – about the night she'd drunk wine with Gareth Box and fallen under his spell and the spell of the house: autumn wine and firelight, the sheer intoxication of it, the first time in weeks that she'd found any *texture* in her life.

And then about last night, walking these streets with Jenny – how weird that had been – discovering that she actually *liked* this manipulator, this hate-figure. Finding that she could understand Jenny's aching need for a true spiritual refuge, somewhere she could feel safe from abuse, safe from hypocrisy.

Not daring, while she was saying all this, even to look at Moira Cairns, who had been, after all, the other significant hate-figure in her recent life.

'Jane.' Moira cut the headlights. 'Seriously. What do you think is happening here?'

'I reckon Gareth Box is in her house, and she's afraid to go back there. She said he'd defiled her chapel.'

'How?'

'I don't know, it was only a message on the machine. She's obviously looking for Mum, but there's nobody in at the vicarage. She doesn't know about this funeral, you see. She thought it was on Friday. She's confused, messed up. You could see that.'

'OK,' Moira said. 'Why don't we just make sure first that your Mum really isnae back yet?'

Jane salvaged a smile. 'Before you stick your head out of the trench?'

'That your house?'

'Just behind those trees.'

'All right. I'll find somewhere safer to park and I'll wait for you here.'

'And then what?'

'Might be a wee bit premature to call the police. We'll go knock on this woman's door.'

'Right.' Jane slid out of the car. She was aware of the sharpness of the wind and the shape of the cobble under her shoe: *texture*.

When they reached the chapel, Merrily was thinking: *Question everything*.

The feeling was confirmed once they were inside the wooden porch and Ingrid had pulled her keys out, while Huw put down his bag of wine and wafers, lurched ahead with his torch and tried the door.

Which, thank God, stayed shut.

'You wanted it to be open, didn't you?' Merrily said in dismay. 'Just like in the stories.'

Huw didn't reply. He levelled his torch beam at the lock so that Ingrid could fit her key. *He wanted it to be open. He wanted someone waiting there for him.*

From just outside the porch door, someone said hesitantly, 'Would this be the one about how, if you find the door open and you go in, something's . . . ?'

'Lol?' Merrily stared at the compact silhouette against the sludgy sky.

'It's just that I've had another long talk with the person who started it all,' Lol said. 'Who was asked by Lynsey Davies to plant the story. As an experiment. She had to sit in a café in Ross, where the schoolkids go, and tell the story to some friends in a very loud voice.'

'That actually *happened*?'

'Must've been all over the school by going-home time,' Lol said. 'What happened after that was that Lynsey would borrow Piers's keys some nights and go down and unlock the chapel door. So that, you know, sometimes it was locked and some-times . . .'

Sometimes kids, like Zoe Franklin and Martin Brinkley, would be able to walk into the hollow vastness of it, and the air would be vibrant with the power of suggestion. Could it be that simple?

Ingrid Sollars sounded relieved. 'I'd never have admitted it, but that scared me. If I had to come down here after dark, I'd get Sam to come with me.' She looked over her shoulder at Lol. 'I'm sorry – I don't even know who you are.'

'This is Lol Robinson,' Merrily said comfortably. 'Him and me – we're like you and Sam, only even more secretive.' She started to laugh.

Huw snarled, '*Shush!*' He turned the handle and slammed his shoulder against the door. 'That changes nowt.' He went in roughly, the door juddering. 'Lights!'

Ingrid followed him in and snapped down the switches. The filaments in the hanging bulbs strained to reveal what they could of the former Underhowle Baptist Chapel in all its shabby splendour – and of the Reverend Huw Owen who, with his dusty, scarecrow hair and his liver-spotted dog collar, was looking suddenly like the minister it deserved.

'In fact,' Huw said, 'what the lad's just said makes it worse. The bitch was trying to feed it.'

He looked around the hacked-at walls, at the dust sheets hanging from the gallery. Then he moved into a shadowed area the size of a carport and came back dragging a plywood tea-chest, which he upturned and placed at the opposite end to the gallery, kicking shards of plaster into the corners.

'Altar,' he said.

The door just opened. As soon as Jane touched the knocker, the door fell away under her hand into the oaky darkness, and she stumbled forward into Chapel House.

Moira's hand came from behind, took hold of Jane's arm above the elbow and pulled her back.

'All I did was touch it.'

'I know,' Moira said soberly.

'Why would she leave it open? I mean, even in Ledwardine.'

'She wouldn't, Jane. She wouldnae do that.'

As they'd walked across the square from the lightless rectory, just a minute ago, Jane had seen Jenny Box at the top of these steps, at the door of Chapel House. She must have rushed in, leaving the door unsecured.

But there were no lights on inside. The wrought-iron lantern over the adjacent alley also remained unlit, just like the other night.

'If you want the absolute truth, Jane,' Moira said, 'I do not like the feel of this.'

Jane held on to the railing and glanced back down the steps. Just a few doors away, the Black Swan was fully lit, a couple of men chatting by the entrance. A car door slammed on the square. The whole situation was absolutely normal.

'Look,' she said, 'we're going to look stupid if we start raising the alarm and then it's nothing. It's not like this is some remote—'

'Shush a minute.' Moira slipped inside.

'Can you hear something?'

'I won't hear a bloody thing if you don't— Just stay there, all right?'

'What are you doing?'

'I'm trying to . . . OK, c'mere a minute.'

Jane stepped into the darkness. She thought for a moment that she could smell the beautiful, sensuous scent of apple wood, but then she couldn't.

'What's that?' Moira said.

'Oh.'

There was this gilded sliver in the middle distance, low down in the darkness.

'Don't move, hen.' She could hear Moira's hand sliding about on the wall, and then the lights came on: subdued, concealed lamps sheening the old oak panels.

Something was lying on the floor. Jane clutched Moira's arm.

'It's a rug,' Moira said, 'rolled up. But what's that alongside?'

The golden bar was a slit in the floor, a light on underneath it.

'Trapdoor,' Jane whispered. 'That has to be her chapel down there.'

Moira called out, 'Hello! You left your front door open!'

Nothing.

Moira went and tapped on the trapdoor. 'Hello down there? Mrs Box?'

'There's a ring handle.'

'Yes, Jane, I can see the ring handle.' Moira sighed and pulled it. The trapdoor came up as easily as the front door had opened, as if it was on a pulley system, uncovering a mellow vault of light.

'I'll go down,' Jane said. 'She knows me.'

'You bloody well will *not* go down.' Moira called out, 'Hello! You OK down there, Mrs Box?' She pulled a face and put a foot on one of the stone steps.

'Be careful.'

'Aye.' Moira went down. She wasn't creeping, she was clattering, which was sensible. If Jenny was holed up in there, expecting trouble, best not to scare her.

Moira was down there like for ever, or that was how it seemed. Jane looked out of the front door, could see the tail lights of a car on the square, could hear voices. 'Yeah, cheers!' someone shouted, and a car horn beeped. Situation normal.

Jane was about to go down the steps when Moira emerged.

'Right, Jane,' she said briskly. 'Let's go, yeah?'

With no make-up, you could tell straightaway how pale she'd gone.

Jane said, 'Oh shit. What?'

'Jane . . .' Moira pointed at the front door. 'Out.'

'*What?*

'Let's keep this nice and quiet, huh? We'll talk about it outside.'

Jane slammed the front door, shutting them in, something welling up in her chest. 'No! I want to know. What's happened to her?'

Moira sighed. 'Isnae her. It's . . . it's him. I guess.'

'Gareth?'

'Big moustache?'

'Yes.' Staring at Moira, Jane moved towards the steps.

Moira pushed down the hatch and stood on it. 'I really don't think so. I . . . it's not that I don't think you can take it, because I'm sure you've seen dead people before—'

'*No!*'

'Just . . .' She had her hands on Jane's shoulders. 'I don't think we should touch anything.'

Jane looked back at the closed front door and pulled away from Moira, ran to another door, flung it open, saw the cold green tint on leaded glass – the room she'd been in with Gareth. Light from the hall showed that the fireplace was dead. She backed out, went to the foot of the oak stairs and shouted up, 'Jenny!'

'Leave it,' Moira hissed. 'For Christ's sake, she's beaten the guy's head in with a bloody great iron cross and there's blood over three walls. Now will you just open that front door and get the—'

'Jenny . . .' Jane ran up the stairs. '*Jenny!*'

Huw stood in front of his tea-chest altar, with the chalice on it and the saucer of wafers, and addressed the five of them: Ingrid, Sam, Fergus, Lol, Merrily.

'We're asking God to cleanse this place of evil.' Over his head, a pale bulb burned coldly on a black flex. 'I want us all to be quite sure what we're about.'

Merrily said, 'I honestly don't see how we *can* be sure.'

'Aye.' Huw looked down at his shoes. 'All right, I've an axe to grind. As Merrily knows, a woman who became a very close friend of mine lost a daughter, it were thought, to Frederick West. Donna Furlowe – found not in the garden or the cellar at Cromwell Street or under Fingerpost field or Letterbox field, but in the Forest of Dean. *Was* it West? Or an imitator? Or was it a person or persons who believed they had . . . let him in?'

Merrily saw that they'd instinctively formed a semicircle around Huw – at one end Lol, looking a little shivery in his alien sweatshirt, and pensive; at the other the lanky, dark-suited Fergus Young.

'Look . . .' Huw pushed out his hands. '*I* don't know who killed Donna. Could very well've been Lynsey Davies, and one day somebody might find the finger bones that were taken away from her, and they might find them here, and then we'll know. But until then, all we know is the source. And the source is the evil that was nurtured in West and in Rosemary West. I'm inclined to say that that were a demonic evil and may eventually have to be dealt with as such.'

'But not yet,' Merrily said. 'Not until we know.'

Huw said nothing.

'Let's be sure about this, Huw. You're saying that the malign, earthbound essence of West, with his beloved 25 Cromwell Street removed from the face of the earth, was . . . invoked here.'

Ingrid broke the semicircle to approach Huw. 'Can I say something?'

'Aye, lass, let's have a debate. We've got all night.'

'Mr Owen, I told you that the people who ran the bottling plant were evasive on the phone last night about the name of the contractor. It was worrying me, so I rang them back this afternoon. Last night I spoke to the man, today I got the woman – and a rather different story. She implied that the contractor was, in fact, a relative, who did the job for cash in hand, and that was why—'

'Did you believe her?'

'I saw no reason not to.'

'I can see every reason. Sergeant Mumford'd certainly heard the rumour about West working here.'

'Huw,' Merrily said, 'you've just heard how *another* rumour was spread. For God's sake, it could be apocryphal! Maybe he was *never* here. This psychotic woman . . . for all we know, she might never even have been at Cromwell Street. So many people here have just lied and lied.'

A moment's silence.

Huw shrugged. 'All right. How would you play it, lass?'

Merrily shook her head. It was one of those situations when this game of Deliverance, the whole of religion, seemed too full of holes and traps to be worth the candle. She looked at Huw – tired-eyed and robbed of redemption.

And then Fergus Young said, 'Do I understand that, in the absence of a person to exorcize of this . . . evil, your options are limited?'

'One way of looking at it,' Huw said.

Fergus moved out and stood in front of the altar and took off his jacket. He was wearing a white shirt.

'I think you'd better exorcize *me*, then.' He looked at Lol. 'I suppose he knows why.'

50

Fuse Your Dreams

'*Don't you?*' The tall guy challenging Lol.

It was like being pushed out on stage all over again, except that the lighting was a little more primitive and, although everybody was staring at him, it was clear that nobody was expecting to be entertained.

Lol had been waiting for this. He could perhaps have made it happen earlier, but it had been a long night, and he'd been hoping it might have been taken out of his hands. Perhaps it had: this Fergus Young had authority. Lol had never seen him before tonight, but he recognized the aura and it had often, in his past, been around men in suits followed by lesser men in white coats. It was the aura of pseudo-sanctity.

'It *is* Tracey you've been speaking to, I assume,' Young said, seeking absolute confirmation.

'Tracey?' Lol said.

'And she's saying I was there.'

'Weren't you?'

'She was very mixed up, that girl.'

'I think *scared to death* might describe it better,' Lol said.

'*I realize,*' Cola had said, in the car on the road to Ross, '*that there's no way of concealing that it was me who told you all this, but just make sure it isn't for nothing. You know what I mean.*'

So Lol was relieved that Fergus Young had raised the issue before he himself was forced into it. Like being pushed out onto the stage. Now he *had* to follow through.

'*Three of them,*' Cola had said. '*Lynsey developed this bond between these three, which was all to do with Ariconium, which had become a kind of dream place. Like Utopia. Atlantis. It was very strong. It gave them focus. "Fuse your dreams," she was saying. "Fuse them inside me!"*'

'Ariconium,' Lol said. 'It became an excuse for everything you did.'

Sam Hall was shaking his head. 'How *could* it be anything good, built inside lines of pylons, this cage of steel shot through with beams and rays?'

'Oh for Christ's sake, Sam,' Fergus snapped, 'do you never get *beyond* that drivel? Look, I want to say I'd have gone with the police – with Piers and Chris. But I guess they thought there was a chance of keeping me out of it. As the one who must be seen to have integrity. The figurehead. If I could survive this, I suppose there was a chance of pulling it together – the e-schools, the book I was writing and that Piers would publish, Ariconium . . . everything.'

Lol looked at Merrily: small and wide-eyed, the old duffel coat hanging open over the alb with the muddied hem. She clearly hadn't been expecting this, but he thought the older woman seemed less shocked.

'*In a way, it all* began *with Fergus,*' Cola had said. '*He was in a sad state. It was his first school as headmaster and they were gonna close it down, and he reckoned he wasn't well in enough to get another school, and his wife was into the status, you know? Oh, he was a real loser, Fergus, the night he showed up on Piers's doorstep – the way people did, the way Piers encouraged them to: your bookseller's your counsellor, shrink, priest, all rolled into one. What an ego. And Fergus would come up some nights, to get away from his wife, and drink too much. And this particular night we were there, Lynsey and me, all of us at a bit of a loose end, and Lynsey suddenly springs up, with her eyes all glittering, and she's going "Let's DO something about it . . ."*'

'It's like Chris said, it was incredible how she seemed to turn things around,' Fergus said. 'How ideas came to you that were clear winners. Came to all of us. In reality, I suppose it was just because it brought the three of us together – people who could help each other and the community coming together in that spirit of . . . release. Outside the rules. And when we managed to pull the school back from the brink of closure and turn it into something extraordinary, it was . . . suddenly it was something bigger than all of us.'

He turned to Huw Owen, who'd started to say something. Huw hadn't taken his eyes off Fergus Young since he'd used the word *exorcize*.

'I suppose *you*'d say there was something slightly Faustian about it and perhaps you'd be right. But we didn't feel that at the time. It was release and not only sexual. To us, she was an extraordinary woman who seemed able to open doors one hadn't even known were there. And look at what we achieved . . . look at it! Look at what we achieved for *everybody*!'

'But look *how* it was achieved,' Merrily said bleakly.

'Look,' Fergus said, 'when we found out about her . . . past associations, we – *I* was determined to get out of it any way I could.'

'*I think, when they thought they were all on top of the situation and maybe they didn't need her any more, that was when they got, you know, a little blasé, a little . . . Well, you didn't ever diss that woman, Lol, not if you valued your peace of mind. What she had was hard won, and nobody was gonna . . . you know, nobody. So maybe that was when she started to be less circumspect. And she was involving Roddy by then, and Roddy was this real wild card. And that was when I started to try and get out of the circle, keep different company, 'cause I could see it going pear-shaped in front of my eyes. I knew what she was and where she'd been and they couldn't see it, not for a long time. They were just too high on it all.*'

Huw Owen said, 'You were here, in this chapel, after Lynsey Davies killed Melanie. With the other two.'

'Yes,' Fergus said.

'Therefore, you were part of the cover-up.'

'I . . .' Fergus's mouth tightened.

'Come on, lad, if you *were*, sooner or later one of the others is going to spill it to the police. You think they won't shop you, but they will. Like young Cody said, it's a murder inquiry now.'

Fergus said, 'We all decided to keep quiet about it, for—'

'The good of the community,' Huw said.

'We were doing *great things*. We had an *energy*!'

'Was she blackmailing you, in the end?' Lol suggested.

'That's nonsense.'

'*Really rubbing their noses in it, Lol. Cromwell Street, the whole bit . . . where she'd come from, and therefore where they were coming from. What they were – by association – now part of. It must have seemed very dirty and repugnant. Maybe Piers could take a little of that, but I'm not sure about the others. I mean, Chris was a street kid, but . . . bloody hell. As for Fergus . . . a primary-school head? A man in charge of developing the minds of little children? But she knew that. I think she knew what it would do to Fergus and that's why she was concentrating on him.*'

'When we found out about her,' Fergus was saying, 'I'm not even going to try to tell you what that was like for me.'

Lol said, 'But your whole future – and the future of the community – was somehow mortgaged to her now. I mean, if she did something again, if she killed somebody, and this time she got caught . . . it would all come out.'

Fergus shook his head. 'Wasn't so much her we were worried about as him – Lodge. She was going round with him, looking for . . . opportunities for him.'

'Like Mrs Pawson?' Lol said. He saw Merrily's face twist.

'I don't know anything about that, but there were other instances. They were becoming totally irresponsible, the pair of them. Like delinquents. Undisciplined. They thought they were protected, invulnerable. Protected by us, in a way, because we were at the centre of the establishment – especially Chris and me. Lodge, by this time, was becoming quite mad, and his condition was worsening – he'd be having blackouts all the time. But he didn't realize, or he didn't care because, in other respects, he was having the time of his life.'

'*Number One,*' Merrily said.

Lol said, '*Satan,*' and Sam Hall looked at him. And so he gave them the explanation of this that he'd had on the phone from Mephisto Jones.

'Sometimes, with EH, you experience dramatic temperature changes, particularly at the extremities. Hands, feet . . . genitals?'

'Holy shit,' Sam Hall said.

'In the days of the witch-hunts, when women would be made to confess to having intercourse with the Devil, they're supposed to have said that they could tell it was him because his penis was so cold.'

Merrily was nodding. 'Yes, and in Roddy's first statement to the police, he said Lynsey liked to call him Satan *because he was hard and cold*. And therefore . . . I mean, maybe she convinced him he could have . . . relations with any woman he wanted. Particularly if she was dead. Maybe in his dreams, I don't—'

'His electric dreams,' Sam said.

'It's quite obscene,' Fergus said. 'Everything we had going here was threatened by this unstable, odious little twerp, his fantasies and his . . . his *keeper*. Yes, I'm afraid we were all immensely relieved when he killed Lynsey. Getting rid of both of them, two people who were beyond the pale, seemed like a kind of cleansing. We could move on now. And if that's a terrible admission to make, I'm facing the truth. I'm facing my demons.'

Not really, though, are you? Lol was thinking.

And maybe Sam wasn't fooled either. 'I wouldn't rule it out, Fergus, that one of you somehow got it over to Roddy that Lynsey murdered his girlfriend, Melanie. How far off the truth would I be there?'

Fergus reared up. '*No.* Certainly not. Being glad at what happened – even grateful – is one thing, but actually conspiring to *make* it happen? No. I couldn't do that. You *know* me. You must realize how deeply, deeply sorry I am for ever becoming involved in something so ultimately obnoxious. I only ask you to believe that it began at a difficult time emotionally for me . . . and that *I did not know* the kind of psychotic individual we were dealing with. And I want to go on serving this community. Because there's so much for me still to do – you know that. Ingrid . . . Sam . . . you *know* that. *We mustn't fall back.*'

Lol looked at him standing there in his white shirt, the local hero, regrettably a little tarnished by an unfortunate choice of friends in adverse circumstances, but humbly seeking redemption: *Here I am, baring my back for the lash.*

Fergus turned to Huw. 'I would like to take communion from you. I would like to confess. To pray for absolution. I would like you to exorcize me.'

Huw didn't respond.

Lol felt suddenly very, very tired, and he just wanted to get this over. 'Mr Young,' he said. 'Why don't you just tell them how you killed Lynsey?'

Jane went timidly into the bedroom, the only one with a light showing under the door. On the bedside table, a small table lamp with a parchment shade was spreading a honey warmth.

The bedlinen was all white. There were magnolia rugs on the oak floorboards. A plain wooden cross hung on the white wall over the bed under oak beams stained almost black. There was an overwhelming silence in here, as thick as candle wax.

Jenny wore a long white nightdress with a high neck. She lay on her back with her hands, loosely clasping a small white prayer book, crossed over her breasts.

Her eyes were open but there was a glaze on them, a blur.

She would always be blurred.

There was a carafe of water on a bedside table and a glass and two small brown bottles with their tops off.

Designer death, Jane thought cynically, for just a moment before she began to cry quietly, going down onto her knees and touching one of the hands, which was like porcelain. And cold.

'Don't, Jane,' Moira said softly. 'Don't touch a thing.'

'She's not a thing,' Jane said.

'No. I'm sorry.'

Jane looked up at Moira. 'I don't understand. She's so cold.'

'She's been dead quite some time, Jane. Since long before we got here.'

'No. She couldn't be. We . . . saw her. On the square. On the cobbles. She . . .'

There was silence. The leaded window was grey-green and mysterious in the subtle lamplight, with just a faint reflection of the room, of Jane herself kneeling by the bed. But Jenny Box was invisible in the reflection and even in reality remained amorphous and indistinct.

'No,' Moira said gently. 'We didn't see her. *You* did.'

Jane's voice rose, querulous. 'You *must've* seen her.'

'No.'

Jane's voice almost vanished. 'Oh God,' she breathed. 'Oh my *God*.'

But what if he was wrong? This had been kicking at Lol's insides ever since he'd watched Lodge up there, edging towards inevitable death, since the night he'd lain in bed with Merrily and said, '*How can anybody feel sorry for a man who killed women?*'

That sense of Lodge as just another loser.

'*What's it like?*' he'd asked Mephisto Jones. '*How long does it last?*'

'*Oh, man, complete disorientation,*' Mephisto said. '*You don't know where you've been or what you've done. It's not like drink, not even quite like dope. You're well out of it, well out of it.*'

The final piece had dropped into place just now in the church, when the computer guy had been spilling it all to Bliss. The thing was, Lol hadn't been able to see either of those two in the role. But this one . . . this one he *could* see.

Cola, trying to conceal the fear, had said, '*Just make sure it isn't for nothing.*'

He looked up at the visceral hanging bulbs, so reminiscent of the dull lights in the hospital corridors of his twenties, and at the drabness of the place. Above all, he hated drabness. His own song was raging in his head now: *Someone's got to pay, now Dr Gascoigne's on his way.* He looked at Fergus and saw Dr Gascoigne whom all the nurses loved.

He took a breath. The air here smelled foul to him now.

He said to Fergus, 'You said Roddy Lodge had blackouts more and more often. He must have had them in front of you a few times, maybe during . . . magical practices. Especially in this chapel – right under the pylon, right here in the middle of the hot spot. How long was he out of it, usually . . . five minutes, ten . . . longer?'

'I never studied it,' Fergus said distantly. 'We tried to *help* him.'

Lol said, 'Why don't you take us through Lynsey's last night? You were there.'

'What are you talking about? You're absolutely crazy,' Fergus said. 'Cola couldn't—'

'I know, Cola *wasn't* there. I didn't get this from Cola. She probably doesn't even have an inkling . . .'

'I don't know what you're talking about.' Fergus turned to the others. 'What's he talking about?'

Lol exploded. 'Oh, you fucking *do* know. I get so pissed *off* with people like you . . . teachers, shrinks . . .'

He squeezed his eyes closed and heard Fergus saying, 'What's the matter with him? Is he on medication?'

Lol felt a merciful warmth, and when he opened his eyes Merrily was next to him, and she was holding his hand, pressing something hot and metallic into it, holding his hand closed over it, holding him together. He put his arm around her. He needed help. He instinctively knew the truth of it, but he couldn't make that final leap.

'Blackouts, huh?' Sam Hall was rubbing his white beard. Lol remembered Sam on the night of the execution: ' . . . *Shit coming off of the power lines. He's gonna be disoriented by now. His balance'll go completely, can't they see that?'* Warning the police about what might happen. Empathizing with the man on the pylon.

'Sam, help me,' Lol said. 'Roddy Lodge wasn't a killer. He probably wasn't a very nice man, especially in the end, but he didn't kill this Melanie, and I really don't think he killed Lynsey Davies, either. But when . . .' He shook his head, trying to clear the fog.

Sam said, 'You're saying that when he came round from a blackout, resulting from heavy electrical bombardment, he might've *thought* he had. Yeah?'

'Yeah,' Lol breathed, and he felt the breath coming out of Merrily, too. 'If you . . . I mean, if there were certain people who knew he'd often have blackouts in a certain situation . . .'

'Say, like in here?'

'They were coming more and more often, I think Mr Young just said. But if they were all ready for it – ready for the next one to happen – and there was another person among them whom they very much needed to kill . . .'

'They'd wait till Roddy was out of it, and then do it.' Sam Hall started to smile. 'And when he came round, with the body at his feet, they'd say, "Jeez, look what you did, you crazy bastard." '

'Or maybe they'd just go out and leave him to come round on his own and find it. He might not remember they'd even been here too.'

'Are you *both* mad?' Fergus Young cried, and Lol could hear the strain, the striving for effect.

'I tell you, though,' Sam said, 'killing like this, by strangulation, not everyone's capable of that. That is ultimate contact-killing. Intimate killing. I never did think Roddy Lodge could do that.'

'But this isn't getting us anywhere, is it?' Huw Owen said, almost brightly. 'This is all daft speculation.' He looked at Fergus. 'You meant what you said about being cleaned out, lad?'

Fergus glanced suspiciously from side to side. 'What kind of set-up—?'

'It's entirely up to you,' Huw said. 'Nobody ever gets forced.'

Lol looked at Fergus – the head teacher, the golden-haired golden boy of Underhowle, the local hero, the man who wore the admiration of the community like a halo – and Fergus looked down at Huw and smiled ruefully.

'Rather set *myself* up for this one, didn't I?' He shrugged. 'All right. Do what you want.'

Huw shook his head regretfully. 'Not me, lad. I'm too close to it.' He turned, putting out an open hand in invitation. 'Merrily?'

51

Sacrificial

Huw moved rapidly, setting up candles on the packing case and lighting them. Sam and Ingrid stood quietly with Lol against the wall, while Fergus prowled restlessly like an actor waiting to be auditioned, going over his lines. When Merrily caught his gaze once he smiled and shook his head. *It's a farce; we both know that.*

'Minor exorcism?' Merrily murmured to Huw. 'You reckon?'

'Aye, but you can't mess about. He's not going to sit still for the whole bit. Have to compress it a little.'

'Is he a Christian?'

'Ask him. No, don't bother. You'll find out.'

'Huw . . . You tricked him.'

'He tricked himself,' Huw said. 'Now put the lights out.'

Merrily took off her coat, knelt at the packing case and prayed. The cold seeped through her alb, and it felt as though her back was naked. She was aware of Huw standing behind her, as if trying to shield the fragile candle flames from an unfelt wind.

She said the Lord's Prayer, muttered St Patrick's Breastplate and wondered what this spontaneous, makeshift ritual, without any of the important preliminaries, could possibly achieve. Was this Huw grabbing his last chance, while Fergus was relaxed enough – or hypocritical enough – to throw himself at the mercy of a God in whom he had probably never believed?

Huw whispered, 'Call him.'

Merrily said, 'Fergus.'

Huw and Lol had dragged over one of the rubber mats and then folded a dust sheet and laid it on top, Lol squeezing her hand and leaving something in it.

'Where do you want me?' Fergus said.

'Might be as well if you just knelt. If that's not too un-comfortable.'

'I try to keep myself flexible, Merrily.'

'Good.'

Fergus knelt. She stood. She still didn't have far to gaze down on his open, bony face, his wide-apart brown eyes. *Had* he? Was any of this even conceivable? She saw how long and bony his hands were, knuckles like ball—

'If you could move a little closer to the altar.' She wanted it so the two candles lit the upper part of his face, so that she could see his eyes.

It was always going to be the eyes.

Very quietly, Huw was removing from the bag two items: the white diary of Lynsey Davies and a small picture, the miniature in its slender frame, and he was edging silently along the dust-sheeted wall towards the entrance. He could leave this to the lass.

He had to.

Huw crept away, to be on his own. He hadn't eaten for more than a day now. He'd awoken at five a.m. in the dark, and had spent nigh on three hours in meditation at the window. His room had faced east – she were thoughtful like that, the lass – and before the dawn came he'd established inside himself a centre of calm to which periodically, during the day, he'd returned.

His head was light now, filled with this quiet incandescence that was still linked to his spine as he padded down the body of the chapel, arriving at the side of the door. Standing there with his back to a hanging dust sheet, looking down to the altar at the opposite end of the chapel where, between the shapes of the people gathered there, he could see the candlelight, as remote from him now as starlight.

He placed the diary on the flagstones at his feet and held the miniature for a few moments in both hands. Too dark to see it, but the image was clear to him. He could see the face of Donna Furlowe sketched by her mother in pale grey pastel on white paper, so that it was like an imprint on a sheet. Or a shroud.

Huw knelt and, clasping the picture to his heart, held it there behind his hands as he put them together to pray.

With the bulbs out, there was a vague ball of light around them; Merrily could barely see anyone else.

'Our Father . . .'

She said the Lord's Prayer, the old exorcism, for the second time, slowly, and she could hear the others joining in, a grounded echo. She saw that Fergus was mouthing some of the words but not all of them, as if finding them difficult to remember. He looked briefly puzzled.

Merrily said, 'Deliver us, merciful Lord, from all evils, past and present and to come, and grant us peace in our day. Keep us free from sin and safe from all distress . . .'

Fergus knelt with his heavy, proud head raised up like the prow of a Viking longboat, his eyes closed. Where was he? Where were his thoughts taking him?

Merrily floundered, sought out Huw's shadow, couldn't see him anywhere, but she thought she heard his whisper: 'Confession.'

Yes, she thought, *of course*.

'Almighty God, in penitence we confess that we have sinned against you, through our own fault, in thought, word and deed . . .'

No penitence, no regrets, 'course there wasn't. He was what he was, no getting round that. He'd scratched it out on the wall of his cream-painted cell at Winson Green: **Freddy the mass murderer from Gloucester.**

Gloucester, not Hereford, them days was long gone. He'd picked Gloucester; made his home there, made it hisself, filled it full of hisself and what he'd took – bringing bits of Gloucester home.

Some nights he'd go back to Number 25 – not to the place it was now, look, emptied and gutted by the bloody coppers, but what it used to be, full of sweat and heat . . . vibrating with it.

Him too. He was strong then, at his peak, ready for anything: work hard, play hard, that was him.

Now he'd lost a lot of weight, didn't feel too good no more. Not here in this shithole, no privacy, nothing to see, nothing to watch. Nothing to watch here but him – *people looking at him all the bloody time, having a laugh, the laughs echoing across the exercise yard* – 'Build us a patio, Fred? Ho ho!'

Days fading into more days, going nowhere, never going nowhere again. Never working for hisself again, no more building things with his hands. Nothing to do with his hands no more.

No women, no more women ever. No wife. When they was in court, she wouldn't look at him – after all he'd done for her, trying to keep her out of it, telling the coppers she didn't know nothing. And she en't talking to them neither. And him . . . he's talked enough. All he's got left now's his secrets – the who and the when and the where. The how-many-times. They don't know next to nothing, when you works it out, en't got the half of it and that's all right by him – Freddy the mystery man. Freddy the mass murderer from Gloucester.

And Huw stood there in the gutted chapel, and he could hear the voice well enough, but he couldn't feel anything. No energy. All he was getting was the husk in the prison cell on New Year's Day, 1995. The day the prison officer couldn't get the cell door open because of what was hanging behind it from a rope made out of – versions differed – a prison blanket, or prison shirts.

This was the very worst crime to be committed against the relatives of every missing girl in Britain: allowing him to do it – letting Fred escape, with all his secrets.

Why hadn't they – the police, the prison authorities – put the psychology together, realized just how depressed he was likely to become without the anticipation of gross and grosser sexual excesses to heat his blood? Had nobody guessed he'd become empty, a husk, insubstantial enough to hang?

Maybe they had. Maybe they just bloody *had*. He'd heard of coppers who'd cheered when they'd heard about the death at Winson Green. A banner going up: *Nice one, Fred* – something as inane as that.

And now nobody would know the who, the where, the how-many. Lynsey had written her secrets down, in the *Magickal Diary*, but amiable, garrulous Fred had been barely literate, and Rose was saying nowt.

Freddy, the man of mystery, and those who followed him: Lynsey and the others, the unknown others who'd lived in Cromwell Street or had just dropped in for an hour or two, and would never be identified now. Out there, with the virus inside them.

Huw stared into the darkest corner of the chapel, listening for the remains of the laughter and the sniggers, the sound of a hammer, thrown from a ladder, clanging on the flags.

He heard nothing but the drone of Merrily's *ad hoc* ritual, useless in itself.

It was all useless. There was nobody watching, nothing worthy of a fight.

Huw held the pastel drawing of Donna, by Julia, close to his aching heart, thinking of all the relatives and friends and lovers of long-missing girls and women who did something like this every night. And he broke down.

At some point, Fergus's eyes opened, and Merrily came in at once with the ritualized question, 'What do you want from God in his Holy Church?'

Fergus, unprepared, made no reply at first. While she waited, she could hear the wind outside, coming down off Howle Hill. Sam Hall's line came into her head: *insidious wind*. Where was Sam? She couldn't see him. Where was Lol? All she could see were Fergus's eyes, looking into hers.

'I want,' Fergus said, 'what I deserve.' He smiled at her.

Merrily felt a hollowness in her stomach. She gripped the angel pendant and felt the weight of her pectoral cross.

'Do you renounce the Devil and all the spiritual forces of wickedness that rebel against God?'

Fergus kept smiling. 'Sure.'

'Do you renounce all the evil powers of this world that corrupt and destroy what God has created?'

'I . . . yes,' Fergus said. 'Of course.'

'Do you renounce all sinful desires that draw you away from the love of God?'

When he hesitated, Merrily saw that he was looking at her breasts. Then he looked up.

'Oh yes,' he said.

The heat from the pendant went right up her arm. She looked into his eyes, then, and knew.

What a cliché that was: *seen it in his eyes, windows of the soul* – all that stuff.

In Fergus's eyes, she saw nothing at all. A void. An absence. It was like opening the doors of a lift and finding that you were looking directly down the shaft. The *absence* that could now only be filled with life and energy when his hands were exploring you, when the eyes were lighting up like little torch bulbs. When he was swimming towards you through a pool of liquid lust.

Merrily knew that she was seeing what Lynsey Davies had seen, been surprised and probably delighted by, in the second before he came for her with . . . what?

A thin belt was the pathologist's suggestion, according to Bliss, but no belt had ever been found. Perhaps it was Roddy's – Fergus bending over the unconscious Roddy, as if to help him, sliding the belt out of his trousers. And then subduing Lynsey with his fists. She saw blood jetting from Lynsey's nose and then the image cut to the belt, each end wrapped around one of Fergus's hands and then its length pulled tight around Lynsey's throat.

Silence soaked her head and then, over it, she heard, quite clearly and crisply:

'*Show you what's what, where the bits goes, you little smart bitch . . .*'

'Do you renounce—?'

'Yes, of course. I renounce everything.' Fergus smiled. 'Is that it?'

'That's up to you,' she said.

'Oh, I'm sure that will do.' Fergus stood up. 'Thank you, Merrily. I imagine we all feel so much better for that.'

And he walked out of the glow and into the darkness.

'Laughing,' Ingrid Sollars said. 'Laughing at us. Didn't you feel that?'

'I didn't feel anything. There wasn't anything to feel.' Merrily turned to the altar and saw that the candles had gone out. But her eyes had long since adjusted; it seemed much lighter in here, and she could see Ingrid and Sam and Lol quite plainly. 'Were we all expecting a confession?'

'He's not that dumb,' Sam said. 'All the people who know the truth are dead. Hell, I can see it *all* now. The panic Roddy musta been in – a killing he didn't recall, a body on the floor right here. What's he gonna do? Maybe they even advised him, Fergus and Piers – you can't bury her here, buddy, all these excavations we're gonna have. Must surely be someplace you've been working lately where you could stash her.'

'Mmm.'

Merrily walked away, looking for Huw, whose idea this had been . . . and what a pointless exercise. She was disappointed in him – which she knew was wrong; he was just a man, with a burden. Perhaps what she was really avoiding was her disappointment in God, into whose hands this had been placed, in the hope of a solution. And there was none, not really. No one had been redeemed.

'Cola French,' Sam Hall mused. 'I recall her now. She'd stay some weekends with Piers, I guess, came along to the village hall with him sometimes. Bright kid. But what I wondered, Lol . . .' He looked around. 'Where'd he go?'

'Lol?'

Merrily could see him across the chapel, quite clearly silhouetted against a dust sheet hanging from the ceiling. Silhouetted because there was a blush on the cloth, a warm glow inside it. Lol was gathering the cloth into his arms and pulling on it.

'What's happening?' Ingrid said.

When the sheet came down, with a shower of dust and plaster fragments, Merrily saw it had concealed a Gothic window that was both tall and wide and had plain glass in it, and what she saw through the glass explained why it was now so bright in here.

Cherry Lodge was wearing her old parka, and her hair was matted to her forehead. She was panting. There was a pile of old tyres beside her and she lifted one quite easily and threw it into the flames.

'We piled some tyres all around, first,' she said. 'I didn't want to *see* him go up, did I?'

A tractor was parked at the edge of the field, not far from the end wall of the Baptist chapel. It had a trailer attached, and there were more tyres on that.

'Left over from the foot-and-mouth pyres,' Cherry said. 'Railway sleepers would've been better but there was no time for that, see. I don't know what'll happen if it goes out before he's all gone.'

The flames, with the wind under them now, lit up the pylon at the bottom of the field. When Merrily and the others had first come out of the chapel, it had looked as though the pylon itself was alight, as though the flames were filling it up inside, turning it into some metal Wicker Man of the new millennium: sacrificial fire.

It had taken Merrily a long time to work out what was happening here. Ingrid Sollars had been the first to realize, showing no shock at all. 'Mr Lomas,' she said drily, 'would be most offended.'

Underneath the stench of diesel and burning rubber, Merrily detected the worst smell of all – barbecue, roast pork, *Nev.*

She coughed into a hand and wondered if Gomer was here, among the small but swelling crowd, the bonfire-night crowd, the villagers who would never in a million years have turned out for Roddy Lodge's funeral.

'The police've sent for the fire brigade.' Cherry Lodge was smiling, tired but triumphant. 'Too late now. Oh, they'll probably think of something to charge us with, but we're only doing what they all wanted, aren't we?'

My fault, Merrily thought. *Should have made sure the church was locked.*

She saw Lol coming back from the chapel, with Huw. They walked across to the other side of the fire, where there were fewer people, and Merrily was sure she saw Huw throw something grey-white into the flames. *The diary?*

'After we left you, we went straight back up to the farm, we did, and piled the tyres on the trailer with the diesel,' Cherry said. A wild exhilaration there now. 'And we built up the pyre, and then we went back to the church and just wheeled the coffin out on Mr Lomas's bier and loaded him on the trailer and brought him back here. Nobody noticed. The police weren't out in force yet, just a couple down by the grave.'

'Your idea?' Merrily asked.

'Bit of both. He was very bitter, Tony was, about that protest, with the banners and the placards. Lived here longer than any of them and he gets treated like dirt. Very bitter, he was. And at Roddy too, of course.'

Let him be cremated. Empty his bloody ashes in the gutter.

Catharsis, Merrily thought, a hand on her pectoral cross.

And the Lodges didn't yet know that he was probably an innocent man.

Redemption.

Really?

She looked away. In the top corner of the field, where it was separated from the land that extended behind Roddy's bungalow . . . was that a woman standing alone there against the wire fence, arms folded, very still, watching Roddy burn?

Or was it just a fence post, with an old, fraying rag caught in the wire, so that it blew back in the wind, like hair?

Epilogue

The skin was softly sepia-toned, the crow's-feet delicately faded out. There was an ethereal light around the head.

Angel of Our Days, it said above the picture of Merrily.

She shuddered. 'I can't even think where she got this one from.'

'Of course, it'll never be wiped now,' Jane said. 'You realize that? You'll go on for ever, making rings around the world.'

'Nothing goes on for ever,' Merrily said. 'Certainly not on the Internet.'

'That's true, in fact,' said Eirion, who'd brought along the printout. 'When somebody stops paying for the site, it'll vanish overnight.'

'You don't know,' Jane said. 'Odd things happen.'

Merrily saw Eirion giving her his famous smile and guessed that they were holding hands under the table. *Odd things happen.* When did the kid last say something like that?

How quickly they recovered. The elasticity of young skin. Whereas crow's feet only got deeper.

She stretched her legs under the table. It was the first time she'd felt able if not to relax, at least to *sag*. Like spending a few moments on a plateau where you could lie on your back and not see the abyss. Maybe this was the most she could hope for: the feeling of not, for a while, having to look into the abyss.

On the printout, underneath her picture, she read:

The Archangel Uriel is at this moment working on earth

through Her servant, The Reverend Merrily Watkins, Deliverance Minister for the Diocese of Hereford on the border of England and Wales.

It is very unusual in the UK, where the women's ministry is itself so very young, for a woman, especially one so youthful, to be elevated to this most important and spiritually crucial role.

We ask for your prayers to aid Merrily in what we believe to be the summit of her endeavour, the task for which she was chosen above all women.

We believe that a satanic male maleficence lives on and will be *passed* on again, unless Merrily Watkins is permitted to exorcize it at the laying down of Roddy Lodge in the village of Underhowle, Herefordshire.

You are requested to commence your prayers for Merrily NOW. By the grace of God, amen.

It was signed: *The Daughters of Uriel*. And the tone was ludicrously apocalyptic, and yet . . .

'I failed her,' Merrily said. 'Don't let anybody say otherwise. I did not get any of this right.'

'You didn't know,' Jane said. 'You couldn't have known.'

'All the praying I do, you'd think there'd've been a little divine intervention,' Merrily said bitterly.

'*Don't*,' Jane said sharply.

'No. I'm sorry.' Maybe there had been. How could any of them know?

Jane said, 'Just because you're a priest, it doesn't have to happen through you. The other thing happened through Lol. I mean, didn't it? It was Lol who exposed that guy.'

'Yes.' Merrily smiled. 'And Lol hated every minute of it.'

Merrily had watched Fergus – or had seemed to – in that frigid flicker of transition between man and monster. Yet he was *not* a monster. He was the best head teacher they'd ever known in Underhowle; he treated kids like equals and he was endlessly enterprising and affable with everybody, only occasionally displaying the steel cord under the velvet, which was so essential to a good *school director*.

Yet already, according to Frannie Bliss, the stories were filtering through, including the rumours about why Fergus's marriage had failed – not because his wife had found out about his evenings of recreational release, but because of what he'd become between the sheets at home: a gradual diminishing of tenderness, the parallel escalation of sexual violence. This indictment had come from Fergus's mother-in-law, who had thought him such a wonderful man that at first she'd accused her daughter of simply being inadequate to his healthy, masculine needs.

How easily and efficiently he'd lied, exactly the way West had lied, revealing nothing until it had already been found out.

Bliss said that if the killing of Lynsey Davies had not happened *exactly* as Lol had suggested, he couldn't have been far out. The way Frannie saw it, the three of them had probably agreed to wait for Roddy's next blackout and then go for it.

Lol had told Merrily about Lynsey's resonant instruction to the three of them: *Fuse your dreams inside me.*

It would be important for all three of them to kill her, fusing the guilt. But when it came to it, Frannie reckoned, Cody and Connor-Crewe would have chickened out. Maybe they didn't have *quite* enough to lose.

Frannie wanted Fergus for this one. He'd said on the phone that they'd now be turning major heat on Cody and Connor-Crewe.

He was confident that, before the day was out, one of them would have pointed the finger. And then he'd start on Fergus.

Huw had gone home to the Beacons. But he and Merrily had arranged to return to the Baptist chapel tomorrow, possibly with Jerome Banks and a chalice of Harvey's Spanish Red and some white wafers. A full exorcism of place would not be underplaying it.

Meanwhile, Huw had been learning more about Lynsey Davies's past and was wondering how much of a coincidence it was that Donna Furlowe's body had been found close to the hamlet where Lynsey had been born, near Lydbrook, in the Forest.

Had Donna been killed by Lynsey and Fred? West had, after all, known the girl. Or was it, as the police had suspected, too late in his murderous career for it to be down to Fred? Lynsey and somebody else, then? Not Roddy Lodge, that was more or less certain now.

Lynsey on her own? Or with another of her old Cromwell Street friends?

Not long after Huw had left, Gomer had arrived with a man who was as close to a cube as anyone Merrily had seen.

Jumbo Humphries had parked his blue and white Cadillac on the square, parallel to the Market Hall, the only spot where it was unlikely to cause an obstruction. Jumbo had curly hair and stubble and he talked a lot. He was from the southern end of the Beacons or the top end of the Valleys, however you wanted to look at it, and he talked fast and emotionally.

'A *wond*erful lady, she was, Mrs Watkins. A de*light*ful woman. I cannot bring myself even to think about it. Asked myself a thousand times, I have, since I yeard: *what* could I have done? How could we have helped her, any of us? How could we have *saved* her?'

Jenny Box.

Jane said now, 'I'm not sure anyone could have saved her. Really, I'm not just saying that. I've been thinking about it all day. She never told you anything *straight out*, did she? She was like so diffuse – is that the word? I mean, sometimes you looked at her and it was like part of her had already left the building. You know what I mean?'

'Yes.' Diffuse. Gone with the fairies. Flying with the angels. Merrily blinked back tears. 'Oh God, if I'd only gone to see her yesterday morning . . .'

'Instead of what? You couldn't do everything. Maybe if *I'd* gone to see her . . . I mean, you've hardly slept this week as it is.' Jane leaned over the table, both hands around her mug.

'Mum, it was so strange, so unearthly, being in that room and her laid out like the Lady of Shalott. I can't . . .'

When she'd come out of Chapel House with Moira Cairns, Eirion had been there on the square, having discreetly followed them back, planning only to hand Jane the *Daughters of Uriel* printout and see what happened then. In the end, he'd stayed all night, had been with Jane when DCI Annie Howe had arrived with the ubiquitous Andy Mumford and the scenes-of-crime investigators – a big overtime night for the Durex suits.

They'd all listened to the message on the vicarage answering machine. *'He's defiled my chapel.'* The only interpretation they could put on this was that the chapel had been defiled by Gareth Box's body and his blood. Why he'd gone down there, why he'd even returned from London, remained a mystery. All that was known for sure was that Jenny had smashed him savagely around the head and face with the heavy gilded iron cross that had stood on the altar.

They'd found Jenny's bloodstained clothes in a bathroom. She'd evidently stripped off everything, taken a shower and then dressed in that long white Edwardian nightdress and gone to lie on the bed with her prayer book, her Bible, a carafe of water and two bottles of sleeping pills.

Andy Mumford had called back, at the end of his extended shift, and Merrily had told him about the woman from the *Mail on Sunday* who'd wanted to speak to her about Jenny Box. Mumford already knew about it. The *Mail* had been cooperative. It seemed that Gareth Box had supplied them with a large package of background information and a long, unattributable interview with himself. The proposed end product: a definitive profile of Jenny Driscoll demonstrating conclusively that Jenny Driscoll had become mad. The paper had been told of her gift of eighty thousand pounds to a woman vicar with whom she had become obsessed – a vicar who, incidentally, was having a secret affair with a rock musician who had 'history'.

Box apparently had said that while this little detail might not turn out to be appropriate to the story, it might, if mentioned, make the vicar more amenable to a frank discussion of Jenny's 'stalking' of her.

'And Jenny found out about this?' Merrily had said. 'She killed him and then herself because she found out he was trying to destroy her in the press, for whatever commercial reasons . . . ? That's *why*?'

'We don't know,' Mumford had said. 'But it's not the weakest motive I've ever come across.'

But then there *was* the other thing.

'Reason I've called, see, Mrs Watkins,' Jumbo Humphries had said, 'is I thought I ought to let you know this small thing.'

'Bugger means *I* thought he oughter let you know,' Gomer said, 'on account of all that stuff about you he pumped out of me unbeknownst, for this lady.'

'What you have to understand, see,' Jumbo said, 'is this issue of client confidentiality. Couldn't breathe a word of this while the client was alive, and I wouldn't be able to tell you now but for—'

''Cept for me twisting the fat bastard's arm,' Gomer said grimly.

'Well, yes. Except for my friendship of many years with Mr Parry. Now, you'll know that I was retained initially through Marquis and Co., the London investigation bureau working on a regular basis for the Vestalia company. However, Mrs Box – so satisfied, she was, with my services that she asked me to undertake separate inquiries on a more personal basis, which of course I was delighted to do. This all come about because of the name of a Midlands-based company which she've noticed in the newspaper in relation to this Underhowle business, see. The name being Efflapure.'

'See?' Gomer said urgently. 'See?'

Merrily blinked, well overburdened with information.

'The reason this name struck a chord,' Jumbo Humphries said, 'was that, although the business side was something she left largely to her husband, she was vaguely aware of some investment he've made in this very company – Efflapure.'

'Bloody hell,' Merrily said.

'As you say. My inquiries at Companies House and other

sources revealed that Mr Gareth Box had invested *substantially* in Efflapure, and was – until his death, of course – a director.'

'See?' Gomer said. 'This feller was keeping Lodge in work.'

'Maybe I'm tired,' Merrily had said, 'but I think there's something I'm missing.'

Eirion finally dragged himself away around six, leaving Merrily and Jane alone in front of the sitting-room fire.

'You're OK?' Merrily asked the kid.

'Yeah. We're OK.' Jane slumped down on the sofa. It was dark outside; the fire of logs and coal was the only light in the room. 'I feel like I've been away. I feel like I'm *still* away.'

'Strange days,' Merrily said, head resting on a cushion.

'I don't know what to say. It's like when Lucy Devenish died. It wasn't real then, and this is different, obviously, because I didn't really know Jenny Driscoll, but I *did*. You know? We just walked the streets in the rain for less than an hour and I *knew* her.'

'Maybe you had more in common than you imagined.'

'She said . . . she was talking about you, and she said, "It's a deep-embedded evil she's confronting. And she needs the angels at her shoulder." What did she mean?'

'She could've meant anything. I don't really know, flower. There are lots of things I wish I knew.' Merrily closed her eyes, thinking of Melanie's angel, all the little connections you could make if you wanted to.

'What will you do with the money?' Jane asked.

'If it turns out that it's mine to give, I think I'm going to find out which charity is supporting research into electro-hypersensitivity.'

'Cool,' Jane said.

'Yes. I'm sure Ted will agree, if threatened.'

'Will the paper still do this story?'

'They've got a much bigger story now, haven't they?'

'I mean you and Lol.'

'I think that's very unlikely, but I don't really care. I think it's time me and Lol . . . came out, as it were.'

'You're just saying that because he's this big star now. Well . . . he is in Hereford.'

'And then the world.'

Jane said, 'I think I saw Jenny Box's ghost.'

Merrily opened her eyes and sat up.

'It was when we got back here, Moira and me. Jenny was walking across the square. She must've been dead some time by then.' Jane gazed into the fire. 'Moira didn't see her at all.'

'Moira didn't know her,' Merrily said softly.

'You couldn't miss her. Who else walked around with a big white scarf over her head? And her face – unclear. Like a face in motion. Like a face painted by . . . who was that guy?'

'Francis Bacon?'

'Yeah, of course.'

'Were you scared?'

'No. Not then. I didn't know what I was seeing.'

'Are you scared now?'

'A bit. When we found her dead, it was . . . it was like somebody had played this awful trick on me. But afterwards . . . I mean it's awesome, isn't it? It's bloody awesome, Mum. The implications, you know? Awesome.'

'Yes. It is, sometimes.'

'And I'm sorry, Mum,' Jane said. 'I'm really *so sorry.*'

It was after nine when Frannie Bliss arrived. Jane had gone to bed. Merrily had fallen asleep on the sofa. She staggered to the door and brought him back into the lounge.

'You look terrible,' she said.

'And you look all sleepy and sexy. And I didn't say that. I'm a married man, just.'

'Have you even seen Kirsty today?'

'Nope.'

'Do you have a job?'

'Bloody right.'

'Do you want coffee?'

'I don't think I will.'

'Heavens,' Merrily said, 'have we entered a parallel universe?'

The fire had burned low. Bliss sat down on the sofa. 'I've nicked Fergus.'

'You sure of him?'

'No. But, by God, I'll try. I want this man so bad I can't breathe when I think about it.'

'Handle him carefully.'

'Merrily, I'll handle him like with those little plastic tongs they give you to shovel a scone onto your plate in these self-service joints. I, er . . . Lol . . . Lol did well.'

'Six numbers and an encore.'

'You know what I mean.'

'Yes, he did.' Merrily shovelled a little coal onto the fire and poked it until a few small flames appeared. 'I think he was probably the only person who, from the very beginning, had a strong feeling that Roddy Lodge was innocent. And he didn't let it go. It was . . . a new Lol.'

'Lot of changes.' Bliss looked very tired. 'Lots still to understand. Lots we never will. Listen.' He moved to the edge of the sofa. 'Couple of things. You were in from the beginning, so I'm telling you. One . . . Melanie Pullman. Missing bones.'

'Oh God.'

'Two toes and an ankle bone from the left foot.'

'They're definitely not . . . ?'

'We went down another metre. Nothing.'

'So what's it tell you?'

'I don't know, Merrily. I don't know what it tells us. The other thing is this.' He brought a folded sheet of paper from his inside pocket. 'It's a photocopy – one of the photocopies I showed you before. Neither of us noticed this, but then why should we?'

Merrily unfolded the paper and held it close to the flames.

INSIDE THE HOUSE OF HORROR
EXCLUSIVE
Former tenants talk for the first time about real life in Twenty-Five Cromwell Street.
By GARETH BOX

'Christ,' she said.

Frannie leaned back in his chair. 'Box started his career in the Gloucester office of the Three Counties News Agency.'

'Yeah, I know Three Counties.'

'They don't pay much, but it's good experience for a young reporter. You get to see your stories in the big papers – usually under somebody else's byline, but it's a start. Also the big papers get to know you. You can make an impression.'

'But he wasn't at the news agency when he wrote this, was he?'

'No, he was in London by then, working on a national, but in quite a lowly position. But then the West story breaks, and he gets them to send him back to his old hunting ground. And he comes up with some heavy dirt. He knew exactly who'd been in Cromwell Street when all the murders were happening, all the torturing in the cellars. He knew exactly who to go to for the inside stuff. His paper was very pleased with him. Never looked back. Within a year he's an assistant editor in features and writing Jenny Box's column, and the rest is . . . as they say.'

'But you think the *real* history . . .'

'Young reporter in Gloucester in the late seventies, finding his way, earning peanuts. In need of some cheap accommodation. Merrily, there is so much . . . *so* much gossip about that place, and he may not have been the only young journalist to have spent some time there. There are – as I'm sure you've heard – even suggestions that some lads who dropped in for an occasional leg-over had to take off their dark blue trousers first. But Box – yeh, we're pretty sure about him.'

'Oh God, Frannie.' Merrily was wide awake. 'He was also a director of Efflapure.'

'Yeh, and Lynsey Davies knew somebody at Efflapure and was thus able to bend somebody's arm to put the area contract Roddy's way.' He did his acid smile. 'The Old Cromwellians, eh?'

'And he liked young girls.'

Bliss nodded.

'You knew all about that?'

'Mrs Box didn't leave a note, and it's always nice to know *why* they do these things, isn't it? The general feeling is that he only married her because . . . well, because she was famous and earning more than him, but also because she still had the look of a teenager who'd been given bad drugs and then beaten up.'

'Yes.'

'By mid-morning, Annie Howe even had the names of four of Box's ex-girlfriends, all with bad memories. And a fifth, who'd . . . disappeared some time ago.'

Merrily poked mindlessly at the fire.

A deep-embedded evil.

She looked up. 'You think he killed? You really think Box killed?'

'One thing you learned at Cromwell Street,' Frannie Bliss said, 'was how easy it could be.'

'And he knew Lynsey . . .'

'And you're thinking about Donna Furlowe.'

She nodded and wondered how much Jenny Box had known, and what else Jumbo Humphries had been able to tell her. The enormous, holistic connections her mystical mind must have made as she waited for Gareth Box, with the iron cross held high.

'Don't you sometimes feel,' Frannie said, 'when these horrible little coincidences occur, that there's a wider plan, and it isn't always constructed by somebody with our best interests at heart?'

'I don't get paid to feel that,' Merrily said uncomfortably.

That night, she prayed by the landing window overlooking the square. She didn't see a woman out there with a white scarf over her head.

But she found she still had Melanie's angel, and she slept with it under her pillow.

CLOSING CREDITS

Nobody who has studied the Cromwell Street case believes it was satisfactorily resolved or even, in the end, fully investigated – there is a limit to police resources. Estimates of the number of West victims still undiscovered range from ten to more than forty. All over Britain, there are relatives of missing women and girls who are unlikely ever to know whether their worst fears are justified. Hardly what you expect in peacetime.

The idea that the guilt extends beyond Fred and Rose is not new but is still rarely spoken of. Researching this book, I was told more unpublished West stories than I could reasonably use. The Black Dai story is true; a thirty-two-year-old man was jailed for life on 4 December 1996. The Terry Crick story is also true.

I owe particular thanks to West's official biographer, Geoffrey Wansell, who knows more about Cromwell Street than anyone should ever have to. For information about the West case, electricity, radiation, EH, septic tanks, Ariconium and other related issues, many thanks also to: Rosemary Aitken, Penny Arnold, Caroline Boots at GPU, Krys and Geoff Boswell, William Corlett, the Courtyard, John Deeley, Paul Devereux, Kate Fenton, Philip Grey, Paul Harrison, Prof. Dennis Henshaw, Michael Howard, Prof. Bernard Knight, Mike Kreciala, Rebecca Lacey, John Mason, John Mayglothling, Ed Richmond, The Electric Shop, Ross, Lisle Ryder, Andrew Taylor, Rebecca Tope, Hereford Samaritans and West Mercia Police at Hereford, who were very accommodating and probably very grateful not to have Frannie Bliss in the CID room. Thanks also to Gruff Rhys, of Super Furry Animals for permission to quote lines from the excellent album *Rings Around the World*.

I leaned heavily on three books on the West Case: *An Evil Love* by Geoffrey Wansell, *Happy Like Murderers* by Gordon Burn and *She Must Have Known* by Brian Masters. Also Paul Britton's *The Jigsaw Man*. The more bizarre effects of electricity and the hot-spot phenomenon are discussed in Albert Budden's *Allergies and Aliens*. You can find out about Ariconium in Brian Cave's *The Countryside Around Weston and Lea (The Roman town of Ariconium and its district)*, which may be out of print now but was published by The Forest Bookshop, Coleford, where I got mine second-hand.

Frankly, this was not exactly an easy book to write, and I relied throughout on the judgment and penetrating editorial skills of my wife Carol, who spent many weeks disentangling it and pulling me back from the brink of excess, before it was deemed fit to pass on to Peter Lavery, my editor at Macmillan, whose fuse-wire sensitivities always react to any hitch or twitch in the flow. Finally, Nick Austin's copy-edit was always thoughtful and perceptive.

One day the whole truth may come out. But I'm not holding my breath.

PHIL RICKMAN

The Wine of Angels

PAN BOOKS

The Revd Merrily Watkins had never wanted a picture-postcard parish – or a huge and haunted vicarage. Nor had she particularly wanted to walk straight into a local dispute over a controversial play about a strange seventeenth-century clergyman accused of witchcraft . . . a story that certain old-established families would rather remained obscure.

But this is Ledwardine, steeped in cider and secrets. A paradise of cobbled streets and timber-framed houses. And also – as Merrily and her teenage daughter Jane discover – a village where horrific murder is a tradition that spans centuries.

'As if an episode of *The Vicar of Dibley* or
The Archers had suddenly turned into *Cracker*'
Sunday Times

'Escalates with all the excitement of a good
thriller and races breathlessly towards the climax . . .
a wonderful, enthralling read'
Daily Express

PHIL RICKMAN

Midwinter of the Spirit

PAN BOOKS

'Exorcism' is a word no longer favoured by the Church of England. Nowadays the term for dealing with cases of possession and paranormal disturbance is 'deliverance ministry'. It sounds less sinister, more caring – so why not a job for a woman?

When offered the post once styled 'diocesan exorcist', the Revd Merrily Watkins – parish priest and single parent – cannot easily refuse. But the retiring exorcist, strongly objecting to women priests, not only refuses to help Merrily but also ensures that she's soon exposed to the job at its most terrifying.

And things get no easier. As an early winter slices through the old city of Hereford, a body is found in the River Wye, an ancient church is desecrated, and there are signs of dark ritual on a hill overlooking the city. Meanwhile, reports of psychic unrest in the cathedral reflect an undying evil lying close to the heart of the Church itself.

Based on true practices, this is the first spiritual-procedural thriller – the electrifying story of a woman who must walk in dark places where an intangible malevolence thrives uncurbed by the forces of law and order.

PHIL RICKMAN

A Crown of Lights

PAN BOOKS

When a redundant country church is bought by a pagan couple, the local evangelical minister reacts with fury. A modern witch-hunt begins and Merrily Watkins, diocesan exorcist, is expected to keep the lid on this cauldron. But when the truth begins to emerge, her loyalty to the Church is seriously tested. Meanwhile, there is the problem of the man who won't be parted from his dead wife, and the ancient mystery of the five local churches dedicated to St Michael, slayer of dragons. Also, a killer with an old tradition to guard.

'A highly sophisticated crime novel. Its complex narrative grips like a clamp. Rickman makes us care about his characters . . . is brilliant at dialogue'
Andrew Taylor, *Crimetime*

'Supernatural events subtly introduced . . . paragraphs like lightning flashes . . . has you ransacking the English language for adequate words of praise. "Faultless" springs to mind . . .'
John Whitbourn, *SFX*

PHIL RICKMAN

The Cure of Souls

Pan Books

In Herefordshire's hop-growing country, where the river flows as dark as beer, a converted kiln is the scene of a savage murder. When the local vicar refuses to help its new owners cope with the aftermath, diocesan exorcist Merrily Watkins is sent in by the bishop. Already involved in the case of a schoolgirl whose deeply religious mother thinks she's possessed by evil, the hesitant Merrily is drawn into a deadly tangle of deceit, corruption and sexual menace as she uncovers the secrets of a village with a past as twisted as the hop-bines that once enclosed it.

'Intrigue, lies, cover-ups, danger and
the unexplainable . . . plot twists around every
corner . . . a most provocative read'
Publishers' Weekly

'Rickman has virtually created a new genre.
Highly entertaining . . . delivered with a panache
we have come to expect'
Crimetime